# CHARITON

LCL 481

# CHARITON

## CALLIRHOE

EDITED AND TRANSLATED BY

## G. P. GOOLD

HARVARD UNIVERSITY PRESS

CAMBRIDGE, MASSACHUSETTS

LONDON, ENGLAND

1995

*Library of Congress Cataloging-in-Publication Data*

Chariton.
[De Chaerea et Callirrhoe. English & Greek]
Callirhoe / Chariton; edited and translated by G. P. Goold.
p.     cm. — (Loeb classical library; 481)
Includes bibliographical references.
ISBN 0–674–99530–9
I. Goold, G. P.     II. Title.     III. Series.
PA3948.C5E5     1994          94–6918
883'.01—dc20          CIP

*Typeset by Chiron, Inc, Cambridge, Massachusetts.
Printed in Great Britain by St Edmundsbury Press Ltd,
Bury St Edmunds, Suffolk, on acid-free paper.
Bound by Hunter & Foulis Ltd, Edinburgh, Scotland.*

# CONTENTS

PREFACE                    vii

INTRODUCTION                 1

SELECT BIBLIOGRAPHY         20

## CALLIRHOE

    BOOK  1                28

    BOOK  2                84

    BOOK  3               132

    BOOK  4               190

    BOOK  5               230

    BOOK  6               280

    BOOK  7               324

    BOOK  8               360

INDEX                      415

MAP                   *follows* p. 7

# PREFACE

The absence of Chariton from the canon of the Loeb Classical Library has always been regrettable, and it was decided many years ago to remedy the omission. Unhappily, economic and other circumstances led to various delays and eventually the plan to include the author was, although never abandoned, for the time being suspended. When it was revived in 1993, the first proposal was simply to revise the edition and translation of W. E. Blake, taking account of new evidence and the considerable critical work that has been done since 1938. I quickly found, however, that far more changes were necessary than would befit a simple revision, and I therefore undertook to produce an entirely new edition and translation.

The need seemed all the greater in that texts of Chariton are few and rather inaccessible; for this reason I have included much information in the introduction, bibliography, and notes that in the case of better served authors would be unnecessary.

This edition has the aim, at once humble and ambitious, of presenting a synthesis of all that the best scholarship has achieved: it is heavily dependent on the editions of D'Orville, Hercher, and Blake; on the brilliancies of individual critics, notably Reiske, Cobet, and Jackson; and on the modern commentators whose works are listed in the bibliography.

But I must also acknowledge a number of personal debts. First, to Bryan Reardon for his encouragement and advice throughout, and for the indispensable help furnished by his books and articles and in particular his superb translation in *Collected Ancient Greek Novels*; to Christopher Jones, who made salutary criticisms of an early draft of the introduction; to Susan Stephens, who gave me the benefit of her insights and freely made available to me the proofs of her and Winkler's *Ancient Greek Novels: The Fragments*; to Paul G. Naiditch for a number of suggestions, which I have gratefully followed; to Kevin Goold for designing and executing the map; and to Margaretta Fulton and Philippa Goold for vigilant attention to the manuscript. But my greatest debt is to Tomas Hägg, who has contributed so much to our understanding of the Greek novel: he has given liberally of his time to this book, and I owe many a correction and improvement to him.

Finally, a special note. Most of the more than fifty conjectures of John Jackson accepted into the text will not be found in his remarkable article "The Greek Novelists." They (and accompanying *loci conferendi*) have been taken from among the three thousand marginalia which in an exquisitely minute but clear and beautiful hand Jackson entered into his copy of Hirschig's *Erotici Scriptores*. The volume was generously given me by my old friend Fred Schreiber when he learned I was preparing this edition, and he not least has my warmest thanks.

South Hadley, Massachusetts         G. P. GOOLD
January 1995

# CALLIRHOE

# INTRODUCTION

### *The Author's Date*

In his opening sentence, wherein he describes his theme as a *Love Story in Syracuse*, the author identifies himself as Chariton of Aphrodisias and his employer as Athenagoras. Of the author's identity nothing is known for certain: inscriptions containing his name and that of Athenagoras but telling us no more have been discovered on the modern site of Aphrodisias. Of the author's date, however, more can be said. At first, because of his pronounced differences from the other novelists (his work was the last major novel to come to light, editio princeps 1750), he was thought to be the latest. As a result Erwin Rohde, then the foremost authority on the Greek novel, stated that Chariton's work was "scarcely to be placed before the beginning of the sixth century [A.D.], at the very earliest in the closing years of the fifth" (p. 489 = p. 522[3]); but Wilhelm Schmid in an appendix to the third edition of Rohde (p. 610) dated it "at latest towards the end of the first century B.C."

This volte-face is correct, or essentially correct. The chief criterion confirming an early date is language. Chariton writes in an educated κοινή, showing no trace of that Atticist movement, begun in Cicero's time by such teachers as Caecilius of Caleacte and enthusiastically promoted by the early imperial schools and teachers of style,

INTRODUCTION

which culminated in the so-called Second Sophistic (second century A.D.). All the other extant Greek novelists are, chronologically, "sophistic": the earliest, Xenophon of Ephesus, refers to the office of irenarch instituted by Trajan, and his work is usually put at about A.D. 125. Of course, the change from κοινή to Atticist Greek was neither quick nor uniform; but it might be thought that a writer like Chariton, who was steeped in the classical authors and needed small encouragement to imitate their language, was more likely to learn of and follow the latest trends than St. Paul, for example. The most detailed investigation of his language, by Antonios Papanikolaou, agrees with Schmid in placing him no later than the second half of the first century B.C., while mention of Chinese arrows in 6.4.2 (see note *ad loc.*) rules out an earlier date.

But whether the dating of Chariton's Greek can be narrowed to fifty years is open to question; even among writers of the same generation one finds a considerable linguistic range, and this makes it difficult, without more comparative material than we possess, to chart the progress of *Atticismus* and locate Chariton within it. Moreover, Chariton's novel reflects less the Hellenistic society of Caria than that obtaining when Roman imperial influence was firmly established, and local law had been superseded by Roman (cf. Plepelits, p. 8); this scarcely happened much, if at all, before the triumvir Octavian could proclaim that of all the cities in the province of Asia Aphrodisias was the one he had chosen to be his own. Thus the range 25 B.C.–A.D. 50 would seem to fix more reliably, if imprecisely, the period within which *Callirhoe* is to be placed.

# INTRODUCTION

## His Popularity

The work, not artificially boosted by being prescribed in an academic curriculum, must have enjoyed a remarkable success. Two papyri of the second century, one of the third, and a parchment of the 6/7th prove a demand for copyists over some hundreds of years. Successful people are always targets for the envious, and the 66th of the *Letters* of Flavius Philostratus (born c. 170) consists of a curt sneer at the lowbrow Chariton: "You fancy that Greece is going to remember your work (λόγων) when you are dead; but what is likely to be the posthumous fate of men who were nobodies even while they were alive?" This is one of Philostratus' imaginary letters addressed to dead persons (cf. *Ep*. 65 to Epictetus and *Ep*. 72 to Caracalla) and initially would convince one that the addressee either was alive or had died in recent years. But Chariton's work had flourished for at least a century. It would seem, then, that the whole genre of light fiction rather than its most renowned exponent is the target of the gibe, and that the sophist is confidently saying "You and your like, Chariton, for all your popular appeal, will *never* be admitted to the select company of the Greek classics!"

## Title of the Novel

Here, too, an early presumption was to prove a stumbling block. The medieval manuscript gives the title as τῶν περὶ χαιρέαν καὶ καλλιρόην ἐρωτικῶν διηγη-μάτων (λόγοι) "The Love Story of Chaereas and Callirhoe," and so most editors. But two considerations might have provoked doubt. In both the opening and the

3

closing sentence of his work Chariton writes authorially in the first person, formally stating his identity and his theme; and the subscription, by its limitation to περὶ Καλλιρόης "of Callirhoe," strongly suggests that only Callirhoe was specified in the title. Another compelling reason emerges from the story, for, as will be discussed below, Callirhoe is the protagonist and does not in this share honors with Chaereas. In the event, clinching proof came from the Michailidis papyrus published in 1955, evidence older than what we had by rather more than a thousand years: this gave the title as τῶν περὶ Καλλιρόην διηγημάτων (λόγοι) "The Story of Callirhoe." One can see how the title was changed. Heliodorus ends his *Aethiopica* by referring to "Theagenes and Clariclea"; the manuscripts of Xenophon Ephesius specify "Anthia and Habrocomes"; Longus, "Daphnis and Chloe"; and Achilles Tatius, "Leucippe and Clitophon." It was natural, though mistaken, to bring Chariton into line with these. The heroine's name alone, on the other hand, better fits the earlier date now postulated, associating Chariton with Hellenistic love elegy and the stories in Parthenius' Ἐρωτικὰ παθήματα.

## Persius 1.134

In the light of the foregoing conclusions, that Chariton's *Callirhoe* was composed no later than the age of the Julio-Claudians and that for more than two centuries it enjoyed a wide circulation, a passage in the Roman satirist Persius now takes on a special significance. His first satire is a savage attack on popular light literature and in the last line (134) he contemptuously says of those who like such stuff: *his mane edictum, post prandia Calliroen do* "To them I recommend the morning's play-bill and after lunch *Callirhoe*." In the Loeb edition G. G. Ramsay explained *Callirhoe* as a "mawkish sentimental" composition, assuming that a poem must be meant. However, in line 13 Persius makes clear that his diatribe includes prose; and line 70 does not exclude Greek. It would be a fantastic coincidence if the satirist were not referring to Chariton's *Callirhoe*, which invites as much as any novel ever did the charge of being mawkish and sentimental. Unless we admit a fantastic coincidence, Persius' *Callirhoe* was none other than Chariton's. Possibly a copy of it had won a place in Persius' home (he lived with his mother, his sister, and his aunt). At all events, that *Callirhoe* had in Neronian Rome already achieved the status of a classic in light literature is guaranteed by the satirist's emphasis in climaxing his poem with this title, a title found nowhere else.

### Summary of the Story

*Book 1.* The main character, CALLIRHOE, represented as the most beautiful girl in the world, is the daughter of HERMOCRATES, ruler of Syracuse. She falls in love with and marries CHAEREAS, who is comparably handsome. But, his jealousy evilly aroused by disappointed suitors, he gives her a vicious kick which causes her apparent death. She is hastily buried. The pirate THERON robs her tomb and, finding Callirhoe alive, takes her aboard his ship; in Miletus he meets LEONAS, steward of the wealthy and eminent DIONYSIUS, and sells Callirhoe to him as a slave.

# INTRODUCTION

*Book 2.* Dionysius, who is in mourning for his wife, meets Callirhoe in a temple of Aphrodite on his estate and falls madly in love with her. His scruples prevent him from taking advantage of the girl, who is entrusted to the care of PLANGON, the wife of his estate manager. A crisis arises when Callirhoe is found to be pregnant. Abortion is considered, but Plangon eventually persuades Callirhoe to marry Dionysius and allow him to think that the child is his.

*Book 3.* Dionysius and Callirhoe are duly married. In Syracuse the tomb robbery is discovered. Coincidences lead to Theron's capture; he is brought to Syracuse, where he confesses at his trial and is crucified. With his friend POLYCHARMUS Chaereas goes to Miletus but is thwarted by PHOCAS, Plangon's husband, who causes Chaereas' ship to be attacked as piratical: Chaereas and Polycharmus are sold as slaves to MITHRIDATES, governor of Caria. From a deceitful account given her by Phocas, Callirhoe (who by this time has given birth to a son) believes Chaereas to be dead.

*Book 4.* Further to convince Callirhoe of Chaereas' death Dionysius holds funeral ceremonies for him and even builds a tomb. Mithridates, who has been invited, instantly falls in love with Callirhoe; on his return to Caria and discovering who Chaereas is, he persuades him to write a letter to Callirhoe. This falls into the hands of Dionysius, who, suspicious of Mithridates' intentions, appeals to ARTAXERXES, king of Persia. The king orders them both to Babylon for trial.

*Book 5.* Callirhoe's beauty creates a stir in Babylon and increases the excitement at the trial. Dionysius confidently accuses Mithridates of planning adultery and forging a letter from the supposedly dead Chaereas; but Mithridates is able to produce him alive, and is acquitted. Artaxerxes is left with the problem of ruling to which husband Callirhoe belongs, but defers a decision and meanwhile places her in the care of his queen STATIRA.

*Book 6.* But the king too has fallen desperately in love with Callirhoe, though like Dionysius he is prevented by his conscience from taking her by force. In this situation he employs the chief eunuch, ARTAXATES, to win her round. This functionary is egregiously unsuccessful, and the impasse has not been resolved when news arrives that Egypt is in revolt. The king marches off to war taking Statira, and thus Callirhoe also, with him. The loyal Dionysius accompanies him.

*Book 7.* Chaereas escapes to the Egyptians and is allowed to select and lead a small company of Greek mercenaries. With them he performs the incredible feat of capturing Tyre. Now he is given a naval command and captures Aradus, where Artaxerxes had, for safety, left Statira and her attendant Persian ladies. But he does not know that Callirhoe is among their number. On the Persian side Dionysius likewise distinguishes himself, so much so that Artaxerxes awards him Callirhoe for his prowess, the Egyptian army having been defeated and their monarch killed.

*Book 8.* (Here the author intervenes with an assurance that his story has a happy ending.) Chaereas quickly discovers Callirhoe among the captive women and the couple are finally reunited. Ending hostilities with Artaxerxes, he sends Statira back to him with an assurance that she has been treated like a queen, and generously settles his troops. Callirhoe contrives to write Dionysius a short

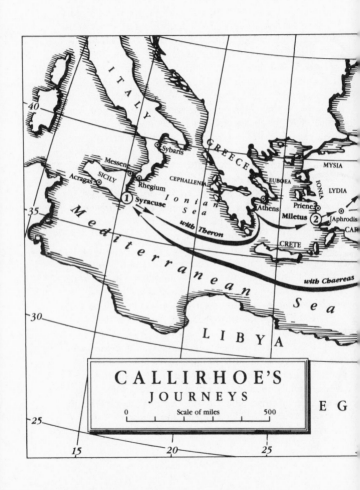

# CALLIRHOE'S
## JOURNEYS

0      Scale of miles      500

Caucasus mountains

Black Sea

Caspian Sea

Euphrates

route of Mithridates

ARMENIA

PERSIA N

RYGIA

Taurus mountains

MEDIA

Bactra 1000 miles

E M P I R E

CILICIA

SYRIA

with Dionysius

Tigris

⊙ Ecbatana

YPRUS

with Artaxerxes

hos ⊙

④ Aradus

Euphrates

Babylon ③

⊙ Susa

Sidon ⊙

COELE

Tyre ⊙

PHOENICIA

SYRIA

Pelusium

e delta

Memphis

A r a b i a n

Persian Gulf

d e s e r t

T

35

40

45

but touching letter, relinquishing her son to him (obviously the time has passed for telling him the child is not his own). Back in Syracuse Chaereas gives a report to the assembled citizens, and Callirhoe slips away to the temple of Aphrodite to give thanks.

## Ancient Light Fiction

The broad category to which *Callirhoe* belongs is more appropriately termed light fiction than popular fiction (as though it were an ancient counterpart of today's mass-produced paperback book). Popular it was, but it was a popularity restricted to the top stratum of society. *Callirhoe* cannot have circulated among the lower classes, who were illiterate, uneducated, and unable to afford the purchase of books. The Greek and Roman critics regarded this light fiction as beneath their professional notice, though for all we know they may have enjoyed it no less than some modern academics derive pleasure not only from reading detective stories but even writing them: there is no compelling reason to deny to the sophist Publius Hordeonius Lollianus authorship of the *Phoenicica*. Nevertheless, as a consequence of academic pride information about ancient light fiction is exiguous and largely limited to extant works, which comprise such diverse productions as those of Chariton, Petronius, Lucian, and Longus. Hitherto the fictional element in literature had been dignified by poetic composition, in epic and drama. But much earlier than any date that can be assigned to Chariton it took on and kept the form of prose. Not that we can point to any inauguration of prose fiction, still less of the novel. Elements we later find in

the Greek novelists are already discernible in the anec-
dotal Herodotus, Xenophon's largely imaginary portrait of
Cyrus—with its love story of Panthea and Abradates, and
Ctesias' fanciful history of Persia. A fragment of the last-
named (early 4th-century B.C.) published in 1954 (POxy
2330) reveals that the affair between Zarina, queen of the
Sacae, and the Median Struangarus is not history but historical romance, just like Chariton's *Callirhoe*.

The city of Miletus, which was well known to Chariton
and is likely to have been for him what Mediolanum was
for Virgil, gave its very name to a class of erotic tales, the
first known example of which is the *Milesiaca* of Aristides
(2nd century B.C.). The appeal of this work was great
enough for it to have been translated into Latin by the
historian Sisenna. (Let it be remarked that Sisennia was
the name of Persius' mother.) A copy of Sisenna's version,
which evidently enjoyed a vogue, was found in the baggage of a Roman officer at Carrhae (Plutarch, *Crassus*
32), and both from Plutarch and from Ovid (*Tristia* 2.413,
443) we learn that the *Milesiaca* were considered inde-
cent. It is doubtful, however, whether they differed much
from the stories retailed by Boccaccio and Chaucer. At
any rate Chariton, who must have known of this type of
prose fiction, quite likely reacted against it. But others
did not and, like the author of the *Iolaus* and Petronius
and Lollianus and Apuleius, were inspired to write about
low life, heroic and grotesque rascals, cult initiations and
magic, and blood-curdling adventures, set in a hard contemporary world. Nor can we simply divide popular
prose into the veristic and the ideal. There will have been
forerunners of utopian fantasy like Antonius Diogenes'
*Marvels beyond Thule* and of hagiography as exemplified

in such diverse works as *Secundus the Silent Philosopher*, Philostratus' *Life of Apollonius of Tyana*, and the much later Christian *Barlaam and Ioasaph*.

## The Historical Element in Chariton

*Callirhoe* differs most obviously from these tales of realism on the one hand and of wild imaginings on the other by being a historical novel (and in this it differs sharply from the novels of the second century). Indeed, all our earliest novels are framed in a historical setting. Foremost is the *Alexander Romance*, fictitiously attributed to Callisthenes and going back to a second century B.C. source. The *Ninus* fragments, perhaps as early as 100 B.C., deal with the love story of the Assyrian prince who founded Nineveh and Semiramis, queen of Babylon; and the author of the *Metiochus and Parthenope* fragment, possibly to be dated in the first century B.C., set his plot at the court of Polycrates in Samos.

Chariton is certainly at pains to fit his story into the glorious past and to associate his characters with persons of eminence; and it looks as if he has attempted to weave a plot out of events which took place in high society at Syracuse.

His heroine is unambiguously identified as the daughter of Hermocrates, the Sicilian statesman who contributed much to the Athenian defeat in 413; Chariton calls her Callirhoe (Lady Lovely Stream), no doubt unhistorically. Hermocrates' daughter did indeed marry a Dionysius (Dionysius I), who shortly after Hermocrates' death in 407 ruled Syracuse from 405 to 367; and he in turn was succeeded not by any Chaereas but by his son,

Dionysius II. This may explain Callirhoe's otherwise inexplicable abandonment of her baby son to Dionysius' care and the suggestion that he would one day succeed his grandfather in Syracuse (3.8.8). Moreover, the real "Callirhoe" never recovered from the vicious assault made on her (not by her husband, but by mutineers), but fades out of history (Plutarch, *Dion* 3.2, says that she committed suicide). Converting her actual death into an apparent one enabled Chariton to resurrect her for adventures abroad just as Euripides resurrected Iphigenia for his Tauric drama. Now while the motif of apparent death (*Scheintod*) is timeless and universal in storytelling, we need to realize that it was forced on Chariton (as on Euripides) by the fixity of the historical material he was working on. The later novelists eagerly borrowed this motif from Chariton without any historical dilemma to prompt it. In the hands of Achilles Tatius and Heliodorus *Scheintod* becomes a conjuring trick and serves only to provide sensational melodrama.

The Persian king has a secure basis in history. Artaxerxes is none other than he of Xenophon's *Anabasis* (1.1.1), whose brother Cyrus rose against him immediately on his accession in 404; he held the throne until his death in 358. Plutarch confirms both the name and the beauty and nobility of his wife, Statira (*Artaxerxes* 5.3; 2.2). But it is the historical romancer Ctesias on whom Chariton has principally drawn for his oriental personages: the names of Rhodogune (5.3.4), Megabyzus and Zopyrus (*ib.*), and Pharnaces (4.1.7) all occur in Book 17 of the *Persica*, where we also meet the King's Paphlagonian eunuch Artaxares (manifestly the model for Artaxates, 5.2.2); and Book 19 tells us that Mithridates, also a historical figure, was appointed satrap (governor) at the insistence of Statira. Even Theron, the villain of the piece, was conceivably a man of flesh and blood, being referred to by Apuleius as a famous criminal (see note on 1.7.1).

The Egyptian revolt against Artaxerxes which brings about the conclusion of the novel bears a striking resemblance to that recorded by Diodorus (15.92) and Cornelius Nepos (12.2): the hero was in real life not Chaereas but Chabrias, an Athenian who was in fact entrusted with the Egyptian naval command. The date (361) is forty years later than fits the novel's chronology, and Chaereas' storming of Tyre is even later, for it can only correspond to Alexander's siege of that city in 332.

Accordingly it is impossible to insist on a precise literary-historical equation, though one may in a loose sense suggest that the dramatic date of the novel is set in the last few years of the fifth century. What is significant is that, while Chariton required a background of historical events for his characters, the background had to fit the characters, not vice versa, and that he was prepared to adapt the record drastically to secure what he wanted.

## The Theme of the Novel

Chariton's theme, however, is not historical at all; it is a love story. While the historical background is essential and performs the important function of providing a background of famous persons, places, and events, it is the fictional element which is paramount; the fictional nature of the work is emphasized by all sorts of fanciful and even amusing exaggerations, and the frequent quotations from Homer (carefully chosen to illustrate the context) help to distance the characters from contemporary reality by clothing them in a mantle of epic grandeur. This is taken further by the allusions to Herodotus, Thucydides, Xenophon, and Demosthenes, which serve to furnish intertextual décor, forcing the reader to date the action of the novel to a bygone age of classical Greece. Just so does Shakespeare in *A Midsummer Night's Dream* enhance his tale of Elizabethan life by locating it in legendary Athens.

The story of *Callirhoe*, as opposed to its setting, is rather akin to the subject matter of New Comedy, and the action, as in those plays, springs from the effects of love upon the various characters (who seem themselves not so much aristocrats as members of middle-class society): the unpredictable whims of Fortune repeatedly foil a natural outcome and lead the cast into strange and complicated situations. Indeed, Chariton's style is less a narrative than a dramatic one: we are not so much told how the characters act as hear them speak (and think) in the course of their actions. No less than 40 percent of the work consists of direct speech, and an equal amount is taken up with setting the stage, as it were. For example, we eavesdrop on Theron and his accomplices deliberating what to do with Callirhoe (1.10); we are told of her conflicting emotions about her pregnancy not by the narrator but by herself in a soliloquy (2.11); Chaereas' last-minute rescue from the cross could have been narrated without any loss of excitement, but instead we learn of it in a dialogue between Polycharmus and Mithridates (4.2.8–4.3). The most thrilling passage in the whole work is the trial scene (5.6ff): we listen to Dionysius and Mithridates delivering their speeches and fairly gasp when Chaereas is resurrected; tension rises to a climax with the angry thrust and parry between him and Dionysius, surely the prose counterpart of tragic stichomythia. Says the author himself (5.8.2): "What dramatist ever staged such an extraordinary situation? You would have thought you were in a theater filled with every conceivable emotion." Some scholars have even attempted to recast the novel in the five acts of a Menandrian drama, but this is precisely to undo what Chariton has done. He has, moreover, deliberately broken away from a dramatic mold by articulating his work in eight parts, not five.

The novel is appropriately called after the heroine, for through her beauty and character Callirhoe controls the whole action. Indeed, it is tempting to regard the novel less as a love story than as a female character study; viewed in this light, *Callirhoe* is the original precursor of Richardson's *Pamela* and *Clarissa* (note the use Chariton makes of the text of letters—not that he dreamed of the lengths to which this device would one day be taken). The men she meets all fall in love with her, bringing about situations which reveal and test every facet of her character. Chaereas is not a satisfactory hero, for in the first half of the work he is culpably intemperate and given to self-pity, while in the second his war exploits are too fantastic and out of character to be other than those of a cardboard Alexander; Dionysius is not only a worthier husband, he is a credible one; even Artaxerxes is convincingly and not unsympathetically portrayed.

## Chariton and His Successors

Historical inconsistencies and difficulties with characterization support the notion, which the absence of contrary indications tends to confirm, that Chariton is a pioneer in a new genre that has yet to acquire a definite

shape. His extravagance in description, whether of Callirhoe's beauty, the lovesickness of her admirers, Theron's
villainy, or anything which diverges from the norm, suggests an enthusiastic innovator (he is hardly writing farce:
his love story is serious from beginning to end); and he is
inexperienced in or has poor models for plot construc-
tion, being too ready to employ Fortune to initiate actions
which had been better brought about through the natural
promptings of an individual's character. We should therefore not be surprised that his successors in prose
romance, while preserving many features of his work,
have discarded the historical upholstery and introduced
innovations of their own. They all fall within the second
century, excepting Heliodorus, who wrote in the late
fourth. Xenophon of Ephesus, a slavish imitator, contrives that after their wedding his couple is also separated: we meet with pirates, *Scheintod*, a similar itinerary
over the Mediterranean, the near crucifixion of Abro-
comes and the real crucifixion of Cyno, and of course the
final reunion of husband and wife. The exigencies of
Chariton's plot demanded that Callirhoe deliberately for-
feit her sexual fidelity to Chaereas: in Xenophon no such
violation is permitted, and perhaps for that very reason
numerous—but unsuccessful—attempts are mounted on
the virtue of hero and heroine (Anthia is for a time kept in
a brothel). In the novels after Chariton this principle is
hardly ever broken: once in Achilles, where as a means to
recovering Leucippe Clitophon allows himself to be
seduced by Melite, and once in Longus (by Daphnis—
and the plot practically compelled this), whose depiction
of the sexual maturation of two young shepherds in Les-
bos is altogether unlike anything else we have.

To pass over the *Babyloniaca* of Iamblichus, of which

15

we possess only the summary of Photius and which seems to conform to the pattern of Xenophon, the works of Achilles Tatius and Heliodorus mark a distinct development not only in an access of fantastic adventure and flamboyant rhetoric but also in the fundamental device of separating hero and heroine before marriage, so that after harrowing vicissitudes they may be united at the end. By universal agreement the *Aethiopica* of Heliodorus, which approaches Dickensian dimensions and contains the finest techniques of storytelling, marks the highest achievement of the Greek novel.

In spite of its strong appeal ancient fiction did not rise above escapist literature; neither the historical nor the romantic novel established itself as a serious genre until an age much closer to our own. Even so, the demands made by Chariton on his readers, in whom he assumed an extensive familiarity with history, geography, and classical literature, as well as the ability to appreciate his fastidious language and his artfully contrived dramatic ironies, would be inexplicable if he wrote for the unlettered or composed merely for a single performance. Like Petronius, he aimed less at impressing his audience than at entertaining it. But for all that there is no hint that he looked down on it or sought less than lasting applause.

## The Text

Chariton is preserved in a single medieval manuscript, but fragments covering just under 6 percent of the text exist in one ancient palimpsest and in three papyri.

F: Codex Florentinus Laur. Conv. Soppr. 627, saec. 13, parchment: *entire*

T: Codex Thebanus, saec. 6/7, parchment: 8.5.9–8.7.3, except for 8.6.1–8 (*see below*), published 1901

$\Pi^1$: Papyrus Fayûmensis 1, saec. 2: 4.2.3–4.3.2 (*fragments*), published 1900

$\Pi^2$: Papyrus Oxyrynchica 1019: 2.3.5–2.4.2 (*fragments*), published 1910; and another part of the same document in POxy 2948, saec. 3: 2.4.5–2.5.1 (*fragments*), published 1972

$\Pi^3$: Papyri Michaelidae 1, saec. 2: 2.11.4–2.11.6 (*fragments*), published 1955

The Florentinus, which also contains Xenophon of Ephesus, Longus, and Achilles Tatius (as far as 4.4.4), was collated in 1725 by Antonio Salvini and again in 1727–28 by Antonio Cocchi; upon their reports (preserved at Leiden) the editio princeps of D'Orville is based. But the manuscript had badly faded, and for his collation of 1843 (also preserved at Leiden) C. G. Cobet used chemicals which have now impaired legibility; the first folio can no longer be read.

Incredibly, none of "The Overtrustful Editors of Chariton" (Blake) ever saw the Florentinus; they relied on the collations specified above. Only with Blake's edition was a reliable account of its readings made available. As first the Thebanus and then the Fayûmensis provided an external check on its text, the quality of the manuscript seemed remarkably good, but later papyri have discredited this rating; the most recent opinion, that of Christina Lucke, is distinctly negative. In any case, F's text is from first book to last pockpitted, to use Jackson's apt word, with haplographies and omissions of the kind 1.1.13 ταύτην <τὴν>, 8.1.3 τό<δε> δεινὸν, and 2.1.4 δέδωκα

17

<. . . -δέδωκε>. Recent decades have sharpened sensitivity to Chariton's language and rhythms; Reeve, for example, using the avoidance of hiatus as a critical tool, has indicated many passages where F is probably corrupt. Further erosion of confidence in F has been caused by the realization that the romantic novels are among those texts which scribes felt at liberty to alter the wording of as they went along (see Reeve, *Longus*, Teubner edition, 1982, p. xi note 7 with other references). The Codex Thebanus (Chariton erased under a Coptic text) was discovered in 1898: for a preliminary transcript Ulrich Wilcken confined himself to deciphering only the flesh side of the parchment, and this is all that survives, for by an unfortunate accident the palimpsest itself was destroyed in a fire on the docks at Hamburg. Wilcken's preliminary transcript, however, is preserved. All agree, however, that while T corrects F on several occasions and gives the correct spelling of Καλλιρόη and Συρακόσιοι (-ρρ- and -ρρακουσ- F throughout), it purveys a capricious text much inferior to F's.

The papyri, on the other hand, provide a larger number of correct readings than F for the portions of the text they cover, though it must be acknowledged that F is occasionally right where they are wrong. But one new reading is of paramount importance, namely the colophon given by the Michailidis at the end of Book 2: this settles the true title of Chariton's novel.

The text here presented embodies my own choice of readings, but in orthographical detail it adheres closely to F and therefore must necessarily often differ from what Chariton intended. It seems in the highest degree unlikely that one who took such pains to avoid hiatus should wish in thousands of places, *but not everywhere*, to employ scriptio plena, writing at 2.5.4 ἐπεὶ δὲ ἧκεν but at 5.1.3 ὡς δ' ἧκεν, at 1.7.1 ἀλλὰ ἐγώ but at 2.9.2 ἀλλ' ἐγώ. One can conceive that he wrote at 1.9.2 ἑκκαίδεκα and at 4.2.5 ἑξκαίδεκα; that at 1.8.3 and elsewhere he wrote ἐδύνατο but at 2.1.7 and elsewhere ἠδύνατο; even that he wrote πράττειν 19 times but πράσσειν once, θάλασσα 69 times but θάλαττα once, and that he fluctuated inconsistently between various other such alternatives. However, when the authority for such minutiae is a manuscript as unreliable as F, it would be absurd to insist on their correctness. Nevertheless, though tempted to do so, I have refrained from standardizing the text. In the case of Chariton this prerogative belongs to the scholar who next produces a full-scale critical edition.

The textual notes in this volume do not aspire to take the place of an apparatus criticus. But they serve to warn the reader when the text of the Florentinus has been rejected in favor of other readings—except that, to save space, I generally give no note when a slight emendation of F's text has won acceptance from Hercher onwards. However, the testimony of the ancient witnesses (unavailable of course to Hercher and his predecessors) calls for a different treatment: I have given a reasonably full account, even including the vagaries of the Theban palimpsest. Finally, at the cost of some disfigurement of the text, I consistently use square brackets when indicating words deemed to be interpolated in F and angle brackets when indicating words deemed to be omitted from it.

# SELECT BIBLIOGRAPHY

Wilhelm Schmid: "Chariton" in Paulys *Real-Encyclopädie der classischen Altertumswissenschaft* III 2 (1899) 2168–2171.

## Editions

J. P. D'Orville: ΧΑΡΙΤΩΝΟΣ Αφροδισιέως τῶν περὶ ΧΑΙΡΕΑΝ καὶ ΚΑΛΛΙΡΡΟΗΝ ΕΡΩΤΙΚΩΝ ΔΙΗΓΗΜΑΤΩΝ ΛΟΓΟΙ Η, Amsterdam 1750. The editio princeps. Between the Greek text and close on 800 pages of erudite adversaria (many on the *Apotelesmatica* of Manetho) come several pages of emendations and a Latin translation by J. J. Reiske.

——— second edition, augmented by critical notes of Abresch, Pierson, and the editor, C. D. Beck, Leipzig 1783.

W. A. Hirschig: *Erotici Scriptores* (Didot edition, with Latin translations, reprinting Reiske's for Chariton), Paris 1856. Also contains P(arthenius), A(chilles) T(atius), L(ongus), X(enophon Ephesius), H(eliodorus), A(ntonius) D(iogenes), I(amblichus), *A(pollonius) of T(yre)*, E(ustathius) M(acrembolites), and N(icetas) E(ugenianus).

R. Hercher: *Erotici Scriptores Graeci* (Vol. 2, Teubner),

Leipzig 1859. Besides Chariton, contains EM, Theo-
dorus Prodromus, NE, and Constantinus Manasses
(Vol. 1 [1858] contains P, AT, I, L, and X).

Warren E. Blake: *Charitonis Aphrodisiensis De Chaerea
et Callirhoe Amatoriarum Narrationum libri octo*,
Oxford 1938. The first critical edition; records all conjectures known to the editor.

Georges Molinié: *Chariton, Le Roman de Chairéas et
Callirhoé* (Budé edition), Paris 1979. Contains introduction, text with apparatus, facing French translation
with brief notes, index, and map. Second edition, cor-
rected by A. Billault, 1989.


*Translations*

(English) Warren E. Blake: *Chariton's Chaereas and Callirhoe*, Ann Arbor 1939. The first English translation to
be made directly from the Greek.

—————— B. P. Reardon (editor and himself the translator of
Chariton): *Collected Ancient Greek Novels*, Berkeley
and Los Angeles 1989. Contains also translation of X,
AT, L, H, Ps(eudo)-Luc(ian), Luc(ian: *Vera Historia*),
Pseudo-Callisthenes, *A of T*; AD and I; and all that is
readable in the papyrus fragments published to date
(*N[inus]*, Loll[ianus: *Phoenicica*], *M[etiochus] and
P[arthenope]*, *Iol[aus]*, *Ses[onchosis]*, *Herp[yllis]*,
*Ch[ione]*, and *Callig[one]*). This work, each section of
which contains its own introduction, bibliography, and
explanatory footnotes, is an indispensable reference
work for all students of the ancient Greek novel.

(French) Pierre Grimal (editor): *Romans Grecs et Latins*
(Bibliothèque de la Pléiade), Paris 1958. Another col-

lection of translations (with introductions, brief notes, and maps): comprises Petr(onius), Ap(uleius), Chariton, H, L, AT, Philostratus (*Life of Apollonius of Tyana*), Luc, and the *Confession of St. Cyprian*.

———— See Molinié's Budé edition, above.

(German) Karl Plepelits: *Chariton von Aphrodisias, Kallirhoe: eingeleitet, übersetzt und erläutert*, Stuttgart 1976. The first work to give the correct title of Chariton's novel.

———— Bernhard Kytzler (editor): *Im Reiche des Eros* (2 vols), Munich 1983. Another collection of translations: vol. 1 comprises L, X, *A of T*, H, and (tr. H. M. Werhahn) Chariton; vol. 2, Petr, AT, Ap, Ps-Luc, Luc; selections from utopian novels (Euhemerus, Theopompus, Hecataeus, Iambulus, AD, I); and fragments (*N*, *M and P*, *Ch*, *Iol*, AD, *Callig*, *Herp*, and Loll).

———— Christina Lucke and Karl-Heinz Schäfer: *Chariton: Callirhoe* (Reclams Universal-Bibliothek 1101), Leipzig 1985: translation, postscript by Heinrich Kuch (serves as introduction), annotations, notes on the textual tradition, a concordance of readings with Blake's text, bibliography; includes 20 one-page line drawings by Wolfgang Teucher of scenes in the novel.

(Italian) Aristide Calderini: *Caritone de Afrodisia: Le Avventure di Cherea e Calliroe*, with extensive *Prolegomeni* (pp. 1–227, a treatise on the Greek romance), Turin 1913.

———— Quintino Cataudella (editor): *Il romanzo classico* (Edizioni Casini), another collection of translations with brief notes and 47 plates: comprises *N*, AD, Chariton (translated by Renzo Nuti), X, I, Luc, Ps-Luc, AT, L, H; and Petr, Ap, and *A of T*. Second edition (*Il romanzo antico greco e latino*), Florence 1973.

# SELECT BIBLIOGRAPHY

(Spanish) Julia Mendoza: *Quéreas y Calírroe* (Biblioteca Clásica Gredos 16), Madrid 1979.

## Text and Transmission

C. G. Cobet: "Annotationes Criticae ad Charitonem," *Mnemosyne* 8 (1859) 229–303. The most gifted Greek scholar ever to deal with Chariton.

S. Heibges: *De clausulis Charitoneis*, Diss. Halle, 1911. Preferred clausulae are (rounded percentages given, with a bracketed figure which includes resolutions): – ⏑ – × = 21 (35); – ⏑ – – × = 18 (26); – ⏑ – – ⏑ × = 7 (21); – ⏑ – ⏑ × = 3 (16). Furnishes a wealth of detail on questions of prosody and cola.

Warren E. Blake: "The Overtrustful Editors of Chariton," *Transactions of the American Philological Association* 62 [1931] 68–77.

John Jackson: "The Greek Novelists," *Classical Quarterly* 29 (1935) 52–57, 96–112. (See Eduard Fraenkel's tribute to Jackson in the latter's posthumous *Marginalia Scaenica*, Oxford 1955.)

M. D. Reeve: "Hiatus in the Greek Novelists," *Classical Quarterly* 21 (1971) 514–539. Determines the nature and circumstances of hiatus in the Greek novelists, shows that Chariton sought to avoid it, and lists all the questionable instances of it in his text.

Antonios Dem. Papanikolaou: *Chariton-Studien: Untersuchungen zur Sprache und Chronologie der griechischen Romane* (Hypomnemata 57), Göttingen 1973. A valuable detailed study. Concludes that Chariton's language is that of the middle or the second half of the first century B.C. and that his work predates Xenophon of Ephesus.

Christina Lucke: "Zum Charitontext auf Papyrus," *Zeitschrift für Papyrologie und Epigraphik* 58 (1985) 21–33. Examines in detail the readings of the three papyri (which cover just under 4 percent of Chariton) and concludes that in the absence of a papyrus control the codex F is likely to be corrupt rather more frequently than has hitherto been suspected.

*Literary*

Erwin Rohde: *Der griechische Roman und seine Vorläufer*, Leipzig (1876[1], 1900[2] seen through the press by Fritz Schöll), 1914[3] with supplementary survey and notes by Wilhelm Schmid. A monumental work of great erudition, still indispensable, but requiring significant modification in the light of papyrus finds and subsequent studies. (1960[4] with an appreciation of Rohde by K. Kerényi; Darmstadt, 1974[5].)

Ben Edwin Perry: "Chariton and His Romance from a Literary-Historical Point of View," *American Journal of Philology* 51 (1930) 93–134. Preliminary to and subsumed in the following work.

———— *The Ancient Romances: A Literary-Historical Account of their Origins* (Sather Classical Lectures 37), Berkeley and Los Angeles 1967. A valuable corrective to Rohde's speculations, treating the romantic novel from the Ninus-fragment to Richardson and Fielding. Chapter 3 (pp. 96–148) deals with "Chariton and the Nature of Greek Romance."

Reinhold Merkelbach: *Roman und Mysterium in der Antike*, Munich 1962. Holds that the Greek novel developed from mystery religions (Isis, Mithras, Dionysus), a view difficult to reconcile with *Callirhoe*, though the attempt was made by his pupil R. Petri (*Ueber den Roman des Chariton*, Meisenheim/Glan 1963).

Tomas Hägg: *Narrative Technique in Ancient Greek Romances: Studies of Chariton, Xenophon Ephesius, and Achilles Tatius*, Stockholm 1971.

—— *The Novel in Antiquity*, Oxford, Berkeley and Los Angeles 1983. Nonpareil. Introduces nonclassicists to the ancient novel (taking in Byzantine times and the Renaissance). Contains 79 illustrations (including a full-page reproduction of a 1775 engraving of the reunited Chaereas and Callirhoe described in Chariton 8.1).

—— "*Callirhoe* and *Parthenope*: The Beginnings of the Historical Novel," *Classical Antiquity* 6 (1987) 184–204.

B. P. Reardon: *Courants littéraires grecs des IIe et IIIe siècles après J.-C.*, Paris 1971, and particularly part 3, chapter 3 (pp. 309–403) "Le roman." The Greek novels in their literary context.

—— "Theme, Structure and Narrative in Chariton," *Yale Classical Studies* 27 (1982) 1–27.

—— *The Form of Greek Romance*, Princeton 1991. An attempt to analyze the genre in terms of ancient literary theory. With extensive bibliography.

Gareth L. Schmeling: *Chariton* (Twayne's World Authors Series), New York 1974. A fine introduction to Chariton and ancient prose fiction (principally addressed to the Greekless).

C. W. Müller: "Chariton von Aphrodisias und die Theorie des Romans in der Antike," *Antike und Abendland* 22 (1976) 115–136.

25

## SELECT BIBLIOGRAPHY

Graham Anderson: *Eros Sophistes: Ancient Novelists at Play* (American Classical Studies, Number 9), Chico 1982. The element of humor in the ancient novelists.

——— *Ancient Fiction: The Novel in the Graeco-Roman World*, London and Sydney 1984. Themes found in earlier oriental texts.

M.-F. Baslez, P. Hoffmann, M. Trédé (editors): *Le monde du roman grec* (Etudes de littérature ancienne 4), Paris 1992. A collection of 28 papers given at a 1987 colloquium: includes Christopher P. Jones, "La personnalité de Chariton," pp. 161–167 and Marie-Françoise Baslez, "De l'histoire au roman: la Perse de Chariton," pp. 199–212.

### Other

*Thesaurus Linguae Graecae: An Alphabetical Keyword-in-context Concordance to the Greek Novelists* (on microfiche), *TLG* Publications VIII, Irvine 1980.

Kenan T. Erim: *Aphrodisias: City of Venus Aphrodite*, introduction by John Julius Norwich, New York 1986. Sumptuously illustrated with color photographs, this volume vividly brings to life Chariton's native city and also its excavator, who died prematurely in 1990.

Susan A. Stephens and John J. Winkler (edd.): *Ancient Greek Novels: The Fragments* (introduction, text, translation, and commentary), Princeton 1995. Part I (novel fragments) includes *N*, *M and P*, AD (to which *Herp* may belong), I, *Ses*, *Callig*, *Anthea*, *Ch*, Loll, *Iol*, and *Daulis*; Part II contains ambiguous fragments.

ΧΑΡΙΤΩΝΟΣ ΑΦΡΟΔΙΣΙΕΩΣ
ΤΑ ΠΕΡΙ ΚΑΛΛΙΡΟΗΝ ΔΙΗΓΗΜΑΤΑ

CHARITON OF APHRODISIAS
THE STORY OF CALLIRHOE

---

τῶν περὶ κα[λλιρόην] διηγημάτω[ν λόγος β'] P³, colophon to
Book 2 (cf. the author's own colophon, 8.8.16: τόσαδε περὶ Καλλιρόης συνέγραψα): τῶν περὶ χαιρέαν καὶ καλλιρρόην ἐρωτικῶν διηγημάτων λόγος α' F, before Book 1 (and similarly
before the other books).

# A

1. Χαρίτων Ἀφροδισιεύς, Ἀθηναγόρου τοῦ ῥήτορος ὑπογραφεύς, πάθος ἐρωτικὸν ἐν Συρακούσαις γενόμενον διηγήσομαι.

Ἑρμοκράτης ὁ Συρακοσίων στρατηγός, οὗτος ὁ νικήσας Ἀθηναίους, εἶχε θυγατέρα Καλλιρόην τοὔνομα, θαυμαστόν τι χρῆμα παρθένου καὶ ἄγαλμα τῆς ὅλης Σικελίας. ἦν γὰρ τὸ κάλλος οὐκ ἀνθρώπινον ἀλλὰ θεῖον, οὐδὲ Νηρηΐδος ἢ Νύμφης τῶν ὀρειῶν ἀλλ᾽ αὐτῆς Ἀφροδίτης [παρθένου]. φήμη δὲ τοῦ παραδόξου θεάματος πανταχοῦ διέτρεχε καὶ μνηστῆρες κατέρρεον εἰς Συρακούσας, δυνάσται τε καὶ παῖδες τυράννων, οὐκ ἐκ Σικελίας μόνον, ἀλλὰ καὶ ἐξ Ἰταλίας καὶ ἠπείρου καὶ ἐθνῶν τῶν ἐν ἠπείρῳ. ὁ δὲ Ἔρως ζεῦγος ἴδιον ἠθέλησε συμπλέξαι. Χαιρέας γάρ τις ἦν μειράκιον εὔμορφον, πάντων ὑπερέχον, οἷον Ἀχιλλέα καὶ Νιρέα καὶ

---

1.1 Συρακούσαις, Συρακοσίων Cobet: Συρρακούσαις, Συρρακουσίων F consistently |
Καλλιρόην Blake: Καλλιρρόην F consistently.
1.2 del. Hercher (intrusion from 1.1).

# BOOK 1

1. I, Chariton of Aphrodisias,[a] clerk of the lawyer Athenagoras, am going to relate a love story which took place in Syracuse.

Hermocrates, ruler of Syracuse, victor over the Athenians,[b] had a daughter named Callirhoe, a marvel of a girl and the idol of all Sicily. In fact her beauty was not so much human as divine, not that of a Nereid or mountain nymph, either, but of Aphrodite herself. Reports of this incredible vision spread far and wide: suitors came pouring into Syracuse, potentates and princes, not only from Sicily, but from Italy,[c] the continent,[d] and the peoples of the continent. But Love[e] wanted to make a match of his own devising. Now there was a certain youth named Chaereas, whose handsomeness surpassed all, resembling the statues and pictures of Achilles and Nireus[f] and Hip-

---

[a] In identifying himself in the opening sentence Chariton follows the lead of Herodotus and Thucydides.

[b] In 413 B.C.; alluded to 1.1.13, 1.11.2, and elsewhere.

[c] I.e. Magna Graecia.

[d] Referring to the Balkan peninsula.

[e] Eros in Greek (Latin Cupid), Aphrodite's child, and represented as her ever-active agent.

[f] The handsomest of the Greeks at Troy after Achilles (Homer, *Iliad* 2.673f).

29

Ἱππόλυτον καὶ Ἀλκιβιάδην πλάσται τε καὶ γραφεῖς
ἀποδεικνύουσι, πατρὸς Ἀρίστωνος τὰ δεύτερα ἐν
Συρακούσαις μετὰ Ἑρμοκράτην φερομένου. καί τις
ἦν ἐν αὐτοῖς πολιτικὸς φθόνος ὥστε θᾶττον ἂν
4 πᾶσιν ἢ ἀλλήλοις ἐκήδευσαν. φιλόνεικος δέ ἐστιν ὁ
Ἔρως καὶ χαίρει τοῖς παραδόξοις κατορθώμασιν·
ἐζήτησε δὲ τοιόνδε τὸν καιρόν.

Ἀφροδίτης ἑορτὴ δημοτελὴς <ἦν>, καὶ πᾶσαι
5 σχεδὸν αἱ γυναῖκες ἀπῆλθον εἰς τὸν νεών. τέως δὲ
μὴ προϊοῦσαν τὴν Καλλιρόην προήγαγεν ἡ μήτηρ,
<Ἔρωτος> κελεύσαντος προσκυνῆσαι τὴν θεόν.
τότε δὲ Χαιρέας ἀπὸ τῶν γυμνασίων ἐβάδιζεν
οἴκαδε στίλβων ὥσπερ ἀστήρ· ἐπήνθει γὰρ αὐτοῦ
τῷ λαμπρῷ τοῦ προσώπου τὸ ἐρύθημα τῆς παλαί-
6 στρας ὥσπερ ἀργύρῳ χρυσός. ἐκ τύχης οὖν περί
τινα καμπὴν στενοτέραν συναντῶντες περιέπεσον
ἀλλήλοις, τοῦ θεοῦ πολιτευσαμένου τήνδε τὴν συν-
οδίαν ἵνα ἑκάτερος τῷ ἑτέρῳ ὀφθῇ. ταχέως οὖν
πάθος ἐρωτικὸν ἀντέδωκαν ἀλλήλοις ....... τοῦ
κάλλους τῇ εὐγενείᾳ συνελθόντος.

7 Ὁ μὲν οὖν Χαιρέας οἴκαδε μετὰ τοῦ τραύματος
μόλις ἀπῄει, καὶ ὥσπερ τις ἀριστεὺς ἐν πολέμῳ
τρωθεὶς καιρίαν, καὶ καταπεσεῖν μὲν αἰδούμενος,
στῆναι δὲ μὴ δυνάμενος. ἡ δὲ παρθένος τῆς Ἀφροδίτης τοῖς ποσὶ προσέπεσε καὶ καταφιλοῦσα, "σύ
μοι, δέσποινα" εἶπε, "δὸς ἄνδρα τοῦτον ὃν ἔδειξας."
8 νὺξ ἐπῆλθεν ἀμφοτέροις δεινή· τὸ γὰρ πῦρ ἐξεκαίετο. δεινότερον δ' ἔπασχεν ἡ παρθένος διὰ τὴν

polytus and Alcibiades. His father was Ariston,[a] second
only to Hermocrates in Syracuse. There was a political
rivalry between the two, so fierce that they would have
made a family alliance with anyone sooner than with each
other. However, Love likes winning and enjoys unexpected triumphs, and he was looking for such just a
chance as the following.

There was a public feast of Aphrodite, and almost
every woman had gone to her temple. Callirhoe had not
appeared in public before, but at the prompting of Love
her mother took her to do homage to the goddess. Just
then Chaereas was walking home from the gymnasium,
radiant as a star. The flush of exercise bloomed on his
beaming face like gold on silver. As chance would have it,
the two walked headlong into each other at the corner of
a narrow intersection—a meeting contrived by the god to
make sure that they saw each other. They fell in love at
first sight: . . . beauty had been matched with nobility.

So smitten, Chaereas could barely make his way home;
like a hero mortally wounded in battle, he was too proud
to fall but too weak to stand. As for the girl, she fell at the
feet of Aphrodite and, kissing them, said, "Lady, give me
as my husband this man you have shown me." The ensuing night brought torment to both, for love's fire was rag-
ing. But the girl's suffering was worse, for she had to keep

[a] Presumably based on the historical Ariston of Corinth,
whose conduct in the battle against the Athenians is given honorable mention by Thucydides, 7.39.2.

---

1.4 add. Richards.
1.5 add. Gerschmann.
1.6 The gap (of 7 letters) is illegible in the manuscript.

σιωπήν, αἰδουμένη κατάφωρος γενέσθαι. Χαιρέας δὲ
νεανίας εὐφυὴς καὶ μεγαλόφρων, ἤδη τοῦ σώματος
αὐτῷ φθίνοντος, ἀπετόλμησεν εἰπεῖν πρὸς τοὺς
γονεῖς ὅτι ἐρᾷ καὶ οὐ βιώσεται τοῦ Καλλιρόης
9 γάμου μὴ τυχών. ἐστέναξεν ὁ πατὴρ ἀκούσας καὶ
"οἴχῃ δή μοι, τέκνον" <ἔφη>· "δῆλον γάρ ἐστιν ὅτι
Ἑρμοκράτης οὐκ ἂν δοίη σοὶ τὴν θυγατέρα
τοσούτους ἔχων μνηστῆρας πλουσίους καὶ βασιλεῖς. οὔκουν οὐδὲ πειρᾶσθαί σε δεῖ, μὴ φανερῶς
ὑβρισθῶμεν." εἶθ' ὁ μὲν πατὴρ παρεμυθεῖτο τὸν
παῖδα, τῷ δὲ ηὔξετο τὸ κακὸν ὥστε μηδὲ ἐπὶ τὰς
10 συνήθεις προϊέναι διατριβάς. ἐπόθει δὲ τὸ γυμνά-
σιον Χαιρέαν καὶ ὥσπερ ἔρημον ἦν. ἐφίλει γὰρ
αὐτὸν ἡ νεολαία. πολυπραγμονοῦντες δὲ τὴν αἰτίαν
ἔμαθον τῆς νόσου, καὶ ἔλεος πάντας εἰσῄει μειρακίου καλοῦ κινδυνεύοντος ἀπολέσθαι διὰ πάθος
ψυχῆς εὐφυοῦς.

11 Ἐνέστη νόμιμος ἐκκλησία. συγκαθεσθεὶς οὖν ὁ
δῆμος τοῦτο πρῶτον καὶ μόνον ἐβόα "καλὸς Ἑρμοκράτης, μέγας στρατηγός, σῷζε Χαιρέαν· τοῦτο
πρῶτον τῶν τροπαίων. ἡ πόλις μνηστεύεται τοὺς γά-
12 μους σήμερον ἀλλήλων ἀξίων." τίς ἂν μηνύσειε τὴν
ἐκκλησίαν ἐκείνην, ἧς ὁ Ἔρως ἦν δημαγωγός; ἀνὴρ
δὲ φιλόπατρις Ἑρμοκράτης ἀντειπεῖν οὐκ ἠδυνήθη
τῇ πόλει δεομένῃ. κατανεύσαντος δὲ αὐτοῦ πᾶς ὁ
δῆμος ἐξεπήδησε τοῦ θεάτρου, καὶ οἱ μὲν νέοι
ἀπῇσαν ἐπὶ Χαιρέαν, ἡ βουλὴ δὲ καὶ οἱ ἄρχοντες
13 ἠκολούθουν Ἑρμοκράτει· παρῆσαν δὲ καὶ αἱ γυναῖ-

silent for shame of being exposed. But when Chaereas, a
well-bred and spirited youth, began to waste away, he had
the courage to tell his parents that he was in love and
could not live without Callirhoe as his wife. At this his
father groaned and said, "I fear you are done for, my son.
Hermocrates will surely never give you his daughter
when he has so many rich and royal suitors for her. You
must not even make the attempt, in case we suffer a public humiliation." His father then tried to comfort the boy,
but the latter's malady grew worse, and he no longer went
out even to his usual pastimes. The gymnasium missed
Chaereas and was virtually deserted, for the young people
loved him. Their curiosity found out the cause of his sickness, and all felt pity for a handsome youth who seemed
likely to die from the passion of an honest heart.

A regular assembly occurred. When the people had
taken their seats, their first and only cry was this, "Excellent Hermocrates, mighty leader, save Chaereas! This will
be your greatest triumph. The city petitions for the
marriage today of a couple worthy of each other." Who
could describe that assembly, at which Love was the
spokesman? The patriotic Hermocrates was unable to
refuse the appeals of the city. When he gave his consent,
the people all rushed from the theater:[a] the young men
went to find Chaereas while the council and magistrates
escorted Hermocrates. Even the women of Syracuse

---

[a] Assemblies were regularly held in the theater.

1.9 add. Zankogiannes | πειρᾶσθαι Blake: πειρᾶσαι F.

κες αἱ Συρακοσίων ἐπὶ τὴν οἰκίαν νυμφαγωγοῦσαι.
ὑμέναιος ᾔδετο κατὰ πᾶσαν τὴν πόλιν· μεσταὶ δὲ αἱ
ῥῦμαι στεφάνων, λαμπάδων· ἐρραίνετο τὰ πρόθυρα
οἴνῳ καὶ μύροις. ἥδιον ταύτην τὴν ἡμέραν ἤγαγον οἱ
Συρακόσιοι τῆς τῶν ἐπινικίων.

14    Ἡ δὲ παρθένος οὐδὲν εἰδυῖα τούτων ἔρριπτο ἐπὶ
τῆς κοίτης ἐγκεκαλυμμένη, κλαίουσα καὶ σιωπῶσα.
προσελθοῦσα δὲ ἡ τροφὸς τῇ κλίνῃ "τέκνον" εἶπε,
"διανίστασο, πάρεστι γὰρ ἡ εὐκταιοτάτη πᾶσιν
ἡμῖν ἡμέρα· ἡ πόλις σε νυμφαγωγεῖ."

τῆς δ' αὐτοῦ λύτο γούνατα καὶ φίλον ἦτορ·

οὐ γὰρ ᾔδει, τίνι γαμεῖται. ἄφωνος εὐθὺς ἦν καὶ
σκότος αὐτῆς τῶν ὀφθαλμῶν κατεχύθη καὶ ὀλίγου
δεῖν ἐξέπνευσεν· ἐδόκει δὲ τοῦτο τοῖς ὁρῶσιν αἰδώς.
15    ἐπεὶ δὲ ταχέως ἐκόσμησαν αὐτὴν αἱ θεραπαινίδες,
τὸ πλῆθος ἐπὶ τῶν θυρῶν ἀπέλιπον· οἱ δὲ γονεῖς τὸν
νυμφίον εἰσήγαγον πρὸς τὴν παρθένον. ὁ μὲν οὖν
Χαιρέας προσδραμὼν αὐτὴν κατεφίλει, Καλλιρόη δὲ
γνωρίσασα τὸν ἐρώμενον, ὥσπερ τι λύχνου φῶς ἤδη
σβεννύμενον ἐπιχυθέντος ἐλαίου πάλιν ἀνέλαμψε
16    καὶ μείζων ἐγένετο καὶ κρείττων. ἐπεὶ δὲ προῆλθεν
εἰς τὸ δημόσιον, θάμβος ὅλον τὸ πλῆθος κατέλαβεν,
ὥσπερ Ἀρτέμιδος ἐν ἐρημίᾳ κυνηγέταις ἐπιστάσης·
πολλοὶ δὲ τῶν παρόντων καὶ προσεκύνησαν. πάντες
δὲ Καλλιρόην μὲν ἐθαύμαζον, Χαιρέαν δὲ ἐμακάρι-

1.16 Χαιρέαν . . . Καλλιρόην F, corr. Hercher.

a Cf. Sappho, fr. 44 LP (the wedding of Andromache).

were there to attend the bride. The marriage hymn
sounded throughout the city; the streets were filled with
garlands and torches, and the doorways sprinkled with
wine and perfume.[a] The Syracusans celebrated this day
with more joy than the day of their victory over the Athenians.

Knowing nothing of this the girl had flung herself on
her bed, buried her head, and was silently weeping. Her
nurse came to her bed and said, "Get up, my child. The
day we have all been looking forward to has arrived. The
city is here to attend your wedding."

At this her knees collapsed and the heart within her,[b]

for she had no idea to whom she was being married. At
once she was unable to speak, darkness covered her eyes,
and she nearly expired—which those who saw her
thought just modesty. As soon as her maids had dressed
her, the crowd at the door made way, and his parents
brought the bridegroom to the girl. Then Chaereas ran
forward and kissed her; recognizing the man she loved,
Callirhoe, like a dying lamp once it is replenished with
oil,[c] flamed into life again and became taller and stronger.
When she came out into the open, all were astounded, as
when Artemis appears to hunters in lonely places.[d] Many
of the onlookers even knelt in homage.[e] All were
entranced by Callirhoe and congratulated Chaereas.

[b] *Odyssey* 4.703 (Penelope) and elsewhere. The formula is
also quoted at 3.6.3 and 4.5.9.   [c] Cf. Xenophon, *Symposium*
2.24.   [d] Cf. Sappho, fr. 44A LP.

[e] As an expression of homage the προσκύνησις (kneeling
and touching the ground with the forehead) was in the Greek
and Roman worlds confined to the gods; but in the Orient it was
commanded by potentates and their wives.

ζον. τοιοῦτον ὑμνοῦσι ποιηταὶ τὸν Θέτιδος γάμον ἐν
Πηλίῳ γεγονέναι. πλὴν καὶ ἐνταῦθά τις εὑρέθη
βάσκανος δαίμων, ὥσπερ ἐκεῖ φασὶ τὴν Ἔριν.

2. Οἱ γὰρ μνηστῆρες ἀποτυχόντες τοῦ γάμου
λύπην ἐλάμβανον μετ᾽ ὀργῆς. τέως οὖν μαχόμενοι
πρὸς ἀλλήλους ὡμονόησαν τότε, διὰ δὲ τὴν ὁμό-
νοιαν, ὑβρίσθαι δοκοῦντες, συνῆλθον εἰς βουλευτή-
ριον κοινόν· ἐστρατολόγει δὲ αὐτοὺς ἐπὶ τὸν κατὰ
2 Χαιρέου πόλεμον ὁ Φθόνος. καὶ πρῶτος ἀναστὰς
νεανίας τις Ἰταλιώτης, υἱὸς τοῦ Ῥηγίνων τυράννου,
τοιαῦτα ἔλεγεν· "εἰ μέν τις ἐξ ἡμῶν ἔγημεν, οὐκ ἂν
ὠργίσθην, ὥσπερ ἐν τοῖς γυμνικοῖς ἀγῶσιν ἕνα δεῖ
νικῆσαι τῶν ἀγωνισαμένων· ἐπεὶ δὲ παρευδοκίμησεν
ἡμᾶς ὁ μηδὲν ὑπὲρ γάμου πονήσας, οὐ φέρω τὴν
3 ὕβριν. ἡμεῖς δὲ ἐτάθημεν αὐλείοις θύραις προσ-
αγρυπνοῦντες καὶ κολακεύοντες τίτθας καὶ θεραπαινίδας καὶ δῶρα πέμποντες τροφοῖς. πόσον χρόνον
δεδουλεύκαμεν; καί, τὸ πάντων χαλεπώτατον, ὡς
ἀντεραστὰς ἀλλήλους ἐμισήσαμεν. ὁ δὲ ἄπορος καὶ
πένης καὶ μηδενὸς κρείττων βασιλέων ἀγωνισα-
4 μένων αὐτὸς ἀκονιτὶ τὸν στέφανον ἤρατο. ἀλλὰ
ἀνόνητον αὐτῷ γενέσθω τὸ ἆθλον καὶ τὸν γάμον
θάνατον τῷ νυμφίῳ ποιήσωμεν."

Πάντες οὖν ἐπήνεσαν, μόνος δὲ ὁ Ἀκραγαντίνων
τύραννος ἀντεῖπεν. "οὐκ εὐνοίᾳ δὲ" εἶπε "τῇ πρὸς
Χαιρέαν κωλύω τὴν ἐπιβουλήν, ἀλλὰ ἀσφαλεστέρῳ
τῷ λογισμῷ· μέμνησθε γὰρ ὅτι Ἑρμοκράτης οὐκ

2.3 ἄπορος Praechter: πόρνος F.

Even such was the wedding of Thetis on Pelion as described by the poets. Yet just as there, they say, was the goddess Discord,[a] so here likewise was found an envious demon.

2. The unsuccessful suitors felt anger as well as disappointment. Hitherto they had competed with one another, but now they were of a single mind, and because of this and a sense of outrage they took counsel together, Malice leading them in their attack on Chaereas. First a young Italian, the prince of Rhegium,[b] got up and spoke as follows: "If any of us had married her, I should not have been angry, for, as in athletic contests, only one of the contestants can win; but since we have been passed over for one who made no effort to win the bride, I cannot bear the insult. We have worn ourselves out, spending sleepless nights before the door of her house, flattering nurses and maids, and sending gifts to her attendants. How long have we been slaves? And worst of all, we have come to hate each other as rivals. Now a ridiculous, poverty-stricken nobody competing with kings has carried off the prize without lifting a finger. Let him not enjoy his success, but let us make sure that the wedding spells death for the groom."

All applauded, only the ruler of Acragas[c] objecting. "It is not," he said, "good will towards Chaereas that makes me oppose your plan, but more prudent reasoning. Remember that Hermocrates is not a man to be trifled

[a] Eris in Greek: not invited to the wedding she threw before the chief three goddesses an apple inscribed "For the fairest," setting in motion the events which led to the Trojan War.

[b] Modern Reggio di Calabria.

[c] Roman Agrigentum, modern Agrigento.

ἔστιν εὐκαταφρόνητος· ὥστε ἀδύνατος ἡμῖν πρὸς
αὐτὸν ἡ ἐκ τοῦ φανεροῦ μάχη, κρείττων δὲ ἡ μετὰ
5 τέχνης· καὶ γὰρ τὰς τυραννίδας πανουργίᾳ μᾶλλον
ἢ βίᾳ κτώμεθα. χειροτονήσατε ἐμὲ τοῦ πρὸς Χαιρέαν πολέμου στρατηγόν· ἐπαγγέλλομαι διαλύσειν
τὸν γάμον· ἐφοπλιῶ γὰρ αὐτῷ Ζηλοτυπίαν, ἥτις
σύμμαχον λαβοῦσα τὸν Ἔρωτα μέγα τι κακὸν δια-
6 πράξεται· Καλλιρόη μὲν οὖν εὐσταθὴς καὶ ἄπειρος
κακοήθους ὑποψίας, ὁ δὲ Χαιρέας, οἷα δὴ γυμνα-
σίοις ἐντραφεὶς καὶ νεωτερικῶν ἁμαρτημάτων οὐκ
ἄπειρος, δύναται ῥᾳδίως ὑποπτεύσας ἐμπεσεῖν εἰς
νεωτερικὴν ζηλοτυπίαν· ἔστι δὲ καὶ προσελθεῖν
ἐκείνῳ ῥᾷον καὶ λαλῆσαι.”

Πάντες ἔτι λέγοντος αὐτοῦ τὴν γνώμην ἐπεψηφί-
σαντο καὶ τὸ ἔργον ἐνεχείρισαν ὡς ἀνδρὶ πᾶν
ἱκανῷ μηχανήσασθαι. τοιαύτης οὖν ἐπινοίας ἐκεῖνος
ἤρξατο.

3. Ἑσπέρα μὲν ἦν, ἧκε δὲ ἀγγέλλων τις ὅτι Ἀρίστων ὁ πατὴρ Χαιρέου πεσὼν ἀπὸ κλίμακος ἐν
ἀγρῷ πάνυ ὀλίγας ἔχει τοῦ ζῆν τὰς ἐλπίδας. ὁ δὲ
Χαιρέας ἀκούσας, καίτοι φιλοπάτωρ ὤν, ὅμως ἐλυ-
πήθη πλέον ὅτι ἔμελλεν ἀπελεύσεσθαι μόνος· οὐ
2 γὰρ οἷόν τε ἦν ἐξάγειν ἤδη τὴν κόρην. ἐν δὲ τῇ
νυκτὶ ταύτῃ φανερῶς μὲν οὐδεὶς ἐτόλμησεν ἐπικωμά-
σαι, κρύφα δὲ καὶ ἀδήλως ἐπελθόντες σημεῖα κώμου
[ἦσαν καὶ] κατέλιπον· ἐστεφάνωσαν τὰ πρόθυρα,
μύροις ἔρραναν, οἴνου πηλὸν ἐποίησαν, δᾷδας ἔρρι-
ψαν ἡμικαύστους.

38

with, so that we cannot engage in an open fight with him. A crafty approach is better, for it is by cunning and not force that we become rulers. Elect me general of the campaign against Chaereas and I undertake to dissolve the marriage. I shall arm Jealousy against him, and she, with Love as her ally, will work serious damage. Callirhoe may be even-tempered and incapable of base suspicion, but Chaereas, brought up in the gymnasium and not unacquainted with youthful follies, can easily be made suspicious and lured into youthful jealousy. Also he is easier to approach and talk to."

Before he had finished he had won unanimous approval for his plan; they entrusted its execution to him as a man equal to anything. This then was the scheme on which he set to work.

3. Evening had fallen when a man came with the news[a] that Ariston, Chaereas' father, had fallen from a ladder on his farm and that there was very little hope of his surviving. Though Chaereas was fond of his father, he was additionally upset when he heard this, because he had to go alone, since it was not yet proper to take his bride with him.[b] That night, while no one dared to serenade her openly, yet they came secretly and unseen and left behind them evidence of reveling. They garlanded the vestibule, sprinkled it with perfumes, soaked the ground with wine, and let drop half-burned torches.

[a] The opening of this sentence is echoed from the dramatic passage in Demosthenes, *De Corona* 169; and again in 8.1.5.

[b] A bride was expected not to engage in travel until she had borne her husband a child.

---

2.5 ἐμὲ Cobet: με F.    3.2 del. Hercher.

3     Διέλαμψεν ἡμέρα, καὶ πᾶς ὁ παριὼν εἱστήκει
κοινῷ τινι πολυπραγμοσύνης πάθει· Χαιρέας δὲ τοῦ
πατρὸς αὐτοῦ ῥᾷον ἐσχηκότος ἔσπευδε πρὸς τὴν
γυναῖκα. ἰδὼν δὲ τὸν ὄχλον πρὸ τῶν θυρῶν τὸ μὲν
πρῶτον ἐθαύμασεν· ἐπεὶ δὲ ἔμαθε τὴν αἰτίαν, ἐνθου-
4     σιῶν εἰστρέχει· καταλαβὼν δὲ τὸν θάλαμον ἔτι κε-
κλεισμένον, ἤρασσε μετὰ σπουδῆς. ἐπεὶ δὲ ἀνέῳξεν
ἡ θεραπαινίς, ἐπιπεσὼν τῇ Καλλιρόῃ τὴν ὀργὴν
μετέβαλεν εἰς λύπην καὶ περιρρηξάμενος ἔκλαιε.
πυνθανομένης δὲ τί γέγονεν, ἄφωνος ἦν, οὔτε ἀπι-
στεῖν οἷς εἶδεν οὔτε πιστεύειν οἷς οὐκ ἤθελε δυνάμε-
5     νος. ἀπορουμένου δὲ αὐτοῦ καὶ τρέμοντος ἡ γυνὴ
μηδὲν ὑπονοοῦσα τῶν γεγονότων ἱκέτευεν εἰπεῖν τὴν
αἰτίαν τοῦ χόλου· ὁ δὲ ὑφαίμοις τοῖς ὀφθαλμοῖς καὶ
παχεῖ τῷ φθέγματι "κλαίω" φησὶ "τὴν ἐμαυτοῦ
τύχην, ὅτι μου ταχέως ἐπελάθου," καὶ τὸν κῶμον
6     ὠνείδισεν. ἡ δὲ οἷα θυγάτηρ στρατηγοῦ καὶ φρονήματος πλήρης πρὸς τὴν ἄδικον διαβολὴν παρω-
ξύνθη καὶ "οὐδεὶς ἐπὶ τὴν πατρῴαν οἰκίαν ἐκώμα-
σεν" εἶπε, "τὰ δὲ σὰ πρόθυρα συνήθη τυχόν ἐστι
τοῖς κώμοις, καὶ τὸ γεγαμηκέναι σε λυπεῖ τοὺς ἐρα-
στάς." ταῦτα εἰποῦσα ἀπεστράφη καὶ συγκαλυψα-
7     μένη δακρύων ἀφῆκε πηγάς. εὔκολοι δὲ τοῖς ἐρῶσιν
αἱ διαλλαγαὶ καὶ πᾶσαν ἀπολογίαν ἡδέως ἀλλήλων
προσδέχονται. μεταβαλλόμενος οὖν ὁ Χαιρέας
ἤρξατο κολακεύειν, καὶ ἡ γυνὴ ταχέως αὐτοῦ τὴν
μετάνοιαν ἠσπάζετο. ταῦτα μᾶλλον ἐξέκαυσε τὸν
ἔρωτα, καὶ οἱ ἀμφοτέρων αὐτῶν γονεῖς μακαρίους

Day dawned and every passerby stopped out of ordinary curiosity. Now that his father was feeling better, Chaereas hurried back to his wife. Seeing the crowd before the door, he was at first astonished, but when he learned the cause, he rushed in as though possessed. Finding the chamber still shut, he banged on the door vigorously. When the maid opened it and he burst in upon Callirhoe, his anger was changed to sorrow and he tore his clothes and shed tears. When she asked him what had happened, he was speechless, being able neither to disbelieve what he had seen, nor yet to believe what he was unwilling to accept. As he stood confused and trembling, his wife, quite unsuspicious of what had happened, begged him to tell her the reason for his anger. With bloodshot eyes and thick voice he said, "It is the fact that you have forgotten me that hurts so much," and he reproached her for the reveling. But she, true daughter of a general and full of pride, was angered by the unjust accusation and said. "No one has come reveling to my father's house. Perhaps your vestibule is used to revels, and your marriage has hurt your boyfriends."[a] Saying this she turned away and, with her head covered, let her tears pour forth. Yet reconciliation between lovers is easy[b] and they gladly accept any apology from each other. Thus Chaereas, changing his tone, began to talk sweetly to her, and his wife quickly welcomed his change of attitude. This increased the ardor of their love all the more, and

[a] Only here in the novel is homosexuality referred to, unless the mention of Patroclus and Achilles in 1.5.2 is to be so interpreted.

[b] The sententiousness and iambic rhythm of this statement suggest that it derives from New Comedy.

41

CHARITON

αὐτοὺς ὑπελάμβανον τὴν τῶν τέκνων ὁρῶντες ὁμό-
νοιαν.

4. Ὁ δὲ Ἀκραγαντῖνος διαπεπτωκυίας αὐτῷ τῆς
πρώτης τέχνης ἥπτετο λοιπὸν ἐνεργεστέρας κατασκευάσας τι τοιοῦτον. ἦν αὐτῷ παράσιτος στωμύλος
καὶ πάσης χάριτος ὁμιλητικῆς ἔμπλεως. τοῦτον ἐκέλευσεν ὑποκριτὴν ἔρωτος γενέσθαι. τὴν ἄβραν γὰρ
τῆς Καλλιρόης καὶ τιμιωτάτην τῶν θεραπαινίδων
2 προσπίπτων φιλεῖν ἐποίει. μόλις οὖν ἐκεῖνος πλὴν
ὑπηγάγετο τὴν μείρακα μεγάλαις δωρεαῖς τῷ τε
λέγειν ἀπάγξεσθαι μὴ τυχὼν τῆς ἐπιθυμίας. γυνὴ δὲ
εὐάλωτόν ἐστιν, ὅταν ἐρᾶσθαι δοκῇ. ταῦτ᾽ οὖν προ-
κατασκευασάμενος ὁ δημιουργὸς τοῦ δράματος ὑποκριτὴν ἕτερον ἐξηῦρεν, οὐκέτι ὁμοίως εὔχαριν, ἀλλὰ
3 πανοῦργον καὶ ἀξιόπιστον λαλῆσαι. τοῦτον προδι-
δάξας ἃ χρὴ πράττειν καὶ λέγειν, ὑπέπεμψεν ἀγνῶτα
τῷ Χαιρέᾳ. προσελθὼν δὲ ἐκεῖνος αὐτῷ περὶ τὰς
παλαίστρας ἀλύοντι "κἀμοὶ" φησὶν "υἱὸς ἦν, ὦ Χαιρέα, σὸς ἡλικιώτης, πάνυ σε θαυμάζων καὶ φιλῶν,
ὅτε ἔζη. τελευτήσαντος δὲ αὐτοῦ σὲ υἱὸν ἐμαυτοῦ
νομίζω, καὶ γὰρ εἶ κοινὸν ἀγαθὸν πάσης Σικελίας
4 εὐτυχῶν. δὸς οὖν μοι σχολάζοντα σεαυτὸν καὶ
ἀκούσῃ μεγάλα πράγματα ὅλῳ τῷ βίῳ σου δια-
φέροντα."

Τοιούτοις ῥήμασιν ὁ μιαρὸς ἐκεῖνος ἄνθρωπος
τοῦ μειρακίου τὴν ψυχὴν ἀνακουφίσας καὶ μεστὸν
ποιήσας ἐλπίδος καὶ φόβου καὶ πολυπραγμοσύνης,
δεομένου λέγειν ὤκνει καὶ προεφασίζετο μὴ εἶναι

the parents of both counted themselves blessed when they saw the mutual devotion of their children.

4. Foiled in his first plan, the suitor from Acragas turned to a more drastic one, devising the following scheme. He had a crony who was smooth-tongued and full of every social grace. He told him to play the role of a lover: he was to pay court to Callirhoe's personal and trusted servant and win her love. After some trouble this person managed to win the girl over with expensive gifts, telling her that he would hang himself if he did not get his desire. A woman is an easy victim when she thinks she is loved.[a] After this preliminary, the producer of the drama recruited another actor, not equally attractive, but cunning and a persuasive talker. When he had coached him in what to do and say, he sent him to waylay Chaereas, who did not know him. Meeting him unoccupied outside the gymnasium he said, "Chaereas, I too had a son of your age who greatly admired and loved you when he was alive. Now that he is dead, I consider you as my son—indeed, your well-being is a common blessing[b] to all Sicily. Spare me a moment and you shall hear of grave concerns affecting your whole life."

With such words the rogue set the young man's heart aflutter and filled him with hope, fear, and curiosity. But when he asked him to speak, the other hesitated and pre-

[a] Cf. Menander, *Nauclerus* fr. 290 K-T.
[b] Cf. Menander, fr. 542 K-T.

---

4.1 κατασκευάσας Lucke-Schäfer: κατασκευῆς F.

τὸν καιρὸν ἐπιτήδειον τὸν παρόντα, δεῖν δὲ ἀνα-
5 βολῆς καὶ σχολῆς μακροτέρας. ἐνέκειτο μᾶλλον ὁ
Χαιρέας, ἤδη τι προσδοκῶν βαρύτερον· ὁ δὲ ἐμβαλὼν αὐτῷ τὴν δεξιὰν ἀπῆγεν εἴς τι χωρίον ἠρεμαῖον,
εἶτα συναγαγὼν τὰς ὀφρῦς καὶ ὅμοιος γενόμενος
λυπουμένῳ, μικρὸν δέ τι καὶ δακρύσας, "ἀηδῶς μὲν"
εἶπεν, "ὦ Χαιρέα, σκυθρωπόν σοι πρᾶγμα μηνύω
καὶ πάλαι βουλόμενος εἰπεῖν ὤκνουν· ἐπεὶ δὲ ἤδη
φανερῶς ὑβρίζῃ καὶ θρυλλεῖται πανταχοῦ τὸ δεινόν,
οὐχ ὑπομένω σιωπᾶν· φύσει τε γὰρ μισοπόνηρός
6 εἰμι καὶ σοὶ μάλιστα εὔνους. γίνωσκε τοίνυν μοι-
χευομένην σου τὴν γυναῖκα, καὶ ἵνα τούτῳ πιστεύ-
σῃς, ἕτοιμος ἐπ' αὐτοφώρῳ τὸν μοιχὸν δεικνύειν."

ὣς φάτο· τὸν δ' ἄχεος νεφέλη ἐκάλυψε μέλαινα,
ἀμφοτέρῃσι δὲ χερσὶν ἑλὼν κόνιν αἰθαλόεσσαν
χεύατο κὰκ κεφαλῆς, χαρίεν δ' ᾔσχυνε πρόσωπον.

7 ἐπὶ πολὺ μὲν οὖν ἀχανὴς ἔκειτο, μήτε τὸ στόμα μήτε
τοὺς ὀφθαλμοὺς ἐπᾶραι δυνάμενος· ἐπεὶ δὲ φωνὴν
οὐχ ὁμοίαν μὲν ὀλίγην δὲ συνελέξατο, "δυστυχῆ
μὲν" εἶπεν "αἰτῶ παρὰ σοῦ χάριν αὐτόπτης γενέσθαι τῶν ἐμῶν κακῶν· ὅμως δὲ δεῖξον, ὅπως εὐλο-
γώτερον ἐμαυτὸν ἀνέλω· Καλλιρόης γὰρ καὶ ἀδικού-
8 σης φείσομαι." "προσποίησαι" φησὶν "ὡς εἰς ἀγρὸν
ἀπιέναι, βαθείας δὲ ἑσπέρας παραφύλαττε τὴν
οἰκίαν· ὄψει γὰρ εἰσιόντα τὸν μοιχόν."

4.5 μηνύω Reiske: μηνύων F.

tended that the present occasion was not suitable: a post-ponement was needed until they should have more time. Chaereas insisted all the more, by now expecting something unpleasant. The other took his arm and led him off to a quiet spot. Then, knitting his brow, assuming a sad expression, and shedding a tear or two, he said, "Chaereas, I am sorry to have to tell you of a shocking matter. I have long been wanting to speak, but have hesitated. But now that you are being publicly reviled and the scandal is being discussed everywhere, I cannot keep quiet. It's my nature to hate wrong, and I have a special sympathy for you. So I have to tell you that your wife is unfaithful and, to convince you, am ready to show you the adulterer in the act."

At these words a black cloud of grief enveloped him,
and with both hands taking sooty dust he poured it
down over his head and defiled his beautiful features.[a]

For a long time he stood in a daze, unable to speak or lift his eyes. When he had recovered, he said in a weak voice unlike his own, "It is a miserable favor to ask of you, to contrive that I witness my own ruination. Yet show it to me so that I may have more reason for killing myself; for I shall spare Callirhoe, even if she is doing me wrong." "Pretend," said he, "that you are going away to the country. But late in the evening keep watch on the house; then you will see her lover go in."

---

[a] *Iliad* 18.22–24 (Achilles learning of Patroclus' death).

---

4.7 δείξον D'Orville: δείξαι F.

# CHARITON

Συνέθεντο ταῦτα, καὶ ὁ μὲν Χαιρέας πέμψας (οὐ γὰρ αὐτὸς ὑπέμεινεν οὐδὲ εἰσελθεῖν) "ἄπειμι" φησὶν "εἰς ἀγρόν·" ὁ δὲ κακοήθης ἐκεῖνος καὶ διάβολος

9  συνέταττε τὴν σκηνήν. ἑσπέρας οὖν ἐπιστάσης ὁ μὲν ἐπὶ τὴν κατασκοπὴν ἦλθεν, ὁ δὲ τὴν ἄβραν τῆς Καλλιρόης διαφθείρας ἐνέβαλεν εἰς τὸν στενωπόν, ὑποκρινόμενος μὲν τὸν λαθραίοις ἔργοις ἐπιχειρεῖν προαιρούμενον, πάντα δὲ μηχανώμενος ἵνα μὴ λάθοι. κόμην εἶχε λιπαρὰν καὶ βοστρύχους μύρων ἀποπνέοντας, ὀφθαλμοὺς ὑπογεγραμμένους, ἱμάτιον μαλακόν, ὑπόδημα λεπτόν· δακτύλιοι βαρεῖς ὑπέστιλβον. εἶτα πολὺ περιβλεψάμενος τῇ θύρᾳ προσῆλθε, κρούσας δὲ ἐλαφρῶς τὸ εἰωθὸς ἔδωκε σημεῖον.

10  ἡ δὲ θεράπαινα καὶ αὐτὴ περίφοβος ἠρέμα παρανοίξασα καὶ λαβομένη τῆς χειρὸς εἰσήγαγε. ταῦτα θεασάμενος Χαιρέας οὐκέτι κατέσχεν ἀλλὰ εἰσέδραμεν ἐπ᾽ αὐτοφώρῳ τὸν μοιχὸν ἀναιρήσων.

11  Ὁ μὲν οὖν παρὰ τὴν αὔλειον θύραν ὑποστὰς εὐθὺς ἐξῆλθεν, ἡ δὲ Καλλιρόη καθῆστο ἐπὶ τῆς κλίνης ποθοῦσα Χαιρέαν καὶ μηδὲ λύχνον ἅψασα διὰ τὴν λύπην· ψόφου δὲ ποδῶν γενομένου πρώτη τοῦ ἀνδρὸς ᾔσθετο τὴν ἀναπνοὴν καὶ χαίρουσα αὐτῷ

12  προσέδραμεν. ὁ δὲ φωνὴν μὲν οὐκ ἔσχεν ὥστε λοιδορήσασθαι, κρατούμενος δὲ ὑπὸ τῆς ὀργῆς ἐλάκτισε προσιοῦσαν. εὐστόχως οὖν ὁ ποὺς κατὰ τοῦ διαφράγματος ἐνεχθεὶς ἐπέσχε τῆς παιδὸς τὴν

4.11 καθῆστο Hercher: ἐκάθητο F | ποθοῦσα Reiske: ζητοῦσα F.

46

## BOOK 1.4

They agreed, and Chaereas sent a message, since he could not bear even to enter the house, saying, "I am going away to the country." Then the wicked villain set the scene of his drama. When evening came, Chaereas took his place of observation while the other man, who had seduced Callirhoe's maid, hurried into the lane, acting as if he was trying to do something in secret, but in everything contriving to be noticed. His hair was glistening with perfumed locks, his eyes were shadowed; he wore a soft cloak and fine slippers; heavy rings sparkled on his fingers. Next, looking carefully around, he approached the door and, knocking softly, gave the usual sign. The maid, herself very nervous, quietly opened the door and, taking him by the hand, led him in. Seeing this, Chaereas could no longer restrain himself but rushed in to kill the lover in the act.[a]

He, however, had hidden beside the courtyard door and made his escape at once. But Callirhoe was sitting on her couch longing for Chaereas and in her unhappiness had not even lighted a lamp. At the sound of footsteps she was the first to recognize her husband by his breathing;[b] joyfully she ran to greet him. He could find no voice with which to reproach her; but overcome by anger, he kicked at her as she ran forward. His foot struck the girl squarely in the diaphragm and stopped her

[a] This would have been perfectly legal (cf. Lysias 1.30).
[b] Recognition by means of breathing recurs at 8.1.7.

47

CHARITON

ἀναπνοήν, ἐρριμμένην δὲ αὐτὴν αἱ θεραπαινίδες
βαστάσασαι κατέκλιναν ἐπὶ τὴν κοίτην.

5. Καλλιρόη μὲν οὖν ἄφωνος καὶ ἄπνους ἐπέκειτο
νεκρᾶς εἰκόνα πᾶσι παρέχουσα, Φήμη δὲ ἄγγελος
τοῦ πάθους καθ' ὅλην τὴν πόλιν διέτρεχεν, οἰμωγὴν
ἐγείρουσα διὰ τῶν στενωπῶν ἄχρι τῆς θαλάττης·
καὶ πανταχόθεν ὁ θρῆνος ἠκούετο, καὶ τὸ πρᾶγμα
ἐῴκει πόλεως ἁλώσει. Χαιρέας δὲ ἔτι τῷ θυμῷ ζέων
δι' ὅλης νυκτὸς ἀποκλείσας ἑαυτὸν ἐβασάνιζε τὰς
θεραπαινίδας, πρώτην δὲ καὶ τελευταίαν τὴν ἅβραν·

2 ἔτι δὲ καιομένων καὶ τεμνομένων αὐτῶν ἔμαθε τὴν
ἀλήθειαν. τότε ἔλεος αὐτὸν εἰσῆλθε τῆς ἀποθανού-
σης καὶ ἀποκτεῖναι μὲν ἑαυτὸν ἐπεθύμει, Πολύχαρμος δὲ ἐκώλυε, φίλος ἐξαίρετος, τοιοῦτος οἷον
Ὅμηρος ἐποίησε Πάτροκλον Ἀχιλλέως. ἡμέρας δὲ
γενομένης οἱ ἄρχοντες ἐκλήρουν δικαστήριον τῷ
φονεῖ, διὰ τὴν πρὸς Ἑρμοκράτην τιμὴν ἐπισπεύδον-
3 τες τὴν κρίσιν. ἀλλὰ καὶ ὁ δῆμος ἅπας εἰς τὴν
ἀγορὰν συνέτρεχεν, ἄλλων ἄλλα κεκραγότων· ἐδη-
μοκόπουν δὲ οἱ τῆς μνηστείας ἀποτυχόντες καὶ ὁ
Ἀκραγαντῖνος ὑπὲρ ἅπαντας, λαμπρός τε καὶ σοβα-
ρός, οἷον διαπραξάμενος ἔργον ὃ μηδεὶς ἂν προσ-
4 εδόκησε. συνέβη δὲ πρᾶγμα καινὸν καὶ ἐν δικαστηρίῳ μηδεπώποτε πραχθέν· ῥηθείσης γὰρ τῆς
κατηγορίας ὁ φονεὺς μετρηθέντος αὐτῷ τοῦ ὕδατος
ἀντὶ τῆς ἀπολογίας αὐτοῦ κατηγόρησε πικρότερον
καὶ πρῶτος τὴν καταδικάζουσαν ψῆφον ἤνεγκεν,

---

ᵃ Cf. Herodotus 3.32. Given *Callirhoe*'s popularity in Nero-

48

breath.[a] She collapsed, and her maidservants, picking her up, laid her on the bed.

5. Thus Callirhoe lay without speech or breath, presenting to all the appearance of death. Rumor ran throughout the city reporting the tragedy and arousing cries of grief through the streets down to the sea. On every side lamentation could be heard, and the scene resembled a captured city. Chaereas, still inwardly seething, locked himself up all night and interrogated the maidservants, first and last Callirhoe's favorite, and he learned the truth in the course of torturing them with fire and whips.[b] Then his heart was filled with pity for his dead wife and he longed to kill himself, but was prevented by Polycharmus, his closest friend, as in Homer Patroclus was of Achilles. When day came, the magistrates empaneled a jury to try the murderer, hurrying the case out of respect for Hermocrates. The whole populace, too, hastened to the marketplace, uttering all sorts of cries. The unsuccessful suitors incited the crowd, especially the ruler of Acragas, who affected the arrogant swagger of one who has accomplished some unexpected feat. But a strange thing now happened, as never before in a courtroom. After the charge had been read and his time[c] had been allotted him, the killer, instead of a defense, accused himself even more savagely and cast the first vote for conviction. He mentioned none of the cir-

nian Rome the charge that Nero in a fit of rage kicked his pregnant wife, Poppaea Sabina, and caused her death may have been fueled by this passage.

[b] In the ancient world the torture of slaves was regularly practised as a means of getting at the truth.

[c] Literally water; waterclocks were regularly used in trials to set a limit to the length of speeches.

49

οὐδὲν εἰπὼν τῶν πρὸς τὴν ἀπολογίαν δικαίων, οὐ τὴν διαβολήν, οὐ τὴν ζηλοτυπίαν, οὐ τὸ ἀκούσιον, ἀλλὰ ἐδεῖτο πάντων "δημοσίᾳ με καταλεύσατε· ἀπ-
5 εστεφάνωσα τὸν δῆμον. φιλάνθρωπόν ἐστιν ἂν παραδῶτέ με δημίῳ. τοῦτο ὤφειλον παθεῖν, εἰ καὶ θεραπαινίδα Ἑρμοκράτους ἀπέκτεινα. τρόπον ζητή-σατε κολάσεως ἀπόρρητον. χείρονα δέδρακα ἱερο-σύλων καὶ πατροκτόνων. μὴ θάψητέ με, μὴ μιάνητε τὴν γῆν, ἀλλὰ τὸ ἀσεβὲς καταποντώσατε σῶμα."
6 Ταῦτα λέγοντος θρῆνος ἐξερράγη, καὶ πάντες ἀφέντες τὴν νεκρὰν τὸν ζῶντα ἐπένθουν. Ἑρμοκρά-της συνηγόρησε Χαιρέᾳ πρῶτος. "ἐγὼ" φησὶν "ἐπί-σταμαι τὸ συμβὰν ἀκούσιον. βλέπω τοὺς ἐπιβου-λεύοντας ἡμῖν. οὐκ ἐφησθήσονται δυσὶ νεκροῖς, οὐδὲ
7 λυπήσω τεθνεῶσαν τὴν θυγατέρα. ἤκουσα λεγού-σης αὐτῆς πολλάκις ὅτι αὐτῆς μᾶλλον θέλει Χαι-ρέαν ζῆν. παύσαντες οὖν τὸ περισσὸν δικαστήριον ἐπὶ τὸν ἀναγκαῖον ἀπίωμεν τάφον. μὴ παραδῶμεν χρόνῳ τὴν νεκράν, μηδὲ ἄμορφον τῇ παρολκῇ ποιή-σωμεν τὸ σῶμα. θάψωμεν Καλλιρόην ἔτι καλήν."
6. Οἱ μὲν οὖν δικασταὶ τὴν ἀπολύουσαν ψῆφον ἔθεσαν, Χαιρέας δὲ οὐκ ἀπέλυεν ἑαυτόν, ἀλλὰ ἐπ-εθύμει θανάτου καὶ πάσας ὁδοὺς ἐμηχανᾶτο τῆς τελευτῆς. Πολύχαρμος δὲ ὁρῶν ἄλλως ἀδύνατον ἑαυτῷ τὴν σωτηρίαν "προδότα" φησὶ "τῆς νεκρᾶς, οὐδὲ θάψαι Καλλιρόην περιμένεις; ἀλλοτρίαις χερσὶ τὸ σῶμα πιστεύεις; καιρός ἐστί σοι νῦν ἐνταφίων ἐπιμελεῖσθαι πολυτελείας καὶ τὴν ἐκκομιδὴν κατα-

cumstances that could have been justly urged in his defense, such as slander, his jealousy, and the lack of premeditation, but begged them all, "Stone me to death in public. I have robbed the people of its chief distinction.[a] It would be merciful to hand me over to the executioner. I should have deserved this, had I only killed Hermocrates' maidservant. Look for some condign form of punishment. I have committed a crime worse than temple-robbing or parricide. Do not bury me. Do not pollute the earth but plunge my wicked body to the bottom of the sea!"

At these words a cry of grief broke forth and everyone forgot the dead woman and mourned the living man. Hermocrates was the first to come to Chaereas' defense. "I know," he said, "that what happened was unintended. I see the men who have intrigued against us. They shall not enjoy the sight of two corpses, nor shall I cause grief to my daughter's spirit. I have often heard her say that she would rather have Chaereas live than herself. Let us stop this futile trial and get on with the necessary funeral. Let us not give up her body to the ravages of time or allow it to lose its beauty through decay. Let us bury Callirhoe while she is still beautiful."

6. So the jury voted for acquittal. Chaereas, however, would not acquit himself but longed for death and looked for every means to bring about his end. Polycharmus, seeing that it was impossible to save him in any other way, said, "Traitor to your dead wife, will you not even wait to bury Callirhoe? Will you trust her body to others' hands? Now is the time for you to bury her with rich offerings and to prepare a princely funeral." His words prevailed,

[a] I.e. Callirhoe.

2 σκευάσαι βασιλικήν." ἔπεισεν οὗτος ὁ λόγος·
ἐνέβαλε γὰρ φιλοτιμίαν καὶ φροντίδα.

Τίς ἂν οὖν ἀπαγγεῖλαι δύναιτο κατ' ἀξίαν τὴν
ἐκκομιδὴν ἐκείνην; κατέκειτο μὲν Καλλιρόη νυμφι-
κὴν ἐσθῆτα περικειμένη καὶ ἐπὶ χρυσηλάτου κλίνης
μείζων τε καὶ κρείττων, ὥστε πάντες εἴκαζον αὐτὴν
3 Ἀριάδνῃ καθευδούσῃ. προῄεσαν δὲ τῆς κλίνης
πρῶτοι μὲν οἱ Συρακοσίων ἱππεῖς αὐτοῖς ἵπποις
κεκοσμημένοι· μετὰ τούτους ὁπλῖται φέροντες σημεῖα τῶν Ἑρμοκράτους τροπαίων· εἶτα ἡ βουλὴ καὶ
ἐν μέσῳ τῷ δήμῳ πά<ντες οἱ ἄρχο>ντες Ἑρμοκράτην δορυφοροῦντες. ἐφέρετο δὲ καὶ Ἀρίστων ἔτι
νοσῶν, θυγατέρα καὶ κυρίαν Καλλιρόην ἀποκαλῶν.
ἐπὶ τούτοις αἱ γυναῖκες τῶν πολιτῶν μελανείμονες·
4 εἶτα πλοῦτος ἐνταφίων βασιλικός· πρῶτος μὲν ὁ τῆς
φερνῆς χρυσός τε καὶ ἄργυρος· ἐσθήτων κάλλος καὶ
κόσμος (συνέπεμψε δὲ Ἑρμοκράτης πολλὰ ἐκ τῶν
λαφύρων)· συγγενῶν τε δωρεαὶ καὶ φίλων. τελευ-
ταῖος ἐπηκολούθησεν ὁ Χαιρέου πλοῦτος· ἐπεθύμει
γάρ, εἰ δυνατὸν ἦν, πᾶσαν τὴν οὐσίαν συγκαταφλέ-
5 ξαι τῇ γυναικί. ἔφερον δὲ τὴν κλίνην οἱ Συρακοσίων ἔφηβοι, καὶ ἐπηκολούθει τὸ πλῆθος. τούτων δὲ
θρηνούντων μάλιστα Χαιρέας ἠκούετο. ἦν δὲ τάφος
μεγαλοπρεπὴς Ἑρμοκράτους πλησίον τῆς θαλάσσης, ὥστε καὶ τοῖς πόρρωθεν πλέουσι περίβλεπτος
εἶναι· τοῦτον ὥσπερ θησαυρὸν ἐπλήρωσεν ἡ τῶν
ἐνταφίων πολυτέλεια. τὸ δὲ δοκοῦν εἰς τιμὴν τῆς

for they awoke in Chaereas a sense of pride and responsibility.

Who could fittingly describe that funeral? Callirhoe, clothed in her bridal dress, lay upon a golden bier, more stately and beautiful than ever, so that all compared her to the sleeping Ariadne.[a] It was preceded first by the Syracusan cavalry, themselves and their horses in full regalia; after them the infantry carrying the standards of Hermocrates' triumphs; then the council and, surrounded by the people, all the magistrates serving as a bodyguard for Hermocrates. Ariston, too, still ill, was carried in a litter, calling Callirhoe his daughter and his lady. After these were the wives of the citizens clad in black; next, a royal abundance of funeral offerings, first the gold and silver of the dowry, a beautiful array of garments (for Hermocrates had contributed much from the spoils of war), and the gifts of relatives and friends. Last of all followed the wealth of Chaereas: he wanted, if it were possible,[b] to burn all his property with his wife's corpse. The youth of Syracuse carried the bier and the rest of the people followed. Of the lamentations those of Chaereas were the loudest. Hermocrates had a magnificent tomb by the shore, visible to people far out at sea. This was filled like a treasure house with costly funeral gifts. But

[a] After her desertion by Theseus; a popular model for painters and sculptors.

[b] Obviously there was no question of putting Callirhoe on a pyre, but the author seems to suggest a comparison with the splendor of Patroclus' funeral in *Iliad* 23.

6.3 οἱ ἄρχοντες add. Lucke-Schäfer (but after δήμῳ).

νεκρᾶς γεγονέναι μειζόνων πραγμάτων ἐκίνησεν ἀρχήν.

7. Θήρων γάρ τις ἦν, πανοῦργος ἄνθρωπος, ἐξ ἀδικίας πλέων τὴν θάλασσαν καὶ λῃστὰς ἔχων ὑφορμοῦντας τοῖς λιμέσιν ὀνόματι πορθμείου, πειρατήριον συγκροτῶν. οὗτος τῇ ἐκκομιδῇ παρατυχὼν ἐπωφθάλμισε τῷ χρυσῷ καὶ νύκτωρ κατακλινεὶς οὐκ ἐκοιμᾶτο λέγων πρὸς ἑαυτὸν "ἀλλὰ ἐγὼ κινδυνεύω μαχόμενος τῇ θαλάσσῃ καὶ τοὺς ζῶντας ἀποκτείνων ἕνεκα λημμάτων μικρῶν, ἐξὸν πλουτῆσαι παρὰ μιᾶς νεκρᾶς; ἀνερρίφθω κύβος· οὐκ ἀφήσω τὸ κέρδος.

2 τίνας δ' οὖν ἐπὶ τὴν πρᾶξιν στρατολογήσω; σκέψαι, Θήρων, τίς ἐπιτήδειος ὢν οἶδας. Ζηνοφάνης ὁ Θούριος; συνετὸς μὲν ἀλλὰ δειλός. Μένων ὁ Μεσσήνιος; τολμηρὸς μὲν ἀλλὰ προδότης."

3 Ἐπεξιὼν δὲ τῷ λογισμῷ καθέκαστον ὥσπερ ἀργυρογνώμων, πολλοὺς ἀποδοκιμάσας, ὅμως ἔδοξέ τινας ἐπιτηδείους. ἔωθεν οὖν διατρέχων εἰς τὸν λιμένα, ἕκαστον αὐτῶν ἀνεζήτει. εὗρε δὲ ἐνίους μὲν ἐν πορνείοις, οὓς δ' ἐν καπηλείοις, οἰκεῖον στρατὸν 4 τοιούτῳ στρατηγῷ. φήσας οὖν ἔχειν τι διαλεχθῆναι πρὸς αὐτοὺς ἀναγκαῖον, κατόπιν τοῦ λιμένος ἀπήγαγε καὶ τούτων ἤρξατο τῶν λόγων· "ἐγὼ θησαυρὸν εὑρὼν ὑμᾶς κοινωνοὺς εἱλόμην ἐξ ἁπάντων· οὐ γάρ ἐστιν ἑνὸς τὸ κέρδος, οὐδὲ πόνου πολλοῦ δεόμενον, ἀλλὰ μία νὺξ δύναται ποιῆσαι πάντας ἡμᾶς 5 πλουσίους. οὐκ ἄπειροι δ' ἐσμὲν τοιούτων ἐπιτηδευμάτων, ἃ παρὰ μὲν τοῖς ἀνοήτοις ἀνθρώποις ἔχει

what was intended to honor the dead girl set off a train of momentous events.

7. There was a cunning rogue named Theron[a] who followed a life of crime upon the sea. He associated with freebooters whose craft rode at anchor in the harbors ostensibly for ferrying: but Theron led them as a pirate crew. Chancing to be present at the funeral he ogled the gold and when he had gone to bed that night, he could not sleep. "Am I to risk my life," he said to himself, "in fighting the sea and murdering the living for paltry gains when I can become rich from one dead girl? Let the die be cast![b] I will not miss this chance of profit. But whom shall I recruit for the operation? Think carefully, Theron. Who of those you know is fit for the job? Zenophanes of Thurii?[c] He is intelligent, but cowardly. Menon of Messene?[d] He is brave, but untrustworthy."

In his mind he examined each one, like a money-changer testing coins, and rejected many; but some he considered suitable. At dawn he ran down to the harbor and sought them all out. Some he found in the brothels and some in the taverns, a suitable army for such a general. Saying that he had something important to tell them, he took them behind the harbor and began with these words: "I have found a treasure, and I have singled you out from all to share it with me. There is too much here for one man, yet not much effort is involved: a single night's work can make us all rich. We have experience in this line of business, which draws condemnation from the

---

[a] Cf. Apuleius, *Metamorphoses* 7.5 *Therone ... latrone inclito*.   [b] A well-known saying: cf. Menander, fr. 59.4 K-T, Plutarch, *Caesar* 32 (Suetonius, *Caesar* 32 *iacta alea est<o>*).

[c] See note on Sybaris (1.12.8).   [d] Roman Messana, modern Messina.

διαβολήν, ὠφέλειαν δὲ τοῖς φρονίμοις δίδωσι."

Συνῆκαν εὐθὺς ὅτι λῃστείαν ἢ τυμβωρυχίαν ἢ
ἱεροσυλίαν καταγγέλλει, καὶ "παῦσαι" ἔφασαν
"<ἀναπείθων> τοὺς πεπεισμένους ἤδη καὶ μόνον
μήνυε τὴν πρᾶξιν, καὶ τὸν καιρὸν μὴ παραπολλύω-
6 μεν." ὁ δὲ Θήρων ἔνθεν ἑλὼν "ἑωράκατε" φησὶ
"χρυσὸν καὶ ἄργυρον τῆς νεκρᾶς. οὗτος ἡμῶν τῶν
ζώντων δικαιότερον γένοιτ᾽ ἄν. δοκεῖ δή μοι νυκτὸς
ἀνοῖξαι τὸν τάφον, εἶτα ἐνθεμένους τῷ κέλητι, πλεύ-
σαντας ὅποι ποτ᾽ ἂν φέρῃ τὸ πνεῦμα διαπωλῆσαι
τὸν φόρτον ἐπὶ ξένης." ἤρεσε. "νῦν μὲν οὖν" φησὶ
"τρέπεσθε ἐπὶ τὰς συνήθεις διατριβάς· βαθείας δὲ
ἑσπέρας ἕκαστος ἐπὶ τὸν κέλητα κατίτω κομίζων
οἰκοδομικὸν ὄργανον."

8. Οὗτοι μὲν δὴ ταῦτα ἔπραττον· τὰ δὲ περὶ
Καλλιρόην δευτέραν ἄλλην ἐλάμβανε παλιγγενε-
σίαν, καί τινος ἀφέσεως ταῖς ἀπολειφθείσαις ἀνα-
πνοαῖς ἐκ τῆς ἀσιτίας ἐγγενομένης, μόλις καὶ κατ᾽
ὀλίγον ἀνέπνευσεν· ἔπειτα κινεῖν ἤρξατο κατὰ μέλη
τὸ σῶμα, διανοίγουσα δὲ τοὺς ὀφθαλμοὺς αἴσθησιν
ἐλάμβανεν ἐγειρομένης ἐξ ὕπνου καὶ ὡς συγκαθεύ-
2 δοντα Χαιρέαν ἐκάλεσεν. ἐπεὶ δὲ οὔτε ὁ ἀνὴρ οὔτε
αἱ θεραπαινίδες ἤκουον, πάντα δὲ ἦν ἐρημία καὶ
σκότος, φρίκη καὶ τρόμος τὴν παῖδα κατελάμβανεν
οὐ δυναμένην τῷ λογισμῷ συμβαλεῖν τὴν ἀλήθειαν.
μόλις δὲ ἀνεγειρομένη στεφάνων προσήψατο καὶ
ταινιῶν· ψόφον ἐποίει χρυσοῦ τε καὶ ἀργύρου·
3 πολλὴ δὲ ἦν ἀρωμάτων ὀσμή. τότ᾽ οὖν ἀνεμνήσθη

foolish but brings profit to the sensible."

They realized at once that he was proposing some piracy or tomb-breaking or temple-robbing and said, "Stop trying to persuade us: we are already persuaded. Just tell us what the job is; let us not miss the chance." Taking up from this point[a] Theron said, "You saw the dead girl's gold and silver. It should more properly belong to us, the living. I plan to open up the tomb at night, then load the cutter, sail wherever the wind takes us, and sell our cargo overseas." They agreed. "For now," said he, "return to normal business. When it gets dark each of you come to the cutter with a builder's tool."

8. Thus then they were occupied, but as for Callirhoe, she experienced a second[b] return to life. When lack of food had led to some loosening of her blocked respiration, she slowly and gradually regained her breath. Then she began to stir, limb by limb, and opening her eyes she regained consciousness as though waking from sleep, and called Chaereas, thinking he was asleep at her side. But when neither husband nor servants answered, and all was dark and lonely, she began to shiver and tremble, unable by reasoning to guess at the truth. As she slowly came to her senses, she touched the funeral wreaths and ribbons, and caused the gold and silver to clink. There was a prevalent odor of spices. She next remembered the kick and

[a] A Homeric tag, *Odyssey* 8.500: also at 5.7.10; 8.7.9.
[b] The first being that described in 1.1.15.

7.5 add. Blake.
8.1 ἀφέσεως Zimmermann: αἱρέσεως F.
8.2 ὀσμή Reiske: εὐνή F.

τοῦ λακτίσματος καὶ τοῦ δι' ἐκεῖνο πτώματος, μόλις
τε τὸν ἐκ τῆς ἀφωνίας ἐνόησε τάφον. ἔρρηξεν οὖν
φωνήν ὅσην ἐδύνατο "ζ<ῶ" βο>ῶσα καὶ "βοηθεῖτε."
ἐπεὶ δὲ πολλάκις αὐτῆς κεκραγυίας οὐδὲν ἐγίνετο
πλέον, ἀπήλπισεν ἔτι τὴν σωτηρίαν καὶ ἐνθεῖσα
τοῖς γόνασι τὴν κεφαλὴν ἐθρήνει λέγουσα "οἴμοι
τῶν κακῶν· ζῶσα κατώρυγμαι μηδὲν ἀδικοῦσα καὶ
ἀποθνῄσκω θάνατον μακρόν. ὑγιαίνουσάν με πεν-
4 θοῦσι. τίνα τίς ἄγγελον πέμψει; ἄδικε Χαιρέα,
μέμφομαί σε οὐχ ὅτι με ἀπέκτεινας, ἀλλ' ὅτι με
ἔσπευσας ἐκβαλεῖν τῆς οἰκίας. οὐκ ἔδει σε ταχέως
θάψαι Καλλιρόην οὐδ' ἀληθῶς ἀποθανοῦσαν. ἀλλ'
ἤδη τάχα τι βουλεύῃ περὶ <ἄλλου> γάμου."

9. Κἀκείνη μὲν ἐν ποικίλοις ἦν ὀδυρμοῖς· ὁ δὲ
Θήρων φυλάξας αὐτὸ τὸ μεσονύκτιον ἀψοφητὶ
προσῄει τῷ τάφῳ, κούφως ταῖς κώπαις ἁπτόμενος
τῆς θαλάσσης. ἐκβαίνων δὲ πρῶτος ἐπέταξε τὴν
2 ὑπηρεσίαν τὸν τρόπον τοῦτον. τέσσαρας μὲν ἀπ-
έστειλεν ἐπὶ κατασκοπήν, εἴ τινες προσίοιεν εἰς τὸν
τόπον, εἰ μὲν δύναιτο, φονεύειν· εἰ δὲ μή, συνθή-
ματι μηνύειν τὴν ἄφιξιν αὐτῶν· πέμπτος δὲ αὐτὸς
προσῄει τῷ τάφῳ. τοὺς δὲ λοιποὺς <ἑπτὰ> (ἦσαν
γὰρ οἱ σύμπαντες ἑκκαίδεκα) μένειν ἐπὶ τοῦ κέλητος
ἐκέλευσε καὶ τὰς κώπας ἔχειν ἐπτερωμένας, ἵνα, ἐάν
τι αἰφνίδιον συμβαίνῃ, ταχέως τοὺς ἀπὸ γῆς ἁρπά-
σαντες ἀποπλεύσωσιν.

3 Ἐπεὶ δὲ μοχλοὶ προσηνέχθησαν καὶ σφοδροτέρα
πληγὴ πρὸς τὴν ἀνάρρηξιν τοῦ τάφου, τὴν Καλλι-

the ensuing fall and eventually realized that as a result of her unconsciousness she had been buried. Then she screamed at the top of her voice, crying out "I am alive!" and "Help!" When after much shouting nothing happened, she gave up all hope of rescue, and bending her head on her knees she sobbed: "Oh, how dreadful! I have been buried alive though I did no wrong, and I am to die a lingering death. They mourn me as dead, though I am well. Who can be found to take a message? Cruel Chaereas, I blame you, not for killing me, but for being so quick to remove me from the house. You should not have buried Callirhoe with such speed, not even if she were really dead. But perhaps you are already thinking of another marriage!"

9. Thus she was bewailing her several sorrows, but Theron, waiting till midnight, quietly approached the tomb, stroking the water lightly with his oars. Jumping ashore first, he disposed his crew as follows. Four men he sent to keep watch in case anyone approached the spot: they were to kill them if possible, otherwise to signal a warning of their presence. He and four more proceeded to the tomb. The remaining seven (for there were sixteen in all) he told to stay on the cutter, keeping the oars poised so that in an emergency they could quickly pick up those on shore and put to sea.

When the crowbars were applied, and the pounding grew louder as they broke into the tomb, Callirhoe was

---

8.3 ἀφωνίας Jackson: ἀγωνίας F | add. Hilberg.
8.4 add. Naber.
9.2 add. Cobet (ζ').

ρόην κατελάμβανεν ὁμοῦ πάντα, φόβος, χαρά,
λύπη, θαυμασμός, ἐλπίς, ἀπιστία. "πόθεν ὁ ψόφος;
ἀρά τις δαίμων κατὰ νόμον κοινὸν τῶν ἀποθνησκόν-
των ἐπ᾽ ἐμὲ παραγίνεται τὴν ἀθλίαν; ἢ ψόφος οὐκ
ἔστιν, ἀλλὰ φωνὴ καλούντων με τῶν ὑποχθονίων
πρὸς αὐτούς; τυμβωρύχους μᾶλλον εἰκὸς εἶναι· καὶ
γὰρ τοῦτό μου ταῖς συμφοραῖς προσετέθη· πλοῦτος
4 ἄχρηστος νεκρῷ." ταῦτα ἔτι λογιζομένης αὐτῆς
προύβαλε τὴν κεφαλὴν ὁ λῃστὴς καὶ κατὰ μικρὸν
εἰσεδύετο. Καλλιρόη δὲ αὐτῷ προσέπεσε, βουλομένη
δεηθῆναι· κἀκεῖνος φοβηθεὶς ἐξεπήδησε. τρέμων δὲ
πρὸς τοὺς ἑταίρους ἐφθέγξατο "φεύγωμεν ἐντεῦθεν·
δαίμων γάρ τις φυλάττει τὰ ἔνδον καὶ εἰσελθεῖν
5 ἡμῖν οὐκ ἐπιτρέπει." κατεγέλασε Θήρων, δειλὸν
εἰπὼν καὶ νεκρότερον τῆς τεθνεώσης. εἶτα ἐκέλευσεν
ἄλλον εἰσελθεῖν. ἐπεὶ δὲ οὐδεὶς ὑπέμενεν, αὐτὸς εἰσῆλθε προβαλλόμενος τὸ ξίφος. λάμψαντος δὲ τοῦ
σιδήρου, δείσασα ἡ Καλλιρόη μὴ φονευθῇ, πρὸς
τὴν γωνίαν ἐξέτεινεν ἑαυτὴν κἀκεῖθεν ἱκέτευε,
λεπτὴν ἀφεῖσα φωνήν, "ἐλέησον, ὅστις ποτ᾽ εἶ, τὴν
οὐκ ἐλεηθεῖσαν ὑπὸ ἀνδρὸς οὐδὲ γονέων· μὴ ἀπο-
κτείνῃς ἣν σέσωκας."
6    Μᾶλλον ἐθάρσησεν ὁ Θήρων καὶ οἷα δεινὸς ἀνὴρ
ἐνόησε τὴν ἀλήθειαν· ἔστη δὲ σύννους καὶ τὸ μὲν
πρῶτον ἐβουλεύσατο κτεῖναι τὴν γυναῖκα, νομίζων
ἐμπόδιον ἔσεσθαι τῆς ὅλης πράξεως· ταχεῖα δὲ διὰ
τὸ κέρδος ἐγένετο μετάνοια καὶ πρὸς αὐτὸν εἶπεν
"ἔστω καὶ αὐτὴ τῶν ἐνταφίων μέρος· πολὺς μὲν

seized with every emotion at once: fear, joy, misery, amazement, hope, disbelief. "What does this noise mean? Has some deity come for me, poor soul, as happens to all at death? Or is this not mere noise, but the voice of the powers below calling me to them? More likely it is tomb robbers. So this, too, has been added to my tribulations! Wealth is no blessing to a corpse." She was reflecting thus when the robber thrust his head in and came a little inside. Callirhoe fell down before him in a suppliant's attitude, but he leaped back in terror and with a quavering voice shouted to his comrades, "Let us get out of here. A ghost is guarding the treasure inside and will not let us in." Theron laughed at him, calling him a coward and more lifeless than the corpse. Then he ordered someone else to go in; but when no one dared, he entered himself with drawn sword. The gleam of steel made Callirhoe afraid she would be killed, and she shrank back into the farthest corner of the tomb, from where she pleaded in a faint voice, "Whoever you are, have mercy on me, for I have obtained no mercy from either husband or parents. Do not kill the girl you have rescued."

Theron became bolder at this and, being a sharp man, realized the truth. He stood and reflected. At first he planned to kill the girl, judging that she would be a hindrance to the whole enterprise. But thinking of the possible profit he quickly changed his mind and said to himself, "Let her too be part of the funeral treasure. Here is

61

ἄργυρος ἐνταῦθα, πολὺς δὲ χρυσός, τούτων δὲ πάν-
7 των τὸ τῆς γυναικὸς τιμιώτερον κάλλος." λαβόμενος
οὖν τῆς χειρὸς ἐξήγαγεν αὐτήν, εἶτα καλέσας τὸν
συνεργὸν "ἰδοὺ" φησὶν "ὁ δαίμων ὃν ἐφοβοῦ· καλός
γε λῃστὴς φοβηθεὶς καὶ γυναῖκα. σὺ μὲν οὖν
φύλαττε ταύτην· θέλω γὰρ αὐτὴν ἀποδοῦναι τοῖς
γονεῦσιν· ἡμεῖς δὲ ἐκφέρωμεν τὰ ἔνδον ἀποκείμενα,
μηκέτι μηδὲ τῆς νεκρᾶς αὐτὰ τηρούσης."

10. Ἐπεὶ δὲ ἐνέπλησαν τὸν κέλητα τῶν λαφύρων,
ἐκέλευσεν ὁ Θήρων τὸν φύλακα μικρὸν ἀποστῆναι
μετὰ τῆς γυναικός· εἶτα βουλὴν προέθηκε περὶ
αὐτῆς. ἐγένοντο δὲ αἱ γνῶμαι διάφοροι καὶ ἀλλήλαις
2 ὑπεναντίαι. πρῶτος γάρ τις εἶπεν "ἐφ' ἕτερα μὲν
ἤλθομεν, ὦ συστρατιῶται, βέλτιον δὲ τὸ παρὰ τῆς
Τύχης ἀποβέβηκε· χρησώμεθα αὐτῷ· δυνάμεθα γὰρ
ἀκινδύνως εἰργάσθαι. δοκεῖ δή μοι τὰ μὲν ἐντάφια
κατὰ χώραν ἐᾶν, ἀποδοῦναι δὲ τὴν Καλλιρόην ἀνδρὶ
καὶ πατρί, φήσαντας ὅτι προσωρμίσθημεν τῷ τάφῳ
κατὰ συνήθειαν ἁλιευτικήν, ἀκούσαντες δὲ φωνὴν
ἠνοίξαμεν κατὰ φιλανθρωπίαν, ἵνα σώσωμεν τὴν
3 ἔνδον ἀποκεκλεισμένην. ὁρκίσωμεν δὲ τὴν γυναῖκα
πάντα ἡμῖν μαρτυρεῖν. ἡδέως δὲ ποιήσει χάριν
ὀφείλουσα τοῖς εὐεργέταις δι' ὧν ἐσώθη. πόσης
οἴεσθε χαρᾶς ἐμπλήσομεν τὴν ὅλην Σικελίαν;
πόσας ληψόμεθα δωρεάς; ἅμα δὲ καὶ πρὸς ἀνθρώπους δίκαια καὶ πρὸς θεοὺς ὅσια ταῦτα ποιήσομεν."
4 Ἔτι δὲ αὐτοῦ λέγοντος ἕτερος ἀντεῖπεν "ἄκαιρε
καὶ ἀνόητε, νῦν ἡμᾶς κελεύεις φιλοσοφεῖν; ἆρά γε τὸ

plenty of silver and gold, but this girl's beauty is worth more than all put together." So taking her by the hand he led her out. Then calling his confederate he said, "Look, here is the ghost that scared you. A fine brigand you are, to be afraid of a woman. So you keep an eye on her, for I should like to give her back to her parents, while the rest of us bring out the treasure inside, now that there is not even the corpse to guard it any more."

10. When they had filled the cutter with the loot, Theron ordered the guard to stand a little to one side with the girl. Then he raised the question what they ought to do with her. Several conflicting suggestions were put forward. The first speaker said, "Comrades, we came for one thing but, as Fortune would have it, something better has turned up. Let us take advantage of it. We can act without risk. I propose we leave the tomb treasure right here and give Callirhoe back to her husband and father. We should say that we anchored near the tomb in the course of our normal fishing, but hearing a cry we opened it out of humanity so as to rescue the girl shut up inside. Let us make her swear to support everything we say. She will be glad to do this in gratitude to the benefactors who rescued her. Just think of the joy we shall bring to all Sicily, and the large rewards we shall get! At the same time we shall be acting justly in men's eyes and piously in the gods'."

But before he had finished, another objected: "You have picked a bad time, you idiot, telling us now to act

τυμβωρυχεῖν ἡμᾶς ἐποίησε χρηστούς; ἐλεήσομεν ἣν
οὐκ ἠλέησεν ἴδιος ἀνὴρ ἀλλὰ ἀπέκτεινεν; οὐδὲν γὰρ
5 ἠδίκηκεν ἡμᾶς· ἀλλὰ ἀδικήσει τὰ μέγιστα. πρῶτον
μὲν γάρ, ἂν ἀποδῶμεν αὐτὴν τοῖς προσήκουσιν,
ἄδηλον ἣν ἕξουσι γνώμην περὶ τοῦ γεγονότος,
καὶ ἀδύνατον μὴ ὑποπτευθῆναι τὴν αἰτίαν δι' ἣν
ἤλθομεν ἐπὶ τὸν τάφον. ἐὰν δὲ καὶ χαρίσωνται τὴν
τιμωρίαν ἡμῖν οἱ τῆς γυναικὸς συγγενεῖς, ἀλλ' οἱ
ἄρχοντες καὶ ὁ δῆμος αὐτὸς οὐκ ἀφήσει τυμβωρύ-
6 χους ἄγοντας κατ' αὐτῶν τὸ φορτίον. τάχα δέ τις
ἐρεῖ λυσιτελέστερον εἶναι πωλῆσαι τὴν γυναῖκα·
τιμὴν γὰρ εὑρήσει διὰ τὸ κάλλος. ἔχει δὲ καὶ τοῦτο
κίνδυνον. ὁ μὲν γὰρ χρυσὸς οὐκ ἔχει φωνήν, οὐδὲ ὁ
ἄργυρος ἐρεῖ πόθεν αὐτὸν εἰλήφαμεν. ἔξεστιν ἐπὶ
7 τούτοις πλάσασθαί τι διήγημα. φορτίον δὲ ἔχον
ὀφθαλμούς τε καὶ ὦτα καὶ γλῶσσαν τίς ἂν ἀποκρύ-
ψαι δύναιτο; καὶ γὰρ οὐδὲ ἀνθρώπινον τὸ κάλλος,
ἵνα λάθωμεν. ὅτι 'δούλην' ἐροῦμεν; τίς αὐτὴν ἰδὼν
τούτῳ πιστεύσει; φονεύσωμεν οὖν αὐτὴν ἐνθάδε, καὶ
μὴ περιάγωμεν καθ' αὐτῶν τὸν κατήγορον."
8 Πολλῶν δὲ τούτοις συντιθεμένων οὐδετέρα γνώμῃ
Θήρων ἐπεψήφισε. "σὺ μὲν γὰρ" εἶπε "κίνδυνον
ἐπάγεις, σὺ δὲ κέρδος ἀπολλύεις. ἐγὼ δὲ ἀποδώσο-
μαι τὴν γυναῖκα μᾶλλον ἢ ἀπολέσω· πωλουμένη μὲν
γὰρ σιγήσει διὰ τὸν φόβον, πραθεῖσα δὲ κατηγο-
ρείτω τῶν μὴ παρόντων. οὐδὲ γὰρ ἀκίνδυνον βίον
ζῶμεν. ἀλλ' ἐμβαίνετε· πλέωμεν· ἤδη γάρ ἐστι πρὸς
ἡμέραν."

like philosophers. Has robbing a tomb made decent people of us? Shall we show her mercy when her own husband refused to do so and killed her? She has done us no harm, you say. But in the future she can do us plenty. To begin with, if we give her back to her kin, there is no telling what attitude they will take about the matter, and they are certain to suspect our real reason for coming to the tomb. Also, even if the girl's relatives waive charges against us, still the magistrates and the people will not let off tomb robbers who are convicted by the property in their possession. Perhaps someone may say that it is more profitable to sell the girl, since she will fetch a high price for her beauty. But this, too, has its dangers. Gold has no voice and silver will not tell where we got it. We can make up some yarn about them. But who can conceal property which has eyes, ears, and a tongue? And besides, hers is no mere human beauty for us to get away with it. Shall we say that she is a slave? Who will believe that, once he sees her? So let us kill her here and not be encumbered with our own prosecutor."

Many supported these proposals, but Theron favored neither. "One of you," he said, "is courting danger, the other is canceling our profits. I will sell the girl rather than kill her. While on sale she will keep quiet out of fear; once sold let her accuse us, when we are no longer there. In any case the life we lead is a risky one. Get on board and let us sail. Dawn is already near."

---

10.6 τι Blake: καὶ F.

11. Ἀναχθεῖσα δὲ ἡ ναῦς ἐφέρετο λαμπρῶς. οὐδὲ γὰρ ἐβιάζοντο πρὸς κῦμα καὶ πνεῦμα τῷ μὴ προκεῖσθαί τινα πλοῦν ἴδιον αὐτοῖς, ἀλλ' ἅπας ἄνεμος οὔριος αὐτοῖς ἐδόκει καὶ κατὰ πρύμναν εἱστήκει. Καλλιρόην δὲ παρεμυθεῖτο Θήρων, ποικίλαις ἐπινοί-
2 αις πειρώμενος ἀπατᾶν. ἐκείνη δὲ ᾐσθάνετο τὰ καθ' ἑαυτῆς καὶ ὅτι ἄλλως ἐσώθη· προσεποιεῖτο δὲ μὴ νοεῖν, ἀλλὰ πιστεύειν, δεδοικυῖα μὴ ἄρα καὶ ἀνέλωσιν αὐτὴν ὡς ὀργιζομένην. εἰποῦσα δὲ μὴ φέρειν τὴν θάλασσαν, ἐγκαλυψαμένη καὶ δακρύσασα "σὺ μὲν" ἔφη, "πάτερ, ἐν ταύτῃ τῇ θαλάσσῃ τριακοσίας ναῦς Ἀθηναίων κατεναυμάχησας, ἥρπασε δέ σου τὴν θυγατέρα κέλης μικρὸς καὶ οὐδέν μοι βοηθεῖς.
3 ἐπὶ ξένην ἄγομαι γῆν καὶ δουλεύειν με δεῖ τὴν εὐγενῆ· τάχα δὲ ἀγοράσει τις τὴν Ἑρμοκράτους θυγατέρα δεσπότης Ἀθηναῖος. πόσῳ μοι κρεῖττον ἦν ἐν τάφῳ κεῖσθαι νεκράν· πάντως ἂν μετ' ἐμοῦ Χαιρέας ἐκηδεύθη· νῦν δὲ καὶ ζῶντες καὶ ἀποθανόντες διεζεύχθημεν."
4 Ἡ μὲν οὖν ἐν τοιούτοις ἦν ὀδυρμοῖς, οἱ δὲ λῃσταὶ νήσους μικρὰς καὶ πόλεις παρέπλεον· οὐ γὰρ ἦν τὰ φορτία πενήτων, ἐζήτουν δὲ πλουσίους ἄνδρας. ὡρμίσαντο δὴ κατ' ἀντικρὺ τῆς Ἀττικῆς ὑπό τινα χηλήν· πηγὴ δὲ ἦν αὐτόθι πολλοῦ καὶ καθαροῦ
5 νάματος καὶ λειμὼν εὐφυής. ἔνθα τὴν Καλλιρόην προαγαγόντες φαιδρύνεσθαι καὶ ἀναπαύσασθαι κατὰ μικρὸν ἀπὸ τῆς θαλάσσης ἠξίωσαν, διασῴζειν θέλοντες αὐτῆς τὸ κάλλος· μόνοι δὲ ἐβουλεύοντο

66

11. When it put to sea, the ship moved splendidly, for they had not to fight against wind and waves, having set themselves no special course. Every wind seemed to favor them and stood at the stern.[a] Theron sought to comfort Callirhoe, trying to deceive her with elaborate explanations. But she realized her plight and that her rescue had brought her no good. She pretended, however, not to understand, but to believe him, afraid that they might kill her if she became petulant. Saying that she could not stand the sea, she covered her head and wept. "In this very sea, father," she said, "you once defeated three hundred ships of Athens. Now a small cutter is carrying off your daughter and you are powerless to help me. I am being taken abroad and, in spite of noble birth, am to become a slave. Perhaps some Athenian master will buy the daughter of Hermocrates! How much better it would be for me to lie dead in the tomb! Then, at all events, Chaereas would have been buried with me. But now we have been parted both in life and in death."

While she thus lamented, the robbers sailed past small islands and towns, since their cargo was not for the poor man, but they were looking for the rich. Presently they anchored in the shelter of a headland across from Attica,[b] where there was an ample spring of pure water and a pleasant meadow. Taking Callirhoe ashore, they told her to wash and to get a little rest from the voyage, wishing to preserve her beauty. When they were alone, they dis-

---

[a] Cf. Thucydides 2.97.1.
[b] I.e. on the southern shore of the Saronic Gulf.

---

11.2 ἄλλως Hercher: ἄλλοις F.

ὅποι χρὴ τὸν στόλον ὁρμῆσαι. καί τις εἶπεν "'Ἀθῆ-
ναι πλησίον, μεγάλη καὶ εὐδαίμων πόλις. ἐκεῖ πλῆθος μὲν ἐμπόρων εὑρήσομεν, πλῆθος δὲ πλουσίων.
ὥσπερ γὰρ ἐν ἀγορᾷ τοὺς ἄνδρας οὕτως ἐν Ἀθήναις

6   τὰς πόλεις ἔστιν ἰδεῖν." ἐδόκει δὴ πᾶσι καταπλεῖν
εἰς Ἀθήνας, οὐκ ἤρεσκε δὲ Θήρωνι τῆς πόλεως ἡ
περιεργία· "μόνοι γὰρ ὑμεῖς οὐκ ἀκούετε τὴν πολυ-
πραγμοσύνην τῶν Ἀθηναίων; δῆμός ἐστι λάλος καὶ
φιλόδικος, ἐν δὲ τῷ λιμένι μυρίοι συκοφάνται
πεύσονται τίνες ἐσμὲν καὶ πόθεν ταῦτα φέρομεν τὰ
φορτία. ὑποψία καταλήψεται πονηρὰ τοὺς κακοήθεις.

7   Ἄρειος πάγος εὐθὺς ἐκεῖ καὶ ἄρχοντες τυράννων
βαρύτεροι. μᾶλλον Συρακουσίων Ἀθηναίους φοβηθῶμεν. χωρίον ἡμῖν ἐπιτήδειόν ἐστιν Ἰωνία, καὶ
γὰρ πλοῦτος ἐκεῖ βασιλικὸς ἐκ τῆς μεγάλης Ἀσίας
ἄνωθεν ἐπιρρέων καὶ ἄνθρωποι τρυφῶντες καὶ
ἀπράγμονες· ἐλπίζω δέ τινας αὐτόθεν εὑρήσειν καὶ

8   γνωρίμους." ὑδρευσάμενοι δὲ καὶ λαβόντες ἀπὸ τῶν
παρο<ρμω>υσῶν ὁλκάδων ἐπισιτισμὸν ἔπλεον εὐθὺ
Μιλήτου, τριταῖοι δὲ κατήχθησαν εἰς ὅρμον ἀπέχον-
τα τῆς πόλεως σταδίους ὀγδοήκοντα, εὐφυέστατον
εἰς ὑποδοχήν.

12.   Ἔνθα δὴ Θήρων κώπας ἐκέλευσεν ἐκφέρειν
καὶ μονὴν ποιεῖν τῇ Καλλιρόῃ καὶ πάντα παρέχειν
εἰς τρυφήν. ταῦτα δὲ οὐκ ἐκ φιλανθρωπίας ἔπραττεν
ἀλλ' ἐκ φιλοκερδίας, ὡς ἔμπορος μᾶλλον ἢ λῃστής.
αὐτὸς δὲ διέδραμεν εἰς ἄστυ παραλαβὼν δύο τῶν
ἐπιτηδείων. εἶτα φανερῶς μὲν οὐκ ἐβουλεύετο ζητεῖν

cussed where they should make for. One said, "Athens is
nearby, a great and prosperous city. There we shall find
lots of dealers and lots of the wealthy. In Athens you can
see as many communities as you can men in a marketplace." Sailing to Athens appealed to them all. But
Theron did not like the inquisitive nature of the city. "Are
you the only ones," he asked, "who have not heard what
busybodies the Athenians are? They are a talkative lot and
fond of litigation, and in the harbor scores of troublemak-
ers will ask who we are and where we got this cargo. The
worst suspicions will fill their evil minds. The Areopagus[a]
is near at hand and their officials are sterner than tyrants.
We should fear the Athenians more than the Syracusans.
The proper place for us is Ionia, where royal riches flow
in from all over Asia and people love luxury and ask no
questions. Besides, I expect to find there some people I
know." So after taking on water and procuring provisions
from merchant ships nearby, they sailed straight for Miletus and two days later moored in an anchorage ten miles[b]
from the city, a perfect natural harbor.

12. Theron then gave orders to stow the oars, to construct a shelter for Callirhoe and provide everything for
her comfort. This he did not out of compassion but from
a desire for gain, more as a dealer than a pirate. He himself hurried to the town with two of his companions.
Then, having no intention of seeking a buyer openly or of

[a] The supreme lawcourt of the Athenians.
[b] Literally eighty stades.

11.8 add. Naber.

τὸν ὠνητὴν οὐδὲ περιβόητον τὸ πρᾶγμα ποιεῖν,
κρύφα δὲ καὶ διὰ χειρὸς ἔσπευδε τὴν πρᾶσιν.
δυσδιάθετον δὲ ἀπέβαινεν· οὐ γὰρ ἦν τὸ κτῆμα πολλῶν οὐδὲ ἑνὸς τῶν ἐπιτυχόντων, ἀλλὰ πλουσίου
τινὸς καὶ βασιλέως, τοῖς δὲ τοιούτοις ἐφοβεῖτο

2 προσιέναι. γινομένης οὖν διατριβῆς μακροτέρας
οὐκέτι φέρειν ὑπέμενε τὴν παρολκήν· νυκτὸς δὲ
ἐπελθούσης καθεύδειν μὲν οὐκ ἐδύνατο, ἔφη δὲ πρὸς
αὑτὸν "ἀνόητος, ὦ Θήρων, εἰ· ἀπολέλοιπας γὰρ ἤδη
τοσαύταις ἡμέραις ἄργυρον καὶ χρυσὸν ἐν ἐρημίᾳ,

3 ὡς <ὢν> μόνος λῃστής. οὐκ οἶδας ὅτι τὴν θάλασσαν καὶ ἄλλοι πλέουσι πειραταί; ἐγὼ δὲ καὶ τοὺς
ἡμετέρους φοβοῦμαι μὴ καταλιπόντες ἡμᾶς ἀπο-
πλεύσωσιν· οὐ δήπου γὰρ τοὺς δικαιοτάτους ἐστρα-
τολόγησας, ἵνα σοι τὴν πίστιν φυλάττωσιν, ἀλλὰ

4 τοὺς πονηροτάτους ἄνδρας ὧν ᾔδεις. νῦν μὲν οὖν"
εἶπεν "ἐξ ἀνάγκης κάθευδε, ἡμέρας δὲ ἐπιστάσης
διαδραμὼν ἐπὶ τὸν κέλητα ῥῖψον εἰς θάλασσαν τὴν
ἄκαιρον καὶ περιττήν σοι γυναῖκα καὶ μηκέτι φορ-

5 τίον ἐπάγου δυσδιάθετον." κοιμηθεὶς δὲ ἐνύπνιον
εἶδε κεκλεισμένας τὰς θύρας. ἔδοξεν οὖν αὐτῷ τὴν
ἡμέραν ἐκείνην ἐπισχεῖν. οἷα δὲ ἀλύων ἐπί τινος
ἐργαστηρίου καθῆστο, ταραχώδης παντάπασι τὴν
ψυχήν.

6  Ἐν δὲ τῷ μεταξὺ παρῄει πλῆθος ἀνθρώπων ἐλευ-
θέρων τε καὶ δούλων, ἐν μέσοις δὲ αὐτοῖς ἀνὴρ ἡλικίᾳ καθεστώς, μελανειμονῶν καὶ σκυθρωπός. ἀναστὰς οὖν ὁ Θήρων (περίεργον γὰρ ἀνθρώπου φύσις)

70

making his business the talk of the town, he tried to make a quick sale privately without intermediaries. But it proved hard to manage, inasmuch as the property was not for ordinary people or for just anyone, but for some wealthy prince, and he was afraid to approach such persons. After much time-wasting he could no longer endure delay. When night came, he was unable to sleep, and said to himself, "Theron, you are a fool. You have left behind your gold and silver all these days now in a deserted place as though you were the only pirate in existence. Do you not know that other pirates, also, sail the sea? Then I am also worried that our own men may desert us and sail away. Naturally you did not recruit the most honest of men, who would remain loyal to you, but rather the biggest rascals you knew. Well," he said, "you had better get some sleep now, but when day comes, hurry down to the cutter and throw overboard that woman, who is an embarrassing nuisance, and do not take on any other cargo so hard to get rid of." When he fell asleep, he dreamed of seeing locked doors, and so he determined to hold on for that day. Wandering about he sat down in a shop, his thoughts very unsettled.

Meanwhile a crowd of men, both free and slave, was passing by, among them a man in his prime, wearing mourning and sad-faced. Theron got up (men are natu-

12.2 add. Richards.
12.5 ἀλύων Jacobs: ἀλγῶν F.

ἐπυνθάνετο ἑνὸς τῶν ἐπακολουθούντων "τίς οὗτος;" ὁ
δὲ ἀπεκρίνατο "ξένος εἶναί μοι δοκεῖς ἢ μακρόθεν
ἥκειν, ὃς ἀγνοεῖς Διονύσιον πλούτῳ καὶ γένει καὶ
παιδείᾳ τῶν ἄλλων Ἰώνων ὑπερέχοντα, φίλον τοῦ
7  μεγάλου βασιλέως." "διατί τοίνυν μελανειμονεῖ;" "ἡ
γυνὴ γὰρ αὐτοῦ τέθνηκεν ἧς ἤρα." ἔτι μᾶλλον
εἴχετο τῆς ὁμιλίας ὁ Θήρων, εὑρηκὼς ἄνδρα πλούσιον καὶ φιλογύναιον. οὐκέτ' οὖν ἀνῆκε τὸν ἄνδρα
ἀλλ' ἐπυνθάνετο "τίνα χώραν ἔχεις παρ' αὐτῷ;"
8  κἀκεῖνος ἀπεκρίνατο "διοικητής εἰμι τῶν ὅλων,
τρέφω δὲ αὐτῷ καὶ τὴν θυγατέρα, παιδίον νήπιον,
μητρὸς ἀθλίας πρὸ ὥρας ὀρφανόν." [Θήρων] "τί σὺ
καλῇ;" "Λεωνᾶς." "εὐκαίρως" φησίν, "ὦ Λεωνᾶ,
<σοὶ> συνέβαλον. ἔμπορός εἰμι καὶ πλέω νῦν ἐξ
Ἰταλίας, ὅθεν οὐδὲν οἶδα τῶν ἐν Ἰωνίᾳ. γυνὴ δὲ
Συβαρῖτις, εὐδαιμονεστάτη τῶν ἐκεῖ, καλλίστην
ἅβραν ἔχουσα διὰ ζηλοτυπίαν ἐπώλησεν, ἐγὼ δὲ
9  αὐτὴν ἐπριάμην. σοὶ οὖν γενέσθω τὸ κέρδος, εἴτε
σεαυτῷ θέλεις τροφὸν κατασχεῖν τοῦ παιδίου
(πεπαίδευται γὰρ ἱκανῶς) εἴτε καὶ ἄξιον ὑπολαμβάνεις χαρίσασθαι τῷ δεσπότῃ. λυσιτελεῖ δέ σοι
μᾶλλον ἀργυρώνητον ἔχειν αὐτόν, ἵνα μὴ τῇ τρο-
10  φίμῃ σου μητρυιὰν ἐπαγάγηται." τούτων ὁ Λεωνᾶς
ἤκουσεν ἀσμένως καὶ "θεός μοί τις" εἶπεν "εὐεργέ-

12.7 τέθνηκε γὰρ αὐτοῦ ἡ γυνὴ ἧς ἤρα F, corr. Reeve.
12.8 del. Reiske | τί σὺ Blake: τίς F | add. Cobet.
12.9 ὑπολαμβάνεις Cobet: -οις F.

rally curious) and asked one of his companions, "Who is this man?" The other replied, "I think you must be a stranger or come from afar[a] if you do not recognize Dionysius, who outranks all other Ionians in wealth, family, and education, and is a friend of the Great King[b] besides." "Then why is he in mourning?" "His dearly beloved wife has died." Theron sought to prolong the conversation further, now that he had found a man who was rich and susceptible to women, so he hung on to him and inquired, "What is your position with him?" "I am the steward of his establishment," he replied, "and also guardian of his daughter, a mere infant, who all too soon has lost her poor mother." "And what is your name?" "Leonas." "How lucky that I met you, Leonas," he said. "I am a merchant just come by sea from Italy, which is why I know nothing of Ionia. A lady of Sybaris,[c] the wealthiest in the city, had a very beautiful maid whom she put up for sale out of jealousy of her, and I bought her. You can profit by this, whether you wish to get a nurse for the child (she is well enough trained for that), or whether you think it worthwhile doing your master a favor. It is more to your advantage for him to have a bought slave: this will avoid his introducing a stepmother for your young ward." Leonas was delighted to hear this and said, "Heaven must have sent you to be my benefactor. You are showing

[a] Cf. *Odyssey* 9.273.

[b] The king of Persia.

[c] A city on the Tarentine Gulf, proverbially known for its wealth and luxury; destroyed in 510 B.C., it was later resettled and named Thurii.

τὴν σε κατέπεμψεν· ἃ γὰρ ὠνειροπόλουν ὕπαρ μοι
δεικνύεις· ἐλθὲ τοίνυν εἰς τὴν οἰκίαν καὶ φίλος ἤδη
γίνου καὶ ξένος· τὴν δὲ περὶ τῆς γυναικὸς αἵρεσιν ἡ
ὄψις κρινεῖ, πότερον δεσποτικόν ἐστι τὸ κτῆμα ἢ
καθ' ἡμᾶς."

13. Ἐπεὶ δὲ ἦκον εἰς τὴν οἰκίαν, ὁ μὲν Θήρων
ἐθαύμαζε τὸ μέγεθος καὶ τὴν πολυτέλειαν (ἦν γὰρ
εἰς ὑποδοχὴν τοῦ Περσῶν βασιλέως παρεσκευασμέ-
νη), Λεωνᾶς δὲ ἐκέλευσε περιμένειν αὐτὸν περὶ τὴν
θεραπείαν τοῦ δεσπότου πρῶτον <γενησόμενον>.
2 ἔπειτα ἐκεῖνον λαβὼν ἀπήγαγεν εἰς τὴν οἴκησιν
τὴν ἑαυτοῦ σφόδρα ἐλευθέριον οὖσαν, ἐκέλευσε δὲ
παραθεῖναι τράπεζαν. καὶ ὁ Θήρων, οἷα πανοῦργος
ἄνθρωπος καὶ πρὸς πάντα καιρὸν ἁρμόσασθαι δει-
νός, ἥπτετο τροφῆς καὶ ἐφιλοφρονεῖτο ταῖς προπό-
σεσι τὸν Λεωνᾶν, τὰ μὲν ἁπλότητος ἐνδείξει, τὸ δὲ
3 πλέον κοινωνίας πίστει. μεταξὺ δὲ ὁμιλία περὶ τῆς
γυναικὸς ἐγίνετο πολλή, καὶ ὁ Θήρων ἐπήνει τὸν
τρόπον μᾶλλον τῆς γυναικὸς ἢ τὸ κάλλος, εἰδὼς ὅτι
τὸ μὲν ἄδηλον συνηγορίας ἔχει χρείαν, ἡ δὲ ὄψις
αὐτὴν συνίστησιν. "ἀπίωμεν οὖν" ἔφη Λεωνᾶς, "καὶ
4 δεῖξον αὐτήν." ὁ δὲ "οὐκ ἐνταῦθά ἐστιν" ἀπεκρίνατο,
"διὰ γὰρ τοὺς τελώνας περιέστημεν τὴν πόλιν, ἀπὸ
ὀγδοήκοντα δὲ σταδίων τὸ πλοῖον ὁρμεῖ," καὶ τὸν
τόπον ἔφραζεν. "ἐν τοῖς ἡμετέροις" φησὶ "χωρίοις
ὡρμίσασθε· καὶ τοῦτο βέλτιον, ἤδη τῆς Τύχης ὑμᾶς
5 ἀγούσης ἐπὶ Διονύσιον. ἀπίωμεν οὖν εἰς τὸν ἀγρόν,
ἵνα καὶ ἐκ τῆς θαλάσσης αὐτοὺς ἀναλάβητε· ἡ γὰρ

me the reality of what I have been dreaming of. So come to my house and be my friend and guest. As to a decision about the woman, a look at her will tell me whether she is an acquisition worthy of my master or is just for the likes of us."

13. When they came to the house, Theron was astonished at its size and magnificence (for it had been prepared to receive the king of Persia). Leonas told him to wait while he first attended to the needs of his master. Then he collected him and took him off to his own quarters, which were just like those of a free man, and ordered a table set. Theron, a cunning rogue and clever at adapting to every situation, began eating and ingratiated himself with Leonas by toasts to his health, partly to show his openness, but chiefly to inspire trust in their partnership. Meanwhile there was much talk about the girl. Theron kept praising her character rather than her beauty, knowing that what cannot be seen requires an advocate whereas seeing is its own recommendation. "Let us go, then," said Leonas, "and you can show her to me." "She is not here," he replied. "We stayed outside the city because of the customs officials and our boat is anchored ten miles away"—and he described the location. "You are anchored on our own estate," said Leonas, "and that is so much the better. Fortune is already guiding you to Dionysius. Let us be off to the farm, then, so that you can all recover

---

13.1 add. Jackson.
13.2 ἀπήγαγεν Cobet: ἀν- F.

6 πλησίον ἔπαυλις κατεσκεύασται πολυτελῶς." ἥσθη
μᾶλλον ὁ Θήρων, εὐκολωτέραν ἔσεσθαι τὴν πρᾶσιν
οὐκ ἐν ἀγορᾷ νομίζων ἀλλ' ἐν ἐρημίᾳ, καὶ "ἔωθεν"
φησὶν "ἀπίωμεν, σὺ μὲν εἰς τὴν ἔπαυλιν, ἐγὼ δὲ εἰς
τὴν ναῦν, κἀκεῖθεν ἄξω τὴν γυναῖκα πρὸς σέ." συνέθεντο ταῦτα καὶ δεξιὰς ἀλλήλοις ἐμβαλόντες ἀπηλλάγησαν. ἀμφοτέροις δὲ ἡ νὺξ ἐδόκει μακρά, τοῦ
μὲν δὴ σπεύδοντος ἀγοράσαι, τοῦ δὲ πωλῆσαι.

7 Τῆς δ' ὑστεραίας ὁ μὲν Λεωνᾶς παρέπλευσεν εἰς
τὴν ἔπαυλιν, ἅμα καὶ ἀργύριον κομίζων ἵνα προ-
καταλάβῃ τὸν ἔμπορον· ὁ δὲ Θήρων ἐπὶ τὴν ἀκτὴν
καὶ σφόδρα ποθοῦσιν ἐπέστη τοῖς συνεργοῖς, διη-
γησάμενος δὲ τὴν πρᾶξιν αὐτοῖς Καλλιρόην κολα-
8 κεύειν ἤρξατο. "κἀγὼ" φησί, "θύγατερ, εὐθὺς μὲν
ἤθελόν σε πρὸς τοὺς σοὺς ἀπαγαγεῖν· ἐναντίου δὲ
ἀνέμου γενομένου διεκωλύθην ὑπὸ τῆς θαλάσσης·
ἐπίστασαι δὲ πόσην σου πεποίημαι πρόνοιαν· καὶ τὸ
μέγιστον, καθαρὰν ἐτηρήσαμεν· ἀνύβριστον ἀπολή-
ψεταί σε Χαιρέας, ὡς ἐκ θαλάμου τοῦ τάφου σωθεῖ-
9 σαν δι' ἡμᾶς. νῦν μὲν οὖν ἀναγκαῖόν ἐστιν ἡμῖν
μέχρι Λυκίας διαδραμεῖν, οὐκ ἀναγκαῖον δὲ καὶ σὲ
μάτην ταλαιπωρεῖν καὶ ταῦτα χαλεπῶς ναυτιῶσαν·
ἐνταῦθα δὲ δὴ παραθήσομαί σε φίλοις πιστοῖς, ἐπ-
ανιὼν δὲ παραλήψομαι καὶ μετὰ πολλῆς ἐπιμελείας
ἄξω λοιπὸν εἰς Συρακούσας. λαβὲ τῶν σῶν εἴ τι δ'
ἂν θέλῃς· σοὶ γὰρ καὶ τὰ λοιπὰ τηροῦμεν."

10 Ἐπὶ τούτῳ πρὸς αὐτὴν ἐγέλασε Καλλιρόη, καίτοι
σφόδρα λυπουμένη (παντελῶς αὐτὸν ἀνόητον ὑπ-

from the voyage. Our country house nearby is splendidly furnished." Theron was still more pleased, thinking that the transaction would be easier in an isolated place than in the open market. "Let us be off at dawn," he said, "you to the country house, and I to my ship, and I will fetch you the girl from there." They agreed to this and after shaking hands parted. The night seemed long to both, the one impatient to buy, the other to sell.

The next day Leonas sailed along the coast to the country house, bringing money with him to secure his option with the dealer. Theron meanwhile returned to the beach and his anxious confederates. After telling them what he had done, he tried to mollify Callirhoe. "My daughter," said he, "at first I too wanted to take you back to your people, but when an adverse wind sprang up, I was prevented by the state of the sea. You know how much care I have taken of you. Most of all, we have kept your person inviolate. Chaereas will receive you back from the tomb as unmolested as if you had just left your own bedroom—thanks to us. Now we must continue our course to Lycia, but there is no need to put you to needless discomfort, especially as you suffer from seasickness. So I am going to leave you with trusted friends here and on my return I will pick you up and take great care to bring you back to Syracuse. Take any of your things you want. We will look after the rest for you."

At this Callirhoe smiled to herself, greatly troubled though she was, thinking him an utter idiot. She knew she

---

13.7 τῆς δ' ὑστεραίας Jackson: τῇ -αίᾳ F.

ελάμβανεν)· ἡ δὲ πωλουμένη <μὲν> ἠπίστατο, τῆς
δὲ ταλαιπωρίας τὴν πρᾶσιν εὐτυχεστέραν ὑπελάμβανεν, ἀπαλλαγῆναι θέλουσα λῃστῶν. καὶ "χάριν
σοι" φησὶν "ἔχω, πάτερ, ὑπὲρ τῆς εἰς ἐμὲ φιλανθρω-
πίας· ἀποδοῖεν δὲ" ἔφη "πᾶσιν ὑμῖν οἱ θεοὶ τὰς
11 ἀξίας ἀμοιβάς. χρήσασθαι δὲ τοῖς ἐνταφίοις
δυσοιώνιστον ὑπολαμβάνω. πάντα μοι φυλάξατε
καλῶς· ἐμοὶ δὲ ἀρκεῖ δακτυλίδιον μικρόν, ὃ εἶχον
καὶ νεκρά." εἶτα συγκαλυψαμένη τὴν κεφαλὴν "ἄγε
με" φησίν, "ὦ Θήρων, ὅποι ποτὲ θέλεις· πᾶς γὰρ
τόπος θαλάσσης καὶ σκάφους κρείσσων."

14. Ὡς δὲ πλησίον ἐγένετο τῆς ἐπαύλεως, ὁ
Θήρων ἐστρατήγησέ τι τοιοῦτον. ἀποκαλύψας τὴν
Καλλιρόην καὶ λύσας αὐτῆς τὴν κόμην, διανοίξας
τὴν θύραν, πρώτην ἐκέλευσεν εἰσελθεῖν. ὁ δὲ Λεωνᾶς
καὶ πάντες οἱ ἔνδον ἐπιστάσης αἰφνίδιον κατεπλάγησαν, οἷα δὴ δοκοῦντες θεὰν ἑωρακέναι· καὶ γὰρ
ἦν τις λόγος ἐν τοῖς ἀγροῖς Ἀφροδίτην ἐπιφαίνε-
2 σθαι. καταπεπληγμένων δὲ αὐτῶν κατόπιν ὁ Θήρων
ἑπόμενος προσῆλθε τῷ Λεωνᾷ καὶ "ἀνάστα" φησὶ
"καὶ γενοῦ περὶ τὴν ὑποδοχὴν τῆς γυναικός· αὕτη
γάρ ἐστιν ἣν θέλεις ἀγοράσαι." χαρὰ καὶ θαυμασ-
3 μὸς ἐπηκολούθησε πάντων. τὴν μὲν οὖν Καλλιρόην
ἐν τῷ καλλίστῳ τῶν οἰκημάτων κατακλίναντες εἴασαν ἡσυχάζειν· καὶ γὰρ ἐδεῖτο πολλῆς ἀναπαύσεως
ἐκ λύπης καὶ καμάτου καὶ φόβου· Θήρων δὲ τῆς
δεξιᾶς λαβόμενος τοῦ Λεωνᾶ "τὰ μὲν παρ' ἐμοῦ σοι"
φησὶ "πιστῶς πεπλήρωται, σὺ δὲ ἔχε μὲν ἤδη τὴν

was being sold, but in her eagerness to be rid of the pirates she regarded the sale as offering a better chance than her present misery. "I thank you, sir," she said, "for your kind consideration toward me. May Heaven grant all of you the reward you deserve. But I think it unlucky to use the funeral offerings. Take care of them all for me. A little ring which I wore even as a corpse will satisfy me." Then covering her head she said, "Theron, take me wherever you want. Any place is better than a boat at sea."

14. When he got near the country house, Theron devised the following scheme. Unveiling Callirhoe and loosening her hair, he opened the door and told her to go in first. Leonas and all in the room were struck with amazement at the sudden apparition, as if they had set eyes on a goddess, for rumor had it that Aphrodite could be seen in the fields. Amid their amazement, Theron, who came in after her, went up to Leonas and said, "Come and prepare to look after the girl. This is the one you want to buy." Joy and wonder was the reaction of all. Sending Callirhoe off to bed in the finest room in the house, they allowed her to rest, for she badly needed to recover from distress, fatigue, and anxiety. Theron then took Leonas by the hand and said, "My part of the bargain has been faithfully carried out. You can take the girl right

---

13.10 add. Cobet | ταλαιπωρίας Cobet: πάλαι εὐγενείας F.
13.11 σκάφους Naber: τάφου F.
14.1 οἷα δὴ Zimmermann: οἱ μὲν F.

γυναῖκα (φίλος γὰρ εἶ λοιπόν), ἧκε δὲ εἰς ἄστυ καὶ
λάμβανε τὰς καταγραφὰς καὶ τότε μοι τιμήν, ἢν
4 θέλεις, ἀποδώσεις." ἀμείψασθαι δὲ θέλων ὁ Λεωνᾶς
"οὐ μὲν οὖν" φησίν, "ἀλλὰ καὶ ἐγώ σοι τὸ ἀργύριον
ἤδη πιστεύω πρὸ τῆς καταγραφῆς," ἅμα δὲ καὶ προ-
καταλαβεῖν ἤθελε, δεδιὼς μὴ ἄρα μετάθηται·
πολλοὺς γὰρ ἐν τῇ πόλει γενέσθαι τοὺς ἐθέλοντας
5 ὠνεῖσθαι. τάλαντον οὖν ἀργυρίου προκομίσας ἠν-
άγκαζε λαβεῖν, ὁ δὲ Θήρων ἀκκισάμενος λαμβάνει.
κατέχοντος δὲ ἐπὶ δεῖπνον αὐτὸν τοῦ Λεωνᾶ (καὶ γὰρ
ἦν ὀψὲ τῆς ὥρας) "βούλομαι" φησὶν "ἀφ' ἑσπέρας
εἰς τὴν πόλιν πλεῦσαι, τῆς δ' ὑστεραίας ἐπὶ τῷ
λιμένι συμβαλοῦμεν."
6    Ἐπὶ τούτοις ἀπηλλάγησαν. ἐλθὼν δὲ ἐπὶ τὴν
ναῦν ὁ Θήρων ἐκέλευσεν ἀραμένους τὰς ἀγκύρας
ἀνάγεσθαι τὴν ταχίστην, πρὶν ἐκπύστους γενέσθαι.
καὶ οἱ μὲν ἀπεδίδρασκον ἔνθα τὸ πνεῦμα ἔφερε,
μόνη δὲ Καλλιρόη γενομένη ἤδη μετ' ἐξουσίας τὴν
ἰδίαν ἀπωδύρετο τύχην. "ἰδοὺ" φησὶν "ἄλλος τάφος,
ἐν ᾧ Θήρων με κατέκλεισεν, ἐρημότερος ἐκείνου
7 μᾶλλον· πατὴρ γὰρ ἂν ἐκεῖ μοι προσῆλθε καὶ
μήτηρ, καὶ Χαιρέας ἐπέπεισε δακρύων· ἠσθόμην
ἂν καὶ τεθνεῶσα. τίνα δὲ ἐνταῦθα καλέσω; διώ-
κουσα, Τύχη βάσκανε, διὰ γῆς καὶ θαλάσσης τῶν

14.5 τῆς δ' ὑστ.] see on 1.13.7.
14.7 ἂν ἐκεῖ μοι Reeve: μοι ἂν ἐκεῖ F | διώκουσα Richards:
γινώσκεις F.

now—for you are now a friend of mine—and go to the city and get the registration papers.[a] Then you can pay me any price you like." But Leonas, wishing to reciprocate the gesture, said, "Not at all. I will trust you with the money now before registration"—he wanted to secure an option to buy in case the other changed his mind, knowing that there were many willing purchasers in the city. So he produced a talent of silver[b] and forced Theron to take it. Theron, with a show of indifference, accepted. But when Leonas tried to detain him for dinner (in fact it was getting late), he said, "I want to sail to the city this evening, but we will meet each other tomorrow at the harbor."

On this they parted. Going to his ship Theron gave orders to weigh anchor and put out to sea at once, before they were found out.[c] While they escaped where the wind carried them, Callirhoe, now left alone, was free to bewail her fate. "Behold," she said, "yet another tomb, in which Theron has locked me up, one more lonely than the first! There my father and mother would have come to see me and Chaereas would have poured forth his tribute of tears. Even in death, I should have sensed that. But whom can I call on here? Envious Fortune, you hound

[a] Enslaving a freeborn citizen being a serious crime, it was important for both seller and buyer of a slave to be able to show documentary title to ownership.

[b] A talent comprised 6000 drachmas, and since at the dramatic date an adult slave could be sold for less than 300 drachmas, the price for Callirhoe would seem to be exceeding high. On the other hand, in 2.4.7 Dionysius speaks of it as absurdly low. Reardon perceptively sees in this Chariton's desire to emphasize Callirhoe's beauty and Dionysius' wealth.

[c] The same phrase at Thucydides 3.30.1.

CHARITON

ἐμῶν κακῶν οὐκ ἐπληρώθης, ἀλλὰ πρῶτον μὲν τὸν
ἐραστήν μου φονέα ἐποίησας· Χαιρέας, ὁ μηδὲ
δοῦλον μηδέποτε πλήξας, ἐλάκτισε καιρίως με τὴν
8 φιλοῦσαν· εἶτά με τυμβωρύχων χερσὶ παρέδωκας
καὶ ἐκ τάφου προήγαγες εἰς θάλασσαν καὶ τῶν
κυμάτων τοὺς πειρατὰς φοβερωτέρους ἐπέστησας.
τὸ δὲ περιβόητον κάλλος εἰς τοῦτο ἐκτησάμην, ἵνα
ὑπὲρ ἐμοῦ Θήρων ὁ λῃστὴς μεγάλην λάβῃ τιμήν.
9 ἐν ἐρημίᾳ πέπραμαι καὶ οὐδὲ εἰς πόλιν ἠνέχθην, ὡς
ἄλλη τις τῶν ἀργυρωνήτων· ἐφοβήθης γάρ, ὦ Τύχη,
μή τις ἰδὼν εὐγενῆ δόξῃ. διὰ τοῦτο ὡς σκεῦος παρεδόθην οὐκ οἶδα τίσιν, Ἕλλησιν ἢ βαρβάροις ἢ
πάλιν λῃσταῖς." κόπτουσα δὲ τῇ χειρὶ τὸ στῆθος
εἶδεν ἐν τῷ δακτυλίῳ τὴν εἰκόνα τὴν Χαιρέου καὶ
καταφιλοῦσα "ἀληθῶς ἀπόλωλά σοι, Χαιρέα" φησί,
10 "τοσούτῳ διαζευχθεῖσα πελάγει. καὶ σὺ μὲν πενθεῖς
καὶ μετανοεῖς καὶ τάφῳ κενῷ παρακάθησαι, μετὰ
θάνατόν μοι τὴν σωφροσύνην μαρτυρῶν, ἐγὼ δὲ ἡ
Ἑρμοκράτους θυγάτηρ, ἡ σὴ γυνή, δεσπότῃ σήμερον ἐπράθην." τοιαῦτα ὀδυρομένη μόλις ὕπνος
ἐπῆλθεν [αὐτῇ].

14.9 ἀπόλωλά Hirschig σοι Zimmermann: ἀπόλωλας ὦ F |
διαζευχθεῖσα Hirschig πελάγει Hercher: διαζευχθεὶς πάθει F.
14.10 del. Cobet.

82

me by land and sea and have not yet had your fill of my misfortunes? First you made my lover my murderer. Chaereas, who had never struck even a slave, gave me, who loved him, a fatal kick. Then you delivered me into the hands of tomb robbers and brought me from the tomb to the sea and subjected me to pirates more awful than the waves. For this I was given my famed beauty, that the pirate Theron might win a high price for me! I have been sold in an isolated place and was not even brought to the city as any other slave might be, for you were afraid, Fortune, that if any saw me, they might judge me nobly born. That is why I have been handed over like a mere chattel to I know not whom, whether Greeks or orientals[a] or brigands once more." As she beat her breast with her fist, she saw on her ring the image of Chaereas, and kissing it, she said, "Chaereas, now I am truly lost to you, separated by so vast a sea. You are repenting in grief as you sit by the empty tomb, bearing witness to my chastity after my death, while I, the daughter of Hermocrates, your wife, have today been sold to a master!" So she lamented, and it was long before sleep finally came.

[a] Translating *barbaroi*, by which the Greeks meant non-Greek speakers; they might be uncultured, but the term does not imply that they were savages. Chariton uses it to describe the orientals who made up the Persian empire.

# B

1. Λεωνᾶς δὲ κελεύσας Φωκᾷ τῷ οἰκονόμῳ πολλὴν ἐπιμέλειαν ἔχειν τῆς γυναικός, αὐτὸς ἔτι νυκτὸς ἐξῆλθεν εἰς τὴν Μίλητον, σπεύδων εὐαγγελίσασθαι τῷ δεσπότῃ τὰ περὶ τῆς νεωνήτου, μεγάλην οἰόμενος αὐτῷ φέρειν τοῦ πένθους παραμυθίαν. εὗρε δὲ ἔτι κατακείμενον τὸν Διονύσιον· ἀλύων γὰρ ὑπὸ τῆς λύπης οὐδὲ προῄει τὰ πολλά, καίτοι ποθούσης αὐτὸν τῆς πατρίδος, ἀλλὰ διέτριβεν ἐν τῷ θαλάμῳ, ὡς ἔτι παρούσης αὐτῷ τῆς γυναικός.

2  Ἰδὼν δὲ τὸν Λεωνᾶν ἔφη πρὸς αὐτὸν "μίαν ταύτην ἐγὼ νύκτα μετὰ τὸν θάνατον τῆς ἀθλίας ἡδέως κεκοίμημαι· καὶ γὰρ εἶδον αὐτὴν ἐναργῶς μείζονά τε καὶ κρείττονα γεγενημένην, καὶ ὡς ὕπαρ μοι συνῆν. ἔδοξα δὲ εἶναι τὴν πρώτην ἡμέραν τῶν γάμων καὶ ἀπὸ τῶν χωρίων μου τῶν παραθαλαττίων αὐτὴν νυμφαγωγεῖν, σοῦ μοι τὸν ὑμέναιον ᾄδοντος."

3  ἔτι δὲ αὐτοῦ διηγουμένου, Λεωνᾶς ἀνεβόησεν "εὐτυχὴς εἶ, δέσποτα, καὶ ὄναρ καὶ ὕπαρ. μέλλεις ἀκούειν ταῦτα, ἃ τεθέασαι." καὶ ἀρξάμενος αὐτῷ διηγεῖται "προσῆλθέ μοί τις ἔμπορος πιπράσκων γυναῖκα καλλίστην, διὰ δὲ τοὺς τελώνας ἔξω τῆς πόλεως ὥρμισε τὴν ναῦν πλησίον τῶν σῶν χωρίων. κἀγὼ

# BOOK 2

1. Leonas told Phocas, the estate manager, to take great care of the girl, and while it was still dark, set out himself for Miletus. He was eager to tell his master the good news of his recent purchase, thinking this would console him considerably for his loss. He found Dionysius still in the bedroom. Overcome with grief, he refused for the most part even to go out, though the city sorely missed him; he remained in his room as if his wife were still with him.

Seeing Leonas he said to him, "This is the first night since my poor wife's death that I have slept well. In fact I dreamed I saw her clearly, grander and lovelier than ever, and it was as if she were actually with me. I thought it was the first day of our married life and I was bringing her home as my bride from my estate by the sea, and you were singing the wedding hymn." Interrupting him Leonas exclaimed, "Sir, you are as lucky awake as asleep. You are now going to hear of the very thing you have dreamed of." And he began his story. "A merchant who had a beautiful girl for sale approached me. Because of the custom officials he had anchored his boat outside the city near your property. By arrangement I went out to the

4 συνταξάμενος ἀπῆλθον εἰς ἀγρόν. ἐκεῖ δὲ συμβα-
λόντες ἀλλήλοις ἔργῳ μὲν τὴν πρᾶσιν ἀπηρτίκαμεν·
ἐγώ τε γὰρ ἐκείνῳ τάλαντον δέδωκα <κἀκεῖνος ἐμοὶ
τὴν γυναῖκα παραδέδωκε>· δεῖ δὲ ἐνταῦθα γενέσθαι
5 νομίμως τὴν καταγραφήν." ὁ δὲ Διονύσιος τὸ μὲν
κάλλος ἡδέως ἤκουσε τῆς γυναικός (ἦν γὰρ φιλο-
γύνης ἀληθῶς), τὴν δὲ δουλείαν ἀηδῶς· ἀνὴρ γὰρ
βασιλικός, διαφέρων ἀξιώματι καὶ παιδείᾳ τῆς ὅλης
Ἰωνίας, ἀπηξίου κοίτην θεραπαινίδος, καὶ "ἀδύνατον" εἶπεν, "ὦ Λεωνᾶ, καλὸν εἶναι σῶμα μὴ πεφυκὸς
ἐλεύθερον. οὐκ ἀκούεις τῶν ποιητῶν ὅτι θεῶν παῖδές
εἰσιν οἱ καλοί, πολὺ δὲ πρότερον ἀνθρώπων εὐγενῶν;
σοὶ δὲ ἤρεσεν ἐπ' ἐρημίας· συνέκρινας γὰρ αὐτὴν
6 ταῖς ἀγροίκοις. ἀλλ' ἐπείπερ ἐπρίω, βάδιζε εἰς τὴν
ἀγοράν· Ἄδραστος δὲ ὁ ἐμπειρότατος τῶν νόμων
διοικήσει τὰς καταγραφάς."

Ἔχαιρεν ὁ Λεωνᾶς ἀπιστούμενος· τὸ γὰρ ἀπροσδόκητον ἔμελλε τὸν δεσπότην μᾶλλον ἐκπλήσσειν.
παριὼν δὲ τοὺς Μιλησίων λιμένας ἅπαντας καὶ τὰς
τραπέζας καὶ τὴν πόλιν ὅλην οὐδαμοῦ Θήρωνα
7 εὑρεῖν ἠδύνατο. ἐμπόρους ἐξήταζε καὶ πορθμεῖς,
ἐγνώριζε δὲ οὐδείς. ἐν πολλῇ τοίνυν ἀπορίᾳ γενόμενος κωπῆρες λαβὼν παρέπλευσεν ἐπὶ τὴν ἀκτὴν
κἀκεῖθεν ἐπὶ τὸ χωρίον· οὐκ ἔμελλε δὲ εὑρήσειν τὸν
ἤδη πλέοντα. μόλις οὖν καὶ βραδέως ἀπῆλθε πρὸς
8 τὸν δεσπότην. ἰδὼν δὲ αὐτὸν ὁ Διονύσιος σκυθρω-

1.4 add. Jackson (after Cobet).

estate. There we came to an agreement, and essentially completed the sale. In fact, I gave him a talent, and in return he gave me the girl. But the purchase has to be legally registered here." Although Dionysius was pleased to hear of the girl's beauty, for he was a great admirer of women, he was not pleased to hear she was a slave. Being an aristocrat and preeminent all over Ionia in rank and culture, he refused to take a slave as concubine. "Leonas," he said, "it is impossible for a person not free-born to be beautiful.[a] Have you not learned from the poets that beautiful people are the children of gods, and all the more likely children of the nobly born? She impressed you in an isolated place. No doubt you compared her with the local women. However, since you have bought her, go to the marketplace, and Adrastus, an experienced lawyer, will arrange the registration."

Leonas was glad to be disbelieved, because the surprise in store for his master would affect him all the more. But though he went round all the harbors[b] of Miletus and the moneychangers' tables and the whole city, he could not find Theron anywhere. He questioned the merchants and boatmen, but no one knew him. Much perplexed he took a small boat and rowed to the beach, and went on from there to the estate. But he was not likely to find a man who was already on the high seas. So slowly and reluctantly he went off to his master. Seeing his gloomy

---

[a] A basic conception of the ancient aristocracy (cf. Menander, *Heros* fr. 2 K-T).

[b] The city had four natural harbors (Strabo 14.1.6).

---

1.5 ταῖς D'Orville: τοῖς F.
1.8 σοι Hercher: σου F.

87

πὸν ἤρετο τί πέπονθεν· ὁ δέ φησιν "ἀπολώλεκά σοι,
ὦ δέσποτα, τάλαντον." "συμβαῖνον" εἶπεν ὁ Διονύσιος "ἀσφαλέστερόν σε τοῦτο πρὸς τὰ λοιπὰ ποιήσει. τί δὲ ὅμως συμβέβηκε; ἢ μή τι ἡ νεώνητος
ἀποδέδρακεν;" "οὐκ ἐκείνη" φησίν, "ἀλλ' ὁ πωλή-
σας." "ἀνδραποδιστὴς ἄρα ἦν, καὶ ἀλλοτρίαν σοι
πέπρακε δούλην διὰ τοῦτ' ἐπ' ἐρημίας. πόθεν δ'
9 ἔλεγε τὴν ἄνθρωπον εἶναι;" "Συβαρῖτιν ἐξ Ἰταλίας,
πραθεῖσαν ὑπὸ δεσποίνης κατὰ ζηλοτυπίαν." "ζήτη-
σον Συβαριτῶν εἴ τινες ἐπιδημοῦσιν· ἐν δὲ τῷ
μεταξὺ ἐκεῖ κατάλιπε τὴν γυναῖκα." τότε μὲν οὖν ὁ
Λεωνᾶς ἀπῆλθε λυπούμενος, ὡς οὐκ εὐτυχοῦς τῆς
πραγματείας αὐτῷ γεγενημένης· ἐπετήρει δὲ καιρὸν
ἀναπεῖσαι τὸν δεσπότην ἐξελθεῖν εἰς τὰ χωρία, λοιπὸν μίαν ἔχων ἐλπίδα τὴν ὄψιν τῆς γυναικός.

2. Πρὸς δὲ τὴν Καλλιρόην εἰσῆλθον αἱ ἄγροικοι
γυναῖκες καὶ εὐθὺς ὡς δέσποιναν ἤρξαντο κολακεύειν. Πλαγγὼν δέ, ἡ τοῦ οἰκονόμου γυνή, ζῷον οὐκ
ἄπρακτον, ἔφη πρὸς αὐτὴν "ζητεῖς μέν, ὦ τέκνον,
πάντως τοὺς σεαυτῆς· ἀλλὰ [καλῶς] καὶ <τοὺς>
ἐνθάδε νόμιζε σούς· Διονύσιος γάρ, ὁ δεσπότης
ἡμῶν, χρηστός ἐστι καὶ φιλάνθρωπος. εὐτυχῶς σε
ἤγαγεν εἰς ἀγαθὴν ὁ θεὸς οἰκίαν· ὥσπερ ἐν πατρίδι
2 διάξεις. ἐκ μακρᾶς οὖν θαλάσσης ἀπόλουσαι τὴν
ἄσιν· ἔχεις θεραπαινίδας." μόλις μὲν καὶ μὴ βουλομένην, προήγαγε δὲ ὅμως εἰς τὸ βαλανεῖον. εἰσελθοῦσαν δὲ ἤλειψάν τε καὶ ἀπέσμηξαν ἐπιμελῶς

2.1 Πλαγγὼν (-όνος etc.) Cobet: Πλάγγων (-ωνος etc.) F

face Dionysius asked what was the matter. He said, "Sir, I have lost you a talent." "This experience will make you more careful in the future," replied Dionysius. "At any rate, what happened? Has the girl you bought run away?" "No, not she, but the seller has," he said. "Then he was a kidnapper and that is why he sold you someone else's slave in an isolated place. Where did he say the girl was from?" "From Sybaris in Italy; her mistress sold her because she was jealous of her." "Find out whether there are any people from Sybaris visiting here. Meanwhile leave the girl there." Thereupon Leonas went off upset that the deal had not turned out a success. However, he waited for a suitable moment to get his master to visit the estate, since the only hope he had left was for him to see the girl.

2. The countrywomen came to visit Callirhoe and at once began to curry favor with her as if she were their mistress. Plangon, the estate manager's wife and a woman of experience, said to her, "My child, you naturally miss your own folk, but you should also consider the people here your own. Dionysius, our master, is decent and kind. You are lucky that Heaven has brought you to a good home. It will be like living in your own country. Wash off the dirt from your long voyage. Here are servants for you." Though Callirhoe was reluctant and unwilling, Plangon managed to get her to the bath. After she had gone in they rubbed her with oil and wiped it off

---

consistently | σεαυτῆς Hercher: ἑαυτῆς F | del. Zimmermann | add. Hercher | ὥσπερ Hercher: ὥστε F.

   2.2 εἰσελθοῦσαν D'Orville: -οῦσαι F.

καὶ μᾶλλον ἀποδυσαμένης κατεπλάγησαν· ὥστε
ἐνδεδυμένης αὐτῆς θαυμάζουσαι τὸ πρόσωπον ὡς
θεῖον, <ἀ>πρόσωπον ἔδοξαν <τἄνδον> ἰδοῦσαι· ὁ
χρὼς γὰρ λευκὸς ἔστιλψεν εὐθὺς μαρμαρυγῇ τινι
ὅμοιον ἀπολάμπων· τρυφερὰ δὲ σάρξ, ὥστε δεδοικέ-
ναι μὴ καὶ ἡ τῶν δακτύλων ἐπαφὴ μέγα τραῦμα
3 ποιήσῃ. ἡσυχῇ δὲ διελάλουν πρὸς ἀλλήλας "καλὴ
μὲν ἡ δέσποινα ἡμῶν καὶ περιβόητος· ταύτης δὲ ἂν
θεραπαινὶς ἔδοξεν." ἐλύπει τὴν Καλλιρόην ὁ ἔπαινος καὶ τοῦ μέλλοντος οὐκ ἀμάντευτος ἦν. ἐπεὶ δὲ
λέλουτο καὶ τὴν κόμην συνεδέσμουν, καθαρὰς αὐτῇ
προσήνεγκαν ἐσθῆτας· ἡ δὲ οὐ πρέπειν ἔλεγε ταῦτα
4 τῇ νεωνήτῳ. "χιτῶνά μοι δότε δουλικόν· καὶ γὰρ
ὑμεῖς ἐστέ μου κρείττονες." ἐνεδύσατο μὲν οὖν τι
τῶν ἐπιτυχόντων· κἀκεῖνο δὲ ἔπρεπεν αὐτῇ καὶ
πολυτελὲς ἔδοξε καταλαμπόμενον ὑπὸ <τοῦ> κάλλους.

5 Ἐπεὶ δὲ ἠρίστησαν αἱ γυναῖκες, εἶπεν ἡ Πλαγγὼν "ἐλθὲ πρὸς τὴν Ἀφροδίτην καὶ εὖξαι περὶ σαυ-
τῆς· ἐπιφανὴς δέ ἐστιν ἐνθάδε ἡ θεός, καὶ οὐ μόνον
οἱ γείτονες, ἀλλὰ καὶ οἱ ἐξ ἄστεος παραγινόμενοι
θύουσιν αὐτῇ. μάλιστα δὲ ἐπήκοος Διονυσίῳ· ἐκεῖ-
6 νος οὐδέποτε παρῆλθεν αὐτήν." εἶτα διηγοῦντο τῆς
θεοῦ τὰς ἐπιφανείας καί τις εἶπε τῶν ἀγροίκων
"δόξεις, ὦ γύναι, θεασαμένη τὴν Ἀφροδίτην εἰκόνα
βλέπειν σεαυτῆς." ἀκούσασα δὲ ἡ Καλλιρόη
δακρύων <ἐν>επλήσθη καὶ λέγει πρὸς ἑαυτὴν "οἴμοι
τῆς συμφορᾶς, καὶ ἐνταῦθά ἐστιν Ἀφροδίτη θεὸς ἡ

carefully, and marveled at her all the more when undressed, for, whereas when she was dressed they admired her face as divine, they had no thoughts for her face when they saw her hidden beauty. Her skin gleamed white, shining just like a shimmering surface, but her flesh was so delicate as to make one afraid that even the touch of one's fingers might cause a serious wound. They whispered to one another, "Our mistress was famed for her beauty, but she would have seemed this girl's maidservant." Their praise troubled Callirhoe and she had a foreboding of what was to come. When she had had her bath and they were fastening up her hair, they brought her clean clothes. But she said that this was not proper for one who had just been bought: "Give me a slave's tunic, for even you are my superiors." So she put on an ordinary dress, but this too suited her and in reflecting her beauty seemed an expensive one.

When the women had eaten, Plangon said to Callirhoe, "Come to Aphrodite's shrine and offer up a prayer for yourself. The goddess makes her appearance here; and, besides our neighbors, people from the city come here to sacrifice to her. She listens especially to Dionysius, and he has never failed to stop at her shrine." They then told her of the appearances of the goddess, and one of the peasant women said, "Lady, when you see Aphrodite you will think you are looking at a picture of yourself." When Callirhoe heard this, her eyes filled with tears, and she said to herself, "What a disaster! Even here

2.2 add. Jackson (cf. Plato, *Charmides* 154D, Aristaenetus 1.3).     2.4 add. Zankogiannes.
2.5 εἶπεν Heibges: λέγει F.     2.6 add. Hercher

μοι πάντων τῶν κακῶν αἰτία. πλὴν ἄπειμι, θέλω
γὰρ αὐτὴν πολλὰ μέμψασθαι."

7      Τὸ δὲ ἱερὸν πλησίον ἦν τῆς ἐπαύλεως παρ' αὐτὴν
τὴν λεωφόρον. προσκυνήσασα δὲ ἡ Καλλιρόη καὶ
τῶν ποδῶν λαβομένη τῆς Ἀφροδίτης "σύ μοι" φησὶ
"πρώτη Χαιρέαν ἔδειξας, συναρμόσασα δὲ καλὸν
ζεῦγος οὐκ ἐτήρησας· καίτοιγε ἡμεῖς σε ἐκοσμοῦ-
8   μεν. ἐπεὶ δὲ οὕτως ἐβουλήθης, μίαν αἰτοῦμαι παρὰ
σοῦ χάριν· μηδενί με ποιήσῃς μετ' ἐκεῖνον ἀρέσαι."
πρὸς τοῦτο ἀνένευσεν ἡ Ἀφροδίτη· μήτηρ γάρ ἐστι
τοῦ Ἔρωτος, καὶ πάλιν ἄλλον ἐπολιτεύετο γάμον, ὃν
οὐδὲ αὐτὸν ἔμελλε τηρήσειν. ἀπαλλαγεῖσα δὲ ἡ
Καλλιρόη λῃστῶν καὶ θαλάσσης τὸ ἴδιον κάλλος
ἀνελάμβανεν, ὥστε θαυμάζειν τοὺς ἀγροίκους καθημέραν εὐμορφοτέρας αὐτῆς βλεπομένης.

3. Ὁ δὲ Λεωνᾶς, καιρὸν ἐπιτήδειον εὑρών, Διονυσίῳ λόγους προσήνεγκε τοιούτους· "ἐν τοῖς παρα-
θαλασσίοις, ὦ δέσποτα, χωρίοις οὐ γέγονας ἤδη
χρόνῳ πολλῷ καὶ ποθεῖ τὰ ἐκεῖ τὴν σὴν ἐπιδημίαν.
ἀγέλας σε δεῖ καὶ φυτείας θεάσασθαι, καὶ ἡ συγκο-
2   μιδὴ τῶν καρπῶν ἐπείγει. χρῆσαι καὶ τῇ πολυτε-
λείᾳ τῶν οἰκιῶν ἃς σοῦ κελεύσαντος ᾠκοδομήσαμεν·
οἴσεις δὲ καὶ τὸ πένθος ἐλαφρότερον ἐκεῖ, περισπώ-
μενος ὑπὸ τῆς τῶν ἀγρῶν ἀπολαύσεως καὶ διοική-
σεως. ἐὰν δέ τινα ἐπαινέσῃς ἢ βουκόλον ἢ ποιμένα,
δώσεις αὐτῷ τὴν νεώνητον γυναῖκα." ἤρεσε τῷ
Διονυσίῳ ταῦτα καὶ προεῖπε τὴν ἔξοδον εἰς ῥητὴν
3   ἡμέραν. παραγγελίας δὲ γενομένης παρεσκεύαζον
ἡνίοχοι μὲν ὀχήματα, ἱπποκόμοι δὲ ἵππους,

Aphrodite reigns, the cause of all my woes. But I will go,
for I have many complaints to lay before her."

The shrine was near the country house, by the main
road. Callirhoe knelt in homage before Aphrodite and
clinging to her feet she said, "You first showed Chaereas
to me, and joined us in a happy union, but you have not
preserved it. Yet we paid you honor! But since that was
your will, I ask one boon of you. After Chaereas grant
that I never attract any man again!" Aphrodite refused
his prayer, for she is the mother of Love and she was lay-
ing her plans for another marriage, though she had no
intention of preserving that, either. So Callirhoe, rid of
pirates and the perils of the sea, regained her natural
beauty, and the country folk marveled when they saw her
growing lovelier every day.

3. Finding a suitable occasion, Leonas made his suggestion to Dionysius in these words, "Sir, it is now a long
time since you visited your estate by the sea, and matters
there require your presence. You must inspect the herds
and the crops. The harvest is close at hand. You should
also make use of the splendid buildings we erected there
on your orders. Moreover, you will bear your grief more
easily there, distracted by the joys and the management
of your estate. If you are pleased with some herdsman or
shepherd, you can give him the girl I have bought."
Dionysius decided to do so, and set a date for their departure. When the order had been given, the muleteers got
ready their wagons, the grooms their horses, the sailors

---

2.6 ἤ μοι Jacobs: ἐμοὶ F | πάντων τῶν Blake: τῶν πάντων
.

3.2 ῥητὴν Reiske: ἦν F.

93

ναῦται δὲ πορθμεῖα· φίλοι παρεκαλοῦντο συνοδεύειι
καὶ πλῆθος ἀπελευθέρων· φύσει γὰρ ἦν ὁ Διονύσιος
4 μεγαλοπρεπής. ἐπεὶ δὲ πάντα ηὐτρέπιστο, τὴν μὲν
παρασκευὴν καὶ τοὺς πολλοὺς ἐκέλευσε διὰ θαλάσσης κομίζεσθαι, τὰ δὲ ὀχήματα ἐπακολουθεῖν ὅται
αὐτὸς προέλθῃ, πενθοῦντί τε γὰρ μὴ πρέπειν πομ-
πήν. ἅμα δὲ τῇ ἕῳ, πρὶν αἰσθέσθαι τοὺς πολλοὺς
ἵππου πέμπτος ἐπέβη· εἷς δὲ ἦν ἐν αὐτοῖς καὶ ὁ
Λεωνᾶς.

5   Ὁ μὲν οὖν Διονύσιος ἐξήλαυνεν εἰς τοὺς ἀγροὺς
ἡ δὲ Καλλιρόη τῆς νυκτὸς ἐκείνης θεασαμένη τὴ
Ἀφροδίτην ἠβουλήθη καὶ πάλιν αὐτὴν προσκυνῆ-
σαι· καὶ ἡ μὲν ἑστῶσα ηὔχετο, Διονύσιος δὲ ἀποπη-
δήσας ἀπὸ τοῦ ἵππου πρῶτος εἰσῆλθεν εἰς τὸν νεών
ψόφου δὲ ποδῶν αἰσθομένη Καλλιρόη πρὸς αὐτὸ
6 ἐπεστράφη. θεασάμενος οὖν ὁ Διονύσιος ἀνεβόησε
"ἵλεως εἴης, ὦ Ἀφροδίτη, καὶ ἐπ᾽ ἀγαθῷ μο
φανείης." καταπίπτοντα δὲ αὐτὸν ἤδη Λεωνᾶς ὑπ
έλαβε καὶ "αὕτη" φησὶν "ἐστίν, ὦ δέσποτα, ἡ νεώ
νητος· μηδὲν ταραχθῇς. καὶ σὺ δέ, ὦ γύναι, πρόσ
ελθε τῷ κυρίῳ." Καλλιρόη μὲν οὖν πρὸς τὸ ὄνομι
τοῦ κυρίου κάτω κύψασα, πηγὴν ἀφῆκε δακρύων ὀψ
μεταμανθάνουσα τὴν ἐλευθερίαν· ὁ δὲ Διονύσιο
πλήξας τὸν Λεωνᾶν "ἀσεβέστατε" εἶπεν, "ὦ
7 ἀνθρώποις διαλέγῃ τοῖς θεοῖς; ταύτην λέγεις ἀργυρώνητον; δικαίως οὖν οὐχ εὗρες τὸν πιπράσκοντα

3.4 ἵππου D'Orville: ἵππῳ F | πέμπτος ἐπέβη εἷς δὲ Jack-
son: ἐπέβη πέμπτος δὲ εἷς F.

94

their boats. Friends were invited to join them on the journey and so were a large number of freedmen, for Dionysius was inclined to be lavish. When all was ready, he ordered the baggage and most of the people to go by sea and the wagons to follow after him when he himself had gone on ahead, since a formal escort was not suitable for a man in mourning. At dawn, before most would notice, he and four companions, of whom one was Leonas, mounted their horses.

While Dionysius was riding out to the country, Callirhoe, having seen a vision of Aphrodite during the night, wanted to pay homage to her once more. She was standing there in prayer when Dionysius jumped down from his horse and entered the shrine ahead of the others. Hearing the sound of footsteps, Callirhoe turned round to face him. At the sight of her Dionysius cried, 'Aphrodite, be gracious to me, and may your presence bless me!" As he was in the act of kneeling, Leonas caught him and said, "Sir, this is the slave just bought. Do not be disturbed. And you, woman, come to meet your master." And so Callirhoe bowed her head at the name of "master" and shed a flood of tears, learning at last what it means to lose one's freedom. But Dionysius struck Leonas and said, "You blasphemer, do you talk to gods as you would to men? Have you the nerve to call her a bought slave? No wonder you were unable to find the man who sold her.

---

3.5 ψόφου] Π² begins | ποδῶν Π², D'Orville: ποθεν F

3.6 ἀνεβόησεν ἵλεως εἴης F: εἵλεως ἔφη Π². | ἐστίν Π²: om. F | κάτω κύψασα] after κυρίου Π²: after δακρύων F.

3.7 ταύτην Π²: σὺ ταύτην F | δικαίως οὖν Π²: καὶ ὡς F

οὐκ ἤκουσας οὐδὲ Ὁμήρου διδάσκοντος ἡμᾶς

καί τε θεοὶ ξείνοισιν ἐοικότες ἀλλοδαποῖσιν
ἀνθρώπων ὕβριν τε καὶ εὐνομίην ἐφορῶσι;"

τότ' οὖν εἶπεν ἡ Καλλιρόη "παῦσαί μου καταγελῶι
καὶ θεὰν ὀνομάζων τὴν οὐδὲ ἄνθρωπον εὐτυχῆ.
8 λαλούσης δὲ αὐτῆς ἡ φωνὴ τῷ Διονυσίῳ θεία τις
ἐφάνη· μουσικὸν γὰρ ἐφθέγγετο καὶ ὥσπερ κιθάρας
ἀπεδίδου τὸν ἦχον. ἀπορηθεὶς οὖν καὶ ἐπὶ πλέον
ὁμιλεῖν καταιδεσθεὶς ἀπῆλθεν εἰς τὴν ἔπαυλιν
φλεγόμενος ἤδη τῷ ἔρωτι.

Μετ' οὐ πολὺ δὲ ἧκεν ἐξ ἄστεος ἡ παρασκευή
9 καὶ ταχεῖα φήμη διέδραμε τοῦ γεγονότος. ἔσπευδοι
οὖν πάντες τὴν γυναῖκα ἰδεῖν, προσεποιοῦντο δε
πάντες τὴν Ἀφροδίτην προσκυνεῖν. αἰδουμένη δὲ ἡ
Καλλιρόη τὸ πλῆθος οὐκ εἶχεν ὅ τι πράξειε· πάντα
γὰρ ἦν αὐτῇ ξένα καὶ οὐκ ἔβλεπεν οὐδὲ τὴν συνήθη
Πλαγγόνα, ἀλλ' ἐκείνη περὶ τὴν ὑποδοχὴν ἐγίνετε
10 τοῦ δεσπότου. προκοπτούσης δὲ τῆς ὥρας καὶ μηδενὸς ἥκοντος εἰς τὴν ἔπαυλιν, ἀλλὰ πάντων ἑστώτων
ἐκεῖ ὡς κεκλημένων, συνῆκεν ὁ Λεωνᾶς τὸ γεγονὸς
καὶ ἀφικόμενος εἰς τὸ τέμενος ἐξήγαγε τὴν Καλλιρόην. τότε δὲ ἦν ἰδεῖν ὅτι φύσει γίνονται βασιλεῖς
ὥσπερ ὁ ἐν τῷ σμήνει τῶν μελισσῶν· ἠκολούθου

3.7 καί τε Homer: καί γε οἱ Π² F | τότ' οὖν εἶπεν ἡ Κ
Blake: τὸ γοῦν λοιπὸν F: [12 letters Κα]λλιρόη Π² | θεὰν Π²
θεὸν F | ὀνο[μάζων] Π²: εἶναι νομίζων F.
3.9 πράξειε Cobet (cf. 7.6.9): πράξει F: [Π²].

96

## BOOK 2.3

Have you not even heard what Homer teaches us?

> Oft in the guise of strangers from distant lands
> the gods watch human insolence and righteousness."[a]

Then Callirhoe spoke. "Stop mocking me," she said, "and calling me a goddess, when I am not even a happy mortal." As she spoke, her voice sounded to Dionysius like that of a goddess, for it had a musical tone and produced a sound like that of a lyre. In great confusion, therefore, and too embarrassed to say more, he went off to the house, already aflame with love.

Not long afterwards his suite arrived from the city, and reports of the incident quickly spread. So all were eager to see the girl, though they all pretended to be paying homage to Aphrodite. In her shyness of the crowd, Callirhoe did not know what to do. Everything was strange to her and she could not even see the familiar Plangon, since the latter was busy with the reception of her master. As time passed and no one came to the house, but all remained there spellbound, Leonas realized what had happened and, coming to the shrine, brought Callirhoe away. Then you could see that royalty comes by birth, as with the king[b] in a swarm of bees, for they all of their own

---

[a] *Odyssey* 17.485, 487 (a protest to Antinous).

[b] By a common mistake not eradicated until modern times Chariton refers to the queen bee in the masculine (his words, however, are taken from Xenophon, *Cyropaedia* 5.1.24).

---

3.10 ὁ Λ. Π²: Λ. F. | τὸ γεγονὸς F: om. Π² | τότε δὲ F: τοὺς δ' Π² | ὁ ἐν τῷ Π², Xenophon: ἐν τῷ F.

γὰρ αὐτομάτως ἅπαντες αὐτῇ καθάπερ ὑπὸ τοῦ
κάλλους δεσποίνῃ κεχειροτονημένῃ.

4. Ἡ μὲν οὖν ἀπῆλθεν εἰς τὴν οἴκησιν τὴν
συνήθη· Διονύσιος δὲ ἐτέτρωτο μέν, τὸ δὲ τραῦμα
περιστέλλειν ἐπειρᾶτο, οἷα δὴ πεπαιδευμένος ἀνὴρ
καὶ ἐξαιρέτως ἀρετῆς ἀντιποιούμενος. μήτε τοῖς
οἰκέταις θέλων εὐκαταφρόνητος δοκεῖν μήτε μειρα-
κιώδης τοῖς φίλοις, διεκαρτέρει παρ' ὅλην τὴν ἑσπέραν, οἰόμενος μὲν λανθάνειν, κατάδηλος δὲ γινόμε-
2 νος μᾶλλον ἐκ τῆς σιωπῆς. μοῖραν δέ τινα λαβὼν
ἀπὸ τοῦ δείπνου "ταύτην" φησὶ "κομισάτω τις τῇ
ξένῃ. μὴ εἴπῃ δὲ 'παρὰ τοῦ κυρίου,' ἀλλὰ 'παρὰ
Διονυσίου.'"

Τὸν μὲν οὖν πότον προήγαγεν ἐπὶ πλεῖστον·
3 ἠπίστατο γὰρ ὅτι οὐ μέλλει καθεύδειν. ἀγρυπνεῖν
οὖν ἐβούλετο μετὰ τῶν φίλων. ἐπεὶ δὲ προέκοπτε τὰ
τῆς νυκτός, διαλύσας ὕπνου μὲν οὐκ ἐλάγχανεν,
ὅλος δὲ ἦν ἐν τῷ τῆς Ἀφροδίτης ἱερῷ καὶ πάντων
ἀνεμιμνήσκετο, τοῦ προσώπου, τῆς κόμης, πῶς
<ἐπ>εστράφη, πῶς ἐνέβλεψε, τῆς φωνῆς, τοῦ σχή-
ματος, τῶν ῥημάτων· ἐξέκαε δὲ αὐτὸν τὰ δάκρυα.

4 Τότ' ἦν ἰδεῖν ἀγῶνα λογισμοῦ καὶ πάθους. καίτοι γὰρ βαπτιζόμενος ὑπὸ τῆς ἐπιθυμίας γενναῖος
ἀνὴρ ἐπειρᾶτο ἀντέχεσθαι. καθάπερ δὲ ἐκ κύματος
ἀνέκυπτε λέγων πρὸς ἑαυτὸν "οὐκ αἰσχύνῃ, Διονύ-

3.10 αὐτομάτως and αὐτῇ P²: om. F | κεχειροτονημένῃ F:
-μενοι Π².
4.1 δὴ Π²: δὲ F | μήτε (. . . μήτε) F: μ[η]δὲ Π² | θέλων

accord followed after her as though she had been elected by her beauty to be their mistress.

4. She retired to her regular quarters, while Dionysius, love-smitten, tried to conceal the wound, as became somebody well-brought up who made especial claim to manliness. Not wanting his servants to look down on him, or his friends to think him immature, he kept a tight rein on himself throughout the evening, thinking he would not be noticed, but making himself more noticeable by his very silence. Selecting a portion of the meal, he said, "Have someone take this to our guest, and let him not say it is from her master, but from Dionysius."

He prolonged the drinking as long as possible since he knew that he would be unable to sleep, and in his wakefulness he needed the company of friends. The night had far advanced before he brought the banquet to an end, but still he could get no sleep. In his mind he was at the shrine of Aphrodite, and he recalled every detail: her face, her hair, how she had turned round and looked at him, her voice, her figure, her words; her very tears were setting him on fire.

Then you could observe a struggle between reason and passion, for although engulfed by desire, as a noble man he tried to resist, and rising above the waves, as it were, he said to himself, "Are you not ashamed, Diony-

---

Π²: ἐθέλων F | οἰόμενος μὲν F: ποιούμενος γὰρ Π² | μᾶλλον Π²: om. F.

4.2 λαβὼν Π²: λαβόμενος F | εἴπῃ Π²: εἴπητε F | ἀλλὰ Π² ἀλλ᾽ ὅτι F | ἠπίστατο] Π² breaks off.

4.3 διαλύσας Hertlein: ἀναλύσας F | add. Jackson (cf. 2.3.6).

σιε, ἀνὴρ ὁ πρῶτος τῆς Ἰωνίας ἕνεκεν ἀρετῆς τε καὶ
δόξης, ὃν θαυμάζουσι σατράπαι καὶ βασιλεῖς καὶ
πόλεις, παιδαρίου πρᾶγμα πάσχων; ἅπαξ ἰδὼν
ἐρᾷς, καὶ ταῦτα πενθῶν, πρὶν ἀφοσιώσασθαι τοὺς
5   τῆς ἀθλίας δαίμονας. τούτου γε <ἕνεκεν> ἧκες εἰς
ἀγρὸν ἵνα μελανείμων γάμους θύσῃς, καὶ γάμους
δούλης, τάχα δὲ καὶ ἀλλοτρίας; οὐκ ἔχεις γὰρ αὐτῆς
οὐδὲ τὴν καταγραφήν." ἐφιλονείκει δὲ ὁ Ἔρως βου-
λευομένῳ καλῶς καὶ ὕβριν ἐδόκει τὴν σωφροσύνην
τὴν ἐκείνου· διὰ τοῦτο ἐπυρπόλει σφοδρότερον
ψυχὴν ἐν ἔρωτι φιλοσοφοῦσαν.

6   Μηκέτ' οὖν φέρων μόνος αὑτῷ διαλέγεσθαι, Λεωνᾶν μετεπέμψατο· κληθεὶς δὲ ἐκεῖνος συνῆκε μὲν τὴν
αἰτίαν, προσεποιεῖτο δὲ ἀγνοεῖν καὶ ὥσπερ τεταραγ-
μένος "τί" φησὶν "ἀγρυπνεῖς, ὦ δέσποτα; μή τι
πάλιν σε λύπη κατείληφε τῆς τεθνηκυίας γυναικός;"
"γυναικὸς μὲν" εἶπεν ὁ Διονύσιος, "ἀλλ' οὐ τῆς
τεθνηκυίας. οὐδὲν δὲ ἀπόρρητόν ἐστί μοι πρὸς σὲ
7   δι' εὔνοιάν τε καὶ πίστιν. ἀπόλωλά σοι, Λεωνᾶ. σύ
μοι τῶν κακῶν αἴτιος. πῦρ ἐκόμισας εἰς τὴν οἰκίαν,
μᾶλλον δὲ εἰς τὴν ἐμὴν ψυχήν. ταράσσει δέ με καὶ
τὸ ἄδηλον τὸ περὶ τῆς γυναικός. μῦθόν μοι διηγῇ,
ἔμπορόν τιν' ὃν οὐκ οἶδας, οὔτε ὁπόθεν ἦλθεν οὔτε
ὅπου πάλιν ἀπῆλθεν. ἔχων δὲ τίς τοιοῦτον κάλλος

4.4 πρᾶγμα Cobet: πράγματα F.
4.5 add. D'Orville | αὐτῆς] Π² recommences | βουλευομένῳ
Zankogiannes: -ου F | ἐπυρπόλει Π², Hercher: -φόρει F.
4.6 μή τι Π², Gasda: μή τις F.

sius, the leader of Ionia in worth and reputation, a man whom governors,[a] kings, and city-states admire—are you not ashamed to be suffering the heartache of a boy? You fall in love at first sight, and that too while still in mourning and before you have propitiated the spirits of your poor wife. Is this why you came to the country, to celebrate a new marriage still clothed in black—and that too with a slave girl who may even belong to another man? Why, you do not even have legal title to her!" But Love snapped his fingers at these sensible thoughts, considering his self-restraint an insult, and for that reason inflamed all the more a heart which attempted to philosophize with love.

When he could no longer endure debating with himself, he sent for Leonas, who well knew the reason for the summons. However, he pretended not to know and said with an air of alarm, "Why are you so sleepless, master? Can it be that sorrow for your dead wife is again troubling you?" "Sorrow, yes, and for a woman," said Dionysius, "but not for her who is dead. Because of your goodwill and loyalty I have no secrets from you. Leonas, I am utterly ruined and you are the cause of my misery. You have brought fire into my house, or rather, into my heart. The very mystery which surrounds the woman worries me. You tell me a fairy story about some merchant whom you do not know, nor where he came from, nor where he

---

[a] Translating *satrapai*: each province of the Persian empire had a satrap or governor, appointed by the king.

---

4.7 ἀπόλωλά σοι Π², Zimmermann: ἀπόλωλας ὦ F | τιν᾿ ὃν Reardon (Π²?): πτηνόν F | οὔτε . . . οὔτε Π² (Hercher οὔθ᾿ twice): οὐδ᾿ . . . οὐδ᾿ F | τοιοῦτον F: -το Π².

ἐν ἐρημίᾳ πιπράσκει καὶ ταλάντου τὴν τῶν βασιλέως χρημάτων ἀξίαν; δαίμων σέ τις ἐξηπάτησεν.
8  ἐπίστησον οὖν καὶ ἀναμνήσθητι τῶν γενομένων.
τίνα εἶδες; τίνι ἐλάλησας; εἰπέ μοι τὸ ἀληθές.
οὐ πλοῖον ἐθεάσω." "οὐκ εἶδον, δέσποτα, ἀλλὰ
ἤκουσα." "τοῦτο ἐκεῖνο· μία Νυμφῶν ἢ Νηρηΐδων
ἐκ θαλάσσης ἀνελήλυθε. καταλαμβάνουσι δὲ καὶ
δαίμονας καιροί τινες εἱμαρμένης ἀνάγκην φέροντες
ὁμιλίας μετ' ἀνθρώπων· ταῦτα ἡμῖν ἱστοροῦσι ποιη-
9  ταί τε καὶ συγγραφεῖς." ἡδέως δ' ἀνέπειθεν αὐτὸν ὁ
Διονύσιος ἀποσεμνύνειν τὴν γυναῖκα καὶ σεβα-
σμιωτέρας ἢ κατὰ ἄνθρωπον ὁμιλίας. Λεωνᾶς δὲ
χαρίσασθαι τῷ δεσπότῃ βουλόμενος εἶπε "τίς μέν
ἐστι, δέσποτα, μὴ πολυπραγμονῶμεν· ἄξω δὲ αὐτήν,
εἰ θέλεις, πρὸς σέ, καὶ μὴ ἔχε λύπην <ὡς> ἀπο-
10  τυγχάνων ἐν ἔρωτος ἐξουσίᾳ." "οὐκ ἂν ποιήσαιμι"
φησὶν ὁ Διονύσιος "πρὶν μαθεῖν τίς ἡ γυνὴ καὶ
πόθεν. ἕωθεν οὖν πυθώμεθα παρ' αὐτῆς τὴν ἀλήθειαν. μεταπέμψωμαι δ' αὐτὴν οὐκ ἐνθάδε, μὴ καὶ
τινος βιαιοτέρου λάβωμεν ὑποψίαν, ἀλλ' ὅπου πρῶτον αὐτὴν ἐθεασάμην, ἐπὶ τῆς Ἀφροδίτης γενέσθω-
σαν ἡμῖν οἱ λόγοι."

5. Ταῦτα ἔδοξε, καὶ τῆς ὑστεραίας ὁ μὲν Διονύσιος παραλαβὼν φίλους τε καὶ ἀπελευθέρους καὶ

4.7 σέ τις Π², Cobet: δὲ τίς F.
4.8 τίνα Π², Hercher: τίνας F | ἐλάλησας F: -ησεν Π².
4.9 ἀνέπειθεν Π², Hercher: ἂν ἔπειθεν F | ἀποσ. F: σ. Π² |
add. Blake.

102

has gone to. What man who owned beauty such as this
would sell her in an isolated spot and take a talent for one
who is worth a king's treasure? A demon has deceived
you. Come now, pay attention and recall what happened.
Who was the man you saw and spoke to? Tell me the
truth. You did not see any boat!" "No, master, I did not
see it, but I heard of it." "Just as I thought. It was some
nymph or Nereid from the sea who made her epiphany.
Some moments of destiny seize hold of even gods and
compel them to associate with mortals.[a] So the poets[b] and
historians tell us." Dionysius found it easy to talk himself
into elevating the woman to a more august company than
that of humans. Wishing to please his master, Leonas
said, "Sir, let us not worry about who she is. I will bring
her to you if you wish, so do not nurse your grief, as
though you lacked the power to compel her love." "That I
cannot do," said Dionysius, "until I learn who the woman
is and where she comes from. In the morning, then, let us
ask her for the truth. To avoid any suspicion of intimida-
tion, I will not call her here, but our interview shall be in
the shrine of Aphrodite, where I first saw her."

5. So it was decided, and on the following day Dionysius took with him some friends and freedmen and the

---

[a] So Aphrodite was fated to associate with Anchises, Thetis
with Peleus.

[b] Pindar relates the story of Thetis at *Isthmians* 8.26ff.

---

5.1 τῆς δ' ύστ. (Π²F)] see on 1.13.7 | τέμενος] Π² ends.

τῶν οἰκετῶν τοὺς πιστοτάτους, ἵνα ἔχῃ καὶ μάρτυρας, ἧκεν εἰς τὸ τέμενος, οὐκ ἀμελῶς σχηματίσας
ἑαυτόν, ἀλλὰ κοσμήσας ἠρέμα τὸ σῶμα, ὡς ἂν ἐρω-
2 μένῃ μέλλων ὁμιλεῖν. ἦν δὲ καὶ φύσει καλός τε καὶ
μέγας καὶ μάλιστα πάντων σεμνὸς ὀφθῆναι. Λεωνᾶς δὲ παραλαβὼν τὴν Πλαγγόνα καὶ μετ' αὐτῆς
τὰς συνήθεις τῇ Καλλιρόῃ θεραπαινίδας ἧκε πρὸς
3 αὐτὴν καὶ λέγει· "Διονύσιος ἀνὴρ δικαιότατός ἐστι
καὶ νομιμώτατος. ἧκε τοίνυν εἰς τὸ ἱερόν, ὦ γύναι,
καὶ πρὸς αὐτὸν εἰπὲ τὴν ἀλήθειαν, τίς οὖσα τυγχά-
νεις· οὐ γὰρ ἀτυχήσεις οὐδεμιᾶς δικαίας βοηθείας.
ἀλλὰ μόνον ἁπλῶς αὐτῷ διαλέγου, καὶ μηδὲν ὑπο-
κρύψῃς τῶν ἀληθῶν· τοῦτο γὰρ αὐτὸν ἐπικαλέσεται
μᾶλλον <πρὸς> τὴν εἰς σὲ φιλανθρωπίαν."

Ἄκουσα μὲν οὖν ἐβάδιζεν ἡ Καλλιρόη, θαρ-
ροῦσα δὲ ὅμως διὰ τὸ ἐν ἱερῷ γενήσεσθαι τὴν
4 ὁμιλίαν αὐτοῖς. ἐπεὶ δὲ ἧκεν, ἔτι μᾶλλον αὐτὴν
ἐθαύμασαν ἅπαντες. καταπλαγεὶς οὖν ὁ Διονύσιος
ἄφωνος ἦν. οὔσης δὲ ἐπὶ πλεῖστον σιωπῆς ὀψέ ποτε
καὶ μόλις ἐφθέγξατο "τὰ μὲν ἐμὰ δῆλά σοι, γύναι,
πάντα. Διονύσιός εἰμι, Μιλησίων πρῶτος, σχεδὸν
δὲ καὶ τῆς ὅλης Ἰωνίας, ἐπ' εὐσεβείᾳ καὶ φιλανθρω-
5 πίᾳ διαβόητος. δίκαιόν ἐστι καὶ σὲ περὶ σεαυτῆς
εἰπεῖν ἡμῖν τὴν ἀλήθειαν· οἱ μὲν γὰρ πωλήσαντές
σε Συβᾶριτιν ἔφασαν κατὰ ζηλοτυπίαν ἐκεῖθεν
πραθεῖσαν ὑπὸ δεσποίνης."

Ἠρυθρίασεν ἡ Καλλιρόη καὶ κάτω κύψασα
ἠρέμα εἶπεν "ἐγὼ νῦν πρῶτον πέπραμαι· Σύβαριν δὲ

most trusted of his slaves, so as to have witnesses, and came to the shrine. He had dressed himself with some care and even added some adornment to his person, seeing that he was to talk with the woman he loved. He was, moreover, naturally handsome and tall and, above all, of dignified appearance. Taking along Plangon and Callirhoe's regular maids, Leonas went to her and said, "Dionysius is a decent and law-abiding man. So come into the shrine, lady, and tell him truthfully who you are; you may be sure of all the help you are entitled to. Just speak with him frankly and hide nothing of the truth. This will rather induce him to have sympathy for you."

Callirhoe went along with a heavy heart, yet relieved that their interview was to take place in the shrine. When she arrived, all admired her still more; Dionysius was speechless with amazement. After a prolonged silence, he eventually managed to say, "All about me, lady, is known to you. I am Dionysius, the foremost citizen of Miletus and probably all Ionia, well known as a devout and kindly man. It is only right for you too to tell us the truth about yourself. Those who sold you said that you were from Sybaris and had been sold by your mistress there because of her jealousy."

Callirhoe blushed, and lowering her gaze said softly, "This is the first time I have been sold. I have never set

CHARITON

6 οὐκ εἶδον." "ἔλεγόν σοι" φησὶ Διονύσιος ἀποβλέψας
πρὸς τὸν Λεωνᾶν "ὅτι οὐκ ἔστι δούλη· μαντεύομαι
δὲ ὅτι καὶ εὐγενής." "εἶπόν μοι, γύναι, πάντα, καὶ
πρῶτόν γε τοὔνομα τὸ σόν." "Καλλιρόη" φησίν
(ἤρεσε Διονυσίῳ καὶ τὸ ὄνομα), τὰ δὲ λοιπὰ ἐσιώπα.
πυνθανομένου δὲ λιπαρῶς "δέομαί σου" φησίν, "ὦ
δέσποτα, συγχώρησόν μοι τὴν ἐμαυτῆς τύχην σιω-
7 πᾶν. ὄνειρος ἦν τὰ πρῶτα καὶ μῦθος, εἰμὶ δὲ νῦν ὃ
γέγονα, δούλη καὶ ξένη." ταῦτα λέγουσα ἐπειρᾶτο
μὲν λανθάνειν, ἐλείβετο δὲ αὐτῆς τὰ δάκρυα κατὰ
τῶν παρειῶν. προήχθη δὲ <καὶ> ὁ Διονύσιος κλαί-
ειν καὶ πάντες οἱ περιεστηκότες· ἔδοξε δ' ἄν τις καὶ
τὴν Ἀφροδίτην αὐτὴν σκυθρωποτέραν γεγονέναι.
Διονύσιος δὲ ἐνέκειτο ἔτι μᾶλλον πολυπραγμονῶν
καὶ "ταύτην" <ἔφη> "αἰτοῦμαι παρά σου χάριν
8 πρώτην. διήγησαί μοι, Καλλιρόη, τὰ σεαυτῆς. οὐ
πρὸς ἀλλότριον ἐρεῖς· ἔστι γάρ τις καὶ τρόπου συγ-
γένεια. μηδὲν φοβηθῇς, μηδ' εἰ πέπρακταί σοί τι
δεινόν."

Ἠγανάκτησεν ἡ Καλλιρόη πρὸς τοῦτο καὶ "μή
με ὕβριζε" εἶπεν, "οὐδὲν γὰρ σύνοιδα ἐμαυτῇ φαῦ-
9 λον. ἀλλ' ἐπεὶ σεμνότερα τἀμὰ τῆς τύχης ἐστὶ τῆς
παρούσης, οὐ θέλω δοκεῖν ἀλαζὼν οὐδὲ λέγειν
διηγήματα ἄπιστα τοῖς ἀγνοοῦσιν· οὐ γὰρ μαρτυρεῖ
τὰ πρῶτα τοῖς νῦν." ἐθαύμασεν ὁ Διονύσιος τὸ
φρόνημα τῆς γυναικὸς καὶ "συνίημι" φησίν "ἤδη,
κἂν μὴ λέγῃς· εἰπὲ δὲ ὅμως· οὐδὲν γὰρ περὶ σεαυτῆς
10 ἐρεῖς τηλικοῦτον, ἡλίκον ὁρῶμεν. πᾶν ἐστί σου
σμικρότερον λαμπρὸν διήγημα."

106

eyes on Sybaris." "I told you she was not a slave," said
Dionysius, looking at Leonas, "and I will guarantee that
she is of noble birth besides. Tell me everything, lady;
first of all, your name." "Callirhoe," she said, and the very
name delighted Dionysius. After that, however, she
remained silent, and when he kept on questioning her,
she said, "Sir, I beg you, allow me to remain silent about
my fortunes. My origins were but a fabulous dream. I am
now what I have become, a slave and a foreigner!" She
said this trying to conceal it, but the tears poured down
her cheeks.[a] Dionysius, too, was moved to tears and all
who stood around. You would have said that even
Aphrodite looked sadder. But Dionysius persisted still
more in his curiosity and said, "This is the first favor I ask
of you. Tell me your story, Callirhoe; you will not be talking to a stranger, for there exists a kinship of character,
too. Have no fear even if you have done something
awful."

Callirhoe became angry at this and said, "Do not insult
me! I have no crime on my conscience. But since my past
history is so much more worthy of respect than my present lot, I do not want to appear boastful or tell a story
which those who do not know me would not believe, for
my early life does not match my condition now." Dionysius was impressed by the girl's spirit and said, "I already
understand you, even if you say no more. But do tell
about it. You can say nothing about yourself which com-
pares with what we see. Any story, however vivid, is
bound to fall short of you."

[a] Cf. Xenophon, *Cyropaedia* 6.4.3.

---

5.7 add. Hercher | add. Zankogiannes.

Μόλις οὖν ἐκείνη τὰ καθ᾽ ἑαυτὴν ἤρξατο λέγειν "Ἑρμοκράτους εἰμὶ θυγάτηρ, τοῦ Συρακοσίων στρατηγοῦ. γενομένην δέ με ἄφωνον ἐξ αἰφνιδίου πτώματος ἔθαψαν οἱ γονεῖς πολυτελῶς. ἤνοιξαν τυμβωρύχοι τὸν τάφον· εὖρον κἀμὲ πάλιν ἐμπνέουσαν· ἤνεγκαν ἐνθάδε καὶ Λεωνᾷ με τούτῳ παρέδωκε
11 Θήρων ἐπ᾽ ἐρημίας." πάντα εἰποῦσα μόνον Χαιρέαν ἐσίγησεν. "ἀλλὰ δέομαί σου, Διονύσιε (Ἕλλην γὰρ εἶ καὶ πόλεως φιλανθρώπου καὶ παιδείας μετείληφας), μὴ γένῃ τοῖς τυμβωρύχοις ὅμοιος μηδὲ ἀποστερήσῃς με πατρίδος καὶ συγγενῶν. μικρόν ἐστί σοι πλουτοῦντι σῶμα ἐᾶσαι· τὴν τιμὴν οὐκ ἀπολέσεις, ἐὰν ἀποδῷς με τῷ πατρί· Ἑρμοκράτης οὐκ ἔστιν ἀχάριστος. τὸν Ἀλκίνοον ἀγάμεθα δὴ καὶ πάντες φιλοῦμεν ὅτι εἰς τὴν πατρίδα ἀνέπεμψε τὸν ἱκέτην· ἱκετεύω σὲ κἀγώ. σῶσον αἰχμάλωτον ὀρφα-
12 νήν. εἰ δὲ μὴ δύναμαι ζῆν ὡς εὐγενής, αἱροῦμαι θάνατον ἐλεύθερον." τούτων ἀκούων δὲ ἔκλαιε προφάσει μὲν Καλλιρόην, τὸ δὲ ἀληθὲς ἑαυτόν· ᾐσθάνετο γὰρ ἀποτυγχάνων τῆς ἐπιθυμίας. "θάρρει δὲ" ἔφη, "Καλλιρόη, καὶ ψυχὴν ἔχε ἀγαθήν· οὐ γὰρ ἀτυχήσεις ὧν ἀξιοῖς· μάρτυν καλῶ τήνδε τὴν Ἀφροδίτην. ἐν δὲ τῷ μεταξὺ θεραπείαν ἕξεις παρ᾽ ἡμῖν δεσποίνης μᾶλλον ἢ δούλης."

6. Καὶ ἡ μὲν ἀπῄει πεπεισμένη μηδὲν ἄκουσα δύνασθαι παθεῖν, ὁ δὲ Διονύσιος λυπούμενος ἧκεν εἰς οἶκον τὸν ἴδιον. καὶ μόνον καλέσας Λεωνᾶν

And so with reluctance she began her story. "I am the daughter of Hermocrates, ruler of Syracuse. When I lost consciousness after a sudden fall, my parents gave me a costly burial. Tomb-robbers opened the tomb. They found me too, breathing again. They brought me to this place and Theron gave me to Leonas here in an isolated spot." She omitted only Chaereas from her account. "But I beg you, Dionysius, since you are a Greek and belong to a civilized city and are cultured, do not behave like those tomb-robbers or deprive me of my country and kinsmen. To a rich man like you it is a small thing to let a person go. You shall not lose my purchase money if you give me back to my father. Hermocrates is not ungrateful. We all admire and love Alcinoüs[a] for sending a suppliant back to his native land. I am your suppliant. Save me, an orphan and a prisoner! But if I cannot live as befits my birth, I choose to die as a free woman." On hearing this, Dionysius wept, ostensibly for Callirhoe, actually for himself,[b] for he saw that he was unsuccessful in his love. "Cheer up, Callirhoe," he said, "and be of good heart. You shall not fail to obtain your desire. I call Aphrodite here to witness. But meantime you shall receive from us the treatment which befits a lady rather than a slave."

6. So she went away assured that nothing would be done to her against her will, but Dionysius went home depressed. He sent for Leonas privately and said, "I am

[a] King of Phaeacia, who gave Odysseus generous hospitality and safe passage back to Ithaca (*Odyssey* Books 6ff and 13).

[b] Cf. *Iliad* 19.301f (and see 8.5.2).

"κατὰ πάντα" φησὶν "ἐγὼ δυστυχής εἰμι καὶ μισού-
μενος ὑπὸ τοῦ Ἔρωτος. τὴν μὲν γαμετὴν ἔθαψα,
φεύγει δὲ ἡ νεώνητος, ἣν ἤλπιζον ἐξ Ἀφροδίτης
εἶναί μοι τὸ δῶρον, καὶ ἀνέπλαττον ἐμαυτῷ βίον
μακάριον ὑπὲρ Μενέλεων τὸν τῆς Λακεδαιμονίας
γυναικός· οὐδὲ γὰρ τὴν Ἑλένην εὔμορφον οὕτως
ὑπολαμβάνω γεγονέναι. πρόσεστι δὲ αὐτῇ καὶ ἡ
2  τῶν λόγων πειθώ. βεβίωταί μοι. τῆς αὐτῆς ἡμέρας
ἀπαλλαγήσεται Καλλιρόη μὲν ἐντεῦθεν, ἐγὼ δὲ τοῦ
ζῆν." πρὸς τοῦτο ἀνέκραγεν ὁ Λεωνᾶς "μὴ σύ γε, ὦ
δέσποτα, μὴ καταράσῃ σεαυτῷ· κύριος γὰρ εἶ καὶ
τὴν ἐξουσίαν ἔχεις αὐτῆς, ὥστε καὶ ἑκοῦσα καὶ
ἄκουσα ποιήσει τὸ σοὶ δοκοῦν· ταλάντου γὰρ αὐτὴν
3  ἐπριάμην." "ἐπρίω σύ, τρισάθλιε, τὴν εὐγενῆ; οὐκ
ἀκούεις Ἑρμοκράτην τὸν στρατηγὸν τῆς ὅλης Σικελίας ἐγκεχαραγμένον μεγάλως, ὃν βασιλεὺς ὁ Περσῶν θαυμάζει καὶ φιλεῖ, πέμπει δὲ αὐτῷ κατ' ἔτος
δωρεάς, ὅτι Ἀθηναίους κατεναυμάχησε τοὺς Περσῶν πολεμίους; ἐγὼ τυραννήσω σώματος ἐλευθέρου,
καὶ Διονύσιος ὁ ἐπὶ σωφροσύνῃ περιβόητος ἄκουσαν ὑβριῶ, ἣν οὐχ ὕβρισεν οὐδὲ Θήρων ὁ λῃστής;"
4      Ταῦτα μὲν οὖν εἶπε πρὸς τὸν Λεωνᾶν, οὐ μὴν οὐδ'
ἀπεγίνωσκε πείσειν, φύσει γὰρ εὔελπίς ἐστιν ὁ
Ἔρως, ἐθάρρει δὲ τῇ θεραπείᾳ κατεργάσασθαι τὴν
ἐπιθυμίαν. καλέσας οὖν τὴν Πλαγγόνα "δέδωκάς
μοι" φησὶν "ἤδη πεῖραν ἱκανὴν τῆς ἐπιμελείας.
ἐγχειρίζω δή σοι τὸ μέγιστον καὶ τιμιώτατόν μου

unlucky in everything and hated by Love. I buried my
wife, and the new slave spurns me. I had hoped that she
was Aphrodite's gift to me, and was dreaming that I
should be happier than Menelaus with his Spartan wife,
for I cannot believe that even Helen was as beautiful. But
besides this she also has the gift of persuasive speech.
Life is over for me. The same day which sees Callirhoe
depart from here will also see me depart from life." At
this Leonas exclaimed, "No, Sir! Do not bring a curse
upon yourself! You are her master, with full power over
her, so she must do your will whether she likes it or not. I
bought her for a talent." "You bought her, you scoundrel?
Her, a high-born girl? Have you never heard of
Hermocrates, the ruler of all Sicily, a man so distinguished that the king of Persia admires and loves him?
Why, every year he sends him presents for having
defeated Persia's enemies, the Athenians, at sea. Am I to
become a tyrant over a freeborn person? Shall I, Dionysius, famed for my self-control, violate an unwilling
woman whom not even the pirate Theron violated?"

These were his words to Leonas. Yet for all that he did
not abandon hope of persuading her, for Love is naturally
optimistic, and he was confident that he could realize his
desire by his attention to her. And so calling Plangon he
said, "You have already given me sufficient proof of your
devotion. Now I entrust you with the greatest and most

---

6.3 ὅλης Hercher: πολλῆς F | οὐχ Jackson (cf. 3.4.18): οὐκ
ἂν F.

τῶν κτημάτων, τὴν ξένην. βούλομαι δὲ αὐτὴν μηδε-
5 νὸς σπανίζειν, ἀλλὰ προϊέναι μέχρι τρυφῆς. κυρίαν
ὑπολάμβανε, θεράπευε καὶ κόσμει καὶ ποίει φίλην
ἡμῖν· ἐπαίνει με παρ' αὐτῇ πολλάκις καὶ οἷον
ἐπίστασαι διηγοῦ. βλέπε μὴ δεσπότην εἴπῃς."
συνῆκεν ἡ Πλαγγὼν τῆς ἐντολῆς, φύσει γὰρ ἦν
ἐντρεχής· ἀφανῆ δὲ λαβοῦσα πρὸς τὸ πρᾶγμα
τὴν διάνοιαν, ἠπείγετο πρὸς τοῦτο. παραγενομένη
τοίνυν πρὸς τὴν Καλλιρόην, ὅτι μὲν κεκέλευσται
θεραπεύειν αὐτὴν οὐκ ἐμήνυσεν, ἰδίαν δὲ εὔνοιαν
ἐπεδείκνυτο· καὶ τὸ ἀξιόπιστον ὡς σύμβουλος
ἤθελεν ἔχειν.

7. Συνέβη δέ τι τοιόνδε. Διονύσιος ἐνδιέτριβε
τοῖς χωρίοις, προφάσει μὲν ἄλλοτε ἄλλη, τὸ δὲ [δὴ]
ἀληθὲς οὔτε ἀπαλλαγῆναι τῆς Καλλιρόης δυνάμενος
οὔτε ἐπάγεσθαι θέλων αὐτήν· ἔμελλε γὰρ περιβόητος ὀφθεῖσα ἔσεσθαι, καὶ τὸ κάλλος ὅλην τὴν
Ἰωνίαν δουλαγωγήσειν ἀναβήσεσθαί τε τὴν φήμην
2 καὶ μέχρι τοῦ μεγάλου βασιλέως. ἐν δὲ τῇ μονῇ
πολυπραγμονῶν ἀκριβέστερον τὰ περὶ τὴν κτῆσιν,
ἐμέμψατό που καί τι περὶ τὸν οἰκονόμον Φωκᾶν· τὸ
δὲ τῆς μέμψεως οὐ περαιτέρω προῆλθεν, ἀλλὰ μέχρι
ῥημάτων. εὗρε δὴ καιρὸν ἡ Πλαγγών, καὶ περίφοβος εἰσέδραμε πρὸς τὴν Καλλιρόην, σπαράσσουσα
τὴν κόμην ἑαυτῆς· λαβομένη δὲ τῶν γονάτων αὐτῆς

6.5 ἀφανῆ Blake: -ῆς F | βαλοῦσα D'Orville: λαβοῦσα F |
ἠπείγετο Anon.: εἴχετο F | σύμβουλος Beck: -ον F.

112

prized of my possessions, the foreign woman. I want her to lack nothing, but rather to enjoy every luxury. Consider her your mistress. Care for her, adorn her, and make her fond of me. Praise me often in her presence. You know the kind of thing to say. And take care not to call me her master." Plangon understood her orders, being naturally shrewd; she discreetly turned her mind to the task, and made a quick start on it. Accordingly she spent all her time with Callirhoe, though not revealing that she had been asked to look after her. Rather she showed a personal friendliness towards her. What she wanted was to gain her confidence as an adviser.

7. Then the following incident took place. Dionysius was prolonging his stay in the country, now on one pretext and now on another. The actual truth was, he was neither able to part from Callirhoe nor yet willing to bring her back with him: for if she were once seen, she was sure to become celebrated and her beauty would then enthrall all Ionia, indeed her fame would even make its way to the Great King. During his stay, in the course of a detailed inspection of his property, he uttered some criticism of the conduct of the estate manager, Phocas. Actually the criticism did not go beyond a verbal rebuke. Yet in it Plangon discovered her opportunity: she ran in to Callirhoe terrified, tearing her hair. Grasping her by the

---

7.1 προφάσει . . . ἄλλῃ Blake: -εις . . . -ας F | del. Reeve.
7.2 τι Naber: τὰ F.

"δέομαί σου" φησί, "κυρία, σῶσον ἡμᾶς· τῷ γὰρ
ἀνδρί μου χαλεπαίνει Διονύσιος· φύσει δέ ἐστι
3 βαρύθυμος, ὥσπερ καὶ φιλάνθρωπος. οὐδεὶς ἂν
ῥύσαιτο ἡμᾶς ἢ μόνη σύ· παρέξει γάρ σοι Διονύσιος ἡδέως αἰτουμένη χάριν πρώτην." ὤκνει μὲν
οὖν ἡ Καλλιρόη βαδίσαι πρὸς αὐτόν, λιπαρούσης
δὲ καὶ δεομένης ἀντειπεῖν οὐκ ἠδυνήθη, προηνεχυ-
ριασμένη ταῖς εὐεργεσίαις ὑπ' αὐτῆς. ἵν' οὖν μὴ
ἀχάριστος δοκῇ, "κἀγὼ μὲν" φησὶν "εἰμὶ δούλη καὶ
οὐδεμίαν ἔχω παρρησίαν, εἰ δὲ ὑπολαμβάνεις δυνή-
σεσθαί τι κἀμέ, συνικετεύειν ἑτοίμη· γένοιτο δὲ
ἡμᾶς τυχεῖν."

4     Ἐπεὶ δὲ ἦλθον, ἐκέλευσεν ἡ Πλαγγὼν τὸν ἐπὶ
ταῖς θύραις εἰσαγγεῖλαι πρὸς τὸν δεσπότην ὅτι
Καλλιρόη πάρεστιν. ἐτύγχανε δὲ Διονύσιος ἐρριμ-
μένος ὑπὸ λύπης, ἐτετήκει δὲ αὐτῷ καὶ τὸ σῶμα.
ἀκούσας οὖν ὅτι Καλλιρόη πάρεστιν, ἄφωνος ἐγένετο, καί τις ἀχλὺς αὐτοῦ <τῶν ὀφθαλμῶν> κατεχύθη πρὸς τὸ ἀνέλπιστον, μόλις δὲ ἀνενεγκὼν
5 "ἡκέτω" φησί. στᾶσα δὲ ἡ Καλλιρόη πλησίον καὶ
κάτω κύψασα πρῶτον μὲν ἐρυθήματος ἐνεπλήσθη,
μόλις δὲ ὅμως ἐφθέγξατο "ἐγὼ Πλαγγόνι ταύτῃ
χάριν ἐπίσταμαι· φιλεῖ γάρ με ὡς θυγατέρα. δέομαι δή σου, κύριε, μὴ ὀργίζου τῷ ἀνδρὶ αὐτῆς, ἀλλὰ
χάρισαι τὴν σωτηρίαν." ἔτι δὲ βουλομένη λέγειν
οὐκ ἐδυνήθη.

6     Συνεὶς οὖν ὁ Διονύσιος τὸ στρατήγημα τῆς
Πλαγγόνος "ὀργίζομαι μὲν" εἶπε, "καὶ οὐδεὶς <ἂν>

114

knees, she said, "Mistress, I beg you, save us! Dionysius is angry with my husband. His nature is to be as severe when angry as he is normally kind. Only you can save us. Dionysius will be glad to grant the first favor you ask for." Callirhoe hesitated to go to him, but when Plangon kept begging and beseeching her, she could not refuse, feeling under prior obligation to her for her kindnesses. So in order not to seem ungrateful, she said, "I, too, am a slave and have not the right to speak freely, but if you think that I can do something, I am ready to support your appeal. I only hope we succeed!"

When they arrived, Plangon told the slave at the door to inform his master that Callirhoe was there. At that moment Dionysius was lying prostrate with grief, and his body too was emaciated. On hearing that Callirhoe was there, he could not speak, and a mist spread over his eyes[a] at the unexpected news. Eventually he pulled himself together and said, "Have her come in." So Callirhoe approached with her head bowed. First she blushed deeply, but eventually she managed to speak. "I owe thanks to Plangon here, for she loves me as her daughter. I beg you, master, do not be angry with her husband, but spare his life." She wanted to say more but could not.

Dionysius saw through Plangon's scheme and said, "I am indeed angry, and no one else could have saved Pho-

---

[a] Cf. *Iliad* 5.696 (see also 3.1.3; 4.5.9).

ἀνθρώπων ἐρρύσατο μὴ ἀπολέσθαι Φωκᾶν καὶ
τὴν Πλαγγόνα τοιαῦτα πεπραχότας· χαρίζομαι δὲ
αὐτοὺς ἡδέως σοί, καὶ γινώσκετε ὑμεῖς ὅτι διὰ Καλλιρόην ἐσώθητε." προσέπεσεν αὐτοῦ τοῖς γόνασιν ἡ
Πλαγγών, καὶ Διονύσιος ἔφη "τοῖς Καλλιρόης
7 προσπίπτετε γόνασιν, αὕτη γὰρ ὑμᾶς ἔσωσεν." ἐπεὶ
δὲ ἡ Πλαγγών ἐθεάσατο τὴν Καλλιρόην χαίρουσαν
καὶ σφόδρα ἡδομένην ἐπὶ τῇ δωρεᾷ "σὺ οὖν" εἶπε
"χάριν ὁμολόγησον ὑπὲρ ἡμῶν Διονυσίῳ" καὶ ἅμα
ὤθησεν αὐτήν. ἡ δὲ τρόπον τινὰ καταπεσοῦσα
περιέπεσε τῇ δεξιᾷ τοῦ Διονυσίου, κἀκεῖνος, ὡς
δῆθεν ἀπαξιῶν τὴν χεῖρα δοῦναι, προσαγ<αγ>όμε-
νος αὐτὴν κατεφίλησεν, εἶτα εὐθὺς ἀφῆκε, μὴ καί
τις ὑποψία γένηται τῆς τέχνης.

8. Αἱ μὲν οὖν γυναῖκες ἀπῄεσαν, τὸ δὲ φίλημα
καθάπερ ἰὸς εἰς τὰ σπλάγχνα Διονυσίου κατεδύετο
καὶ οὔτε ὁρᾶν ἔτι οὔτε ἀκούειν ἐδύνατο, πανταχόθεν
δὲ ἦν ἐκπεπολιορκημένος, οὐδεμίαν εὑρίσκων θεραπείαν τοῦ ἔρωτος· οὔτε διὰ δώρων, ἑώρα γὰρ τῆς
γυναικὸς τὸ μεγαλόφρον· οὔτε δι᾽ ἀπειλῆς ἢ βίας,
πεπεισμένος ὅτι θάνατον αἱρήσεται θᾶττον ἢ
βιασθήσεται. μίαν οὖν βοήθειαν ὑπελάμβανε τὴν
Πλαγγόνα καὶ μεταπεμψάμενος αὐτὴν "τὰ μὲν
πρῶτά σοι" φησὶν "ἐστρατήγηται, καὶ χάριν ἔχω
τοῦ φιλήματος· ἐκεῖνο δέ με σέσωκεν ἢ ἀπολώλεκε·
2 σκόπει δὴ πῶς γυνὴ γυναικὸς περιγένῃ, σύμμαχον
ἔχουσα κἀμέ. γίνωσκε δὲ ἐλευθερίαν σοι προκειμέ-
νην τὸ ἆθλον καὶ ὃ πέπεισμαί σοι πολὺ ἥδιον εἶναι

cas and Plangon from death after what they have done. Yet I am glad to pardon them as a favor to you. I want you two to know that it is for Callirhoe's sake that you have been spared." Plangon fell at his feet, but Dionysius said, "You should kneel before Callirhoe; it is she who has saved you." When Plangon saw Callirhoe's great delight and pleasure at this favor, she said to her, "Then it is for you to express our thanks to Dionysius," and at the same time she pushed her forward. Somehow she stumbled and clutched at Dionysius' hand, and he, as if it were ungallant just to give her his hand, drew her to him and kissed her. Then he quickly let her go lest she suspect there was some guile.

8. The women then went away, but that kiss sank deep into Dionysius' heart like poison and he could no longer see or hear. He was completely taken by storm, and could find no remedy for his love. He could not offer her gifts, since he had seen the woman's proud spirit; he could not use threats or force, since he was sure that she would prefer death to being violated. Realizing then that Plangon was his only resource, he sent for her and said, "The campaign has started well. I am grateful to you for the kiss; it is either my salvation or my ruin. So now look for some way to get the better of her, woman to woman, with me as your ally. Know that freedom is the prize which I set before you and, what I am sure is much dearer to you

---

7.7 add. Cobet.

8.1 Διονυσίου] after σπλάγχνα Hercher: after φίλημα F.

8.2 δὴ Cobet: ἂν F.

τῆς ἐλευθερίας, τὸ ζῆν Διονύσιον." κελευσθεῖσα δὲ ἡ
Πλαγγὼν πᾶσαν πεῖραν καὶ τέχνην προσέφερεν·
ἀλλ᾽ ἡ Καλλιρόη πανταχόθεν ἀήττητος ἦν καὶ ἔμενε
3 Χαιρέᾳ μόνῳ πιστή. κατεστρατηγήθη δ᾽ ὑπὸ τῆς
Τύχης, πρὸς ἣν μόνην οὐδὲν ἰσχύει λογισμὸς
ἀνθρώπου· φιλόνεικος γὰρ ἡ δαίμων, καὶ οὐδὲν
ἀνέλπιστον παρ᾽ αὐτῇ. καὶ τότ᾽ οὖν πρᾶγμα παράδοξον, μᾶλλον δὲ ἄπιστον κατώρθωκεν.

4    Ἄξιον δὲ ἀκοῦσαι τὸν τρόπον <ὃν> ἐπεβούλευ-
σεν ἡ Τύχη τῇ σωφροσύνῃ τῆς γυναικός· ἐρωτικὴν
γὰρ ποιησόμενοι τὴν πρώτην σύνοδον τοῦ γάμου
Χαιρέας καὶ Καλλιρόη, παραπλησίαν ἔσχον ὁρμὴν
πρὸς τὴν ἀπόλαυσιν ἀλλήλων, ἰσόρροπος δὲ ἐπιθυ-
5 μία τὴν συνουσίαν ἐποίησεν οὐκ ἀργήν. ὀλίγον οὖν
πρὸ τοῦ πτώματος ἡ γυνὴ συνέλαβεν. ἀλλὰ διὰ
τοὺς κινδύνους καὶ τὴν ταλαιπωρίαν τὴν ὕστερον οὐ
ταχέως συνῆκεν ἐγκύμων γενομένη· τρίτου δὲ μηνὸς
ἀρχομένου, προέκοπτεν ἡ γαστήρ· ἐν δὲ τῷ λουτρῷ
συνῆκεν ἡ Πλαγγών, ὡς δὴ πεῖραν ἔχουσα τῶν
6 γυναικείων. εὐθὺς μὲν οὖν ἐσίγησε διὰ τὸ πλῆθος
τῶν θεραπαινίδων· περὶ δὲ τὴν ἑσπέραν σχολῆς
γενομένης, παρακαθίσασα ἐπὶ τῆς κλίνης "ἴσθι
φησίν, "ὦ τέκνον, ὅτι ἐγκύμων ὑπάρχεις." ἀνέκλαυ-
σεν ἡ Καλλιρόη καὶ ὀλολύζουσα καὶ τίλλουσα τὴν
κεφαλὴν "ἔτι καὶ τοῦτό μου" φησί "ταῖς συμφοραῖς,
ὦ Τύχη, προστέθεικας, ἵνα καὶ τέκω δοῦλον."
7 τύπτουσα δὲ τὴν γαστέρα εἶπεν "ἄθλιον πρὸ τοῦ
γεννηθῆναι γέγονας ἐν τάφῳ, καὶ χερσὶ λῃστῶν

118

than freedom, the very life of Dionysius." With these orders, Plangon brought to bear all her experience and skill, but Callirhoe proved completely invincible and remained faithful to Chaereas alone. Yet she was overcome by the stratagems of Fortune, against whom alone human reason is powerless. She is a deity who likes to win and is capable of anything. So now she contrived a situation that was unexpected, not to say incredible.

It is worth hearing how Fortune laid her plans to attack the girl's chastity. On the point of consummating their marriage, Chaereas and Callirhoe had experienced identical eagerness to enjoy each other, and the equal ardor of their passion had rendered their union not unfruitful. So a short while before her fall the girl had become pregnant, but, because of the dangers and miseries which followed, she did not immediately realize her condition. At the beginning of the third month, however, her stomach began to swell. Plangon, with her experience of women's matters, realized this on seeing her in the bath. At first she said nothing in view of the many servants around, but in the evening when all was quiet she sat down beside her on the couch and said, "My child, you ought to know you are pregnant." Callirhoe burst into tears and cries of grief. Tearing her hair, she exclaimed, "Fortune, you have added to my misery that I should also become the mother of a slave!" Then, striking her womb, she said, "Poor thing, before being born you were buried

---

8.4 add. Cobet | ποιησόμενοι Cobet: -σάμενοι F.
8.5 δὴ Cobet: ἂν ἤδη F.

παρεδόθης. εἰς ποῖον παρέρχῃ βίον; ἐπὶ ποίαις
ἐλπίσι μέλλω σε κυοφορεῖν, ὀρφανὲ καὶ ἄπολι
καὶ δοῦλε; πρὸ τῆς γενέσεως πειράθητι θανάτου."
κατέσχε δὲ αὐτῆς τὰς χεῖρας ἡ Πλαγγών, ἐπαγγει-
λαμένη τῆς ὑστεραίας εὐκολωτέραν [αὐτῇ] ἔκτρωσιν
παρασκευάσειν.

9. Γενομένη δὲ καθ᾽ ἑαυτὴν ἑκατέρα τῶν γυναικῶν ἰδίους ἐλάμβανε λογισμούς· ἡ μὲν Πλαγγὼν ὅτι
"καιρὸς ἐπιτήδειος πέφηνεν εἰς τὸ κατεργάσασθαι
τὸν ἔρωτα τῷ δεσπότῃ, συνήγορον ἐχούσῃ τὸ κατὰ
γαστρός· εὕρηται πειθοῦς ἐνέχυρον· νικήσει σωφροσύνην γυναικὸς μητρὸς φιλοστοργία." καὶ ἡ μὲν
2 πιθανῶς τὴν πρᾶξιν συνετίθει. Καλλιρόη δὲ τὸ
τέκνον ἐβουλεύετο φθεῖραι, λέγουσα πρὸς ἑαυτὴν
"ἀλλ᾽ ἐγὼ τέκω δεσπότῃ τὸν Ἑρμοκράτους ἔκγονον
καὶ προενέγκω παιδίον, οὗ μηδεὶς οἶδε πατέρα; τάχα
δὲ ἐρεῖ τις τῶν φθονούντων ‘ἐν τῷ λῃστηρίῳ Καλλι-
3 ρόη συνέλαβεν.’ ἀρκεῖ μόνην ἐμὲ δυστυχεῖν. οὐ
συμφέρει σοι, παιδίον, εἰς βίον ἄθλιον παρελθεῖν,
ὃν ἔδει καὶ γεννώμενον φυγεῖν. ἄπιθι ἐλεύθερος,
ἀπαθὴς κακῶν. μηδὲν ἀκούσῃς τῶν περὶ τῆς μητρὸς
διηγημάτων." πάλιν δὲ μετενόει καί πως ἔλεος
αὐτὴν τοῦ κατὰ γαστρὸς εἰσήει. "βουλεύῃ τεκνο-
κτονῆσαι; πασῶν ἀσεβ<εστάτη, μ>αίνῃ καὶ Μη-
4 δείας λαμβάνεις λογισμούς. ἀλλὰ καὶ τῆς Σκυθίδος
ἀγριωτέρα δόξεις· ἐκείνη μὲν γὰρ ἐχθρὸν εἶχε τὸν

8.7 del. Goold.

and handed over to pirates! What sort of life will you face? To what future shall I bear you, without father or country, and a slave? You had better die before your birth." But Plangon held her back, promising that on the next day she would provide an easier means of abortion.

9. Left alone, each of the women pursued her own line of reasoning. Plangon thought, "Here you have a fine chance to to satisfy your master's love, with the unborn child as an advocate. You have found a sure means of persuasion. Mother love will overcome her wifely virtue." So she devised a plausible line of action. Callirhoe, on the other hand, planned to destroy the child, arguing with herself, "Am I to allow a descendant of Hermocrates to be born a slave? Shall I produce a child whose father no one knows? Perhaps some malicious person will say, 'Callirhoe became pregnant among pirates.' It is enough for me alone to suffer. There is no advantage for you, my child, in entering a life of misery you ought to escape from even if you are born. Depart in freedom while still untouched by woe! May you never hear what they say about your mother!" Then again she changed her mind, and pity for the unborn child came over her. "Are you planning to kill your child?" she said. "You wicked woman, you are mad and thinking like a Medea.[a] And you will seem even more barbaric than the Scythian, for it was her husband she hated, while you want to kill

[a] Wife of Jason, the classic example of a mother who killed her children: daughter of Aeetes, king of Colchis, she was not strictly a Scythian, though this inexactitude emphasizes her barbarity.

---

9.1 ἐχούσῃ Cobet: ἔχουσα F.
9.3 ἀσεβεστάτη Reiske μαίνῃ Jackson: ἀσεβαίνῃ F.

ἄνδρα, σὺ δὲ τὸ Χαιρέου τέκνον θέλεις ἀποκτεῖναι
καὶ μηδὲ ὑπόμνημα τοῦ περιβοήτου γάμου καταλιπεῖν. τί δ' ἂν υἱὸς ᾖ; τί δ' ἂν ὅμοιος τῷ πατρί; τί δ'
ἂν εὐτυχέστερος ἐμοῦ; μήτηρ ἀποκτείνῃ τὸν ἐκ τάφου
5  σωθέντα καὶ λῃστῶν; πόσους ἀκούομεν θεῶν παῖδας
καὶ βασιλέων ἐν δουλείᾳ γεννηθέντας ὕστερον
ἀπολαβόντας τὸ τῶν πατέρων ἀξίωμα, τὸν Ζῆθον
καὶ τὸν Ἀμφίονα καὶ Κῦρον; πλεύσῃ μοι καὶ σύ,
τέκνον, εἰς Σικελίαν· ζητήσεις πατέρα καὶ πάππον,
καὶ τὰ τῆς μητρὸς αὐτοῖς διηγήσῃ. ἀναχθήσεται
στόλος ἐκεῖθεν ἐμοὶ βοηθῶν. σύ, τέκνον, ἀλλήλοις
6  ἀποδώσεις τοὺς γονεῖς." ταῦτα λογιζομένη δι' ὅλης
νυκτὸς ὕπνος ἐπῆλθε πρὸς ὀλίγον. ἐπέστη δὲ [αὐτῇ]
εἰκὼν Χαιρέου πάντα αὐτῷ [ὁμοία]

μέγεθός τε καὶ ὄμματα κάλ' ἔϊκυῖα,
καὶ φωνήν, καὶ τοῖα περὶ χροῒ εἵματα ἔστο.

ἑστὼς δὲ "παρατίθεμαί σοι" φησίν, "ὦ γύναι, τὸν
υἱόν." ἔτι δὲ βουλομένου λέγειν ἀνέθορεν ἡ Καλλιρόη, θέλουσα αὐτῷ περιπλακῆναι. σύμβουλον οὖν
τὸν ἄνδρα νομίσασα θρέψαι τὸ παιδίον ἔκρινε.

10.  Τῆς δ' ὑστεραίας ἐλθούσῃ Πλαγγόνι τὴν
αὑτῆς γνώμην ἐδήλωσεν. ἡ δὲ τὸ ἄκαιρον τῆς βουλῆς οὐ παρέλιπεν, ἀλλ' "ἀδύνατόν ἐστί σοι" φησίν,

9.5 πόσους Cobet: πόσων F.
9.6 del. Goold | del. Abresch.
10.1 παρέλιπεν Zankogiannes: παρέλαβεν F.

Chaereas' child and not even leave behind any memorial of that famous marriage. What if it should be a boy? What if he should be like his father? What if he should be luckier than I? Are you, his mother, going to kill him when he has been saved from the tomb and from pirates? Think of all the sons of gods and kings we hear of that were born in slavery and later regained the rank of their fathers, like Zethus and Amphion[a] and Cyrus![b] You too, my child, will sail to Sicily. You will search for your father and grandfather and tell them your mother's story. A fleet will set out from there to come to my aid. You, my child, will restore your parents to each other." Thus she reasoned with herself the whole night long, but for a few moments sleep came over her. An apparition of Chaereas stood before her, in all things

> like unto him, in stature and bright eyes,
> and voice, and wearing the same garments on his body.[c]

As he stood there he said, "My wife, I entrust our son to you." He wanted to continue, but Callirhoe leapt up, eager to embrace him. In the belief, therefore, that her husband had counseled her, she determined to bring up the child.

10. The next day, when Plangon came, she explained her intention to her. But Plangon did not fail to point out how inopportune the decision was. "My dear," she said,

[a] Sons of Antiope by Zeus they were exposed at birth and not until much later came into their inheritance.

[b] Grandson of Astyages, king of Media, who had him exposed; brought up by a shepherdess he subsequently defeated Astyages and founded the Persian Empire (cf. Herodotus 1.107ff); Xenophon's *Cyropaedia* is a fictional biography.

[c] *Iliad* 23.66f (the ghost of Patroclus).

CHARITON

"ὦ γύναι, τέκνον θρέψαι παρ' ἡμῖν· ὁ γὰρ δεσπότης
ἡμῶν ἐρωτικῶς σου διακείμενος ἄκουσαν μὲν οὐ
βιάσεται δι' αἰδῶ καὶ σωφροσύνην, θρέψαι δὲ
παιδίον οὐκ ἐπιτρέψει διὰ ζηλοτυπίαν, ὑβρίζεσθαι
δοκῶν εἰ τὸν μὲν ἀπόντα περισπούδαστον ὑπολαμ-
2  βάνεις, ὑπερορᾷς δὲ παρόντος αὐτοῦ. κρεῖττον οὖν
μοι δοκεῖ πρὸ τοῦ γεννηθῆναι τὸ παιδίον ἢ γεννηθὲν
ἀπολέσθαι· κερδανεῖς γὰρ ὠδῖνας ματαίας καὶ κυο-
φορίαν ἄχρηστον. ἐγὼ δέ σε φιλοῦσα συμβουλεύω
τἀληθῆ."

Βαρέως ἤκουσεν ἡ Καλλιρόη καὶ προσπεσοῦσα
τοῖς γόνασιν αὐτῆς ἱκέτευεν ὅπως συνεξεύρῃ τινὰ
3  τέχνην, δι' ἧς τὸ παιδίον θρέψει. πολλὰ τοίνυν
ἀρνησαμένη, δύο καὶ τρεῖς ἡμέρας ὑπερθεμένη τὴν
ἀπόκρισιν, ἐπειδὴ μᾶλλον ἐξέκαυσεν αὐτὴν πρὸς
τὰς δεήσεις ἀξιοπιστοτέρα γενομένη, πρῶτον μὲν
αὐτὴν ἐξώρκισε μηδενὶ κατειπεῖν τὴν τέχνην, ἔπειτα
συναγαγοῦσα τὰς ὀφρῦς καὶ τρίψασα τὰς χεῖρας
"τὰ μεγάλα" φησί "τῶν πραγμάτων, ὦ γύναι, μεγάλαις ἐπινοίαις κατορθοῦται· κἀγὼ διὰ τὴν εὔνοιαν
4  τὴν πρὸς σὲ προδίδωμι τὸν δεσπότην. ἴσθι τοίνυν
ὅτι δεήσει δυοῖν θάτερον, ἢ παντάπασιν ἀπολέσθαι
τὸ παιδίον ἢ γεννηθῆναι πλουσιώτατον Ἰώνων,
κληρονόμον τῆς λαμπροτάτης οἰκίας. καὶ σὲ τὴν
μητέρα ποιήσει μακαρίαν. ἑλοῦ δέ, πότερον θέλεις."
"καὶ τίς οὕτως" εἶπεν "ἀνόητος, ἵνα τεκνοκτονίαν
ἀντ' εὐδαιμονίας ἕληται; δοκεῖς δέ μοί τι ἀδύνατον
καὶ ἄπιστον λέγειν, ὥστε σαφέστερον αὐτὸ δήλω-

"it is quite impossible to bring up a baby here with us. Our master is in love with you, and while his respect for you and his own good sense will prevent him from forcing you against your will, still his jealousy will not permit you to rear a child: he would consider it an insult that you hold so dear the father who is not present and disregard himself who is. It seems much better to me for the child to die before its birth rather than after. In that way you will profit by avoiding unnecessary labor pains as well as a futile pregnancy. I give you this frank advice because of my affection for you."

Callirhoe listened with a heavy heart, and falling at her feet she begged her to help devise some means of rearing the child. Plangon, however, repeatedly refused and then postponed her answer for two or three days. Then, when she had aroused Callirhoe to more ardent supplications and increased her influence with her, she first made her swear to tell no one of her plan. Thereupon, knitting her brow and rubbing her hands, she said, "My girl, great things are accomplished by great ideas. Now I am going to betray my master because of my affection for you. You must realize that one of two things is necessary, either that the child is destroyed once and for all or that he is born the wealthiest of Ionians and the heir of a most glorious house. Yes, he shall make you, his mother, happy too. Choose now which you wish." "Who is so foolish," said Callirhoe, "as to prefer child-murder to good fortune? However, I think what you say is impossible and

125

5 σον." ἤρετο γοῦν ἡ Πλαγγὼν "πόσον δοκεῖς χρόνον
ἔχειν τῆς συλλήψεως;" ἡ δὲ "δύο μῆνας" εἶπεν. "ὁ
χρόνος οὖν ἡμῖν βοηθεῖ· δύνασαι γὰρ δοκεῖν ἑπτα-
μηνιαῖον ἐκ Διονυσίου τετοκέναι." πρὸς τοῦτο ἀν-
6 έκραγεν ἡ Καλλιρόη "μᾶλλον ἀπολέσθω." καὶ ἡ
Πλαγγὼν κατειρωνεύσατο αὐτῆς "καλῶς, ὦ γύναι,
φρονεῖς βουλομένη μᾶλλον ἐκτρῶσαι. τοῦτο πράτ-
τωμεν· ἀκινδυνότερον γὰρ ἢ ἐξαπατᾶν δεσπότην.
πανταχόθεν ἀπόκοψόν σου τὰ τῆς εὐγενείας ὑπομνή-
7 ματα, μηδ᾽ ἐλπὶς ἔστω σοι πατρίδος. συνάρμοσαι
τῇ παρούσῃ τύχῃ καὶ ἀκριβῶς γενοῦ δούλη."

Ταῦτα τῆς Πλαγγόνος παραινούσης οὐδὲν ὑπώπτευε Καλλιρόη, μεῖραξ εὐγενὴς καὶ πανουργίας
ἄπειρος δουλικῆς· ἀλλ᾽ ὅσῳ μᾶλλον ἐκείνη τὴν
φθορὰν ἔσπευδε, τοσούτῳ μᾶλλον αὐτὴ τὸ κατὰ
γαστρὸς ἠλέει καὶ "δός μοι" φησὶ "καιρὸν εἰς σκέ-
ψιν· περὶ τῶν μεγίστων γάρ ἐστιν ἡ αἵρεσις,
8 σωφροσύνης ἢ τέκνου." πάλιν τοῦτο ἐπήνεσεν ἡ
Πλαγγών, ὅτι μὴ προπετῶς αἱρεῖται τὸ ἕτερον· "πι-
θανὴ γὰρ εἰς ἑκάτερον ἡ ῥοπή· τὸ μὲν γὰρ ἔχει
πίστιν γυναικός, τὸ δὲ μητρὸς φιλοστοργίαν. καιρὸς δὲ οὐκ ἔστιν ὅμως μακρᾶς ἀναβολῆς, ἀλλὰ τῆς
ὑστεραίας δεῖ πάντως θάτερον ἑλέσθαι, πρὶν ἔκ-
πυστόν σου τὴν γαστέρα γενέσθαι." συνέθεντο
ταῦτα καὶ ἀπηλλάγησαν ἀλλήλων.

11. Ἀνελθοῦσα δὲ εἰς τὸ ὑπερῷον ἡ Καλλιρόη
καὶ συγκλείσασα τὰς θύρας τὴν εἰκόνα Χαιρέου τῇ
γαστρὶ προσέθηκε καὶ "ἰδού" φησι "τρεῖς γεγόνα-

unrealistic; please explain it more clearly." So Plangon asked, "How long do you think you have been with child?" "Two months," she answered. "Then time is on our side. You can make it look as if you gave birth to Dionysius' child after seven months." At this Callirhoe cried out in protest, "I would rather have the child die!" Plangon pretended to agree: "Yes, my girl, you are quite right to prefer an abortion. Let us do it that way. It is less dangerous than deceiving our master. Discard every trace of your noble birth. Abandon all hope of returning home. Adjust to your present situation and really become a slave!"

Callirhoe was quite unsuspicious of Plangon's advice, since she was a well-bred young girl and ignorant of servile cunning. But the more Plangon urged her to destroy the unborn child, the greater became her pity for it. "Give me time to consider," she said. "My choice lies between two vital matters, my honor or the life of my child." Plangon again praised her for not choosing hastily, saying, "A decision either way can be justified, in the one case by a wife's fidelity, in the other by a mother's love. But this is no time for protracted delay. By tomorrow at the latest you must choose one or the other, before your condition becomes known." They agreed to this and went their ways.

11. Going upstairs to her room and shutting the door, Callirhoe held the image of Chaereas against her womb and said, "Behold, we are three—husband, wife, and

---

10.8 θάτερον ἑλέσθαι Schmidt: θατέρον ἔχεσθαι F.

μεν, ἀνὴρ καὶ γυνὴ καὶ τέκνον. βουλευσώμεθα περὶ
τοῦ κοινῇ συμφέροντος. ἐγὼ μὲν οὖν πρώτη τὴν
ἐμὴν γνώμην ἀποφαίνομαι· θέλω γὰρ ἀποθανεῖν
Χαιρέου μόνου γυνή. τοῦτό μοι καὶ γονέων ἥδιον
καὶ πατρίδος καὶ τέκνου, πεῖραν ἀνδρὸς ἑτέρου μὴ
2 λαβεῖν. σὺ δέ, παιδίον, ὑπὲρ σεαυτοῦ τί αἱρῇ; φαρ-
μάκῳ τελευτῆσαι πρὶν τὸν ἥλιον ἰδεῖν καὶ μετὰ τῆς
μητρὸς ἐρρίφθαι, τάχα δὲ μηδὲ ταφῆς ἀξιωθῆναι, ἢ
ζῆν καὶ δύο πατέρας ἔχειν, τὸν μὲν Σικελίας, τὸν δὲ
Ἰωνίας πρῶτον; ἀνὴρ δὲ γενόμενος γνωρισθήσῃ
ῥᾳδίως ὑπὸ τῶν συγγενῶν· πέπεισμαι γὰρ ὅτι
ὅμοιόν σε τέξομαι τῷ πατρί· καὶ καταπλεύσεις λαμπρῶς ἐπὶ τριήρους Μιλησίας, ἡδέως δὲ Ἑρμοκράτης
ἔκγονον ἀπολήψεται, στρατηγεῖν ἤδη δυνάμενον.
3 ἐναντίαν μοι φέρεις, τέκνον, ψῆφον καὶ οὐκ ἐπι-
τρέπεις ἡμῖν ἀποθανεῖν. πυθώμεθά σου καὶ τοῦ
πατρός. μᾶλλον δὲ εὔρηκεν· αὐτὸς γάρ μοι παραστὰς ἐν τοῖς ὀνείροις 'παρατίθεμαί σοι' φησὶ 'τὸν
υἱόν.' μαρτύρομαί σε, Χαιρέα, σύ με Διονυσίῳ
νυμφαγωγεῖς."
4    Ταύτην μὲν οὖν τὴν ἡμέραν καὶ τὴν νύκτα ἐν
τούτοις ἦν τοῖς λογισμοῖς καὶ οὐ δι' αὑτὴν ἀλλὰ διὰ
τὸ βρέφος ἐπείθετο ζῆν· τῆς δὲ ὑστεραίας ἐλθοῦσα
ἡ Πλαγγὼν πρῶτον μὲν καθῆστο σκυθρωπὴ καὶ
σχῆμα συμπαθὲς ἐπεδείξατο, σιγῇ δὲ ἦν ἀμφοτέ-

11.1 ἀνδρὸς ἑτέρου Jackson (cf. 3.7.5): ἑ. ἀ. F.
11.4 ταύτην] Π³ begins.

child! Let us plan together what is best for us all. I first shall reveal my purpose. I wish to die as the wife of Chaereas alone. This is dearer to me than parents, homeland, and child[a]—not to have experience of another husband. But you, my child, what do you choose for yourself? Death by poison before seeing the sun, being cast out with your mother, and perhaps even denied a grave? Or rather to live and have two fathers, one the leader of Sicily, the other of Ionia? And when you become a man, you will easily be recognized by your relatives, for I am sure that I shall bear you in the likeness of your father. And you will sail home in splendor on a Milesian warship,[b] and Hermocrates shall receive his grandson with joy, now ready to be a general. It is a contrary vote which you cast against me, my child, and you do not permit us to die. Let us inquire also of your father. But no: he has already spoken, for he himself stood at my side in a dream and said, 'I entrust our son to you.' I call on you, Chaereas, to bear witness that it is you who make me the bride of Dionysius!"

Thus she spent that day and night in such reflections and was persuaded to live, not for her own sake but for her child's. The next day Plangon came back, and first sat down beside her, looking sad and presenting a sympathetic figure; both remained silent. After a long time

[a] Cf. *Odyssey* 9.34 (and see 3.8.4).

[b] Translating the Greek *trieres* (Latinized as trireme), the standard ancient warship; a reconstruction in recent times achieved a top speed of over 21 knots. See J. S. Morrison and J. F. Coates, *The Athenian Trireme*, Cambridge 1986.

5 ρων. ἐπεὶ δὲ μακρὸς ἐγίνετο χρόνος, ἡ Πλαγγὼν
ἐπύθετο "τί σοι δέδοκται; τί ποιοῦμεν; καιρὸς γὰρ
οὐκ ἔστι τοῦ μέλλειν." Καλλιρόη δὲ ἀποκρίνασθαι
μὲν ταχέως οὐκ ἐδύνατο κλαίουσα καὶ συνεχομένη,
μόλις δὲ εἶπε "τὸ τέκνον με προδίδωσιν ἀκούσης
ἐμοῦ· σὺ πρᾶττε τὸ συμφέρον. δέδοικα δὲ μή, κἂν
ὑπομείνω τὴν ὕβριν, Διονύσιός μου καταφρονήσῃ
τῆς τύχης καὶ ὡς παλλακὴν μᾶλλον ἢ γυναῖκα
νομίσας οὐ θρέψῃ τὸ ἐξ ἄλλου γεννώμενον κἀγὼ
6 μάτην ἀπολέσω τὴν σωφροσύνην." ἔτι λεγούσης ἡ
Πλαγγὼν ὑπέλαβεν "κἀγὼ περὶ τούτων προτέρα
σου βεβούλευμαι· σὲ γὰρ τοῦ δεσπότου μᾶλλον
ἤδη φιλῶ. πιστεύω μὲν οὖν Διονυσίου τῷ τρόπῳ,
χρηστὸς γάρ ἐστιν· ἐξορκιῶ δὲ ὅμως αὐτόν, κἂν
δεσπότης ᾖ· δεῖ πάντα ἡμᾶς ἀσφαλῶς πράττειν,
καὶ σύ, τέκνον, ὀμόσαντι πίστευσον. ἄπειμι δὲ ἐγὼ
τὴν πρεσβείαν κομίζουσα."

11.5 κἂν F: καὶ νῦν Π³ | καὶ ὡς Π³: καὶ F | ἢ Π³, Beck: οὐ
F | γεννώμενον F: γενόμενον Π³.
11.6 ὑπέλαβεν κἀγὼ Π³: ὑπολαβοῦσα ἔγωγε φησί F |
πιστεύω Abresch: πιστεύσω Π³: πίστευε F | καὶ σύ . . .
πίστευσον F: om. Π³ | ὀμόσαντι πίστευσον Cramer: ὅμως
ἀντιπίστευσον F | Π³ ends with colophon to Book 2, for which
see half title page.

130

Plangon inquired, "What have you decided? What shall we do? This is no time for delay." Callirhoe could not answer immediately because of her tears and distress, but at length she said, "The child betrays me, but such is not my wish. Do what you consider best. But I am afraid that even if I yield to his passion, Dionysius may look down on my misfortune and, thinking me a concubine rather than a wife, refuse to rear another man's child. Thus I shall have surrendered my honor for nothing." While she was still speaking, Plangon interrupted her and said, "I have considered that possibility even before you. By now I love you more than I do my master. Therefore though I trust Dionysius' character—for he is a good man—and master though he is, I will still have him swear an oath. We must take every precaution, and when he swears, you, my child, should trust him. Now I am off on my mission."

# Γ

1.  Διονύσιος δὲ ἀποτυγχάνων τοῦ Καλλιρόης ἔρωτος, μηκέτι φέρων ἀποκαρτερεῖν ἐγνώκει καὶ διαθήκας ἔγραφε τὰς τελευταίας, ἐπιστέλλων πῶς ταφῇ. παρεκάλει δὲ Καλλιρόην ἐν τοῖς γράμμασιν ἵνα αὐτῷ προσέλθῃ κἂν νεκρῷ. Πλαγγὼν δὲ ἐβούλετο μὲν εἰσελθεῖν πρὸς τὸν δεσπότην, διεκώλυσε δὲ αὐτὴν ὁ θεράπων κεκελευσμένος μηδένα δέχεσθαι. μαχομέ-

2  νων δὲ αὐτῶν πρὸς ταῖς θύραις ἀκούσας ὁ Διονύσιος ἤρετο τίς ἐνοχλοίη. τοῦ δὲ θεράποντος εἰπόντος ὅτι Πλαγγών, "ἀκαίρως μὲν" εἶπε "πάρεστιν" (οὐκέτι γὰρ οὐδὲ ὑπόμνημα τῆς ἐπιθυμίας ἤθελεν ἰδεῖν),

3  "κάλεσον δὲ ὅμως." ἀνοίξασα δὲ ἐκείνη τὰς θύρας "τί κατατρύχῃ" φησίν, "ὦ δέσποτα, λυπῶν σεαυτὸν ὡς ἀποτυγχάνων. Καλλιρόη γάρ σε ἐπὶ τὸν γάμον παρακαλεῖ. λαμπρεῖμόνει, θῦε, προσδέχου νύμφην, ἧς ἐρᾷς." ἐξεπλάγη πρὸς τὸ ἀνέλπιστον ὁ Διονύσιος καὶ ἀχλὺς αὐτοῦ τῶν ὀφθαλμῶν κατεχύθη, παντάπασι δὲ ὢν ἀσθενὴς φαντασίαν παρέσχε θανάτου. κωκύσασα δὲ ἡ Πλαγγὼν συνδρομὴν ἐποίησε, καὶ ἐφ᾽ ὅλης τῆς οἰκίας ὡς τεθνεὼς ὁ δεσπότης ἐπενθεῖτο.

4  οὐδὲ Καλλιρόη τοῦτο ἤκουσεν ἀδακρυτί· τοσαύτη <γὰρ λύπη πάντων> ἦν, ὥστε κἀκείνη [Διονύσιον] ἔκλαιε τὸν ἄνδρα.

# BOOK 3

1. Frustrated in his love for Callirhoe, Dionysius could endure no longer: he had resolved on suicide by starvation and was drawing up his will with directions for his burial. In it he begged Callirhoe to visit him even if dead. But Plangon was seeking an interview with her master and had been turned away by his attendant, whose orders were to admit no one. Dionysius heard them arguing at the door and asked who was making the uproar. When the attendant told him that it was Plangon, he replied, "This is a bad time for her to come," having no further desire to see anyone who would remind him of his passion, "but call her in anyway!" So she opened the door and said, "Sir, why are you breaking your heart as though all were lost? Callirhoe invites you to marry her. Put on your best clothes, offer sacrifice, and welcome the bride you love!" At this unexpected news Dionysius was paralyzed; a mist covered his eyes[a] and, completely losing consciousness, he looked just like a dead man. Plangon's shriek caused a rush to the spot, and throughout the house the master was mourned as dead. Nor could Callirhoe remain dry-eyed on hearing the news, for such was the universal grief that she too fell to mourning him.

[a] Cf. on 2.7.4.

---

1.4 add. Reiske, D'Orville | del. D'Orville.

133

Ὀψὲ δὲ καὶ μόλις ἐκεῖνος ἀνανήψας ἀσθενεῖ
φωνῇ "τίς με δαιμόνων" φησὶν "ἀπατᾷ βουλόμενος
ἀναστρέψαι τῆς προκειμένης ὁδοῦ; ὕπαρ ἢ ὄναρ
ταῦτα ἤκουσα; θέλει μοι Καλλιρόη γαμηθῆναι, ἡ μὴ
5 θέλουσα μηδὲ ὀφθῆναι;" παρεστῶσα δὲ ἡ Πλαγγὼν
"παῦσαι" φησὶ "μάτην σεαυτὸν ὀδυνῶν καὶ τοῖς ἰδί-
οις ἀγαθοῖς ἀπιστῶν· οὐ γὰρ ἐξαπατῶ μου τὸν
δεσπότην, ἀλλ' ἔπεμψέ με Καλλιρόη πρεσβεῦσαι
περὶ γάμων." "πρέσβευε τοίνυν" εἶπεν ὁ Διονύσιος
6 "καὶ λέγε αὐτὰ τὰ ἐκείνης ῥήματα. μηδὲν ἀφέλῃς
μηδὲ προσθῇς, ἀλλ' ἀκριβῶς μνημόνευσον." "ἐγὼ"
φησὶν 'οἰκίας οὖσα τῆς πρώτης ἐν Σικελίᾳ δεδυστύ-
χηκα μέν, ἀλλ' ἔτι τὸ φρόνημα τηρῶ. πατρίδος,
γονέων ἐστέρημαι, μόνην οὐκ ἀπολώλεκα τὴν εὐγέ-
νειαν. εἰ μὲν οὖν ὡς παλλακὴν θέλει με Διονύσιος
ἔχειν καὶ τῆς ἰδίας ἀπολαύειν ἐπιθυμίας, ἀπάγξομαι
μᾶλλον ἢ ὕβρει δουλικῇ παραδώσω τὸ σῶμα· εἰ δὲ
γαμετὴν κατὰ νόμους, κἀγὼ γενέσθαι θέλω μήτηρ,
7 ἵνα διάδοχον ἔχῃ τὸ Ἑρμοκράτους γένος. βουλευ-
σάσθω περὶ τούτου Διονύσιος μὴ μόνος μηδὲ
ταχέως, ἀλλὰ μετὰ φίλων καὶ συγγενῶν, ἵνα μή τις
ὕστερον εἴπῃ πρὸς αὐτὸν "σὺ θρέψεις παιδία ἐκ τῆς
8 ἀργυρωνήτου καὶ καταισχυνεῖς σου τὸν οἶκον;" εἰ
μὴ θέλει πατὴρ γενέσθαι, μηδὲ ἀνὴρ ἔστω.'" ταῦτα
τὰ ῥήματα μᾶλλον ἐξέκαυσε Διονύσιον καί τινα
ἔσχεν ἐλπίδα κούφην ἀντερᾶσθαι δοκῶν· ἀνατείνας
δὲ τὰς χεῖρας εἰς τὸν οὐρανὸν "εἰ γὰρ ἴδοιμι" φησίν,
"ὦ Ζεῦ καὶ Ἥλιε, τέκνον ἐκ Καλλιρόης· τότε μακα-

When at length he managed to regain consciousness, he said in a weak voice, "Who among the powers above is deceiving me and wants to turn me back from the path before me? Is what I heard a dream or is it real? Does Callirhoe want to become my wife when she does not even wish to be seen?" "Stop," said Plangon, coming to his side. "There is no point in torturing yourself and refusing to believe your own good fortune. I am not deceiving my master. Callirhoe has sent me to talk about marriage." "Do so, then," said Dionysius, "and tell me her very words. Do not add or subtract anything, but quote her exactly." "She said, 'I belong to the first family in Syracuse. I have been the victim of misfortune, but I still have my pride. I have been deprived of country and parents, but the one thing I have not lost is my noble birth. So, if Dionysius merely wants me as a concubine to satisfy his passion, I will hang myself rather than submit to being treated like a slave. But if he wishes me as his legal wife, then I am willing to become a mother, so that the line of Hermocrates may have a descendant. Let Dionysius think this over, not by himself and not in haste, but in company with his friends and relatives. Then no one can say to him afterwards, "Do you intend to rear children of a bought slave and shame your house?" If he does not wish to become a father, let him not become a husband.'" These words excited Dionysius all the more, and he conceived a faint hope that he was loved in return. Stretching his hands towards heaven, he said, "O Zeus and Sun,[a] if only I might see a child born of Callirhoe!

---

[a] This double invocation is practically unique in Greek literature, but the Sun god was often prayed to about personal matters.

ριώτερος δόξω τοῦ μεγάλου βασιλέως. ἀπίωμεν
πρὸς αὐτήν· ἄγε με, Πλαγγόνιον φιλοδέσποτον."

2. Ἀναδραμὼν δὲ εἰς τὰ ὑπερῷα τὸ μὲν πρῶτον
ὥρμησε τοῖς Καλλιρόης γόνασι προσπεσεῖν, κατέσχε δὲ ὅμως ἑαυτὸν καὶ καθεσθεὶς εὐσταθῶς
"ἦλθόν σοι" φησίν, "ὦ γύναι, χάριν γνῶναι περὶ τῆς
ἐμαυτοῦ σωτηρίας· ἄκουσαν μὲν γὰρ οὐκ ἔμελλόν
σε βιάσεσθαι, μὴ τυχὼν δὲ ἀποθανεῖν διεγνώκειν.
2  ἀναβεβίωκα διὰ σέ. μεγίστην δέ σοι χάριν ἔχων
ὅμως τι καὶ μέμφομαι· σὺ γὰρ ἠπίστησας ὅτι ἔξω
σε γαμετὴν παίδων ἐπ' ἀρότῳ κατὰ νόμους Ἑλληνι-
κούς. εἰ γὰρ μὴ ἤρων, οὐκ ἂν ηὐξάμην τοιούτου
γάμου τυχεῖν. σὺ δ', ὡς ἔοικε, μανίαν μου κατέγνω-
κας, εἰ δόξω δούλην τὴν εὐγενῆ καὶ ἀνάξιον υἱὸν
ἐμαυτοῦ τὸν Ἑρμοκράτους ἔκγονον. 'βούλευσαι'
3  λέγεις. βεβούλευμαι. φοβῇ φίλους ἐμοὺς ἢ
φιλτάτη πάντων; τολμήσει δὲ τίς εἰπεῖν ἀνάξιον τὸ
ἐξ ἐμοῦ γεννώμενον, κρείττονα τοῦ πατρὸς ἔχον τὸν
πάππον;" ταῦτα ἅμα λέγων καὶ δακρύων προσῆλθεν αὐτῇ· ἡ δὲ ἐρυθριάσασα ἠρέμα κατεφίλησεν
αὐτὸν καὶ "σοὶ μὲν" εἶπε "πιστεύω, Διονύσιε,
ἀπιστῶ δὲ τῇ ἐμῇ τύχῃ, καὶ γὰρ πρότερον ἐκ μειζό-
4  νων ἀγαθῶν δι' αὐτὴν κατέπεσον. φοβοῦμαι μὴ
οὐδέπω μοι διήλλακται. σὺ τοίνυν, καίπερ ὢν
χρηστὸς καὶ δίκαιος, μάρτυρας ποίησαι τοὺς θεοὺς
οὐ διὰ σαυτόν, ἀλλὰ διὰ τοὺς πολίτας καὶ συγγε-

2.1 βιάσεσθαι Cobet: βιάσασθαι F.

136

Then I should count myself more fortunate than the Great King. Let us go to her. Lead the way, devoted Plangon."

2. His first impulse, after running upstairs, was to throw himself at Callirhoe's feet, but he kept a check on himself and sat down with composure. "I have come, my dear," he said, "to thank you for saving my life. I did not intend to force you against your will, and if I had not won you, I was determined to die. You have restored me to life. Yet, though I am deeply grateful, I have a complaint to make. You did not believe that I would consider you my wife 'for the begetting of children'[a] according to Greek law. If I were not in love with you, I should not have prayed for such a marriage. You seem to have thought me mad enough to consider a nobly-born girl a slave, and a descendant of Hermocrates unworthy to be my son. 'Think it over,' you say. I have done so. Do you fear my friends—you who are dearest of all to me? Who shall dare call any child of mine unworthy, when it has a grandfather even greater than his father?" Saying this all in tears, he approached her, and she, blushing, gently kissed him and said, "I believe you, Dionysius, but I cannot trust Fortune, for through her I have already fallen from a happier state and I am afraid that she is not yet finished with me. Therefore, though you are a good and just man, swear by the powers of Heaven—not because of yourself, but because of your fellow citizens and rela-

---

[a] The regular formula in marriage contracts; cf. Menander, *Dyscolus* 842, *Periciromene* 435f, *Samia* 727.

---

2.3 τὸ ... ἔχον D'Orville: τὸν ... ἔχων F.

νεῖς, ἵνα μή τις ἔτι κακοηθέστερον εἰς ἐμέ τι συμ-
βουλεῦσαι δυνηθῇ, γινώσκων ὅτι ὀμώμοκας. εὐ-

5 καταφρόνητόν ἐστι γυνὴ μόνη καὶ ξένη." "ποίους"
φησὶ "θέλεις ὅρκους θεῶν; ἕτοιμος γὰρ ὀμνύναι, εἰ
δυνατόν, εἰς τὸν οὐρανὸν ἀναβὰς καὶ ἁψάμενος
αὐτοῦ τοῦ Διός." "ὅμοσόν μοι" φησὶ "τὴν θάλασσαν τὴν κομίσασάν με πρὸς σὲ καὶ τὴν Ἀφροδίτην
τὴν δείξασάν μέ σοι καὶ τὸν Ἔρωτα τὸν νυμφαγω-
γόν." ἤρεσε ταῦτα καὶ ταχέως ἐγένετο.

6 Τὸ μὲν οὖν ἐρωτικὸν πάθος ἔσπευδε [δὲ] καὶ ἀναβολὴν οὐκ ἐπέτρεπε τοῖς γάμοις· ταμιεύεσθαι γὰρ
δύσκολον ἐξουσίαν ἐπιθυμίας. Διονύσιος δὲ ἀνὴρ
πεπαιδευμένος κατείληπτο μὲν ὑπὸ χειμῶνος καὶ τὴν
ψυχὴν ἐβαπτίζετο, ὅμως δὲ ἀνακύπτειν ἐβιάζετο

7 καθάπερ ἐκ τρικυμίας τοῦ πάθους. καὶ τότε οὖν ἐπ-
έστησε τοιούτοις λογισμοῖς· "ἐν ἐρημίᾳ μέλλω
γαμεῖν ὡς ἀληθῶς ἀργυρώνητον· οὐχ οὕτως εἰμὶ
ἀχάριστος, ἵνα μὴ ἑορτάσω τοὺς Καλλιρόης
γάμους. ἐν τούτῳ πρώτῳ τιμῆσαί με δεῖ τὴν
γυναῖκα. φέρει δέ μοι ἀσφάλειαν καὶ πρὸς τὰ μέλ-
λοντα· πάντων γὰρ πραγμάτων ὀξύτατόν ἐστιν ἡ
Φήμη· δι' ἀέρος ἄπεισιν ἀκωλύτους ἔχουσα τὰς
ὁδούς· διὰ ταύτην οὐδὲν δύναται παράδοξον λαθεῖν·
ἤδη τρέχει φέρουσα τὸ καινὸν εἰς Σικελίαν διήγημα
'ζῇ Καλλιρόη, καὶ τυμβωρύχοι διορύξαντες τὸν
τάφον ἔκλεψαν αὐτήν, καὶ ἐν Μιλήτῳ πέπραται.'

8 καταπλεύσουσιν ἤδη τριήρεις Συρακοσίων καὶ
Ἑρμοκράτης στρατηγὸς ἀπαιτῶν τὴν θυγατέρα. τί

tives—so that in the future no one can devise some yet more wicked plot against me, knowing that you have taken your oath. A lonely woman in a strange land is of little account." "What gods do you want me to swear by?" he said. "I am ready to climb even to heaven, if that were possible, and swear with my hand upon Zeus himself." "Swear," she said, "by the sea that brought me to you, and by Aphrodite who showed me to you, and by Love who makes me your bride." This was agreed and the oath was sworn at once.

His passion mounted and brooked no delay to the marriage: control is irksome when desire can be indulged. Though well brought up, Dionysius was caught in the tempest and his heart was engulfed. Yet he forced himself to rise above the billows of his passion. And so he then gave himself over to the following reflections: "Am I to marry her in this isolated spot, as though she really were a bought slave? No, I am not so ungrateful as not to celebrate my marriage to Callirhoe in style. In this above all I must honor my wife. Moreover, it will insure me against the future. Rumor is the swiftest of all things. She flits through the air and no way is closed to her. Because of her, nothing unusual can remain secret. Already she is hurrying to Sicily with the news— 'Callirhoe is alive! Tomb robbers opened the tomb and stole her and she has been sold in Miletus.' Soon Syracusan warships will be here with the general, Hermocrates,

---

2.6 del. Jackson (dittography).

μέλλω λέγειν· Θήρων μοι πέπρακε·' Θήρων δὲ ποῦ;
καί, κἂν πιστευθῶ, τὴν ἀλήθειαν, ὑποδοχεύς εἰμι
λῃστοῦ; μελέτα, Διονύσιε, τὴν δίκην. τάχα δὲ ἐρεῖς
αὐτὴν ἐπὶ τοῦ μεγάλου βασιλέως. ἄριστον οὖν τότε
λέγειν 'ἐγὼ γυναῖκα ἐλευθέραν ἐπιδημήσασαν οὐκ
οἶδ' ὅπως ἤκουσα· ἐκδομένην ἑαυτὴν ἐν τῇ πόλει
9 φανερῶς κατὰ νόμους ἔγημα.' πείσω δὲ ταύτῃ μᾶλλον καὶ τὸν πενθερὸν ὡς οὐκ ἀνάξιός εἰμι τῶν
γάμων. καρτέρησον, ψυχή, προθεσμίαν σύντομον,
ἵνα τὸν πλείω χρόνον ἀπολαύσῃς ἀσφαλοῦς ἡδονῆς.
ἰσχυρότερος γενήσομαι πρὸς τὴν κρίσιν, ἀνδρός, οὐ
δεσπότου νόμῳ χρώμενος."

10 Ἔδοξεν οὕτως καὶ καλέσας Λεωνᾶν "ἄπιθι"
φησὶν "εἰς τὴν πόλιν· μεγαλοπρεπῶς ἑτοίμασον τὰ
πρὸς τὸν γάμον· ἐλαυνέσθωσαν ἀγέλαι· σῖτος καὶ
οἶνος διὰ γῆς καὶ θαλάσσης κομιζέσθω· δημοσίᾳ
11 τὴν πόλιν εὐωχῆσαι προῄρημαι." πάντα διατάξας
ἐπιμελῶς τῆς ὑστεραίας αὐτὸς μὲν ἐπὶ ὀχήματος
ἐποιεῖτο τὴν πορείαν, τὴν δὲ Καλλιρόην (οὐδέπω
γὰρ ἐβούλετο δεικνύναι <τοῖς> πολλοῖς) ἐκέλευσε
περὶ τὴν ἑσπέραν διὰ πορθμείου κομισθῆναι μέχρι
τῆς οἰκίας ἥτις ἦν ἐπ' αὐτοῦ τοῦ λιμένος τοῦ Δοκί-
μου λεγομένου· Πλαγγόνι δὲ τὴν ἐπιμέλειαν αὐτῆς
ἐνεχείρισε.

12 Μέλλουσα τοίνυν ἀπαλλάσσεσθαι τῶν ἀγρῶν ἡ
Καλλιρόη τῇ Ἀφροδίτῃ πρῶτον ἐπηύξατο καὶ εἰσελ-

2.11 add. Hercher.

demanding back his daughter. What am I going to say? 'Theron sold her to me?' But where is Theron? Even if I am believed in this, do I tell them the truth, that I am a receiver of stolen goods from a pirate? Dionysius, you had better get your story ready. Possibly you will have to plead it before the Great King. If so, it will be best to say, 'I somehow heard that a freeborn girl had taken up residence here. She gave herself to be my wife and I married her in the city, openly and according to the law.' Thus I shall more likely persuade even my father-in-law that I am not unworthy of the marriage. So be patient, my heart, for a little while, and then you can safely enjoy your pleasure all the longer. In a trial I shall have a stronger case, if I claim the rights of a husband and not of a master."

Having made up his mind he called Leonas and said, "Go to the city and prepare for the wedding in style. Have flocks of sheep driven in and food and wine brought by land and sea. I have decided to give the city a public banquet." After carefully giving full instructions, he himself made the journey in a chariot on the following day, but since he did not want to display Callirhoe to the general public as yet, he arranged for her to be brought in the evening by boat to his house which lay right on the so-called harbor of Docimus,[a] and he entrusted Plangon with her care.

Before Callirhoe left the farm, she first prayed to Aphrodite. Entering the shrine, she made everybody

[a] See C. P. Jones, "Hellenistic History in Chariton of Aphrodisias," *Chiron* 22 (1992) 91–102.

141

# CHARITON

θοῦσα εἰς τὸν νεών, πάντας ἐκβαλοῦσα, ταῦτα εἶπε
πρὸς τὴν θεόν· "δέσποινα Ἀφροδίτη, μέμψομαί σοι
δικαίως ἢ χάριν γνῶ; σύ με οὖσαν παρξένον ἔζευ-
ξας Χαιρέᾳ καὶ νῦν μετ᾽ ἐκεῖνον ἄλλῳ με νυμφαγω-
13  γεῖς. οὐκ ἂν ἐπείσθην σὲ ὀμόσαι καὶ τὸν σὸν υἱόν,
εἰ μή με προύδωκε τοῦτο τὸ βρέφος," δείξασα τὴν
γαστέρα. "ἱκετεύω δέ σε" φησὶν "οὐχ ὑπὲρ ἐμαυτῆς, ἀλλ᾽ ὑπὲρ τούτου. ποίησόν μου λαθεῖν τὴν
τέχνην. ἐπεὶ τὸν ἀληθῆ τοῦτο πατέρα οὐκ ἔχει,
δοξάτω Διονυσίου παιδίον, τραφὲν γὰρ κἀκεῖνον
14  εὑρήσει." βαδίζουσαν δὲ αὐτὴν ἀπὸ τοῦ τεμένους ἐπὶ
τὴν θάλασσαν ἰδόντες οἱ ναῦται δείματι κατεσχέθη-
σαν, ὡς τῆς Ἀφροδίτης αὐτῆς ἐρχομένης ἵνα ἐμβῇ,
καὶ ὥρμησαν ἀθρόοι προσκυνῆσαι· προθυμίᾳ δὲ τῶν
ἐρεσσόντων λόγου θᾶττον ἡ ναῦς κατέπλευσεν εἰς
τὸν λιμένα.

15  Ἅμα δὲ τῇ ἕῳ πᾶσα ἦν ἡ πόλις ἐστεφανωμένη.
ἔθυεν ἕκαστος πρὸ τῆς ἰδίας οἰκίας, οὐκ ἐν μόνοις
τοῖς ἱεροῖς. λογοποιίαι δὲ ἦσαν τίς ἡ νύμφη· τὸ δὲ
δημωδέστερον πλῆθος ἀνεπείθετο διὰ τὸ κάλλος καὶ
τὸ ἄγνωστον τῆς γυναικὸς ὅτι Νηρηῒς ἐκ θαλάσσης
ἀναβέβηκεν ἢ ὅτι θεὰ πάρεστιν ἐκ τῶν Διονυσίου
16  κτημάτων· τοῦτο γὰρ οἱ ναῦται διελάλουν. μία δὲ
πάντων ἦν ἐπιθυμία Καλλιρόην θεάσασθαι, καὶ περὶ
τὸ ἱερὸν τῆς Ὁμονοίας ἠθροίσθη τὸ πλῆθος, ὅπου
πάτριον ἦν τοῖς γαμοῦσι τὰς νύμφας παραλαμβά-
νειν. τότε πρῶτον ἐκοσμήσατο μετὰ τὸν τάφον· κρί-
νασα γὰρ ἅπαξ γαμηθῆναι καὶ πατρίδα καὶ γένος

142

leave; then she spoke to the goddess as follows: "Lady Aphrodite, ought I to blame or thank you? You married me to Chaereas when I was a girl, but now you make me the bride of another man after him. I should never have agreed to swear by you and your son, had not this child betrayed me" (and here she pointed to her womb); "I implore you," she continued, "not for my sake but for his: allow my guile to pass undetected. Since this child does not have his real father, let him be considered the son of Dionysius. When he is grown to manhood, he will find his real father, too." As she made her way from the shrine to the sea, the boatmen were overwhelmed with awe on seeing her, as though Aphrodite herself were coming to embark, and with one accord they hastened to kneel in homage. So ardently did they row that in less time than it takes to tell the ship sailed into the harbor.

By dawn the whole city was adorned with garlands. Every man offered sacrifice before his own house, and not only in the shrines. There was speculation about the bride's identity. Because the woman was beautiful and unknown, the humbler folk were persuaded that she was a Nereid who had risen from the sea or a goddess who had come from Dionysius' estate: this was the gossip of the boatmen. All, however, had but one desire, and that was to see Callirhoe; and the crowd was massed about the temple of Concord where it was the tradition for bridegrooms to receive their brides. Then for the first time since her burial Callirhoe arrayed herself in finery, for once she had resolved upon marriage, she considered that her beauty constituted her country and lineage. After

143

τὸ κάλλος ἐνόμισεν. ἐπεὶ δὲ ἔλαβε Μιλησίαν στολὴν καὶ στέφανον νυμφικόν, ἀπέβλεψεν εἰς τὸ πλῆ-
17 θος. πάντες οὖν ἀνεβόησαν "ἡ Ἀφροδίτη γαμεῖ."
πορφυρίδας ὑπεστρώννυον καὶ ῥόδα καὶ ἴα, μύρον
ἔρραινον βαδιζούσης, οὐκ ἀπελείφθη ἐν ταῖς οἰκίαις
οὐ παιδίον, οὐ γέρων, ἀλλ' οὐδ' ἐν αὐτοῖς τοῖς
λιμέσι· μέχρι κεράμων ἀνέβη τὸ πλῆθος στενοχω-
ρούμενον. ἀλλ' ἐνεμέσησε καὶ ταύτῃ τῇ ἡμέρᾳ
πάλιν ὁ βάσκανος δαίμων ἐκεῖνος· ὅπως δέ, μικρὸν
ὕστερον ἐρῶ. βούλομαι δὲ εἰπεῖν πρῶτον τὰ γενό-
μενα ἐν Συρακούσαις κατὰ τὸν αὐτὸν χρόνον.

3. Οἱ μὲν γὰρ τυμβωρύχοι τὸν τάφον περιέκλει-
σαν ἀμελῶς, οἷα δὴ σπεύδοντες ἐν νυκτί· Χαιρέας δὲ
φυλάξας αὐτὸ τὸ περίορθρον ἧκεν ἐπὶ τὸν τάφον
προφάσει μὲν στεφάνους καὶ χοὰς ἐπιφέρων, τὸ δὲ
ἀληθὲς γνώμην ἔχων ἑαυτὸν ἀνελεῖν· οὐ γὰρ ὑπέμενε Καλλιρόης ἀπεζεῦχθαι, μόνον δὲ τὸν θάνατον
τοῦ πένθους ἰατρὸν ἐνόμιζε· παραγενόμενος δὲ εὗρε
τοὺς λίθους κεκινημένους καὶ φανερὰν τὴν εἴσοδον.
2 ὁ μὲν οὖν ἰδὼν ἐξεπλάγη καὶ ὑπὸ δεινῆς ἀπορίας
κατείχετο τοῦ γεγονότος χάριν· ἄγγελος δὲ Φήμη
ταχεῖα Συρακοσίοις ἐμήνυσε τὸ παράδοξον. πάντες
οὖν συνέτρεχον ἐπὶ τὸν τάφον, ἐτόλμα δὲ οὐδεὶς
ἔνδον παρελθεῖν, πρὶν ἐκέλευσεν Ἑρμοκράτηω. ὁ δὲ
3 εἰσπεμφθεὶς πάντα ἀκριβῶς ἐμήνυσεν. ἄπιστον
ἐδόκει τὸ μηδὲ τὴν νεκρὰν κεῖσθαι. τότ' οὖν ἠξίωσε
Χαιρέας αὐτὸς <εἰσελθεῖν> ἐπιθυμίᾳ τοῦ πάλιν
Καλλιρόην ἰδεῖν κἂν νεκράν· ἐρευνῶν δὲ τὸν τάφον

putting on a Milesian dress[a] and a bridal wreath, she looked out at the assembled crowd. Everyone shouted, "Aphrodite is the bride!" Beneath her feet they spread purple cloth and roses and violets. As she passed they sprayed her with perfume. Not a person, young or old, was left inside the houses or even at the harbors. Cramped for space, the crowd climbed up to the rooftops. But on this day, too, the demon Envy again showed his malice. Just how, I shall describe a little later, but I first want to tell of events in Syracuse during this period.

3. Hurrying in the dark the tomb robbers had been careless in shutting the tomb. Chaereas waited for dawn to visit the tomb, ostensibly to bring wreaths and libations, but really in order to kill himself. He could not bear separation from Callirhoe and considered death the only cure for his sorrow. When he arrived, he discovered that the stones had been moved and that the entrance was wide open. He was astonished at the sight and seized by a fearful bewilderment at what had happened. Rumor swiftly brought the shocking news to Syracuse, and everyone hastened to the tomb, but no one ventured to go inside until Hermocrates gave the order. The man sent in gave a full and true account. It seemed unbelievable that not even the corpse was lying there. Then Chaereas himself decided to go in, eager to see Callirhoe once more even though she was dead, but on searching the tomb he

[a] Of wool, Miletus being famed for the softness, elegance, and beauty of its woolen wares from the 6th century B.C.; see Gow on Theocritus 15.126f.

3.3 add. Cobet.

4 οὐδὲν εὑρεῖν ἠδύνατο. πολλοὶ μετ' αὐτὸν εἰσῆλθον
ὑπ' ἀπιστίας· ἀμηχανία δὲ κατέλαβε πάντας, καί τις
εἶπεν <ἐν>εστὼς "τὰ ἐντάφια σεσύληται, τυμβωρύχων τὸ ἔργον· ἡ νεκρὰ δὲ ποῦ;"

Λογοποίαι πολλαὶ καὶ διάφοροι τὸ πλῆθος
κατεῖχον. Χαιρέας δὲ ἀναβλέψας εἰς τὸν οὐρανὸν
καὶ τὰς χεῖρας ἀνατείνας "τίς ἄρα θεῶν ἀντεραστής
μου γενόμενος Καλλιρόην ἀπενήνοχε καὶ νῦν ἔχει
μεθ' αὑτοῦ μὴ θέλουσαν, ἀλλὰ βιαζομένην ὑπὸ
5 κρείττονος μοίρας; διὰ τοῦτο καὶ αἰφνίδιον ἀπέθα-
νεν, ἵνα μὴ νοσήσῃ. οὕτω καὶ Θησέως Ἀριάδνην
ἀφείλετο Διόνυσος καὶ <Ἀκταίωνος> Σεμέλην ὁ
Ζεύς· μὴ γὰρ οὐκ ᾔδειν ὅτι θεὰν εἶχον γυναῖκα καὶ
κρείττων ἦν ἢ καθ' ἡμᾶς. ἀλλ' οὐκ ἔδει ταχέως
αὐτὴν οὐδὲ μετὰ τοιαύτης προφάσεως ἐξ ἀνθρώπων
6 ἀπελθεῖν. ἡ Θέτις θεὰ μὲν ἦν, ἀλλὰ Πηλεῖ παρ-
έμεινε καὶ υἱὸν ἔσχεν ἐκεῖνος ἐξ αὐτῆς, ἐγὼ δὲ ἐν
ἀκμῇ τοῦ ἔρωτος ἀπελείφθην. τί πάθω; τί γένωμαι,
δυστυχής; ἐμαυτὸν ἀνέλω; καὶ μετὰ τίνος ταφῶ;
ταύτην γὰρ εἶχον ἐλπίδα τῆς συμφορᾶς· εἰ θάλαμον
μετὰ Καλλιρόης κοινὸν οὐκ ἐτήρησα, τάφον αὐτῇ
7 κοινὸν εὑρήσω. ἀπολογοῦμαί σοι, δέσποινα, τῆς
ἐμῆς ψυχῆς. σύ με ζῆν ἀναγκάζεις· ζητήσω γάρ σε
διὰ γῆς καὶ θαλάσσης, κἂν εἰς αὐτὸν ἀναβῆναι τὸν
ἀέρα δύνωμαι. τοῦτο δέομαί σου, γύναι, σύ με μὴ

<hr/>

3.4 add. Naber.     3.5 αἰφνιδίως F, corr. Hercher |
νοσήσῃ d'Orville: νοήσῃ F | add. Rose.

could find nothing. Many others entered incredulously after him. All were baffled, and one of those inside said, "The funeral offerings have been stolen! This is the work of tomb robbers. But where is the corpse?"

Many different speculations were entertained by the crowd. But Chaereas, looking up to heaven, stretched forth his hands and said, "Which of the gods has become my rival and carried off Callirhoe and now keeps her with him, against her will but compelled by a mightier fate? Is this then why she died suddenly, that she might not succumb to disease? So did Dionysus once steal Ariadne from Theseus and Zeus Semele from Actaeon.[a] Or can it be that I had a goddess as my wife and did not know it, and she was above our human lot? But, even so, she should not have disappeared from the world so quickly or for such a reason. Thetis, too, was a goddess, but she remained with Peleus and bore him a son, while I have been deserted at the very peak of my love. What is my fate? What will become of me, poor wretch? Shall I kill myself? With whom shall I be buried? For this was my hope in my misfortune, that if I could no longer share my bed with Callirhoe, at least I would share her grave. My lady, I offer you my defense for staying alive: you compel me to live. I shall search for you over land and sea—yes, if I may, I shall even rise into the sky. Only I beg you, my

[a] Cf. Apollodorus 3.4.4, but this is not the usual story told of Actaeon; nor this the usual account of Ariadne, who was not stolen from Theseus but abandoned by him. Reardon well observes that Chariton's reason for instancing the two women is that they were mortals who were deified.

3.7 γύναι Hercher: γυνή F.

φύγης." θρῆνον τὸ πλῆθος ἐξέρρηξεν ἐπὶ τούτοις
καὶ πάντες ὡς ἄρτι τεθνεῶσαν Καλλιρόην ἤρξαντο
θρηνεῖν.

8 Τριήρεις εὐθὺς κατεσπῶντο καὶ τὴν ζήτησιν πολλοὶ διενέμοντο· Σικελίαν μὲν γὰρ αὐτὸς Ἑρμοκράτης ἠρεύνα, Χαιρέας δὲ Λιβύην· εἰς Ἰταλίαν τινὲς
ἐξεπέμποντο, καὶ ἄλλοι περαιοῦσθαι τὸν Ἰόνιον
ἐκελεύσθησαν. ἡ μὲν οὖν ἀνθρωπίνη βοήθεια
παντάπασιν ἦν ἀσθενής, ἡ Τύχη δὲ ἐφώτισε τὴν
ἀλήθειαν, ἧς χωρὶς ἔργον οὐδὲν τέλειον· μάθοι δ' ἄν
τις ἐκ τῶν γενομένων.

9 Πωλήσαντες γὰρ οἱ τυμβωρύχοι τὸ δυσδιάθετον
φορτίον [τὴν γυναῖκα] Μίλητον μὲν ἀπέλιπον, ἐπὶ
Κρήτης δὲ τὸν πλοῦν ἐποιοῦντο, νῆσον ἀκούοντες
εὐδαίμονα καὶ μεγάλην, ἐν ᾗ τὴν διάπρασιν τῶν
10 φορτίων ἤλπισαν ἔσεσθαι ῥᾳδίαν. ὑπολαβὼν δὲ
αὐτοὺς ἄνεμος σφοδρὸς εἰς τὸν Ἰόνιον ἐξέωσεν,
κἀκεῖ λοιπὸν ἐπλανῶντο ἐν ἐρήμῳ θαλάσσῃ. βρον-
ταὶ δὲ καὶ ἀστραπαὶ καὶ νὺξ μακρὰ κατελάμβανε
τοὺς ἀνοσίους, ἐπιδεικνυμένης τῆς Προνοίας ὅτι τότε
διὰ Καλλιρόην ηὐπλόουν. ἐγγὺς γινομένους ἑκά-
στοτε τοῦ θανάτου ταχέως οὐκ ἀπήλλαττεν ὁ θεὸς
11 τοῦ φόβου, μακρὸν αὐτοῖς ποιῶν τὸ ναυάγιον. γῆ
μὲν οὖν τοὺς ἀνοσίους οὐκ ἐδέχετο, θαλαττεύοντες δὲ
πολὺν χρόνον ἐν ἀπορίᾳ κατέστησαν τῶν ἀναγκαίων, μάλιστα δὲ τοῦ ποτοῦ, καὶ οὐδὲν αὐτοὺς

3.8 ἠρεύνα Reiske: ἐρευνᾷ F.    3.9 del. Cobet.

148

darling, do not flee from me." At these words the crowd broke into lamentation, and all began to mourn for Callirhoe as though she had just died.

Warships were immediately launched and many shared in the search. Hermocrates himself explored Sicily, and Chaereas, Libya.[a] Some were sent off to Italy and others were ordered to cross the Ionian Sea.[b] However, human effort proved utterly ineffective, and it was Fortune who brought the truth to light—Fortune, without whom no work is ever brought to completion, as may be learned from what happened.

After selling their embarrassing cargo,[c] the tomb robbers left Miletus and sailed for Crete. They had heard that it was a great and prosperous island and hoped that there the disposal of their wares would be easy. But a violent wind caught them and drove them out into the Ionian Sea, where they drifted in deserted waters. Thunder and lightning and prolonged darkness overtook the villains, Providence revealing that they had enjoyed fair sailing earlier only through Callirhoe's presence. Each time they came close to death God would not grant them a quick release from their fear of it, but prolonged their shipwreck. Dry land refused to accept such villains and so, long tossed on the sea, they were reduced to shortage of provisions, especially of water. Their ill-gotten gains

[a] I.e. the north coast of Africa.

[b] The sea between Sicily (and the boot of Italy) and the Greek peninsula: in spite of the apparent similarity the name (Ἰόνιος) has no connection with Ionia (Ἰωνία), the Greek seaboard of Asia Minor.

[c] Cf. Menander, fr. 18 K-T.

ὠφέλει πλοῦτος ἄδικος, ἀλλὰ διψῶντες ἀπέθνησκον
ἐν χρυσῷ. βραδέως μὲν οὖν μετενόουν ἐφ' οἷς ἐτόλ-
μησαν, ὅτι "οὐδὲν ὄφελος" ἐγκαλοῦντες ἀλλήλοις.
12 οἱ μὲν οὖν ἄλλοι πάντες ἔθνησκον ὑπὸ δίψους,
Θήρων δὲ καὶ ἐν ἐκείνῳ τῷ καιρῷ πανοῦργος ἦν·
ὑποκλέπτων γὰρ τοῦ ποτοῦ καὶ τοὺς συλλῃστὰς
ἐλῄστευεν. ᾤετο μὲν οὖν τεχνικόν τι πεποιηκέναι, τὸ
δὲ ἄρα τῆς Προνοίας ἔργον ἦν βασάνοις καὶ
σταυρῷ τὸν ἄνδρα τηρούσης.

13 Ἡ γὰρ τριήρης ἡ Χαιρέαν κομίζουσα πλανωμένῳ
τῷ κέλητι περιπίπτει καὶ τὸ μὲν πρῶτον ὡς πειρατι-
κὸν ἐξένευσεν· ἐπεὶ δ' ἀκυβέρνητος ἐφάνη, πρὸς τὰς
τῶν κυμάτων ἐμβολὰς εἰκῇ φερόμενος, ἐκ τῆς τριήρους τις ἀνέκραγεν "οὐκ ἔχει τοὺς ἐμπλέοντας· μὴ
φοβηθῶμεν, ἀλλὰ πλησιάσαντες ἱστορήσωμεν τὸ
14 παράδοξον." ἤρεσε τῷ κυβερνήτῃ· Χαιρέας μὲν γὰρ
ἐν κοίλῃ νηΐ συγκεκαλυμμένος ἔκλαεν. ἐπεὶ δὲ
ἐπλησίασαν, τὸ μὲν πρῶτον τοὺς ἔνδον ἐκάλουν· ὡς
δὲ ὑπήκουεν οὐδείς, ἀνέβη τις ἀπὸ τῆς τριήρους,
εἶδε δὲ οὐδὲν ἕτερον ἢ χρυσὸν καὶ νεκρούς. ἐμήνυσε
τοῖς ναύταις· ἔχαιρον, εὐτυχεῖς ἐνόμιζον ἑαυτούς, ὡς
15 ἐν θαλάσσῃ θησαυρὸν εὑρόντες. θορύβου δὲ γενομένου Χαιρέας ἤρετο τίς ἡ αἰτία. μαθὼν οὖν καὶ
αὐτὸς ἠβουλήθη τὸ καινὸν θεάσασθαι. γνωρίσας δὲ
τὰ ἐντάφια περιερρήξατο καὶ μέγα καὶ διωλύγιον
ἀνεβόησεν "οἴμοι, Καλλιρόη· ταῦτά ἐστι τὰ σά.
στέφανος οὗτος, ὃν ἐγώ σοι περιέθηκα· τοῦτο ὁ
πατήρ σοι δέδωκε, τοῦτο ἡ μήτηρ· αὕτη στολὴ

availed them naught, and they began to die of thirst in the midst of gold. Gradually they repented of their deeds, and reproached each other with the futility of it all. Now all the rest were dying of thirst, but even in this plight Theron proved a rogue. He secretly stole from the water, and thus robbed his fellow robbers. He thought he had done something clever, but this was the design of Providence, preserving him for torture and the cross.

The warship with Chaereas on board fell in with the cutter as it drifted, and at first they avoided it, thinking it was a pirate vessel; but when it became clear that it had no pilot and was floating to and fro under the impact of the waves, someone from the warship shouted, "There is no one on board! No need to be afraid! Let us get close and look into the mystery." The pilot agreed, for Chaereas was below deck weeping, his head covered up. Drawing alongside they first hailed the crew; when no one answered, a man from the warship went on board and could see nothing but gold and corpses. He reported to his mates, who were delighted and congratulated themselves on finding treasure at sea. Hearing the disturbance, Chaereas asked what the trouble was, and, on being told, wanted to look at the strange sight himself. When he recognized the funeral offerings, he tore his clothes in grief and in a loud and piercing voice he exclaimed, "Alas, Callirhoe! These are your things! This is the wreath which I put about your head; your father gave you this; and this is from your mother; and here is your

---

3.12 δίψους Hercher: δίψης F.

16  νυμφική. τάφος σοι γέγονεν ἡ ναῦς. ἀλλὰ τὰ μὲν
σὰ βλέπω, σὺ δὲ ποῦ; μόνη τοῖς ἐνταφίοις ἡ νεκρὰ
λείπει."

Τούτων ἀκούσας ὁ Θήρων ἔκειτο ὅμοιος τοῖς
νεκροῖς, καὶ γὰρ ἦν ἡμιθανής. πολλὰ μὲν οὖν ἐβουλεύσατο [τὸ] μηδ᾽ ὅλως φωνὴν ἀφεῖναι μηδὲ κινεῖ-
σθαι· τὸ γὰρ μέλλον οὐκ ἦν ἀπροόρατον αὐτῷ·
φύσει δὲ φιλόζωόν ἐστιν ἄνθρωπος καὶ οὐδὲ ἐν ταῖς
ἐσχάταις συμφοραῖς ἀπελπίζει τὴν πρὸς τὸ βέλτιον
μεταβολήν, τοῦ δημιουργήσαντος θεοῦ τὸ σόφισμα
τοῦτο πᾶσιν ἐγκατασπείραντος, ἵνα μὴ φύγωσι βίον
17  ταλαίπωρον. κατεχόμενος οὖν τῷ δίψει ταύτην πρώτην ἀφῆκε φωνὴν "ποτόν." ἐπεὶ δὲ αὐτῷ προση-
νέχθη καὶ πάσης ἔτυχεν ἐπιμελείας, παρακαθεσθεὶς
αὐτῷ [ὁ] Χαιρέας ἤρετο "τίνες ἐστέ; καὶ ποῦ πλεῖτε;
καὶ πόθεν ταῦτα; καὶ τί τὴν κυρίαν αὐτῶν πεποιή-
κατε;" Θήρων δὲ ἐμνημόνευεν ἑαυτοῦ πανοῦργος
ἄνθρωπος καὶ "Κρὴς" εἶπεν "εἰμί, πλέω δὲ εἰς
Ἰωνίαν ἀδελφὸν ἐμαυτοῦ ζητῶν στρατευόμενον.
18  ταχείας δὲ τῆς ἀναγωγῆς γενομένης κατελείφθην
ὑπὸ τῶν ἐπὶ τῆς νεὼς ἐν Κεφαλληνίᾳ. ἐκεῖθεν ἐπέβην τοῦδε τοῦ κέλητος παραπλέοντος εὐκαίρως.
ἐξαισίοις δὲ πνεύμασιν ἐξεώσθημεν εἰς ταύτην τὴν
θάλασσαν· εἶτα γαλήνης μακρᾶς γενομένης δίψει

3.16 del. Reiske.
3.17 del. Jackson (cf. 3.3.15) | ζητῶν Reiske: ζητῶ F.
3.18 ταχ. . . . γεν.] after στρατ. Jackson: after Κεφ. F.

bridal dress. This ship has become your tomb. I can see your things, but where are you? Of all the contents of the tomb, the corpse alone is missing!"

On hearing this, Theron lay like one of the dead, and he was indeed half dead. He had firmly resolved not to utter a word or make a movement, for he was aware what was coming to him. Yet man is by nature a life-loving creature and even in the worst misfortunes does not despair of a change for the better, since the god who created men has implanted this illusion in all so that they should not run away from the misery of life. Tormented by thirst the first word he uttered was "Water!" When it had been brought him and he had received every attention, Chaereas sat down beside him and asked: "What people are you? Where are you sailing? Where did these things come from? What have you done with the woman they belong to?" True to his nature the cunning rogue replied: "I am a Cretan, sailing to Ionia in search of my brother in the army there. I was left behind in Cephallenia[a] by the ship's crew when they left in a hurry. From there I got on board this cutter which was conveniently sailing past. Violent winds drove us into this part of the sea. Then came a prolonged calm, and all died

[a] The largest of the Ionian islands, facing Ithaca off the west coast of Greece, and lying in the opposite direction from a voyage from Crete to Ionia. Chariton was perhaps confused over the name Ionian (see note on 3.3.10 above); in any case Theron's story is a pale reflection of the deceptive yarns spun by Odysseus—who also feigns to be Cretan—(*Odyssey* 13.256ff, 14.199ff, 17.419ff, 19.172ff).

πάντες ἀνῃρέθησαν, ἐγὼ δὲ μόνος ἐσώθην ὑπὸ τῆς ἐμῆς εὐσεβείας." ἀκούσας οὖν ὁ Χαιρέας ἐκέλευσεν ἐξάψαι τὸν κέλητα τῆς τριήρους, ἕωθεν δὲ εἰς τοὺς Συρακοσίων λιμένας κατέπλευσε.

4. Προεπεδήμησε δὲ ἡ Φήμη φύσει μὲν οὖσα ταχεῖα, τότε δὲ μᾶλλον σπεύσασα μηνῦσαι πολλὰ παράδοξα καὶ καινά. πάντες οὖν ἐπὶ τὴν θάλασσαν συνέτρεχον, καὶ ἦν ὁμοῦ πάθη ποικίλα κλαόντων, θαυμαζόντων, πυνθανομένων, ἀπιστούντων· ἐξ-
2 έπληττε γὰρ αὐτοὺς τὸ καινὸν διήγημα. ἰδοῦσα δὲ ἡ μήτηρ τὰ ἐντάφια τῆς θυγατρὸς ἀνεκώκυσεν "ἐπι-γινώσκω πάντα· σύ, τέκνον, μόνη λείπεις. ὦ καινῶν τυμβωρύχων· τὴν ἐσθῆτα καὶ τὸν χρυσὸν φυλάξαν-τες μόνην ἔκλεψάν μου τὴν θυγατέρα." συνήχησαν δὲ αἰγιαλοὶ καὶ λιμένες κοπτομέναις ταῖς γυναιξί,
3 καὶ γῆν καὶ θάλασσαν ἐνέπλησαν οἰμωγῆς. Ἑρμο-κράτης δὲ ἔφη, στρατηγικὸς ἀνὴρ καὶ πραγμάτων ἐπιστήμων, "οὐκ ἐνταῦθα χρὴ ζητεῖν, ἀλλὰ νομιμω-τέραν ποιήσασθαι τὴν ἀνάκρισιν. ἀπίωμεν εἰς τὴν ἐκκλησίαν. τίς οἶδεν εἰ χρεία γένοιτο καὶ δικα-στῶν;"

4  οὔπω πᾶν εἴρητο ἔπος

καὶ ἤδη μεστὸν ἦν τὸ θέατρον. ἐκείνην τὴν ἐκκλη-σίαν ἀνήγαγον καὶ γυναῖκες.

Ὁ μὲν οὖν δῆμος μετέωρος καθῆστο, Χαιρέας δὲ πρῶτος εἰσῆλθε μελανείμων, ὠχρός, αὐχμῶν, οἷος

154

of thirst. I alone was saved because of my piety." On hearing this, Chaereas gave orders for the cutter to be towed by the warship, and at dawn he reached harbor in Syracuse.

4. But Rumor arrived there first: naturally swift, on that occasion she made extra speed to report this extraordinary situation. So everyone quickly assembled on the seashore, and every kind of emotion was expressed at the same time: people wept, marveled, inquired, and disbelieved, astounded at the strange tale. When Callirhoe's mother saw her daughter's funeral offerings, she shrieked "I recognize them all, but you, my child, are the one thing missing! A strange sort of tomb robbers! They have left the clothing and the gold and have stolen only my daughter!" The shores and harbors echoed with women beating their breasts; and they filled land and sea with lamentation. But Hermocrates, a man used to giving orders and experienced in politics, said, "We must not examine the matter here but conduct an inquiry more in accordance with law. Let us go to the assembly. Perhaps we may need a jury."

Not yet was the whole word spoken,[a]

when already the theater was filled. In that assembly women also participated.

The citizens sat in suspense. Chaereas entered first, clad in black, pale, disheveled, just as when he accompa-

---

[a] *Odyssey* 16.11 and elsewhere (formula).

---

3.18 ἔωθεν δὲ Jackson: ἔως F.

ἐπὶ τὸν τάφον ἠκολούθησε τῇ γυναικί, καὶ ἐπὶ μὲν τὸ
βῆμα οὐκ ἠθέλησεν ἀναβῆναι, κάτω δέ που στὰς τὸ
μὲν πρῶτον ἐπὶ πολὺν ἔκλαε χρόνον καὶ φθέγξασθαι
θέλων οὐκ ἠδύνατο· τὸ δὲ πλῆθος ἐβόα "θάρρει καὶ
5 λέγε." μόλις οὖν ἀναβλέψας "ὁ μὲν παρὼν" εἶπε
"καιρὸς οὐκ ἦν δημηγοροῦντος ἀλλὰ πενθοῦντος,
ἐγὼ δὲ ὑπὸ τῆς αὐτῆς ἀνάγκης καὶ λέγω καὶ ζῶ,
μέχρις ἂν ἐξεύρω Καλλιρόης τὴν ἀναίρεσιν. διὰ
τοῦτο δὲ ἐντεῦθεν ἐκπλεύσας οὐκ οἶδα πότερον
6 εὐτυχῆ τὸν πλοῦν ἢ δυστυχῆ πεποίημαι. πλοῖον
γὰρ ἐθεασάμην ἐν εὐδίᾳ πλανώμενον, ἰδίου χειμῶνος
γέμον καὶ βαπτιζόμενον ἐν γαλήνῃ. θαυμάσαντες
ἤλθομεν πλησίον. ἔδοξα τὸν τῆς ἀθλίας μου γυναικὸς τάφον ἰδεῖν, πάντα ἔχοντα τὰ ἐκείνης, πλὴν
ἐκείνης. νεκρῶν μὲν ἦν πλῆθος, ἀλλοτρίων δὲ πάντων. ὅδε δέ τις ἐν αὐτοῖς ἡμιθανὴς εὑρέθη. τοῦτον
ἐγὼ μετὰ πάσης ἐπιμελείαω ἀνεκτησάμην καὶ ὑμῖν
ἐτήρησα."

7 Μεταξὺ δὲ οἰκέται δημόσιοι τὸν Θήρωνα δεδεμένον εἰς τὸ θέατρον ἦγον μετὰ πομπῆς ἐκείνῳ
πρεπούσης. ἐπηκολούθει γὰρ αὐτῷ τροχὸς καὶ
καταπέλτης καὶ πῦρ καὶ μάστιγες, ἀποδιδούσης
8 αὐτῷ τῆς Προνοίας τὰ ἔπαθλα τῶν ἀγώνων. ἐπεὶ δὲ
ἐν μέσοις ἔστη, τῶν ἀρχόντων εἷς ἀνέκρινεν αὐτόν·
"τίς εἶ;" "Δημήτριος" εἶπε. "πόθεν;" "Κρής." "τί
οἶδας; εἰπέ." "πρὸς ἀδελφὸν ἐμαυτοῦ πλέων εἰς
Ἰωνίαν ἀπελείφθην νεώς, εἶτα κέλητος ἐπέβην

nied his wife to the tomb. He declined to mount the plat-
form, but, standing below, at first he wept for a long time
and, though wishing to speak, could not. The crowd
shouted, "Courage! Speak!" At last he looked up and said,
"This is a time for mourning, not for speech. The same
purpose compels me to speak as to live, namely to dis-
cover how Callirhoe disappeared. That was why I set sail
from here, and I do not know whether my voyage was
successful or not. I saw a boat drifting about in fair
weather, laboring under a tempest of its own, and sinking
in a calm. Puzzled by this, we drew closer, and it seemed
as if I was looking at the tomb of my poor wife. Everything of hers was there, except herself. There were a
great many corpses, but all of strangers. This fellow was
found among them half dead. I spared no pains to revive
him and have brought him to show you!"

Meanwhile constables[a] brought Theron into the theater in chains with an escort he well deserved. The wheel
and the rack and fire and whips accompanied him, since
Providence was now meting out to him the reward for his
endeavors. When he had taken his place in the assembly,
one of the magistrates asked him, "Who are you?" "Demetrius," he said. "Where do you come from?" "Crete,"
he said. "What do you know? Speak!" "On my way to
meet my brother in Ionia, I was left behind by my ship,
and then I boarded a cutter sailing by. At the time I

[a] Literally 'state slaves': enjoying a salary and greater freedom than private slaves they served as policemen, prison guards,
and executioners.

---

4.8 μέσοις Jackson: μέσῳ F | ἀδελφὸν ἐμαυτοῦ Jackson (cf.
3.3.17): ἐμ. ἀδ. F.

παραπλέοντος. τότε μὲν οὖν ὑπελάμβανον ἐμπό-
9 ρους εἶναι, νῦν δὲ τυμβωρύχους. θαλαττεύοντες δὲ
χρόνον μακρὸν οἱ μὲν ἄλλοι πάντες διεφθάρησαν
ἀπορίᾳ τοῦ ποτοῦ, μόνος δὲ ἐγὼ σέσωσμαι διὰ τὸ
μηδὲν ἐν τῷ βίῳ δεδρακέναι πονηρόν. μὴ οὖν ὑμεῖς,
ὦ Συρακόσιοι, δῆμος ἐπὶ φιλανθρωπίᾳ περιβόητος,
10 γένησθέ μοι καὶ δίψους καὶ θαλάσσης ἀγριώτεροι.
ταῦτα λέγοντος οἰκτρῶς ἔλεος εἰσῆλθε τὰ πλήθη,
καὶ τάχα ἂν ἔπεισεν, ὥστε κἂν ἐφοδίων τυχεῖν, εἰ μὴ
δαίμων τις τιμωρὸς Καλλιρόης ἐνεμέσησεν αὐτῷ
τῆς ἀδίκου πειθοῦς. ἔμελλε γὰρ τὸ σχετλιώτατον
ἔσεσθαι πάντων πραγμάτων, πεισθῆναι Συρακοσίους ὅτι μόνος ἐσώθη διὰ εὐσέβειαν ὁ μόνος σωθεὶς
δι᾿ ἀσέβειαν, ἵνα ἐπὶ πλέον κολασθῇ.

11 Καθεζόμενος οὖν ἐν τῷ πλήθει τις ἁλιεὺς ἐγνώρισεν αὐτὸν καὶ ἡσυχῇ πρὸς τοὺς <παρα>καθεζομέ-
νους εἶπε "τοῦτον ἐγὼ καὶ πρότερον εἶδον περὶ τὸν
λιμένα τὸν ἡμέτερον στρεφόμενον." ταχέως οὖν ὁ
λόγος εἰς πλείονας διεδόθη, καί τις ἐξεβόησε "ψεύ-
12 δεται." πᾶς οὖν ὁ δῆμος ἐπεστράφη, καὶ προσέταξαν
οἱ ἄρχοντες καταβῆναι τὸν πρῶτον εἰπόντα· ἀρνου-
μένου δὲ Θήρωνος ὁ ἁλιεὺς μᾶλλον ἐπιστεύθη
βασανισταὶ εὐθὺς ἐκάλουν καὶ μάστιγες προσεφέ-
ροντο τῷ δυσσεβεῖ· καιόμενος δὲ καὶ τεμνόμενος
ἀντεῖχεν ἐπὶ πλέον καὶ μικροῦ δεῖν ἐνίκησε τὰς
13 βασάνους. ἀλλὰ μέγα τὸ συνειδὸς ἑκάστῳ καὶ
παγκρατὴς ἡ ἀλήθεια· μόλις μὲν γὰρ καὶ βραδέως
ἀλλ᾿ ὡμολόγησεν ὁ Θήρων. ἤρξατο οὖν διηγεῖσθαι

thought they were traders, but now I know they were
tomb robbers. After a long time at sea all the others died
for want of water, and I alone was saved because never in
my life have I done any wrong. Men of Syracuse, city
famed for humanity, do not be more cruel to me than
thirst and the sea!" At his pathetic words the crowd was
seized with pity, and he might have persuaded them even
to arrange his passage home, had not some divine avenger
of Callirhoe been angered by his glib lying. It would have
been the worst outrage ever, if the Syracusans had
believed that he alone had been saved by his piety, when
he alone was saved by his impiety, but saved only for a
harsher penalty.

Now among the crowd was a fisherman who recognized him and said quietly to those sitting beside him, "I
have seen this fellow before, hanging around our harbor."
This remark was quickly passed on to others, and someone shouted, "He is lying!" All the people turned round,
and the magistrates ordered the man who had spoken first
to come down. When Theron denied the charge, it was
the fisherman who was believed. Immediately they summoned the torturers, and the villain was whipped. Yet,
though burned and cut, he held out for a long time and
almost succeeded in overcoming the tortures. But conscience is a powerful force in everyone, and truth prevails
in the end. Though he did so reluctantly and slowly,
Theron owned up, and began his story. "I saw the trea-

---

4.9 μόνος Hercher: μόγις F | γένησθέ Naber: γένεσθέ F.
4.11 add. Cobet.

"πλοῦτον θαπτόμενον ἰδὼν συνήγαγον λῃστάς.

14 ἠνοίξαμεν τὸν τάφον· εὕρομεν ζῶσαν τὴν νεκράν·
πάντα συλήσαντες ἐνεθήκαμεν τῷ κέλητι· πλεύσαντες εἰς Μίλητον μόνην ἐπωλήσαμεν τὴν γυναῖκα, τὰ
δὲ λοιπὰ διεκομίζομεν εἰς Κρήτην· ἐξωσθέντες δὲ εἰς
τὸν Ἰόνιον ὑπὸ ἀνέμων ἃ πεπόνθαμεν καὶ ὑμεῖς
ἑωράκατε." πάντα εἰπὼν μόνον τοὔνομα οὐκ ἐμνημόνευσε τοῦ πριαμένου.

15 Ῥηθέντων δὲ τούτων χαρὰ καὶ λύπη πάντας
εἰσῆλθε· χαρὰ μὲν ὅτι ζῇ Καλλιρόη, λύπη δὲ ὅτι
πέπραται. Θήρωνι μὲν οὖν θανάτου ψῆφος ἠνέχθη,
Χαιρέας δὲ ἱκέτευε μηδέπω θνήσκειν τὸν ἄνθρωπον,
"ἵνα μοι" φησὶν "ἐλθὼν μηνύσῃ τοὺς ἀγοράσαντας·
λογίσασθέ μου τὴν ἀνάγκην· συνηγορῶ τῷ πωλή-

16 σαντί μου τὴν γυναῖκα." τοῦτο Ἑρμοκράτης ἐκώ-
λυσε γενέσθαι "βέλτιον" εἰπὼν "ποιήσασθαι τὴν
ζήτησιν ἐπιπονωτέραν ἢ λυθῆναι τοὺς νόμους. δέομαι δὲ ὑμῶν, ἄνδρες Συρακόσιοι, μνησθέντας στρατηγίας τῆς ἐμῆς καὶ τροπαίων ἀποδοῦναί μοι τὴν
χάριν εἰς τὴν θυγατέρα. πέμψατε πρεσβείαν ὑπὲρ

17 αὐτῆς <ἵνα> τὴν ἐλευθέραν ἀπολάβωμεν." ἔτι
λέγοντος ὁ δῆμος ἀνεβόησε "πάντες πλεύσωμεν,"
ἐκ δὲ τῆς βουλῆς ὑπέστησαν ἐθελονταὶ τὸ πλεῖστον
μέρος· ὁ δὲ Ἑρμοκράτης "τῆς μὲν τιμῆς" ἔφη,
"χάριν ἐπίσταμαι πᾶσιν, ἀρκοῦσι δὲ πρεσβευταὶ
δύο μὲν ἀπὸ τοῦ δήμου, δύο δὲ ἀπὸ τῆς βουλῆς·
πλεύσεται δὲ Χαιρέας πέμπτος αὐτός."

18 Ἔδοξε ταῦτα καὶ ἐκυρώθη, διέλυσέ τε ἐπὶ τούτοις

160

sure that was being buried and got together my gang. We opened the tomb. We found the corpse alive. We took everything and transferred it to our cutter. We sailed to Miletus and there we sold only the girl and were taking all the rest to Crete. But winds drove us off course into the Ionian Sea, and what we suffered you yourselves have seen." In all his story the only thing he left out was the name of Callirhoe's purchaser.

At his words all were filled with joy and grief—joy because Callirhoe was alive, and grief because she had been sold. Sentence of death against Theron was passed, but Chaereas begged that he not be executed yet. "Let him come," he said, "and show me the men who bought her. Think what I am forced to do—plead for the man who sold my wife!" This Hermocrates vetoed, saying, "It is better to make our search more difficult than to condone the violation of the law. Men of Syracuse, I beg you, in memory of my services as general and of my triumphs, thank me by recovering my daughter. Send a mission for her, so that we may recover one who is freeborn." Before he had finished speaking, the members of the assembly shouted, "Let us all sail!" —and most of the council volunteered to go. But Hermocrates said, "I thank you all for this honor, but two envoys from the assembly and two from the council will be sufficient, and Chaereas himself shall sail as the fifth."

This was agreed and ratified, whereupon he dismissed

---

4.16  add. Naber.

τὴν ἐκκλησίαν. ἀπαγομένῳ δὲ Θήρωνι μέγα μέρος
τοῦ πλήθους ἐπηκολούθησεν. ἀνεσκολοπίσθη δὲ
πρὸ τοῦ Καλλιρόης τάφου καὶ ἔβλεπεν ἀπὸ τοῦ
σταυροῦ τὴν θάλασσαν ἐκείνην, δι' ἧς αἰχμάλωτον
ἔφερε τὴν Ἑρμοκράτους θυγατέρα, ἣν οὐκ ἔλαβον
οὐδὲ Ἀθηναῖοι.

5. Τοῖς μὲν οὖν ἄλλοις ἅπασιν ἐδόκει περιμένειν
τὴν ὥραν τοῦ πλοῦ καὶ ἔαρος ὑπολάμψαντος ἀνάγε-
σθαι· τότε γὰρ ἔτι χειμὼν εἰστήκει καὶ παντάπασιν
ἀδύνατον ἐδόκει τὸν Ἰόνιον περαιοῦσθαι· Χαιρέας δὲ
ἔσπευδεν, ἕτοιμος ὢν διὰ τὸν ἔρωτα ζεύξας σχεδίαν
εἰς τὸ πέλαγος ἑαυτὸν ἀφεῖναι τοῖς ἀνέμοις φέρε-
2 σθαι. οὔκουν οὐδὲ οἱ πρέσβεις ἤθελον βραδύνειν
ὑπ' αἰδοῦς τῆς τε πρὸς ἐκεῖνον καὶ μάλιστα πρὸς
Ἑρμοκράτην, ἀλλ' ἡτοιμάζοντο πλεῖν. Συρακόσιοι
δὲ δημοσίᾳ τὸν στόλον ἐξέπεμψαν, ἵνα καὶ τοῦτο εἰς
3 ἀξίωμα προστεθῇ τῆς πρεσβείας. καθείλκυσαν οὖν
ἐκείνην τὴν τριήρη τὴν στρατηγικήν, ἔχουσαν ἔτι
τὰ σημεῖα τῆς νίκης. ἐπεὶ δὲ ἧκεν ἡ κυρία τῆς ἀναγωγῆς ἡμέρα, τὸ πλῆθος εἰς τὸν λιμένα συνέδρα-
μεν, οὐκ ἄνδρες μόνον, ἀλλὰ καὶ γυναῖκες καὶ
παῖδες, καὶ ἦσαν ὁμοῦ δάκρυα, εὐχαί, στεναγμοί,
4 παραμυθία, φόβος, θάρσος, ἀπόγνωσις, ἐλπίς. Ἀρίστων δέ, ὁ Χαιρέου πατήρ, ἐσχάτῳ γήρᾳ καὶ νόσῳ
φερόμενος, περιέφυ τῷ τραχήλῳ τοῦ παιδὸς καὶ
ἀνακρεμάμενος αὐτοῦ [τοῦ τραχήλου] κλαίων ἔλεγε
"τί με καταλείπεις, ὦ τέκνον, ἡμιθνῆτα πρεσβύτην;
5 ὅτι μὲν γὰρ οὐκέτι σε ὄψομαι δῆλον. ἐπίμεινον δὲ

the assembly. Many of the crowd went with Theron as he was taken away; he was crucified in front of Callirhoe's tomb and from the cross gazed out upon that sea over which he had carried Hermocrates' daughter captive, whom not even the Athenians had captured.

5. Now all the others thought they should wait for the sailing season and put to sea at the first sign of spring, because it was still winter then and it seemed quite impossible to cross the Ionian Sea. But Chaereas was impatient to start. Because of his love he was prepared to fit a raft together, and to launch himself on the sea for the winds to carry. The envoys were also unwilling to wait, out of respect for him and especially for Hermocrates, and so they got ready to sail. The Syracusans sent out the expedition at public expense so that this too might add to the mission's prestige. So they launched the famous flagship which still carried the standards of their victory. When the appointed day for departure arrived, the people flocked to the harbor, not only men but also women and children, and there simultaneously occurred tears and prayers, moaning and encouragement, terror and courage, resignation and hope. Ariston, Chaereas' father, was carried because of advanced age and sickness. He flung his arms about the neck of his son, and clinging to him wept and said, "Why are you leaving me, my son, an old man and almost dead? I shall certainly never see you again. Just wait a few days so that I can die in your

---

5.3 δάκρυα εὐχαί Jackson: εὐχαί δάκρυα F.
5.4 del. Hercher | τί Cobet: τίνι F.

κἂν ὀλίγας ἡμέρας, ὅπως ἐν ταῖς χερσὶ ταῖς σαῖς
ἀποθάνω· θάψον δέ με καὶ ἄπιθι." ἡ δὲ μήτηρ τῶν
γονάτων αὐτοῦ λαβομένη "ἐγὼ δέ σου δέομαι"
φησίν, "ὦ τέκνον, μή με ἐνταῦθα καταλίπῃς ἔρημον,
ἀλλ' ἐμβαλοῦ τριήρει φορτίον κοῦφον· ἂν δὲ ὦ
βαρεῖα καὶ περιττή, ῥίψατέ με εἰς τὴν θάλασσαν ἣν
6  σὺ πλεῖς." ταῦτα λέγουσα περιερρήξατο τὴν ἐσθῆτα
καὶ προτείνουσα τὰς θηλὰς "τέκνον" φησί,

> "τάδ' αἴδεο καί μ' ἐλέησον
> αὐτήν, εἴ ποτέ τοι λαθικηδέα μαζὸν ἐπέσχον."

Κατεκλάσθη Χαιρέας πρὸς τὰς τῶν γονέων
ἱκεσίας καὶ ἔρριψεν ἑαυτὸν ἀπὸ τῆς νεὼς εἰς τὴν
θάλασσαν, ἀποθανεῖν θέλων, ἵνα φύγῃ δυοῖν θάτερον, ἢ [τὸ] μὴ ζητεῖν Καλλιρόην ἢ [τὸ] λυπῆσαι
τοὺς γονεῖς· ταχέως δὲ ἀπορρίψαντες οἱ ναῦται
7  μόλις αὐτὸν ἀνεκούφισαν. ἐνταῦθα Ἑρμοκράτης
ἀπεσκέδασε τὸ πλῆθος καὶ ἐκέλευσε τῷ κυβερνήτῃ
λοιπὸν ἀνάγεσθαι. συνέβη δέ τι καὶ ἄλλο φιλίας
ἔργον οὐκ ἀγεννές. Πολύχαρμος γάρ, ἑταῖρος τοῦ
Χαιρέου, παραυτὰ μὲν οὐκ ὤφθη ἐν τῷ μέσῳ, ἀλλὰ
καὶ πρὸς τοὺς γονεῖς ἔφη "φίλος μέν, φίλος Χαιρέας, οὐ μὴν ἄχρι τούτου γε ὥστε καὶ περὶ τῶν
ἐσχάτων αὐτῷ συγκινδυνεύειν. διόπερ, ἕως ἀποπλεῖ,
8  ὑπεκστήσομαι." ἡνίκα δὲ ἀπεσάλευσε τῆς γῆς τὸ
πλοῖον, ἀπὸ τῆς πρύμνης αὐτοὺς ἀπησπάσατο, ἵνα
μηκέτι αὐτὸν δύνωνται κατασχεῖν.

9  Ἐξελθὼν δὲ τοῦ λιμένος Χαιρέας καὶ ἀποβλέψας

164

arms; then bury me and go." His mother, too, clasped his knees and said, "I beg you, my child, do not leave me here all alone, but put me on the boat. I shall be a light load, but if I prove a burden and a nuisance, throw me into the sea you sail on." So saying she tore open her dress and said, holding out her breasts,

> "Son, have respect for these and take pity upon me
> if ever I gave you the teat to soften your sorrows." [a]

Chaereas was shattered by his parents' appeals, and he threw himself overboard, wishing to die so as to avoid having to choose between giving up his search for Callirhoe and causing pain to his parents. At once the sailors jumped in after him, and had a hard time bringing him out. At that point Hermocrates dispersed the crowd and told the pilot to sail forthwith. Another noble act of friendship occurred as well. For a while Polycharmus, Chaereas' comrade, was nowhere to be seen. Actually he had said to his parents, "I am Chaereas' friend, of course, but not to the extent of staking my life on him. So until he sails, I shall keep out of sight." But when the boat drew away from the shore, he waved farewell to his parents from the stern, in order that they might no longer be able to hold him back.

Leaving the harbor Chaereas looked over the open

---

[a] *Iliad* 22.82f (Hecuba to Hector).

5.6 περιερρηξε F, corr. Cobet | τὴν ἐσθῆτα Gasda: τὸ στῆθος F | del. Hilberg (twice).

5.7 ὤφθη ἐν] the hiatus is suspect.

εἰς τὸ πέλαγος "ἄγε με" φησίν, "ὦ θάλασσα, τὸν
αὐτὸν δρόμον ὃν καὶ Καλλιρόης ἤγαγες. εὔχομαί
σοι, Πόσειδον, ἢ κἀκείνην μεθ' ἡμῶν ἢ μηδὲ ἐμὲ
χωρὶς ἐκείνης ἐνταῦθα. εἰ μὴ γὰρ δύναμαι τὴν
γυναῖκα τὴν ἐμὴν ἀπολαβεῖν, θέλω κἂν δουλεύειν
μετ' αὐτῆς."

6. Πνεῦμα δὲ φορὸν ὑπέλαβε τὴν τριήρη καὶ
ὥσπερ κατ' ἴχνος τοῦ κέλητος ἔτρεχεν. ἐν δὲ ταῖς
ἴσαις ἡμέραις εἰς Ἰωνίαν ἧκον καὶ ὡρμίσαντο ἐπὶ
2 τῆς αὐτῆς ἀκτῆς ἐν τοῖς Διονυσίου χωρίοις. οἱ μὲν
οὖν ἄλλοι κεκμηκότες ἐκβάντες εἰς τὴν γῆν περὶ τὴν
ἀνάληψιν ἐγίνοντο τὴν ἑαυτῶν, σκηνάς τε πηγνύμε-
νοι καὶ παρασκευάζοντες εὐωχίαν, Χαιρέας δὲ μετὰ
Πολυχάρμου περινοστῶν "πῶς νῦν" φησὶ "Καλλιρόην εὑρεῖν δυνάμεθα; μάλιστα μὲν γὰρ φοβοῦμαι
μὴ Θήρων ἡμᾶς διεψεύσατο καὶ τέθνηκεν ἡ δυστυχής. εἰ δ' ἄρα καὶ ἀληθῶς πέπραται, τίς οἶδεν ὅπου;
3 πολλὴ γὰρ ἡ Ἀσία." μεταξὺ δὲ ἀλύοντες περιέπεσον
τῷ νεῷ τῆς Ἀφροδίτης. ἔδοξεν οὖν αὐτοῖς προσκυνῆσαι τὴν θεόν, καὶ προσδραμὼν τοῖς γόνασιν
αὐτῆς Χαιρέας "σύ μοι, δέσποινα" <φησί>, "πρώτη
Καλλιρόην ἔδειξας ἐν τῇ σῇ ἑορτῇ· σὺ καὶ νῦν
ἀπόδος, ἣν ἐχαρίσω." μεταξὺ δ' ἀνακύψας εἶδε
παρὰ τὴν θεὸν εἰκόνα Καλλιρόης χρυσῆν, ἀνάθημα
Διονυσίου.

τοῦ δ' αὐτοῦ λύτο γούνατα καὶ φίλον ἦτορ.

4 κατέπεσεν οὖν σκοτοδινιάσας· θεασαμένη δὲ αὐτὸν

waters and prayed, "Take me, O sea, on the same course as you took Callirhoe. Grant, Poseidon, that either she returns with us or that I not come back without her. If I cannot get my wife back, I should prefer to be a slave with her."

6. A favorable breeze wafted the warship on and it ran as if in the tracks of the cutter. They reached Ionia in just the same number of days and anchored at the same beach on the estate of Dionysius. Now the others were worn out when they landed and set about reviving themselves, putting up tents and preparing a feast. Chaereas, however, walking about with Polycharmus said, "How can we find Callirhoe now? I am awfully afraid that Theron lied to us and that my poor wife is dead. If she really has been sold, who knows where? Asia is huge." Meanwhile in their wanderings they came upon the shrine of Aphrodite. So they decided to pay homage to the goddess, and Chaereas, throwing himself at her feet, said, "Lady, you first showed Callirhoe to me at your festival. Now give me back the woman you granted me." Just then he looked up and saw beside the goddess a golden statue of Callirhoe, the offering of Dionysius.

At this his knees collapsed and the heart within him,[a]

and he fell in a swoon. Seeing him, the shrine attendant

---

[a] *Iliad* 21.114 (Lycaon) and see note on 1.1.14.

---

6.2 ἐγίνοντο Anon. Leid.: ἠπείγοντο F.
6.3 add. Blake.

ἡ ζάκορος ὕδωρ προσήνεγκε καὶ ἀνακτωμένη τὸν
ἄθλιον εἶπε "θάρρει, τέκνον· καὶ ἄλλους πολλοὺς ἡ
θεὸς ἐξέπληξεν· ἐπιφανὴς γάρ ἐστι καὶ δείκνυσιν
ἑαυτὴν ἐναργῶς. ἀλλ' ἀγαθοῦ μεγάλου τοῦτ' ἔστι
σημεῖον. ὁρᾷς εἰκόνα τὴν χρυσῆν; αὕτη δούλη μὲν
ἦν, ἡ δὲ Ἀφροδίτη πάντων ἡμῶν κυρίαν πεποίηκεν
5 αὐτήν." "τίς γάρ ἐστιν" ὁ Χαιρέας εἶπεν, "αὕτη;"
"ἡ δέσποινα τῶν χωρίων τούτων, ὦ τέκνον, Διονυσίου γυνή, τοῦ πρώτου τῶν Ἰώνων." ἀκούσας ὁ
Πολύχαρμος, οἷα δὴ σωφρονῶν αὐτός, οὐδὲν εἴασεν
ἔτι τὸν Χαιρέαν εἰπεῖν, ἀλλ' ὑποβαστάσας ἐξήγαγεν
ἐκεῖθεν, οὐ βουλόμενος ἐκπύστους γενέσθαι τίνες
εἰσί, πρὶν ἅπαντα βουλεύσασθαι καλῶς καὶ συντά-
ξαι πρὸς ἀλλήλους.

6     Ὁ δὲ Χαιρέας τῆς ζακόρου παρούσης οὐδὲν εἶπεν
ἀλλὰ πρῶτον μὲν ἐσίγησεν ἐγκρατῶς, πλὴν ὅσον
αὐτομάτως ἐξεπήδησεν αὐτοῦ τὰ δάκρυα· πόρρω δὲ
ἀπελθὼν ἐπὶ γῆς μόνος ἔρριψεν ἑαυτὸν καὶ "ὦ
θάλασσα" φησὶ "φιλάνθρωπε, τί με διέσωσας; ἢ
ἵνα εὐπλοήσας ἴδω Καλλιρόην ἄλλου γυναῖκα;
τοῦτο οὐκ ἤλπισα γενέσθαι ποτὲ οὐδὲ ἀποθανόντος
7 Χαιρέου. τί ποιήσω, δυστυχής; παρὰ δεσπότου μὲν
γὰρ ἤλπιζόν σε κομίσασθαι καὶ τοῖς λύτροις
ἐπίστευον ὅτι πείσω τὸν ἀγοράσαντα· νῦν δὲ εὕρηκά
σε πλουσίαν, τάχα καὶ βασιλίδα. πόσῳ δ' ἂν εὐτυχέστερος ὑπῆρχον, εἴ σε <πτω>χεύουσαν εὑρήκειν.
εἴπω Διονυσίῳ προσελθὼν 'ἀπόδος μοι τὴν γυ-
8 ναῖκα'; τοῦτο δὲ λέγει τίς γεγαμηκότι; ἀλλ' οὐδ', ἂν

brought water and reviving the poor boy said, "Be not alarmed, my son; the goddess has frightened many besides you: for she appears in person and lets herself be clearly seen. However, this is a sign of good luck. Do you see this golden statue? This girl was once a slave, and Aphrodite has made her the mistress of us all." "Who is she?" said Chaereas. "She is the lady of this whole estate, my son, and the wife of Dionysius, the first man in Ionia." On hearing this, Polycharmus as a sensible fellow would not let Chaereas say any more, but helping him up took him away, since he did not wish it known who they were until they had talked over the situation thoroughly and were agreed on a course of action.

Chaereas said nothing in front of the attendant, and at first kept a strict silence, except that the tears spontaneously flowed from him. But withdrawing to a distance all alone he threw himself upon the ground and exclaimed, "Kindly sea, why have you preserved me? Was it so that after a safe voyage I should see Callirhoe the wife of another? I never imagined that this would happen, not even after Chaereas' death! What shall I do, unhappy man? I hoped to get you back from some master and I was relying on winning over the man who bought you with ransom money. But now I have found you wealthy, perhaps even a queen. How much happier I should be, had I found you a beggar! Shall I go to Dionysius and say, 'Give me back my wife'? Who can say that to

6.4 ἄθλιον Naber: ἄνθρωπον F.
6.6 πρῶτον μὲν Headlam: ἅμα F (from α' μὲν).
6.7 add. Hercher.

169

ἀπαντήσω, δύναμαί σοι προσελθεῖν, ἀλλ' οὐδέ, τὸ κοινότατον, ὡς πολίτης ἀσπάσασθαι. κινδυνεύσω τάχα καὶ ὡς μοιχὸς τῆς ἐμῆς γυναικὸς ἀπολέσθαι." ταῦτα ὀδυρόμενον παρεμυθεῖτο Πολύχαρμος.

7. Ἐν δὲ τῷ μεταξὺ Φωκᾶς, ὁ οἰκονόμος Διονυσίου, θεασάμενος τριήρη ναύμαχον οὐκ ἀδεὴς καθειστήκει· ναύτην δέ τινα ὑποκορισάμενος μανθάνει παρ' αὐτοῦ τὴν ἀλήθειαν, τίνες εἰσὶ καὶ πόθεν καὶ διὰ τίνα πλέουσι. συνῆκεν οὖν ὅτι μεγάλην συμφορὰν ἡ τριήρης αὕτη κομίζει Διονυσίῳ καὶ οὐ
2 βιώσεται Καλλιρόης ἀποσπασθείς. οἷα δὲ φιλοδέσποτος ἐθελήσας προλαβεῖν τὸ δεινὸν καὶ σβέσαι πόλεμον μέγαν μὲν οὔ, οὐδὲ κοινόν, ἀλλὰ τῆς Διονυσίου μόνης οἰκίας, διὰ τοῦτο ἀφιππασάμενος εἴς τι φρούριον βαρβάρων, ἀνήγγειλεν ὅτι τριήρης πολεμία λανθάνει, τάχα μὲν ἐπὶ κατασκοπήν, τάχα δὲ καὶ διὰ λῃστείαν ὑφορμοῦσα, συμφέρει δὲ τοῖς βασιλέως πράγμασιν ἀνάρπαστον αὐτὴν γενέσθαι
3 πρὶν ἀδικεῖν. ἔπεισε τοὺς βαρβάρους καὶ συντεταγμένους ἤγαγεν. ἐπιπεσόντες οὖν μέσῃ νυκτὶ καὶ πῦρ ἐμβαλόντες τὴν μὲν τριήρη κατέφλεξαν, ὅσους δὲ ζῶντας ἔλαβον δήσαντες εἰς τὸ φρούριον ἀνήγαγον. νεμήσεως δὲ τῶν αἰχμαλώτων γενομένης ἱκέτευσαν Χαιρέας καὶ Πολύχαρμος ἑνὶ δεσπότῃ πραθῆναι. καὶ ὁ λαβὼν αὐτοὺς ἐπώλησεν εἰς Καρίαν. ἐκεῖ δὲ πέδας σύροντες παχείας εἰργάζοντο τὰ Μιθριδάτου.
4 Καλλιρόῃ δὲ ὄναρ ἐπέστη Χαιρέας δεδεμένος καὶ θέλων αὐτῇ προσελθεῖν, ἀλλὰ μὴ δυνάμενος· ἀνεκώ-

a husband? Supposing I meet you, I cannot even come up to you, or greet you as my fellow citizen, the commonest of courtesies. Perhaps I shall even risk being killed as a seducer of my own wife!" Amid these complaints Polycharmus tried to comfort him.

7. Meanwhile Phocas, Dionysius' estate manager, had caught sight of the warship and become somewhat alarmed. Striking up a friendship with one of the crew he learned exactly who they were, where they had come from, and for whose sake they had made the voyage. He realized then that the warship brought great misfortune for Dionysius, who could not live if separated from Callirhoe. As a loyal servant, he was eager to forestall disaster and extinguish a conflict which, though not intense or widespread, would however damage the house of his master Dionysius alone. So he rode off to a garrison of orientals and reported that an enemy warship was hiding at anchor, perhaps on a mission of spying, perhaps intending a raid, and that it was in the king's interests to seize it before it did any harm. He convinced the orientals and brought them out in battle order. At midnight they fell upon the warship, set it on fire and destroyed it. Such as survived they put in chains and brought them back to the garrison. When the prisoners were distributed, Chaereas and Polycharmus begged to be sold to the same master. The man who got them sold them to a buyer in Caria and there, with heavy chains on their feet, they labored on the estate of Mithridates.

Now Callirhoe had a dream in which Chaereas appeared before her, chained and wanting to approach

---

7.2 ἀφιππασάμενος Cobet: ἀφιππευσ- F.

# CHARITON

κυσε δὴ μέγα καὶ διωλύγιον ἐν τοῖς ὕπνοις "Χαιρέα,
δεῦρο." τότε πρῶτον Διονύσιος ἤκουσεν ὄνομα Χαιρέου καὶ τῆς γυναικὸς συνταραχθείσης ἐπύθετο "τίς,
ὃν ἐκάλεις;" προύδωκε δὲ αὐτὴν τὰ δάκρυα καὶ τὴν
λύπην οὐκ ἠδυνήθη κατασχεῖν, ἀλλ' ἔδωκε παρρη-
5  σίαν τῷ πάθει. "δυστυχὴς" φησὶν "ἄνθρωπος, ἐμὸς
ἀνὴρ ἐκ παρθενίας, οὐδὲ ἐν τοῖς ὀνείροις εὐτυχής·
εἶδον γὰρ αὐτὸν δεδεμένον. ἀλλὰ σὺ μέν, ἄθλιε,
τέθνηκας ζητῶν ἐμὲ (δηλοῖ γὰρ θάνατόν σου τὰ
δεσμά), ἐγὼ δὲ ζῶ καὶ τρυφῶ, κατάκειμαι δὲ ἐπὶ
χρυσηλάτου κλίνης μετὰ ἀνδρὸς ἑτέρου. πλὴν οὐκ
6  εἰς μακρὰν ἀφίξομαι πρὸς σέ. εἰ καὶ ζῶντες ἀλλήλων οὐκ ἀπηλαύσαμεν, ἀποθανόντες ἀλλήλους
ἕξομεν." τούτων τῶν λόγων ἀκούσας ὁ Διονύσιος
ποικίλας ἐλάμβανε γνώμας· ἥπτετο μὲν γὰρ αὐτοῦ
ζηλοτυπία διότι καὶ νεκρὸν ἐφίλει Χαιρέαν, ἥπτετο
δὲ καὶ φόβος μὴ ἑαυτὴν ἀποκτείνῃ· ἐθάρρει δὲ ὅμως
ὅτι ὁ πρῶτος ἀνὴρ ἐδόκει τεθνηκέναι τῇ γυναικί· μὴ
γὰρ ἀπολείψειν αὐτὴν Διονύσιον, οὐκ ὄντος ἔτι Χαι-
7  ρέου. παρεμυθεῖτο τοίνυν ὡς δυνατὸν μάλιστα τὴν
γυναῖκα καὶ ἐπὶ πολλὰς ἡμέρας παρεφύλαττε, μὴ
ἄρα τι δεινὸν ἑαυτὴν ἐργάσηται. περιέσπασε δὲ τὸ
πένθος ἐλπὶς τοῦ τάχα ζῆν ἐκεῖνον καὶ ψευδόνειρον
αὐτὴν γεγονέναι· τὸ δὲ πλεῖον ἡ γαστήρ· ἑβδόμῳ
γὰρ μηνὶ μετὰ τοὺς γάμους υἱὸν ἔτεκε τῷ μὲν δοκεῖν
ἐκ Διονυσίου, Χαιρέου δὲ ταῖς ἀληθείαις. ἑορτὴν
μεγίστην ἤγαγεν ἡ πόλις καὶ πρεσβεῖαι ἀφίκοντο
πανταχόθεν Μιλησίοις συνηδομένων ὅτι τὸ γένος

172

her, but unable to do so. In her sleep she uttered a loud, piercing cry, "Chaereas, come to me." Then for the first time did Dionysius hear the name of Chaereas, and he asked his wife in her distress, "Who is this man you called?" Her tears betrayed her and she could not check her grief, but gave free rein to her feelings. "An unfortunate man," she said, "whom I married as a girl. Even in my dream he was not happy; I saw him in chains. Poor husband, so you died while looking for me, for the chains signify your death. Meanwhile I am living in luxury and lie upon a gilded bed with another husband! But it will not be long before I come to you. Though in life we could not enjoy each other's company, yet we shall have each other in death." On hearing these words Dionysius was visited by conflicting thoughts. He was gripped by jealousy because she loved Chaereas even dead, and also by the fear that she might kill herself. Still he was heartened by the thought that she believed her first husband dead and surely would not desert Dionysius now that Chaereas was no longer alive. Comforting her as much as he could he kept watch on her for several days to see that she did herself no harm. Callirhoe's grief was mitigated by the hope that perhaps Chaereas was alive and the dream had been false; and still more by her child. In the seventh month after the wedding she gave birth to a son, ostensibly of Dionysius, but in reality of Chaereas. The city put on a splendid festival and delegations arrived from all quarters to share with the Milesians their joy that the

---

7.4 δὴ Zankogiannes: δέ F | συνταρ- Blake: οὖν ταρ- F.

αὔξει τὸ Διονυσίου. κἀκεῖνος ὑπὸ τῆς χαρᾶς πάντων παρεχώρησε τῇ γυναικὶ καὶ δέσποιναν αὐτὴν ἀπέδειξε τῆς οἰκίας, ἀναθημάτων ἐνέπλησε τοὺς ναούς, πανδημεὶ τὴν πόλιν εἱστία θυσίαις.

8. Ἀγωνιῶσα δὲ Καλλιρόη μὴ προδοθῇ τὸ ἀπόρρητον αὐτῆς, ἠξίωσεν ἐλευθερωθῆναι Πλαγγόνα, τὴν μόνην αὐτῇ συνειδυῖαν ὅτι πρὸς Διονύσιον ἦλθεν ἐγκύμων, ἵνα μὴ μόνον ἐκ τῆς γνώμης ἀλλὰ καὶ ἐκ τῆς τύχης ἔχῃ τὸ πιστὸν παρ' αὐτῆς. "ἀσμένως" εἶπεν ὁ Διονύσιος "ἀμείβομαι Πλαγγόνα
2  διακονίας ἐρωτικῆς. ἄδικον δὲ ποιοῦμεν εἰ τὴν <μὲν> θεραπαινίδα τετιμήκαμεν, οὐκ ἀποδώσομεν δὲ τὴν χάριν τῇ Ἀφροδίτῃ, παρ' ᾗ πρῶτον ἀλλήλους εἴδομεν." "κἀγὼ" φησὶν ἡ Καλλιρόη "σοῦ θέλω μᾶλλον· ἔχω γὰρ αὐτῇ μείζονα χάριν. νῦν μὲν οὖν λεχὼς ἔτι εἰμί, περιμείναντες δὲ ὀλίγας ἡμέρας ἀσφαλέστερον ἀπίωμεν εἰς τοὺς ἀγρούς."

3  Ταχέως δὲ αὐτὴν ἀνέλαβεν ἐκ τοῦ τόκου καὶ κρείττων ἐγένετο καὶ μείζων, οὐκέτι κόρης, ἀλλὰ γυναικὸς ἀκμὴν προσλαβοῦσα. παραγενομένων δὲ αὐτῶν εἰς τὸν ἀγρὸν μεγαλοπρεπεῖς θυσίας παρεσκεύασε Φωκᾶς· καὶ γὰρ πλῆθος ἐπηκολούθησεν ἐξ ἄστεος. καταρχόμενος οὖν ὁ Διονύσιος ἑκατόμβης "δέσποινα" φησὶν "Ἀφροδίτη, σύ μοι πάντων
4  <τῶν> ἀγαθῶν αἰτία. παρὰ σοῦ Καλλιρόην ἔχω, παρὰ σοῦ τὸν υἱόν, καὶ ἀνήρ εἰμι διὰ σὲ καὶ πατήρ. ἐμοὶ μὲν ἤρκει Καλλιρόη, καὶ πατρίδος μοι καὶ

family of Dionysius had received an heir. In his happiness he deferred to his wife in everything; he made her the mistress of his household, filled the temples with offerings, and gave sacrificial feasts to everyone in the city.

8. Callirhoe was afraid of her secret being divulged, and asked that Plangon be given her freedom, since she was the only other one to know she was already pregnant when she came to Dionysius. She hoped that Plangon's improved fortunes in addition to her natural affection would secure her loyalty. "I am glad," replied Dionysius, "to repay Plangon for the service she did our love, but we should be wrong to reward the servant and not thank Aphrodite at whose shrine we first saw each other." "I am even more eager than you," said Callirhoe, "since I have greater cause to thank her. But now I am still in childbed. Let us wait for a few days, and then I shall be well enough to go to the estate."

She soon recovered from the birth and became stronger and bigger, no longer a girl but a mature woman. When they arrived at the farm, Phocas prepared a magnificent sacrificial feast, for a large number of people had followed them from town. In opening the ceremonial banquet, Dionysius prayed as follows: "Lady Aphrodite, you are the cause of all my blessings. From you I have Callirhoe, and from you I have a son. Through you I am a husband and a father. Though Callirhoe was enough for me and dearer to me than my country and parents,[a] yet I

---

[a] Cf. *Odyssey* 9.34.

---

8.2 add. Cobet.     8.3 add. Cobet.

γονέων γλυκυτέρα, φιλῶ δὲ τὸ τέκνον ὅτι μοι τὴν
μητέρα βεβαιοτέραν πεποίηκεν. ὅμηρον ἔχω τῆς
εὐνοίας τῆς πρὸς αὑτῆς. ἱκετεύω σε, δέσποινα, σῷζε
5 ἐμοὶ μὲν Καλλιρόην, Καλλιρόη δὲ τὸν υἱόν." ἐπευ-
φήμησε τὸ πλῆθος τῶν περιεστηκότων καὶ οἱ μὲν
ῥόδοις, οἱ δὲ ἴοις, οἱ δὲ αὐτοῖς στεφάνοις ἐφυλλοβό-
λησαν αὐτούς, ὥστε πλησθῆναι τὸ τέμενος ἀνθῶν.
Διονύσιος μὲν οὖν πάντων μὲν ἀκουόντων εἶπε τὴν
εὐχήν, Καλλιρόη δὲ ἠθέλησε μόνη πρὸς τὴν Ἀφρο-
6 δίτην λαλῆσαι. πρῶτον μὲν οὖν τὸν υἱὸν εἰς τὰς
αὑτῆς ἀγκάλας ἐνέθηκε, καὶ ὤφθη θέαμα κάλλιστον,
οἷον οὔτε ζωγράφος ἔγραψεν οὔτε πλάστης ἔπλασεν
οὔτε ποιητὴς ἱστόρησε μέχρι νῦν· οὐδεὶς γὰρ αὐτῶν
ἐποίησεν Ἄρτεμιν ἢ Ἀθηνᾶν βρέφος ἐν ἀγκάλαις
κομίζουσαν. ἔκλαυσεν ὑφ' ἡδονῆς Διονύσιος ἰδὼν
καὶ ἡσυχῇ τὴν Νέμεσιν προσεκύνησε. μόνην δὲ
Πλαγγόνα προσμεῖναι κελεύσασα τοὺς λοιποὺς
προέπεμψεν εἰς τὴν ἔπαυλιν.
7 Ἐπεὶ δὲ ἀπηλλάγησαν, στᾶσα πλησίον τῆς
Ἀφροδίτης καὶ ἀνατείνασα χερσὶ τὸ βρέφος "ὑπὲρ
τούτου σοι" φησίν, "ὦ δέσποινα, γινώσκω τὴν
χάριν· ὑπὲρ ἐμαυτῆς γὰρ οὐκ οἶδα. τότ' ἄν σοι καὶ
περὶ ἐμαυτῆς ἠπιστάμην χάριν, εἴ μοι Χαιρέαν ἐτή-
ρησας· πλὴν εἰκόνα μοι δέδωκας ἀνδρὸς φιλτάτου
8 καὶ ὅλον οὐκ ἀφείλω μου Χαιρέαν. δὸς δή μοι γενέσθαι τὸν υἱὸν εὐτυχέστερον μὲν τῶν γονέων, ὅμοιον
δὲ τῷ πάππῳ· πλεύσειε δὲ καὶ οὗτος ἐπὶ τριήρους
στρατηγικῆς, καί τις εἴποι, ναυμαχοῦντος αὐτοῦ,

love the child because he has made his mother more surely mine. I have in him a pledge of her affection for me. Lady, I beg you, preserve Callirhoe for my sake and preserve my son for Callirhoe's." The crowd that stood about him applauded his prayer and showered them both with flowers, some with roses, others with violets, and still others with whole garlands, so that the precinct was filled with flowers. Dionysius had uttered his prayer in the hearing of all, but Callirhoe wished to speak to Aphrodite by herself. So first she took her son in her arms, and thus afforded a beautiful sight, the like of which no painter has ever yet portrayed, nor sculptor fashioned, nor poet described before now; for none of them has represented Artemis or Athena with a baby in her arms.[a] On seeing her, Dionysius wept for very joy and quietly paid homage to Nemesis.[b] She then asked only Plangon to remain with her and sent the others on ahead to the house.

When they had gone, she stood close to Aphrodite and, holding up her child in her arms, she prayed, "Lady, for this child I give you thanks; for myself I am not sure. Had you preserved Chaereas for me, then I should be grateful for my own sake as well. But at least you have given me this image of my dear husband, and so have not taken Chaereas from me altogether. Grant that my son be happier than his parents and the equal of his grandsire. May he, too, sail on a flagship, and may men say of his prowess on the sea, 'Hermocrates' grandson is greater

[a] Both being virgin goddesses.

[b] The goddess of retributive justice, who penalizes an excess of good fortune among mortals.

---

8.5 ἠθέλησε μόνη Jackson: μ. ἠ. F.

'κρείττων Ἑρμοκράτους ὁ ἔκγονος·' ἡσθήσεται μὲν
γὰρ καὶ ὁ πάππος ἔχων τῆς ἀρετῆς διάδοχον, ἡσθη-
9  σόμεθα δὲ οἱ γονεῖς αὐτοῦ καὶ τεθνεῶτες. ἱκετεύω
σε, δέσποινα, διαλλάγηθί μοι λοιπόν· ἱκανῶς γάρ
μοι δεδυστύχηται. τέθνηκα, ἀνέζηκα, λελήστευμαι,
πέφευγα, πέπραμαι, δεδούλευκα· τίθημι δὲ καὶ τὸν
δεύτερον γάμον ἔτι μοι τούτων βαρύτερον. ἀλλὰ
μίαν ἀντὶ πάντων αἰτοῦμαι χάριν παρὰ σοῦ καὶ διὰ
σοῦ παρὰ τῶν ἄλλων θεῶν· σῶζέ μου τὸν ὀρφανόν.'
ἔτι βουλομένην λέγειν ἐπέσχε τὰ δάκρυα.

9.  Μικρὸν οὖν διαλιποῦσα καλεῖ τὴν ἱέρειαν· ἡ
δὲ πρεσβῦτις ὑπακούσασα "τί κλάεις" εἶπεν, "ὦ
παιδίον, ἐν ἀγαθοῖς τηλικούτοις; ἤδη γὰρ καὶ σὲ ὡς
θεὰν οἱ ξένοι προσκυνοῦσι. πρώην ἦλθον ἐνθάδε
δύο νεανίσκοι καλοὶ παραπλέοντες· ὁ δὲ ἕτερος
αὐτῶν θεασάμενός σου τὴν εἰκόνα, μικροῦ δεῖν ἐξ-
έπνευσεν. οὕτως ἐπιφανῆ σε ἡ Ἀφροδίτη πεποίη-
2  κεν." ἔπληξε τὴν καρδίαν τῆς Καλλιρόης τοῦτο καὶ
οὕτως, ὥσπερ ἐμμανὴς γενομένη, στήσασα τοὺς
ὀφθαλμοὺς ἀνέκραγε "τίνες ἦσαν οἱ ξένοι; πόθεν
ἔπλεον; τί σοι διηγοῦντο;" δείσασα δὲ ἡ πρεσβῦτις
τὸ μὲν πρῶτον ἄφωνος εἱστήκει, μόλις δὲ ἐφθέγξατο
3  "μόνον εἶδον αὐτούς, οὐδὲν ἤκουσα." "ποταποὺς τὸ
εἶδος; ἀναμνήσθητι τὸν χαρακτῆρα αὐτῶν." ἔφρα-
σεν ἡ γραῦς οὐκ ἀκριβῶς μέν, ὑπώπτευσε δὲ ὅμως
ἐκείνη τὴν ἀλήθειαν. ὃ γὰρ βούλεται τοῦθ' ἕκαστος

8.8 πάππος Jakob: πατὴρ F.

than he.'[a] His grandsire, too, will be happy to have a suc-
cessor in his valor, and we, his parents, shall feel that
delight even though we are dead. I beg you, Lady, from
now on be reconciled to me, for I have suffered enough. I
have died, and been resurrected; I have been kidnapped
and taken into exile; I have been sold and made a slave. I
add also my second marriage, even harder to bear. To
make up for all this I ask one favor from you, and through
you from the other gods: save my orphan child!" She
would have said more, but her tears forbade.

9. A little later she called the priestess. The old
woman came in answer and said, "My child, why are you
crying amid such blessings? Why, even strangers are paying you homage now as a goddess. The other day two fine
young men sailed by here, and one of them nearly expired
at the sight of your statue, so like a goddess on earth has
Aphrodite made you." Callirhoe's heart was pierced by
these words, and with staring eyes, like one possessed,
she cried, "Who were the strangers? Where had they
sailed from? What did they say?" At first the old woman
was speechless with fright but at last she managed to say,
"I only saw them. I heard nothing." "What did they look
like? Try to remember their features." Though the old
woman's account was vague, still Callirhoe suspected the
truth, for people are apt to believe what they want to.[b]

[a] Cf. Homer, *Iliad* 6.479, and Sophocles, *Ajax* 550f.
[b] Cf. Demosthenes, *Olynthiacs* 3.19 (also echoed 6.5.1).

---

8.9 ἀνέζηκα Naber: ἀνέζησα F.
9.2 οὕτως ὥσπερ Reiske: οὕτωσπερ F.
9.3 τὸ εἶδος Naber: εἶδες F.

καὶ οἴεται. βλέψασα δὲ πρὸς Πλαγγόνα "δύναται"
φησὶν "ὁ δυστυχὴς Χαιρέας πλανώμενος ἐνθάδε
παρεῖναι. τί οὖν ἐγένετο; ζητήσωμεν αὐτόν, ἀλλὰ
σιγῶσαι."

4 Ἀφικομένη τοίνυν πρὸς Διονύσιον τοῦτο μόνον
εἶπεν, ὅπερ ἤκουσε παρὰ τῆς ἱερείας· ἠπίστατο γὰρ
ὅτι φύσει περίεργός ἐστιν ὁ Ἔρως κἀκεῖνος δι᾽ ἑαυτὸν πολυπραγμονήσει περὶ τῶν γεγονότων. ὅπερ
οὖν καὶ συνέβη. πυθόμενος γὰρ ὁ Διονύσιος εὐθὺς
ἐνεπλήσθη ζηλοτυπίας καὶ πόρρω μὲν ἦν τοῦ
Χαιρέαν ὑποπτεύειν, ἔδεισε δὲ μή τις ἄρα λανθάνῃ
κατὰ τοὺς ἀγροὺς ἐπιβουλὴ μοιχική· πάντα γὰρ
ὑποπτεύειν αὐτὸν καὶ δεδιέναι τὸ κάλλος ἀνέπειθε
5 τῆς γυναικός. ἐφοβεῖτο δὲ οὐ μόνον τὰς παρὰ
ἀνθρώπων ἐπιβουλάς, ἀλλὰ προσεδόκα τάχα αὐτῷ
καταβήσεσθαι καὶ θεὸν ἐξ οὐρανοῦ ἀντεραστήν.

Καλέσας τοίνυν Φωκᾶν διηρεύνα "τίνες εἰσὶν οἱ
νεανίσκοι καὶ πόθεν; ἆρά γε πλούσιοι καὶ καλοί;
διατί δὲ τὴν ἐμὴν Ἀφροδίτην προσεκύνουν; τίς ἐμή-
6 νυσεν αὐτοῖς; τίς ἐπέτρεψεν;" ὁ δὲ Φωκᾶς ἀπέκρυπτε
τὴν ἀλήθειαν, οὐ Διονύσιον δεδοικώς, γινώσκων δὲ
ὅτι Καλλιρόη καὶ αὐτὸν ἀπολεῖ καὶ τὸ γένος αὐτοῦ,
πυθομένη περὶ τῶν γεγονότων. ἐπεὶ οὖν ἔξαρνος ἦν
ἐπιδεδημηκέναι τινάς, οὐκ εἰδὼς ὁ Διονύσιος τὴν
αἰτίαν ὑπώπτευσε βαρυτέραν ἐπιβουλὴν καθ᾽ ἑαυτοῦ
7 συνίστασθαι. διοργισθεὶς οὖν μάστιγας ᾔτει καὶ
τροχὸν ἐπὶ Φωκᾶν, καὶ οὐ μόνον ἐκεῖνον ἀλλὰ καὶ
τοὺς ἐν τοῖς ἀγροῖς ἅπαντας συνεκάλει μοιχείαν
πεπεισμένος ζητεῖν.

Looking at Plangon she said, "Perhaps poor Chaereas has come here in his wanderings. What can have happened to him? Let us look for him; but do keep quiet about it."

Rejoining Dionysius, she told him only what she had heard from the priestess, fully aware that love is naturally curious and that Dionysius himself would try to ferret out what had taken place. And this is exactly what happened. On learning the facts, Dionysius was immediately consumed with jealousy, and, while he was far from suspecting Chaereas, he was afraid that a plot to seduce his wife was secretly afoot at the farm. Indeed, the beauty of his wife induced him to suspect and fear the worst. Not only was he afraid of human designs on her, he even expected that perhaps some god would come down from heaven to compete for her love.[a]

He therefore called Phocas and questioned him closely: "Who are these young men and where did they come from? Are they rich and handsome? Why were they paying homage to my Aphrodite? Who told them about her? Who gave them permission?" Phocas tried to conceal the truth, not so much from fear of Dionysius, but he knew that Callirhoe would ruin him and his family if she found out what had happened. So when he said that there had been no visitors, Dionysius, unaware of his reason, suspected that a still more serious plot was being laid against himself. Much angered he called for whips and the torture-wheel for Phocas, and summoned not only him but all the people at the farm, convinced he was investigating a plot for seduction.

---

[a] As, for example, Zeus came down to Amphitryon's wife.

9.4 μή τις ἄρα Cobet: ἄρα μή τις F.

Αἰσθόμενος δὲ Φωκᾶς οἷ καθέστηκε δεινοῦ καὶ λέγων καὶ σιωπῶν "σοὶ" φησί, "δέσποτα, ἐρῶ μόνῳ 8 τὴν ἀλήθειαν." ὁ δὲ Διονύσιος πάντας ἀποπέμψας "ἰδού" φησὶ "μόνοι γεγόναμεν. μηδὲν ἔτι ψεύσῃ, λέγε τἀληθὲς κἂν φαῦλον ᾖ." "φαῦλον μὲν" εἶπεν "οὐδέν ἐστιν, ὦ δέσποτα, μεγάλων γὰρ ἀγαθῶν φέρω σοι διηγήματα· εἰ δὲ σκυθρωπότερά ἐστιν αὐτοῦ τὰ πρῶτα, διὰ τοῦτο μηδὲν ἀγωνιάσῃς μηδὲ λυπηθῇς, ἀλλὰ περίμεινον, ἕως οὗ πάντα ἀκούσῃς· 9 χρηστὸν γὰρ ἔχει σοι τὸ τέλος." μετέωρος οὖν ὁ Διονύσιος πρὸς τὴν ἐπαγγελίαν γενόμενος καὶ ἀναρτήσας ἑαυτὸν τῆς ἀκροάσεως "μὴ βράδυνε" φησὶν "ἀλλ' ἤδη διηγοῦ."

Τότ' οὖν ἤρξατο λέγειν "τριήρης ἐνθάδε κατ-έπλευσεν ἐκ Σικελίας καὶ πρέσβεις Συρακοσίων 10 παρὰ σοῦ Καλλιρόην ἀπαιτούντων." ἐξέθανεν ὁ Διο-νύσιος ἀκούσας καὶ νὺξ αὐτοῦ τῶν ὀφθαλμῶν κατε-χύθη· φαντασίαν γὰρ ἔλαβεν ὡς ἐφεστηκότος αὐτῷ Χαιρέου καὶ Καλλιρόην ἀποσπῶντος. ὁ μὲν οὖν ἔκειτο καὶ σχῆμα καὶ χρῶμα νεκροῦ παριστάς, Φωκᾶς δὲ ἐν ἀπορίᾳ καθειστήκει, καλέσαι μὲν οὐδένα θέλων, ἵνα μή τις αὐτῷ μάρτυς γένηται τῶν ἀπορρήτων· μόλις δὲ καὶ κατ' ὀλίγον αὐτὸς τὸν δεσπότην ἀνεκτήσατο "θάρρει" λέγων, "Χαιρέας 11 τέθηκεν· ἀπόλωλεν ἡ ναῦς· οὐδεὶς ἔτι φόβος." ταῦτα τὰ ῥήματα ψυχὴν ἐνέθηκε Διονυσίῳ, καὶ κατ' ὀλίγον πάλιν ἐν ἑαυτῷ γενόμενος ἀκριβῶς ἐπυνθά-νετο πάντα, καὶ Φωκᾶς διηγεῖτο τὸν ναύτην τὸν

But perceiving that he was in a tight spot, whether he spoke or remained silent, Phocas said, "Sir, I will tell you the truth in private." Dionysius then sent them all away and said, "Well, here we are alone. Tell me no more lies. Speak the truth, even if it is bad." "It is nothing bad, master," he answered. "In fact I bring you excellent news. If the beginning is rather unpleasant, do not let that worry or upset you. Wait till you have heard it all; there is a happy ending in store for you." Excited at the promised news, Dionysius hung upon his words, and said, "Hurry up! Tell me now!"

So he then began: "A warship has arrived from Sicily with ambassadors from the Syracusans demanding Callirhoe back from you." When he heard this, Dionysius fainted, and darkness covered his eyes; he had a vision of Chaereas standing before him, trying to tear Callirhoe away from him. So he lay there presenting the appearance and color of a corpse. Phocas was at a loss what to do, not wishing to call anyone for fear of having a witness to his secret. At length he gradually restored his master by saying, "Cheer up. Chaereas is dead. His ship has been destroyed. There is nothing to fear." These words put life into Dionysius, and gradually returning to his senses he asked for full details. Phocas told him about the

---

9.8 ἔχει σοι Naber: ἔχουσι F.

μηνύσαντα πόθεν ἡ τριήρης καὶ διὰ τίνα πλέουσι καὶ τίνες οἱ παρόντες, τὸ στρατήγημα τὸ ἴδιον ἐπὶ τοὺς βαρβάρους, τὴν νύκτα, τὸ πῦρ, τὸ ναυάγιον, τὸν φόνον, τὰ δεσμά.

Καθάπερ οὖν νέφος ἢ σκότος ἀπεκάλυψε τῆς ψυχῆς Διονύσιος, καὶ περιπτυξάμενος Φωκᾶν "σὺ" φησὶν "εὐεργέτης ἐμός, σὺ κηδεμὼν ἀληθὴς καὶ 12 πιστότατος ἐν τοῖς ἀπορρήτοις. διὰ σὲ Καλλιρόην ἔχω καὶ τὸν υἱόν· ἐγὼ μὲν οὐκ ἄν σοι προσέταξα Χαιρέαν ἀποκτεῖναι, σοῦ δὲ ποιήσαντος οὐ μέμφομαι· τὸ γὰρ ἀδίκημα φιλοδέσποτον. τοῦτο μόνον ἀμελῶς ἐποίησας· οὐκ ἐπολυπραγμόνησας πότερον ἐν τοῖς τεθνηκόσι Χαιρέας ἐστὶν ἢ ἐν τοῖς δεδεμένοις. ἔδει ζητῆσαι τὸν νεκρόν· καὶ γὰρ ἐκεῖνος ἂν ἔτυχε τάφου κἀγὼ βεβαιότερον ἔσχον τὸ θαρρεῖν. οὐ δύναμαι δὲ νῦν ἀμερίμνως εὐτυχεῖν διὰ τοὺς δεδεμένους· οὐδὲ γὰρ τοῦτο ἴσμεν, ὅπου τις αὐτῶν ἐπράθη."

10. Προστάξας δὲ Φωκᾷ τὰ μὲν ἄλλα τῶν γεγονότων φανερῶς διηγεῖσθαι, δύο δὲ ταῦτα σιγᾶν, τὸ ἴδιον στρατήγημα καὶ ὅτι ἐκ τῆς τριήρους τινὲς ἔτι ζῶσι, παραγίνεται πρὸς Καλλιρόην σκυθρωπός· εἶτα συνεκάλεσε πεισθέντας τοὺς ἀγροίκους, ἵνα ἡ γυνὴ πυθομένη τὰ συμβάντα βεβαιοτέραν ἤδη 2 λάβῃ περὶ Χαιρέου τὴν ἀπόγνωσιν. ἐλθόντες δὲ διηγοῦντο πάντες ἅπερ ᾔδεσαν, ὅτι "βάρβαροί ποθεν λῃσταὶ νυκτὸς καταδραμόντες ἐνέπρησαν

9.11 Διονύσιος Reiske: -ιον F.

184

sailor who had informed him where the warship came from, for whose sake they had made the voyage, and who were on board. He also explained his own scheme of calling the orientals in, the happenings of the night, the fire, the shipwreck, the killing, and the taking of prisoners.

Then Dionysius lifted a black cloud, as it were, from his mind, and embracing Phocas he said, "You are my benefactor; you are my true guardian and my most loyal supporter in confidential affairs. It is through you that I possess Callirhoe and my son. I would not myself have ordered you to kill Chaereas, but I do not blame you for having done so. The fault was that of a loyal servant. But you were careless about this one point; you did not inquire whether Chaereas was among the dead or among the prisoners. You should have looked for his body. Then he would have secured burial and I would have had firmer ground for confidence. As it is, because of the prisoners I cannot enjoy my good luck without some anxiety; and we do not even know where any of them has been sold."

10. He instructed Phocas to speak freely of all else that had happened, but to keep silent on two matters: first, the stratagem he had employed, and, second, the fact that some of the men on the warship were still alive. Grim-faced he went to Callirhoe; then he summoned countryfolk whom he had primed, in the hope that on learning what had happened his wife would become firmly reconciled to the loss of Chaereas. They came and each of them reported what he knew: "During the night

---

10.1 Φωκᾷ Richards: -ᾶν F | συνεκάλεσε Calderini: συγκακέσας F | πεισθέντας Reiske: πεισθέντα F.

10.2 ἅπερ Goold, after Reiske: δὲ F.

Ἑλληνικὴν τριήρη τῆς προτεραίας ὁρμισθεῖσαν ἐπὶ
τῆς ἀκτῆς· καὶ μεθ' ἡμέραν εἴδομεν αἵματι με-
μιγμένον ὕδωρ καὶ νεκροὺς ὑπὸ τῶν κυμάτων
φερομένους."

3    Ἀκούσασα ἡ γυνὴ τὴν ἐσθῆτα περιερρήξατο,
κόπτουσα δὲ τοὺς ὀφθαλμοὺς καὶ τὰς παρειὰς ἀν-
έδραμεν εἰς τὸν οἶκον, ὅπου τὸ πρῶτον εἰσῆλθε πραθεῖσα. Διονύσιος δὲ ἐξουσίαν ἔδωκε τῷ πάθει,
φοβούμενος μὴ γένηται φορτικός, ἂν ἀκαίρως παρῇ.
πάντας οὖν ἐκέλευσεν ἀπαλλαγῆναι, μόνην δὲ
προσεδρεύειν Πλαγγόνα, μὴ ἄρα τι δεινὸν αὐτὴν
ἐργάσηται.

4    Καλλιρόη δὲ ἐρημίας λαβομένη, χαμαὶ καθε-
σθεῖσα καὶ κόνιν τῆς κεφαλῆς καταχέασα, τὰς
κόμας σπαράξασα τοιούτων ἤρξατο γόων "ἐγὼ μὲν
προαποθανεῖν ἢ συναποθανεῖν ηὐξάμην σοι, Χαι-
ρέα· πάντως δέ μοι κἂν ἐπαποθανεῖν ἀναγκαῖον· τίς
γὰρ ἔτι λείπεται ἐλπὶς ἐν τῷ ζῆν με κατέχουσα;
5    δυστυχοῦσα μέχρι νῦν ἐλογιζόμην 'ὄψομαί ποτε
Χαιρέαν καὶ διηγήσομαι αὐτῷ πόσα πέπονθα δι'
ἐκεῖνον· ταῦτά με ποιήσει τιμωτέραν αὐτῷ. πόσης
ἐμπλησθήσεται χαρᾶς, ὅταν ἴδῃ τὸν υἱόν.' ἀνόνητά
μοι πάντα γέγονε, καὶ τὸ τέκνον ἤδη περισσόν·
6    προσετέθη γάρ μου τοῖς κακοῖς ὀρφανός. ἄδικε
Ἀφροδίτη, σὺ μόνη Χαιρέαν εἶδες, ἐμοὶ δὲ οὐκ ἔδειξας αὐτὸν ἐλθόντα· λῃστῶν χερσὶ παρέδωκας τὸ
σῶμα τὸ καλόν· οὐκ ἠλέησας τὸν πλεύσαντα διὰ σέ.
τοιαύτῃ θεῷ τίς ἂν προσεύχοιτο, ἥτις τὸν ἴδιον

oriental brigands came out of nowhere and set fire to a
Greek warship which had anchored by the beach on the
previous day, and when daylight came, we saw the waters
stained with blood and corpses floating on the waves."

On hearing this, Callirhoe ripped her clothes, and
beating her eyes and cheeks, she ran back into the house
she had first entered when sold as a slave. Dionysius
allowed her grief to run its course, fearing that his presence at such a time might prove irksome. He therefore
told everyone to get out of her way; only Plangon was to
keep watch on her so as to prevent her harming herself.

When Callirhoe had found some privacy, she sat upon
the ground and sprinkled dust upon her head; she tore
her hair, and began to utter this lament: "Chaereas, it had
been my prayer to die before you or to die with you. Now
it is indeed imperative for me to die, even if after you; for
what hope is left any more to keep me alive? Until now I
used to think in my misfortune, 'Some day I shall see
Chaereas and tell him all that I have suffered for him, and
this will endear me to him. How overjoyed he will be to
see our son!' All has proved to no purpose. Even the
child is now an extra burden, an orphan added to my
woes. Cruel Aphrodite, only you saw Chaereas when he
came and you never showed him to me! You delivered his
fair body into the hands of brigands. You had no pity on
him who sailed the sea in your service. Who could pray to

---

10.3 μὴ ἄρα τι Jackson (cf. 4.1.2): μή τι ἄρα F.
10.4 ἐρημίας Naber: ἠρεμίας F | γόων Hirschig: βοῶν F.

7 ἱκέτην ἀπέκτεινας; οὐκ ἐβοήθησας ἐν νυκτὶ φοβερᾷ
φονευόμενον ἰδοῦσα πλησίον σου μειράκιον καλόν,
ἐρωτικόν· ἀφείλω μου τὸν ἡλικιώτην, τὸν πολίτην,
8 τὸν ἐραστήν, τὸν ἐρώμενον, τὸν νυμφίον. ἀπόδος
αὐτοῦ μοι κἂν τὸν νεκρόν. τίθημι ὅτι ἐγεννήθημεν
ἡμεῖς ἀτυχέστατοι πάντων· τί δὲ καὶ ἡ τριήρης ἠδί-
κησεν, ἵνα βάρβαροι κατέκαυσαν αὐτήν, ἧς οὐκ
ἐκράτησαν οὐδὲ Ἀθηναῖοι; νῦν ἡμῶν ἀμφοτέρων οἱ
γονεῖς τῇ θαλάσσῃ παρακάθηνται, τὸν ἡμέτερον
κατάπλουν περιμένοντες, καὶ ἥτις ἂν ναῦς πόρρωθεν
ὀφθῇ, λέγουσι 'Χαιρέας Καλλιρόην ἄγων ἔρχεται.'
τὴν κοίτην ἡμῖν εὐτρεπίζουσι τὴν νυμφικήν, κοσμεῖ-
ται δὲ θάλαμος οἷς ἴδιος οὐδὲ τάφος ὑπάρχει.
θάλασσα μιαρά, σὺ καὶ Χαιρέαν εἰς Μίλητον
ἤγαγες φονευθῆναι καὶ ἐμὲ πραθῆναι."

10.8 ἵνα Cobet: καὶ F.

such a goddess, who killed her own suppliant? On that dreadful night you saw a fair young lover murdered near you, and you did not help him. You have robbed me of my companion, my countryman, my lover, my darling, my husband! At least give me back his corpse! Granted that we were born the unluckiest of mankind, what crime had the warship committed for orientals to burn it, which not even the Athenians could vanquish? At this moment the parents of both of us are sitting by the sea longing and waiting for our return, and whenever a ship is seen in the distance they say, 'Chaereas is bringing Callirhoe home!' They are preparing our marriage bed and a chamber is being adorned for us, who lack even a tomb of our own. Cruel sea! You brought Chaereas to Miletus to be killed, and me to be sold into slavery."

## Δ

1. Ταύτην μὲν οὖν τὴν νύκτα Καλλιρόη διῆγεν ἐν θρήνοις, Χαιρέαν ἔτι ζῶντα πενθοῦσα· μικρὸν δὲ καταδραθεῖσα ὄναρ ἑώρα λῃστήριον βαρβάρων πῦρ ἐπιφέροντας, ἐμπιπραμένην δὲ τριήρη, Χαιρέᾳ δὲ

2 βοηθοῦσαν ἑαυτήν. ὁ δὲ Διονύσιος ἐλυπεῖτο μὲν ὁρῶν τρυχομένην τὴν γυναῖκα, μὴ ἄρα τι καὶ τοῦ κάλλους αὐτῇ παραπόληται, λυσιτελεῖν δὲ ὑπελάμβανεν εἰς τὸν ἴδιον ἔρωτα τὸν πρότερον ἄνδρα βε-

3 βαίως αὐτὴν ἀπογνῶναι. θέλων οὖν ἐνδείξασθαι στοργὴν καὶ μεγαλοψυχίαν ἔφη πρὸς αὐτὴν "ἀνά-στηθι, ὦ γύναι, καὶ τάφον κατασκεύασον τῷ ταλαι-πώρῳ. τί τὰ μὲν ἀδύνατα σπεύδεις, ἀμελεῖς δὲ τῶν ἀναγκαίων; νόμιζε ἐφεστηκότα σοι λέγειν αὐτὸν

'θάπτε με, ὅττι τάχιστα πύλας Ἀίδαο περήσω.'

καὶ γὰρ εἰ μὴ τὸ σῶμα εὕρηται τοῦ δυστυχοῦς, ἀλλὰ νόμος οὗτος ἀρχαῖος Ἑλλήνων, ὥστε καὶ τοὺς ἀφανεῖς τάφοις κοσμεῖν."

4 Ἔπεισε ταχέως, τὸ γὰρ πρὸς ἡδονὴν εἶχεν ἡ συμβουλία. φροντίδος οὖν ἐμπεσούσης ἐλώφησεν ἡ

# BOOK 4

1. So Callirhoe spent that night in lamentation, mourning for Chaereas who was still alive. But briefly dozing she dreamed that she saw a host of oriental brigands with torches setting the warship on fire, while she herself tried to help Chaereas. Although Dionysius was sorry to see his wife in such distress, fearing also that her beauty might be impaired, still he considered that his own love would benefit if she gave up all hope of her former husband. So, wishing to demonstrate his affection and magnanimity, he said to her, "Get up, my dear, and build a tomb for the poor boy. Why hanker after the impossible, and neglect the things you have to do? Imagine him at your side and saying,

'bury me that at once I may enter the portals of Hades.'[a]

Even though the unhappy man's body has not been found, it is an old Greek custom to honor with a tomb even those who are missing."

He soon persuaded her, for the advice was to her liking. As the thought took hold, her grief abated, and

---

[a] *Iliad* 23.71 (Patroclus to Achilles).

1.2 εἰς . . . ἔρωτα] before τὸν Hercher: before λυσ. F.

λύπη, καὶ διαναστᾶσα τῆς κλίνης κατεσκόπει
χωρίον, ἐν ᾧ ποιήσει τὸν τάφον. ἤρεσε δὲ αὐτῇ
πλησίον τοῦ νεὼ τῆς Ἀφροδίτης, ὥστε καὶ τοὺς
5 αὖθις ἔχειν ἔρωτος ὑπόμνημα. Διονύσιος δὲ ἐφθό-
νησε Χαιρέᾳ τῆς γειτνιάσεως καὶ τὸν τόπον τοῦτον
ἐφύλαττεν ἑαυτῷ. θέλων οὖν ἅμα καὶ τριβὴν ἐγγε-
νέσθαι τῇ φροντίδι "βαδίζωμεν, ὦ γύναι" φησίν,
"εἰς ἄστυ, κἀκεῖ πρὸ τῆς πόλεως ὑψηλὸν καὶ ἀρί-
δηλον κατασκευάσωμεν τάφον,

ὥς κεν τηλεφανὴς ἐκ ποντόφιν ἀνδράσιν εἴη.

καλοὶ δὲ Μιλησίων εἰσὶ λιμένες, εἰς οὓς καθορμίζον-
ται καὶ Συρακόσιοι πολλάκις. οὔκουν οὐδὲ παρὰ
τοῖς πολίταις ἀκλεᾶ τὴν φιλοτιμίαν ἕξεις."

6 Ὁ λόγος ἤρεσε Καλλιρόῃ, καὶ τότε μὲν ἐπέσχε
τὴν σπουδήν· ἐπειδὴ δὲ ἧκεν εἰς τὴν πόλιν, ἐπί τινος
ὑψηλῆς ἠϊόνος οἰκοδομεῖν ἤρξατο τάφον, πάντα
ὅμοιον τῷ ἰδίῳ τῷ ἐν Συρακούσαις, τὸ σχῆμα, τὸ
μέγεθος, τὴν πολυτέλειαν, καὶ οὗτος δὲ ὡς ἐκεῖνος
ζῶντος. ἐπεὶ δὲ ἀφθόνοις ἀναλώμασι καὶ πολυχει-
ρίᾳ ταχέως τὸ ἔργον ἠνύσθη, τότε ἤδη καὶ τὴν ἐκκο-
7 μιδὴν ἐμιμήσατο τὴν ἐφ' αὑτῇ. προήγγελτο μὲν
γὰρ ἡμέρα ῥητή, συνῆλθε δὲ εἰς ἐκείνην οὐ μόνον τὸ
Μιλησίων πλῆθος ἀλλὰ καὶ τῆς Ἰωνίας σχεδὸν
ὅλης. παρῆσαν δὲ καὶ δύο σατράπαι κατὰ καιρὸν
ἐπιδημοῦντες, Μιθριδάτης ὁ ἐν Καρίᾳ καὶ Φαρνάκης

1.6 ἐφ' αὑτῇ Hägg: ἐπ' αὐτῷ F.
1.7 προήγγελτο Cobet: προηγγέλλετο F.

getting up from her couch she went to look for a site on which to build the tomb. A place near the shrine of Aphrodite attracted her, so that posterity also might have a reminder of her love. But Dionysius begrudged Chaereas such proximity, wishing to reserve this site for himself. At the same time he wanted her interest to continue, so he said, "My dear, let us go to the city, and there before the walls let us construct an imposing and conspicuous memorial

that from afar it may be visible to men on the waters.[a]

Miletus has excellent harbors and Syracusans, too, often anchor in them. So even with your own countrymen you will be known for the honor you do him."

The proposal delighted Callirhoe, and for the moment she kept her eagerness in check. But when she came to the city, she began to build on a mound by the shore a tomb in every way similar to her own in Syracuse in shape, size, and opulence. And this, like that, was for a living person. When the work had been quickly completed by a vast labor force with no expense spared, she at once copied her own funeral as well. The day appointed had been announced, and on it assembled the population, not only of Miletus, but also of practically all Ionia. Two governors, who were visitors at the time, Mithridates of

[a] *Odyssey* 24.83 (the tomb of Achilles).

8 δὲ ὁ Λυδίας. ἡ μὲν οὖν πρόφασις ἦν τιμῆσαι Διονύσιον, ἡ δὲ ἀλήθεια Καλλιρόην ἰδεῖν. ἦν δὴ καὶ
κλέος μέγα τῆς γυναικὸς ἐπὶ τῆς Ἀσίας πάσης καὶ
ἀνέβαινεν ἤδη μέχρι τοῦ μεγάλου βασιλέως ὄνομα
Καλλιρόης, οἷον οὐδὲ Ἀριάδνης οὐδὲ Λήδας. τότε
δὲ καὶ τῆς δόξης εὑρέθη κρείττων· προῆλθε γὰρ
μελανείμων, λελυμένη <μὲν> τὰς τρίχας, ἀστρά-
πτουσα δὲ τῷ προσώπῳ· καὶ παραγυμνοῦσα τοὺς
βραχίονας <καὶ τὰς κνήμας> ὑπὲρ τὴν Λευκώλενον
καὶ Καλλίσφυρον ἐφαίνετο τὰς Ὁμήρου.

9 Οὐδεὶς μὲν οὖν οὐδὲ τῶν ἄλλων τὴν μαρμαρυγὴν
ὑπήνεγκε τοῦ κάλλους, ἀλλ' οἱ μὲν ἀπεστράφησαν,
ὡς ἀκτῖνος ἡλιακῆς ἐμπεσούσης, <οἱ δὲ> καὶ προσεκύνησαν. ἔπαθόν τι καὶ παῖδες. Μιθριδάτης δέ, ὁ
Καρίας ὕπαρχος, ἀχανὴς κατέπεσεν, ὥσπερ τις ἐξ
ἀπροσδοκήτου σφενδόνῃ βληθείς, καὶ μόλις αὐτὸν
10 οἱ θεραπευτῆρες ὑποβαστάζοντες ἔφερον. ἐπόμπευε
δ' εἴδωλον Χαιρέου πρὸς τὴν ἐν τῷ δακτυλίῳ σφρα-
γῖδα διατυπωθέν· καλλίστην δὲ οὖσαν τὴν εἰκόνα
προσέβλεψεν οὐδεὶς Καλλιρόης παρούσης, ἀλλ'
ἐκείνη μόνη τοὺς ἁπάντων ἐδημαγώγησεν ὀφθαλμούς.

11 Πῶς ἄν τις διηγήσηται κατ' ἀξίαν τὰ τελευταῖα
τῆς πομπῆς; ἐπεὶ γὰρ ἐγένοντο τοῦ τάφου πλησίον,
οἱ μὲν κομίζοντες τὴν κλίνην ἔθηκαν, ἀναβᾶσα δὲ
ἐπ' αὐτὴν ἡ Καλλιρόη Χαιρέα περιεχύθη καὶ κατα-

1.8 add. Cobet | add. Cobet.
1.9 add. Reiske | ὕπαρχος Cobet: ἔπαρχος F.

Caria and Pharnaces of Lydia,[a] were also present. They
let out that they were honoring Dionysius, but the truth
was that they wanted to see Callirhoe. Her great fame
had spread all over Asia, and already the name of Callirhoe had come to the attention of the Great King as one
excelling even Ariadne and Leda.[b] On this occasion, however, she surpassed all expectation. She appeared dressed
in black, her hair loose and her face radiant; with her
bare arms and feet she seemed more beautiful than the
Homeric goddesses "of the white arms"[c] and "of the fair
ankles."[d]

In fact not a single one there could withstand her daz-
zling beauty. Some turned their heads away as though the
sun's rays shone into their eyes, and others actually knelt
in homage; even children were affected. Mithridates, the
governor of Caria, fell speechless to the ground like a
man unexpectedly struck by a missile, and his attendants
barely managed to hold him up. In the procession was
carried a statue of Chaereas modeled on the seal of Callirhoe's ring. Yet handsome though the likeness was, no
one looked at it with Callirhoe present, but she alone held
every eye in thrall.

How could one do justice to the completion of the
funeral? When they reached the tomb, those who were
carrying the bier set it down, and Callirhoe mounted it,
put her arms about the image of Chaereas, and kissing it

[a] Caria is the Persian province to the east of Miletus, Lydia
that to the north. Subsequently (4.6.1 and 3; 5.6.8) Pharnaces'
territory is specified as also including Ionia (the coastal strip).

[b] By Zeus the mother of Helen.

[c] A regular epithet of Hera, *Iliad* 1.55 and often.

[d] Ino Leucothea, *Odyssey* 5.333; Hebe, *Odyssey* 11.603.

φιλοῦσα τὴν εἰκόνα "σὺ μὲν ἔθαψας ἐμὲ πρῶτος ἐν
12 Συρακούσαις, ἐγὼ δὲ ἐν Μιλήτῳ πάλιν σέ. μὴ γὰρ
μεγάλα μόνον, ἀλλὰ καὶ παράδοξα δυστυχοῦμεν·
ἀλλήλους ἐθάψαμεν. οὐκ ἔχει δ' ἡμῶν οὐδέτερος
οὐδὲ τὸν νεκρόν. Τύχη βάσκανε, καὶ ἀποθανοῦσιν
ἡμῖν ἐφθόνησας κοινῇ γῆν ἐπιέσασθαι καὶ φυγάδας
ἡμῶν ἐποίησας καὶ τοὺς νεκρούς." θρῆνον ἐξέρρηξε
τὸ πλῆθος καὶ πάντες οὐχ ὅτι τέθνηκε Χαιρέαν
ἠλέουν, ἀλλ' ὅτι τοιαύτης γυναικὸς ἀφῄρητο.

2. Καλλιρόη μὲν οὖν ἐν Μιλήτῳ Χαιρέαν ἔθαπτε,
Χαιρέας δὲ ἐν Καρίᾳ δεδεμένος εἰργάζετο. σκάπτων
δὲ τὸ σῶμα ταχέως ἐξετρυχώθη· πολλὰ γὰρ αὐτὸν
ἐβάρει, κόπος, ἀμέλεια, τὰ δεσμά, καὶ τούτων μᾶλλον ὁ ἔρως. ἀποθανεῖν δὲ βουλόμενον αὐτὸν οὐκ εἴα
2 λεπτή τις ἐλπίς, ὅτι τάχα ποτὲ Καλλιρόην ὄψεται.
Πολύχαρμος οὖν, ὁ συναλοὺς αὐτῷ φίλος, βλέπων
Χαιρέαν ἐργάζεσξαι μὴ δυνάμενον, ἀλλὰ πληγὰς
λαμβάνοντα καὶ προπηλακιζόμενον αἰσχρῶς, λέγει
πρὸς τὸν ἐργοστόλον "χωρίον ἡμῖν ἀπομέρισον
ἐξαίρετον, ἵνα μὴ τὴν τῶν ἄλλων δεσμωτῶν ῥαθυ-
μίαν ἡμῖν καταλογίζῃ· τὸ δὲ ἴδιον μέτρον αὐτοὶ
3 ἀποδώσομεν πρὸς ἡμέραν." πείθεται καὶ δίδωσιν. ὁ
δὲ Πολύχαρμος, οἷα δὴ νεανίας ἀνδρικὸς τὴν φύσιν
καὶ μὴ δουλεύων Ἔρωτι, χαλεπῷ τυράννῳ, τὰς δύο
μοίρας αὐτὸς σχεδὸν εἰργάζετο [μόνος], πλεονεκτῶν
ἐν τοῖς πόνοις ἡδέως, ἵνα περισώσῃ τὸν φίλον.

4 Καὶ οὗτοι μὲν ἦσαν ἐν τοιαύταις συμφοραῖς, ὀψὲ

said, "You first buried me in Syracuse, and now I, in turn, do the same for you in Miletus! Our misfortunes are as unbelievable as they are enormous. We have buried each other, yet neither of us possesses even the other's dead body. Envious Fortune, you have begrudged us even in death the shroud of a common grave[a] and exiled our very corpses!" The crowd burst into tears and all felt pity for Chaereas, not because he was dead, but because he had been deprived of such a wife.

2. While Callirhoe was burying Chaereas in Miletus, Chaereas himself was working in chains in Caria. He was soon physically exhausted from digging, and there was much to depress his spirits: fatigue, neglect, chains, and more than these, his love. Though he longed for death, still some slight hope that perhaps one day he would see Callirhoe again kept him alive. Then his friend Polycharmus, who had been captured with him, seeing that Chaereas, incapable of work, was being beaten and cruelly ill-treated, said to their overseer, "Measure off a special area for us so that you do not charge us with the laziness of the other prisoners, and we will complete our own daily quota." The overseer agreed and granted his request. So Polycharmus, being young and naturally robust and not enslaved to the cruel tyrant Love, practically performed a double portion by himself, glad to do most of the work in order to save his friend.

With the pair in this sorry plight and finally aware of

[a] Cf. Xenophon, *Cyropaedia* 6.4.6.

---

1.12 κοινὴν γῆν ἐπιθέσθαι F, corr. D'Orville.
2.3 del. Cobet | πλεονεκτῶν] Π[1] begins.

μεταμανθάνοντες τὴν ἐλευθερίαν· ὁ δὲ Μιθριδάτης ὁ
σατράπης ἐπανῆλθεν εἰς Καρίαν οὐ τοιοῦτος, ὁποῖος
εἰς Μίλητον ἐξῆλθεν, ἀλλ' ὠχρός τε καὶ λεπτός, οἷα
δὴ τραῦμα ἔχων ἐν τῇ ψυχῇ θερμόν τε καὶ δριμύ.
5  τηκόμενος δὲ ὑπὸ τοῦ Καλλιρόης ἔρωτος πάντως ἂν
ἐτελεύτησεν, εἰ μὴ τοιᾶσδέ τινος ἔτυχε παραμυθίας.
τῶν ἐργατῶν τινες τῶν ἅμα Χαιρέᾳ δεδεμένων (ἑξκαίδεκα δὲ ἦσαν τὸν ἀριθμὸν ἐν οἰκίσκῳ σκοτεινῷ
καθειργμένοι) νύκτωρ διακόψαντες τὰ δεσμὰ τὸν
ἐπιστάτην ἀπέσφαξαν, εἶτα δρασμὸν ἐπεχείρουν.
6  ἀλλ' οὐ διέφυγον, οἱ γὰρ κύνες ὑλάσσοντες ἐμήνυ-
σαν αὐτούς. φωραθέντες οὖν ἐκείνης τῆς νυκτὸς
ἐδέθησαν ἐπιμελέστερον ἐν ξύλῳ πάντες, μεθ' ἡμέραν δὲ ὁ οἰκονόμος ἐμήνυσε Μιθριδάτῃ τὸ συμβάν,
κἀκεῖνος οὐδὲ ἰδὼν αὐτοὺς οὐδὲ ἀπολογουμένων
ἀκούσας εὐθὺς ἐκέλευσε τοὺς ἑξκαίδεκα τοὺς ὁμο-
7  σκήνους ἀνασταυρῶσαι. προήχθησαν οὖν πόδας τε
καὶ τραχήλους συνδεδεμένοι, καὶ ἕκαστος αὐτῶν τὸν
σταυρὸν ἔφερε· τῇ γὰρ ἀναγκαίᾳ τιμωρίᾳ καὶ τὴν
ἔξωθεν φαντασίαν σκυθρωπὴν προσέθεσαν οἱ κολά-
ζοντες εἰς φόβου παράδειγμα τοῖς ὁμοίοις.

Χαιρέας μὲν οὖν συναπαγόμενος ἐσίγα, Πολύχαρμος δὲ τὸν σταυρὸν βαστάσας "διὰ σὲ" φησίν,
"ὦ Καλλιρόη, ταῦτα πάσχομεν. σὺ πάντων ἡμῖν
8  τῶν κακῶν αἰτία." τοῦτον δὴ τὸν λόγον ὁ οἰκονόμος
ἀκούσας ἔδοξεν εἶναί τινα γυναῖκα τὴν συνειδυῖαν
τοῖς τετολμημένοις. ὅπως οὖν κἀκείνη κολασθῇ καὶ

their loss of freedom, the governor Mithridates returned
to Caria, not the man he had been on his departure for
Miletus, but pale and thin from the hot piercing wound in
his heart. Pining with love for Callirhoe, he would surely
have died had he not met with some consolation as follows. Some of those chained with Chaereas (sixteen in all
shut up in a gloomy cell) broke through their chains in the
night, murdered the overseer, and then attempted a get-
away. But they did not escape, as the dogs' barking
betrayed them. They were discovered and all securely
fastened in the stocks for the night, and when day came
the estate manager told Mithridates what had happened.
Without even seeing them or listening to their defense he
immediately ordered the sixteen cell-mates to be crucified. They were duly brought out, chained together at
foot and neck, each carrying his own cross. The executioners added this grim public spectacle to the requisite
penalty as a deterrent to others so minded.

Now Chaereas said nothing as he was led off with the
others, but on taking up his cross Polycharmus exclaimed,
"It is your fault, Callirhoe, that we are in this mess. You
are responsible for all our troubles!" Hearing this remark,
the estate manager thought that a woman was implicated
in the crime. So that she too might be punished and an

---

2.4 ὅποιος Π¹: οἷος F | δριμύ Π¹: γλυκύ F.

2.5 ἔτυχε Π¹: ἐτύγχανε F | δὲ ἦσαν F: ἦσαν Π¹.

2.6 Μιθριδάτῃ Π¹: τῷ δεσπότῃ F.

2.7 γὰρ Π¹: δὲ F | σκυθρωπὴν Π¹: -ῆς F | προσέθεσαν
Π¹: -έθηκαν F | βαστάσας Π¹: βαστάζων F | συναπ- Π¹: ἀπ-
F.

2.8 τοῦτον Π¹: τοσοῦτον F | κἀκείνη F: -νῃ Π¹.

199

ζήτησις γένηται τῆς ἐπιβουλῆς, ταχέως τὸν
Πολύχαρμον ἀπορρήξας τῆς κοινῆς ἁλύσεως πρὸς
Μιθριδάτην ἤγαγεν. ὁ δ' ἐν παραδείσῳ κατέκειτο
μόνος ἀλύων καὶ Καλλιρόην ἀναπλάττων ἑαυτῷ τοιαύτην, ὁποίαν εἶδε πενθοῦσαν· ὅλος δὲ ὢν ἐπὶ τῆς

9 ἐννοίας ἐκείνης καὶ τὸν οἰκέτην ἀηδῶς ἐθεάσατο. "τί
γάρ μοι" φησὶ "παρενοχλεῖς;" "ἀναγκαῖον" εἶπεν,
"ὦ δέσποτα· τὴν γὰρ πηγὴν ἀνεύρηκα τοῦ μεγάλου
τολμήματος, καὶ οὗτος ὁ κατάρατος ἐπίσταται
γυναῖκα μιαρὰν συμπράξασαν τῷ φόνῳ." ἀκούσας ὁ
Μιθριδάτης συνήγαγε τὰς ὀφρῦς καὶ δεινὸν βλέπων
"λέγε" φησὶ "τὴν συνειδυῖαν καὶ κοινωνὸν ὑμῖν τῶν

10 ἀδικημάτων." ὁ δὲ Πολύχαρμος ἔξαρνος ἦν εἰδέναι,
μηδὲ γὰρ ὅλως τῆς πράξεως κεκοινωνηκέναι.
μάστιγες ᾐτοῦντο καὶ πῦρ ἐπεφέρετο καὶ βασανι-
στηρίων ἦν παρασκευή, καί τις ἤδη καὶ τοῦ σώματος ἁπτόμενος αὐτοῦ "λέγε" φησὶ "τοὔνομα τῆς
γυναικός, ἣν αἰτίαν ὡμολόγησας εἶναί σοι τῶν
κακῶν." "Καλλιρόην" εἶπεν ὁ Πολύχαρμος.

11 Ἔπληξε τοὔνομα Μιθριδάτην, καὶ ἀτυχῆ τινα
ἔδοξεν ὁμωνυμίαν τῶν γυναικῶν. οὐκέτ' οὖν προθύμως ἤθελεν ἐξελέγχειν, δεδοικὼς μὴ καταστῇ ποτε
εἰς ἀνάγκην ὑβρίσαι τὸ ἥδιστον ὄνομα· τῶν δὲ
φίλων καὶ τῶν οἰκετῶν εἰς ἔρευναν ἀκριβεστέραν

12 παρακαλούντων "ἡκέτω" φησὶ "Καλλιρόη." παίοντες
οὖν τὸν Πολύχαρμον ἠρώτων τίς ἐστι καὶ πόθεν

2.8 παραδείσῳ Π¹: παραδείσῳ τινὶ F.

investigation made into the plot, he at once detached
Polycharmus from the chained group and brought him to
Mithridates. The latter was reclining alone in his garden,
depressed and imagining Callirhoe as he had seen her in
her sorrow. Absorbed in the thought of her, he regarded
even his servant with displeasure. "What do you mean by
disturbing me?" he said. "I must, master," the other
replied. "I have discovered the source of that awful outrage. This damned rogue knows of a horrible woman who
was an accomplice to the murder." On hearing this,
Mithridates scowled and said with a forbidding look, "Tell
me about the woman who was implicated and helped you
in the crime." But Polycharmus denied knowing any such
person or even having taken any part in it at all. Whips
were called for, fire brought, and the torture instruments
made ready. Then one of them seized him and said, "Tell
us the name of that woman who you admitted was responsible for your troubles." "Callirhoe," said Polycharmus.

The name startled Mithridates, and he assumed that
by some unhappy coincidence the women had the same
name. He was therefore no longer keen to investigate,
fearing that he might later have to deal harshly with the
beloved name. But when his friends and servants recom-
mended a thorough inquiry, he said, "Have Callirhoe
come here." So they began to hit Polycharmus, asking

---

2.9 μοι Π¹ | om. F | τόλμήματος Π¹, Cobet: αἵματος F |
κατά]ρατο[ς Π¹ κατάρατος ἄνθρωπος F | ὁ M. Π¹: οὖν ὁ M.
F.

2.10 ἐπεφέρετο Π¹: ἐφέρετο F | ἤδη καὶ Π¹: ἤδη F.

2.11 τῶν γυναικῶν Π¹: ἔχειν ἐκείνῃ γυναῖκα F | ἤθελεν
ἐξελέγχειν Π¹: ἐξ. ἤθ. F.

ἄγωσιν αὐτήν. ὁ δὲ ἄθλιος ἐν ἀμηχανίᾳ γενόμενος
καταψεύσασθαι μὲν οὐδεμιᾶς ἤθελε· "τί δὲ μάτην"
εἶπε "θορυβεῖσθε ζητοῦντες τὴν οὐ παροῦσαν;
Καλλιρόης ἐγὼ Συρακοσίας ἐμνημόνευσα, θυγατρὸς
13 Ἑρμοκράτους τοῦ στρατηγοῦ." ταῦτα ἀκούσας ὁ
Μιθριδάτης ἐρυθήματος ἐνεπλήσθη καὶ ἴδρου τὰ
ἔνδον, καί που καὶ δάκρυον αὐτοῦ μὴ θέλοντος
προύπεσεν, ὥστε καὶ τὸν Πολύχαρμον διασιωπῆσαι
καὶ πάντας ἀπορεῖν τοὺς παρόντας. ὀψὲ δὲ καὶ
μόλις ὁ Μιθριδάτης συναγαγὼν ἑαυτὸν "τί δὲ σοὶ"
φησὶ "πρᾶγμα πρὸς Καλλιρόην ἐκείνην, καὶ διατί
μέλλων ἀποθνήσκειν ἐμνημόνευσας αὐτῆς;" ὁ δὲ
ἀπεκρίνατο "μακρὸς ὁ μῦθος, ὦ δέσποτα, καὶ πρὸς
14 οὐδὲν ἔτι χρήσιμός μοι. οὐκ ἐνοχλήσω δέ σοι
λήρων ἀκαίρως, ἅμα δὲ καὶ δέδοικα μή, ἐὰν βρα-
δύνω, φθάσῃ με ὁ φίλος· θέλω δὲ αὐτῷ καὶ συναποθανεῖν." ἐπεκλάσθησαν αἱ ὀργαὶ τῶν ἀκουόντων καὶ
ὁ θυμὸς εἰς ἔλεον μετέπεσε, Μιθριδάτης δὲ ὑπὲρ
πάντας συνεχύθη καὶ "μὴ δέδιθι" φησίν, "οὐ γὰρ
ἐνοχλήσεις μοι διηγούμενος· ἔχω γὰρ ψυχὴν φιλάν-
15 θρωπον. λέγε πάντα θαρρῶν καὶ μηδὲν παραλίπῃς.
τίς εἶ καὶ πόθεν, καὶ πῶς ἦλθες εἰς Καρίαν καὶ διατί
σκάπτεις δεδεμένος; μάλιστα δέ μοι διήγησαι περὶ
Καλλιρόης καὶ τίς ὁ φίλος."

3. Ἤρξατο οὖν ὁ Πολύχαρμος λέγειν "ἡμεῖς, οἱ
δύο δεσμῶται, Συρακόσιοι γένος ἐσμέν. ἀλλ᾽ ὁ μὲν
ἕτερος νεανίσκος πρῶτος Σικελίας δόξῃ τε καὶ
πλούτῳ καὶ εὐμορφίᾳ ποτέ, ἐγὼ δὲ εὐτελὴς μέν,

him who she was and where they could get her. Though at his wits' end the poor man did not want any woman falsely accused and said, "It is no use making a fuss, looking for a woman who is not here. I meant Callirhoe of Syracuse, daughter of the ruler Hermocrates." At this Mithridates blushed deeply and broke into a sweat all over, and somehow in spite of himself a tear actually dropped from his eyes, so that Polycharmus too became silent, and everyone present felt at a loss. After some time Mithridates managed to pull himself together and said, "What is your connection with that Callirhoe and why on the point of execution did you mention her?" "Sir," he replied, "it is a long story, and it will no longer do me any good. I will not bother you with chatter at the wrong time. Besides, I am afraid that if I dally my friend will pass on ahead of me, and I want to die with him." The mood of his listeners turned full circle: anger changed to pity, and Mithridates was more moved than the rest. "Have no fear," he said, "you will not bother me with your story. I have a kindly heart. Be brave and tell everything. Leave nothing out. Who are you and where do you come from? How did you come to Caria, and why are you digging in a chain gang? Most important, tell me about Callirhoe, and who your friend is."

3. So Polycharmus started on his story. "We, the two prisoners, are Syracusans. The other one was once the most distinguished youth in Sicily, in reputation, wealth, and handsomeness. I by contrast, his companion and

---

2.12 ἄγωσιν Cobet: ἄγουσιν F: [Π¹].
2.13 ἐμνημόνευσας Π¹, Reiske: -σεν F.
2.14 δέ σοι Blake: δέ σε F (σ[ Π¹).

2 συμφοιτητὴς δὲ ἐκείνου καὶ φίλος. καταλιπόντες
οὖν τοὺς γονεῖς ἐξεπλεύσαμεν τῆς πατρίδος, ἐγὼ μὲν
δι᾽ ἐκεῖνον, ἐκεῖνος δὲ διὰ γυναῖκα Καλλιρόην τοὔνομα, ἥν, δόξασαν ἀποτεθνηκέναι, ἔθαψε πολυτελῶς. τυμβωρύχοι δὲ ζῶσαν εὑρόντες εἰς Ἰωνίαν
ἐπώλησαν. τοῦτο γὰρ ἡμῖν ἐμήνυσε δημοσίᾳ
3 βασανιζόμενος Θήρων ὁ λῃστής. ἔπεμψεν οὖν ἡ
πόλις <ἡ> Συρακοσίων τριήρη καὶ πρέσβεις τοὺς
ἀναζητήσοντας τὴν γυναῖκα. ταύτην τὴν τριήρη
νυκτὸς ὁρμοῦσαν ἐνέπρησαν βάρβαροι καὶ τοὺς μὲν
πολλοὺς ἀπέσφαξαν, ἐμὲ δὲ καὶ τὸν φίλον δήσαντες
ἐπώλησαν ἐνταῦθα. ἡμεῖς μὲν οὖν σωφρόνως ἐφέ-
ρομεν τὴν συμφοράν· ἕτεροι δέ τινες τῶν ἡμῖν συν-
δεδεμένων, οὓς ἀγνοοῦμεν, διαρρήξαντες τὰ δεσμὰ
φόνον εἰργάσαντο· καὶ σοῦ κελεύσαντος τὴν ἐπὶ τὸν
4 σταυρὸν ἠγόμεθα πάντες. ὁ μὲν οὖν φίλος οὐδὲ
ἀποθνῄσκων ἐνεκάλει τῇ γυναικί, ἐγὼ δὲ προήχθην
αὐτῆς μνημονεῦσαι καὶ τῶν κακῶν αἰτίαν εἰπεῖν
ἐκείνην, δι᾽ ἣν ἐπλεύσαμεν." ἔτι λέγοντος αὐτοῦ Μι-
5 θριδάτης ἀνεβόησε "πῶς λέγεις τὸν φίλον;" <"Χαιρέαν"> εἶπεν ὁ Πολύχαρμος· "ἀλλὰ δέομαί σου,
δέσποτα, κέλευσον τῷ δημίῳ μηδὲ τοὺς σταυροὺς
ἡμῶν διαζεῦξαι." δάκρυα καὶ στεναγμὸς ἐπηκολούθησε τῷ διηγήματι, καὶ πάντας ἔπεμψε Μιθριδάτης
ἐπὶ Χαιρέαν, ἵνα μὴ φθάσῃ τελευτήσας. εὗρον δὲ
τοὺς μὲν ἄλλους ἀνηρτημένους, ἄρτι δὲ ἐκεῖνον ἐπι-
6 βαίνοντα τοῦ σταυροῦ. πόρρωθεν οὖν ἐκεκράγεσαν
ἄλλος ἄλλο τι "φεῖσαι," "κατάβηθι," "μὴ τρώσῃς,"

friend, am of no consequence. Leaving our parents we sailed away from our country, I because of him, and he because of his wife, named Callirhoe. Thinking her dead, he buried her sumptuously. But grave robbers discovered her alive and sold her in Ionia. We learned this from the pirate Theron who confessed to it publicly under torture. Then the city of Syracuse sent out a warship with envoys to recover the woman. One night, as the ship lay at anchor, orientals set it on fire and killed most of us, but taking me and my friend prisoner they sold us here. Now we endured our misfortune with resignation, but some of our fellow prisoners, whom we do not know, broke their chains and committed murder. Then on your orders we were all taken out to be crucified. Even in his last moments my friend would not reproach his wife, but I could not refrain from mentioning her name and calling her the cause of our troubles, since it was for her sake that we made the voyage." While he was still speaking, Mithridates exclaimed, "Do you mean Chaereas?" "Yes—my friend," said Polycharmus. "But I beg you, sir, tell the executioner not to separate even our crosses." Tears and groans greeted his story, and Mithridates sent them all to save Chaereas before he died. They found the others already hanging on their crosses, and he was just mounting his. From far off they each shouted appeals: "Spare

---

3.2 δόξασαν Π¹: δόξας F | ἐπώλησαν] Π¹ ends.

3.3 add. Cobet.

3.4 ἐγὼ δὲ προήχθην Cobet: προήχθην δὲ F | πῶς Jackson: Χαιρέαν F.

3.5 add. Jackson | ἀνηρτημένους Naber: ἀνῃρημένους F.

"ἄφες." ὁ μὲν οὖν δήμιος ἐπέσχε τὴν ὁρμήν· Χαιρέας δὲ λυπούμενος κατέβαινε τοῦ σταυροῦ· χαίρων
γὰρ ἀπηλλάσσετο βίου πονηροῦ καὶ ἔρωτος ἀτυχοῦς.

Ἀγομένῳ δὲ αὐτῷ Μιθριδάτης ἀπήντησε καὶ
περιπτυξάμενος εἶπεν "ἀδελφὲ καὶ φίλε, μικροῦ με
ἐνήδρευσας ἔργον ἀσεβὲς ἐργάσασθαι διὰ τὴν
7  ἐγκρατῆ μὲν ἀλλ᾽ ἄκαιρόν σου σιωπήν." εὐθὺς οὖν
προσέταξε τοῖς οἰκέταις ἄγειν ἐπὶ λουτρὰ καὶ τὰ
σώματα θεραπεῦσαι, λουσαμένοις δὲ περιθεῖναι χλα-
μύδας Ἑλληνικὰς πολυτελεῖς· αὐτὸς δὲ γνωρίμους
εἰς [τὸ] συμπόσιον παρεκάλει καὶ ἔθυε Χαιρέου
σωτήρια. πότος ἦν μακρὸς καὶ ἡδεῖα φιλοφρόνησις
8  καὶ θυμηδίας οὐδὲν ἐνέδει. προκοπτούσης δὲ
τῆς εὐωχίας θερμανθεὶς Μιθριδάτης οἴνῳ καὶ ἔρωτι
"μὴ γὰρ τὰ δεσμὰ καὶ τὸν σταυρὸν ἐλεῶ σου, Χαιρέα" φησίν, "ἀλλ᾽ ὅτι τοιαύτης γυναικὸς ἀφῃρέ-
θης." ἐκπλαγεὶς οὖν ὁ Χαιρέας ἀνέκραγε "ποῦ γὰρ
σὺ Καλλιρόην εἶδες τὴν ἐμήν;" "οὐκέτι σὴν" εἶπεν ὁ
Μιθριδάτης, "ἀλλὰ Διονυσίου τοῦ Μιλησίου νόμῳ
γαμηθεῖσαν· ἤδη δὲ καὶ τέκνον ἐστὶν αὐτοῖς."

9  Οὐκ ἐκαρτέρησεν ὁ Χαιρέας ἀκούσας, ἀλλὰ τοῖς
γόνασι Μιθριδάτου προσπεσὼν "ἱκετεύω σε, πάλιν,
ὦ δέσποτα, τὸν σταυρόν μοι ἀπόδος. χεῖρόν με
βασανίζεις, ἐπὶ τοιούτῳ διηγήματι ζῆν ἀναγκάζων.
10  ἄπιστε Καλλιρόη καὶ πασῶν ἀσεβεστάτη γυναικῶν,
ἐγὼ μὲν ἐπράθην διὰ σὲ καὶ ἔσκαψα καὶ σταυρὸν
ἐβάστασα καὶ δημίου χερσὶ παρεδόθην, σὺ δὲ ἐτρύ-

him!" "Come down!" "Do not hurt him!" "Let him go!"
So the executioner stopped his work, and Chaereas
descended from the cross, regretfully, for he had been
glad to be leaving his miserable life and unhappy love.

He was taken to Mithridates, who greeted him with an
embrace. "My dear brother," he said, "you almost
trapped me into committing a sacrilege because of your
heroic but misguided silence." At once he ordered his
slaves to take them to the baths and see to their physical
well-being, and after the bath to clothe them in expensive
Greek mantles. He himself invited his friends to a banquet celebrating the rescue of Chaereas. The drinking
was extensive, the entertainment generous, and there was
no lack of jollity. As the feasting progressed, Mithridates,
inflamed with wine and passion, said, "Chaereas, it is not
the chains and the cross for which I pity you, but rather
for losing such a wife." "And where have you seen my Callirhoe?" cried Chaereas in astonishment. "Not yours any
more," said Mithridates, "for she is the lawful wife of
Dionysius of Miletus, and besides they now have a child."

Chaereas could not restrain himself at this but fell at
the knees of Mithridates and said, "I implore you, sir,
send me back to the cross. You are inflicting a worse torture, compelling me to live in the face of such news.
Faithless Callirhoe, wickedest of all women! Because of
you I have been sold, have wielded a shovel, have carried
a cross and been delivered into the hands of the execu-

---

3.7 ἐς F | del. Cobet.

CHARITON

φας καὶ γάμους ἔθυες ἐμοῦ δεδεμένου. οὐκ ἤρκεσεν
ὅτι γυνὴ γέγονας ἄλλου Χαιρέου ζῶντος, γέγονας δὲ
11 καὶ μήτηρ." κλάειν ἤρξαντο πάντες καὶ μετέβαλε τὸ
συμπόσιον εἰς σκυθρωπὴν ὑπόθεσιν. μόνος ἐπὶ τούτοις Μιθριδάτης ἔχαιρεν, ἐλπίδα τινὰ λαμβάνων
ἐρωτικήν, ὡς δυνάμενος ἤδη καὶ λέγειν καὶ πράττειν
12 τι περὶ Καλλιρόης, ἵνα δοκῇ φίλῳ βοηθεῖν. "ἄρτι
μὲν οὖν" ἔφη, "νὺξ γάρ ἐστιν, ἀπίωμεν, τῇ δ᾽ ὑστεραίᾳ νήφοντες βουλευώμεθα περὶ τούτων· δεῖται γὰρ
ἡ σκέψις σχολῆς μακροτέρας." ἐπὶ τούτοις ἀναστὰς
διέλυσε τὸ συμπόσιον καὶ αὐτὸς μὲν ἀνεπαύετο
καθάπερ ἦν ἔθος αὐτῷ, τοῖς δὲ Συρακοσίοις νεανί-
σκοις θεραπείαν τε καὶ οἶκον ἐξαίρετον ἀπέδειξε.

4. Νὺξ ἐκείνη φροντίδων μεστὴ πάντας κατελάμβανε καὶ οὐδεὶς ἐδύνατο καθεύδειν· Χαιρέας μὲν γὰρ
ὠργίζετο, Πολύχαρμος δὲ παρεμυθεῖτο, Μιθριδάτης
δὲ ἔχαιρεν ἐλπίζων ὅτι καθάπερ ἐν τοῖς ἀγῶσι τοῖς
γυμνικοῖς ἔφεδρος μένων μεταξὺ Χαιρέου τε καὶ
Διονυσίου αὐτὸς ἀκονιτὶ τὸ ἆθλον [Καλλιρόην]
ἀποίσεται.

2     Τῆς δ᾽ ὑστεραίας προτεθείσης τῆς γνώμης ὁ μὲν
Χαιρέας εὐθὺς ἠξίου βαδίζειν εἰς Μίλητον καὶ Διονύσιον ἀπαιτεῖν τὴν γυναῖκα· μὴ γὰρ ἂν μηδὲ Καλλιρόην ἐμμένειν ἰδοῦσαν αὐτόν· ὁ δὲ Μιθριδάτης
"ἐμοῦ μὲν ἕνεκα" φησὶν "ἄπιθι, βούλομαι γάρ σε
μηδὲ μίαν ἡμέραν ἀπεζεῦχθαι τῆς γυναικός· ὄφελον
μηδὲ Σικελίας ἐξήλθετε, μηδὲ συνέβη τι δεινὸν ἀμ-
φοῖν· ἐπεὶ δὲ ἡ φιλόκαινος Τύχη δρᾶμα σκυθρωπὸν

4.1 del. Cobet.
208

tioner. And you were living in luxury and celebrating your marriage while I was in chains! It was not enough for you to become the wife of another while Chaereas was alive, but you had to become a mother as well!" All began to shed tears, and the feast was transformed into a scene of gloom. Mithridates alone was pleased at this, conceiving some hope for his love, since he could now speak and act in regard to Callirhoe with the appearance of helping a friend. "Well," he said, "it is night now, so let us break up; but tomorrow, when we are sober, we had better discuss the position. Its consideration will take some time." Thereupon he got up and brought the party to an end. He himself went to bed as usual, after providing special service and a room for the young Syracusans.

4. That night was filled with anxiety for them all: not one of them could sleep. Chaereas was angry, while Polycharmus tried to comfort him. Mithridates, in turn, was happy in the hope that he might, as it were, sit on the sidelines[a] during the contest between Chaereas and Dionysius and then carry off the prize himself without a struggle.

On the following day, when discussion began, Chaereas at once asked to go to Miletus and claim his wife from Dionysius: he was sure that Callirhoe would not stay there once she had seen him. "So far as I am concerned," said Mithridates, "you may go. I do not want you to be parted from your wife even for a single day. I wish that you had never left Sicily and that misfortune had not befallen either of you. But since fickle Fortune has

[a] In certain athletic combats the *ephedros*, a third party, stood by and challenged the winner, cf. Aristophanes, *Frogs* 792.

ὑμῖν περιτέθεικε, βουλεύσασθαι δεῖ περὶ τῶν ἑξῆς
φρονιμώτερον· νῦν γὰρ σπεύδεις πάθει μᾶλλον ἢ
3 λογισμῷ, μηδὲν τῶν μελλόντων προορώμενος. μόνος καὶ ξένος εἰς πόλιν ἀπέρχῃ τὴν μεγίστην, καὶ
ἀνδρὸς πλουσίου καὶ πρωτεύοντος ἐν Ἰωνίᾳ θέλεις
ἀποσπάσαι γυναῖκα ἐξαιρέτως αὐτῷ συναφθεῖσαν;
ποίᾳ δυνάμει πεποιθώς; μακρὰν Ἑρμοκράτης σου
καὶ Μιθριδάτης οἱ μόνοι σύμμαχοι, πενθῆσαι δυνά-
4 μενοί σε μᾶλλον ἢ βοηθῆσαι. φοβοῦμαι καὶ τὴν
τύχην τοῦ τόπου. δεινὰ μὲν ἐκεῖ πέπονθας ἤδη·
δόξει δέ σοι τὰ τότε <χρυσός>. φιλανθρωποτέρα
τότε Μίλητος ἦν. ἐδέθης μέν, ἀλλὰ ἔζησας· ἐπρά-
θης, ἀλλὰ ἐμοί. νῦν δέ, ἂν αἴσθηται Διονύσιός
<σε> ἐπιβουλεύοντα τοῖς γάμοις αὐτοῦ, τίς σε θεῶν
δυνήσεται σῶσαι; παραδοθήσῃ γὰρ ἀντεραστῇ
τυράννῳ, καὶ τάχα μὲν οὐδὲ πιστευθήσῃ Χαιρέας
εἶναι, κινδυνεύσεις δὲ μᾶλλον, κἂν ἀληθῶς εἶναί σε
5 νομίσῃ. σὺ μόνος ἀγνοεῖς τὴν φύσιν τοῦ Ἔρωτος,
ὅτι οὗτος ὁ θεὸς ἀπάταις χαίρει καὶ δόλοις; δοκεῖ δέ
μοι πρῶτον ἀποπειραθῆναί σε τῆς γυναικὸς διὰ
γραμμάτων εἰ μέμνηταί σου καὶ Διονύσιον θέλει
καταλιπεῖν ἢ

κείνου βούλεται οἶκον ὀφέλλειν, ὅς κεν ὀπυίῃ.

ἐπιστολὴν γράψον αὐτῇ· λυπηθήτω, χαρήτω, ζητη-
σάτω, καλεσάτω· τῆς δὲ τῶν γραμμάτων διαπομπῆς
ἐγὼ προνοήσομαι. βάδιζε καὶ γράφε."
6   Πείθεται Χαιρέας καὶ μόνος ἐπ' ἐρημίας γενόμε-

involved you in a grim drama, you must carefully consider
the next step. Your present haste springs more from emotion than reason, and you do not foresee what is likely to
happen. Alone and abroad are you planning to go to a
capital city and appropriate the wife of a wealthy man, the
most prominent in Ionia, when she has the closest of ties
with him? What power do you command? Hermocrates
and Mithridates, your only allies, are a long way off, more
able to provide sympathy than help. I also fear the place
is unlucky for you. You have already come to grief there;
but that disaster is going to seem like heaven. Miletus
was kinder to you then. True, you were put in chains, but
your life was spared. You were sold, but to me. And now,
if Dionysius realizes that you are planning to break up his
marriage, no god will be able to save you. You will be
delivering yourself into the hands of a powerful rival.
Perhaps he will not even believe that you are Chaereas;
and if he does, your danger will be all the greater. You
must be strangely ignorant of the ways of Love not to
know that this god delights in deceit and trickery. I think
it is best for you to try out the woman by letter first and
find out if she remembers you and is willing to leave
Dionysius or

wishes to prosper the house of whoever shall wed her.[a]

Write her a letter: make her sad; make her happy; make
her seek you; make her summon you. I will arrange for
the letter to be delivered. Go now and write to her."

Chaereas took his advice, and when he was quite

[a] *Odyssey* 15.21 (Athena to Telemachus).

---

4.4 τὰ τότε φιλανθρωπότερα F, corr. Jackson | add. Blake.

νος ἤθελε γράφειν, ἀλλ' οὐκ ἠδύνατο, δακρύων
ἐπιρρεόντων καὶ τῆς χειρὸς αὐτοῦ τρεμούσης. ἀποκλαύσας δὲ τὰς ἑαυτοῦ συμφορὰς μόλις ἤρξατο τοιαύτης ἐπιστολῆς·

7     Καλλιρόη Χαιρέας· ζῶ, καὶ ζῶ διὰ Μιθριδάτην, τὸν ἐμὸν εὐεργέτην, ἐλπίζω δὲ καὶ
<τὸν> σόν· ἐπράθην γὰρ εἰς Καρίαν ὑπὸ
βαρβάρων, οἵτινες ἐνέπρησαν τριήρη τὴν
καλήν, τὴν στρατηγικήν, τὴν τοῦ σοῦ
πατρός· ἐξέπεμψε δὲ ἐπ' αὐτῆς ἡ πόλις
πρεσβείαν ὑπὲρ σοῦ. τοὺς μὲν οὖν ἄλλους
πολίτας οὐκ οἶδ' ὅ τι γεγόνασιν, ἐμὲ δὲ καὶ
Πολύχαρμον τὸν φίλον ἤδη μέλλοντας
φονεύεσθαι σέσωκεν ἔλεος δεσπότου.

8     Πάντα δὲ Μιθριδάτης εὐεργετήσας τοῦτό
με λελύπηκεν ἀντὶ πάντων, ὅτι μοι τὸν σὸν
γάμον διηγήσατο· θάνατον μὲν γὰρ ἄνθρωπος ὢν προσεδόκων, τὸν δὲ σὸν γάμον οὐκ
ἤλπισα. ἀλλ' ἱκετεύω, μετανόησον. κατα-
σπένδω τούτων μου τῶν γραμμάτων
9     δάκρυα καὶ φιλήματα. ἐγὼ Χαιρέας εἰμὶ ὁ
σὸς ἐκεῖνος ὃν εἶδες παρθένος εἰς Ἀφροδίτης βαδίζουσα, δι' ὃν ἠγρύπνησας. μνή-
σθητι τοῦ θαλάμου καὶ τῆς νυκτὸς τῆς
μυστικῆς, ἐν ᾗ πρῶτον σὺ μὲν ἀνδρός,
ἐγὼ δὲ γυναικὸς πεῖραν ἐλάβομεν. ἀλλὰ
ἐζηλοτύπησα. τοῦτο ἴδιόν ἐστι φιλοῦντος.

alone, he longed to write, but could not because of floods of tears and a trembling hand. But after bewailing his misfortunes, he finally began the following letter:

To Callirhoe from Chaereas: I am alive, and this thanks to Mithridates, my benefactor and, I hope, yours too. I was taken to Caria and sold by orientals who set fire to that glorious vessel, the flagship of your father. On it our city had sent out a mission to recover you. I do not know what has become of the rest of my fellow citizens, but when my friend Polycharmus and I were about to be executed, the mercy of our master saved us.

Yet though Mithridates has rendered me every kindness, he has by telling me of your marriage given me such pain as to cancel all. Death, to be sure, I expected, since I am human, but this marriage of yours I had never imagined. Change your mind, I implore you! I pour my tears and kisses over this letter. I am your own Chaereas, whom once you saw when you went as a maiden to Aphrodite's temple and for whom you spent sleepless nights. Remember our marriage chamber and that mystic night when you first had experience of a husband and I of a wife. You say I was jealous. That is not

---

4.7 add. Naber.
4.9 Ἀφροδίτης Jakob: -την F.

δέδωκά σοι δίκας. ἐπράθην, ἐδούλευσα,

10    ἐδέθην. μή μοι μνησικακήσῃς τοῦ λακτίσματος τοῦ προπετοῦς· κἀγὼ γὰρ ἐπὶ σταυρὸν ἀνέβην διὰ σέ, σοὶ μηδὲν ἐγκαλῶν. εἰ
μὲν οὖν ἔτι μνημονεύσειας, οὐδὲν ἔπαθον· εἰ
δὲ ἄλλο τι φρονεῖς, θανάτου μοι δώσεις
ἀπόφασιν.

5. Ταύτην τὴν ἐπιστολὴν ἔδωκε <Μιθριδάτης>
Ὑγίνῳ τῷ πιστοτάτῳ, ὃν καὶ διοικητὴν εἶχεν ἐν
Καρίᾳ τῆς ὅλης οὐσίας, παραγυμνώσας αὐτῷ καὶ
τὸν ἴδιον ἔρωτα. ἔγραψε δὲ καὶ αὐτὸς πρὸς Καλλιρόην, εὔνοιαν ἐπιδεικνύμενος αὐτῇ καὶ κηδεμονίαν,
ὅτι δι' ἐκείνην Χαιρέαν ἔσωσε, καὶ συμβουλεύων μὴ
ὑβρίσαι τὸν πρῶτον ἄνδρα, ὑπισχνούμενος αὐτὸς
στρατηγήσειν ὅπως ἀλλήλους ἀπολάβωσιν, ἂν καὶ
2    τὴν ἐκείνης προσλάβῃ ψῆφον. συνέπεμψε δὲ τῷ
Ὑγίνῳ τρεῖς ὑπηρέτας καὶ δῶρα πολυτελῆ καὶ χρυσίον συχνόν· εἴρητο δὲ πρὸς τοὺς ἄλλους οἰκέτας
ὅτι πέμπει ταῦτα Διονυσίῳ, πρὸς τὸ ἀνύποπτον.
κελεύει δὲ τὸν Ὑγῖνον, ἐπειδὰν ἐν Πριήνῃ γένηται,
τοὺς μὲν ἄλλους αὐτοῦ καταλιπεῖν, μόνον δὲ αὐτόν,
ὡς Ἴωνα (καὶ γὰρ ἡλλήνιζε τὴν φωνήν) κατάσκοπον
εἰς τὴν Μίλητον πορευθῆναι· εἶτ' ἐπειδὰν μάθῃ πῶς
ἂν χρήσαιτο τοῖς πράγμασι, τότε τοὺς ἐκ Πριήνης
εἰς Μίλητον ἀπαγαγεῖν.

3    Ὁ μὲν οὖν ἀπῄει καὶ ἔπραττε τὰ κεκελευσμένα, ἡ

5.1 add. Beck.

214

unusual in a lover. I have paid the penalty; I was sold, enslaved, chained. Do not hold against me the impulsive kick. Because of you I have ascended the cross and uttered not a word of reproach. If you should still remember me, then my sufferings are nothing; but if you are otherwise disposed, then you sentence me to death.

5. Mithridates gave this letter to Hyginus, his trusted servant, whom he had made the steward of all his property in Caria, and to whom he had also revealed his love. He also wrote to Callirhoe himself, emphasizing his sympathy and concern for her, saying that he had saved Chaereas for her sake. He counseled her not to treat her former husband harshly and promised her that he himself would contrive to restore them to each other, if he had her agreement. He sent three slaves with Hyginus, as well as costly gifts and a large amount of money; but, to disarm suspicion, he told the other servants that he was sending these things to Dionysius. He ordered Hyginus on arrival at Priene[a] to leave the other servants there and, representing himself as an Ionian (since he could speak Greek), to go on by himself to Miletus and spy out the land. Then when he had learned how to manage the situation, he should bring to Miletus those he had left behind in Priene.

So off he set, and was carrying out his orders,[b] but

---

[a] A small town about ten miles north of Miletus. Plepelits makes the interesting suggestion that since Hyginus evidently traveled to Miletus from the east Mithridates' residence may even have been Chariton's home town Aphrodisias.

[b] The phrase occurs in Xenophon, *Cyropaedia* 4.1.3.

Τύχη δὲ οὐχ ὅμοιον τῇ γνώμῃ τὸ τέλος ἐβράβευσεν, ἀλλὰ μειζόνων πραγμάτων ἐκίνησεν ἀρχήν. ἐπειδὴ γὰρ Ὑγῖνος εἰς Μίλητον ἀπηλλάγη, καταλειφθέντες οἱ δοῦλοι τοῦ προεστηκότος ἔρημοι πρὸς ἀσωτίαν

4 ὥρμων, ἔχοντες χρυσίον ἄφθονον. ἐν πόλει δὲ μικρᾷ καὶ περιεργίας Ἑλληνικῆς πλήρει ξενικὴ πολυτέλεια τοὺς πάντων ἐπέστρεψεν ὀφθαλμούς· ἄγνωστοι γὰρ ἄνθρωποι καὶ τρυφῶντες ἔδοξαν αὐτοῖς μάλιστα μὲν λῃσταί, δραπέται δὲ πάντως.

5 ἧκεν οὖν εἰς τὸ πανδοχεῖον ὁ στρατηγὸς καὶ διερευνώμενος εὗρε χρυσίον καὶ κόσμον πολυτελῆ. φώρια δὲ νομίσας ἀνέκρινε τοὺς οἰκέτας τίνες εἶεν καὶ πόθεν ταῦτα. φόβῳ δὲ βασάνων κατεμήνυσαν τὴν ἀλήθειαν, ὅτι Μιθριδάτης ὁ Καρίας ὕπαρχος δῶρα πεπόμφει Διονυσίῳ, καὶ τὰς ἐπιστολὰς ἐπεδείκνυ-

6 σαν. ὁ δὲ στρατηγὸς τὰ μὲν γράμματα οὐκ ἔλυσεν, ἦν γὰρ ἔξωθεν κατασεσημασμένα, δημοσίοις δὲ παραδοὺς ἅπαντα μετὰ τῶν οἰκετῶν ἔπεμψε πρὸς Διονύσιον, εὐεργεσίαν εἰς αὐτὸν κατατίθεσθαι νομίζων.

7 Ἐτύγχανε μὲν οὖν ἑστιῶν τοὺς ἐπιφανεστάτους τῶν πολιτῶν καὶ λαμπρὸν τὸ συμπόσιον ἦν, ἤδη δέ που καὶ αὐλὸς ἐφθέγγετο καὶ [δι'] ᾧ δῆς ἠκούετο μέλος. μεταξὺ δὲ ἐπέδωκέ τις αὐτῷ τὴν ἐπιστολήν·

8 Στρατηγὸς Πριηνέων Βίας εὐεργέτῃ Διονυσίῳ χαίρειν· δῶρα καὶ γράμματα κομιζό-

5.7 del. Cobet.

216

Fortune determined a sequel other than that intended, and started a train of momentous events. When Hyginus had departed for Miletus, the slaves who had been left behind in Priene, no longer under the control of their supervisor, embarked on a licentious life with the plentiful money they had. In a small city imbued with typical Greek curiosity this extravagance on the part of strangers drew all eyes upon them. They were naturally unknown, and by their lavishness suggested to the townsfolk that they were probably robbers and certainly runaway slaves. So the chief magistrate came to their inn and after a search found the money and costly ornament. Suspecting a robbery, he asked the slaves who they were and where these things came from. For fear of torture they told the truth, namely that Mithridates, governor of Caria, had sent these gifts to Dionysius, and they also showed him the letters. However, the magistrate did not open them, since they were sealed, but handing over everything, including the slaves, to public officials sent them on to Dionysius, thinking that he was doing him a good service.

As it happened, Dionysius was entertaining at dinner the foremost of his fellow citizens. The banquet was splendid and had reached the stage where a flute was playing and melodious song heard. At that moment someone handed him this letter:

> Bias,[a] chief magistrate of Priene, to his benefactor, Dionysius—Greetings! Certain gifts and

[a] One of the Seven Wise Men was a Bias of Priene (Strabo 14.1.12).

CHARITON

μενά σοι παρὰ Μιθριδάτου τοῦ Καρίας
ὑπάρχου δοῦλοι πονηροὶ κατέφθειρον, οὓς
ἐγὼ συλλαβὼν ἀνέπεμψα πρὸς σέ.

Ταύτην τὴν ἐπιστολὴν ἐν μέσῳ τῷ συμποσίῳ
Διονύσιος ἀνέγνω, καλλωπιζόμενος ἐπὶ ταῖς βασιλι-
καῖς δωρεαῖς· ἐντεμεῖν δὲ τὰς σφραγῖδας κελεύσας
ἐντυγχάνειν ἐπειρᾶτο τοῖς γράμμασιν. εἶδεν οὖν
"Καλλιρόῃ Χαιρέας· ζῶ."

9          τοῦ δ' αὐτοῦ λύτο γούνατα καὶ φίλον ἦτορ,

εἶτα σκότος τῶν ὀφθαλμῶν αὐτοῦ κατεχύθη. καὶ
μέντοι λιποθυμήσας ὅμως ἐκράτησε τὰ γράμματα,
φοβούμενος ἄλλον αὐτοῖς ἐντυχεῖν. θορύβου δὲ καὶ
συνδρομῆς γενομένης ἐπηγέρθη, καὶ συνεὶς τοῦ
πάθους ἐκέλευσε τοῖς οἰκέταις μετενεγκεῖν αὐτὸν εἰς
ἕτερον οἰκίσκον, ὡς δῆθεν βουλόμενος ἐρημίας
10  μετασχεῖν. τὸ μὲν οὖν συμπόσιον σκυθρωπῶς δι-
ελύθη (φαντασία γὰρ ἀποπληξίας αὐτοὺς ἔσχε),
Διονύσιος δὲ καθ' ἑαυτὸν γενόμενος πολλάκις ἀνεγίνωσκε τὰς ἐπιστολάς. κατελάμβανε δὲ αὐτὸν πάθη
ποικίλα, θυμός, ἀθυμία, φόβος, ἀπιστία. ζῆν μὲν
οὖν Χαιρέαν οὐκ ἐπίστευε (τοῦτο γὰρ οὐδὲ ὅλως
ἤθελε), σκῆψιν δὲ μοιχικὴν ὑπελάμβανε Μιθριδάτου
διαφθεῖραι θέλοντος Καλλιρόην ἐλπίδι Χαιρέου.

6. Μεθ' ἡμέραν οὖν τήρησιν ἐποιεῖτο τῆς γυναικὸς ἀκριβεστέραν, ἵνα μή τις αὐτῇ προσέλθῃ μηδὲ

5.9 ἐρημίας Naber: ἠρεμίας F.

218

letters on their way to you from Mithridates, governor of Caria, were being appropriated by dishonest slaves. I arrested them and am sending them on to you.

Dionysius read the letter without interrupting the banquet, taking pride in the mention of the princely gifts. Giving orders to break the seals he proceeded to read the letters. His eyes fell upon the words: "To Callirhoe from Chaereas: I am alive."

At this his knees collapsed and the heart within him,[a]

and darkness spread over his eyes.[b] But even in his fainting condition he kept hold of the letters for fear that another might find them. During the alarm and bustle he revived and, realizing what had happened, told his servants to carry him into another room since he wanted to be alone. Thus the banquet broke up in some gloom, since they imagined that he had had a fit. When Dionysius was by himself, he read over the letters several times and was seized with a variety of emotions—anger, depression, fear, disbelief. He refused to believe that Chaereas was alive, because that was the last thing he wanted; rather he suspected a plan for adultery on the part of Mithridates who, by raising her hopes for Chaereas, was proposing to seduce Callirhoe.

6. So, when day came, he had his wife more carefully guarded in case anyone visited her or told her any of the

[a] *Iliad* 21.114 (Lycaon). See note on 1.1.14.
[b] Cf. *Iliad* 5.696.

CHARITON

ἀπαγγείλη τι τῶν ἐν Καρίᾳ διηγημάτων· αὐτὸς δὲ
ἄμυναν ἐπενόησε τοιαύτην. ἐπεδήμει κατὰ καιρὸν ὁ
Λυδίας καὶ Ἰωνίας ὕπαρχος Φαρνάκης, ὃς δὴ καὶ
μέγιστος εἶναι δοκεῖ τῶν ὑπὸ βασιλέως καταπεμπο-
μένων ἐπὶ θάλατταν. ἐπὶ τοῦτον ἦλθεν ὁ Διονύσιος,
ἦν γὰρ αὐτῷ φίλος, καὶ ἰδιολογίαν ἠτήσατο. μόνος
<δὲ μετὰ μόνου γενόμενος>, "ἱκετεύω σε" φησίν, "ὦ
δέσποτα, βοήθησον ἐμοί τε καὶ σεαυτῷ. Μιθριδάτης γάρ, ὁ κάκιστος ἀνθρώπων, καὶ σοὶ φθονῶν,
ξένος μοι γενόμενος ἐπιβουλεύει μου τῷ γάμῳ
καὶ πέπομφε γράμματα μοιχικὰ μετὰ χρυσίου πρὸς
2   τὴν γυναῖκα τὴν ἐμήν." ἐπὶ τούτοις ἀνεγίνωσκε τὰς
ἐπιστολὰς καὶ διηγεῖτο τὴν τέχνην. ἀσμένως
ἤκουσε Φαρνάκης τῶν λόγων τὰ μὲν καὶ διὰ Μιθριδάτην (ἐγεγόνει γὰρ αὐτοῖς οὐκ ὀλίγα προσκρούσ-
ματα διὰ τὴν γειτνίασιν), τὸ δὲ πλέον διὰ τὸν
ἔρωτα· καὶ γὰρ αὐτὸς ἐκάετο τῆς Καλλιρόης καὶ δι'
αὐτὴν ἐπεδήμει τὰ πολλὰ Μιλήτῳ, καλῶν ἐπὶ τὰς
3   ἑστιάσεις Διονύσιον μετὰ τῆς γυναικός. ὑπέσχετο
οὖν βοηθήσειν αὐτῷ κατὰ τὸν δυνατὸν τρόπον καὶ
γράφει δι' ἀπορρήτων ἐπιστολήν.

Βασιλεῖ Βασιλέων Ἀρταξέρξῃ σατράπης
Λυδίας καὶ Ἰωνίας Φαρνάκης ἰδίῳ δεσπότῃ
4   χαίρειν. Διονύσιος ὁ Μιλήσιος δοῦλός ἐστι
σὸς ἐκ προγόνων πιστὸς καὶ πρόθυμος εἰς
τὸν σὸν οἶκον. οὗτος ἀπωδύρατο πρός με
ὅτι Μιθριδάτης ὁ Καρίας ὕπαρχος ξένος

news from Caria. For himself he adopted the following method of protecting his interests. Very conveniently Pharnaces, the governor of Lydia and Ionia, was in town, a man ranking as the most important official sent by the king to rule the coastal districts. Dionysius, being a friend, went to him and asked for a private interview. When they were alone together, he said, "Sir, please help me and at the same time help yourself. Mithridates, a scoundrel and jealous of you, is after enjoying my hospitality now trying to break up my marriage, sending my wife lover's letters and money." Here he read the letters aloud and explained the plot. Pharnaces was glad to hear this story, partly on account of Mithridates, since they had had not a few squabbles as neighbors, but still more so because of his own passion. In fact he too was ardently in love with Callirhoe, and she was the reason that he often visited Miletus, inviting Dionysius to banquets together with his wife. So he promised he would help him in every way possible; and he wrote this confidential letter:

> Pharnaces, governor of Lydia and Ionia, to his master Artaxerxes, King of Kings—Greetings! Dionysius of Miletus is your slave, like his ancestors, loyal and zealous to your house. He has complained to me that Mithridates, governor of Caria, after being his guest, is trying to

---

6.1 add. Jackson | ἀνθρώπων Cobet: ἀνδρῶν F | μοι Cobet: ιου F.

6.2 τὰ μὲν Cobet: τάχα μὲν F.

6.3 οὖν Hercher: δ᾽ οὖν F.

αὐτῷ γενόμενος διαφθείρει τὴν γυναῖκα
αὐτοῦ. φέρει δὲ μεγάλην ἀδοξίαν εἰς τὰ σὰ
πράγματα, μᾶλλον δὲ ταραχήν· πᾶσα μὲν
γὰρ παρανομία σατράπου μεμπτή, μάλιστα
δὲ αὕτη. καὶ γὰρ ὁ Διονύσιός ἐστι δυνατώτατος Ἰώνων καὶ τὸ κάλλος τῆς γυναικὸς
περιβόητον, ὥστε τὴν ὕβριν μὴ δύνασθαι
λαθεῖν.

5    Ταύτην τὴν ἐπιστολὴν κομισθεῖσαν ὁ βασιλεὺς
ἀνέγνω τοῖς φίλοις καὶ τί χρὴ πράττειν ἐβουλεύετο
γνῶμαι δὲ ἐρρήθησαν διάφοροι· τοῖς μὲν γὰρ Μιθριδάτῃ φθονοῦσιν ἢ τὴν σατραπείαν αὐτοῦ μνωμέ-
νοις ἐδόκει μὴ περιορᾶν ἐπιβουλὴν εἰς γάμον ἀνδρὸς
ἐνδόξου, τοῖς δὲ ῥᾳθυμοτέροις τὰς φύσεις ἢ τιμῶσι
τὸν Μιθριδάτην (εἶχε δὲ πολλοὺς <τοὺς> προεστη-
κότας) οὐκ ἤρεσκεν ἀνάρπαστον ἐκ διαβολῆς ποιεῖν
6    ἄνδρα δόκιμον. ἀγχωμάλων δὲ τῶν γνωμῶν γενομένων ἐκείνης μὲν τῆς ἡμέρας οὐδὲν ἐπεκύρωσεν
ὁ βασιλεύς, ἀλλ' ὑπερέθετο τὴν σκέψιν· νυκτὸς
δὲ ἐπελθούσης ὑπεδύετο αὐτὸν μισοπονηρία μὲν
διὰ τὸ τῆς βασιλείας εὐπρεπές, εὐλάβεια δὲ περὶ
τοῦ μέλλοντος· ἀρχὴν γὰρ ἔχειν τὸν Μιθριδάτην
καταφρονήσεως.

7    Ὥρμησεν οὖν καλεῖν ἐπὶ τὴν δίκην αὐτόν· ἄλλο
δὲ πάθος παρῄνει μεταπέμπεσθαι καὶ τὴν γυναῖκα
τὴν καλήν· σύμβουλοι μὲν οὖν <οἶνος> καὶ σκότος
ἐν ἐρημίᾳ γενόμενον καὶ τούτου τοῦ μέρους τῆς ἐπι-

seduce his wife. This is causing serious criticism of your rule, and actually unrest. Any wrongdoing by a governor should be censured, and especially this, for Dionysius is the most powerful of the Ionians, and the beauty of his wife is so well known that this outrage cannot be hushed up.

When this letter was delivered, the Great King read it to his friends and discussed what to do. Different opinions were voiced. Those who envied Mithridates or sought his governorship thought that a plot to break up the marriage of so prominent a man should not be overlooked. Those who were more easygoing or who respected Mithridates—and he had many champions— objected to the ruin of a distinguished man on account of a whisper of scandal. Since opinions were evenly balanced, the king made no decision that day, but postponed the inquiry. When night came, he was filled on the one hand with indignation at this wrong because of the threat to his royal authority and on the other with apprehension about the future, since Mithridates might regard this as cause for defiance.

He decided therefore to bring him to trial. Then another feeling prompted him to send for the beautiful wife as well. Wine and darkness had been the king's counselors in his loneliness and reminded him of the

---

6.4 τὴν γυναῖκα αὐτοῦ Jackson: αὐτ. τ. γ. F.
6.5 add. Jackson, Morel (F has a space of 4 letters).
6.7 add. D'Orville | γενόμενον Jackson: -μενοι F.

στολῆς ἀνεμίμνησκον βασιλέα, προσηρέθιζε δὲ κα
φήμη, Καλλιρόην τινὰ καλλίστην ἐπὶ τῆς Ἰωνία
εἶναι· καὶ τοῦτο μόνον ἐμέμφετο βασιλεὺς Φαρνά
κην, ὅτι οὐ προσέγραψεν ἐν τῇ ἐπιστολῇ τοὔνομα
8 τῆς γυναικός. ὅμως δὲ ἐπ' ἀμφιβόλῳ τοῦ τάχα κα
κρείττονα τυγχάνειν τῆς φημιζομένης ἑτέραν ἔδοξ
καλέσαι καὶ τὴν γυναῖκα. γράφει δὲ [καὶ] πρὸ
Φαρνάκην "Διονύσιον, ἐμὸν δοῦλον, Μιλήσιον
πέμψον, <καὶ τὴν γυναῖκα δὲ αὐτοῦ σύμπεμψον>.
πρὸς δὲ Μιθριδάτην "ἧκε ἀπολογησόμενος ὅτι οὐ
ἐπεβούλευσας γάμῳ Διονυσίου."

7. Καταπλαγέντος δὲ τοῦ Μιθριδάτου καὶ ἀπο
ροῦντος τὴν αἰτίαν τῆς διαβολῆς, ὑποστρέψας
Ὑγῖνος ἐδήλωσε τὰ πεπραγμένα περὶ τοὺς οἰκέτας
προδοθεὶς οὖν ὑπὸ τῶν γραμμάτων ἐβουλεύετο μ
βαδίζειν ἄνω, δεδοικὼς τὰς διαβολὰς καὶ τὸν θυμὸ
τὸν βασιλέως, ἀλλὰ Μίλητον μὲν καταλαβὼν κα
Διονύσιον ἀνελὼν τὸν αἴτιον, Καλλιρόην δὲ ἁρπά
2 σας ἀποστῆναι βασιλέως. "τί γὰρ σπεύδεις" φησ
"παραδοῦναι δεσπότου χερσὶ τὴν ἐλευθερίαν; τάχε
δὲ καὶ κρατήσεις ἐνθάδε μένων· μακρὰν γάρ ἐστ
βασιλεὺς καὶ <φαύλους> ἔχει στρατηγούς· εἰ δὲ κα
ἄλλως <σε> ἀθετήσειεν, οὐδὲν δυνήσῃ χεῖρο
παθεῖν. ἐν τοσούτῳ δὲ σὺ μὴ προδῷς δύο τ
κάλλιστα, ἔρωτα καὶ ἀρχήν. ἐντάφιον ἔνδοξον
ἡγεμονία καὶ μετὰ Καλλιρόης θάνατος ἡδύς."

6.7 τοὔνομα D'Orville: ὄνομα F.
6.8 τοῦ D'Orville: τῷ F I del. Hercher I add. Cobet.

part of the letter mentioning her. He was also stimulated by the rumor that a certain Callirhoe was the most beautiful woman in Ionia; this was the only criticism the king had to make of Pharnaces, that in his letter he had not mentioned the wife's name. However, on the possibility that perhaps another woman might prove even more beautiful than the one people were talking of, he decided to summon the wife too. So he wrote to Pharnaces, "Send my slave Dionysius of Miletus and send his wife with him"; and to Mithridates, "Come and defend yourself on the charge of plotting to wreck Dionysius' marriage."

7. Mithridates was panic-stricken, and remained baffled about the source of the accusation until Hyginus returned and reported what had happened to the servants. And so, compromised by the letters, he thought about not going to Babylon, fearing the charges and the king's wrath; instead he would capture Miletus and kill Dionysius, the cause of his troubles, then seize Callirhoe and revolt against the king. "Why be in a hurry to surrender your liberty to the hands of a master?" he said to himself. "Perhaps you can win by staying right here. The king is far away, and his generals are incompetent; even if he should try another way of getting rid of you, you can be no worse off. In this situation do not surrender those two greatest of blessings, love and power. Authority is a glorious memorial,[a] and death would be sweet with Callirhoe!"

[a] Cf. Isocrates 6.45.

---

7.1 τὸν β. Hercher: τοῦ β. F | καταλαβεῖν . . . ἀνελεῖν F, corr. Naber.    7.2 σπεύδεις Hercher: σπεύδω F | ἐνθάδε Cobet: τοι ἅδε F | add. D'Orville | add. Blake.

3    Ἔτι ταῦτα βουλευομένου καὶ παρασκευαζομένου
πρὸς ἀπόστασιν ἧκέ τις ἀγγέλλων ὡς Διονύσιος
ἐξώρμηκε Μιλήτου καὶ Καλλιρόην ἐπάγεται. τοῦτο
λυπηρότερον ἤκουσε Μιθριδάτης ἢ τὸ πρόσταγμα
τὸ καλοῦν ἐπὶ τὴν δίκην· ἀποκλαύσας δὲ τὴν ἑαυτοῦ
συμφορὰν "ἐπὶ ποίαις" φησὶν "ἐλπίσιν ἔτι μένω;
4    προδίδωσί με πανταχόθεν ἡ Τύχη. τάχα γὰρ
ἐλεήσει με βασιλεὺς μηδὲν ἀδικοῦντα· εἰ δὲ ἀποθανεῖν δεήσειε, πάλιν ὄψομαι Καλλιρόην· κἂν [ἐν] τῇ
κρίσει Χαιρέαν ἔξω μετ᾽ ἐμαυτοῦ καὶ Πολύχαρμον
οὐ συνηγόρους μόνον, ἀλλὰ καὶ μάρτυρας." πᾶσαν
οὖν τὴν θεραπείαν κελεύσας συνακολουθεῖν ἐξώρμησε Καρίας, ἀγαθὴν ἔχων ψυχὴν ἐκ τοῦ μηδὲν ἀδικεῖν ἂν δόξαι· ὥστε οὐδὲ μετὰ δακρύων προέπεμψαν
αὐτόν, ἀλλὰ μετὰ θυσιῶν καὶ πομπῆς.

5    Ἕνα μὲν οὖν στόλον τοῦτον ἐκ Καρίας ἔστελλεν
ὁ Ἔρως, ἐξ Ἰωνίας δὲ ἐνδοξότερον ἄλλον· ἐπιφανέ-
στερον γὰρ καὶ βασιλικώτερον ἦν τὸ κάλλος. προ-
έτρεχε γὰρ τῆς γυναικὸς ἡ Φήμη, καταγγέλλουσα
πᾶσιν ἀνθρώποις ὅτι Καλλιρόη παραγίνεται, τὸ
περιβόητον ὄνομα, τὸ μέγα τῆς φύσεως κατόρθωμα,

Ἀρτέμιδι ἰκέλη ἢ χρυσείη Ἀφροδίτη.

ἐνδοξοτέραν αὐτὴν ἐποίει καὶ τὸ τῆς δίκης διήγημα.
6    πόλεις ἀπήντων ὅλαι καὶ τὰς ὁδοὺς ἐστενοχώρουν οἱ
συντρέχοντες ἐπὶ τὴν θέαν· ἐδόκει δὲ [τοῖς] πᾶσι
τῆς φήμης ἡ γυνὴ κρείττων. μακαριζόμενος δὲ
Διονύσιος ἐλυπεῖτο, καὶ δειλότερον αὐτὸν ἐποίει τῆς

While he was still pondering these matters and medi-
tating revolt, a message came that Dionysius had set out
from Miletus and was bringing Callirhoe with him. This
upset Mithridates more than the summons to trial.
Bewailing his lot he said, "What have I to hope for if I
stay? Fortune turns on me in every way. Well, perhaps
the king will take pity on me since I have done no wrong;
and if I should have to die, I shall see Callirhoe once
more. At the trial I shall keep Chaereas and Polycharmus
with me, not only as advocates, but as witnesses, too."
Accordingly he ordered all his household to accompany
him, and set out from Caria in good spirits, confident that
he would not be found guilty of any crime. So they saw
him off, not with tears but with sacrificial rites and a
solemn escort.

In addition to this expedition from Caria Love was dis-
patching another, a more celebrated one, from Ionia, for
its beauty was more striking and majestic. Indeed, the
woman's fame ran on before her, announcing to everybody the arrival of Callirhoe, the renowned Callirhoe, the
masterpiece of Nature,

like unto Artemis or to Aphrodite the golden.[a]

Talk of the trial only increased her celebrity. Whole cities
came out to meet her. The streets were crowded with
those that ran to see her; and all thought the woman more
beautiful than report had made her. The congratulations
heaped upon Dionysius caused him pain, and the extent

[a] *Odyssey* 17.37 = 19.54 (Penelope).

---

7.4 del. D'Orville (dittography).

7.5 χρυσείη Reiske: χρυσῇ F (ἠὲ χρυσῇ Homer and perhaps Chariton). 7.6 del. Blake.

εὐτυχίας τὸ μέγεθος· ἀνὴρ γὰρ πεπαιδευμένος ἐν-
εθυμεῖτο ὅτι φιλόκαινός ἐστιν ὁ Ἔρως· διὰ τοῦτο
καὶ τόξα καὶ πῦρ ποιηταί τε καὶ πλάσται περιτεθεί-
7 κασιν αὐτῷ, τὰ κουφότατα καὶ στῆναι μὴ θέλοντα.
μνήμη δὲ ἐλάμβανεν αὐτὸν παλαιῶν διηγημάτων,
ὅσαι μεταβολαὶ γεγόνασι τῶν καλῶν γυναικῶν.
πάντα οὖν Διονύσιον ἐφόβει, πάντας ἔβλεπεν ὡς
ἀντεραστάς, οὐ τὸν ἀντίδικον μόνον, ἀλλ᾽ αὐτὸν τὸν
δικαστήν, ὥστε καὶ μετενόει προπετέστερον Φαρνάκῃ ταῦτα μηνύσας,

    ἐξὸν καθεύδειν τήν τ᾽ ἐρωμένην ἔχειν·

οὐ γὰρ ὅμοιον ἐν Μιλήτῳ φυλάττειν Καλλιρόην καὶ
8 ἐπὶ τῆς Ἀσίας ὅλης. διεφύλαττε δὲ ὅμως τὸ ἀπόρρητον μέχρι τέλους, καὶ τὴν αἰτίαν οὐχ ὡμολόγει
πρὸς τὴν γυναῖκα, ἀλλ᾽ ἡ πρόφασις ἦν ὅτι βασιλεὺς
αὐτὸν μεταπέμπεται, βουλεύσασθαι θέλων περὶ τῶν
ἐν Ἰωνίᾳ πραγμάτων. ἐλυπεῖτο δὲ Καλλιρόη,
μακρὰν στελλομένη θαλάσσης Ἑλληνικῆς· ἕως γὰρ
τοὺς Μιλησίων λιμένας ἑώρα, Συρακούσας ἐγγὺς
ἐδόκει τυγχάνειν· μέγα δὲ εἶχε παραμύθιον καὶ τὸν
Χαιρέου τάφον ἐκεῖ.

    7.6 ἀνὴρ γὰρ F (according to Guida; conjectured by Jack-
son).
    7.8 ἐγγὺς ἐδόκει Jackson: ἐδ. ἐγγ. F.

of his good fortune made him all the more fearful, for as
an educated man he was aware that Love is fickle. That is
why poets and sculptors equip him with bow and flame, of
all things the most light and unstable. He was visited by
the remembrance of ancient stories which told of the
inconstant ways of beautiful women. In fact, everything
frightened Dionysius. He looked on all men as his rivals,
not merely his adversary in the trial, but the very judge,
so that he regretted his haste in telling Pharnaces of the
affair,

when he could be in bed, embracing his beloved.[a]

It was one thing to keep an eye on Callirhoe in Miletus,
and quite another to do so throughout all Asia. However,
he kept his secret to the end and did not confide to his
wife the true reason for their journey, but pretended that
the king had summoned him for a consultation about
affairs in Ionia. Callirhoe was unhappy to travel so far
from the Mediterranean; so long as she could see the harbors of Miletus she considered Syracuse near. Moreover
she derived much comfort from Chaereas' tomb there.

[a] Actually "when I . . . my beloved," from Thrasonides' opening speech in Menander's *Misumenus* (A9 Sandbach).

# E

1. Ὡς μὲν ἐγαμήθη Καλλιρόη Χαιρέᾳ, καλλίστη γυναικῶν ἀνδρῶν καλλίστῳ, πολιτευσαμένης Ἀφροδίτης τὸν γάμον, καὶ ὡς δι᾽ ἐρωτικὴν ζηλοτυπίαν Χαιρέου πλήξαντος αὐτὴν ἔδοξε τεθνάναι, ταφεῖσαν δὲ πολυτελῶς εἶτα ἀνανήψασαν ἐν τῷ τάφῳ τυμβωρύχοι νυκτὸς ἐξήγαγον ἐκ Σικελίας, πλεύσαντες δὲ εἰς Ἰωνίαν ἐπώλησαν Διονυσίῳ, καὶ τὸν ἔρωτα τὸν Διονυσίου καὶ τὴν Καλλιρόης πρὸς Χαιρέαν πίστιν καὶ τὴν ἀνάγκην τοῦ γάμου διὰ τὴν γαστέρα καὶ τὴν Θήρωνος ὁμολογίαν καὶ Χαιρέου πλοῦν ἐπὶ ζήτησιν τῆς γυναικὸς ἅλωσίν τε αὐτοῦ καὶ πρᾶσιν
2 εἰς Καρίαν μετὰ Πολυχάρμου τοῦ φίλου, καὶ ὡς Μιθριδάτης ἐγνώρισε Χαιρέαν μέλλοντα ἀποθνήσκειν καὶ ὡς ἔσπευδεν ἀλλήλοις ἀποδοῦναι τοὺς ἐρῶντας, φωράσας δὲ τοῦτο Διονύσιος ἐξ ἐπιστολῶν διέβαλεν αὐτὸν πρὸς Φαρνάκην, ἐκεῖνος δὲ πρὸς βασιλέα, βασιλεὺς δὲ ἀμφοτέρους ἐκάλεσεν ἐπὶ τὴν κρίσιν —ταῦτα ἐν τῷ πρόσθεν λόγῳ δεδήλωται· τὰ δὲ ἑξῆς νῦν διηγήσομαι.

1.1 ἀνδρῶν Naber: ἀνδρὶ F.

# BOOK 5

1. How Callirhoe, the most beautiful of women, married Chaereas, the handsomest of men, through the management of Aphrodite; how, when Chaereas struck her in a lover's fit of jealousy, she apparently died and then, after a sumptuous funeral, returned to consciousness in the tomb; how next grave robbers carried her away from Sicily by night and, sailing to Ionia, sold her to Dionysius; after that, the love of Dionysius and the fidelity of Callirhoe to Chaereas; the compulsion to marry because of her pregnancy; the confession of Theron and the voyage of Chaereas in search of his wife; how he was captured, sold, and taken to Caria with his friend Polycharmus; how Mithridates identified Chaereas on the point of death and endeavored to restore the lovers to each other; how Dionysius, discovering this from letters, denounced him to Pharnaces, and he to the king; and how the king summoned them both to trial: all this has been set forth in the preceding account.[a] I shall now relate what happened next.

[a] This recapitulation, modeled on the summaries introducing Books 2, 3, 4, 5, and 7 of Xenophon's *Anabasis*, has suggested that *Callirhoe* was conceived as a publication in two rolls, Book 5 beginning the second. See also 8.1.1.

3　　Καλλιρόη μὲν γὰρ μέχρι Συρίας καὶ Κιλικίας
κούφως ἔφερε τὴν ἀποδημίαν· καὶ γὰρ Ἑλλάδος
ἤκουε φωνῆς καὶ θάλασσαν ἔβλεπε τὴν ἄγουσαν εἰς
Συρακούσας· ὡς δ' ἧκεν ἐπὶ ποταμὸν Εὐφράτην,
μεθ' ὃν ἤπειρός ἐστι μεγάλη, ἀφετήριον εἰς τὴν
βασιλέως γῆν τὴν πολλήν, τότε ἤδη πόθος αὐτὴν
ὑπεδύετο πατρίδος τε καὶ συγγενῶν <καὶ> ἀπόγνω-
4　σις τῆς εἰς τοὔμπαλιν ὑποστροφῆς. στᾶσα δὲ ἐπὶ
τῆς ἠϊόνος καὶ πάντας ἀναχωρῆσαι κελεύσασα
πλὴν Πλαγγόνος τῆς μόνης πιστῆς, τοιούτων
ἤρξατο λόγων· "Τύχη βάσκανε καὶ μιᾶς γυναικὸς
προσφιλονεικοῦσα πολέμῳ, σύ με κατέκλεισας ἐν
τάφῳ ζῶσαν, κἀκεῖθεν ἐξήγαγες οὐ δι' ἔλεον, ἀλλ'
5　ἵνα λῃσταῖς με παραδῷς. ἐμερίσαντό μου τὴν
φυγὴν θάλασσα καὶ Θήρων· ἡ Ἑρμοκράτους
θυγάτηρ ἐπράθην καί, τὸ τῆς ἀφιλίας μοι βαρύτερον, ἐφιλήθην, ἵνα ζῶντος Χαιρέου ἄλλῳ γαμηθῶ.
σὺ δὲ καὶ τούτων ἤδη μοι φθονεῖς· οὐκέτι γὰρ εἰς
Ἰωνίαν με φυγαδεύεις. ξένην μέν, πλὴν Ἑλληνικὴν
ἐδίδους γῆν, ὅπου μεγάλην εἶχον παραμυθίαν, ὅτι
θαλάσσῃ παρακάθημαι· νῦν δὲ ἔξω με τοῦ συνήθους
ῥίπτεις ἀέρος καὶ τῆς πατρίδος ὅλῳ διορίζομαι
6　κόσμῳ. Μίλητον ἀφείλω μου πάλιν, ὡς πρότερον
Συρακούσας· ὑπὲρ τὸν Εὐφράτην ἀπάγομαι καὶ
βαρβάροις ἐγκλείομαι μυχοῖς ἢ νησιῶτις, ὅπου
μηκέτι θάλασσα. ποίαν ἔτ' ἐλπίσω ναῦν ἐκ Σικελίας καταπλέουσαν; ἀποσπῶμαι καὶ τοῦ σοῦ τάφου,

1.3 add. Blake.　　1.5 ἀφιλίας Abresch: φιλίας F.

232

As far as Syria and Cilicia[a] Callirhoe readily put up
with the journey, for she still heard Greek spoken and
could look upon the sea which led to Syracuse. But when
she arrived at the River Euphrates, the starting point of
the Great King's empire, beyond which lies the vast continent, then she was filled with longing for her home and
family and despaired of ever returning again. So standing
on the river bank and telling all to withdraw save Plangon,
her one loyal friend, she began to speak as follows: "Envious Fortune, happy to persecute a lone female, you
immured me alive in a tomb, releasing me not from pity,
but to place me in the clutches of pirates. Theron and the
sea between them sent me into exile, and I, the daughter
of Hermocrates, was sold into slavery! Then, a thing even
harder to bear than being unloved, I aroused a man's love
and so, while Chaereas was still alive, became the wife of
another. But even this you now grudge me, for you no
longer banish me to Ionia. There the land which you gave
me, though foreign, was still Greek, and I had the great
consolation of living by the sea. But now you cast me
forth from familiar surroundings and I am separated from
my home by a whole world. This time you take Miletus
from me, as before you took Syracuse. Carried off
beyond the Euphrates, I, an islander born, am enclosed in
the depths of a barbarian continent where no sea exists.
What ship searching for me from Sicily can I now expect?
I am torn away even from your tomb, Chaereas. Who is

[a] The order is misleading, since she had to pass through Cilicia before reaching Syria.

233

7 Χαιρέα. τίς ἐπενέγκῃ σοι χοάς, δαῖμον ἀγαθέ;
Βάκτρα μοι καὶ Σοῦσα λοιπὸν οἶκος καὶ τάφος.
ἅπαξ, Εὐφρᾶτα, μέλλω σε διαβαίνειν· φοβοῦμαι
γὰρ οὐχ οὕτως τὸ μῆκος τῆς ἀποδημίας ὡς μὴ δόξω
κἀκεῖ καλή τινι." ταῦτα ἅμα λέγουσα τὴν γῆν κατεφίλησεν, εἶτα ἐπιβᾶσα τῆς πορθμίδος διεπέρασεν.

8 Ἦν μὲν οὖν καὶ Διονυσίῳ χορηγία πολλή· πλου-
σιώτατα γὰρ ἐπεδείκνυτο τῇ γυναικὶ τὴν παρα-
σκευήν· βασιλικωτέραν δὲ τὴν ὁδοιπορίαν αὐτοῖς
παρεσκεύασεν ἡ τῶν ἐπιχωρίων φιλοφρόνησις· δῆμος παρέπεμπεν εἰς δῆμον, καὶ σατράπης παρεδίδου
τῷ μεθ' αὑτόν, πάντας γὰρ ἐδημαγώγει τὸ κάλλος.
καὶ ἄλλη δέ τις ἐλπὶς ἔθαλπε τοὺς βαρβάρους, ὅτι
ἥδε ἡ γυνὴ μέγα δυνήσεται, καὶ διὰ τοῦτο ἕκαστος
ἔσπευδε ξένια διδόναι ἢ πάντως τινὰ χάριν εἰς
αὐτὴν ἔχειν ἀποκειμένην.

2. Καὶ οἱ μὲν ἦσαν ἐν τούτοις· ὁ δὲ Μιθριδάτης
δι' Ἀρμενίας ἐποιεῖτο τὴν πορείαν σφοδροτέραν,
μάλιστα μὲν δεδοικὼς μὴ καὶ τοῦτο ἐπαίτιον αὐτῷ
γένηται πρὸς βασιλέως, ὅτι κατ' ἴχνος ἐπηκολούθει
τῇ γυναικί, ἅμα δὲ καὶ σπεύδων προεπιδημῆσαι καὶ
2 συγκροτῆσαι τὰ πρὸς τὴν δίκην. ἀφικόμενος οὖν
εἰς Βαβυλῶνα (βασιλεὺς γὰρ αὐτόθι διέτριβεν)
ἐκείνην μὲν τὴν ἡμέραν ἡσύχασε παρ' ἑαυτῷ·
πάντες γὰρ οἱ σατράπαι σταθμοὺς ἔχουσιν ἀποδε-

1.8 ξένια D'Orville: ξενίας F.
2.1 ἐπαίτιον Cobet: αἴτιον F.

234

to pour libations for you, dear soul?[a] Henceforth Bactra and Susa[b] are to be my home, and my tomb. I shall cross your stream but once, Euphrates! I fear not so much the length of the journey, but rather that there too someone will think me beautiful." With these words she kissed the ground and then, boarding the ferry, crossed to the other side.

Now Dionysius was accompanied by a large retinue, for he wanted to impress his wife with the great wealth at his disposal. However, their journey was made still more princely by the welcome given them by the local people. One community would escort them to the next, and each governor would entrust them to his neighbor: everybody succumbed to her beauty. But something else encouraged the orientals, the presumption that this woman would acquire great power; as a result each eagerly offered her gifts or tried in some way to gain her goodwill for the future.

2. So things stood with them. Mithridates, on the other hand, took the more arduous route through Armenia, chiefly because he feared that the king might also criticize him if he followed in Callirhoe's footsteps; but at the same time he was eager to get there first and prepare for the trial. On arrival in Babylon (that is where the king was staying) he spent the day quietly in his own quarters, for all the governors have lodgings assigned to them

[a] Derived from δαίμονες ἀγαθοί, a rendering of Latin *di manes* (never in the singular) 'departed spirit.'

[b] Important cities of the Persian Empire, Susa (a royal residence) over 200 miles east of Babylon, Bactra (in modern Afghanistan) well over 1000 miles northeast of Susa.

CHARITON

δειγμένους· τῆς δ' ὑστεραίας ἐπὶ θύρας ἐλθὼν τὰς
βασιλέως, ἠσπάσατο μὲν Περσῶν τοὺς ὁμοτίμους,
Ἀρταξάτην δὲ τὸν εὐνοῦχον ὃς μέγιστος ἦν παρὰ
βασιλεῖ καὶ δυνατώτατος πρῶτον μὲν δώροις ἐτίμη-
σεν, εἶτα "ἀπάγγειλον" εἶπε "βασιλεῖ· Μιθριδάτης
ὁ σὸς δοῦλος πάρεστιν ἀπολύσασθαι διαβολὴν Ἕλ-
3  ληνος ἀνδρὸς καὶ προσκυνῆσαι.'" μετ' οὐ πολὺ δὲ
ἐξελθὼν ὁ εὐνοῦχος ἀπεκρίνατο ὅτι "ἔστι βασιλεῖ
βουλομένῳ Μιθριδάτην μηδὲν ἀδικεῖν· κρίνῃ δὲ
ἐπειδὰν καὶ Διονύσιος παραγένηται." προσκυνήσας
οὖν ὁ Μιθριδάτης ἀπηλλάττετο, μόνος δὲ γενόμενος
ἐκάλεσε Χαιρέαν καὶ ἔφη πρὸς αὐτὸν "ἐγὼ κρίνομαι
καὶ ἀποδοῦναί σοι θελήσας Καλλιρόην ἐγκαλοῦμαι·
τὴν γὰρ σὴν ἐπιστολήν, ἣν ἔγραψας πρὸς τὴν
γυναῖκα, Διονύσιος ἐμέ φησι γεγραφέναι καὶ μοιχείας ἀπόδειξιν ἔχειν ὑπολαμβάνει· πέπεισται γὰρ
σὲ τεθνάναι, καὶ πεπείσθω μέχρι τῆς δίκης, ἵνα
4  αἰφνίδιον ὀφθῇς. ταύτην ἀπαιτῶ σε τῆς εὐεργεσίας
τὴν ἀνταμοιβήν· ἀπόκρυψον σεαυτόν· μήτε ἰδεῖν
Καλλιρόην μήτ' ἐξετάσαι τι περὶ αὐτῆς καρτέρησον."

Ἄκων μέν, ἀλλὰ ἐπείθετο Χαιρέας καὶ λανθάνειν
μὲν ἐπειρᾶτο, ἐλείβετο δὲ αὐτοῦ τὰ δάκρυα κατὰ τῶν
παρειῶν· εἰπὼν δὲ "ποιήσω, δέσποτα, ἃ προστάτ-
τεις," ἀπῆλθεν εἰς τὸ δωμάτιον ἐν ᾧ κατήγετο μετὰ
Πολυχάρμου τοῦ φίλου, καὶ ῥίψας ἑαυτὸν εἰς τὸ
ἔδαφος, περιρρηξάμενος τὸν χιτῶνα,

there, but the next day he presented himself in the king's antechambers and greeted the Persian peers.[a] Then after first presenting gifts to Artaxates, the most important and influential of the king's eunuchs, he said, "Announce my presence to the king and say, 'Your slave Mithridates is here to rebut a slanderous charge made by a Greek, and to pay homage.'" The eunuch shortly returned and replied, "The king hopes that Mithridates is guiltless. He will deliver judgment when Dionysius is also present." Mithridates knelt in homage and left. When he was by himself, he called Chaereas and said to him, "I have been put on trial: for offering to restore Callirhoe to you I am charged with a crime. Dionysius claims that the letter which you wrote to your wife was written by me and thinks he has proof of adultery. He is convinced that you are dead. Let him remain so convinced until the trial, so that you can make a sudden appearance. What I ask in return for my kindness to you is this: stay out of sight, and force yourself not to see Callirhoe or make any inquiry about her."

Much against his will Chaereas consented. He tried to hide his feelings, but the tears ran down his cheeks. However, he said, "Sir, I shall do your bidding," and went off to the room which he was sharing with his friend Polycharmus. There, throwing himself on the floor and tearing his clothes,

[a] A group of nobles close to the king, cf. Xenophon, *Cyropaedia* 2.1.9.

---

2.3 δὲ ἐξελθὼν Reiske: διεξελθὼν F | κρίνομαι Hirschig: καίομαι F.

ἀμφοτέραις χερσὶ περιελὼν κόνιν αἰθαλόεσσαν
χεύατο κὰκ κεφαλῆς, χαρίεν δ' ᾔσχυνε πρόσωπον.

εἶτα ἔλεγε κλάων "ἐγγύς ἐσμεν, ὦ Καλλιρόη, καὶ
5 οὐχ ὁρῶμεν ἀλλήλους. σὺ μὲν οὖν οὐδὲν ἀδικεῖς· οὐ
γὰρ οἶδας ὅτι Χαιρέας ζῇ· πάντων δὲ ἀσεβέστατος
ἐγώ, μὴ βλέπειν σε κεκελευσμένος, καὶ ὁ δειλὸς καὶ
φιλόζωος μέχρι τοσούτου φέρω τυραννούμενος. σοὶ
δὲ εἴ τις τοῦτο προσέταξεν, οὐκ ἂν ἔζησας."

6 Ἐκεῖνον μὲν οὖν παρεμυθεῖτο Πολύχαρμος, ἤδη
δὲ καὶ Διονύσιος πλησίον ἐγένετο Βαβυλῶνος καὶ ἡ
Φήμη προκατελάμβανε τὴν πόλιν, ἀπαγγέλλουσα
πᾶσιν ὅτι παραγίνεται γυνή, [κάλλος οὐκ ἀνθρώπινον ἀλλά τι θεῖον] ὁποίαν ἐπὶ γῆς ἄλλην ἥλιος οὐχ
ὁρᾷ· φύσει δέ ἐστι τὸ βάρβαρον γυναιμανές, ὥστε
πᾶσα οἰκία καὶ πᾶς στενωπὸς ἐπεπλήρωτο τῆς
δόξης· ἀνέβαινε δὲ ἡ φήμη μέχρις αὐτοῦ τοῦ βασιλέως, ὥστε καὶ ἤρετο Ἀρταξάτην τὸν εὐνοῦχον εἰ
7 πάρεστιν ἡ Μιλησία. Διονύσιον δὲ καὶ πάλαι μὲν
ἐλύπει τὸ περιβόητον τῆς γυναικὸς (οὐ γὰρ εἶχεν
ἀσφάλειαν), ἐπεὶ δὲ εἰς Βαβυλῶνα ἔμελλεν εἰσιέναι,
τότ' ἤδη καὶ μᾶλλον ἐνεπίμπρατο, στενάξας δὲ ἔφη
πρὸς ἑαυτὸν "οὐκέτι ταῦτα Μίλητός ἐστι, Διονύσιε,
ἡ σὴ πόλις· κἀκεῖ δὲ τοὺς ἐπιβουλεύοντας ἐφυλάτ-
8 του. τολμηρὲ καὶ τοῦ μέλλοντος ἀπροόρατε, εἰς

2.4 ἀμφοτέρῃσι δὲ χερσὶν ἑλὼν Homer and perhaps
Chariton (cf. 1.4.6).

238

with both hands taking sooty dust he poured it
down over his head and defiled his beautiful features.[a]

Then he sobbed, "Callirhoe, we are so close, and yet we
are not to see each other! But you have done nothing
wrong, for you do not know that Chaereas is alive.
Rather, I am the wickedest man in the world. I was
ordered not to set eyes on you and, coward and intent on
life as I am, I submit to such tyranny! If someone had told
you to do this, you would have refused to live."

While Polycharmus was trying to comfort Chaereas,
Dionysius in turn reached the outskirts of Babylon.
Rumor reached the city first, announcing to all the coming of a woman whose peer was not to be found under the
sun. Now, orientals are by nature intensely fond of
women, so that every house and every street was full of
talk about her. News about her reached the king himself
and he even asked the eunuch Artaxates whether the
Milesian woman had yet arrived. His wife's celebrity had
long troubled Dionysius, causing him to feel uneasy; but
on the point of entering Babylon he became still more
agitated. With a sigh he said to himself, "Dionysius, this
is no longer your own city, Miletus, though there too you
had to guard against schemers. It was risky and short-
sighted to bring Callirhoe to Babylon, where there are so

[a] *Iliad* 18.23f (Achilles learning of Patroclus' death). See
1.4.6.

---

2.6 del. Cobet (interpolated from 1.1.2) | ἀνέβαινε Cobet:
διέβαινε F.

CHARITON

Βαβυλῶνα Καλλιρόην ἄγεις, ὅπου Μιθριδάται
τοσοῦτοι; Μενέλαος ἐν τῇ σώφρονι Σπάρτῃ τὴν
Ἑλένην οὐκ ἐτήρησεν, ἀλλὰ παρευδοκίμησε καὶ
βασιλέα βάρβαρος ποιμήν· πολλοὶ Πάριδες ἐν Πέρσαις. οὐχ ὁρᾷς τοῦ κινδύνου τὰ προοίμια; πόλεις
9 ἡμῖν ἀπαντῶσι καὶ θεραπεύουσι σατράπαι. σοβα-
ρωτέρα γέγονεν ἤδη, καὶ οὔπω βασιλεὺς ἑώρακεν
αὐτήν. μία τοίνυν σωτηρίας ἐλπὶς διακλέψαι τὴν
γυναῖκα· φυλαχθήσεται γάρ, ἂν δυνηθῇ λαθεῖν.᾽
ταῦτα λογισάμενος ἵππου μὲν ἐπέβη, τὴν δὲ Καλλιρόην εἴασεν ἐπὶ τῆς ἀρμαμάξης καὶ συνεκάλυψε τὴν
σκηνήν. τάχα δ᾽ ἂν καὶ προεχώρησεν ὅπερ ἤθελεν,
εἰ μὴ συνέβη τι τοιοῦτον.

3. Ἦκον παρὰ Στάτειραν τὴν γυναῖκα τὴν βασιλέως τῶν ἐνδοξοτάτων Περσῶν αἱ γυναῖκες καί τις
εἶπεν ἐξ αὐτῶν "ὦ δέσποινα, γύναιον Ἑλληνικὸν
ἐπιστρατεύεται ταῖς ἡμετέραις οἰκείαις, ἃς καὶ
πάλαι μὲν πάντες ἐθαύμαζον ἐπὶ τῷ κάλλει, κινδυ-
νεύει δὲ ἐφ᾽ ἡμῶν ἡ δόξα τῶν Περσίδων γυναικῶν
καταλυθῆναι. φέρ᾽ οὖν σκεψώμεθα πῶς μὴ παρ-
ευδοκιμηθῶμεν ὑπὸ τῆς ξένης."

2 Ἐγέλασεν ἡ βασιλὶς ἀπιστοῦσα τῇ φήμῃ, ἅμα
δὲ εἶπεν "ἀλαζόνες εἰσὶν Ἕλληνες καὶ πτωχοὶ καὶ
διὰ τοῦτο καὶ τὰ μικρὰ θαυμάζουσι μεγάλως. οὕτως
φημίζουσι Καλλιρόην καλὴν ὡς καὶ Διονύσιον
πλούσιον. μία τοίνυν ἐξ ἡμῶν, ἐπειδὰν εἰσίῃ
φανήτω μετ᾽ αὐτῆς, ἵνα ἀποσβέσῃ τὴν πενιχρὰν τε
3 καὶ δούλην." προσεκύνησαν πᾶσαι τὴν βασιλίδα

240

many men like Mithridates! Menelaus could not keep
Helen safe in respectable Sparta, but an oriental shepherd boy outwitted him, king though he was. There is
many a man like Paris in Persia. Can you not recognize
the prelude to danger? Cities welcome us and governors
give us hospitality. She has already begun to put on airs,
and the king has not yet seen her. My only hope of safety
lies in keeping my wife hidden. She will be secure if she
can stay out of sight." Reasoning thus, he mounted his
horse, but left Callirhoe in the carriage and closed the
curtains.[a] Perhaps his wishes might have been realized,
had it not been for the following incident.

3. The wives of the foremost Persians went to the
king's consort, Statira, and one of them said, "Madam, a
Greek female is waging a campaign against our women,
whom the world has long admired for their beauty; there
is a danger that in our time the renown of Persian women
will be ended. Let us consider how we can avoid humiliation by the foreigner."

Not believing the rumor the queen laughed and said,
"The Greeks are braggarts and beggars, which is why they
so much admire even small things. They make out that
Callirhoe is beautiful just as they do that Dionysius is
wealthy. So when she comes, let one of us appear beside
her and eclipse this poor slave." All the women knelt in

[a] Cf. Xenophon, *Cyropaedia* 6.4.11 (and on 5.3.10 below).

2.8 τοῦ κινδύνου Cobet: τοὺς κινδύνους οὐ F.
3.1 οἰκείαις ἃς Blake: οἰκίαις ὃ F.

CHARITON

καὶ τῆς γνώμης ἀπεθαύμασαν καὶ τὸ μὲν πρῶτον ὡς
ἐξ ἑνὸς στόματος ἀνεβόησαν "εἴθε δυνατὸν ἦν
ὀφθῆναι σέ, δέσποινα·" εἶτα διεχέθησαν αἱ γνῶμαι
4 καὶ τὰς ἐνδοξοτάτας ὠνόμαζον ἐπὶ κάλλει. χειροτο-
νία δὲ ἦν ὡς ἐν θεάτρῳ, καὶ προεκρίθη Ῥοδογούνη,
θυγάτηρ μὲν Ζωπύρου, γυνὴ δὲ Μεγαβύζου, μέγα
τι χρῆμα <κάλλους> καὶ περιβόητον· οἷον τῆς
Ἰωνίας Καλλιρόη, τοιοῦτο τῆς Ἀσίας ἡ Ῥοδογούνη.
λαβοῦσαι δὲ αὐτὴν αἱ γυναῖκες ἐκόσμουν, ἑκάστη τι
παρ' αὑτῆς συνεισφέρουσα εἰς κόσμον· ἡ δὲ βασιλὶς ἔδωκε περιβραχιόνια καὶ ὅρμον.
5    Ἐπεὶ τοίνυν εἰς τὸν ἀγῶνα καλῶς αὐτὴν κατ-
εσκεύασαν, ὡς δῆθεν εἰς ἀπάντησιν Καλλιρόης
παρεγίνετο· καὶ γὰρ εἶχε πρόφασιν οἰκείαν, ἐπειδήπερ ἦν ἀδελφὴ Φαρνάκου τοῦ γράψαντος βασιλεῖ
6 περὶ Διονυσίου. ἐξεχεῖτο δὲ πᾶσα Βαβυλὼν ἐπὶ τὴν
θέαν καὶ τὸ πλῆθος ἐστενοχώρει τὰς πύλας. ἐν δὲ
τῷ περιφανεστάτῳ παραπεμπομένη βασιλικῶς ἡ
Ῥοδογούνη περιέμενεν· εἱστήκει δὲ ἁβρὰ καὶ θρυπτ-
ομένη καὶ ὡς προκαλουμένη, πάντες δὲ εἰς αὐτὴν
ἀπέβλεπον καὶ διελάλουν πρὸς ἀλλήλους "νενικήκα-
7 μεν· ἡ Περσὶς ἀποσβέσει τὴν ξένην. εἰ δύναται,
συγκριθήτω· μαθέτωσαν Ἕλληνες ὅτι εἰσὶν ἀλαζόνες." ἐν τούτῳ δὲ ἐπῆλθεν ὁ Διονύσιος καὶ μηνυθέν-
τος αὐτῷ τὴν Φαρνάκου συγγενίδα παρεῖναι,
καταπηδήσας ἀπὸ τοῦ ἵππου προσῆλθεν αὐτῇ φιλο-

3.4 add. Hercher.

242

homage to the queen and expressed their admiration of her plan, and at first with one accord they cried, "Madam, if only you could be seen yourself!" After that their opinions differed and they proceeded to name the women considered to be the most beautiful. A vote was taken as in the theater, and their first choice was Rhodogune, the daughter of Zopyrus and the wife of Megabyzus, a woman famed for her great beauty. What Callirhoe was to Ionia, Rhodogune was to Asia. The women took her and dressed her, each one contributing something of her own to her adornment. The queen, too, gave her bracelets and a necklace.

So when they had carefully groomed her for the contest, she appeared on the pretext of welcoming Callirhoe. In fact, she had a suitable excuse, since she was the sister of the Pharnaces who had written to the king about Dionysius. All Babylon poured out to the spectacle and the crowd blocked the gates. With a royal escort Rhodogune waited in the most conspicuous position. There she stood, lovely and confident in her loveliness as if challenging competition, and as they looked at her all murmured to each other, "We have won! The Persian will eclipse the foreign woman. Let her stand comparison if she can. The Greeks must realize that they are only braggarts." In the meantime Dionysius had arrived, and when he was informed that the kinswoman of Pharnaces was there, he dismounted and approached her with a friendly

---

3.5 ἐπειδήπερ Jackson: ἐπειδὴ F (cf. 7.5.6).
3.7 ἀπὸ Cobet: ἐκ F.

CHARITON

8 φρονούμενος. ἐκείνη δὲ ὑπερυθριῶσα "θέλω" φησὶ
"τὴν ἀδελφὴν ἀσπάσασθαι," καὶ ἅμα τῇ ἁρμαμάξῃ
προσῆλθεν. οὔκουν δυνατὸν ἦν αὐτὴν ἔτι μένειν
κεκαλυμμένην, ἀλλὰ Διονύσιος μὲν ἄκων καὶ στένων
ὑπ' αἰδοῦς τὴν Καλλιρόην προελθεῖν ἠξίωσεν· ἅμα
δὲ πάντες οὐ μόνον τοὺς ὀφθαλμοὺς ἀλλὰ καὶ τὰς
ψυχὰς ἐξέτειναν καὶ μικροῦ δεῖν ἐπ' ἀλλήλους κατέπεσον, ἄλλος πρὸ ἄλλου θέλων ἰδεῖν καὶ ὡς δυνα-
9 τὸν ἐγγυτάτω γενέσθαι. ἐξέλαμψε δὲ τὸ Καλλιρόης
πρόσωπον, καὶ μαρμαρυγὴ κατέσχε τὰς ἁπάντων
ὄψεις, ὥσπερ ἐν νυκτὶ βαθείᾳ πολλοῦ φωτὸς αἰφνίδιον φανέντος· ἐκπλαγέντες δὲ οἱ βάρβαροι προσεκύνησαν καὶ οὐδεὶς ἐδόκει Ῥοδογούνην παρεῖναι.
συνῆκε δὲ καὶ ἡ Ῥοδογούνη τῆς ἥττης, καὶ μήτε
ἀπελθεῖν δυναμένη μήτε βλέπεσθαι θέλουσα ὑπέδυ
τὴν σκηνὴν μετὰ τῆς Καλλιρόης, παραδοῦσα αὐτὴν
10 τῷ κρείττονι φέρειν. ἡ μὲν <οὖν> ἁρμάμαξα προῄει
συγκεκαλυμμένη, οἱ δὲ ἄνθρωποι, μηκέτι ἔχοντες
Καλλιρόην ὁρᾶν, κατεφίλουν τὸν δίφρον.

Βασιλεὺς δὲ ὡς ἤκουσεν ἀφῖχθαι Διονύσιον,
ἐκέλευσεν Ἀρταξάτην τὸν εὐνοῦχον ἀπαγγεῖλαι
πρὸς αὐτὸν "ἐχρῆν μέν σε κατηγοροῦντα ἀνδρὸς
ἀρχὴν μεγάλην πεπιστευμένου μὴ βραδύνειν·
ἀφίημι δέ σοι τὴν αἰτίαν, ὅτι μετὰ γυναικὸς ἐβάδι-
11 ζες. ἐγὼ δὲ νῦν μὲν ἑορτὴν ἄγω καὶ πρὸς ταῖς θυσίαις εἰμί· τριακοστῇ δὲ ὕστερον ἡμέρᾳ τῆς δίκης
ἀκροάσομαι." προσκυνήσας ὁ Διονύσιος ἀπηλλάγη.

greeting. With a blush she said, "I should like to welcome my sister," and at the same time she came up to the carriage. As a result it was no longer possible for Callirhoe to remain concealed, and Dionysius, against his will and chafing at the embarrassment, asked her to come out. At that moment everyone strained not only their eyes but their very souls, and nearly fell over each other in their eagerness to be first to see and get as near as possible. Callirhoe's face shone with a radiance which dazzled the eyes of all, just as when on a dark night a blinding flash is seen. Struck with amazement, the Persians knelt in homage, and no one noticed the presence of Rhodogune. The latter herself recognized her defeat: unable to leave and unwilling to be looked at, she passed inside with Callirhoe, submitting to be led by her superior. The carriage then moved on with curtains drawn, and the people, no longer able to see Callirhoe, sought to kiss the vehicle itself.[a]

When the king heard that Dionysius had arrived, he told the eunuch Artaxates to take him the following message: "Since you are bringing a charge against a man trusted with high office, you should not have been so slow. But I excuse you the lapse since you were traveling with your wife. Now, however, I am celebrating a holy festival and am occupied with the sacrifices. I will hear the case thirty days from now." Dionysius knelt in homage and withdrew.

---

[a] Recalling Panthea's farewell to Abradates, cf. Xenophon, *Cyropaedia* 6.4.10.

---

3.8 ἀλλὰ Δ. Cobet: ἀλλ' ὁ Δ. F.     3.10 add. Cobet.
3.11 τῆς δίκης ἀκρ. Jackson: ἀκρ. τῆς δίκης F.

CHARITON

4. Παρασκευὴ οὖν ἐντεῦθεν ἐγίνετο ἐπὶ τὴν δίκην
παρ' ἑκατέρων ὥσπερ ἐπὶ πόλεμον τὸν μέγιστον.
ἐσχίσθη δὲ τὸ πλῆθος τῶν βαρβάρων καὶ ὅσον μὲν
ἦν σατραπικὸν Μιθριδάτῃ προσέθετο· καὶ γὰρ ἦν
ἀνέκαθεν ἐκ Βάκτρων, εἰς Καρίαν δὲ ὕστερον μετ-
ῳκίσθη· Διονύσιος δὲ τὸ δημοτικὸν εἶχεν εὔνουν·
ἐδόκει γὰρ ἀδικεῖσθαι παρὰ τοὺς νόμους εἰς γυναῖκα

2 ἐπιβουλευθείς, καὶ ὃ μεῖζόν ἐστι, τοιαύτην. οὐ μὴν
οὐδ' ἡ γυναικωνῖτις ἡ Περσῶν ἀμέριμνος ἦν, ἀλλὰ
καὶ ἐνταῦθα διῃρέθησαν αἱ σπουδαί· τὸ μὲν γὰρ
αὐτῶν ἐπ' εὐμορφίᾳ μέγα φρονοῦν ἐφθόνει τῇ Καλλιρόῃ καὶ ἤθελεν αὐτὴν ἐκ τῆς δίκης ὑβρισθῆναι, τὸ
δὲ πλῆθος ταῖς οἰκείαις φθονοῦσαι τὴν ξένην εὐδο-

3 κιμῆσαι συνηύχοντο. τὴν νίκην δὲ ἑκάτερος αὑτῶν
ἐν ταῖς χερσὶν ἔχειν ὑπελάμβανε· Διονύσιος μὲν
θαρρῶν ταῖς ἐπιστολαῖς αἷς ἔγραψε Μιθριδάτης
πρὸς Καλλιρόην ὀνόματι Χαιρέου (ζῆν γὰρ οὐδέποτε Χαιρέαν προσεδόκα), Μιθριδάτης δὲ Χαιρέαν
ἔχων δεῖξαι πέπειστο ἁλῶναι μὴ δύνασθαι. προσεποιεῖτο δὲ δεδιέναι καὶ συνηγόρους παρεκάλει, ἵνα
διὰ τὸ ἀπροσδόκητον λαμπροτέραν τὴν ἀπολογίαν

4 ποιήσηται. ταῖς δὲ τριάκοντα ἡμέραις Πέρσαι καὶ
Περσίδες οὐδὲν ἕτερον διελάλουν ἢ τὴν δίκην ταύτην, ὥστε, εἰ χρὴ τἀληθὲς εἰπεῖν, ὅλη [ἡ] Βαβυλὼν
δικαστήριον ἦν. ἐδόκει δὲ πᾶσιν ἡ προθεσμία
μακρὰ καὶ οὐ τοῖς ἄλλοις μόνον ἀλλὰ καὶ αὐτῷ τῷ
βασιλεῖ. ποῖος ἀγὼν Ὀλυμπικὸς ἢ νύκτες Ἐλευσί-

4. From then on preparations for the trial were made by both sides as though for the most crucial of battles. The oriental populace was split. All those who supported the governors sided with Mithridates—he came from Bactra and had only later moved to Caria. Dionysius, on the other hand, enjoyed the sympathy of the common people, since they considered that he had been illegally wronged by this plot against his wife, who—and this was what counted most—was so beautiful. Moreover, not even the female half of the Persian population was unaffected, but there, too, passions were divided. Those of them who plumed themselves on their good looks were jealous of Callirhoe and wanted her to be humiliated by the trial. But the majority, who were envious of their local rivals, combined in praying for the foreign woman's success. Each of the two men felt he had victory in his grasp: Dionysius relied on the letter that Mithridates wrote to Callirhoe in the name of Chaereas (for of course he never imagined that Chaereas was alive); Mithridates, on the other hand, being able to produce Chaereas, was sure that he could not be convicted. However, he pretended to be afraid and consulted advocates, so as to render his defense more striking by its element of surprise. During the thirty days men and women in Persia talked of nothing but this trial, and, to tell the truth, all Babylon became a courthouse. Everyone found the adjournment too long, the king himself no less than the others. What

---

4.4 del. Reeve.

νιαι προσδοκίαν τοσαύτης ἔσχον σπουδῆς;

5 Ἐπεὶ δὲ ἧκεν ἡ κυρία τῶν ἡμερῶν, ἐκαθέσθη
βασιλεύς. ἔστι δὲ οἶκος ἐν τοῖς βασιλείοις ἐξαίρετος, ἀποδεδειγμένος εἰς δικαστήριον, μεγέθει κα
κάλλει διαφέρων· ἔνθα μέσος μὲν ὁ θρόνος κεῖτα
βασιλεῖ, παρ' ἑκάτερα δὲ τοῖς φίλοις οἳ τοῖς ἀξιώ-
μασι καὶ ταῖς ἀρεταῖς ὑπάρχουσιν ἡγεμόνες ἡγεμό-
6 νων. περιεστᾶσι δὲ κύκλῳ τοῦ θρόνου λοχαγοὶ κα
ταξίαρχοι καὶ τῶν βασιλέως ἐξελευθέρων τὸ ἐντιμό-
τατον, ὥστε ἐπ' ἐκείνου τοῦ συνεδρίου καλῶς ἂ
εἴποι τις·

  οἱ δὲ θεοὶ πὰρ Ζηνὶ καθήμενοι ἠγορόωντο.

7 παράγονται δὲ οἱ δικαζόμενοι μετὰ σιγῆς καὶ δέους
τότε οὖν ἕωθεν μὲν πρῶτος ἧκε Μιθριδάτης, δορυφο-
ρούμενος ὑπὸ φίλων καὶ συγγενῶν, οὐ πάνυ τι λαμ-
πρὸς οὐδὲ φαιδρός, ἀλλ', ὡς ὑπεύθυνος, ἐλεεινός
ἐπηκολούθει δὲ καὶ Διονύσιος Ἑλληνικῷ σχήματ
Μιλησίαν στολὴν ἀμπεχόμενος, τὰς ἐπιστολὰς τῇ
8 χειρὶ κατέχων. ἐπεὶ δὲ εἰσήχθησαν, προσεκύνησαν
ἔπειτα βασιλεὺς ἐκέλευσε τὸν γραμματέα τὰς ἐπιστολὰς ἀναγνῶναι, τήν τε Φαρνάκου καὶ ἣν ἀντ
ἔγραψεν αὐτός, ἵνα μάθωσιν οἱ συνδικάζοντες πῶ
εἰσῆκται τὸ πρᾶγμα. ἀναγνωσθείσης δὲ τῆς ἐπιστολῆς ἔπαινος ἐξερράγη πολὺς τὴν σωφροσύνη

4.5 οἳ Blake (καὶ οἳ Beck): καὶ F.
4.7 δικαζόμενοι Blake: καθεζόμενοι F.
4.8 ἐκέλευσε Cobet: ἐκέλευε F.

Olympic games or Eleusinian nights[a] ever promised such excitement?

When the appointed day came, the king took his place. In the palace is a room of special size and beauty set aside as a court; the king's throne is placed in the middle, and seats on either side for his friends who, because of their rank and ability, are styled "leaders of leaders." Round about the throne stand captains and commanders and the foremost of the king's freedmen, so that one might well say of that tribunal:

The gods sat beside Zeus and were holding assembly.[b]

Those summoned to judgment are brought forward in silence and trepidation. On this occasion Mithridates appeared first, early in the morning, escorted by friends and relatives. He looked by no means bright and cheerful but, as befits an accused man, pitiable. Dionysius followed after him, dressed in Greek fashion with a Milesian mantle and holding the letters in his hand. On being ushered in, they knelt in homage. Then the king ordered the clerk to read the letters, both that of Pharnaces and the one which he himself had written in reply, so that his fellow judges might know how the case had come about. After his letter had been read out, there came a loud

[a] Every year in September the great festival of Demeter took place in Athens and culminated on the fifth day with a spectacular torchlight procession to Eleusis, followed by all-night revelry. Of the connected initiations and mysteries we know practically nothing.

[b] *Iliad* 4.1 (debate on the fate of Troy).

249

καὶ δικαιοσύνην θαυμαζόντων τὴν βασιλέως.

9 Σιωπῆς δὲ γενομένης ἔδει μὲν ἄρξασθαι τοῦ
λόγου Διονύσιον τὸν κατήγορον, καὶ πάντες εἰς ἐκεῖνον ἀπέβλεψαν. ἔφθη δὲ Μιθριδάτης· "οὐ προλαμ-
βάνω" φησί, "δέσποτα, τὴν ἀπολογίαν, ἀλλ' οἶδα
τὴν τάξιν· δεῖ δὲ πρὸ τῶν λόγων ἅπαντας παρεῖναι
τοὺς ἀναγκαίους ἐν τῇ δίκῃ· ποῦ τοίνυν ἡ γυνή, περὶ
ἧς ἡ κρίσις; ἔδοξας δ' αὐτὴν ἀναγκαίαν διὰ τῆς ἐπι-
10 στολῆς καὶ ἔγραψας παρεῖναι, καὶ πάρεστι. μὴ οὖν
Διονύσιος ἀποκρυπτέτω τὸ κεφάλαιον καὶ τὴν αἰτίαν
ὅλου τοῦ πράγματος." πρὸς ταῦτα ἀπεκρίνατο Διονύσιος "καὶ τοῦτο μοιχοῦ παράγειν εἰς ὄχλον ἀλλοτρίαν γυναῖκα οὐ θέλοντος ἀνδρός, οὔτε ἐγκαλοῦσαν
11 οὔτε ἐγκαλουμένην αὐτή. εἰ μὲν οὖν διεφθάρη, ὡς
ὑπεύθυνον ἔδει παρεῖναι· νῦν δὲ σὺ ἐπεβούλευσας
ἀγνοούσῃ, καὶ οὔτε μάρτυρι χρῶμαι τῇ γυναικὶ οὔτε
συνηγόρῳ. τί οὖν ἀναγκαῖον παρεῖναι τὴν κατ'
οὐδὲν μετέχουσαν τῆς δίκης;"

Ταῦτα δικανικῶς μὲν εἶπεν ὁ Διονύσιος, πλὴν
οὐδένα ἔπειθεν· ἐπεθύμουν γὰρ πάντες Καλλιρόην
12 ἰδεῖν. αἰδουμένου δὲ κελεῦσαι βασιλέως πρόφασιν
ἔσχον οἱ φίλοι τὴν ἐπιστολήν· ἐκλήθη γὰρ ὡς
ἀναγκαία. "πῶς οὖν οὐκ ἄτοπον" ἔφη τις "ἐξ
Ἰωνίας μὲν ἐλθεῖν, ἐν Βαβυλῶνι δὲ οὖσαν ὑστερεῖν;"
13 ἐπεὶ τοίνυν ὡρίσθη καὶ Καλλιρόην παρεῖναι, οὐδὲ
αὐτῇ προειρηκὼς ὁ Διονύσιος, ἀλλὰ μέχρι παντὸς

4.9 ἔφθη Jackson: ἔφη F.

250

burst of applause from those who admired the restraint and justice of the king.

When silence was restored, Dionysius as the plaintiff was due to speak first, and all turned their eyes upon him. But Mithridates anticipated him: "Sire," he said, "I am not trying to speak out of turn, but I know the rules of order. Before the speeches everyone who is essential to the trial must be present. Where, then, is the woman the case is about? You considered her essential because of the letter; you wrote for her to be present, and she is present. Do not let Dionysius conceal the chief participant and cause of this whole affair." To this Dionysius objected, "This too is a seducer's behavior, bringing another man's wife before the public contrary to his wishes, when she is neither the plaintiff nor the defendant. If she had actually been seduced, then she would have to appear to give her testimony, but as it is, she knows nothing of your schemes against her, and I do not need my wife as a witness or to support my case. Why, then, must she be here, since she has no actual part in the trial?"

Dionysius' contention was technically true, but failed to persuade anyone, since they were all dying to see Callirhoe. When the king hesitated to command her presence, his friends pointed out to him as justification the letter he had written: she had been summoned as an essential witness. "How ridiculous it is," was the argument, "for her to have come all the way from Ionia and then, when she is in Babylon, not to show up!" Thus it was decided that Callirhoe, too, should appear at the trial. But so far Dionysius had told her nothing, having all

251

ἀποκρυψάμενος τὴν αἰτίαν τῆς εἰς Βαβυλῶνα ὁδοῦ,
φοβηθεὶς αἰφνίδιον εἰσαγαγεῖν εἰς δικαστήριον
οὐδὲν εἰδυῖαν (εἰκὸς γὰρ ἦν καὶ ἀγανακτῆσαι τὴν
γυναῖκα ὡς ἐξηπατημένην) εἰς τὴν ὑστεραίαν ὑπερέθετο τὴν δίκην.

5. Καὶ τότε μὲν οὕτως διελύθησαν· ἀφικόμενος
δὲ εἰς τὴν οἰκίαν ὁ Διονύσιος, οἷα δὴ φρόνιμος ἀνὴρ
καὶ πεπαιδευμένος, λόγους τῇ γυναικὶ προσήνεγκεν
ὡς ἐν τοιούτοις πιθανωτάτους, ἐλαφρῶς τε καὶ
πράως ἕκαστα διηγούμενος. οὐ μὴν ἀδακρυτί γε
ἤκουεν ἡ Καλλιρόη, πρὸς τὸ ὄνομα δὲ τὸ Χαιρέου
πολλὰ ἀνέκλαυσε καὶ πρὸς τὴν δίκην ἐδυσχέραινε.
2 "τοῦτο γὰρ" φησὶ "μόνον ἔλιπέ μου ταῖς συμφοραῖς, εἰσελθεῖν εἰς δικαστήριον. τέθνηκα, [καὶ]
κεκήδευμαι, τετυμβωρύχημαι, πέπραμαι, δεδού-
λευκα· ἰδού, Τύχη, καὶ κρίνομαι. οὐκ ἤρκει σοι δια-
βαλεῖν ἀδίκως με πρὸς Χαιρέαν, ἀλλ' ἔδωκάς μοι
3 παρὰ Διονυσίῳ μοιχείας ὑπόθεσιν. τότε μου τὴν
διαβολὴν ἐπόμπευσας τάφῳ, νῦν δὲ βασιλικῷ δικαστηρίῳ. διήγημα καὶ τῆς Ἀσίας καὶ τῆς Εὐρώπης
γέγονα. ποίοις ὀφθαλμοῖς ὄψομαι τὸν δικαστήν;
ποίων ἀκοῦσαί με δεῖ ῥημάτων; κάλλος ἐπίβουλον,
εἰς τοῦτο μόνον ὑπὸ τῆς φύσεως δοθέν, ἵνα μου πλη-
4 σθῇ γῆ διαβολῶν. Ἑρμοκράτους θυγάτηρ κρίνεται
καὶ τὸν πατέρα συνήγορον οὐκ ἔχει· οἱ μὲν [γὰρ]
ἄλλοι ἐπὰν εἰς δικαστήριον εἰσίωσιν, εὔνοιαν εὔχον-
ται καὶ χάριν, ἐγὼ δὲ φοβοῦμαι μὴ ἀρέσω τῷ
δικαστῇ."

along suppressed the reason for their journey to Babylon; as a result he was afraid to bring his wife without warning into court after keeping her in the dark, for she was bound to be furious at having been deceived. So he had the case postponed to the following day.

5. In this way, then, the court adjourned. Returning home Dionysius, as a sensible and cultivated man, spoke to his wife as persuasively as the circumstances allowed, going into all the details gently and tactfully. Even so, Callirhoe could not refrain from tears as she listened, and when Chaereas' name was mentioned, she burst into sobs, and bitterly condemned the trial. "This is the one thing," she said, "which was yet lacking to my misfortunes—to be dragged into court! I have died, I have been buried, I have been the victim of tomb robbers, I have been sold, I have been a slave, and now, here I am, on trial! Was it not enough for you, Fortune, to have unjustly accused me to Chaereas? Have you also given Dionysius grounds for suspecting me of adultery? Then your slanders led me to the grave; now it is to the lawcourt of the king. I have become the gossip of both Asia and Europe. How can I bear to face the judge? What dreadful things must I hear? O treacherous beauty, given me by nature only that earth might be filled with slanders about me! The daughter of Hermocrates is being brought to trial and has not her father to defend her! When others enter the courtroom they beg for kindness and sympathy, but my fear is that I may please the eye of the judge."

---

5.2 del. Jackson.
5.3 ποίων Blake: οἵων F | πληοθῇ γῇ Goold, after Morel: πληοθήσῃ τῶν F.    5.4 del. Richards.

5 Τοιαῦτα ὀδυρομένη τὴν ἡμέραν ὅλην ἀθύμως διήγαγε καὶ μᾶλλον ἐκείνης Διονύσιος· νυκτὸς δὲ ἐπελθούσης ὄναρ ἔβλεπεν αὐτὴν ἐν Συρακούσαις παρθένον εἰς τὸ τῆς Ἀφροδίτης τέμενος εἰσιοῦσαν κἀκεῖθεν ἐπανιοῦσαν, ὁρῶσαν Χαιρέαν καὶ τὴν τῶν γάμων ἡμέραν· ἐστεφανωμένην τὴν πόλιν ὅλην καὶ προπεμπομένην αὐτὴν ὑπὸ πατρὸς καὶ μητρὸς εἰς

6 τὴν οἰκίαν τοῦ νυμφίου. μέλλουσα δὲ καταφιλεῖν Χαιρέαν ἐκ τῶν ὕπνων ἀνέθορε καὶ καλέσασα Πλαγγόνα (Διονύσιος γὰρ ἔφθη προεξαναστάς, ἵνα μελετήσῃ τὴν δίκην) τὸ ὄναρ διηγεῖτο. καὶ ἡ Πλαγγὼν ἀπεκρίνατο "θάρρει, δέσποινα, καὶ χαῖρε· καλὸν ἐνύπνιον εἶδες· πάσης ἀπολυθήσῃ φροντίδος·

7 ὥσπερ γὰρ ὄναρ ἔδοξας, οὕτως καὶ ὕπαρ. ἄπιθι εἰς τὸ βασιλέως δικαστήριον ὡς ἱερὸν Ἀφροδίτης, ἀναμνήσθητι σαυτῆς, ἀναλάμβανε τὸ κάλλος τὸ νυμφικόν." [καὶ] ταῦτα ἅμα · λέγουσα ἐνέδυε καὶ ἐκόσμει τὴν Καλλιρόην, ἡ δὲ αὐτομάτως ψυχὴν εἶχεν ἱλαράν, ὥσπερ προμαντευομένη τὰ μέλλοντα.

8 Ἕωθεν οὖν ὠθισμὸς ἦν περὶ τὰ βασίλεια καὶ μέχρις ἔξω πλήρεις οἱ στενωποί· πάντες γὰρ συνέτρεχον τῷ μὲν δοκεῖν ἀκροαταὶ τῆς δίκης, τὸ δὲ ἀληθὲς Καλλιρόης θεαταί· τοσούτῳ δὲ ἔδοξε κρείττων ἑαυτῆς, ὅσῳ τὸ πρότερον τῶν ἄλλων γυναικῶν.

9 εἰσῆλθεν οὖν εἰς τὸ δικαστήριον, οἵαν ὁ θεῖος ποιητὴς τὴν Ἑλένην ἐπιστῆναί φησι τοῖς

ἀμφὶ Πρίαμον καὶ Πάνθοον ἠδὲ Θυμοίτην

She spent the whole day miserably making such complaints, and Dionysius was even more downcast than she. When night came, she dreamed of herself, once more a girl in Syracuse, entering the sacred precinct of Aphrodite and returning from it; her first meeting with Chaereas and her wedding day; the whole city was decked with garlands and she herself was being conducted by her father and mother to her bridegroom's home. Just as she was about to kiss Chaereas, she started up from sleep. Calling Plangon (for Dionysius had already risen to prepare himself for the trial) she told her about the dream, and Plangon replied, "Cheer up, mistress, and rejoice! Your dream bodes well. You are about to be rid of all your worries, for what you have dreamed is really going to happen. Go to the king's court as if to Aphrodite's temple. Be true to your real self and recover the beauty you had as a bride." With these words, she dressed and groomed Callirhoe, who instinctively felt cheerful, as though foreseeing what was to come.

In the morning a jostling crowd gathered about the palace, and the streets were thronged to the city limits. Everyone flocked together, ostensibly to listen to the trial, but really to see Callirhoe, who, just as she had formerly surpassed the beauty of the other women, so now appeared to surpass herself. Consequently, when she entered the courtroom she looked just as the divine poet describes Helen, when she appeared to them that were

about Priam and Panthous and also Thymoetes,[a]

[a] *Iliad* 3.146 (Helen on the wall).

---

5.7 del. Hercher.

δημογέρουσιν· ὀφθεῖσα δὲ θάμβος ἐποίησε καὶ σιωπήν,

πάντες δ᾽ ἠρήσαντο παραὶ λεχέεσσι κλιθῆναι·

καὶ εἴγε Μιθριδάτην ἔδει πρῶτον εἰπεῖν, οὐκ ἂν ἔσχε
φωνήν· ὥσπερ γὰρ ἐπὶ τραύματι παλαιῷ σφοδροτέραν αὖθις ἐλάμβανε πληγήν.

6.    Ἤρξατο δὲ Διονύσιος τῶν λόγων οὕτως
"χάριν ἔχω σοι τῆς τιμῆς, βασιλεῦ, ἣν ἐτίμησας
κἀμὲ καὶ <τὴν τῆσδε> σωφροσύνην καὶ τοὺς πάντων γάμους· οὐ γὰρ περιεῖδες ἄνδρα ἰδιώτην ἐπι-
βουλευθέντα ὑπὸ ἡγεμόνος, ἀλλὰ ἐκάλεσας, ἵνα ἐπ᾽
ἐμοῦ μὲν ἐκδικήσῃς τὴν ἀσέλγειαν καὶ ὕβριν, ἐπὶ
2   τῶν ἄλλων δὲ κωλύσῃς. μείζονος δὲ τιμωρίας ἄξιον
τὸ ἔργον γέγονε καὶ διὰ τὸν ποιήσαντα. Μιθριδάτης γάρ, οὐκ ἐχθρὸς ὢν ἀλλὰ ξένος ἐμὸς καὶ φίλος,
ἐπεβούλευσέ μοι, καὶ οὐκ εἰς ἄλλο τι τῶν κτημάτων,
ἀλλὰ εἰς τὸ τιμιώτερον ἐμοὶ σώματός τε καὶ ψυχῆς,
3   τὴν γυναῖκα· ὃν ἐχρῆν, εἰ καί τις ἄλλος ἐπλημμέλη-
σεν εἰς ἡμᾶς, αὐτὸν βοηθεῖν, εἰ καὶ μὴ δι᾽ ἐμὲ τὸν
φίλον, ἀλλὰ διὰ σὲ τὸν βασιλέα. σὺ γὰρ ἐνεχείρι-
σας αὐτῷ τὴν μεγίστην ἀρχήν, ἧς ἀνάξιος φανεὶς
κατῄσχυνε, μᾶλλον δὲ προέδωκε τὸν πιστεύσαντα
4   τὴν ἀρχήν. τὰς μὲν οὖν δεήσεις τὰς Μιθριδάτου καὶ
τὴν δύναμιν καὶ τὴν παρασκευήν, ὅσῃ χρῆται πρὸς

5.9 ἐπί τι θαῦμα ἐρωτικὸν τὴν παλαιὰν ἐπιθυμίαν σφ. F,
corr. Jackson (cf. 8.5.6).

elders of the people. The sight of her brought admiration and silence, and

they all prayed for the prize of sleeping beside her.[a]

Indeed, if Mithridates had been compelled to plead first, he would have been unable to speak, for on the old wound, as it were, he had received another, more violent, blow.

6. Dionysius opened his statement as follows: "Your Majesty, I thank you for the regard you pay to me, my wife's chastity, and the institution of marriage. You have not allowed a private citizen to be ruined by a governor's intrigue but have summoned him here, so that by punishing his immoral and vicious behavior towards me you may stop it in other cases. The crime merits an even greater penalty because of the standing of the perpetrator. For Mithridates, no enemy but a guest and friend, schemed against me not for some other of my possessions but for that which is dearer to me than body and soul: my wife. This is the man whose duty it was, had anyone else thus injured me, to come to my aid himself, if not out of friendship to me, at least out of respect for you, his king. You have delegated to him the highest authority, and he has proved himself unfit by shaming it; worse still, he has betrayed you who trusted him with it. I am fully aware of the appeals and influence and resources that Mithridates brings to this case, and that I do not stand on the same

---

[a] *Odyssey* 1.366 = 18.213 (the suitors and Penelope).

---

6.1 add. Jackson.
6.2 ἐπεβούλευσέ μοι Cobet: ἐπίβουλος ἐμοί F.

τὸν ἀγῶνα, <καὶ> ὅτι οὐκ ἐξ ἴσου καθεστήκαμεν,
οὐδὲ αὐτὸς ἀγνοῶ· θαρρῶ δέ, βασιλεῦ, τῇ σῇ
δικαιοσύνῃ [καὶ τοῖς γάμοις] καὶ τοῖς νόμοις, οὓς
5 ὁμοίως σὺ πᾶσι τηρεῖς. εἰ γὰρ μέλλεις αὐτὸν
ἀφιέναι, πολὺ βέλτιον ἦν μηδὲ καλέσαι· τότε μὲν
γὰρ ἐφοβοῦντο πάντες, ὡς κολασθησομένης τῆς
ἀσελγείας, ἐὰν εἰς κρίσιν εἰσέλθῃ· καταφρονήσει δὲ
λοιπόν, ἐάν κριθεὶς παρὰ σοὶ μὴ κολασθῇ.

"Ὁ δὲ ἐμὸς λόγος σαφής ἐστι καὶ σύντομος.
ἀνήρ εἰμι Καλλιρόης ταύτης, ἤδη δὲ ἐξ αὐτῆς καὶ
πατήρ, γήμας οὐ παρθένον, ἀλλὰ ἀνδρὸς προτέ<ρον
ἑτέ>ρου γενομένην, Χαιρέου τοὔνομα, πάλαι τεθνεῶ-
6 τος, οὗ καὶ τάφος ἐστὶ παρ' ἡμῖν. Μιθριδάτης οὖν
ἐν Μιλήτῳ γενόμενος καὶ θεασάμενός μου τὴν
γυναῖκα διὰ τὸ τῆς ξενίας δίκαιον, τὰ μετὰ ταῦτα
οὐκ ἔπραξεν οὔτε ὡς φίλος οὔτε ὡς ἀνὴρ σώφρων
καὶ κόσμιος, ὁποίους σὺ εἶναι βούλει τοὺς τὰς σὰς
πόλεις ἐγκεχειρισμένους, ἀλλ' ἀσελγὴς ὤφθη καὶ
7 τυραννικός. ἐπιστάμενος δὲ τὴν σωφροσύνην καὶ
φιλανδρίαν τῆς γυναικὸς λόγοις μὲν ἢ χρήμασι
πεῖσαι αὐτὴν ἀδύνατον ἔδοξε, τέχνην δὲ ἐξεῦρεν ἐπιβουλῆς, ὡς ᾤετο, πιθανωτάτην· τὸν γὰρ πρότερον
αὐτῆς ἄνδρα Χαιρέαν ὑπεκρίνατο ζῆν καὶ πλάσας
ἐπιστολὰς ἐπὶ τῷ ὀνόματι τῷ ἐκείνου πρὸς Καλλι-
8 ρόην ἔπεμψε διὰ δούλων. ἡ δὲ σὴ τύχη, βασιλεῦ,
ἄξιον ὄντα <κριτήν σε> κατέστησε καὶ ἡ πρόνοια
τῶν ἄλλων θεῶν φανερὰς ἐποίησε τὰς ἐπιστολάς·
τοὺς γὰρ δούλους μετὰ τῶν ἐπιστολῶν ἔπεμψε πρὸς

footing, but I have confidence, Your Majesty, in your justice and in the laws which you administer impartially to all. If you are going to acquit him, it would be much better not to have summoned him at all. Until now everyone has lived in fear of improper conduct being punished if one were brought to trial. But if when tried before you one is not punished, he will thereafter hold you in contempt.

"My story is clear and brief. I am the husband of Callirhoe here, and by her I have now been made a father. When I married her, she was not a virgin but had been previously married to another man, Chaereas by name, who is now long dead; his very tomb stands near our home. When Mithridates came to Miletus and met my wife in the course of customary hospitality, he proceeded to act not like a friend or a decent and respectable man, such as you wish those to be to whom you entrust the rule of your cities, but showed himself lewd and presumptuous. Sensing the chastity and fidelity of my wife, he realized it was impossible to win her with talk or bribes, so he devised a cunning trick which he thought would persuade her. He pretended that her former husband, Chaereas, was still alive and forged letters in his name, which he sent to Callirhoe through his slaves. But your destiny, Sire, appointed in you a worthy judge, and the providence of the other gods brought those letters to light. Bias, the chief magistrate of Priene, dispatched these slaves

---

6.4 add. Cobet | del. Cobet (dittography of καὶ τοῖς νόμοις).
6.5 add. Cobet.
6.6 εἶναι βούλει Jackson: β. εἶν. F.
6.8 add. Richards.

ἐμὲ Βίας ὁ στρατηγὸς Πριηνέων, ἐγὼ δὲ φωράσας ἐμήνυσα τῷ σατράπῃ Λυδίας καὶ Ἰωνίας Φαρνάκῃ, ἐκεῖνος δὲ σοί.

9    "Τὸ μὲν διήγημα εἴρηκα τοῦ πράγματος, περὶ οὗ δικάζεις· αἱ δὲ ἀποδείξεις ἄφυκτοι· δεῖ γὰρ δυοῖν θάτερον, ἢ Χαιρέαν ζῆν, ἢ Μιθριδάτην ἠλέγχθαι μοιχόν. καὶ γὰρ οὐδὲ τοῦτο δύναται λέγειν, ὅτι τεθνηκέναι Χαιρέαν ἠγνόει· τούτου γὰρ ἐν Μιλήτῳ παρόντος ἐχώσαμεν ἐκείνῳ τὸν τάφον, καὶ συνεπέν-
10  θησεν ἡμῖν. ἀλλ' ὅταν μοιχεῦσαι θέλῃ Μιθριδάτης, ἀνίστησι τοὺς νεκρούς. παύομαι τὴν ἐπιστολὴν ἀναγνούς, ἣν οὗτος διὰ τῶν ἰδίων δούλων ἔπεμψεν εἰς Μίλητον ἐκ Καρίας. λέγε λαβών· 'Χαιρέας ζῶ.' τοῦτο ἀποδειξάτω Μιθριδάτης καὶ ἀφείσθω. λόγισαι δέ, βασιλεῦ, πῶς ἀναίσχυντός ἐστι μοιχός, ὅπου καὶ νεκροῦ καταψεύδεται."

11   Ταῦτα εἰπὼν ὁ Διονύσιος παρώξυνε τοὺς ἀκούοντας καὶ εὐθὺς εἶχε τὴν ψῆφον. θυμωθεὶς δὲ ὁ βασιλεὺς εἰς Μιθριδάτην πικρὸν καὶ σκυθρωπὸν ἀπέβλεψε.

7. Μηδὲν οὖν καταπλαγεὶς ἐκεῖνος "δέομαί σου" φησί, "βασιλεῦ, δίκαιος γὰρ εἶ καὶ φιλάνθρωπος, μὴ καταγνῷς μου, πρὶν ἀκούσῃς τῶν λόγων ἑκατέρωθεν, μηδὲ ἄνθρωπος Ἕλλην, πανούργως συνθεὶς κατ' ἐμοῦ ψευδεῖς διαβολάς, πιθανώτερος γένηται
2    παρὰ σοὶ τῆς ἀληθείας. συνίημι δὲ ὅτι βαρεῖ με πρὸς ὑποψίαν τὸ κάλλος τῆς γυναικός· οὐδενὶ γὰρ ἄπιστον φαίνεται θελῆσαί τινα Καλλιρόην διαφθεῖ-

together with the letters to me, and I, detecting villainy afoot, reported them to Pharnaces, governor of Lydia and Ionia, and he reported them to you.

"I have told the story of the case which you are judging. The argument is undeniable. One of two things must be true: either Chaereas is still alive or Mithridates is shown to be a seducer. He cannot even claim that he was ignorant of Chaereas' death, because we built his tomb while Mithridates was there in Miletus and he joined in our mourning. However, when he wishes to commit adultery, he brings the dead to life! I conclude by reading the letter which he sent from Caria to Miletus by the hands of his own servants. Take[a] the letter and read: 'From Chaereas: I am alive.' Let Mithridates make that good and gain his acquittal. Just think, Your Majesty, how shameless an adulterer is, when he even impersonates the dead!"

This speech of Dionysius impressed his audience and he had them with him at once. Moved to anger the king looked at Mithridates with a severe and forbidding expression.

7. Not a bit disconcerted, the latter said, "Your Majesty, you are just and compassionate; do not condemn me, I beg you, until you have heard both sides of the story. Do not allow a mere Greek, who has cunningly put together false slanders against me, to have more credit with you than the truth. I am aware that the beauty of this woman lends weight to suspicions of me, for it can surprise no one that a man should wish to seduce Cal-

[a] Addressed to the clerk of the court, who (not Dionysius) would read out the words of the letter (4.4.7). We are evidently to imagine that the trial was conducted in Greek.

ραι. ἐγὼ δὲ καὶ τὸν ἄλλον βίον ἔζηκα σωφρόνως
καὶ πρώτην ταύτην ἔσχηκα διαβολήν· εἰ δέ γε καὶ
ἀκόλαστος καὶ ἀσελγὴς ἐτύγχανον, ἐποίησεν ἄν με
βελτίω τὸ παρὰ σοῦ τοσαύτας πόλεις πεπιστεῦσθαι.
3 τίς οὕτως ἐστὶν ἀνόητος, ἵνα ἕληται τὰ τηλικαῦτα
ἀγαθὰ μιᾶς ἡδονῆς ἕνεκεν ἀπολέσαι καὶ ταύτης
αἰσχρᾶς; εἰ δὲ ἄρα τι καὶ συνῄδειν ἐμαυτῷ πονηρόν,
ἐδυνάμην καὶ παραγράψασθαι τὴν δίκην· Διονύσιος
γὰρ οὐχ ὑπὲρ γυναικὸς ἐγκαλεῖ κατὰ νόμους αὐτῷ
γαμηθείσης, ἀλλὰ πωλουμένην ἠγόρασεν αὐτήν· ὁ
4 δὲ τῆς μοιχείας νόμος οὐκ ἔστιν ἐπὶ δούλων. ἀνα-
γνώτω σοι πρῶτον τὸ γραμμάτιον τῆς ἀπελευθερώ-
σεως, εἶτα τότε γάμον εἰπάτω. γυναῖκα τολμᾷς ὀνο-
μάζειν, ἣν ἀπέδοτό σοι ταλάντου Θήρων ὁ λῃστής,
κἀκεῖνος ἁρπάσας ἐκ τάφου; 'ἀλλὰ' φησὶν 'ἐλευθέραν οὖσαν ἐπριάμην.' οὐκοῦν ἀνδραποδιστὴς εἶ σὺ
5 καὶ οὐκ ἀνήρ. πλὴν ὡς ἀνδρὶ νῦν ἀπολογήσομαι.
γάμον ὀνόμαζε τὴν πρᾶσιν καὶ προῖκα τὴν τιμήν·
Μιλησία σήμερον ἡ Συρακοσία δοξάτω. μάθε,
δέσποτα, ὅτι οὔτε Διονύσιον ὡς ἄνδρα οὔτε ὡς
κύριον ἠδίκηκα. πρῶτον μὲν γὰρ οὐ γενομένην,
ἀλλ' ὡς μέλλουσαν μοιχείαν ἐγκαλεῖ, καὶ πρᾶξιν
6 οὐκ ἔχων εἰπεῖν ἀναγινώσκει γράμματα κενά. τὰς
δὲ τιμωρίας οἱ νόμοι τῶν ἔργων λαμβάνουσι. προ-
φέρεις ἐπιστολήν. ἐδυνάμην εἰπεῖν 'οὐ γέγραφα·
χεῖρα ἐμὴν οὐκ ἔχεις· Καλλιρόην Χαιρέας ζητεῖ·

7.2 ἔζηκα Naber: ἔζησα F.

lirhoe. For myself, all my life I have lived virtuously, and this is the first charge to be brought against me. But if I actually were a lewd and dissolute person, still the fact that I have been entrusted by you with the government of so many cities would have made me a better man. Who is so senseless as to choose to lose such blessings for the sake of a moment's base pleasure? Furthermore, if I had had a guilty conscience, I could have raised an objection to the indictment, seeing that Dionysius is not bringing suit on behalf of a wife legally married to him. Rather, he bought her when she was offered for sale, and the law which deals with adultery does not apply to slaves. Let him first read to you the certificate of her emancipation and then let him talk of marriage. Do you dare to call her your wife, whom the pirate Theron sold you for a talent after snatching her from a tomb? 'But,' he will say, 'she was free when I bought her.' Then you are a kidnapper, not a husband. Still, I shall now plead my case as though you were her husband. Call the purchase a marriage, and the price paid her dowry. For today, let the Syracusan woman pass for a Milesian. Now, Sire, I shall show that I have done no wrong to Dionysius either as her husband or her master. In the first place, he charges me with adultery, not committed, but, as he says, intended, and being unable to specify any deed, he reads us irrelevant letters. Yet the laws exact punishment only for actual deeds. You produce a letter. I could say, 'I did not write it. That is not my handwriting. It is Chaereas who is looking for

---

7.5 ὀνόμαζε Naber: νόμιζε F (cf. 2.3.7).

κρῖνε τοίνυν μοιχείας ἐκεῖνον.' 'ναὶ' φησίν. 'ἀλλὰ
Χαιρέας μὲν τέθνηκε, σὺ δὲ ὀνόματι τοῦ νεκροῦ τὴν
7 γυναῖκά μου διέφθειρες.' προκαλῇ με, Διονύσιε,
πρόκλησιν οὐδαμῶς <σοι> συμφέρουσαν. μαρτύ-
ρομαι· φίλος εἰμί σοι καὶ ξένος. ἀπόστηθι τῆς
κατηγορίας· συμφέρει σοι. βασιλέως δεήθητι
παραπέμψαι τὴν δίκην. παλινῳδίαν εἰπὲ 'Μιθριδάτης οὐδὲν ἀδικεῖ· μάτην ἐμεμψάμην αὐτόν.' ἂν δὲ
ἐπιμείνῃς, μετανοήσεις· κατὰ σαυτοῦ τὴν ψῆφον
οἴσεις. προλέγω σοι, Καλλιρόην ἀπολέσεις. οὐκ
ἐμὲ βασιλεὺς ἀλλὰ σὲ μοιχὸν εὑρήσει."

8 Ταῦτα εἰπὼν ἐσίγησεν· ἅπαντες δὲ εἰς Διονύσιον
ἀπέβλεψαν θέλοντες μαθεῖν, αἱρέσεως αὐτῷ προτεθείσης, πότερον ἀφίσταται τῆς κατηγορίας ἢ
βεβαίως ἐμμένει. τὸ γὰρ αἰνιττόμενον ὑπὸ Μιθριδάτου τί ποτε ἦν αὐτοὶ μὲν οὐ συνίεσαν, Διονύσιον
δὲ ὑπελάμβανον εἰδέναι. κἀκεῖνος δὲ ἠγνόει, μηδέ-
9 ποτ' ἂν ἐλπίσας ὅτι Χαιρέας ζῇ. ἔλεγεν οὖν· "εἰπὲ"
φησὶν "ὅτι ποτὲ καὶ θέλεις· οὐδὲ γὰρ ἐξαπατήσεις
με σοφίσμασι καὶ ἀξιοπίστοις ἀπειλαῖς, οὐδ' εὑρε-
θήσεταί ποτε Διονύσιος συκοφαντῶν."

10 Ἔνθεν ἑλὼν ὁ Μιθριδάτης φωνὴν ἐπῆρε καὶ
ὥσπερ ἐπὶ θειασμοῦ "θεοὶ" φησὶ "βασίλειοι ἐπου-
ράνιοί τε καὶ ὑποχθόνιοι, βοηθήσατε ἀνδρὶ ἀγαθῷ,
πολλάκις ὑμῖν εὐξαμένῳ δικαίως καὶ θύσαντι μεγα-
λοπρεπῶς· ἀπόδοτέ μοι τὴν ἀμοιβὴν τῆς εὐσεβείας
συκοφαντουμένῳ· χρήσατέ μοι κἂν εἰς τὴν δίκην

Callirhoe; try him therefore for adultery.' 'Yes,' he will say, 'but Chaereas is dead, and you tried to seduce my wife in the name of a dead man.' Dionysius, your challenge to me is not in your interest. I swear I am your friend and ally. Withdraw your charge. This is in your interest. Ask the king to dismiss the suit. Recant, and say, 'Mithridates has done no wrong. I blamed him without cause.' If you persist, you will regret it. You will stand self-condemned. I warn you, you will lose Callirhoe. The king will find not me, but you, the adulterer!"

With these words he fell silent. All looked at Dionysius to see whether, offered the choice, he would withdraw his accusation or resolutely stick by it; for what this riddle of Mithridates meant they did not know, but they supposed that Dionysius did. Yet he, too, had no idea, since he never dreamed that Chaereas was still alive. So he replied: "Say whatever you want, you will not deceive me with your hair-splitting and your sham threats. Dionysius shall never be convicted of making false accusations."

Taking up from this point,[a] Mithridates[b] raised his voice and uttered as though under divine inspiration, "Ye majestic deities who rule Heaven and Hell, come to the aid of a virtuous man! Often have I duly prayed and made sumptuous sacrifice to you. Render me, then, the reward for my piety now that I am falsely accused. Grant to me

[a] Cf. *Odyssey* 8.500 (and note on 1.7.6).
[b] The theatrical Asianic style of Mithridates is in designed contrast with the restrained Atticism of Dionysius.

7.6 διέφθειρες Zankogiannes: διέφθειρας F.
7.7 add. Abresch ǀ εἰμί σοι Cobet: εἰμί σου F.

265

Χαιρέαν. φάνηθι, δαῖμον ἀγαθέ· καλεῖ σε ἡ σὴ
Καλλιρόη· μεταξὺ δὲ ἀμφοτέρων, ἐμοῦ τε καὶ Διονυσίου στὰς εἶπον βασιλεῖ τίς ἐστιν ἐξ ἡμῶν μοιχός."

8. Ἔτι δὲ λέγοντος (οὕτω γὰρ ἦν διατεταγμένον)
προῆλθε Χαιρέας αὐτός. ἰδοῦσα δὲ ἀνέκραγεν ἡ
Καλλιρόη "Χαιρέα, ζῇς;" καὶ ὥρμησεν αὐτῷ προσ-
δραμεῖν· κατέσχε δὲ Διονύσιος καὶ μέσος γενόμενος
2 οὐκ εἴασεν ἀλλήλοις περιπλακῆναι. τίς ἂν φράσῃ
κατ' ἀξίαν ἐκεῖνο τὸ σχῆμα τοῦ δικαστηρίου; ποῖος
ποιητὴς ἐπὶ σκηνῆς παράδοξον μῦθον οὕτως εἰσ-
ήγαγεν; ἔδοξας ἂν ἐν θεάτρῳ παρεῖναι μυρίων
παθῶν πλήρει· πάντα ἦν ὁμοῦ, δάκρυα, χαρά, θάμ-
3 βος, ἔλεος, ἀπιστία, εὐχαί. Χαιρέαν ἐμακάριζον,
Μιθριδάτῃ συνέχαιρον, συνελυποῦντο Διονυσίῳ,
περὶ Καλλιρόης ἠπόρουν. μάλιστα γὰρ ἦν ἐκείνη
τεθορυβημένη καὶ ἄναυδος εἱστήκει, μόνον ἀνα-
πεπταμένοις τοῖς ὀφθαλμοῖς εἰς Χαιρέαν ἀποβλέ-
πουσα· δοκεῖ δ' ἄν μοι καὶ βασιλεὺς τότε θέλειν
Χαιρέας εἶναι.

4 Συνήθης μὲν οὖν καὶ πρόχειρος πᾶσι τοῖς ἀντ-
ερασταῖς πόλεμος· ἐκείνοις δὲ καὶ μᾶλλον <πρὸς>
ἀλλήλους ἐξῆψε φιλονεικίαν τὸ ἆθλον βλεπόμενον,
ὥστε, εἰ μὴ διὰ τὴν αἰδῶ τὴν πρὸς βασιλέα, καὶ χεῖ-
5 ρας ἀλλήλοις προσέβαλον. προῆλθε δὲ μέχρι
ῥημάτων. Χαιρέας μὲν ἔλεγε "πρῶτός εἰμι ἀνήρ,"
Διονύσιος δὲ "ἐγὼ βεβαιότερος." "μὴ γὰρ ἀφῆκά
μου τὴν γυναῖκα;" "ἀλλὰ ἔθαψας αὐτήν." "δεῖξόν
γάμου διάλυσιν." "τὸν τάφον ὁρᾷς μοι." "πατὴρ

Chaereas, if only for this trial. Appear, noble spirit! Your Callirhoe summons you! Take your stand between the two of us, myself and Dionysius, and tell the king which of us is the adulterer."

8. While he was still speaking (for so it had been arranged) Chaereas himself stepped forward. Callirhoe, on seeing him, cried out, "Chaereas, are you really alive?" and started to run to him. But Dionysius stopped her and, standing between them, would not allow them to embrace. What reporter could do justice to the scene in that courtroom? What dramatist ever staged such an extraordinary situation? An observer would have thought himself in a theater filled with every conceivable emotion. All were there at once—tears, joy, astonishment, pity, disbelief, prayer. They blessed Chaereas and rejoiced with Mithridates; they grieved with Dionysius; about Callirhoe they were baffled. She herself was totally confused and stood there speechless, gazing with eyes wide open only at Chaereas: I think that on that occasion even the king would have wished to be Chaereas.

However, warfare between rivals in love is natural and spontaneous, and for these two the very sight of the prize provoked their antagonism all the more, so that, had not their respect for the king forbidden, they would have come to blows. As it was, their fight was confined to words. "I am her first husband," said Chaereas. "But I am the more constant," retorted Dionysius. "Did I divorce my wife?" "No, but you buried her." "Show the divorce papers!" "You can see her tomb!" "Her father

---

8.2 φράσῃ Blake: φράσοι F.
8.3 δοκεῖ Naber: ἐδόκει F.     8.4 add. Cobet.

267

CHARITON

ἐξέδωκεν." "ἐμοὶ δὲ ἑαυτήν." "ἀνάξιος εἶ τῆς Ἑρμοκράτους θυγατρός." "σὺ μᾶλλον ὁ παρὰ Μιθριδάτῃ
δεδεμένος." "ἀπαιτῶ Καλλιρόην." "ἐγὼ δὲ κατέχω."
"σὺ τὴν ἀλλοτρίαν κρατεῖς." "σὺ τὴν σὴν ἀπέκτει-
6   νας." "μοιχέ." "φονεῦ." ταῦτα πρὸς ἀλλήλους μαχό-
μενοι· οἱ δ᾽ ἄλλοι πάντες ἤκουον οὐκ ἀηδῶς.

Καλλιρόη μὲν εἱστήκει κάτω βλέπουσα καὶ κλαίουσα, Χαιρέαν φιλοῦσα, Διονύσιον αἰδουμένη·
βασιλεὺς δὲ μεταστησάμενος ἅπαντας, ἐβουλεύετο
μετὰ τῶν φίλων οὐκέτι περὶ Μιθριδάτου, λαμπρῶς
γὰρ ἀπελογήσατο, ἀλλὰ εἰ χρὴ διαδικασίαν προθεῖ-
7   ναι περὶ τῆς γυναικός. καὶ τοῖς μὲν ἐδόκει μὴ βασι-
λικὴν εἶναι τὴν κρίσιν· "τῆς μὲν γὰρ Μιθριδάτου
κατηγορίας εἰκότως ἤκουσας, σατράπης γὰρ ἦν·
τούτους δὲ ἰδιώτας πάντας εἶναι." οἱ δὲ πλείονες
τἀναντία συνεβούλευον καὶ διὰ τὸν πατέρα τῆς γυναικὸς οὐκ ἄχρηστον γενόμενον τῇ βασιλέως οἰκίᾳ
καὶ ὅτι οὐκ ἔξωθεν ἐκάλει τὴν κρίσιν ἐφ᾽ αὑτόν
ἀλλὰ σχεδὸν μέρος οὖσαν ἧς ἐδίκαζεν ἤδη· τὴν γὰρ
ἀληθεστάτην αἰτίαν οὐκ ἤθελον ὁμολογεῖν, ὅτι τὸ
Καλλιρόης κάλλος δυσαπόσπαστον τοῖς ὁρῶσι.

8   Πάλιν οὖν προσκαλεσάμενος οὓς μετεστήσατο
"Μιθριδάτην μὲν" εἶπεν "ἀφίημι, καὶ δῶρα παρ᾽ ἐμοῦ
λαβὼν ἀπίτω τῆς ὑστεραίας ἐπὶ τὴν σατραπείαν
τὴν ἰδίαν· Χαιρέας δὲ καὶ Διονύσιος λεγέτωσαν
ἑκάτερος ἅπερ ἔχει δίκαια περὶ τῆς γυναικός·
προνοεῖσθαι γάρ με δεῖ τῆς θυγατρὸς Ἑρμοκράτους
τοῦ καταπολεμήσαντος Ἀθηναίους τοὺς ἐμοί τε κα-

gave her to me." "Yes, but she gave herself to me." "You are unworthy of Hermocrates' daughter." "More so you, who were a slave of Mithridates." "I demand Callirhoe back." "And I am keeping her." "You are detaining another man's wife." "You killed your own." "Adulterer!" "Murderer!" Such was their thrust and parry, and the audience listened with no small pleasure.

Callirhoe, her eyes cast down, stood and wept, loving Chaereas, respecting Dionysius; but the king dismissed everyone and took counsel with his friends, no longer on the case of Mithridates, for he had defended himself brilliantly, but whether he should issue a ruling about the woman. Some thought that this was not a decision for the king. "It was natural," they said, "for you to listen to the charge against Mithridates, because he was a governor" ; but the people now involved were all private citizens. The majority, however, gave the opposite advice, because the woman's father had rendered service to the royal house, and because this was not a separate case that the king had introduced but was virtually part of the one already before him. However they did not admit the real reason, which was that it was hard to tear themselves away from the sight of Callirhoe's beauty.

So he recalled those whom he had dismissed and said, "I acquit Mithridates: after receiving gifts from me he is to return to his own governorship tomorrow. Chaereas and Dionysius are each to plead their claims to this woman, since I am bound to protect the interests of the daughter of Hermocrates, victor over the Athenians, who

---

8.8 ἀπίτω δῶρα τ. ὑ. παρ' ἐμοῦ λαβὼν F, corr. Hercher.

9 Πέρσαις ἐχθίστους." ῥηθείσης δὲ τῆς ἀποφάσεως
Μιθριδάτης μὲν προσεκύνησεν, ἀπορία δὲ τοὺς ἄλλους κατέλαβεν. ἰδὼν δὲ ὁ βασιλεὺς ἀμηχανοῦντας
αὐτοὺς "οὐκ ἐπείγω" φησίν "ὑμᾶς, ἀλλὰ συγχωρῶ
παρασκευασαμένους ὑμᾶς ἐπὶ τὴν δίκην ἥκειν.
δίδωμι δὲ πέντε ἡμερῶν διάστημα· ἐν δὲ τῷ μεταξὺ
Καλλιρόης ἐπιμελήσεται Στάτειρα ἡ ἐμὴ γυνή· οὐ
γάρ ἐστι δίκαιον μέλλουσαν αὐτὴν κρίνεσθαι περὶ
ἀνδρός, μετὰ ἀνδρὸς ἥκειν ἐπὶ τὴν κρίσιν."

10 Ἐξῇεσαν οὖν τοῦ δικαστηρίου οἱ μὲν ἄλλοι πάντες σκυθρωποί, μόνος δὲ Μιθριδάτης γεγηθώς.
λαβὼν δὲ τὰ δῶρα καὶ τὴν νύκτα καταμείνας ἕωθεν
εἰς Καρίαν ἐξώρμησε λαμπρότερος ἢ πρόσθεν.

9. Τὴν δὲ Καλλιρόην εὐνοῦχοι παραλαβόντες
ἤγαγον πρὸς τὴν βασιλίδα, μηδὲν αὐτῇ προειπόν-
τες· ὅταν γὰρ πέμψῃ βασιλεύς, οὐκ ἀπαγγέλλεται.
θεασαμένη δὲ αἰφνίδιον ἡ Στάτειρα τῆς κλίνης ἀνέθορε δόξασα Ἀφροδίτην ἐφεστάναι, καὶ γὰρ ἐξαι-
2 ρέτως ἐτίμα τὴν θεόν· ἡ δὲ προσεκύνησεν. ὁ δὲ
εὐνοῦχος νοήσας τὴν ἔκπληξιν αὐτῆς "Καλλιρόη"
φησὶν "ἐστὶν αὕτη· πέπομφε δὲ αὐτὴν βασιλεύς, ἵνα
παρὰ σοὶ φυλάττηται μέχρι τῆς δίκης." ἀσμένη
τοῦτο ἤκουσεν ἡ Στάτειρα καὶ πᾶσαν ἀφεῖσα γυναι-
κείαν φιλονεικίαν εὐνουστέρα τῇ Καλλιρόῃ διὰ τὴν
3 τιμὴν ἐγένετο· ἠγάλλετο γὰρ τῇ παρακαταθήκῃ.
λαβομένη δὲ τῆς χειρὸς αὐτῆς "θάρρει" φησίν,
"ὦ γύναι, καὶ παῦσαι δακρύουσα· χρηστός ἐστι
βασιλεύς. ἕξεις ἄνδρα ὃν θέλεις· ἐντιμότερον μετὰ

are my worst enemy and Persia's." When the acquittal was pronounced, Mithridates knelt in homage. But the others were taken aback, and the king, realizing their perplexity, said, "I will not press you, but allow you to come to trial prepared. I grant a postponement of five days. Meanwhile my queen, Statira, will take care of Callirhoe, since it would not be right for her to be accompanied in court by a husband, when it remains to be decided who that husband is."

All the others were downcast when they left the courtroom, and Mithridates alone was happy. After collecting his gifts and staying overnight he set out at dawn for Caria, a more imposing figure than before.

9. The king's eunuchs took Callirhoe and brought her to the queen without prior warning, for there is no announcement when the king acts. Seeing her unexpectedly Statira started up from her couch, thinking that Aphrodite stood before her, for she held that goddess in special honor. Callirhoe in turn knelt in homage, and the eunuch, noticing the queen's amazement, said, "This is Callirhoe. The king has sent her to be in your care until the trial begins." Statira was delighted to hear this and, completely putting aside the jealousy a woman might feel, became very friendly to Callirhoe because of the honor shown her: in fact, she preened herself on the commission. Taking her by the hand, she said, "Take courage, my girl, and cease weeping. The king is a good man. You will

---

9.2 ἐστὶν αὕτη Goold: αὔτ. ἐστ. F.

τὴν κρίσιν γαμηθῇσῃ. βάδιζε δὲ καὶ ἀναπαύου νῦν,
κέκμηκας γάρ, ὡς ὁρῶ, καὶ ἔτι τὴν ψυχὴν ἔχεις
τεταραγμένην." ἡδέως ἡ Καλλιρόη τοῦτο ἤκουσεν,
4 ἐπεθύμει γὰρ ἐρημίας. ὡς οὖν κατεκλίθη καὶ εἴασαν
αὐτὴν ἡσυχάζειν, ἀψαμένη τῶν ὀφθαλμῶν "εἴδετε"
φησὶ "Χαιρέαν ὑμεῖς ἀληθῶς; ἐκεῖνος ἦν Χαιρέας ὁ
ἐμός, ἢ καὶ τοῦτο πεπλάνημαι; τάχα γὰρ Μιθριδάτης
διὰ τὴν δίκην εἴδωλον ἔπεμψε· λέγουσι γὰρ ἐν
5 Πέρσαις εἶναι μάγους. ἀλλὰ καὶ ἐλάλησε καὶ πάντα
εἶπεν ὡς εἰδώς. πῶς οὖν ὑπέμεινέ μοι μὴ περιπλακῆναι; μηδὲ καταφιλήσαντες ἀλλήλους διελύθημεν."
ταῦτα διαλογιζομένης ἠκούετο ποδῶν ψόφος καὶ
κραυγαὶ γυναικῶν· πᾶσαι γὰρ συνέτρεχον πρὸς τὴν
βασιλίδα, νομίζουσαι πολλὴν ἐξουσίαν ἔχειν Καλλι-
6 ρόην ἰδεῖν. ἡ δὲ Στάτειρα εἶπεν "ἀφῶμεν αὐτήν· διά-
κειται γὰρ πονήρως· ἔχομεν δὲ πέντε ἡμέρας καὶ
βλέπειν καὶ ἀκούειν καὶ λαλεῖν." λυπούμεναι δὲ ἀπῇε-
σαν καὶ τῆς ὑστεραίας ἕωθεν ἀφικνοῦνται· καὶ τοῦτο
πάσαις ταῖς ἡμέραις ἐπράττετο μετὰ σπουδῆς, ὥστε
πολυανθρωποτέραν γενέσθαι τὴν βασιλέως οἰκίαν.
7 ἀλλὰ καὶ ὁ βασιλεὺς πρὸς τὰς γυναῖκας εἰσῄει
συνεχέστερον, ὡς δῆθεν πρὸς Στάτειραν. ἐπέμπετο
δὲ Καλλιρόῃ δῶρα πολυτελῆ· ἡ δὲ παρ' οὐδενὸς
ἐλάμβανε, φυλάττουσα τὸ σχῆμα γυναικὸς ἀτυχού-
σης, μελανείμων, ἀκόσμητος καθημένη. ταῦτα καὶ
λαμπροτέραν αὐτὴν ἀπεδείκνυε. πυθομένης δὲ τῆς
βασιλίδος ὁπότερον ἄνδρα βούλοιτο μᾶλλον, οὐδὲν
ἀπεκρίνατο, ἀλλὰ μόνον ἔκλαυσε.

get the husband you wish, and after the trial you will be married with all the greater honor. Go now and rest. I can see you are worn out and your soul still perturbed." Callirhoe was relieved to hear this, for she was longing to be by herself. Then, when she lay on her couch, and they had left her to rest, she put her hands to her eyes and said, "Have you really seen Chaereas? Was that my Chaereas, or is this too an illusion? Perhaps Mithridates conjured up a ghost for the trial. They say there are magicians among the Persians. And yet he spoke and told everything with the assurance of one who knew. So how could he bear not to embrace me? We parted without even a kiss." Amid these thoughts, she heard footsteps and women's upraised voices. All were flocking to the queen, thinking they had a wonderful opportunity of seeing Callirhoe. But Statira said, "We must let her be. She is not feeling well. We have five days in which to see and hear and talk with her." Regretfully they left but were back early the next morning. This happened with the same fervor every day, so that the palace became thronged with people. Moreover, the king, too, visited the women more often, under the pretext of seeing Statira. Rich gifts were sent to Callirhoe, but she would not accept them from anyone, and maintained her appearance of a woman in distress, sitting there dressed in black and without adornment. This only made her look still more striking. But when the queen asked her which husband she preferred she made no answer but only wept.

---

9.3 ἐρημίας Naber: ἠρεμίας F.      9.4 εἴασαν αὐτὴν
Hercher: ἔασεν αὐτὴν F.      9.6 δὲ πέντε (δὲ ε´) Cobet: δὲ
F.      9.7 ἡ δὲ Cobet: καὶ F (< ἠδὲ).

8    Καλλιρόη μὲν <οὖν> ἐν τούτοις ἦν, Διονύσιος δὲ
ἐπειρᾶτο μὲν φέρειν τὰ συμβαίνοντα γενναίως διά τε
φύσεως εὐστάθειαν καὶ διὰ παιδείας ἐπιμέλειαν, τὸ
δὲ παράδοξον τῆς συμφορᾶς καὶ τὸν ἀνδρειότατον
9    ἐκστῆσαι δυνατὸν ὑπῆρχεν· ἐξεκάετο γὰρ σφοδρότερον ἢ ἐν Μιλήτῳ. ἀρχόμενος γὰρ τῆς ἐπιθυμίας
μόνου τοῦ κάλλους ἐραστὴς ἦν, τότε δὲ πολλὰ
προσεξῆπτε τὸν ἔρωτα, συνήθεια καὶ τέκνων εὐεργε-
σία καὶ ἀχαριστία καὶ ζηλοτυπία καὶ μάλιστα τὸ
ἀπροσδόκητον.

10.  Ἐξαίφνης γοῦν ἀνεβόα [πολλάκις] "ποῖος
οὗτος ἐπ' ἐμοῦ Πρωτεσίλεως ἀνεβίω; τίνα τῶν ὑποχθονίων θεῶν ἠσέβησα, ἵνα εὕρω μοι νεκρὸν ἀντεραστήν, οὗ τάφον ἔχωσα; δέσποινα Ἀφροδίτη, σύ
με ἐνήδρευσας, ἣν ἐν τοῖς ἐμοῖς ἱδρυσάμην, ᾗ θύω
πολλάκις. τί γὰρ ἔδειξάς μοι Καλλιρόην, ἣν
φυλάττειν οὐκ ἔμελλες; τί δὲ πατέρα ἐποίεις τὸν οὐδὲ
ἄνδρα ὄντα;"

2    Μεταξὺ δὲ περιπτυξάμενος τὸν υἱὸν ἔλεγε κλάων
"τέκνον ἄθλιον, πρότερον μὲν εὐτυχῶς δοκοῦν μοι
γεγονέναι, νῦν δὲ ἀκαίρως· ἔχω γάρ σε μητρὸς κλη-
3    ρονομίαν καὶ ἔρωτος ἀτυχοῦς ὑπόμνημα. παιδίον
μὲν εἶ, πλὴν οὐ παντελῶς ἀναίσθητον ὢν ὁ πατήρ
σου δυστυχεῖ. κακὴν ἀποδημίαν ἤλθομεν· οὐκ ἔδει

9.8 add. Hercher | ἀνδρεῖον ... δυνατώτατον F, corr.
Hilberg.
10.1 del. Jackson (anticipation from farther on) | ἔχωσα
Jackson: ἔχω F (cf. 5.6.9).

Such was Callirhoe's plight. Through his steadfast character and disciplined training Dionysius endeavored to face the situation with dignity. Yet this incredible misfortune was enough to drive even the bravest man out of his mind. His love burned more fiercely even than in Miletus; for while at the beginning he had been in love only with her beauty, now many things increased the flame: their intimacy, the blessing of children, as well as her lack of gratitude and his jealousy, and above all the unexpected turn events had taken.

10. At any rate he suddenly began to shout, "What sort of Protesilaus[a] is this who has come back from the dead to attack me? What power of Hell have I offended that I should find a rival lover in a dead man whose tomb I built? Lady Aphrodite, I have been cheated by you, for whom I set up a shrine on my estate and make frequent sacrifices! Why did you show Callirhoe to me, if you did not mean to keep her for me? Why did you make me a father when I am not even a husband?"

Meanwhile he took his son in his arms and weeping said, "Poor child, I once thought your birth a blessing, but now it is a burden. In you I have a legacy from your mother and a reminder of my unhappy love. Though but a child, you are not wholly unaware of your father's unhappiness. It is a sorry journey on which we have

[a] The first Greek to be killed at Troy; his bride Laodamia was so distraught that the gods permitted him to return from the dead for a day, after which she took her own life.

275

Μίλητον καταλιπεῖν· Βαβυλὼν ἡμᾶς ἀπολώλεκε.
τὴν μὲν πρώτην δίκην νενίκημαι, <ἣν> Μιθριδάτης
μου κατηγόρει· περὶ δὲ τῆς δευτέρας μᾶλλον φοβοῦ-
μαι· ὅδε γὰρ μείζων ὁ κίνδυνος, δύσελπιν δέ με
4 πεποίηκε τῆς δίκης τὸ προοίμιον. ἄκριτος ἀφήρη-
μαι γυναικὸς καὶ περὶ τῆς ἐμῆς ἀγωνίζομαι πρὸς
ἕτερον, καί, τὸ τούτου χαλεπώτερον, οὐκ οἶδα Καλλιρόη τίνα θέλει. σὺ δέ, τέκνον, ὡς παρὰ μητρὸς
δύνασαι μαθεῖν. καὶ νῦν ἄπελθε καὶ ἱκέτευσον ὑπὲρ
5 τοῦ πατρός. κλαῦσον, καταφίλησον, εἰπὲ "μῆτερ, ὁ
πατήρ μου φιλεῖ σε," ὀνειδίσῃς δὲ μηδέν. τί λέγεις,
παιδαγωγέ; οὐδεὶς ἡμᾶς ἐᾷ τοῖς βασιλείοις εἰσελθεῖν; ὦ τυραννίδος δεινῆς. ἀποκλείουσιν υἱὸν
πρὸς μητέρα πατρὸς ἥκοντα πρεσβευτήν."

6 Διονύσιος μὲν οὖν διέτριβεν ἄχρι τῆς κρίσεως
μάχην βραβεύων ἔρωτος καὶ λογισμοῦ, Χαιρέαν δὲ
πένθος κατεῖχεν ἀπαρηγόρητον. προσποιησάμενος
οὖν νοσεῖν ἐκέλευσε Πολυχάρμῳ παραπέμψαι Μιθριδάτην, ὡς εὐεργέτην ἀμφοῖν· μόνος δὲ γενόμενος
ἧψε βρόχον, καὶ μέλλων ἐπ᾽ αὐτὸν ἀναβαίνειν
"εὐτυχέστερον μὲν" εἶπεν "ἀπέθνησκον, εἰ ἐπὶ τὸν
σταυρὸν ἀνέβαινον, ὃν ἔπηξέ μοι κατηγορία ψευδὴς
ἐν Καρίᾳ δεδεμένῳ· τότε μὲν γὰρ ἀπηλλαττόμην
ζωῆς ἠπατημένος ὑπὸ Καλλιρόης φιλεῖσθαι, νῦν δὲ
ἀπολώλεκα οὐ μόνον τὸ ζῆν, ἀλλὰ καὶ τοῦ θανάτου
7 τὴν παραμυθίαν. Καλλιρόη με ἰδοῦσα οὐ προσῆλθεν, οὐ κατεφίλησεν· ἐμοῦ παρεστῶτος ἄλλον
ᾐδεῖτο. μηδὲν δυσωπείσθω· φθάσω τὴν κρίσιν· οὐ

come. We should not have left Miletus. Babylon has brought our ruin. I met defeat in the first trial in which Mithridates turned the accusation against me; the second encounter I dread still more. The danger this time is greater, and the prelude to the trial has left me without hope. I have been deprived of my wife without a hearing, and I am competing for my own wife with another man. To make matters worse, I do not know which of us Callirhoe prefers. But you, my child, can learn this from her as your mother. So go now and plead for your father. Weep and kiss her and say, 'Mother, my father loves you,' but offer no reproaches. Tutor, what is that you say? They will not allow us to enter the palace? What monstrous despotism! They shut the door upon a son who comes to intercede for his father with his mother!"

While Dionysius spent his time before the trial deciding between passion and reason, Chaereas was seized with an inconsolable grief. Feigning sickness he told Polycharmus to say good-bye to Mithridates, as the benefactor of them both. Then, left alone, he fastened a noose and as he was about to climb up to use it, he said, "I should die more happy, if I were ascending the cross to which a false accusation condemned me when I was a slave in Caria. Then I was taking leave of life under the delusion that Callirhoe loved me, but now I lose not only life but even the consolation of death. When Callirhoe saw me, she did not come and kiss me. Though I stood at her side, she felt shame before another man. She need

---

10.3 add. Cobet | κατηγόρει Reiske: κατηγορεῖ F | ὅδε Cobet: οὐδὲ F.

περιμένω τέλος ἄδοξον. οἶδα ὅτι μικρὸς ἀνταγωνι-
στής εἰμι Διονυσίου, ξένος ἄνθρωπος καὶ πένης καὶ
ἀλλότριος ἤδη. σὺ μὲν εὐτυχοίης, ὦ γύναι· γυναῖκα
γάρ σε καλῶ, κἂν ἕτερον φιλῇς. ἐγὼ δὲ ἀπέρχομαι
καὶ οὐκ ἐνοχλῶ τοῖς σοῖς γάμοις. πλούτει καὶ
8 τρύφα καὶ τῆς Ἰωνίας ἀπόλαυε πολυτελείας. ἔχε ὃν
θέλεις. ἀλλὰ νῦν ἀληθῶς ἀποθανόντος Χαιρέου
αἰτοῦμαί σε, Καλλιρόη, χάριν τελευταίαν. ὅταν
ἀποθάνω, πρόσελθέ μου τῷ νεκρῷ καὶ εἰ μὲν
δύνασαι κλαῦσον· τοῦτο γὰρ ἐμοὶ καὶ ἀθανασίας
γενήσεται μεῖζον· εἰπὲ δὲ προσκύψασα τῇ στήλῃ,
κἂν ἀνὴρ καὶ βρέφος ὁρῶσιν, ʽοἴχῃ, Χαιρέα, νῦν
ἀληθῶς. νῦν ἀπέθανες· ἐγὼ γὰρ ἔμελλον ἐπὶ βασι-
9 λέως αἱρεῖσθαι σέ.ʼ ἀκούσομαί σου, γύναι· τάχα καὶ
πιστεύσω. ἐνδοξότερόν με ποιήσεις τοῖς κάτω
δαίμοσιν.

εἰ δὲ θανόντων περ καταλήθοντ᾽ εἰν Ἀΐδαο
αὐτὰρ ἐγὼ καὶ κεῖθι φίλης μεμνήσομαί σου.ʺ

τοιαῦτα ὀδυρόμενος κατεφίλει τὸν βρόχον ʺσύ μοιʺ
λέγων ʺπαραμυθία καὶ συνήγορος· διὰ σὲ νικῶ· σύ
10 με Καλλιρόης μᾶλλον ἔστερξας.ʺ ἀναβαίνοντος
αὐτοῦ καὶ τῷ αὐχένι περιάπτοντος ἐπέστη Πολύχαρμος ὁ φίλος καὶ ὡς μεμηνότα κατεῖχε, λοιπὸν μηκέτι
παρηγορεῖν δυνάμενος. ἤδη δὲ καὶ ἡ προθεσμία
τῆς δίκης καθειστήκει.

not be embarrassed! I shall anticipate the decision. I shall not wait for an ignominious end. I know that I am a weak rival to Dionysius, being foreign, poor, and already alienated. Good luck, my wife, for wife I call you, even if you love another! I am going away and will not get in the way of your marriage. Be rich! Live in comfort! Enjoy the luxury of Ionia! Keep the man you want! But one last favor, Callirhoe, I beg of you, now that your Chaereas is truly dead. When I am gone, pay a visit to my corpse and, if you can, weep over it. For me this will be better than immortality. As you bend over the tombstone, say, even if your husband and child are looking on, 'Now, Chaereas, you are really gone. Now you are dead. At the king's tribunal I would have chosen you.' I shall hear you, wife; perhaps even believe you. You will raise my standing with the gods below.

> Even if in Hades' halls men forget the departed,
> yet shall I even there remember you, my dear." [a]

So repining he kissed the noose and said, "You are my comforter and defender. Through you I win. You have loved me more than Callirhoe." He had climbed up and was putting the noose round his neck when in came the faithful Polycharmus, who, no longer able to console him with words, forcibly restrained his frantic struggles. Meanwhile the day fixed for the trial came round.

[a] Adapted from *Iliad* 22.389f (Achilles on Patroclus).

---

10.8 κἂν ἀνὴρ D'Orville: κἀνὴρ F | ὁρῶσιν Jackson: ὁρῶ F.
10.9 φίλου μεμνήσομ' ἑταίρου Homer.

ς

1. Ἐπεὶ δὲ ἔμελλε βασιλεὺς τῇ ὑστεραίᾳ δικά-
ζειν πότερον Χαιρέου γυναῖκα Καλλιρόην εἶναι δεῖ
ἢ Διονυσίου, μετέωρος ἦν πᾶσα Βαβυλών, καὶ ἐν
οἰκίαις τε πρὸς ἀλλήλους καὶ ἐν τοῖς στενωποῖς οἱ
ἀπαντῶντες ἔλεγον "αὔριον τῆς Καλλιρόης οἱ γάμοι.
2 τίς εὐτυχέστερος ἄρα;" διέσχιστο δὲ ἡ πόλις, καὶ οἱ
μὲν Χαιρέᾳ σπεύδοντες ἔλεγον "πρῶτος ἦν ἀνήρ,
παρθένον ἔγημεν ἐρῶσαν ἐρῶν· πατὴρ ἐξέδωκεν
αὐτῷ, πατρὶς ἔθαψε· τοὺς γάμους οὐκ ἀπέλιπεν· οὐκ
ἀπελείφθη. Διονύσιος δὲ ἠγόρασεν, οὐκ ἔγημεν.
λῃσταὶ <μὲν> ἐπώλησαν· οὐκ ἐξὸν δὲ τὴν ἐλευθέραν
3 ἀγοράσαι." οἱ δὲ Διονυσίῳ σπεύδοντες ἀντέλεγον
πάλιν "ἐξήγαγε πειρατηρίου τὴν μέλλουσαν φονεύ-
εσθαι· τάλαντον ἔδωκεν ὑπὲρ τῆς σωτηρίας αὐτῆς·
πρῶτον ἔσωσεν, εἶτα ἔγημε· Χαιρέας δὲ γήμας
ἀπέκτεινε· μνημονεύειν ὀφείλει Καλλιρόη τοῦ τάφου·
μέγιστον δὲ Διονυσίῳ πρόσεστιν εἰς τὸ νικᾶν ὅτι
4 καὶ τέκνον ἔχουσι κοινόν." ταῦτα μὲν οὖν οἱ ἄνδρες·
αἱ δὲ γυναῖκες οὐκ ἐρρητόρευον μόνον, ἀλλὰ καὶ
συνεβούλευον ὡς παρούσῃ Καλλιρόῃ "μὴ παρῇς
τὸν παρθένιον· ἑλοῦ τὸν πρῶτον φιλήσαντα, τὸν

1.2 ἠγόρασεν Reiske: οὐκ ἔπρασεν F | add. Jackson.

280

# BOOK 6

1. When, on the following day, the king was about to rule whether Callirhoe should be the wife of Chaereas or of Dionysius, all Babylon was at fever pitch: people at home and meeting each other in the streets were saying, "Tomorrow is Callirhoe's wedding. Who will be the lucky man?" The city was divided, and the supporters of Chaereas argued, "He was her first husband; she was a virgin when he married her, and each loved the other. Her father gave her to him; her country buried her. He did not desert his bride; he was not deserted by her. Dionysius bought her; he did not marry her. Pirates put her up for sale; but it is not permissible to buy a freeborn woman." The supporters of Dionysius, on the other hand, retorted, "He rescued her from a pirate band when she was about to be killed; he paid a talent to save her. First he saved her, then he married her; but Chaereas married her and then killed her. Callirhoe ought to remember her tomb. But the chief point favoring Dionysius' victory is that they have a child in common." Such were the arguments of the men. But the women not only made speeches, but actually offered advice to Callirhoe as though she were listening. "Do not pass over your maiden love; take the man who loved you first, your

---

1.3 τάφου Naber: γάμου F | μέγιστον D'Orville: γνωστὸν F.

# CHARITON

πολίτην, ἵνα καὶ τὸν πατέρα ἴδῃς· εἰ δὲ μή, ζήσεις
5 ἐπὶ ξένης ὡς φυγάς·" αἱ δ' ἕτεραι "τὸν εὐεργέτην
ἑλοῦ, τὸν σώσαντα, μὴ τὸν ἀποκτείναντα· τί δὲ ἂν
πάλιν ὀργισθῇ Χαιρέας; πάλιν τάφος; μὴ προδῷς
τὸν υἱόν· τίμησον τὸν πατέρα τοῦ τέκνου." τοιαῦτα
διαλαλούντων ἦν ἀκούειν, ὥστε εἶπεν ἄν τις
ὅλην Βαβυλῶνα εἶναι δικαστήριον.

6 Νὺξ ἐκείνη τελευταία πρὸ τῆς δίκης ἐφειστήκει·
κατέκειντο δὲ οἱ βασιλεῖς οὐχ ὁμοίους λαμβάνοντες
λογισμούς, ἀλλὰ ἡ μὲν βασιλὶς ηὔχετο ἡμέραν
γενέσθαι τάχιον, ἵνα ἀπόθηται τὴν παρακαταθήκην
ὡς φορτίον· ἐβάρει γὰρ αὐτὴν τὸ κάλλος τῆς γυναικὸς ἀντισυγκρινόμενον ἐγγύς· ὑπώπτευε δὲ καὶ
βασιλέως τὰς πυκνὰς εἰσόδους καὶ τὰς ἀκαίρους
7 φιλοφροσύνας. πρότερον μὲν γὰρ σπανίως εἰς τὴν
γυναικωνῖτιν εἰσῄει· ἀφ' οὗ δὲ Καλλιρόην εἶχεν
ἔνδον, συνεχῶς ἐφοίτα. παρεφύλαττε δὲ αὐτὸν καὶ
ἐν ταῖς ὁμιλίαις ἡσυχῇ Καλλιρόην ὑποβλέποντα,
καὶ τοὺς ὀφθαλμοὺς κλέπτοντας μὲν τὴν θέαν, αὐτο-
8 μάτως δὲ ἐκεῖ φερομένους. Στάτειρα μὲν οὖν ἡδεῖαν
ἡμέραν ἐξεδέχετο, βασιλεὺς δὲ οὐχ ὁμοίαν, ἀλλ'
ἠγρύπνει δι' ὅλης νυκτὸς

ἄλλοτ' ἐπὶ πλευρὰς κατακείμενος, <ἄλλοτε δ' αὖτε
ὕπτιος,> ἄλλοτε δὲ πρηνής,

ἐννοούμενος καθ' αὑτὸν καὶ λέγων "πάρεστιν ἡ
κρίσις· ὁ γὰρ προπετὴς ἐγὼ σύντομον ἔδωκα

282

countryman, so that you can also see your father. If not, you will live an exile in a foreign land." But the other women said, "Choose your benefactor, the man who saved you, not the one who killed you. What if Chaereas should again get angry? Do you want the tomb again? Do not betray your son. Honor the father of your child." This was the sort of talk to be heard, so that one might say that all Babylon was a courtroom.

The last night before the trial arrived. The royal couple lay pondering very different thoughts. The queen prayed for day to come more quickly so that she could get rid of her burdensome charge. In truth the woman's beauty, which could be compared at first hand with her own, was depressing her. Moreover, she had become suspicious of the frequent visits of the king and his untimely attentions. Whereas previously he seldom came into the women's quarters, now, since Callirhoe had been there, he had been a constant visitor. Besides, she had observed him even when talking to her looking sideways at Callirhoe, his eyes stealing glances and unconsciously straying in that direction. So Statira looked forward with pleasure to the coming day. Not so the king. He stayed awake all night long,

> sometimes lying on his side, and again sometimes
> on his back, and sometimes lying upon his face,[a]

reflecting with himself and saying, "The moment for decision has come; I was too hasty in granting a short post-

---

[a] *Iliad* 24.10f (Achilles after the death of Patroclus).

1.8 add. Hercher.

προθεσμίαν. τί οὖν μέλλομεν πράττειν ἕωθεν;
ἄπεισι Καλλιρόη λοιπὸν εἰς Μίλητον ἢ εἰς Συρακού-
9 σας. ὀφθαλμοὶ δυστυχεῖς, μίαν ὥραν ἔχετε λοιπὸν
ἀπολαῦσαι τοῦ καλλίστου θεάματος· εἶτα γενήσεται
δοῦλος ἐμὸς εὐτυχέστερος ἐμοῦ. σκέψαι τί σοι
πρακτέον ἐστίν, ὦ ψυχή· κατὰ σαυτὴν γενοῦ· συμ-
βουλον οὐκ ἔχεις ἄλλον· ἐρῶντος σύμβουλός ἐστιν
10 αὐτὸς ὁ Ἔρως. πρῶτον οὖν ἀπόκριναι σεαυτῷ. τίς
εἶ; Καλλιρόης ἐραστὴς ἢ δικαστής; μὴ ἐξαπάτα
σεαυτόν. ἀγνοεῖς μέν, ἀλλὰ ἐρᾷς· ἐλεγχθήσῃ δὲ
μᾶλλον, ὅταν αὐτὴν μὴ βλέπῃς. τί οὖν σεαυτὸν
θέλεις λυπεῖν; Ἥλιος προπάτωρ σὸς ἐξεῖλέ σοι
τοῦτο τὸ ζῷον, κάλλιστον ὧν αὐτὸς ἐφορᾷ· σὺ δὲ
11 ἀπελαύνεις τὸ δῶρον τοῦ θεοῦ; πάνυ γοῦν ἐμοὶ μέλει
Χαιρέου καὶ Διονυσίου, δούλων ἐμῶν ἀδόξων, ἵνα
βραβεύω τοὺς ἐκείνων γάμους καὶ ὁ μέγας βασιλεὺς
ἔργον διαπράττωμαι προμνηστρίας γραῖδος. ἀλλὰ
ἔφθην ἀναδέξασθαι τὴν κρίσιν καὶ πάντες τοῦτο
12 ἴσασι. μάλιστα δὲ Στάτειραν αἰδοῦμαι. μήτε οὖν
δημοσίευε τὸν ἔρωτα μήτε τὴν δίκην ἀπάρτιζε.
ἀρκεῖ σοι Καλλιρόην κἂν βλέπειν· ὑπέρθου τὴν
κρίσιν· τοῦτο γὰρ ἔξεστι καὶ ἰδιώτῃ δικαστῇ."

2. Ἡμέρας οὖν φανείσης οἱ μὲν ὑπηρέται τὸ
βασιλικὸν ἡτοίμαζον δικαστήριον· τὸ δὲ πλῆθος
συνέτρεχεν ἐπὶ τὰ βασίλεια, καὶ ἐδονεῖτο πᾶσα
Βαβυλών. ὥσπερ δὲ ἐν Ὀλυμπίοις τοὺς ἀθλητὰς
ἔστι θεάσασθαι παραγινομένους ἐπὶ τὸ στάδιον
μετὰ παραπομπῆς, οὕτω δὴ κἀκείνους. τὸ μὲν

ponement. What am I to do in the morning? In any case
Callirhoe will go away, either to Miletus or to Syracuse.
Unhappy eyes, you have only a single hour left to enjoy
that loveliest of visions; then any slave of mine will be
happier than I. Consider, my soul, what you must do.
Return to your senses. You have no other counselor.
Love himself is the lover's counselor. First, then, answer
this: who are you, Callirhoe's lover or her judge? Do not
deceive yourself. You may not know it, but you are in
love, and this will become more evident when you no
longer see her. Then, should you cause yourself pain?
Your ancestor, the Sun,[a] chose this creature for you, the
fairest of those he looks upon: are you going to reject the
god's gift? I must care much for my humble slaves
Chaereas and Dionysius to arbitrate their marriages and,
Great King that I am, act as a bride-broker like an old
woman! Yet I was too quick to accept the office of judge
and all men know it. Most of all, I am ashamed when I
think of Statira. Well then, do not make your love obvious
and do not bring the trial to an end. It would be enough
for you just to look at Callirhoe. Put off the decision.
Even an ordinary judge can do that."

2. When daylight appeared, the servants made ready
the king's courtroom, the people flocked to the palace,
and all Babylon was in a ferment.[b] Just as at the Olympic
games you can see the athletes arriving at the stadium
with an escort of their supporters, so it was with these

[a] According to Plutarch, *Artaxerxes* 1.2, the name Cyrus
means Sun.

[b] The verb is taken from Herodotus 7.1.1.

2.1 ἔστι Reiske: ἔδει F.

δοκιμώτατον Περσῶν πλῆθος παρέπεμπε Διονύσιον,

2 ὁ δὲ δῆμος Χαιρέαν. συνευχαὶ δὲ καὶ ἐπιβοήσεις
μυρίαι τῶν σπευδόντων ἑκατέροις, ἐπευφημούντων
"σὺ κρείττων, σὺ νικᾷς." ἦν δὲ τὸ ἆθλον οὐ κότινος,
οὐ μῆλα, οὐ πίτυς, ἀλλὰ κάλλος τὸ πρῶτον, ὑπὲρ οὗ
δικαίως ἂν ἤρισαν καὶ θεοί. βασιλεὺς δὲ καλέσας
τὸν εὐνοῦχον Ἀρταξάτην, ὃς ἦν <παρ'> αὐτῷ μέγιστος, "ὄναρ μοι" φησὶν "ἐπιστάντες βασίλειοι θεοὶ
θυσίας ἀπαιτοῦσι καὶ δεῖ με πρῶτον ἐκτελέσαι τὸ

3 τῆς εὐσεβείας. παράγγειλον οὖν τριάκοντα ἡμερῶν
ἱερομηνίαν ἑορτάζειν πᾶσαν τὴν Ἀσίαν ἀφειμένην
δικῶν τε καὶ πραγμάτων." ὁ δὲ εὐνοῦχος τὸ προσ-
ταχθὲν ἀπήγγειλε, πάντα δὲ εὐθὺς μεστὰ θυόντων

4 ἐστεφανωμένων. αὐλὸς ἤχει καὶ σύριγξ ἐκελάδε
καὶ ᾄδοντος ἠκούετο μέλος· ἐθυμιᾶτο <τὰ> πρόθυρα
καὶ <πᾶσα οἰκία καὶ> πᾶς στενωπὸς συμπόσιον ἦν

κνίση δ' οὐρανὸν ἷκεν ἑλισσομένη περὶ καπνῷ·

βασιλεὺς δὲ μεγαλοπρεπεῖς θυσίας παρέστησε τοῖς
βωμοῖς. τότε πρῶτον καὶ Ἔρωτι ἔθυσε καὶ πολλὰ
παρεκάλεσεν Ἀφροδίτην, ἵνα αὐτῷ βοηθῇ πρὸς τὸν
υἱόν.

2.2 add. Cobet | ἐπιστάντες D'Orville: ἐπιστὰν F | θυσία
Naber: θυσίαν F.
2.3 ἀφειμένην Naber: ἀφεμένην F.
2.4 add. Hercher | add. Hilberg.

contestants. Dionysius was escorted by a host of the Persian nobility, Chaereas by the populace. Prayers and endless cheers of encouragement came from those on either side, as they shouted, "You are the better man! You will win!" The prize, however, was not a wild olive wreath, not apples, not a pine wreath,[a] but rather supreme beauty, for which even the gods might fitly have competed. The king called the eunuch Artaxates, his most influential adviser, and said, "The royal gods have appeared to me in a dream and are demanding sacrifices, so I must first fulfill my religious duties. Proclaim, therefore, a sacred month[b] to be celebrated by all Asia, suspending both legal and public business." The eunuch made the announcement as he had been told, and immediately the whole land was filled with men offering sacrifice and wearing garlands. There was the sound of the flute and the piping of the syrinx, and the melody of song was heard. Doorways smoked with incense, every house and every street held a banquet, and

the savor rose unto heaven, eddying amid the smoke.[c]

The king set up magnificent sacrifices at the altars, and then for the first time offered sacrifice to Love as well and often invoked Aphrodite to intercede for him with her son.

[a] The prizes mentioned are those awarded at the Olympian (olive), Pythian (apples), and Isthmian (pine) games. Cf. Lucian, *Anacharsis* 9.

[b] A peculiarly Greek institution during which the great festivals were held (e.g. those specified in note on 6.2.2) and hostilities suspended.

[c] *Iliad* 1.317 (the savor of a hecatomb).

5   Πάντων δὲ ἐν θυμηδίαις ὄντων μόνοι τρεῖς ἐλυ-
πоῦντο, Καλλιρόη, Διονύσιος, καὶ πρὸ τούτων Χαιρέας. Καλλιρόη δὲ οὐκ ἠδύνατο λυπεῖσθαι φανερῶς
ἐν τοῖς βασιλείοις, ἀλλ' ἡσυχῇ καὶ λανθάνουσα
ὑπέστενε καὶ τῇ ἑορτῇ κατηρᾶτο· Διονύσιος δ' ἑαυτῷ, διότι Μίλητον κατέλιπε. "φέρε" φησίν, "ὦ
τλῆμον, τὴν ἑκούσιον συμφοράν· σαυτῷ γὰρ αἴτιος
6   τούτων. ἐξῆν σοι Καλλιρόην ἔχειν καὶ Χαιρέου
ζῶντος. σὺ ἧς ἐν Μιλήτῳ κύριος, καὶ οὐδὲ ἡ ἐπι-
στολὴ Καλλιρόῃ τότε σοῦ μὴ θέλοντος ἐδόθη. τί
ἂν εἶδε; τίς ἂν προσῆλθε; φέρων δὲ σεαυτὸν εἰς
7   μέσους ἔρριψας τοὺς πολεμίους. καὶ εἴθε σεαυτὸ
μόνον· νῦν δὲ καὶ τὸ τῆς ψυχῆς σου τιμιώτερο
κτῆμα. διὰ τοῦτο πανταχόθεν σοι πόλεμος κεκίνη-
ται. τί δοκεῖς, ἀνόητε, Χαιρέαν ἀντίδικον ἔχειν
κατεσκεύασας σεαυτῷ δεσπότην ἀντεραστήν. νῦ
βασιλεὺς καὶ ὀνείρατα βλέπει, καὶ ἀπαιτοῦσιν αὐτὸ
8   θυσίας οἷς καθημέραν θύει. ὦ τῆς ἀναισχυντίας
παρέλκει τις τὴν κρίσιν, ἔνδον ἔχων ἀλλοτρίαν
γυναῖκα, καὶ ὁ τοιοῦτος εἶναι λέγει δικαστής."

Τοιαῦτα μὲν ὠδύρετο Διονύσιος, Χαιρέας δὲ οὐχ
ἥπτετο τροφῆς, οὐδὲ ὅλως ἤθελε ζῆν. Πολυχάρμου
δὲ τοῦ φίλου κωλύοντος αὐτὸν ἀποκαρτερεῖν "σύ μο
πάντων" εἶπε "πολεμιώτατος ὑπάρχεις φίλου σχή-
ματι· βασανιζόμενον γάρ με κατέχεις καὶ ἡδέω
9   κολαζόμενον ὁρᾷς. εἰ δὲ φίλος ἧς, οὐκ ἂν ἐφθόνει

2.5 σαυτῷ Jackson: ἑαυτῷ F.

288

While all were engaged in merrymaking, three alone were sad—Callirhoe, Dionysius, and especially Chaereas. Callirhoe could not openly show her sadness in the palace, but quietly, without being noticed, she sighed and cursed the festival. As for Dionysius, he cursed himself for ever having left Miletus. "You wretch," he exclaimed, "you must put up with this disaster you brought on yourself: you have no one but yourself to blame for it. You could have kept Callirhoe, even with Chaereas alive. You were the master in Miletus, and then the letter would never even have reached Callirhoe against your will. Who would have seen her? Who would have approached her? But you rushed to fling yourself into the midst of your enemies. Would it were only yourself alone! But you also flung the possession more precious than your life. That is why you are attacked on every side. Fool, why do you suppose you have Chaereas as your opponent in this trial? It is because you have made your master your rival in love. Now the king is even seeing visions, and the gods to whom he makes offerings every day are demanding sacrifices from him! The shamelessness of it! A man drags out the trial, while keeping at home another man's wife, and such a person claims to be a judge!"

While Dionysius was complaining in this fashion, Chaereas would not touch food and gave up all desire to live. When his friend Polycharmus sought to prevent him from starving himself to death, he said, "You are my worst enemy and pretend to be my friend! You keep me here in torment and delight to see me suffering. If you were my friend, you would not begrudge me my freedom from

---

2.7 ἔχειν Cobet: ἔχεις F.

μοι τῆς ἐλευθερίας ὑπὸ δαίμονος κακοῦ τυραννου-
μένῳ. πόσους μου καιροὺς εὐτυχίας ἀπολώλεκας;
μακάριος ἦν, εἰ ἐν Συρακούσαις θαπτομένῃ Καλλιρόη συνετάφην· ἀλλὰ καὶ τότε σύ με βουλόμενον
ἀποθανεῖν ἐκώλυσας καὶ ἀφείλω καλῆς συνοδίας·
τάχα γὰρ οὐκ ἂν ἐξῆλθε τοῦ τάφου καταλιποῦσα
10  τὸν νεκρόν. εἰ δ' οὖν, ἐκείμην ταύτῃ τὰ μετὰ ταῦτα
κερδήσας, τὴν πρᾶσιν, τὸ λῃστήριον, τὰ δεσμά, τὸν
<σταυρόν, τὸν> τοῦ σταυροῦ χαλεπώτερον βασιλέα.
ὦ θανάτου καλοῦ, μεθ' ὃν ἤκουσα τὸν δεύτερον Καλλιρόης γάμον. οἷον πάλιν καιρὸν ἀπώλεσάς μου
11  τῆς ἀποκαρτερήσεως, τὸν μετὰ τὴν δίκην. ἰδὼν
Καλλιρόην οὐ προσῆλθον, οὐ κατεφίλησα. ὦ και-
νοῦ καὶ ἀπίστου πράγματος· κρίνεται Χαιρέας εἰ
Καλλιρόης ἀνήρ ἐστιν. ἀλλ' οὐδὲ τὴν ὁποιανδήποτε
κρίσιν ὁ βάσκανος δαίμων ἐπιτρέπει τελεσθῆναι.
καὶ ὄναρ καὶ ὕπαρ οἱ θεοί με μισοῦσι." ταῦτα λέγων
ὥρμησεν ἐπὶ ξίφος, κατέσχε δὲ τὴν χεῖρα Πολύχαρμος καὶ μονονουχὶ δήσας παρεφύλαττεν αὐτόν.

3.  Βασιλεὺς δὲ καλέσας τὸν εὐνοῦχον, ὃς ἦν
αὐτῷ πιστότατος ἁπάντων, τὸ μὲν πρῶτον ᾐδεῖτο
κἀκεῖνον· ἰδὼν δὲ αὐτὸν Ἀρταξάτης ἐρυθήματος
μεστὸν καὶ βουλόμενον εἰπεῖν <τι>, "τί κρύπτεις"
ἔφη, "δέσποτα, δοῦλον σόν, εὔνουν σοι καὶ σιωπᾶν
δυνάμενον; τί τηλικοῦτον συμβέβηκε δεινόν; ὡς
ἀγωνιῶ μή τινα ἐπιβουλὴν—" <"ἐπιβουλὴν"> εἶπε
βασιλεύς, "καὶ μεγίστην, ἀλλ' οὐχ ὑπ' ἀνθρώπων,
2  ἀλλ' ὑπὸ θεοῦ. τίς γὰρ ἔστιν Ἔρως πρότερον

persecution by a malign power. How many times have
you destroyed my chances for happiness? How happy I
should be if only I had been buried together with Callirhoe in Syracuse! But then too, though I wanted to die,
you prevented me and so robbed me of her dear compan-
ionship. Perhaps she might not have deserted my corpse
and come forth from the tomb. In any case, I should now
be lying there, spared my subsequent sufferings—
enslavement, pirates, chains, the cross, and the king more
cruel than the cross. O happy death I might have had
before I heard of Callirhoe's second marriage! And again,
after the trial, what an opportunity for ending my sufferings you have ruined! I saw Callirhoe and I did not go to
her; I did not kiss her. O strange and incredible fact! A
trial to establish whether Chaereas is Callirhoe's husband!
And yet the demon Envy does not permit even this trial,
such as it is, to be completed. Whether I am awake or
asleep, the gods hate me." Saying this he made to seize his
sword, but Polycharmus held back his hand and, all but
putting him in chains, kept him under constraint.

3. The king then summoned the eunuch, whom he
trusted more than anyone else, and to begin with showed
some embarrassment even before him. But Artaxates,
seeing that he was blushing and wanted to speak, said,
"Sir, what are you hiding from your servant? I am devoted
to you and I can be discreet. What has happened to upset
you so? I worry if some plot—" "Yes, a plot," said the king,
"and a big one, although laid not by men but by a god.
Long ago I heard in stories and poems who Love is, and

---

2.10 ταύτῃ τὰ D'Orville: ταύτην F ǀ add. Hilberg.
3.1 add. Cobet ǀ add. Reiske.

ἤκουον ἐν μύθοις τε καὶ ποιήμασιν, ὅτι κρατεῖ πάντων τῶν θεῶν καὶ αὐτοῦ τοῦ Διός· ἠπίστουν δὲ ὅμως
ὅτι δύναταί τις παρ᾽ ἐμὲ γενέσθαι δυνατώτερος.
ἀλλὰ πάρεστιν ὁ θεός· ἐνδεδήμηκεν εἰς τὴν ἐμὴν
ψυχὴν πολὺς καὶ σφοδρὸς Ἔρως· δεινὸν μὲν ὁμολογεῖν, ἀληθῶς δὲ ἑάλωκα."

3    Ταῦτα ἅμα λέγων ἐνεπλήσθη δακρύων, ὥστε
μηκέτι <τι> δύνασθαι προσθεῖναι τοῖς λόγοις· ἀπο-
σιωπήσαντος δὲ εὐθὺς μὲν Ἀρταξάτης ἠπίστατο
πόθεν ἐτρώθη. οὐδὲ γὰρ πρότερον ἀνύποπτος ἦν,
ἀλλὰ ἠσθάνετο μὲν τυφομένου τοῦ πυρός, ἔτι γε μὴν
οὐδὲ ἀμφίβολον ἦν οὐδὲ ἄδηλον ὅτι Καλλιρόης
4    παρούσης οὐκ ἂν ἄλλου τινὸς ἠράσθη· προσεποιεῖτο δὲ ὅμως ἀγνοεῖν καὶ "ποῖον" ἔφη "κάλλος δύναται τῆς σῆς κρατῆσαι, δέσποτα, ψυχῆς, ᾧ τὰ καλὰ
πάντα δουλεύει, χρυσός, ἄργυρος, ἐσθής, ἵπποι,
πόλεις, ἔθνη; καλαὶ μὲν μυρίαι σοι γυναῖκες, ἀλλὰ
καὶ Στάτειρα καλλίστη τῶν ὑπὸ τὸν ἥλιον, ἧς ἀπο-
λαύεις μόνος. ἐξουσία δὲ ἔρωτα καταλύει, πλὴν εἰ
μή τις ἐξ οὐρανοῦ καταβέβηκε τῶν ἄνωθεν ἢ ἐκ
5    θαλάττης ἀναβέβηκεν ἄλλη Θέτις. πιστεύω γὰρ ὅτι
καὶ θεοὶ τῆς σῆς ἐρῶσι συνουσίας."

Ἀπεκρίνατο βασιλεὺς "τοῦτο ἴσως ἀληθές ἐστιν,
ὃ λέγεις, ὅτι θεῶν τίς ἐστιν ἥδε ἡ γυνή· οὐδὲ γὰρ
ἀνθρώπινον τὸ κάλλος· πλὴν οὐχ ὁμολογεῖ· προσ-

---

3.2 παρ᾽ ἐμὲ Hilberg: παρ᾽ ἐμοὶ ἐμοῦ F | Ἔρως Blake: ερω.
F.    3.3 add. Blake | ἠράσθη Jacobs: ἐρασθῇ F.

292

that he rules all the gods, even Zeus himself.[a] However, I did not believe that in a match with me anyone could come out on top. But the god has come. With irresistible might Love has invaded my heart. It is hard to admit, but I am truly his captive."

As he said this, his eyes filled with tears and he was unable to continue speaking. His abrupt silence made Artaxates aware at once of the nature of his wound. Even earlier he had formed suspicions, and perceived the fire that was smoldering. Besides, there was no doubt or uncertainty that, with Callirhoe about, the king would not have fallen in love with anyone else. Nevertheless he pretended ignorance, and said, "Sir, what beauty is there that can gain control of your soul, when all that is beautiful is at your command—gold and silver and clothes and horses, cities, peoples? You have countless beautiful women, and Statira, moreover, whom you alone enjoy, is the most beautiful under the sun. Having whatever you want puts an end to love, unless some goddess has descended from heaven above or risen from the sea, like another Thetis: for I feel sure that even goddesses crave your company."

"What you say is perhaps true," replied the king, "that this woman is a goddess; certainly her beauty is more than human. Yet she does not admit it, but pretends to be a

[a] Cf. Menander, *Heros* fr. 1K.

---

3.4 μυρίαι σοι Blake: μυρι[ . . . . ] F.

CHARITON

ποιεῖται δὲ Ἑλληνὶς εἶναι Συρακοσία. καὶ τοῦτο δὲ
6 τῆς ἀπάτης ἐστὶ σημεῖον. ἐλεγχθῆναι γὰρ οὐ βούλεται πόλιν εἰποῦσα [οὐ] μίαν τῶν ὑφ' ἡμᾶς, ἀλλ'
ὑπὲρ τὸν Ἰόνιον καὶ τὴν πολλὴν θάλασσαν τὸν περὶ
αὑτῆς μῦθον ἐκπέμπει. προφάσει δὲ δίκης ἦλθεν ἐπ'
ἐμὲ καὶ ὅλον τὸ δρᾶμα τοῦτο ἐκείνη κατεσκεύασε.
θαυμάζω δέ σε πῶς ἐτόλμησας Στάτειραν λέγειν
7 καλλίστην ἁπασῶν, Καλλιρόην βλέπων. σκεπτέον
οὖν πῶς ἂν ἀπαλλαγείην τῆς ἀνίας. ζήτει πανταχόθεν εἴ τι ἄρα δυνατόν ἐστιν εὑρεῖν φάρμακον."
"εὕρηται" φησὶ "φάρμακον, βασιλεῦ, καὶ παρ' Ἕλ-
λησι καὶ βαρβάροις, τοῦτο ὅπερ ζητεῖς. φάρμακον
γὰρ ἕτερον ἔρωτος οὐδέν ἐστι πλὴν αὐτὸς ὁ ἐρώμε-
νος· τοῦτο δὲ ἄρα καὶ τὸ ᾀδόμενον λόγιον ἦν ὅτι ὁ
τρώσας αὐτὸς ἰάσεται." κατηδέσθη βασιλεὺς τὸν
λόγον καὶ "μὴ σύ γε" ἔφη "τοιοῦτο μηδὲν εἴπῃς, ἵνα
8 γυναῖκα ἀλλοτρίαν διαφθείρω. μέμνημαι νόμων οὓς
αὐτὸς ἔθηκα <καὶ> δικαιοσύνης ἣν ἐν ἅπασιν ἀσκῶ.
μηδεμίαν μου καταγνῷς ἀκρασίαν. οὐχ οὕτως
ἑαλώκαμεν." δείσας Ἀρταξάτης ὡς εἰπών τι προπε-
τές, μετέβαλε τὸν λόγον εἰς ἔπαινον. "σεμνῶς" ἔφη
"διανοῇ, βασιλεῦ. μὴ τὴν ὁμοίαν τοῖς ἄλλοις ἀνθρώποις θεραπείαν τῷ ἔρωτι προσαγάγῃς, ἀλλὰ τὴν
κρείττονα καὶ βασιλικήν, ἀνταγωνιζόμενος σεαυτῷ·
δύνασαι γάρ, ὦ δέσποτα, σὺ μόνος κρατεῖν καὶ
9 θεοῦ. ἄπαγε δὴ τὴν σεαυτοῦ ψυχὴν εἰς πάσας

3.6 del. Hercher.

294

Greek from Syracuse. This, too, is an indication of deception: for she does not want to be caught out by naming one of the cities subject to us, but sets the scene of her story beyond the Ionian Sea, far across the water. Using this trial as an excuse she has come for me, and has produced the whole drama. But I am surprised that you ventured to call Statira the most beautiful of women when you look at Callirhoe. Well, we must consider how to relieve me of my pain. Look everywhere and see if you can find a remedy." "Your Majesty," he replied, "the remedy you seek has already been found by Greeks as well as Persians. There is no other remedy for love except the loved one. This after all is the meaning of the famous oracle, 'He who wounded shall heal.'"[a] The king was shocked at these words and said, "Never suggest such a thing as seducing another man's wife. I am mindful of the laws I have myself imposed and the justice I dispense in all matters. Do not accuse me of lacking self-control. I am not overcome to that extent." Fearing he had spoken too hastily Artaxates switched to a complimentary tone. "That is a noble thought, Your Majesty," he replied. "Do not apply to your love the same remedy that other men use, but rather the more potent and kingly one of fighting against yourself. For you alone, master, can overcome even a god. So distract your thoughts with every plea-

[a] On his way to Troy Achilles dealt Telephus, king of Mysia, a wound which would not heal: the Delphic oracle pronounced the quoted words, and eventually Telephus was cured with rust from Achilles' spear.

---

3.8 add. Cobet | σεαυ- Hercher -τῷ D'Orville: ἑαυτοῦ F.

ἡδονάς. μάλιστα δὲ κυνηγεσίοις ἐξαιρέτως χαίρεις·
οἶδα γάρ σε ὑφ᾽ ἡδονῆς διημερεύοντα ἄβρωτον,
ἄποτον. ἐν θήρᾳ δὲ ἐνδιατρίβειν <βέλτιον> ἢ τοῖς
βασιλείοις καὶ ἐγγὺς εἶναι τοῦ πυρός."

4. Ταῦτα ἤρεσε καὶ θήρα κατηγγέλλετο μεγαλοπρεπής. ἐξήλαυνον ἱππεῖς κεκοσμημένοι καὶ Περσῶν
οἱ ἄριστοι καὶ τῆς ἄλλης στρατιᾶς τὸ ἐπίλεκτον.
πάντων δὲ ὄντων ἀξιοθεάτων διαπρεπέστατος ἦν

2   αὐτὸς ὁ βασιλεύς. καθῆστο γὰρ ἵππῳ Νισαίῳ
καλλίστῳ καὶ μεγίστῳ χρύσεον ἔχοντι χαλινόν,
χρύσεα δὲ φάλαρα καὶ προμετωπίδια καὶ προστερ-
νίδια· πορφύραν δὲ ἠμφίεστο Τυρίαν (τὸ δὲ ὕφασμα
Βαβυλώνιον) καὶ τιάραν ὑακινθινοβαφῆ· χρύσεον δὲ
ἀκινάκην ὑπεζωσμένος δύο ἄκοντας ἐκράτει, καὶ
φαρέτρα καὶ τόξον αὐτῷ παρήρτητο, Σηρῶν ἔργον

3   πολυτελέστατον. καθῆστο δὲ σοβαρός· ἔστι γὰρ
ἴδιον ἔρωτος τὸ φιλόκοσμον· ἤθελε δὲ σεμνὸς ὑπὸ
Καλλιρόης ὁραθῆναι, καὶ διὰ τῆς πόλεως ἁπάσης
ἐξιὼν περιέβλεπεν εἴ που κἀκείνη θεᾶται τὴν πομ-
πήν. ταχέως δὲ ἐνεπλήσθη τὰ ὄρη βοώντων, θεόν-
των, κυνῶν ὑλασσόντων, ἵππων χρεμετιζόντων,

4   θηρῶν ἐλαυνομένων. ἡ σπουδὴ καὶ ὁ θόρυβος ἐκεῖνος αὐτῶν ἐξέστησεν ἂν καὶ τὸν Ἔρωτα· τέρψις γὰρ

3.9 add. Cobet.
4.1 αὐτὸς Beck: αὐτοῖς F.
4.3 σεμνὸς Schmidt: μέσος F.

---

[a] The language echoes Xenophon, *Cyropaedia* 7.5.53.

sure. You are especially fond of hunting. In fact I have known you to go all day without food or drink[a] when you have been enjoying yourself. It is better to spend your time hunting than in the palace and close to love's fire."[b]

4. This won the king's approval, and a magnificent hunt was announced. On horseback in full splendor rode forth the Persian nobility and the army's elite. All were worth seeing, but the most conspicuous figure was the king himself. His mount was a beautiful large Nisaean[c] horse fitted out with a bridle and cheek pieces, as well as frontlet and breastplate, all of gold. He was dressed in Tyrian purple of Babylonian weave, and wore a turban[d] of hyacinth hue. Girt with a golden dagger, he carried two javelins, and slung about his shoulder was a bow and quiver of the finest Chinese[e] craftsmanship. He preened himself in the saddle, for fondness for adornment is characteristic of love. He wanted to look majestic to Callirhoe, and as he rode all through the city, he kept glancing round in case she too were watching the parade. Soon the mountains were filled with shouting and running, with barking dogs and whinnying horses and fleeing game. The bustle and uproar would have driven Love himself out of his senses, for delight was mingled with

[b] For the hunt as an antidote to love see, for example, Euripides, *Hippolytus* 215ff.

[c] The plain of Nisa, northeast of Ecbatana in Media, was famous for its horses (Herodotus 3.106; Strabo 11.13.7).

[d] The distinctive headdress of the Persian kings (cf. Xenophon, *Cyropaedia* 8.3.13); later affected by Alexander.

[e] The Chinese made contact with the Greco-Roman world in the second half of the 1st century B.C., and Horace mentions Chinese arrows in *Odes* 1.29.9.

ἦν μετ' ἀγωνίας, καὶ χαρὰ μετὰ φόβου, καὶ κίνδυνος
ἡδύς.

Ἀλλὰ βασιλεὺς οὔτε ἵππον ἔβλεπε τοσούτων ἱπ-
πέων αὐτῷ παραθεόντων, οὔτε θηρίον τοσούτων διω-
κομένων· οὔτε κυνὸς ἤκουε τοσούτων ὑλακτούντων,
5   οὔτε ἀνθρώπου πάντων βοώντων. ἔβλεπε δὲ Καλλιρόην μόνην τὴν μὴ παροῦσαν, καὶ ἤκουεν ἐκείνης
τῆς μὴ λαλούσης. συνεξῆλθε γὰρ ἐπὶ τὴν θήραν ὁ
Ἔρως αὐτῷ, καί, ἅτε δὴ φιλόνεικος θεός, ἀντιταττό-
μενον ἰδὼν καὶ βεβουλευμένον, ὡς ᾤετο, καλῶς, εἰς
τοὐναντίον τὴν τέχνην περιέτρεψεν αὐτῷ καὶ δι'
αὐτῆς τῆς θεραπείας ἐξέκαυσε τὴν ψυχήν, ἔνδον
παρὼν καὶ λέγων "οἷον ἦν ἐνθάδε Καλλιρόην ἰδεῖν,
κνήμας ἀνεζωσμένην καὶ βραχίονας γεγυμνωμένην,
πρόσωπον ἐρυθήματος πλῆρες, στῆθος ἀστάθμητον.
6   ἀληθῶς

οἵη δ' Ἄρτεμις εἶσι κατ' οὔρεος ἰοχέαιρα,
ἢ κατὰ Τηγετον περιμήκετον ἢ Ἐρύμανθον,
τερπομένη κάπροισι καὶ ὠκείης ἐλάφοισι."

7   ταῦτα ἀναζωγραφῶν καὶ ἀναπλάττων ἐξεκαίετο
σφόδρα.

\*    \*    \*    \*    \*

Ταῦτα λέγοντος Ἀρταξάτης ὑπολαβὼν "ἐπιλέλη-
σαι" φησί, "δέσποτα, τῶν γεγονότων· Καλλιρόη

4.4 ἀνθρώπου Hercher: ἀνθρώπων F.

anxiety, joy with fear, and danger was spiced with excitement.

Yet the king saw no horse, though many riders raced with him; no beast, though many were pursued: he heard no hound, though many were baying; no man, though all were shouting. He saw only Callirhoe, though she was not there; he heard only her, though she was not speaking. In fact Love had accompanied him to the hunt, and being a god who likes to win and seeing that the king was opposing him with well-laid plans, as he thought, Love turned his own strategy against him, and used the very cure to set his heart on fire. Love entered his mind and said, "How wonderful it would be to see Callirhoe here, with her dress tucked up to her knees and her arms bared, with flushed face and heaving bosom. Truly

> even so roves the archer Artemis over the mountains,
> along the ridges of Taygetus or Erymanthus,
> as she delights in the hunt of boar or speedy deer."[a]

As the king so pictured and imagined her, his passion flared up.

\* \* \* \* \*[b]

While he was uttering these words, Artaxates interrupted and said, "Sir, you have forgotten what has happened. Callirhoe in fact has no husband, and the trial

---

[a] *Odyssey* 6.102–4 (of Nausicaa).

[b] See critical note: in the lacuna the beginning of the conversation with Artaxates will have been described.

---

4.5 ἐρυθήματος στῆθος ἀσταθμήτου πλῆρες F, corr. D'Orville.

4.7 After σφόδρα F has a lacuna of 21 lines.

γὰρ ἄνδρα οὐκ ἔχει, μένει δὲ ἡ κρίσις, τίνι ὀφείλει
γαμηθῆναι. μέμνησο οὖν ὅτι χήρας ἐρᾷς· ὡς μήτε
τοὺς νόμους αἰδοῦ, κεῖνται γὰρ ἐπὶ τοῖς γάμοις, μήτε
μοιχείαν, δεῖ γὰρ πρῶτον εἶναι ἄνδρα τὸν ἀδικούμε-
8   νον, εἶτα τὸν ἀδικοῦντα μοιχόν." ἤρεσεν ὁ λόγος τῷ
βασιλεῖ, πρὸς ἡδονὴν γὰρ ἦν, καὶ προσλαβόμενος
ὑπὸ χεῖρα τὸν εὐνοῦχον κατεφίλησε καὶ "δικαίως
ἄρα σε ἐγὼ" ἔφη "πάντων προτιμῶ· σὺ γὰρ εὐνού-
στατος καὶ φύλαξ ἀγαθὸς ἐμοί. ἄπιθι δὴ καὶ Καλλιρόην ἄγε. δύο δέ σοι προστάσσω, μὴ ἄκουσαν,
μήτε φανερῶς· θέλω γάρ σε καὶ πεῖσαι καὶ λαθεῖν."

9   Εὐθὺς οὖν ἀνακλητικὸν τῆς θήρας σύνθημα
διεδόθη καὶ πάντες ἀνέστρεφον· βασιλεὺς δὲ ἀνηρ-
τημένος ταῖς ἐλπίσιν εἰσήλαυνεν εἰς τὰ βασίλεια
10   χαίρων ὡς τὸ κάλλιστον θήραμα θηράσας. καὶ
Ἀρταξάτης δὲ ἔχαιρε νομίζων προϋπηρεσίαν ὑπ-
εσχῆσθαι, βραβεύσειν δὲ λοιπὸν ἅρμα βασιλικόν,
χάριν εἰδότων ἀμφοτέρων αὐτῷ, Καλλιρόης δὲ μᾶλ-
λον· ἔκρινε γὰρ τὴν πρᾶξιν ῥᾳδίαν, ὡς εὐνοῦχος, ὡς
δοῦλος, ὡς βάρβαρος. οὐκ ᾔδει δὲ φρόνημα Ἑλληνικὸν εὐγενὲς καὶ μάλιστα τὸ Καλλιρόης τῆς
σώφρονος καὶ φιλάνδρου.

5. Καιρὸν οὖν ἐπιτηρήσας ἧκε πρὸς αὐτὴν καὶ
μόνης λαβόμενος "μεγάλων" εἶπεν "ἀγαθῶν, ὦ
γύναι, θησαυρόν σοι κεκόμικα· καὶ σὺ δὲ μνημόνευέ
μου τῆς εὐεργεσίας· εὐχάριστον γὰρ εἶναί σε
πιστεύω." πρὸς τὴν ἀρχὴν τοῦ λόγου Καλλιρόη
περιχαρὴς ἐγένετο· φύσει γὰρ ἄνθρωπος, ὃ βούλε-

to decide whom she should marry is still impending. Remember that it is a widow you love. So do not worry about breaking the law, since that is designed to protect marriage, or about committing adultery, since there must first be a husband to be wronged before there can be an adulterer to wrong him." This argument pleased the king, since it agreed with his desires. So, placing his arm about the eunuch, he kissed him and said, "I am right to regard you above everyone else. You are indeed my kindest friend and true guardian. Go now and bring Callirhoe; but I attach two conditions: do not act against her will nor yet openly. I want you to talk her round but to do so without anyone's knowing."

At once the signal recalling the hunt was given, and they all turned back. The king, now in high hopes, rode back to the palace as happy as if he had captured the finest game. Artaxates, too, rejoiced in the thought that he had rendered him a true service and that from then on he would hold the reins at court, seeing that they would both be grateful to him, especially Callirhoe. As a eunuch, slave, and oriental, he reckoned the task would be easy, having no idea of the pride and nobility of a Greek and especially of the chaste and faithful Callirhoe.

5. So, seizing his chance, he approached her, and finding her alone, he said, "Lady, I have brought you a treasure house of great gains. And for your part, remember my kindness; I am sure you are appreciative." At his opening words Callirhoe was overjoyed, for people are

2 ται, τοῦτο καὶ οἴεται. τάχ᾽ οὖν ἔδοξεν ἀποδίδοσθαι
Χαιρέα καὶ ἔσπευδε τοῦτο ἀκοῦσαι, [καὶ] τῶν εὐαγ-
γελίων ἀμείψασθαι τὸν εὐνοῦχον ὑπισχνουμένη.
πάλιν δὲ ἐκεῖνος ἀναλαβὼν ἀπὸ προοιμίων ἤρξατο
"σύ, γύναι, κάλλος μὲν θεῖον εὐτύχησας, μέγα δέ τι

3 ἀπ᾽ αὐτοῦ καὶ σεμνὸν οὐκ ἐκαρπώσω. τὸ διὰ γῆς
πάσης ἔνδοξον καὶ περιβόητον ὄνομα μέχρι σήμερον οὐχ εὗρεν οὔτ᾽ ἄνδρα κατ᾽ ἀξίαν οὔτ᾽ ἐραστήν,
ἀλλ᾽ ἐνέπεσεν εἰς δύο, νησιώτην πένητα, καὶ ἕτερον,

4 δοῦλον βασιλέως. τί σοι γέγονεν ἐκ τούτων μέγα
καὶ λαμπρόν; ποίαν χώραν ἔχεις εὔφορον; ποῖον
κόσμον πολυτελῆ; τίνων πόλεων ἄρχεις; πόσοι
δοῦλοί σε προσκυνοῦσι; γυναῖκες Βαβυλώνιαι
θεραπαινίδας ἔχουσι πλουσιωτέρας σου. πλὴν οὐκ

5 ἠμελήθης εἰς πάντα, ἀλλὰ κήδονταί σου θεοί. διὰ
τοῦτό σε ἐνθάδε ἤγαγον, πρόφασιν εὑρόντες τὴν
δίκην, ἵνα σε ὁ μέγας βασιλεὺς θεάσηται. καὶ
τοῦτο πρῶτον εὐαγγέλιον ἔχεις· ἡδέως σε εἶδε.
κἀγὼ δὲ αὐτὸν ἀναμιμνήσκω καὶ ἐπαινῶ σε παρ᾽
ἐκείνῳ." τοῦτο δὲ προσέθηκεν· εἴωθε γὰρ πᾶς δοῦλος, ὅταν διαλέγηταί τινι περὶ τοῦ δεσπότου, καὶ
ἑαυτὸν συνιστᾶν, ἴδιον ἐκ τῆς ὁμιλίας μνώμενος
κέρδος.

6 Καλλιρόη δὲ εὐθὺς τὴν καρδίαν ἐπλήγη καθάπερ
ὑπὸ ξίφους τοῦ λόγου· προσεποιεῖτο δὲ μὴ συνιέναι
καὶ "θεοὶ" φησὶν "ἵλεῳ βασιλεῖ διαμένοιεν, σοὶ
δὲ ἐκεῖνος, ὅτι ἐλεεῖτε γυναῖκα δυστυχῆ. δέομαι,

5.2 del. Hercher.     5.5 τοῦτο δὲ Hercher: τοῦτο γὰρ F.

naturally inclined to believe what they wish.[a] She thought that she would soon be restored to Chaereas, and, eager to hear that, promised the eunuch his reward for the good news. Resuming the initiative he started with this overture: "Lady, though you have been blessed with heavenly beauty, yet you have reaped no profit or distinction from it. Your name is known and famed throughout the world, but until today it has not gained you a worthy husband or lover. Instead, it has stumbled on two men, one a poor islander, and the other a servant of the king. What notable distinction have you derived from them? What fertile land do you own? What costly jewelry? What cities do you rule? How many servants pay homage to you? Women of Babylon have maids richer than you! Yet you have not been altogether neglected. The gods are providing for you; that is why they brought you here, discovering in the trial a pretext for the Great King to look upon you. This is the first of my good news: he has looked upon you with pleasure. I keep reminding him of you and speak well of you to him." He could not refrain from adding this bit. Indeed every slave, when he speaks to anyone about his master, has to give prominence to himself as well, in the hope of profiting personally from the conversation.

These words pierced Callirhoe's heart like a sword-thrust, but she pretended not to understand, and said, "May the gods continue to be gracious to the king, and he to you, for taking pity on an unfortunate girl. I beg

[a] See note on 3.9.3.

---

5.6 καθάπερ Jackson: ὥσπερ F.

θᾶττον ἀπαλλαξάτω με τῆς φροντίδος, ἀπαρτίσας
τὴν κρίσιν, ἵνα μηκέτι ἐνοχλῶ μηδὲ τῇ βασιλίδι."
δόξας δὲ ὁ εὐνοῦχος ὅτι ἀσαφῶς εἴρηκεν ὃ ἤθελε καὶ
7 οὐ νενόηκεν ἡ γυνή, φανερώτερον ἤρξατο λέγειν.
"αὐτὸ τοῦτο εὐτύχηκας, ὅτι οὐκέτι δούλους καὶ πένη-
τας ἔχεις ἐραστὰς ἀλλὰ τὸν μέγαν βασιλέα, τὸν
δυνάμενόν σοι Μίλητον αὐτὴν καὶ ὅλην Ἰωνίαν καὶ
Σικελίαν καὶ ἄλλα ἔθνη μείζονα χαρίσασθαι. θῦε
δὴ τοῖς θεοῖς καὶ μακάριζε σεαυτήν, καὶ ἄνυτε ὅπως
ἀρέσῃς μᾶλλον αὐτῷ, καὶ ὅταν πλουτ<ήσ>ῃς ἐμοῦ
μνημόνευε."
8 Καλλιρόη δὲ τὸ μὲν πρῶτον ὥρμησεν, εἰ δυνατόν,
καὶ τοὺς ὀφθαλμοὺς ἐξορύξαι τοῦ διαφθείροντος
αὐτήν, οἷα δὲ γυνὴ πεπαιδευμένη καὶ φρενήρης,
ταχέως λογισαμένη καὶ τὸν τόπον καὶ τίς ἐστιν
αὐτὴ καὶ τίς ὁ λέγων, τὴν ὀργὴν μετέβαλε καὶ
9 κατειρωνεύσατο λοιπὸν τοῦ βαρβάρου. "μὴ γὰρ
οὕτω" φησί "μαινοίμην, ἵνα ἐμαυτὴν ἀξίαν εἶναι
πεισθῶ τοῦ μεγάλου βασιλέως. εἰμὶ δὲ θεραπαινί-
σιν ὁμοία Περσίδων γυναικῶν. μὴ σύ, δέομαί σου,
μνημονεύσῃς ἔτι περὶ ἐμοῦ πρὸς τὸν δεσπότην. καὶ
γὰρ ἂν ἐν τῷ παραυτίκα μηδὲν ὀργισθῇ, μετὰ ταῦτά
σοι χαλεπανεῖ, λογισάμενος ὅτι τὸν γῆς ἁπάσης
10 κύριον ὑπέρριψας Διονυσίου δούλῃ. θαυμάζω δὲ
πῶς συνετώτατος ὑπάρχων ἀγνοεῖς τὴν βασιλέως
φιλανθρωπίαν, ὅτι οὐκ ἐρᾷ δυστυχοῦς γυναικὸς
ἀλλὰ ἐλεεῖ. παυσώμεθα τοίνυν λαλοῦντες, μὴ καὶ
βασιλίδι τις ἡμᾶς διαβάλῃ." καὶ ἡ μὲν ἀπέδραμεν,

him to free me at once from worry by concluding the trial, so that I need no longer be a burden on the queen." The eunuch, thinking that he had failed to express his meaning clearly, and that the girl had not understood, began to speak more plainly. "Your good fortune lies in precisely this, that you no longer have slaves and poor men as your lovers, but the Great King instead, who can freely give you Miletus itself and all Ionia and Sicily and other still greater nations. Sacrifice then to the gods and count yourself happy. Contrive to please him still more, and when you become rich, remember me."

Callirhoe's first impulse was, if she could, to pluck out the eyes of this corrupter; but as a polite and intelligent woman, she quickly remembered where she was, who she was, and who was talking to her. So she restrained her anger and gave the oriental an evasive reply. "May I never be so mad," she said, "as to consider myself worthy of the Great King! Indeed I am no better than the maid-servants of Persian ladies. Please make no further mention of me to your master. I assure you that even if he is not angry now, he will deal with you severely later, when he reflects that you have flung the ruler of the world at a slave of Dionysius. I am surprised, too, that for one so intelligent you fail to recognize the king's humanity, and that he is not in love with an unfortunate woman, but rather pities her. So let us put an end to this conversation, in case someone gossips about us to the queen." On this

---

5.7 δὴ Gasda: δὲ F | ἄνυτε D'Orville: νύττε F | πλουτήσῃς Cobet: πλουτῆς F.

5.10 διαβάλῃ Cobet: διαβαλεῖ F.

ἔστη δὲ ὁ εὐνοῦχος ἀχανής· οἷα γὰρ ἐν μεγάλῃ
τυραννίδι τεθραμμένος οὐδὲν ἀδύνατον ὑπελάμβανεν, οὐ βασιλεῖ μόνον, ἀλλ' οὐδ' ἑαυτῷ.

6. Καταλειφθεὶς οὖν καὶ μηδὲ ἀποκρίσεως κατ-
αξιωθεὶς ἀπηλλάττετο μυρίων παθῶν μεστός, ὀργι-
ζόμενος μὲν Καλλιρόῃ, λυπούμενος δὲ ἐφ' ἑαυτῷ
φοβούμενος δὲ βασιλέα· τάχα γὰρ οὐδὲ πιστεύσει
αὐτὸν ὅτι ἀτυχῶς μέν, ἀλλὰ διελέχθη· δόξει δὲ
καταπροδιδόναι τὴν ὑπηρεσίαν χαριζόμενος τῇ βασι-
2 λίδι. ἐδεδοίκει δὲ μὴ καὶ πρὸς ἐκείνην Καλλιρόη
κατείπῃ τοὺς λόγους· Στάτειραν δὲ βαρυθυμοῦσαν
μέγα τι βουλεύσειν αὐτῷ κακὸν ὡς οὐχ ὑπηρετοῦντι
μόνον ἀλλὰ καὶ κατασκευάζοντι τὸν ἔρωτα.

Καὶ ὁ μὲν εὐνοῦχος ἐσκέπτετο πῶς ἂν ἀσφαλῶς
ἀπαγγείλῃ βασιλεῖ περὶ τῶν γεγονότων· Καλλιρόη
δὲ καθ' ἑαυτὴν γενομένη "ταῦτα" φησὶν "ἐγὼ προ-
3 εμαντευόμην. ἔχω σε μάρτυν, Εὐφρᾶτα. προεῖπον
ὅτι οὐκέτι σε διαβήσομαι. ἔρρωσο, πάτερ, καὶ σύ
μῆτερ, καὶ Συρακοῦσαι πατρίς· οὐκέτι γὰρ ὑμᾶς
ὄψομαι. νῦν ὡς ἀληθῶς Καλλιρόη τέθνηκεν. ἐκ τοῦ
τάφου μὲν ἐξῆλθον, οὐκ ἐξάξει δέ με ἐντεῦθεν λοιπὸν
4 οὐδὲ Θήρων ὁ λῃστής. ὦ κάλλος ἐπίβουλον, σύ μο
πάντων κακῶν αἴτιον. διὰ σὲ ἀνηρέθην, διὰ σὲ
ἐπράθην, διὰ σὲ ἔγημα μετὰ Χαιρέαν, διὰ σὲ εἰς
Βαβυλῶνα ἤχθην, διὰ σὲ παρέστην δικαστηρίῳ.
πόσοις με παρέδωκας; λῃσταῖς, θαλάττῃ, τάφῳ
δουλείᾳ, κρίσει. πάντων δέ μοι βαρύτατον ὁ ἔρως
5 βασιλέως. καὶ οὔπω λέγω τὴν τοῦ βασιλέως

she hurried off and the eunuch stood there, mouth wide open. Brought up under rigid despotism he could not believe anything impossible for the king or even himself.

6. So, left alone and denied even an answer, he went away feeling all kinds of emotion—anger at Callirhoe, sorrow for himself, and fear of the king. Indeed it was quite possible that the king would not believe that he had interviewed her at all, even unsuccessfully, and that he might seem to be betraying his trust to the king by currying favor with the queen. He also feared that Callirhoe would report their conversation to her, and that in her anger Statira would get him into serious trouble for not only supporting but even encouraging the king's passion.

While the eunuch was considering how he might safely report to the king, Callirhoe said, as soon as she was alone, "This is what I predicted. Euphrates, you are my witness. I prophesied that I should not cross your stream again. Farewell, father, and you, too, mother, and you, my native Syracuse: I shall not see you again! Now Callirhoe really is dead. Once I came back from the grave, but from here not even the pirate Theron can take me. O treacherous beauty, you are the cause of all my woes! Because of you, I was killed; because of you, I was sold as a slave; because of you, I married another after Chaereas; because of you, I was brought to Babylon; because of you, I stood before the tribunal. To how many ordeals have you surrendered me—to pirates, the sea, the tomb, slavery, the courtroom! But hardest of all to bear is the king's love. And I still do not mention the king's anger: more

ὀργήν· φοβερωτέραν ἡγοῦμαι τὴν τῆς βασιλίδος
ζηλοτυπίαν· ἣν οὐκ ἤνεγκε Χαιρέας, ἀνὴρ Ἕλλην,
τί ποιήσει γυναῖκα καὶ δέσποιναν βάρβαρον; ἄγε
δή, Καλλιρόη, βούλευσαί τι γενναῖον, Ἑρμοκράτους
ἄξιον· ἀπόσφαξον σεαυτήν. ἀλλὰ μήπω· μέχρι γὰρ
νῦν ὁμιλία πρώτη καὶ παρ' εὐνούχου· ἂν δὲ βιαιότε-
ρόν τι γένηται, τότε ἔσται σοι καιρὸς ἐπιδεῖξαι Χαιρέα παρόντι τὴν πίστιν."

6    Ὁ δ' εὐνοῦχος ἐλθὼν πρὸς τὸν βασιλέα τὴν μὲν
ἀλήθειαν ἀπέκρυπτε τῶν γεγονότων, ἀσχολίαν δὲ
ἐσκήπτετο καὶ τήρησιν ἀκριβῆ τῆς βασιλίδος, ὥστε
μηδὲ δύνασθαι Καλλιρόῃ προσελθεῖν· "σὺ δὲ
ἐκέλευσάς μοι, δέσποτα, προνοεῖσθαι τοῦ λαθεῖν.
7    ὀρθῶς δὲ προσέταξας· ἀνείληφας γὰρ τὸ σεμνότα-
τον πρόσωπον τοῦ δικαστοῦ καὶ θέλεις παρὰ Πέρσαις εὐδοκιμεῖν. διὰ τοῦτό σε πάντες ὑμνοῦσιν.
Ἕλληνες δέ εἰσι μικραίτιοι καὶ λάλοι. περιβόητον
αὐτοὶ ποιήσουσι τὴν πρᾶξιν, Καλλιρόη μὲν ὑπ'
ἀλαζονείας ὅτι αὐτῆς βασιλεὺς ἐρᾷ, Διονύσιος δὲ
8    καὶ Χαιρέας ὑπὸ ζηλοτυπίας. οὐκ ἔστι δὲ ἄξιον
οὐδὲ τὴν βασιλίδα λυπῆσαι <διὰ γυναῖκα ξένην>,
ἣν εὐμορφοτέραν ἐποίησεν ἡ δίκη δόξαι." ταύτην δὲ
παρέμισγε τὴν παλινῳδίαν, εἴ πως ἀποστρέψαι
δύναιτο τὸν βασιλέα τοῦ ἔρωτος, καὶ ἑαυτὸν ἐλευθε-
ρῶσαι διακονίας δυσχεροῦς.

7. Παραυτίκα μὲν οὖν ἔπεισε, πάλιν δὲ νυκτὸς
γενομένης ἀνεκάετο, καὶ ὁ Ἕρως αὐτὸν ἀνεμίμνη-
σκεν οἵους μὲν ὀφθαλμοὺς ἔχει Καλλιρόη, πῶς δὲ

frightening I consider the queen's jealousy. Even Chaereas, a man and a Greek, could not control jealousy: what will it do to a woman and an oriental queen at that? Come, Callirhoe, decide on some heroic deed, worthy of Hermocrates. Kill yourself! But wait—not yet! So far you have only had this first approach, and that from a eunuch. But if things take a more violent turn, then will be the time to show Chaereas, in his presence, the proof of your loyalty."

The eunuch went to the king and concealed what had really taken place, alleging that lack of time and the queen's close guard had prevented him from approaching Callirhoe: "Sir, you told me to be sure to act discreetly. You were right to do so. You have assumed the majestic role of judge and are keen to enjoy the good opinion of the Persians. This is why everybody praises of you. But the Greeks are complainers and chatterers, and will themselves broadcast the matter everywhere, Callirhoe boasting that the king is her lover, and Dionysius and Chaereas venting their jealousy. It would not be right to hurt the queen because of a foreign woman whose beauty the trial has caused to be exaggerated." He sought to introduce this recantation in the hope that he might turn the king away from his passion and relieve himself of an uncongenial duty.

7. He persuaded him for the moment, but when night came, the king was again on fire, and Love kept reminding him of Callirhoe's sparkling eyes and beautiful face;

---

6.5 γυνὴ καὶ δέσποινα βάρβαρος F, corr. Jackson Ι ἔσται Cobet: ἐστί F.

6.8 add. Rose Ι δόξαι Cobet: δόξης F.

καλὸν τὸ πρόσωπον· τὰς τρίχας ἐπήνει, τὸ βάδισμα,
τὴν φωνήν· οἷα μὲν εἰσῆλθεν εἰς τὸ δικαστήριον, οἷα
δὲ ἔστη, πῶς ἐλάλησε, πῶς ἐσίγησε, πῶς ἠδέσθη,

2 πῶς ἔκλαυσε. διαγρυπνήσας δὲ τὸ πλεῖστον μέρος
καὶ τοσοῦτον καταδραθὼν ὅσον καὶ ἐν τοῖς ὕπνοις
Καλλιρόην ἰδεῖν, ἕωθεν καλέσας τὸν εὐνοῦχον
"ἄπιθι" φησὶ "καὶ παραφύλαττε δι' ὅλης τῆς ἡμέ-
ρας· πάντως γὰρ καιρὸν εὑρήσεις κἂν βραχύτατον
ὁμιλίας λανθανούσης. εἰ γὰρ ἤθελον φανερῶς καὶ
βίᾳ περιγενέσθαι τῆς ἐπιθυμίας, εἶχον δορυφό-

3 ρους." προσκυνήσας ὁ εὐνοῦχος ὑπέσχετο· οὐδενὶ
γὰρ ἔξεστιν ἀντειπεῖν βασιλέως κελεύοντος. εἰδὼς
δὲ ὅτι Καλλιρόη καιρὸν οὐ δώσει, διακρούσεται δὲ
τὴν ὁμιλίαν ἐξεπίτηδες συνοῦσα τῇ βασιλίδι, τοῦτο
δὲ θεραπεῦσαι θέλων ἔτρεψε τὴν αἰτίαν οὐκ εἰς τὴν

4 φυλαττομένην ἀλλ' εἰς τὴν φυλάττουσαν, καὶ "ἄν
σοι δοκῇ" φησίν, "ὦ δέσποτα, μετάπεμψαι Στάτειραν, ὡς ἰδιολογήσασθαί τι βουλόμενος πρὸς αὐτήν·
ἐμοὶ γὰρ ἡ ἐκείνης ἀπουσία Καλλιρόης ἐξουσίαν
δώσει." "ποίησον οὕτως" εἶπε βασιλεύς.

5 Ἐλθὼν δὲ Ἀρταξάτης καὶ προσκυνήσας τὴν
βασιλίδα "καλεῖ σε" φησίν, "ὦ δέσποινα, ὁ ἀνήρ."
ἀκούσασα ἡ Στάτειρα προσεκύνησε καὶ μετὰ σπουδῆς ἀπῄει πρὸς αὐτόν. ὁ δὲ εὐνοῦχος ἰδὼν τὴν Καλλιρόην μόνην ἀπολελειμμένην, ἐμβαλὼν τὴν δεξιάν,
ὡς δή τις φιλέλλην καὶ φιλάνθρωπος, ἀπήγαγε τοῦ

6 πλήθους τῶν θεραπαινίδων. ἡ δὲ ἠπίστατο μὲν καὶ
εὐθὺς ὠχρά τε ἦν καὶ ἄφωνος, ἠκολούθει δὲ ὅμως.

he praised her hair, her walk, her voice, how she walked into the courtroom, the way she stood, her speech, her silence, her embarrassment, her weeping. After remaining awake for most of the night and sleeping only long enough to see Callirhoe even in his dreams, when dawn came he called the eunuch and said, "Go and be on the look-out all day. You will surely find an opportunity for talking with her, however briefly, without anyone noticing. If I wanted to satisfy my desire openly and take her by force, I had guards available." Kneeling in homage the eunuch promised his aid, for no one can demur when the king commands. He knew, however, that Callirhoe would give him no opportunity but would block any conversation by purposely staying close to the queen; and wishing to provide for that possibility he diverted blame from the protected to the protector and said, "Sir, if you please, send for Statira and say that you want to talk privately with her. Her absence will give me a chance to speak to Callirhoe." "Do that," said the king.

So Artaxates came and knelt in homage to the queen. "Madam," he said, "your husband calls you." When Statira heard this, she knelt in homage and hurried off to him. Then the eunuch, seeing that Callirhoe was left alone, took her hand, as if he were fond of Greeks and all mankind, and led her away from her group of attendants. Though she knew what he was up to and at once became pale and silent, she followed him. When they were by

ἐπεὶ δὲ κατέστησαν μόνοι, λέγει πρὸς αὐτὴν "ἑώρα-
κας τὴν βασιλίδα πῶς ἀκούσασα τὸ βασιλέως
ὄνομα προσεκύνησε καὶ τρέχουσα ἄπεισι· σὺ δέ, ἡ
δούλη, τὴν εὐτυχίαν οὐ φέρεις, οὐδὲ ἀγαπᾷς ὅτι σε
7    παρακαλεῖ κελεῦσαι δυνάμενος. ἀλλ' ἐγὼ (τιμῶ
γάρ σε) πρὸς ἐκεῖνον οὐ κατηγόρευσα τὴν μανίαν
τὴν σήν, τοὐναντίον δέ, ὑπεσχόμην ὑπὲρ σοῦ. πάρεστιν οὖν σοι δυοῖν ὁδοῖν ὁποτέραν βούλει τρέπε-
σθαι. μηνύσω δὲ ἀμφοτέρας· πεισθεῖσα μὲν βασιλεῖ δῶρα λήψῃ τὰ κάλλιστα καὶ ἄνδρα ὃν θέλεις· οὐ
δήπου γάρ σε αὐτὸς μέλλει γαμεῖν ἀλλὰ πρόσκαι-
ρον αὐτῷ χάριν δώσεις· εἰ δὲ μὴ πεισθῇς, ἀκούεις ἃ
πάσχουσιν οἱ βασιλέως ἐχθροί· μόνοις γὰρ τούτοις
οὐδὲ ἀποθανεῖν θέλουσιν ἔξεστι."

8    Κατεγέλασε Καλλιρόη τῆς ἀπειλῆς καὶ ἔφη "οὐ
νῦν πρῶτον πείσομαί τι δεινόν· ἔμπειρός εἰμι τοῦ
δυστυχεῖν. τί με δύναται βασιλεὺς ὢν πέπονθα
διαθεῖναι χαλεπώτερον; ζῶσα κατεχώσθην· παντὸς
δεσμωτηρίου τάφος ἐστὶ στενότερος. λῃστῶν χερσὶ
9    παρεδόθην. ἄρτι τὸ μέγιστον τῶν κακῶν πάσχω·
παρόντα Χαιρέαν οὐ βλέπω." τοῦτο τὸ ῥῆμα προ-
έδωκεν αὐτήν· ὁ γὰρ εὐνοῦχος δεινὸς ὢν τὴν φύσιν
ἐνόησεν ὅτι ἐρᾷ. "ὢ" φησὶ "πασῶν ἀνοητοτάτη
γυναικῶν, τοῦ βασιλέως τὸν Μιθριδάτου δοῦλον
προτιμᾷς;" ἠγανάκτησε Καλλιρόη Χαιρέου λοιδορη-
10    θέντος καὶ "εὐφήμησον" εἶπεν, "ἄνθρωπε. Χαιρέας

7.7 πάρεισιν . . . δύο ὁδοί F, corr. Cobet.

themselves, he said to her, "You saw how the queen knelt in homage on hearing the king's name and went off in haste. But you, his slave, do not appreciate your good fortune, nor are you pleased that he invites you when he could command. However, I have not complained to him of your folly, for I respect you. Instead I have done the opposite; I have made a promise to him on your behalf. It is up to you which one of two courses you decide to take.[a] Let me tell you what they are. On the one hand, if you obey the king, you will receive splendid presents from him and have the husband you desire; for, of course, he does not intend to marry you himself, but you will afford him occasional pleasure. If you do not comply—well, you know what happens to the king's enemies: they alone are not permitted to die though they long to."[b]

Callirhoe laughed at his threat and said, "This will not be the first time that I have suffered. I am acquainted with misfortune. What can the king devise for me that is worse than what I have already endured? I was buried alive, and a tomb is narrower than any prison; I was delivered into the hands of pirates. And now I am suffering the greatest of my misfortunes: though Chaereas is here, I cannot see him." This remark gave her away, for the eunuch, who was naturally shrewd, realized that she was in love. "You silly woman," he said, "do you prefer Mithridates' slave to the king?" Callirhoe was maddened by this insult to Chaereas and said, "Keep quiet, fellow!

[a] Echoing Herodotus 1.11.2.
[b] Cf. Xenophon, *Anabasis* 3.1.29.

εὐγενής ἐστι, πόλεως πρῶτος, ἣν οὐκ ἐνίκησαν
οὐδὲ Ἀθηναῖοι οἱ ἐν Μαραθῶνι καὶ Σαλαμῖνι νική-
σαντες τὸν μέγαν σου βασιλέα." ταῦτα ἅμα
λέγουσα δακρύων πηγὰς ἀφῆκεν· ὁ δὲ εὐνοῦχος ἐπ-
έθετο μᾶλλον καὶ "σεαυτῇ" φησὶ "τῆς βραδυτῆτος
11  αἰτία γίνῃ. πῶς οὐκ εὐμενῆ τὸν δικαστὴν σχεῖν
κάλλιον, ἵνα καὶ τὸν ἄνδρα κομίσῃ; τάχα μὲν οὐδὲ
Χαιρέας γνοίη τὸ πραχθέν, ἀλλὰ καὶ γνοὺς οὐ
ζηλοτυπήσει τὸν κρείττονα· δόξει δέ σε τιμιωτέραν,
12  ὡς ἀρέσασαν βασιλεῖ." τοῦτο δὲ προσέθηκεν οὐχὶ
δι' ἐκείνην ἀλλὰ καὶ αὐτὸς οὕτω φρονῶν· καταπε-
πλήγασι γὰρ πάντες οἱ βάρβαροι καὶ θεὸν φανερὸν
νομίζουσι τὸν βασιλέα. Καλλιρόη δὲ καὶ αὐτοῦ τοῦ
Διὸς οὐκ ἂν ἠσπάσατο γάμους, οὐδὲ ἀθανασίαν
προετίμησεν ἂν ἡμέρας μιᾶς τῆς μετὰ Χαιρέου.
13  μηδὲν οὖν ἀνύσαι δυνάμενος ὁ εὐνοῦχος "δίδωμί
σοι" φησίν, "ὦ γύναι, σκέψεως καιρόν. σκέπτου
δὲ μὴ περὶ σεαυτῆς μόνης, ἀλλὰ καὶ Χαιρέου κινδυνεύοντος ἀπολέσθαι τὸν οἴκτιστον μόρον· οὐ γὰρ
ἀνέξεται βασιλεὺς ἐν ἔρωτι παρευδοκιμούμενος."
κἀκεῖνος μὲν ἀπηλλάγη, τὸ δὲ τελευταῖον τῆς
ὁμιλίας ἥψατο Καλλιρόης.

8.  Πᾶσαν δὲ σκέψιν καὶ πᾶσαν ἐρωτικὴν ὁμιλίαν
ταχέως μετέβαλεν ἡ Τύχη, καινοτέρων εὑροῦσα
πραγμάτων ὑπόθεσιν· βασιλεῖ γὰρ ἧκον ἀπαγγέλ-
λοντες Αἴγυπτον ἀφεστάναι μετὰ μεγάλης παρα-
2  σκευῆς. τὸν μὲν γὰρ σατράπην τὸν βασιλικὸν τοὺς
Αἰγυπτίους ἀνῃρηκέναι, κεχειροτονηκέναι δὲ βασιλέα

Chaereas is of noble birth, and the foremost man in a city
which not even the Athenians could defeat—and they
defeated your Great King at Marathon and Salamis." As
she said this, she burst into floods of tears. But the
eunuch pressed her all the more. "You yourself," he said,
"are responsible for the delay. Is it not better to gain the
judge's goodwill and get back your husband as well? Possibly Chaereas might not even know what happened, and
even if he did, he would not be jealous of his superior. He
will think all the more of you for having pleased the king."
This he added not so much to convince her, but because
he really believed it: for all orientals stand in blind awe of
the king and consider him to be a god on earth. But Callirhoe would not have welcomed marriage even with Zeus
himself,[a] nor counted even immortality better than a single day with Chaereas. So the eunuch, unable to achieve
his purpose, said, "I will allow you, my lady, time for
reflection. Think not only of yourself but of Chaereas as
well, since he runs the risk of a horrible death. The king
will not tolerate being bested in love." On this he left, but
his parting words remained fixed in Callirhoe's mind.

8.  However, Fortune quickly put an end to all
thoughts and talk of love by contriving a scenario of
extraordinary events. Messengers came to the king with
the report that a large-scale revolt had taken place in
Egypt: the Egyptians had killed the royal governor and

---

[a] Cf. Catullus 70.2 and 72.2.

---

7.11 οὐκ . . . σχεῖν Wifstrand: οὖν . . . ἕξεις ἤ σχεῖν F.

τῶν ἐπιχωρίων, ἐκεῖνον δὲ ἐκ Μέμφεως ὁρμώμενον
διαβεβηκέναι μὲν Πηλούσιον, ἤδη δὲ Συρίαν καὶ
Φοινίκην κατατρέχειν, ὡς μηκέτι τὰς πόλεις ἀντ-
έχειν, ὥσπερ χειμάρρου τινὸς ἢ πυρὸς αἰφνίδιον

3 ἐπιρρυέντος αὐταῖς. πρὸς δὲ τὴν φήμην ἐταράχθη
μὲν ὁ βασιλεύς, κατεπλάγησαν δὲ Πέρσαι· κατ-
ήφεια δὲ πᾶσαν ἔσχε Βαβυλῶνα. τότε καὶ ὄναρ
βασιλέως λογοποιοὶ καὶ μάντεις ἔφασκον τὰ μέλλοντα προειρηκέναι· θυσίας γὰρ ἀπαιτοῦντας τοὺς
θεοὺς κίνδυνον μὲν ἀλλὰ καὶ νίκην προσημαίνειν.

4 πάντα μὲν τὰ εἰωθότα συμβαίνειν καὶ ὅσα εἰκὸς ἐν
ἀπροσδοκήτῳ πολέμῳ, καὶ ἐλέγετο καὶ ἐγίνετο·
κίνησις γὰρ μεγάλη <πᾶσαν τὴν> Ἀσίαν κατέλαβε. συγκαλέσας οὖν ὁ βασιλεὺς Περσῶν τοὺς
ὁμοτίμους καὶ ὅσοι παρῆσαν ἡγεμόνες τῶν ἐθνῶν,
μεθ' ὧν εἰώθει τὰ μεγάλα χρηματίζειν, ἐβουλεύετο
περὶ τῶν καθεστηκότων καὶ ἄλλος ἄλλο τι παρῄνει·

5 πᾶσι δὲ ἤρεσκε τὸ σπεύδειν καὶ μηδὲ μίαν ἡμέραν,
εἰ δυνατόν, ἀναβαλέσθαι δυοῖν ἕνεκεν· ἵνα καὶ τοὺς
πολεμίους ἐπίσχωσι τῆς πρὸς τὸ πλεῖον αὐξήσεως
καὶ τοὺς φίλους εὐθυμοτέρους ποιήσωσι, δείξαντες
αὐτοῖς ἐγγύθεν τὴν βοήθειαν· βραδυνόντων δὲ εἰς
τοὐναντίον ἅπαντα χωρήσειν· τοὺς μὲν γὰρ πολεμίους καταφρονήσειν ὡς δεδιότων, τοὺς δὲ οἰκείους

6 ἐνδώσειν ὡς ἀμελουμένους. εὐτύχημα δὲ μέγιστον

8.4 add. Jackson.
8.5 μηδὲ μίαν Blake: μηδεμίαν F.

316

elected a pharaoh[a] from their own number; he had set out from Memphis,[b] crossed the Nile at Pelusium,[c] and was now overrunning Syria and Phoenicia, with the result that the cities were no longer offering any opposition; it was as though some torrent or conflagration had suddenly swept down upon them. The news threw the king into confusion, and the Persians were struck with terror. Gloom descended on the whole of Babylon. Then rumor mongers and prophets declared that the king's dream[d] had forecast the future; in demanding sacrifices the gods foretold danger, but victory as well. Everything was said and done which is customary and natural at the unexpected outbreak of war, for all Asia was gripped by profound stirrings. So the king convened the Persian nobles and the chiefs of the other nations who were in Babylon, with whom he usually discussed matters of importance, and considered the situation. Various courses were suggested, but all saw the need to act promptly and if possible not to delay even for a single day. There were two reasons for this, first, to prevent the enemy from augmenting his forces, and secondly, to hearten their friends by showing them that help was near. If they delayed, everything would tend to the opposite result: their enemies would despise them as cowards, and their allies would give in for lack of support. It was very fortu-

[a] So translated for clarity: literally 'a king.' See note on 7.1.4.
[b] At the head of the Nile delta, and in pre-Alexandrian times the capital city of Egypt.
[c] See on 7.3.3.
[d] Cf. 6.2.2.

βασιλεῖ γεγονέναι τὸ μήτε ἐν Βάκτροις μήτε ἐν
Ἐκβατάνοις, ἀλλὰ ἐν Βαβυλῶνι κατειλῆφθαι
πλησίον τῆς Συρίας· διαβὰς γὰρ τὸν Εὐφράτην
εὐθὺς ἐν χερσὶν ἕξει τοὺς ἀφεστῶτας. ἔδοξεν οὖν
τὴν μὲν ἤδη περὶ αὐτὸν δύναμιν ἐξάγειν, διαπέμψαι
δὲ πανταχόσε κελεύοντα τὴν στρατιὰν ἐπὶ ποταμὸν
Εὐφράτην ἀθροίζεσθαι. ῥᾴστη δέ ἐστι Πέρσαις ἡ
7  παρασκευὴ τῆς δυνάμεως. συντέτακται γὰρ ἀπὸ
Κύρου, τοῦ πρώτου Περσῶν βασιλεύσαντος, ποῖα
μὲν τῶν ἐθνῶν εἰς πόλεμον ἱππείαν καὶ πόσην τὸν
ἀριθμὸν δεῖ παρέχειν, ποῖα δὲ πεζὴν στρατιὰν καὶ
πόσην, τίνας δὲ τοξότας καὶ πόσα ἑκάστους ἅρματα
ψιλά τε καὶ δρεπανηφόρα, καὶ ἐλέφαντας ὁπόθεν καὶ
πόσους, καὶ χρήματα παρ' ὧντινων, ποῖα καὶ πόσα·
τοσούτῳ δὲ παρασκευάζεται χρόνῳ πάντα ὑπὸ
πάντων, ὅσῳ κἂν εἷς ἀνὴρ παρεσκεύασε.

9. Τῇ δὲ πέμπτῃ τῶν ἡμερῶν μετὰ τὴν ἀγγελίαν
ἐξήλαυνε Βαβυλῶνος ὁ βασιλεύς, κοινῷ παραγγέλ-
ματι πάντων αὐτῷ συνακολουθούντων, ὅσοι τὴν
στρατεύσιμον εἶχον ἡλικίαν. ἐν δὲ τούτοις ἐξῆλθε
καὶ Διονύσιος· Ἴων γὰρ ἦν καὶ οὐδενὶ τῶν ὑπηκόων
2  μένειν ἐξῆν. κοσμησάμενος δὲ ὅπλοις καλλίστοις
καὶ ποιήσας στῖφος οὐκ εὐκαταφρόνητον ἐκ τῶν
μεθ' ἑαυτοῦ, ἐν τοῖς πρώτοις καὶ φανερωτάτοις κατ-
έταξεν ἑαυτὸν καὶ δῆλος ἦν πράξων τι γενναῖον, οἷα
δὴ καὶ φύσει φιλότιμος ἀνὴρ καὶ οὐ πάρεργον τὴν
3  ἀρετὴν τιθέμενος, ἀλλὰ τῶν καλλίστων ἀξιῶν. τότ-

nate for the king that this news had reached him, not in Bactra or in Ecbatana, but in Babylon, close to Syria, for once he had crossed the Euphrates, he would have the rebels in his power. He decided, therefore, to take the field with the forces he had with him, and to send out the order to all provinces for the army to assemble at the river Euphrates. Now the mobilization of the Persian forces is very easily effected. The system was drawn up by Cyrus, the first Persian king: which communities are to supply cavalry for a war and how great a number; also which of them are to supply infantry, and how many; likewise who must supply archers, and how many chariots apiece, both ordinary and scythe-bearing; where the elephants are to come from, and how many; and from whom money is to come, in what currency and how much.[a] All these preparations take the whole empire only as much time as one man would need to get ready.

9. On the fifth day after the news of the revolt, the king marched out from Babylon, issuing a general order for all of military age to follow him. Dionysius also was among those who left, for he was an Ionian, and none of the king's subjects was permitted to stay behind. Equipped in his best armor and forming a far from negligible company of his retainers, he stationed himself conspicuously in the front ranks. He made it plain that he would serve with distinction, since he was naturally ambitious, and far from considering bravery a secondary virtue he counted it as one of the noblest. Moreover, on this

[a] For the whole passage cf. Xenophon, *Cyropaedia* 6.1.30.

---

8.7 πόσην τὸν Hercher: πόσον τὸν F | κἂν Cobet: καὶ F.

δὲ καὶ ἐλπίδος εἶχέ τι κούφης, ὅτι <ἂν> χρήσιμος
ὢν ἐν τῷ πολέμῳ φανῇ, λήψεται παρὰ τοῦ βασιλέως
καὶ δίχα κρίσεως ἆθλον τῆς ἀριστείας τὴν γυναῖκα.

4    Καλλιρόην δὲ ἡ μὲν βασιλὶς οὐκ ἤθελεν ἐπάγε-
σθαι· διὰ τοῦτο οὐδὲ ἐμνημόνευσεν αὐτῆς πρὸς
βασιλέα οὐδὲ ἐπύθετο τί κελεύει γενέσθαι περὶ τῆς
ξένης· ἀλλὰ καὶ Ἀρταξάτης κατεσιώπησεν, ὡς δῆτα
μὴ θαρρῶν ἐν κινδύνῳ τοῦ δεσπότου καθεστηκότος
παιδιᾶς ἐρωτικῆς μνημονεύειν, τὸ δὲ ἀληθὲς ἄσμενος
ἀπηλλαγμένος καθάπερ ἀγρίου θηρίου· ἐδόκει δ᾽ ἅι
μοι καὶ χάριν ἔχειν τῷ πολέμῳ διακόψαντι τὴι
βασιλέως ἐπιθυμίαν ὑπὸ ἀργίας τρεφομένην.

5    Οὐ μὴν Καλλιρόης ἐπελέληστο βασιλεύς, ἀλλὰ
ἐν ἐκείνῳ τῷ ἀδιηγήτῳ ταράχῳ μνήμη τις αὐτὸν εἰσῆλθε τοῦ κάλλους· ᾐδεῖτο δὲ εἰπεῖν τι περὶ αὐτῆς, μὴ
δόξῃ παιδαριώδης εἶναι παντάπασιν, ἐν πολέμῳ
τηλικούτῳ γυναικὸς εὐμόρφου μνημονεύων. βιαζο-
μένης δὲ τῆς ὁρμῆς πρὸς μὲν Στάτειραν αὐτὴν οὐδὲι
εἶπεν, ἀλλ᾽ οὐδὲ πρὸς τὸν εὐνοῦχον, ἐπειδήπερ αὐτῷ
6    συνῄδει τὸν ἔρωτα, ἐπενόησε δέ τι τοιοῦτον. ἔθος
ἐστὶν αὐτῷ τε βασιλεῖ καὶ Περσῶν τοῖς ἀρίστοις
ὅταν εἰς πόλεμον ἐξίωσιν, ἐπάγεσθαι καὶ γυναῖκας
καὶ τέκνα καὶ χρυσὸν καὶ ἄργυρον καὶ ἐσθῆτα καὶ
εὐνούχους καὶ παλλακίδας καὶ κύνας καὶ τραπέζας
7    καὶ πλοῦτον πολυτελῆ καὶ τρυφήν. τὸν οὖν ἐπ᾽

9.3 ἂν χ. ὢν Reiske: χ. ἦν F.
9.4 δ᾽ ἄν Blake: δέ F.

occasion, he felt some slight hope that, if he proved himself useful in the war, he would be given his wife by the king as a reward for his valor without a trial taking place.

The queen did not want Callirhoe taken along, and for that reason she did not mention her to the king and did not even ask what his orders were respecting the foreign woman. Artaxates, too, kept silent, apparently because he was afraid to remind his master of a love affair now that he found himself in a parlous situation, but the fact was that he was as glad to escape from her as from a savage beast. Indeed I can well imagine that he was grateful to the war for having cut short this passion of the king which had been fed by idleness.

However, the king had not forgotten Callirhoe, and even in that indescribable confusion[a] the recollection of her beauty came to his mind. Still, he was embarrassed to say anything about her for fear of appearing so utterly juvenile as to be thinking of a pretty girl during a major war. Even so, his passion did not abate. Though he said nothing to Statira herself nor to the eunuch who was privy to his love, he devised the following plan. It is the custom for the king himself and the nobles of Persia, when they go to war, to take along with them their wives and children, their gold and silver and clothes, their eunuchs and mistresses, their dogs and tables, and precious treasures

[a] Cf. Xenophon, *Cyropaedia* 7.1.32.

---

9.5 τι περὶ Cobet: τὸ περὶ F | ἐπειδήπερ Hercher: ἐπειδὴ F (cf. 7.5.6).

τούτων διάκονον καλέσας ὁ βασιλεύς, πολλὰ πρῶτον εἰπὼν καὶ τὰ ἄλλα διατάξας ὡς ἕκαστον ἔδει γενέσθαι, τελευταίας ἐμνημόνευσε Καλλιρόης ἀξιοπίστῳ τῷ προσώπῳ, ὡς οὐδὲν αὐτῷ μέλον. "κἀκεῖνο" φησὶ "τὸ γύναιον τὸ ξένον, περὶ οὗ τὴν κρίσιν ἀνεδεξάμην, σὺν ταῖς ἄλλαις γυναιξὶν ἀκολουθείτω."

8    Καὶ Καλλιρόη μὲν οὕτως ἐξῆλθε Βαβυλῶνος οὐκ ἀηδῶς, ἤλπιζε γὰρ καὶ Χαιρέαν ἐξελεύσεσθαι· πολλὰ μὲν οὖν φέρειν πόλεμον καὶ ἄδηλα, καὶ μεταβολὰς τοῖς δυστυχοῦσι βελτίονας, τάχα δὲ καὶ τὴν δίκην ἕξειν τέλος ἐκεῖ ταχείας εἰρήνης γενομένης.

9.8 πόλεμον καὶ Blake: καὶ πόλεμον F.

and luxuries.[a] Accordingly the king summoned the steward in charge of these matters and first embarked on a lengthy discussion and detailed instructions for the handling of everything. Then finally he mentioned Callirhoe, with a casual air as though a matter of indifference to him. "As for the little foreign woman," he said, "the one whose case I undertook to judge, let her come along with the other women."

And so Callirhoe left Babylon, without regret, because she supposed that Chaereas would be leaving too: war brought with it much which could not be foreseen and changes which, to those in distress, could only be for the better; perhaps after a speedy peace the trial would also be concluded there.

[a] Cf. Xenophon, *Cyropaedia* 4.2.2.

# Z

1. Πάντων δὲ ἐξιόντων μετὰ βασιλέως ἐπὶ τὸν πόλεμον τὸν πρὸς τοὺς Αἰγυπτίους Χαιρέᾳ παρήγγειλεν οὐδείς· βασιλέως γὰρ δοῦλος οὐκ ἦν, ἀλλὰ τότε μόνος ἐν Βαβυλῶνι ἐλεύθερος. ἔχαιρε δὲ ἐλπίζων ὅτι καὶ Καλλιρόη μένει. τῆς οὖν ὑστεραίας

2 ἦλθεν ἐπὶ τὰ βασίλεια, ζητῶν τὴν γυναῖκα. κεκλεισμένα δὲ ἰδὼν καὶ πολλοὺς ἐπὶ θύραις τοὺς φυλάσσοντας περιῄει τὴν πόλιν ὅλην ἐξερευνώμενος καὶ συνεχῶς καθάπερ ἐμμανὴς Πολυχάρμου τοῦ φίλου πυνθανόμενος "Καλλιρόη δὲ ποῦ; τί γέγονεν; οὐ δήπου γὰρ καὶ αὐτὴ στρατεύεται."

3 Μὴ εὑρὼν δὲ Καλλιρόην ἐζήτει Διονύσιον τὸν ἀντεραστὴν καὶ ἧκεν ἐπὶ τὴν οἰκίαν τὴν ἐκείνου. προῆλθεν οὖν τις ὥσπερ οἰκουρὸς καὶ εἶπεν ἅπερ ἦν δεδιδαγμένος. θέλων γὰρ ὁ Διονύσιος ἀπελπίσαι Χαιρέαν τὸν Καλλιρόης γάμον καὶ μηκέτι μένειν

4 τὴν δίκην, ἐπενόησέ τι στρατήγημα τοιοῦτον. ἐξιὼν ἐπὶ τὴν μάχην κατέλιπε τὸν ἀπαγγελοῦντα πρὸς Χαιρέαν ὅτι βασιλεὺς ὁ Περσῶν χρείαν ἔχων συμμάχων πέπομφε Διονύσιον ἀθροῖσαι στρατιὰν ἐπὶ τὸν Αἰγύπτιον καί, ἵνα πιστῶς αὐτῷ καὶ προθύμως

1.3 οἰκουρὸς Jackson: ἄκαιρος F.

324

# BOOK 7

1. When everyone accompanied the king to the war against the Egyptians, Chaereas was given no orders, for he was not the king's slave, but at that moment the only free person in Babylon. He was glad of this, supposing that Callirhoe was also remaining behind. So the next day he came to the palace in search of his wife. Seeing it shut and many guards at the gates, he went about the whole city searching, and like one possessed kept asking his friend Polycharmus, "Where is Callirhoe? What has become of her? Surely she, too, has not taken the field?"

Not finding Callirhoe, he looked for his rival Dionysius, and went to his house; someone purporting to be a housekeeper came out and told the story he had been primed with. Dionysius had in fact devised the following scheme, desiring Chaereas to give up hopes of regaining Callirhoe and no longer wait for the trial. When he started out for battle, he had left someone behind to tell Chaereas that the king of Persia, having need of allies, had sent Dionysius to raise an army against the pharaoh,[a] and that he had given him Callirhoe to guarantee his

[a] Literally 'the Egyptian' (cf. Xenophon, *Cyropaedia*, which refers to oriental kings simply as 'the Armenian,' 'the Assyrian,' etc.). And so often below; but at 8.2.3 the expression is used twice, referring to two different persons. See note on 6.8.2.

ἐξυπηρετῆται, Καλλιρόην ἀπέδωκε.

Ταῦτα ἀκούσας Χαιρέας ἐπίστευσεν εὐθύς· εὐεξ-
5 απάτητον γὰρ ἄνθρωπος δυστυχῶν. καταρρηξάμε-
νος οὖν τὴν ἐσθῆτα καὶ σπαράξας τὰς τρίχας, τὸ
στέρνον ἅμα παίων ἔλεγεν "ἄπιστε Βαβυλών, κακὴ
ξενοδόχε, ἐπ' ἐμοῦ δὲ καὶ ἐρήμη. ὦ καλοῦ δικαστοῦ·
προαγωγὸς γέγονεν ἀλλοτρίας γυναικός. ἐν πολέμῳ γάμοι. καὶ ἐγὼ μὲν ἐμμελετῶν τὴν δίκην καὶ
πάνυ πεπείσμην δίκαια ἐρεῖν· ἐρήμην δὲ κατεκρίθην
6 καὶ Διονύσιος νενίκηκε σιγῶν. ἀλλ' οὐδὲν ὄφελος
αὐτῷ τῆς νίκης· οὐ γὰρ ζήσεται Καλλιρόη παρόντος
διαζευχθεῖσα Χαιρέου· καὶ τὸ πρῶτον ἐξηπάτησεν
αὐτὴν τῷ δοκεῖν ἐμὲ τεθνηκέναι. τί οὖν ἐγὼ βρα-
δύνω καὶ οὐκ ἀποσφάζω πρὸ τῶν βασιλείων ἐμαυ-
τόν, προχέας τὸ αἷμα ταῖς θύραις τοῦ δικαστοῦ;
γνώτωσαν Πέρσαι καὶ Μῆδοι, πῶς βασιλεὺς ἐδίκα-
σεν ἐνταῦθα."

7 Πολύχαρμος δὲ ἰδὼν ἀπαρηγόρητον αὐτῷ τὴν
συμφορὰν καὶ ἀδύνατον σωθῆναι Χαιρέαν "πάλαι
μὲν" ἔφη "παρεμυθούμην σε, φίλτατε, καὶ πολλάκις
ἀποθανεῖν ἐκώλυσα, νῦν δέ μοι δοκεῖς καλῶς βεβου-
λεῦσθαι· καὶ τοσοῦτον ἀποδέω τοῦ σε κωλύειν, ὥστε
καὶ αὐτὸς ἤδη συναποθανεῖν ἕτοιμος. σκεψώμεθα
δὲ θανάτου τρόπον, ὅστις ἂν γένοιτο, βέλτιον· ὃν
γὰρ σὺ διανοῇ, φέρει μέν τινα φθόνον βασιλεῖ καὶ
πρὸς τὸ μέλλον αἰσχύνην, οὐ μεγάλην δὲ ἐκδικίαν
8 ὧν πεπόνθαμεν. δοκεῖ δέ μοι τὸν ἅπαξ ὡρισμένον
θάνατον ὑφ' ἡμῶν εἰς ἄμυναν καταχρήσασθαι

326

faithful and enthusiastic service.

Chaereas readily believed what he heard, for an unhappy man is easily deceived. He rent his clothes and tore his hair, and beating his breast exclaimed, "Treacherous Babylon! What a cruel host you are, and to me a veritable desert! What a fine judge to become the procurer of another man's wife! A wedding in time of war! And I was carefully preparing my case, confident of receiving justice when I made my defense. Now I have lost by default, and Dionysius has won without saying a word. But he shall not profit by his victory. Callirhoe will not live, if she is separated from Chaereas when he is near. At the beginning he was only able to deceive her by pretending I was dead. Why do I hesitate and not cut my throat in front of the palace, pouring forth my blood at the very gates of the judge? Let the Persians and the Medes know what kind of justice the king has dispensed here!"

Polycharmus, seeing that he could provide no consolation for this disaster, and that it was impossible to save Chaereas, said, "My dearest friend, in the past I have tried to comfort you and often prevented your death, but now I think your decision is right. And so far am I from preventing you that now I too am ready to die with you. But let us consider more carefully what sort of death it should be. The one which you propose may raise some ill-feeling against the king and cause him shame in the future, but it is not much of a retribution for our sufferings. I think that once we have decided on death we

---

1.5 ἐπεπείσμην F, corr. Jackson.
1.7 βέλτιον Jackson (cf. 4.4.2): βελτίων F.

τοῦ τυράννου· καλὸν γὰρ λυπήσαντας αὐτὸν ἔργῳ
ποιῆσαι μετανοεῖν, ἔνδοξον καὶ τοῖς ὕστερον
ἐσομένοις διήγημα καταλείποντας ὅτι δύο Ἕλληνες
ἀδικηθέντες ἀντελύπησαν τὸν μέγαν βασιλέα καὶ
ἀπέθανον ὡς ἄνδρες."

9     "Πῶς οὖν" εἶπε Χαιρέας "ἡμεῖς οἱ <δύο> μόνοι
καὶ πένητες καὶ ξένοι τὸν κύριον τηλικούτων καὶ
τοσούτων ἐθνῶν καὶ δύναμιν ἔχοντα ἣν ἑωράκαμεν
λυπῆσαι δυνάμεθα; τοῦ μὲν γὰρ σώματος αὐτῷ
φυλακαὶ καὶ προφυλακαί, κἂν ἀποκτείνωμεν δέ τινα
τῶν ἐκείνου, κἂν ἐμπρήσωμέν τι τῶν ἐκείνου κτημά-
10    των, οὐκ αἰσθήσεται τῆς βλάβης." "ὀρθῶς ἂν" ἔφη
Πολύχαρμος "ταῦτα ἔλεγες, εἰ μὴ πόλεμος ἦν· νῦν
δὲ ἀκούομεν Αἴγυπτον μὲν ἀφεστάναι, Φοινίκην δὲ
ἑαλωκέναι, Συρίαν δὲ καταδρέχεσθαι. βασιλεῖ δὲ ὁ
πόλεμος ἀπαντήσει καὶ πρὸ τοῦ διαβῆναι τὸν
11    Εὐφράτην. οὐκ ἐσμὲν οὖν οἱ δύο μόνοι, τοσούτους
δὲ ἔχομεν συμμάχους ὅσους ὁ Αἰγύπτιος ἄγει,
τοσαῦτα ὅπλα, τοσαῦτα χρήματα, τοσαύτας τριήρεις. χρησόμεθα ἀλλοτρίᾳ δυνάμει πρὸς τὴν ὑπὲρ
ἑαυτῶν ἄμυναν."

οὔπω πᾶν εἴρητο ἔπος

καὶ Χαιρέας ἀνεβόησε "σπεύδωμεν, ἀπίωμεν. δίκας
ἐν τῷ πολέμῳ λήψομαι παρὰ τοῦ δικαστοῦ."

2. Ταχέως τοίνυν ἐξορμήσαντες ἐδίωκον βασιλέα,
προσποιούμενοι θέλειν ἐκείνῳ συστρατεύεσθαι· διὰ
γὰρ ταύτης τῆς προφάσεως ἤλπιζον ἀδεῶς διαβή-

should use it to wreak vengeance on the tyrant. It would be a fine thing to cause him enough pain to make him sorry, and bequeath to posterity the legend of two Greeks who made the Great King suffer for the injustice he did them and died like heroes."

"But," said Chaereas, "we are only two men, poor, and strangers here. How can we inflict pain on the master of all these powerful nations? We have seen the resources that he possesses. He has bodyguards and sentries, and even if we do succeed in killing one of those men or in setting fire to some of his property, he will not even notice the damage." "What you say would be true," said Polycharmus, "if there were no war; but now we hear that Egypt has revolted, Phoenicia been captured, and Syria overrun. The war will catch up with the king even before he crosses the Euphrates. Therefore we are not two men alone. Rather we have as allies all those whom the pharaoh commands, and all his arms, resources, and warships. Let us use another man's power to effect our own vengeance."

Not yet was the whole word spoken,[a]

when Chaereas exclaimed, "Hurry! Let us go! I shall get judgment from the war against this judge."

2. So they set out in haste after the king on the pretense of wanting to join his forces, since by this device

[a] *Odyssey* 16.11 and elsewhere (formula); cf. 3.4.4.

---

1.9 add. Zankogiannes.
2.1 ἐθέλειν F, corr. Hercher.

σεσθαι τὸν Εὐφράτην. κατέλαβον δὲ τὴν στρατιὰν
ἐπὶ τῷ ποταμῷ καὶ προσμίξαντες τοῖς ὀπισθοφύλα-
ξιν ἠκολούθουν. ἐπεὶ δὲ ἧκον εἰς Συρίαν, ηὐτομόλη-
σαν πρὸς τὸν Αἰγύπτιον. λαβόντες δὲ αὐτοὺς οἱ
φύλακες ἐξήταζον τίνες εἶεν· σχῆμα γὰρ πρεσβευ-
τῶν οὐκ ἔχοντες ὑπωπτεύοντο κατάσκοποι μᾶλλον.
ἔνθα κἂν παρεκινδύνευσαν, εἰ μὴ εἷς γέ τις Ἕλλην
ἐκεῖ κατὰ τύχην εὑρεθεὶς συνῆκε τῆς φωνῆς· ἠξίουν
δὲ ἄγεσθαι πρὸς τὸν βασιλέα, ὡς μέγα ὄφελος αὐτῷ
κομίζοντες. ἐπεὶ δὲ ἤχθησαν, Χαιρέας εἶπεν "ἡμεῖς
Ἕλληνές ἐσμεν Συρακόσιοι τῶν εὐπατριδῶν. οὗτος
μὲν οὖν εἰς Βαβυλῶνα φίλος ἐμὸς ὢν ἦλθε δι' ἐμέ,
ἐγὼ δὲ διὰ γυναῖκα, τὴν Ἑρμοκράτους θυγατέρα, εἴ
τινα Ἑρμοκράτην ἀκούεις στρατηγὸν <τὸν> Ἀθηναίους καταναυμαχήσαντα." ἐπένευσεν ὁ Αἰγύπτιος,
οὐδὲν γὰρ ἔθνος ἄπυστον ἦν τῆς Ἀθηναίων δυστυ-
χίας, ἣν ἐδυστύχησαν ἐν τῷ πολέμῳ τῷ Σικελικῷ.
"τετυράννηκε δὲ ἡμῶν Ἀρταξέρξης," καὶ πάντα διηγήσατο. "φέροντες οὖν ἑαυτοὺς δίδομέν σοι φίλους
πιστούς, δύο τὰ προτρεπτικώτατα εἰς ἀνδρείαν ἔχοντες, θανάτου καὶ ἀμύνης ἔρωτα· ἤδη γὰρ ἐτεθνήκειν
ὅσον ἐπὶ ταῖς συμφοραῖς, λοιπὸν δὲ ζῶ μόνον εἰς τὸ
λυπῆσαι τὸν ἐχθρόν.

μὴ μὰν ἀσπουδί γε καὶ ἀκλειῶς ἀπολοίμην,
ἀλλὰ μέγα ῥέξας τι καὶ ἐσσομένοισι πυθέσθαι."

2.2 κἂν Jackson: καὶ F.
2.3 add. Cobet.

they hoped to cross the Euphrates without danger. They
came upon the army at the river bank, and joining in with
the rearguard followed along. Once they arrived in
Syria,[a] however, they deserted to the pharaoh. His guards
seized them and inquired who they were, for the fact that
they were not dressed as ambassadors aroused the suspicion that they were probably spies. Then they would have
been in trouble, had a Greek who chanced to be present
not understood their speech. They asked to be taken to
the monarch, since they had something to offer him
greatly to his advantage. When they were brought to him,
Chaereas said, "We are Greeks and belong to the Syracusan aristocracy. My friend here came to Babylon for my
sake, and I came for the sake of my wife, who is the
daughter of Hermocrates, if you have heard of
Hermocrates, the general who defeated the Athenians at
sea." The pharaoh nodded, for there was no nation that
had not heard of the disaster suffered by the Athenians in
the Sicilian war. "Artaxerxes has treated us like a tyrant,"
they said, and told him the whole story. "So we have
come to offer ourselves to you as loyal friends. We have
the two greatest incentives to bravery, desire for death
and desire for revenge. In fact I am as good as dead in
view of my misfortunes; I continue to live only in order to
inflict pain on my enemy.

Let me not die without a struggle, no, not without glory,
but after a feat that even men to be born shall hear of."[b]

[a] I.e. after crossing the Euphrates.
[b] *Iliad* 22.304f (Hector at his last fight).

---

2.4 διηγήσατο Hercher: διηγήσαντο F | μόνον εἰς Jackson:
εἰς μόνον F.

5 ταῦτα ἀκούσας ὁ Αἰγύπτιος ἥσθη καὶ τὴν δεξιὰν
ἐμβαλὼν "εἰς καιρὸν ἥκεις" φησίν, "ὦ νεανία, σεαυτῷ τε κἀμοί." παραυτίκα μὲν οὖν αὐτοῖς ἐκέλευσεν
ὅπλα δοθῆναι καὶ σκηνήν, μετ᾽ οὐ πολὺ δὲ καὶ ὁμο-
τράπεζον ἐποιήσατο Χαιρέαν, εἶτα καὶ σύμβουλον·
ἐπεδείκνυτο γὰρ φρόνησίν τε καὶ θάρσος, μετὰ τούτων δὲ καὶ πίστιν, οἷα δὴ καὶ φύσεως ἀγαθῆς καὶ
6 παιδείας οὐκ ἀπρονόητος. ἐπήγειρε δὲ μᾶλλον
αὐτὸν καὶ διαπρεπέστερον ἐποίησεν ἡ πρὸς βασιλέα
φιλονεικία καὶ τὸ δεῖξαι θέλειν ὅτι οὐκ ἦν εὐκαταφρόνητος, ἀλλ᾽ ἄξιος τιμῆς.

Εὐθὺς οὖν ἔργον ἐπεδείξατο μέγα. τῷ μὲν Αἰγυπτίῳ τὰ μὲν ἄλλα προκεχωρήκει ῥᾳδίως καὶ κύριος
ἐγεγόνει τῆς Κοίλης Συρίας ἐξ ἐπιδρομῆς, ὑποχεί-
7 ριος δὲ ἦν αὐτῷ καὶ Φοινίκη πλὴν Τύρου. Τύριοι δὲ
φύσει γένος εἰσὶ μαχιμώτατον καὶ κλέος ἐπ᾽ ἀνδρείᾳ
θέλουσι κεκτῆσθαι, μὴ δόξωσι καταισχύνειν τὸν
Ἡρακλέα, φανερώτατον θεὸν παρ᾽ αὐτοῖς καὶ ᾧ
μόνῳ σχεδὸν ἀνατεθείκασι τὴν πόλιν. θαρροῦσι δὲ
8 καὶ ὀχυρότητι τῆς οἰκήσεως. ἡ μὲν γὰρ πόλις ἐν
θαλάσσῃ κατῴκισται, λεπτὴ δὲ εἴσοδος αὐτὴν
συνάπτουσα τῇ γῇ κωλύει τὸ μὴ νῆσον εἶναι· ἔοικε
δὲ νηὶ καθωρμισμένῃ καὶ ἐπὶ γῆς τεθεικυίᾳ τὴν ἐπι-
9 βάθραν. πανταχόθεν οὖν αὐτοῖς τὸν πόλεμον ἀπο-
κλεῖσαι ῥᾴδιον· τὴν μὲν πεζὴν στρατιὰν ἐκ τῆς
θαλάσσης, ἀρκούσης αὐτῇ πύλης μιᾶς, τὸν δὲ ἐπί-

2.7 εἰσὶ Reiske: ἐστὶ F.

332

The pharaoh was delighted to hear this and held out his hand and said, "Young man, you have come at just the right time for both of us." Then he ordered armor and a tent to be given them at once. Not long after he made Chaereas first his messmate, and then his adviser, for he displayed intelligence and courage, and trustworthiness besides, for he was not without a noble character and education. But what drove him on all the more and gave him prominence was his desire to defeat the king and show that he was not to be taken lightly, but was worthy of respect.

He immediately demonstrated his ability with a remarkable achievement. On the whole the pharaoh's advance had proceeded smoothly: he had occupied Coele Syria[a] by storm, and Phoenicia was also in his hands. But Tyre held out. The Tyrians are by nature a most warlike race, eager to maintain a reputation for bravery lest they be thought to disgrace Heracles,[b] who is their chief deity, and to whom almost exclusively they have dedicated their city. They also rely on the natural impregnability of the site. The city is actually built in the sea, and only a narrow approach unites it with the shore and keeps it from being an island. It is like a ship at anchor with its gangplank resting upon the land. Thus they can easily shut out an enemy from any direction, a land force by their position in the sea, as they need only a single gate, and the attack

[a] Literally 'Hollow Syria,' originally the district between Mt. Libanus and Mt. Antilibanus, but later extended to cover all Syria west of the Euphrates, excluding the seaboard (Phoenicia).

[b] The Semitic Melkart ('King of the City,' Melicertes, Moloch), but long since identified with the Greek Heracles.

πλοῦν τῶν τριηρῶν τείχεσιν, ὀχυρῶς ᾠκοδομημένης τῆς πόλεως καὶ λιμέσι κλειομένης ὥσπερ οἰκίας.

3. Πάντων οὖν τῶν πέριξ ἑαλωκότων μόνοι Τύριοι τῶν Αἰγυπτίων κατεφρόνουν, τὴν εὔνοιαν καὶ πίστιν τῷ Πέρσῃ φυλάττοντες. ἐπὶ τούτῳ δυσχεραίνων ὁ Αἰγύπτιος συνήγαγε βουλήν. τότε πρῶτον Χαιρέαν παρεκάλεσεν εἰς τὸ συμβούλιον καὶ ἔλεξεν ὧδε.

2    "Ἄνδρες σύμμαχοι, δούλους γὰρ οὐκ ἂν εἴποιμι τοὺς φίλους, ὁρᾶτε τὴν ἀπορίαν ὅτι ὥσπερ ναῦς ἐπὶ πολὺ εὐπλοήσασα ἐναντίῳ <τῷ> ἀνέμῳ λαμβανόμεθα καὶ Τύρος ἡ παγχάλεπος κατέχει σπεύδοντας ἡμᾶς· ἐπείγεται δὲ καὶ βασιλεύς, ὡς πυνθανόμεθα. τί οὖν χρὴ πράττειν; οὔτε γὰρ ἑλεῖν Τύρον ἔνεστιν, οὔτε ὑπερβῆναι, καθάπερ δὲ τεῖχος ἐν μέσῳ κειμένη τὴν Ἀσίαν ἡμῖν πᾶσαν ἀποκλείει. δοκεῖ δέ μοι τὴν ταχίστην ἐντεῦθεν ἀπιέναι, πρὶν ἢ τὴν Περσῶν

3    δύναμιν Τυρίοις προσγενέσθαι. κίνδυνος δὲ καταληφθεῖσιν ἡμῖν ἐν τῇ πολεμίᾳ. τὸ δὲ Πηλούσιον ὀχυρόν, ἔνθα οὔτε Τυρίους οὔτε Μήδους οὔτε πάντας ἀνθρώπους ἐπιόντας δεδοίκαμεν· ψάμμος τε γὰρ ἀδιόδευτος καὶ εἴσοδος ὀλίγη καὶ θάλασσα ἡμετέρα καὶ Νεῖλος Αἰγυπτίους φιλῶν." ταῦτα εἰπόντος λίαν εὐλαβῶς σιωπὴ πάντων ἐγένετο καὶ κατήφεια· μόνος δὲ Χαιρέας ἐτόλμησεν εἰπεῖν·

4    "Ὦ βασιλεῦ, σὺ γὰρ ἀληθῶς βασιλεύς, οὐχ ὁ Πέρσης, ὁ κάκιστος ἀνθρώπων· λελύπηκάς με σκεπτόμενος περὶ φυγῆς ἐν ἐπινικίοις· νικῶμεν γάρ, ἂν

of warships by their walls, as the city is strongly fortified and is locked up like a house by its harbors.

3. Thus, after the whole area had been subdued, the Tyrians alone defied the Egyptians and maintained their loyalty and allegiance to the Persian king. Vexed at this, the pharaoh summoned his council. This was the first meeting to which he invited Chaereas, and he made the following speech.

"My allies, for I should not dream of calling my friends 'slaves,' you see the difficulty. Like a ship, we have long enjoyed smooth sailing, but now we are caught by an adverse wind, and it is impregnable Tyre which checks our victorious advance. We also learn that the king is pressing hard upon us. What, then, must we do? It is not possible to capture Tyre, nor yet to pass beyond it. It lies like a wall in our path and shuts us off from all Asia. I think we should withdraw from here as quickly as possible, before the Persian army joins the Tyrians. It is dangerous for us to be caught on enemy soil. But Pelusium[a] is strongly fortified and there we need have no fear of Tyrians or Medes or anyone else who may attack us. The desert there is impassable, the approach is narrow, the sea is ours, and the Nile is Egypt's friend." At these overcautious words, all sat silent and depressed. Chaereas alone dared to speak.

"Your Majesty," said he, "for true majesty belongs to you and not to that wicked Persian—it pains me to hear you considering flight on the very eve of victory. With

---

[a] A coastal fortress on the easternmost tributary of the Nile.

3.2 add. Jackson.

θεοὶ θέλωσι, καὶ οὐ μόνον Τύρον ἕξομεν, ἀλλὰ καὶ
Βαβυλῶνα. πολλὰ δὲ ἐν πολέμῳ [καὶ] τὰ ἐμπόδια
γίνεται, πρὸς ἃ δεῖ μὴ παντάπασιν ἀποκνεῖν, ἀλλὰ
5 ἐγχειρεῖν προβαλλομένους ἀεὶ τὴν ἀγαθὴν ἐλπίδα.
τούτους δὲ ἐγώ σοι τοὺς Τυρίους, τοὺς νῦν κατα-
γελῶντας, γυμνοὺς ἐν πέδαις παραστήσω. εἰ δὲ
ἀπιστεῖς, ἐμὲ προθυσάμενος ἀπέρχου· ζῶν γὰρ
οὐ κοινωνήσω φυγῆς. ἂν δὲ καὶ πάντως θέλῃς,
ὀλίγους ἐμοὶ κατάλιπε τοὺς ἑκουσίως μενοῦντας·

νῶι δ', ἐγὼ Πολύχαρμός τε μαχησόμεθα . . .
. . . σὺν γὰρ θεῷ εἰλήλουθμεν."

6  Ἠιδέσθησαν πάντες μὴ συγκαταθέσθαι τῇ
Χαιρέου γνώμῃ· βασιλεὺς δὲ θαυμάσας αὐτοῦ τὸ
φρόνημα συνεχώρησεν ὁπόσον βούλεται τῆς
στρατιᾶς ἐπίλεκτον λαβεῖν. ὁ δὲ οὐκ εὐθὺς εἵλετο,
ἀλλὰ καταμίξας ἑαυτὸν εἰς τὸ στρατόπεδον καὶ
Πολύχαρμον κελεύσας τὸ αὐτό, πρῶτον ἀνηρεύνα εἴ
7  τινες εἶεν Ἕλληνες ἐν τῷ στρατοπέδῳ. πλείονες μὲν
οὖν εὑρέθησαν οἱ μισθοφοροῦντες, ἐξελέξατο δὲ
Λακεδαιμονίους καὶ Κορινθίους καὶ τοὺς ἄλλους
Πελοποννησίους· εὗρε δὲ καὶ ὡς εἴκοσι Σικελιώτας.
ποιήσας οὖν τριακοσίους τὸν ἀριθμὸν ἔλεξεν ὧδε·
8  ""Ἄνδρες Ἕλληνες, ἐμοὶ τοῦ βασιλέως ἐξουσίαν
παρασχόντος ἐπιλέξασθαι τῆς στρατιᾶς τοὺς ἀρίστους, εἱλόμην ὑμᾶς· καὶ γὰρ αὐτὸς Ἕλλην εἰμί,
Συρακόσιος, γένος Δωριεύς. δεῖ δὲ ἡμᾶς μὴ μόνον

Heaven's will we shall win, and we shall take not only Tyre, but Babylon as well. Many are the setbacks which occur in war: we must never flinch before them, but tackle them, ever holding before us like a shield the hope of success. As for these Tyrians who are now mocking us, I shall bring them before you stripped and in chains. If you do not believe me, then kill me first before you go, for while I am alive I shall never share your flight. If you are going anyway, then leave a few volunteers to stay with me.

Yet will we two, I and Polycharmus, fight on . . .
. . . for we have come with the blessing of heaven."[a]

They were all too ashamed not to accept Chaereas' proposal, and the pharaoh, astonished at his bold spirit, gave him permission to take as many picked soldiers as he wished. However, he did not choose them immediately, but joining the throng in the camp and bidding Polycharmus to do likewise, he first tried to find out whether there were any Greeks at hand. Sure enough, a great many were found serving as mercenaries, and from these he selected Spartans and Corinthians and others who were Peloponnesians. He also discovered about twenty Sicilians. Having thus made up a band of three hundred men he addressed them as follows:

"Fellow Greeks, when his Majesty gave me authority to select the best soldiers in the army, I chose you. I am Greek myself, from Syracuse, of Dorian stock. We must

[a] *Iliad* 9.48f (Diomedes in defiance: adapted).

3.4 del. Hercher.

εὐγενείᾳ τῶν ἄλλων ἀλλὰ καὶ ἀρετῇ διαφέρειν.

9 μηδεὶς οὖν καταπλαγῇ τὴν πρᾶξιν ἐφ' ἣν ὑμᾶς
παρακαλῶ, καὶ γὰρ δυνατὴν εὑρήσομεν καὶ ῥᾳδίαν,
δόξῃ μᾶλλον ἢ πείρᾳ δύσκολον. Ἕλληνες ἐν
Θερμοπύλαις τοσοῦτοι Ξέρξην ὑπέστησαν. Τύριοι
δὲ οὐκ εἰσὶ πεντακόσιαι μυριάδες, ἀλλὰ ὀλίγοι καὶ
καταφρονήσει μετ' ἀλαζονείας, οὐ φρονήματι μετ'

10 εὐβουλίας χρώμενοι. γνώτωσαν οὖν πόσον Ἕλληνες Φοινίκων διαφέρουσιν. ἐγὼ δὲ οὐκ ἐπιθυμῶ
στρατηγίας, ἀλλ' ἕτοιμος ἀκολουθεῖν ὅστις ἂν ὑμῶν
ἄρχειν θέλῃ· πειθόμενον γὰρ εὑρήσει, ἐπεὶ καὶ
δόξης οὐκ ἐμῆς ἀλλὰ κοινῆς ὀρέγομαι." πάντες ἐπεβόησαν "σὺ στρατήγει."

11 "Βουλομένων" ἔφη "στρατηγῶ καὶ τὴν ἀρχήν μοι
ὑμεῖς δεδώκατε· διὰ τοῦτο πειράσομαι πάντα πράττειν, ὥστε ὑμᾶς μὴ μετανοεῖν τὴν πρὸς ἐμὲ εὔνοιάν
τε καὶ πίστιν ᾑρημένους. ἀλλ' ἔν τε τῷ παρόντι σὺν
θεοῖς ἔνδοξοι καὶ περίβλεπτοι γενήσεσθε καὶ πλου-
σιώτατοι τῶν συμμάχων, εἴς τε τὸ μέλλον ὄνομα
καταλείψετε τῆς ἀρετῆς ἀθάνατον, καὶ πάντες ὑμνή-
σουσιν, ὡς τοὺς μετὰ Ὀθρυάδου τριακοσίους ἢ τοὺς
μετὰ Λεωνίδου, οὕτως καὶ τοὺς μετὰ Χαιρέου [ἀνευ-

3.11 Ὀθρυάδου D'Orville: Μιθριδάτου | del. D'Orville.

show that we surpass the others not only in noble origin
but also in courage.[a] No one should be alarmed at the
venture which I am asking you to undertake; in fact we
shall find it both possible and easy, seeming more difficult
than it really is. This same number of Greeks once stood
up against Xerxes at Thermopylae. The Tyrians, however,
are no five million[b] in number, but only a few, and they
rely upon impudence and bragging, not upon resolution
and prudence. Let them realize the difference between
Greeks and Phoenicians. Now I do not crave to be your
general, but I am ready to follow any man of you who may
wish to hold command. He will find me obedient, since I
am ambitious not for personal glory but for the common
glory of us all." They all shouted, "You must be our general!"

"Since you wish it," he said, "I will be your general,
and this command is your gift to me. For that reason I
shall do all I can to ensure that you do not regret confer-
ring this mark of favor and confidence upon me. Indeed
with Heaven's help you shall gain present glory and fame
as well as the greatest wealth among the allies, and, for
the future, you shall leave behind an undying memory of
heroism, and just as all men commemorate the three hundred of Othryades or Leonidas,[c] so they will the three

[a] Playing on Pericles' glorification of the Athenians in the
Funeral Speech (Thucydides 2.35ff); cf. 7.3.9 below with Thucydides 2.37.1.

[b] The figure given by Herodotus (7.186) for the Persians at
Thermopylae.

[c] Two Spartans who each led bands of three hundred, Othryades in succoring Croesus (Herodotus 1.82), Leonidas the
hero of Thermopylae.

φημήσουσιν]." ἔτι λέγοντος πάντες ἀνέκραγον
"ἡγοῦ," καὶ πάντες ὥρμησαν ἐπὶ τὰ ὅπλα.

4. Κοσμήσας δὲ αὐτοὺς ὁ Χαιρέας ταῖς καλ-
λίσταις πανοπλίαις ἤγαγεν ἐπὶ τὴν βασιλέως σκηνήν. ἰδὼν δὲ ὁ Αἰγύπτιος ἐθαύμασε καὶ ἄλλους
ὁρᾶν ὑπελάμβανεν, οὐ τοὺς συνήθεις, ἐπηγγείλατο
2  δὲ αὐτοῖς μεγάλας δωρεάς. "ταῦτα μὲν" ἔφη Χαιρέας "πιστεύομεν· σὺ δὲ ἔχε τὴν ἄλλην στρατιὰν ἐν
τοῖς ὅπλοις καὶ μὴ πρότερον ἐπέλθῃς τῇ Τύρῳ, πρὶν
κρατήσωμεν αὐτῆς καὶ ἀναβάντες ἐπὶ τὰ τείχη
καλέσωμεν ὑμᾶς." "οὕτως" ἔφη "ποιήσειαν οἱ θεοί."
3  συνεσπειραμένους οὖν ὁ Χαιρέας ἐκείνους ἤγαγεν
ἐπὶ τὴν Τύρον, ὥστε πολὺ ἐλάττονας δόξαι· καὶ ὡς
ἀληθῶς

ἀσπὶς ἄρ' ἀσπίδ' ἔρειδε, κόρυς κόρυν, ἀνέρα δ' ἀνήρ.

καὶ τὸ μὲν πρῶτον οὐδὲ καθεωρῶντο ὑπὸ τῶν πολε-
μίων· ὡς δ' ἐγγὺς ἦσαν, βλέποντες αὐτοὺς <οἱ> ἀπὸ
τῶν τειχῶν ἐσήμαινον τοῖς ἔνδον, πάντα μᾶλλον
4  <ἢ> πολεμίους εἶναι προσδοκῶντες. τίς γὰρ ἂν καὶ
προσεδόκησε τοσούτους ὄντας ἐπὶ τὴν δυνατωτάτην
πόλιν παραγίνεσθαι, πρὸς ἣν οὐδέποτε ἐθάρρησεν
ἐλθεῖν οὐδὲ πᾶσα ἡ τῶν Αἰγυπτίων δύναμις· ἐπεὶ δὲ
τοῖς τείχεσιν ἐπλησίαζον, ἐπυνθάνοντο τίνες εἶεν
5  καὶ τί βούλοιντο. Χαιρέας δὲ ἀπεκρίνατο "ἡμεῖς

4.2 καλέσωμεν Gasda: καλῶμεν F.
4.3 καὶ ὡς Hercher: ὡς καὶ F | add. Hercher | πάντα Blake:
ὅτι F | add. D'Orville.

340

hundred of Chaereas." Before he had finished, all shouted, "Lead on," and they all rushed for their arms.

4. Chaereas then equipped them with the finest armor and took them to the royal tent. The pharaoh was surprised to see them, thinking that instead of his familiar troops he must be looking at others, and he promised them large rewards. "We are sure of that," said Chaereas, "but you must keep the rest of the army under arms and not attack Tyre until we have gained possession of it and have climbed on the walls and called you." "Heaven bring this to fulfillment," said he. So Chaereas led his men against Tyre, keeping them closely massed so that their numbers seemed much smaller; and in very truth

shield pressed on shield, helmet on helmet, man on man.[a]

At first they were not even observed by the enemy, but when they drew near, the men on the walls spotted them and signaled to those inside, though the last thing they expected was that they were the enemy. Indeed, who could have guessed that so small a number was coming to attack this most powerful city, against which not even the entire might of Egypt had ever dared to move? Instead, when they were close to the walls, the Tyrians asked who they were and what they wanted. "We are Greek mercenaries," replied Chaereas, "who have not received our pay

[a] *Iliad* 13.131 = 16.215 (fierce fighting).

Ἕλληνες μισθοφόροι παρὰ τοῦ Αἰγυπτίου τὸν
μισθὸν οὐκ ἀπολαμβάνοντες ἀλλὰ καὶ ἐπιβουλευ-
θέντες ἀπολέσθαι πάρεσμεν πρὸς ὑμᾶς, μεθ᾽ ὑμῶν
6 ἀμύνεσθαι θέλοντες τὸν κοινὸν ἐχθρόν." ἐμήνυσέ τις
ταῦτα τοῖς ἔνδον καὶ ἀνοίξας τὰς πύλας προῆλθεν ὁ
στρατηγὸς μετ᾽ ὀλίγων. τοῦτον πρῶτον Χαιρέας
ἀποκτείνας ὥρμησεν ἐπὶ τοὺς ἄλλους,

τύπτε δ᾽ ἐπιστροφάδην· τῶν δὲ στόνος ὤρνυτ᾽ ἀεικής.

ἄλλος δὲ ἄλλον ἐφόνευεν, ὥσπερ λέοντες εἰς ἀγέλην
βοῶν ἐμπεσόντες ἀφύλακτον· οἰμωγὴ δὲ καὶ θρῆνος
κατεῖχε τὴν πόλιν ἅπασαν, ὀλίγων μὲν τὸ γινόμενον
7 ὁρώντων, πάντων δὲ θορυβουμένων. καὶ ὄχλος
ἄτακτος ἐξεχεῖτο διὰ τῆς πύλης, βουλόμενος θεάσασθαι τὸ συμβεβηκός. τοῦτο μάλιστα τοὺς Τυρίους
8 ἀπώλεσεν. οἱ μὲν γὰρ ἔνδοθεν ἐξελθεῖν ἐβιάζοντο,
οἱ δὲ ἔξω παιόμενοι καὶ κεντούμενοι ξίφεσι καὶ
λόγχαις εἴσω πάλιν ἔφευγον, ἀπαντῶντες δὲ ἀλλήλοις ἐν στενοχωρίᾳ πολλὴν ἐξουσίαν παρεῖχον τοῖς
φονεύουσιν. οὔκουν οὐδὲ τὰς πύλας δυνατὸν ἦν
κλεῖσαι, σεσωρευμένων ἐν αὐταῖς τῶν νεκρῶν.

9 Ἐν δὲ τῷ ἀδιηγήτῳ τούτῳ ταράχῳ μόνος
ἐσωφρόνησε Χαιρέας· βιασάμενος γὰρ τοὺς ἀπαν-
τῶντας καὶ εἴσω τῶν πυλῶν γενόμενος ἀνεπήδησεν
ἐπὶ τὰ τείχη δέκατος αὐτὸς καὶ ἄνωθεν ἐσήμαινε
καλῶν τοὺς Αἰγυπτίους. οἱ δὲ λόγου θᾶττον παρ-
10 ῆσαν καὶ Τύρος ἑαλώκει. Τύρου δὲ ἁλούσης οἱ μὲν

BOOK 7.4

from the pharaoh, and there is a plot to kill us besides.
We have come here wishing to join with you in getting
revenge on our common foe." Someone reported this to
those inside and the commandant opened the gates and
came out with a few men. Chaereas killed him first and
rushed upon the others, and he

smote them right and left: there arose a hideous groaning.[a]

Each picked his man for slaughter, like lions falling on an
unguarded herd of cattle. Shrieking and moaning filled
the whole city, for though few saw what was going on, all
were thrown into a panic. A crowd out of control poured
through the gate, wanting to see what had happened.
This in particular doomed the Tyrians. While those on
the inside were forcing their way out, those outside,
struck and pierced[b] with swords and spears, were trying
to get back inside. The result was that they met each
other at the narrow entrance, and created an excellent
opportunity for the attackers; furthermore, it was not
even possible to shut the gates since the corpses were
piled so high there.

In this indescribable confusion[c] Chaereas alone kept
calm. Forcing a way through those in his path and getting
inside the gates, he and nine others leaped upon the walls
and from above signaled to the Egyptians to come. In no
time they arrived, and Tyre was captured. While all the

[a] *Iliad* 10.483 (Diomedes among the Thracians); Chariton
proceeds to echo the following simile, *Iliad* 10.485f.

[b] Cf. Xenophon, *Anabasis* 3.1.29.

[c] The phrase is taken verbatim from Xenophon, *Cyropaedia*
7.1.32 (and see also note on 6.9.5).

343

ἄλλοι πάντες ἑώρταζον, μόνος δὲ Χαιρέας οὔτε
ἔθυσεν οὔτε ἐστεφανώσατο. "τί γάρ μοι ὄφελος
ἐπινικίων, ἂν σύ, Καλλιρόη, μὴ βλέπῃς; οὐκέτι
στεφανώσομαι μετ᾽ ἐκείνην τὴν γαμήλιον νύκτα.
εἴτε γὰρ τέθνηκας, ἀσεβῶ, εἴτε καὶ ζῇς, πῶς ἑορτάζειν δύναμαι δίχα σοῦ κατακείμενος;"

11    <Καὶ οἱ μὲν ἦσ>αν ἐν τούτοις, βασιλεὺς δὲ ὁ
Περσῶν διαβὰς τὸν Εὐφράτην ἔσπευδεν ὡς τάχιστα
τοῖς πολεμίοις συμμίξαι. πυθόμενος γὰρ Τύρον
ἑαλωκέναι περὶ Σιδῶνος ἐφοβεῖτο καὶ τῆς ὅλης
12    Συρίας, ὁρῶν τὸν πολέμιον ἀντίπαλον ἤδη. διὰ
τοῦτο ἔδοξεν αὐτῷ μηκέτι μετὰ πάσης τῆς θεραπείας
ὁδεύειν, ἀλλὰ εὐζωνότερον, ἵνα μηδὲν ἐμπόδιον ᾖ τῷ
τάχει. παραλαβὼν δὲ τῆς στρατιᾶς τὸ καθαρώτατον
τὴν ἄχρηστον ἡλικίαν αὐτοῦ κατέλιπε μετὰ τῆς
βασιλίδος καὶ τὰ χρήματα καὶ τὰς ἐσθῆτας καὶ τὸν
13    πλοῦτον τὸν βασιλικόν. ἐπεὶ δὲ πάντα θορύβου καὶ
ταραχῆς ἐπέπληστο καὶ μέχρις Εὐφράτου τὰς
πόλεις κατειλήφει [ὁ] πόλεμος, ἔδοξεν ἀσφαλέστερον εἶναι τοὺς καταλειπομένους εἰς Ἄραδον ἀποθέ-
σθαι.

5. Νῆσος δέ ἐστιν αὕτη τῆς ἠπείρου σταδίους
ἀπέχουσα τριάκοντα, παλαιὸν ἱερὸν ἔχουσα Ἀφροδίτης. ὥσπερ οὖν ἐν οἰκίᾳ, μετὰ πάσης ἀδείας αἱ

4.10 κατακείμενος Zankogiannes: κατακειμένης F.
4.11 ἂν ἐν τοιούτοις F, add. and corr. Jackson.
4.13 del. Jackson.

others were celebrating the fall of Tyre, Chaereas alone neither sacrificed nor wore a garland. "What good is a victory celebration to me," he said, "if you, Callirhoe, cannot see it? After our wedding night, I shall never wear a garland again. If you are dead, it would be sacrilege, and even if you are alive, how can I recline at the feast without you at my side?"

So things were with them, but the king of Persia had crossed the Euphrates and was hurrying to engage the enemy with all speed. On learning that Tyre was captured, he feared for Sidon[a] and the whole of Syria, seeing that the enemy was already a match for him. Therefore he decided not to proceed any farther with the whole of his entourage but to advance in light marching order to remove any hindrance to his speed. Accordingly he took with him the elite of his army, and left behind with the queen those of an age unsuitable for service, as well as stores, clothing, and the royal treasure. And since alarm and confusion reigned everywhere and the cities west of the Euphrates were gripped by war, he thought it safer to put those he was leaving behind on Aradus[b] out of danger.

5. Now Aradus is an island three and a half miles[c] from the mainland, possessing an ancient shrine of Aphrodite. There the women could feel completely

[a] The chief city of Phoenicia after Tyre, and about forty miles north of it.
[b] An island off the coast some 120 miles north of Tyre.
[c] Literally thirty stades.

---

5.1 ἀπέχουσα] after σταδίους Jackson: after αὕτη F.

2  γυναῖκες ἐνταῦθα διῆγον. θεασαμένη δὲ Καλλιρόη τὴν Ἀφροδίτην, στᾶσα καταντικρὺ τὸ μὲν πρῶτον ἐσιώπα καὶ ἔκλαιεν, ὀνειδίζουσα τῇ θεῷ τὰ δάκρυα· μόλις δὲ ὑπεφθέγξατο ''ἰδοὺ καὶ ''Αραδος, μικρὰ νῆσος ἀντὶ τῆς μεγάλης Σικελίας καὶ οὐδεὶς ἐνταῦθα

3  ἐμός. ἀρκεῖ, δέσποινα. μέχρι πού με πολεμεῖς; εἰ καὶ ὅλως σοι προσέκρουσα, τετιμώρησαί με· εἰ καὶ νεμεσητὸν ἔδοξέ σοι τὸ δυστυχὲς κάλλος, ὀλέθρου μοι γέγονεν αἴτιον. ὃ μόνον ἔλιπέ μου ταῖς συμ-

4  φοραῖς, ἤδη καὶ πολέμου πεπείραμαι. πρὸς τὴν σύγκρισιν τῶν παρόντων ἦν μοι καὶ Βαβυλὼν φιλάνθρωπος. ἐγγὺω ἐκεῖ Χαιρέας ἦν. νῦν δὲ πάν- τως τέθνηκεν· ἐμοῦ γὰρ ἐξελθούσης οὐκ ἂν ἔζησεν.

5  ἀλλ᾽ οὐκ ἔχω παρὰ τίνος πύθωμαι τί γέγονε. πάντες ἀλλότριοι, πάντες βάρβαροι, φθονοῦντες, μισοῦντες, τῶν δὲ μισούντων χείρονες οἱ φιλοῦντες. σύ μοι, δέσποινα, δήλωσον εἰ Χαιρέας ζῇ.'' ταῦτα λέγουσα ἔτι ἀπήει. ἐπιστᾶσα δὲ <παρεμυθεῖτο> Ῥοδογούνη, Ζωπύρου μὲν θυγάτηρ, γυνὴ δὲ Μεγαβύζου, καὶ πατρὸς καὶ ἀνδρὸς Περσῶν ἀρίστων. αὕτη δὲ ἦν ἡ Καλλιρόη ἀπαντήσασα πρώτη Περσίδων, ὅτε εἰς Βαβυλῶνα εἰσῄει.

6  Ὁ δὲ Αἰγύπτιος ἐπειδήπερ ἤκουσε βασιλέα πλη- σίον ὄντα καὶ παρεσκευασμένον κατὰ γῆν καὶ κατὰ θάλασσαν, καλέσας Χαιρέαν εἶπε ''τὰ μὲν πρῶτά σου τῶν κατορθωμάτων ἀμείψασθαι καιρὸν οὐκ ἔσχον· σὺ γάρ μοι Τύρον ἔδωκας· περὶ δὲ τῶν ἑξῆς παρακαλῶ, μὴ ἀπολέσωμεν ἕτοιμα ἀγαθά, ὧν

unafraid, as though at home. When Callirhoe caught sight of the statue of Aphrodite, she took her stand in front of it; first she remained silent and wept, reproaching the goddess with her tears; but at length she spoke: "So now I am on Aradus, a tiny island compared with mighty Sicily, and without a friend! My Lady, this is enough! How long will you treat me as an enemy? If indeed I offended you, you have had your revenge. If my wretched beauty has aroused your indignation, still it has caused my ruin. Now I have experienced the one misfortune which was still left for me: war. Compared to my present state, even Babylon was kindly; there Chaereas was near. But now he is dead for sure; he could not have survived after I left. Yet I have no one to ask what has happened to him. All are strangers, orientals who envy and hate me; and those who love me are worse than those who hate! Lady, reveal to me if Chaereas still lives." With these words on her lips she went away. Rhodogune came to comfort her, she who was the daughter of Zopyrus and the wife of Megabyzus, her father and husband both being Persian nobles. She had been the first Persian woman to meet Callirhoe on her arrival in Babylon.

When the pharaoh heard that the king was near and was ready for action on land and sea, he called Chaereas and said, "Though I have not had a chance to reward you for your first success in delivering Tyre into my hands, I ask your help for the next step. We must not lose our

---

5.5 add. Morel.

7 κοινωνόν σε ποιήσομαι. ἐμοὶ μὲν γὰρ Αἴγυπτος
ἀρκεῖ, σοὶ δὲ γενήσεται κτῆμα Συρία. φέρ᾽ οὖν σκεψώμεθα τί ποιητέον· ἐν ἀμφοτέροις γὰρ τοῖς στοι-
χείοις ὁ πόλεμος ἀκμάζει. σοὶ δὲ ἐπιτρέπω τὴν
αἵρεσιν, εἴτε τῆς πεζῆς θέλεις στρατηγεῖν εἴτε τῆς
8 ναυτικῆς δυνάμεως. οἴομαι δὲ οἰκειότερόν σοι εἶναι
τὴν θάλασσαν· ὑμεῖς γὰρ οἱ Συρακόσιοι καὶ Ἀθηναίους κατεναυμαχήσατε. σήμερον δὲ ἀγών ἐστί
σοι πρὸς Πέρσας τοὺς ὑπὸ Ἀθηναίων νενικημένους.
ἔχεις τριήρεις Αἰγυπτίας, μείζονας καὶ πλείονας τῶν
Σικελικῶν· μίμησαι τὸν κηδεστὴν Ἑρμοκράτην ἐν
τῇ θαλάσσῃ." Χαιρέας δὲ ἀπεκρίνατο "πᾶς ἐμοὶ κίνδυνος ἡδύς· ὑπὲρ σοῦ δὲ ἀναδέξομαι τὸν πόλεμον
9 καὶ πρὸς τὸν ἔχθιστον ἐμοὶ βασιλέα. δὸς δέ μοι
μετὰ τῶν τριηρῶν καὶ τοὺς τριακοσίους τοὺς ἐμούς."
"ἔχε" φησὶ "καὶ τούτους καὶ ἄλλους, ὅσους ἂν
θέλῃς."

Καὶ εὐθὺς ἔργον ἐγένετο ὁ λόγος· κατήπειγε γὰρ
ἡ χρεία. καὶ ὁ μὲν Αἰγύπτιος ἔχων τὴν πεζὴν στρατιὰν ἀπηντᾶτο τοῖς πολεμίοις, ὁ δὲ Χαιρέας ναύαρ-
10 χος ἀπεδείχθη. τοῦτο πρῶτον ἀθυμοτέρους ἐποίησε
τοὺς πεζούς, ὅτι μετ᾽ αὐτῶν οὐκ ἐστρατεύσατο Χαιρέας, καὶ γὰρ ἐφίλουν αὐτὸν ἤδη καὶ ἀγαθὰς εἶχον
ἐλπίδας ἐκείνου στρατηγοῦντος· ἔδοξεν οὖν ὥσπερ
11 ὀφθαλμὸς ἐξῃρῆσθαι μεγάλου σώματος. τὸ δὲ
ναυτικὸν ἐπήρθη ταῖς ἐλπίσι καὶ φρονήματος
ἐνεπλήσθησαν, ὅτι τὸν ἀνδρειότατον καὶ κάλλιστον
εἶχον ἡγούμενον. ὀλίγον τε ἐπενόουν οὐδέν, ἀλλὰ

present gains, which I shall share with you. Egypt is enough for me, and Syria shall be yours. Now let us consider what to do. The war is at its climax on both elements. I offer you your choice, to command either the infantry or the fleet, whichever you wish. But I believe that the sea is more familiar to you, for it was you Syracusans who defeated even the Athenians on the sea. Today your enemy is the Persians who were once defeated by the Athenians. Available to you are Egyptian warships larger and more numerous than those of the Sicilians. Emulate the prowess of your father-in-law Hermocrates on the sea." "Any danger is agreeable to me," replied Chaereas. "I will undertake this war to serve you and to oppose the king, whom I detest. But together with the warships give me my three hundred soldiers as well." "Take them and as many others as you wish," he said.

The plan was at once put into effect, for necessity drove them. So the pharaoh went out with the infantry to engage the enemy, while Chaereas was appointed admiral. At first, the infantry were rather downcast because Chaereas had not joined their ranks, for he had already won their affection and they had high hopes under his leadership: it was just like a powerful body losing an eye. In the fleet, on the other hand, morale rose high, and the men were filled with optimism now that they had their bravest and noblest leader. In fact their minds were set

---

5.7 Αἴγυπτος ἀρκεῖ Reeve: ἀ. Αἴ. F.
5.10 πρῶτον D'Orville: πρότερον F.

ὥρμηντο καὶ τριήραρχοι καὶ κυβερνῆται καὶ ναῦται
καὶ στρατιῶται πάντες ὁμοίως, τίς προθυμίαι
ἐπιδείξεται Χαιρέᾳ πρῶτος.

12   Τῆς δὲ αὐτῆς ἡμέρας καὶ κατὰ γῆν καὶ κατὰ
θάλασσαν ἡ μάχη συνήφθη. χρόνον μὲν οὖν πολὺ
[πολὺν] ἀντέσχεν ἡ πεζὴ στρατιὰ τῶν Αἰγυπτίωι
Μήδοις τε καὶ Πέρσαις, εἶτα πλήθει βιασθέντες ἐν-
έδωκαν. καὶ βασιλεὺς <μὲν ἠπείγετο φεύγων
βασιλεὺς> δὲ ἔφιππος διώκων. σπουδὴ δὲ ἦν τοῦ
Αἰγυπτίου καταφυγεῖν εἰς Πηλούσιον, τοῦ δὲ Πέρ-
σου θᾶττον καταλαβεῖν· τάχα δ' ἂν καὶ διέφυγεν, εἰ
13   μὴ Διονύσιος ἔργον θαυμαστὸν ἐπεδείξατο· κἂν τῇ
συμβολῇ <γὰρ> ἠγωνίσατο λαμπρῶς, ἀεὶ μαχόμενος πλησίον βασιλέως, ἵνα αὐτὸν βλέπῃ, καὶ πρῶτος ἐτρέψατο τοὺς καθ' αὑτόν· τότε δὲ τῆς φυγῆς
μακρᾶς οὔσης καὶ συνεχοῦς ἡμέραις τε καὶ νυξὶν
ὁρῶν ἐπὶ τούτοις λυπούμενον βασιλέα "μὴ λυποῦ"
φησίν, "ὦ δέσποτα· κωλύσω γὰρ ἐγὼ τὸν Αἰγύπτιοι
14   διαφυγεῖν, ἄν μοι δῷς ἱππεῖς ἐπιλέκτους." ἐπήνεσε
βασιλεὺς καὶ δίδωσιν· ὁ δὲ πεντακισχιλίους λαβὼν
συνῆψε σταθμοὺς δύο ἡμέρᾳ μιᾷ, καὶ νυκτὸς ἐπιπεσὼν τοῖς Αἰγυπτίοις ἀπροσδόκητος πολλοὺς μὲν
ἐζώγρησε, πλείονας δὲ ἀπέκτεινεν. ὁ δὲ Αἰγύπτιος
ζῶν καταλαμβανόμενος ἀπέσφαξεν ἑαυτὸν καὶ Διο-
15   νύσιος τὴν κεφαλὴν ἐκόμισε πρὸς βασιλέα. θεασάμενος δὲ ἐκεῖνος "ἀναγράφω σε" εἶπεν "εὐεργέτηι

5.12 del. Reiske (dittography) | add. Jackson.

on nothing petty,[a] but all alike, captains and pilots and sailors and marines, set out to see who should be the first to demonstrate his zeal to Chaereas.

On the same day battle was joined both on land and on sea. The Egyptian infantry held out a long time against the Medes and Persians, but finally, overwhelmed by superior numbers, they gave in.[b] One monarch made haste to flee and the other came riding in pursuit. The Egyptian strove hard to escape to Pelusium, the Persian to catch him first. He might perhaps have escaped, too, had Dionysius not performed a remarkable feat, for even in the engagement he had conducted himself valiantly, always fighting near the king so as to catch his attention and being the first to rout the enemy in front of him. Now when the retreat was prolonged for several days and nights on end and he saw that the king was worried by this, he said, "Do not worry, Sire; I shall prevent the pharaoh from escaping if you will give me some picked cavalrymen." The king approved, and gave them to him. Then with five thousand of them, he completed two days' march in a single day, and falling upon the Egyptians unexpectedly by night, captured many of them, and slaughtered more. The pharaoh, though captured alive, killed himself, and Dionysius brought his head to the Great King. On seeing it, the latter said, "I appoint

---

[a] A quotation from Thucydides 2.8.1.

[b] Cf. Thucydides 4.44.1.

---

5.13 κἂν Jackson: καὶ ἐν F | add. Jackson.

εἰς τὸν οἶκον τὸν ἐμὸν καὶ ἤδη σοι δίδωμι δῶρον τὸ
ἥδιστον, οὗ μάλιστα πάντων αὐτὸς ἐπιθυμεῖς, Καλλιρόην γυναῖκα. κέκρικε τὴν δίκην ὁ πόλεμος
ἔχεις τὸ κάλλιστον ἆθλον τῆς ἀριστείας." Διονύσιος
δὲ προσεκύνησε καὶ ἰσόθεον ἔδοξεν ἑαυτόν, πεπεισμένος ὅτι βεβαίως ἤδη Καλλιρόης ἀνήρ ἐστι.

6. Καὶ ἐν μὲν τῇ γῇ ταῦτα ἐπράσσετο· ἐν δὲ τῇ
θαλάσσῃ Χαιρέας ἐνίκησεν, ὥστε μηδὲ ἀντίπαλοι
αὐτῷ γενέσθαι τὸ πολέμιον ναυτικόν· οὔτε γὰρ τὰς
ἐμβολὰς ἐδέξαντο τῶν Αἰγυπτίων τριηρῶν, οὔτε
ὅλως ἀντίπρωροι κατέστησαν, ἀλλὰ αἱ μὲν εὐθὺς
ἀνετράπησαν, ἃς δὲ καὶ πρὸς τὴν γῆν ἐξενεχθείσας
ἐζώγρησεν αὐτάνδρους· ἐνεπλήσθη δὲ ἡ θάλασσα
2   ναυαγίων Μηδικῶν. ἀλλ' οὔτε βασιλεὺς ἐγίνωσκε
τὴν ἧτταν τὴν ἐν τῇ θαλάσσῃ τῶν ἰδίων οὔτε Χαιρέας τὴν ἐν τῇ γῇ τῶν Αἰγυπτίων, ἐνόμιζε δὲ ἑκάτερος κρατεῖν ἐν ἀμφοτέροις. ἐκείνης οὖν τῆς ἡμέρας
ἧς ἐναυμάχησε καταπλεύσας εἰς Ἄραδον ὁ Χαιρέας
τὴν μὲν νῆσον ἐκέλευσε περιπλέοντας ἐν κύκλῳ
παραφυλάττειν

*   *   *   *   *

3   ὡς αὐτοὺς ἀποδώσοντας λόγον τῷ δεσπότῃ. κἀκεῖ-
νοι τοὺς μὲν εὐνούχους καὶ θεραπαινίδας καὶ πάντα
τὰ εὐωνότερα σώματα συνήθροισαν εἰς τὴν ἀγορὰν

6.1 αἱ Blake: αἰ F.
6.2 Gasda recognized the lacuna here: its size is unclear.

you as a Benefactor[a] of my house, and here and now I award you the most pleasing of gifts, the one which you yourself desire above all others—Callirhoe as your wife. War has pronounced the decision. You have the fairest prize for your valor." Dionysius knelt in homage and deemed himself an equal of the gods, convinced that now surely he was Callirhoe's husband.

6. So much for what took place on land. On the sea Chaereas was so victorious that the enemy fleet was no match for him. They neither withstood the ramming of the Egyptian warships nor faced them at all prow to prow. Instead, some fled immediately, and others were forced ashore, and captured, crews and all. The sea was filled with the wreckage of Median ships. Yet the king was not aware of the defeat of his forces at sea, nor Chaereas of the defeat of the Egyptians on land, but each of them thought that he had the upper hand on both elements. So, on the same day on which the battle was fought Chaereas sailed along to Aradus and gave orders to circle the island and secure it.

\* \* \* \* \*[b]

for them to give an account to their master.[c] Likewise they collected the eunuchs, the maidservants, and all the meaner slaves into the marketplace, since there was

---

[a] A Persian title; cf. Herodotus 8.85, Thucydides 1.129.3.

[b] The lacuna, which may have explained why Chaereas moved against Aradus, must have described the occupation of the island, the collection of booty, and the selection of a few prisoners to open negotiations with the enemy.

[c] The king of Persia.

αὕτη γὰρ εὐρυχωρίαν εἶχε. τοσοῦτο δὲ ἦν τὸ πλῆθος, ὥστε οὐ μόνον ἐν ταῖς στοαῖς, ἀλλὰ καὶ
4 ὑπαίθριοι διενυκτέρευσαν. τοὺς δ' ἀξιώματός τι μετέχοντας εἰς οἴκημα τῆς ἀγορᾶς εἰσήγαγον, ἐν ᾧ συνήθως οἱ ἄρχοντες ἐχρημάτιζον. αἱ δὲ γυναῖκες χαμαὶ καθέζοντο περὶ τὴν βασιλίδα καὶ οὔτε πῦρ ἀνῆψαν οὔτε τροφῆς ἐγεύσαντο· πεπεισμέναι γὰρ ἦσαν ἑαλωκέναι μὲν βασιλέα καὶ ἀπολωλέναι τὰ Περσῶν πράγματα, τὸν δὲ Αἰγύπτιον πανταχοῦ νικᾶν.
5 Ἡ νὺξ ἐκείνη καὶ ἡδίστη καὶ χαλεπωτάτη κατέσχεν Ἄραδον. Αἰγύπτιοι μὲν γὰρ ἔχαιρον ἀπηλλαγμένοι πολέμου καὶ δουλείας Περσικῆς, οἱ δὲ ἑαλωκότες Περσῶν δεσμὰ καὶ μάστιγας καὶ ὕβρεις καὶ σφαγὰς προσεδόκων, τὸ φιλανθρωπότατον δέ, δουλείαν· ἡ δὲ Στάτειρα ἐνθεῖσα τὴν κεφαλὴν εἰς τὰ γόνατα Καλλιρόης ἔκλαιεν· ἐκείνη γάρ, ὡς ἂν Ἑλληνὶς καὶ πεπαιδευμένη καὶ οὐκ ἀμελέτητος κακῶν, παρεμυθεῖτο μάλιστα τὴν βασιλίδα.
6 Συνέβη δέ τι τοιοῦτον. Αἰγύπτιος στρατιώτης, ὁ πεπιστευμένος φυλάττειν τοὺς ἐν τῷ οἰκήματι, γνοὺς ἔνδον εἶναι τὴν βασιλίδα, κατὰ τὴν ἔμφυτον θρησκείαν τῶν βαρβάρων πρὸς τὸ ὄνομα τὸ βασιλικὸν ἐγγὺς μὲν αὐτῇ προσελθεῖν οὐκ ἐτόλμησε, στὰς δὲ
7 παρὰ τῇ θύρᾳ κεκλεισμένῃ "θάρρει, δέσποινα" εἶπε, "νῦν μὲν γὰρ οὐκ οἶδεν ὁ ναύαρχος ὅτι καὶ σὺ μετὰ τῶν αἰχμαλώτων ἐνταῦθα κατεκλείσθης, μαθὼν δὲ προνοήσεταί σου φιλανθρώπως· οὐ μόνον γὰρ

plenty of room there. Indeed, so great was the crowd that they spent the night not only in the colonnades, but even under the open sky. Those who had some special value were brought into a building in the marketplace where the town council was accustomed to hold its meetings. The women sat on the ground round the queen without lighting a fire or tasting food, convinced that the king had been captured, that the Persian cause was lost, and that the pharaoh was everywhere triumphant.

That night brought the greatest joy and the deepest misery to Aradus. The Egyptians exulted in their deliverance from war and Persian domination, while the captured Persians awaited chains and whips, outrage and death, with slavery the mildest fate. Statira was weeping with her head resting in Callirhoe's lap. Indeed, the latter could best comfort the queen, since she was a cultured Greek lady and not without experience of misfortune.

Then occurred the following incident. An Egyptian soldier who had been told to guard the people in the building discovered that the queen was inside, but did not dare to come too close to her because of the instinctive reverence which orientals feel at the name of royalty. Instead, he stood by the closed door and said, "Courage, Your Majesty! The admiral does not yet know that you too are imprisoned here with the captives, but when he is told, he will look after you with all kindness. He is not

---

6.4 καθέζοντο Jackson: ἐκαθέζοντο F.

ἀνδρεῖος, ἀλλὰ καὶ

\* \* \* \* \*

γυναῖκα ποιήσεται· φύσει γάρ ἐστι φιλογύναιος."
ταῦτα ἀκούσασα ἡ Καλλιρόη μέγα ἀνεκώκυσε καὶ
τὰς τρίχας ἐσπάραττε λέγουσα "νῦν ἀληθῶς
αἰχμάλωτός εἰμι. φόνευσόν με μᾶλλον ἢ ταῦτα ἐπ-
8 αγγέλλου. γάμον οὐχ ὑπομένω· θάνατον εὔχομαι.
κεντείτωσαν καὶ καέτωσαν· ἐντεῦθεν οὐκ ἀναστήσο-
μαι· τάφος ἐμός ἐστιν οὗτος ὁ τόπος. εἰ δέ, ὡς
λέγεις, φιλάνθρωπός ἐστιν ὁ στρατηγός, ταύτην μοι
δότω τὴν χάριν· ἐνταῦθά με ἀποκτεινάτω."
9 Δεήσεις αὐτῇ πάλιν ἐκεῖνος προσέφερεν, ἡ δ' οὐκ
ἀνίστατο, ἀλλὰ συγκεκαλυμμένη πεσοῦσα ἐπὶ τῆς
γῆς ἔκειτο. σκέψις προύκειτο τῷ Αἰγυπτίῳ τί καὶ
πράξειε· βίαν μὲν γὰρ οὐκ ἐτόλμα προσφέρειν,
πεῖσαι δὲ πάλιν οὐκ ἐδύνατο. διόπερ ὑποστρέψας
10 προσῆλθε τῷ Χαιρέᾳ σκυθρωπός. ὁ δὲ ἰδὼν "τοῦτο
ἄλλο" φησὶν "ἦν. κλέπτουσί τινες τὰ κάλλιστα τῶν
λαφύρων; ἀλλ' οὐ χαίροντες αὐτὸ πράξουσιν." ὡς
οὖν εἶπεν ὁ Αἰγύπτιος "οὐδεμία γέγονε κάκη,
δέσποτα· τὴν γὰρ γυναῖκα, ἣν εὗρον ἐν πλαταγαῖς
τεταμένην, οὐ βούλεται <προσ>ελθεῖν, ἀλλ'

6.7 Hilberg recognized the lacuna here, perhaps of a page.
6.10 πλαταιαῖς F, corr. Plepelits
6.10 τεταγμένην F, corr. D'Orville | add. Jackson (cf. 8.1.6).

only a brave but also[a] [*an honorable man.*" *The Egyptian*
*reports to Chaereas that the queen is among the captives.*
*He is told to treat her as befits her rank, and on returning*
*to arrange this discovers that one of the prisoners is a*
*woman of extraordinary beauty. Chaereas, informed of*
*this, becomes curious to see her. She, however, is far from*
*cooperative and the Egyptian tries to overcome her resis-*
*tance by guaranteeing kind treatment from the admiral,*
*finally promising that "he*] will make you his wife, for he
has a chivalrous nature." On hearing this, Callirhoe
uttered a loud cry of grief and tearing her hair, she said,
"Now I really am a prisoner! Kill me rather than bring
me a message like that! I will not submit to marriage. I
pray rather for death. They can goad me and burn me. I
will not move from here. This place shall be my tomb. If,
as you say, your leader is a kind man, let him grant me this
favor; let him kill me here!"

Again he pleaded with her, but she refused to move,
and, covering her head, she sank to the ground and lay
there. The Egyptian was confronted with the problem
what he should do. He did not dare to apply force, and on
the other hand he could not persuade her; he therefore
left and went with a gloomy face to Chaereas. On seeing
him, the latter said, "So this was for nothing! Are people
stealing the most beautiful of the spoils? Well, they will
regret it!" "No harm has been done, master," replied the
Egyptian. "Only, the woman I found grieving without
restraint refuses to come to you; she has thrown herself

---

[a] Hilberg and others have established with fair certainty the
general contents of the lacuna, summarized in the text; its conclusion has been modeled on Xenophon, *Cyropaedia* 5.1.6,
where Cyrus is similarly commended to Panthea.

ἔρριπται χαμαί, ξίφος αἰτοῦσα καὶ ἀποθανεῖν
βουλομένη."

Γελάσας ὁ Χαιρέας εἶπεν "ὦ πάντων ἀνθρώπων
ἀφυέστατε, οὐκ οἶδας πῶς μεθοδεύεται γυνὴ παρα-
κλήσεσιν, ἐπαίνοις, ἐπαγγελίαις, μάλιστα δέ, ἂν
ἐρᾶσθαι δοκῇ; σὺ δὲ βίαν ἴσως προσῆγες καὶ
11 ὕβριν." "οὔ" ἔφη, "δέσποτα· πάντα δὲ ταῦτα, ὅσα
λέγεις, πεποίηκα ἐν διπλῷ μᾶλλον, καὶ γάρ σου
κατεψευσάμην ὅτι ἕξεις αὐτὴν γυναῖκα· ἡ δὲ πρὸς
12 τοῦτο μάλιστα ἠγανάκτησεν." ὁ δὲ Χαιρέας "ἐπ-
αφρόδιτος ἄρα" φησὶν "εἰμὶ καὶ ἐράσμιος, εἰ καὶ
πρὶν ἰδεῖν ἀπεστράφη με καὶ ἐμίσησεν. ἔοικε δὲ
φρόνημα εἶναι τῆς γυναικὸς οὐκ ἀγεννές. μηδεὶς
αὐτῇ προσφερέτω βίαν, ἀλλὰ ἐᾶτε διάγειν ὡς
προῄρηται· πρέπει γάρ μοι σωφροσύνην τιμᾶν. καὶ
αὐτὴ γὰρ ἴσως ἄνδρα πενθεῖ."

on the ground, is asking for a sword, and wants to die."

Chaereas laughed and said, "You are a perfect simple-ton! Do you not know that one must handle a woman with appeals and flattery and promises, and above all by making her think she is loved? You were probably violent and highhanded." "Not at all, master," said he, "I tried everything you said, and in fact went twice as far. I even misrepresented you by saying that you would take her as your wife. She was particularly annoyed at that." "I must be a very attractive and charming person," said Chaereas, "if she rejects and hates me before even seeing me. There seems to be a proud spirit in this woman which is rather noble. Let no one use violence against her, but let her carry on as she wishes. I, for one, should respect chastity. Perhaps she, too, is mourning for a husband."

# H

1. Ὡς μὲν οὖν Χαιρέας ὑποπτεύσας Καλλιρόην
Διονυσίῳ παραδεδόσθαι, θέλων ἀμύνασθαι βασιλέα
πρὸς τὸν Αἰγύπτιον ἀπέστη καὶ ναύαρχος ἀποδειχθεὶς ἐκράτησε τῆς θαλάσσης, νικήσας δὲ κατέσχεν
Ἄραδον, ἔνθα βασιλεὺς καὶ τὴν γυναῖκα τὴν ἑαυτοῦ
καὶ πᾶσαν τὴν θεραπείαν ἀπέθετο καὶ Καλλιρόην,
ἐν τῷ πρόσθεν λόγῳ δεδήλωται.

2  Ἔμελλε δὲ ἔργον ἡ Τύχη πράττειν οὐ μόνον
παράδοξον, ἀλλὰ καὶ σκυθρωπόν, ἵνα ἔχων Καλλιρόην Χαιρέας ἀγνοήσῃ καὶ τὰς ἀλλοτρίας γυναῖκας
ἀναλαβὼν ταῖς τριήρεσιν ἀπ<αγ>άγῃ, μόνην δὲ τὴν
ἰδίαν ἐκεῖ καταλίπῃ οὐχ ὡς Ἀριάδνην καθεύδουσαν,
οὐδὲ Διονύσῳ νυμφίῳ, λάφυρον δὲ τοῖς ἑαυτοῦ πολε-
3  μίοις. ἀλλὰ ἔδοξε τό<δε> δεινὸν Ἀφροδίτῃ· ἤδη
γὰρ αὐτῷ διηλλάττετο, πρότερον ὀργισθεῖσα χαλεπῶς διὰ τὴν ἄκαιρον ζηλοτυπίαν, ὅτι δῶρον παρ'
αὐτῆς λαβὼν τὸ κάλλιστον, οἷον οὐδὲ Ἀλέξανδρος ὁ
Πάρις, ὕβρισεν εἰς τὴν χάριν. ἐπεὶ δὲ καλῶς ἀπελογήσατο τῷ Ἔρωτι Χαιρέας ἀπὸ δύσεως εἰς ἀνατο-
λὰς διὰ μυρίων παθῶν πλανηθείς, ἠλέησεν αὐτὸν

1.2 add. Hercher.
1.3 add. Cobet.

# BOOK 8

1. How Chaereas, suspecting that Callirhoe had been handed over to Dionysius and desiring to revenge himself on the king, had deserted to the pharaoh; how he had been appointed admiral and gained control of the sea; how after his victory he captured Aradus, where the king had secluded his wife and all her retinue, Callirhoe included: this has been described in the preceding book.[a]

Fortune was now planning a blow as grim as incredible: though in possession of Callirhoe, Chaereas was to remain ignorant of the fact and, sailing away with other men's wives aboard his warships, was to leave his wife there alone, not, like Ariadne, asleep, nor for a Dionysus[b] to marry, but as booty for his enemies. But Aphrodite thought this excessive; by now she was becoming reconciled to Chaereas, though earlier she had been intensely angered at his intemperate jealousy; for, having received from her the fairest of gifts, surpassing even that[c] given to Alexander surnamed Paris,[d] he had repaid her favor with insult. Since Chaereas had now made full amends to Love by his wanderings from west to east amid countless

---

[a] See note on 5.1.1.     [b] After her desertion by Theseus Ariadne was married by the god Dionysus.

[c] Helen.     [d] Helen's seducer; surnamed Paris, he is said to have been dubbed Alexander ('Defender') by the shepherds among whom he grew up, and this is what Homer normally calls him. Only rarely are the two names found together.

Ἀφροδίτη καὶ ὅπερ ἐξ ἀρχῆς δύο τῶν καλλίστων
ἥρμοσε ζεῦγος, γυμνάσασα διὰ γῆς καὶ θαλάσσης,
πάλιν ἠθέλησεν ἀποδοῦναι.

4    Νομίζω δὲ καὶ τὸ τελευταῖον τοῦτο σύγγραμμα
τοῖς ἀναγινώσκουσιν ἥδιστον γενήσεσθαι· καθάρ-
σιον γάρ ἐστι τῶν ἐν τοῖς πρώτοις σκυθρωπῶν.
οὐκέτι λῃστεία καὶ δουλεία καὶ δίκη καὶ μάχη καὶ
ἀποκαρτέρησις καὶ πόλεμος καὶ ἅλωσις ἐν τούτῳ,
5 ἀλλὰ ἔρωτες δίκαιοι <καὶ> νόμιμοι γάμοι. πῶς οὖν
ἡ θεὸς ἐφώτισε τὴν ἀλήθειαν καὶ τοὺς ἀγνοουμένους
ἔδειξεν ἀλλήλοις λέξω.

   Ἑσπέρα μὲν ἦν, ἔτι δὲ πολλὰ τῶν αἰχμαλώτων
καταλέλειπτο. κεκμηκὼς οὖν ὁ Χαιρέας ἀνίσταται,
6 ἵνα διατάξηται τὰ πρὸς τὸν πλοῦν. παριόντι δὲ
αὐτῷ τὴν ἀγορὰν ὁ Αἰγύπτιος ἔλεξεν "ἐνταῦθά ἐστιν
ἡ γυνή, δέσποτα, ἡ μὴ βουλομένη προσελθεῖν, ἀλλὰ
ἀποκαρτεροῦσα· τάχα δὲ σὺ πείσεις αὐτὴν ἀναστῆ-
ναι· τί γάρ σε δεῖ καταλείπειν τὸ κάλλιστον τῶν
λαφύρων;" συνεπελάβετο καὶ Πολύχαρμος τοῦ
λόγου, βουλόμενος ἐμβαλεῖν αὐτόν, εἴ πως δύναιτο,
εἰς ἔρωτα καινὸν καὶ Καλλιρόης παραμύθιον.
"εἰσέλθωμεν" ἔφη, "Χαιρέα."

7    Ὑπερβὰς οὖν τὸν οὐδὸν καὶ θεασάμενος ἐρριμμένην καὶ ἐγκεκαλυμμένην εὐθὺς ἐκ τῆς ἀναπνοῆς καὶ
τοῦ σχήματος ἐταράχθη τὴν ψυχὴν καὶ μετέωρος
ἐγένετο· πάντως δ' ἂν καὶ ἐγνώρισεν, εἰ <μὴ>

1.4 ἐν τούτῳ] after ἅλωσις Goold: after δίκαιοι F.
1.7 add. Cocchi.

tribulations, Aphrodite took pity on him, and, as she had originally brought together this handsome pair, so now, having harassed them over land and sea, she resolved to unite them again.

Moreover, I think that this last book will prove the most enjoyable for my readers,[a] as an antidote to the grim events in the preceding ones. No more piracy or slavery or trials or fighting or suicide or war or captivity in this one, but honest love and lawful marriage! How then the goddess brought the truth to light and revealed the unsuspecting lovers to each other, I shall now relate.

Evening had fallen,[b] but much of the captured material was still left on shore. Wearily Chaereas got up to give orders for embarkation. As he passed through the marketplace, the Egyptian said to him, "Sir, here is that woman who would not come to you, but is bent on suicide. Perhaps you can persuade her to get up, for you ought not to leave behind the most beautiful of the spoils." Polycharmus also supported the suggestion, since he wished, if possible, to involve Chaereas in a new love which might console him for the loss of Callirhoe. "Let us go in, Chaereas," he said.

So he crossed the threshold into the room. The moment he saw her, lying down and wrapped up though she was, his heart was stirred by the way she breathed and looked, and he was seized with excitement. He would certainly have recognized her, had he not been utterly

[a] Other authorial comments are found at 3.2.17; 5.8.3; 6.9.4 (and questions at 5.4.4; 5.8.2).

[b] See note on 1.3.1.

363

σφόδρα πέπειστο Καλλιρόην ἀπειληφέναι Διονύ-
8 σιον. ἠρέμα δὲ προσελθὼν "θάρρει" φησίν, "ὦ
γύναι, ἥτις ἂν ᾖς, οὐ γάρ σε βιασόμεθα· ἕξεις δὲ
ἄνδρα, ὃν θέλεις." ἔτι λέγοντος ἡ Καλλιρόη γνωρίσασα τὴν φωνὴν ἀπεκαλύψατο καὶ ἀμφότεροι συνε-
βόησαν "Χαιρέα," "Καλλιρόη." περιχυθέντες δὲ
9 ἀλλήλοις, λιποψυχήσαντες ἔπεσον. ἄφωνος δὲ καὶ
Πολύχαρμος τὸ πρῶτον εἱστήκει πρὸς τὸ παράδοξον, χρόνου δὲ προϊόντος "ἀνάστητε" εἶπεν, "ἀπει-
λήφατε ἀλλήλους· πεπληρώκασιν οἱ θεοὶ τὰς ἀμφοτέρων εὐχάς. μέμνησθε δὲ ὅτι οὐκ ἐν πατρίδι ἐστέ,
ἀλλ' ἐν πολεμίᾳ γῇ, καὶ δεῖ ταῦτα πρότερον οἰκονο-
10 μῆσαι καλῶς, ἵνα μηδεὶς ἔτι ὑμᾶς διαχωρίσῃ." τοιαῦτα ἐμβοῶντος, ὥσπερ τινὲς ἐν φρέατι βαθεῖ
βεβαπτισμένοι μόλις ἄνωθεν φωνὴν ἀκούσαντες,
βραδέως ἀνήνεγκαν, εἶτα ἰδόντες ἀλλήλους καὶ
καταφιλήσαντες πάλιν παρείθησαν καὶ δεύτερον καὶ
τρίτον τοῦτο ἔπραξαν, μίαν φωνὴν ἀφιέντες "ἔχω
σε, εἰ ἀληθῶς εἶ Καλλιρόη· εἰ ἀληθῶς εἶ Χαιρέας."
11     Φήμη δὲ διέτρεχεν ὅτι ὁ ναύαρχος εὕρηκε τὴν
γυναῖκα. οὐ στρατιώτης ἔμεινεν ἐν σκηνῇ, οὐ ναύ-
της ἐν τριήρει, οὐ θυρωρὸς ἐν οἰκίᾳ· πανταχόθεν
συνέτρεχον λαλοῦντες "ὦ γυναικὸς μακαρίας,
εἴληφε τὸν εὐμορφότατον ἄνδρα." Καλλιρόης δὲ
φανείσης οὐδεὶς ἔτι Χαιρέαν ἐπήνεσεν, ἀλλ' εἰς ἐκεί-
12 νην πάντες ἀφεώρων, ὡς μόνην οὖσαν. ἐβάδιζε δὲ
σοβαρά, Χαιρέου καὶ Πολυχάρμου μέσην αὐτὴν
δορυφορούντων. ἄνθη καὶ στεφάνους <ἐπ>έβαλλον

convinced that Dionysius had recovered Callirhoe. Quietly going to her, he said, "Courage, my dear, whoever you are! We are not going to use force on you. You shall have the husband you want." While he was still speaking, Callirhoe recognized his voice and uncovered her face. At the same instant they both cried out: "Chaereas!" "Callirhoe!" As they rushed into each other's arms they fainted and fell to the floor. At first Polycharmus, too, stood speechless at this miracle, but after a while he said, "Stand up! You have recovered each other; the gods have granted the prayers of you both. But remember, you are not at home, but in an enemy country, and first you must take good care that no one separates you again." He had to shout: they were like people plunged in a deep well barely able to hear a voice from above. Gradually they recovered; then after gazing at each other and kissing, they swooned again, and this happened a second and a third time. The only thing they could say was, "Are you really Callirhoe whom I hold in my arms?" and "Are you really Chaereas?"

The rumor swiftly spread that the admiral had found his wife. No soldier remained in his tent, no sailor on his ship, no janitor at his door, but from all sides they flocked together exclaiming, "What a lucky woman to have gained so handsome a husband!" Nevertheless when Callirhoe appeared, no one praised Chaereas any more, but all turned their gaze on her, as though only she were there. She moved with dignity, escorted by Chaereas and Polycharmus on either side. Flowers and wreaths were show-

---

1.12 add. Cobet.

αὐτοῖς, καὶ οἶνος καὶ μύρα πρὸ τῶν ποδῶν ἐχεῖτο, καὶ πολέμου καὶ εἰρήνης ἦν ὁμοῦ τὰ ἥδιστα, ἐπινίκια καὶ γάμοι.

13 Χαιρέας δὲ εἴθιστο μὲν ἐν τριήρει καθεύδειν καὶ νυκτὸς καὶ μεθ’ ἡμέραν πολλὰ πράττων· τότε δὲ Πολυχάρμῳ πάντα ἐπιτρέψας, αὐτὸς οὐδὲ νύκτα περιμείνας εἰσῆλθεν εἰς τὸν θάλαμον τὸν βασιλικόν· καθ’ ἑκάστην γὰρ πόλιν οἶκος ἐξαίρετος ἀπο-
14 δέδεικται τῷ μεγάλῳ βασιλεῖ. κλίνη μὲν ἔκειτο χρυσήλατος, στρωμνὴ δὲ Τυρία πορφύρα, ὕφασμα Βαβυλώνιον.

Τίς ἂν φράσῃ τὴν νύκτα ἐκείνην πόσων διηγημάτων μεστή, πόσων δὲ δακρύων ὁμοῦ καὶ φιλημάτων; πρώτη μὲν ἤρξατο Καλλιρόη διηγεῖσθαι, πῶς ἀνέζησεν ἐν τῷ τάφῳ, πῶς ὑπὸ Θήρωνος ἐξήχθη, πῶς
15 ἔπλευσε, πῶς ἐπράθη. μέχρι τούτων Χαιρέας ἀκούων ἔκλαεν· ἐπεὶ δὲ ἦκεν εἰς Μίλητον τῷ λόγῳ, Καλλιρόη μὲν ἐσιώπησεν αἰδουμένη, Χαιρέας δὲ τῆς ἐμφύτου ζηλοτυπίας ἀνεμνήσθη, παρηγόρησε δὲ αὐτὸν τὸ περὶ τοῦ τέκνου διήγημα. πρὶν δὲ πάντα ἀκοῦσαι, "λέγε μοι" φησὶ "πῶς εἰς Ἄραδον ἦλθες καὶ ποῦ Διονύσιον καταλέλοιπας καὶ τί σοι πέπρα-
16 κται πρὸς βασιλέα." ἡ δ’ εὐθὺς ἀπώμνυτο μὴ ἑωρα-κέναι Διονύσιον μετὰ τὴν δίκην· βασιλέα δὲ ἐρᾶν μὲν αὐτῆς, μὴ κεκοινωνηκέναι δὲ αὐτῷ μηδὲ μέχρι φιλήματος. "ἄδικος οὖν" ἔφη Χαιρέας "ἐγὼ καὶ ὀξὺς εἰς ὀργήν, τηλικαῦτα δεινὰ διατεθεικὼς βασιλέα μηδὲν ἀδικοῦντά σε· σοῦ γὰρ ἀπαλλαγεὶς εἰς

ered upon them; wine and myrrh were poured at their feet, and the sweetest fruits of war and peace, the triumph and the wedding, were there combined.

It was Chaereas' custom to sleep on board the warship, being busy night and day. Now, however, he turned everything over to Polycharmus, and as for himself did not even wait until evening before coming to the royal chamber: for in every city a special house is reserved for the Great King. In it stood a bed of beaten gold, with a coverlet of Tyrian dye and Babylonian weave.

Who could describe that night—the many stories with which it was filled, the many tears and kisses? Callirhoe first began her story—how she had revived in the tomb, been brought out by Theron, crossed the sea, and been sold into slavery. Up to this point Chaereas wept as he listened, but when her narrative reached Miletus, Callirhoe fell silent with embarrassment, and Chaereas felt the stirrings of his innate jealousy. However, the news about his child comforted him. Not waiting to hear everything he said, "Tell me how you came to Aradus, where you left Dionysius, and what you had to do with the king." She immediately swore that she had not seen Dionysius since the trial. The king was in love with her, but she had had no dealings with him, not even a kiss. "Then," said Chaereas, "I was unjust and too quick-tempered in treating the king so badly when he had done you no wrong, for when I was separated from you, I felt obliged to desert

17 ἀνάγκην κατέστην αὐτομολίας. ἀλλ' οὐ κατῄσχυνά
σε· πεπλήρωκα γῆν καὶ θάλασσαν τροπαίων." καὶ
πάντα ἀκριβῶς διηγήσατο, ἐναβρυνόμενος τοῖς
κατορθώμασιν. ἐπεὶ δὲ ἅλις ἦν δακρύων καὶ διηγημάτων, περιπλακέντες ἀλλήλοις

ἀσπάσιοι λέκτροιο παλαιοῦ θεσμὸν ἵκοντο.

2. Ἔτι δὲ νυκτὸς κατέπλευσέ τις Αἰγύπτιος οὐ
τῶν ἀφανῶν, ἐκβὰς δὲ τοῦ κέλητος μετὰ σπουδῆς
ἐπυνθάνετο ποῦ Χαιρέας ἐστίν. ἀχθεὶς οὖν πρὸς
Πολύχαρμον ἑτέρῳ μὲν οὐδενὶ ἔφη τὸ ἀπόρρητον
δύνασθαι εἰπεῖν, ἐπείγειν δὲ τὴν χρείαν ὑπὲρ ἧς
2 ἀφῖκται. καὶ ἐπὶ πολὺ μὲν ἀνεβάλλετο Πολύχαρμος
τὴν πρὸς Χαιρέαν εἴσοδον, ἐνοχλεῖν ἀκαίρως οὐ
θέλων· ἐπεὶ δὲ ὁ ἄνθρωπος κατήπειγε, παρανοίξας
τοῦ θαλάμου τὴν θύραν ἐμήνυσε τὴν σπουδήν. ὡς
δὲ στρατηγὸς ἀγαθὸς Χαιρέας "κάλει" φησί· "πόλε-
3 μος γὰρ ἀναβολὴν οὐ περιμένει." εἰσαχθεὶς δὲ ὁ
Αἰγύπτιος, ἔτι σκότους ὄντος, τῇ κλίνῃ παραστὰς
"ἴσθι" φησὶν "ὅτι βασιλεὺς ὁ Περσῶν ἀνῄρηκε τὸν
Αἰγύπτιον καὶ τὴν στρατιὰν τὴν μὲν εἰς Αἴγυπτον
πέπομφε καταστησομένην τὰ ἐκεῖ, τὴν δὲ λοιπὴν
ἄγει πᾶσαν ἐνθάδε καὶ ὅσον οὔπω πάρεστι· πεπυσ-
μένος γὰρ Ἄραδον ἑαλωκέναι λυπεῖται μὲν καὶ
περὶ τοῦ πλούτου παντὸς ὃν ἐνθάδε καταλέλοιπεν,
ἀγωνιᾷ δὲ μάλιστα περὶ τῆς Στατείρας τῆς γυναικός."

from him. But I have not shamed you. I have filled land and sea with my triumphs," and he gave her an exact account of it all, proud of his achievements. When they had had their fill of tears and tales, embracing each other,

they gladly came to the ancient rite of the bed.[a]

2. While it was still dark, an Egyptian of distinction landed and, stepping ashore from his cutter, urgently asked where Chaereas was. He was taken to Polycharmus, but declared that he could reveal his mission to no one else, except that the matter which brought him was an urgent one. For some time Polycharmus kept putting off his meeting with Chaereas, unwilling to disturb him at an inconvenient time, but when the man kept insisting, he slightly opened the bedroom door, and informed Chaereas of the emergency. Like a good general, Chaereas said, "Call him in; war permits no delay." When the Egyptian had been brought in—it was still dark—he stood by the bed and said, "I have to report that the Persian king has killed the pharaoh, and has dispatched some of his army to Egypt to establish control there; the remainder he is leading in this direction, and is almost here. He has learned of the capture of Aradus, and so is not only worrying about all the wealth which he left here, but is especially anxious about the safety of his wife, Statira."

---

[a] *Odyssey* 23.296 (the reunion of Odysseus and Penelope).

2.3 πάρεστι Cobet: παρέσται F.

4 Ταῦτα ἀκούσας Χαιρέας ἀνέθορε· Καλλιρόη δὲ
αὐτοῦ λαβομένη "ποῦ σπεύδεις" εἶπε "πρὶν βουλεύσασθαι περὶ τῶν ἐφεστηκότων; ἂν γὰρ τοῦτο δημο-
σιεύσῃς, μέγαν πόλεμον κινήσεις σεαυτῷ, πάντων
ἐπισταμένων ἤδη καὶ καταφρονούντων· πάλιν δὲ ἐν
χερσὶ γενόμενοι πεισόμεθα τῶν πρώτων βαρύτερα."
5 ταχέως ἐπείσθη τῇ συμβουλῇ καὶ τοῦ θαλάμου προῆλθε μετὰ τέχνης. κρατῶν γὰρ τῆς χειρὸς τὸν
Αἰγύπτιον, συγκαλέσας τὸ πλῆθος "νικῶμεν,
ἄνδρες" εἶπε, "καὶ τὴν πεζὴν στρατιὰν τὴν βασι-
λέως· οὗτος γὰρ ὁ ἀνὴρ τὰ εὐαγγέλια ἡμῖν φέρει καὶ
γράμματα παρὰ τοῦ Αἰγυπτίου· δεῖ δὲ τὴν ταχίστην
ἡμᾶς πλεῖν, ἔνθα ἐκεῖνος ἐκέλευσε. συσκευασάμενοι
οὖν πάντες ἐμβαίνετε."
6 Ταῦτα εἰπόντος ὁ σαλπιστὴς τὸ ἀνακλητικὸν εἰς
τὰς τριήρεις ἐσήμαινε. λάφυρα δὲ καὶ αἰχμαλώτους
τῆς προτεραίας ἦσαν ἐντεθειμένοι, καὶ οὐδὲν ἐν τῇ
νήσῳ καταλέλειπτο, πλὴν εἰ μή τι βαρὺ καὶ ἄχρη-
7 στον. ἔπειτα ἔλυον τὰ ἀπόγεια καὶ ἀγκύρας ἀν-
ῄρουν καὶ βοῆς καὶ ταραχῆς ὁ λιμὴν πεπλήρωτο καὶ
ἄλλος ἄλλο τι ἔπραττε. παριὼν δὲ Χαιρέας εἰς τὰς
τριήρεις σύνθημα λεληθὸς τοῖς τριηράρχαις διέδωκεν ἐπὶ Κύπρου κρατεῖν, ὡς δῆτα ἀναγκαῖον ἔτι
ἀφύλακτον οὖσαν αὐτὴν προκαταλαβεῖν· πνεύματι
δὲ φορῷ χρησάμενοι τῆς ὑστεραίας κατήχθησαν εἰς
8 Πάφον, ἔνθα ἐστὶν ἱερὸν Ἀφροδίτης. ἐπεὶ δὲ ὡρμί-

2.7 διέδωκεν Cobet: δέδωκεν F.

On hearing this Chaereas started to his feet; but Callirhoe held him back and said, "Where are you off to in such a hurry before considering the situation? If you make this news public, you will have a revolt on your hands; when people know the facts, they will lose confidence in you. And if we are captured a second time, our troubles will be worse than before." Chaereas was soon convinced by her advice, and left the bedroom with a plan ready. Taking the Egyptian by the hand, he assembled his whole force and said, "Men, we are victorious over the land forces of the king as well. This man has brought us the good news together with letters from the pharaoh, and we must set sail at once to where he has ordered us. So all of you are to pack up and get on board."

At these words the trumpeter sounded the recall to the ships. On the previous day they had put on board the spoils and prisoners, and nothing was left on the island except what was cumbersome or useless. Then they proceeded to cast off and weigh anchor; the harbor was filled with shouting and uproar as each performed his task. Chaereas passed from ship to ship and gave secret orders to each captain to head for Cyprus, on the grounds that they had to capture that island while it was still unguarded. Meeting with a favorable breeze, on the following day they put in at Paphos,[a] where there is a temple

[a] On the southwestern coast of the island (actually a few miles inland); Aphrodite had been worshipped there from the earliest times.

371

σαντο, Χαιρέας, πρὶν ἐκβῆναί τινα τῶν τριηρῶν,
πρώτους ἐξέπεμψε τοὺς κήρυκας εἰρήνην καὶ σπον-
δὰς τοῖς ἐπιχωρίοις καταγγεῖλαι. δεξαμένων δὲ
αὐτῶν ἐξεβίβασε τὴν δύναμιν ἅπασαν εἰς γῆν καὶ
ἀναθήμασι τὴν Ἀφροδίτην ἐτίμησε· πολλῶν δὲ
9   ἱερείων συναχθέντων εἰστίασε τὴν στρατιάν. σκε-
πτομένου δὲ αὐτοῦ περὶ τῶν ἑξῆς ἀπήγγειλαν οἱ
ἱερεῖς (οἱ αὐτοὶ δέ εἰσι καὶ μάντεις) ὅτι καλὰ γέγονε
τὰ ἱερά. τότε οὖν θαρρήσας ἐκάλεσε τοὺς τριηράρ-
χας καὶ τοὺς Ἕλληνας τοὺς τριακοσίους καὶ ὅσους
τῶν Αἰγυπτίων εὔνους ἑώρα πρὸς αὐτὸν καὶ ἔλεξεν
ὧδε·

10  "" Ἄνδρες συστρατιῶται καὶ φίλοι, κοινωνοὶ
μεγάλων κατορθωμάτων, ἐμοὶ καὶ εἰρήνη καλλίστη
καὶ πόλεμος ἀσφαλέστατος μεθ' ὑμῶν· πείρᾳ γὰρ
μεμαθήκαμεν ὅτι ὁμονοοῦντες ἐκρατήσαμεν τῆς
θαλάσσης· καιρὸς δὲ ὀξὺς ἐφέστηκεν ἡμῖν εἰς τὸ
βουλεύσασθαι περὶ τοῦ μέλλοντος ἀσφαλῶς· ἴστε
γὰρ ὅτι ὁ μὲν Αἰγύπτιος ἀνήρηται μαχόμενος, κρατεῖ δὲ βασιλεὺς ἁπάσης τῆς γῆς, ἡμεῖς δὲ ἀπειλήμ-
11  μεθα ἐν μέσοις τοῖς πολεμίοις. εἶτ' οὖν συμβου-
λεύει τις ἡμῖν ἀπιέναι πρὸς τὸν βασιλέα καὶ εἰς τὰς
ἐκείνου χεῖρας φέροντας αὐτοὺς ἐμβαλεῖν;" ἀνεβόησαν εὐθὺς ὡς πάντα μᾶλλον ἢ τοῦτο ποιητέον.

"Ποῦ τοίνυν ἄπιμεν; πάντα γάρ ἐστιν ἡμῖν
πολέμια καὶ οὐκέτι οὐδὲ τῇ θαλάττῃ προσήκει
πιστεύειν, τῆς γῆς κρατουμένης ὑπὸ τῶν πολεμίων·
οὐ δήπου γε ἀναπτῆναι δυνάμεθα."

of Aphrodite. When they had anchored, and before anyone had disembarked, Chaereas first dispatched heralds
to proclaim peace and make a pact with the inhabitants;
when this had been accepted, he landed his whole force
and rendered homage to Aphrodite with offerings. Then,
collecting a large number of sacrificial animals, he prepared a feast for his whole force. While he was considering his next step, the priests, who are also prophets,
reported that the omens of sacrifice were good. Encouraged by this, he summoned the captains, his three hundred Greeks, and all the Egyptians he saw to be loyal to
him, and spoke as follows:

"Fellow soldiers and friends, partners in mighty
accomplishments, for me peace is fairest and war is safest
when I have you at my side. We have learned by experience that united in spirit we could gain mastery of the
sea. But a critical moment has arisen when we must
deliberate about our future safety. The fact is that the
pharaoh has been killed in battle and the king is in control
of all the land, while we are cut off in the enemy's midst.
So, then, does anyone recommend going to the king and
throwing ourselves on his mercy?" They cried at once that
anything was better than that.

"Then where shall we go? Every quarter is hostile to
us; it is no longer reasonable even to trust the sea, now
that the land is under the control of our enemies; and
obviously we cannot fly away!"

---

2.11 εἶτ' D'Orville, Cobet: εἴτε F.

CHARITON

12  Σιωπῆς ἐπὶ τούτοις γενομένης Λακεδαιμόνιος
ἀνήρ, Βρασίδου συγγενής, κατὰ μεγάλην ἀνάγκην
τῆς Σπάρτης ἐκπεσών, πρῶτος ἐτόλμησεν εἰπεῖν "τί
δὲ ζητοῦμεν ποῦ φύγωμεν βασιλέα; ἔχομεν γὰρ
θάλασσαν καὶ τριήρεις· ἀμφότερα δὲ ἡμᾶς εἰς Σικελίαν ἄγει καὶ Συρακούσας, ὅπου μὴ μόνον Πέρσας
13  οὐκ ἂν δείσαιμεν, ἀλλ' οὐδὲ Ἀθηναίους." ἐπήνεσαν
πάντες τὸν λόγον· μόνος Χαιρέας προσεποιεῖτο μὴ
συγκατατίθεσθαι, τὸ μῆκος τοῦ πλοῦ προφασιζόμε-
νος, τὸ δὲ ἀληθὲς ἀποπειρώμενος εἰ βεβαίως αὐτοῖς
δοκεῖ. σφόδρα δὲ ἐγκειμένων καὶ πλεῖν ἤδη θελόν-
των, "ἀλλ' ὑμεῖς μέν, ἄνδρες Ἕλληνες, βουλεύεσθε
καλῶς καὶ χάριν ὑμῖν ἔχω τῆς εὐνοίας τε καὶ
πίστεως· οὐκ ἐάσω δὲ ὑμᾶς μετανοῆσαι, θεῶν ὑμᾶς
14  προσλαμβανομένων. τῶν δὲ Αἰγυπτίων πολλοὶ
πάρεισιν οὓς οὐ προσήκεν ἄκοντας βιάζεσθαι· καὶ
γὰρ γυναῖκας καὶ τέκνα ἔχουσιν οἱ πλείους, ὧν οὐκ
ἂν ἡδέως ἀποσπασθεῖεν. κατασπαρέντες οὖν εἰς τὸ
πλῆθος διαπυνθάνεσθαι ἑκάστου σπεύσατε, ἵνα
μόνον τοὺς ἑκόντας παραλάβωμεν."

3. Ταῦτα μέν, ὡς ἐκέλευσεν, ἐγίνετο· Καλλιρόη
δὲ λαβομένη Χαιρέου τῆς δεξιᾶς, μόνον αὐτὸν ἀπ-
αγαγοῦσα "τί" ἔφη "βεβούλευσαι, Χαιρέα; καὶ Στάτειραν ἄγεις εἰς Συρακούσας καὶ Ῥοδογούνην τὴν
καλήν;" ἠρυθρίασεν ὁ Χαιρέας καὶ "οὐκ ἐμαυτοῦ"
φησὶν "ἕνεκα ἄγω ταύτας, ἀλλὰ σοὶ θεραπαινίδας."

2.12 μὴ Reeve: οὐ F.

374

In the ensuing silence, a man from Lacedaemon, a relative of Brasidas,[a] who had been forced into exile from Sparta, was the first who had the courage to speak. "Why are we looking for a place to escape from the king?" he said. "We have the sea and warships; both afford us passage to Sicily and Syracuse, where we need not fear the Persians or even the Athenians." Everyone applauded his words. Chaereas alone pretended not to agree; he professed that the journey was too long, but he really wanted to test their strength of purpose.[b] When they strongly insisted and were keen to sail at once, he said, "Fellow Greeks, your advice is good, and I thank you for your kindness and loyalty; with the gods standing by you, I shall see that you do not regret it. But there are many Egyptians here whom we should not force against their will: most of them have wives and children from whom they would hate to be separated. You must fan out among their number and be sure to make inquiries of each, so that we take with us only those who wish to come."

3. This was done as he ordered. Callirhoe, however, took Chaereas' hand and, leading him off to one side, said, "What have you in mind, Chaereas? Are you also taking Statira and the beautiful Rhodogune to Syracuse?" Chaereas blushed and said, "It is not for my sake that I am taking them, but as servants for you." "May the gods not

[a] A Spartan general, much admired by Thucydides, who inflicted several defeats on the Athenians (died 422 B.C.).

[b] Like Agamemnon at Homer, *Iliad* 2.73f.

---

2.14 τοὺς δὲ Αἰγυπτίους πολλοὶ γάρ εἰσιν F, corr. Cobet.

2 ἀνέκραγεν ἡ Καλλιρόη "μὴ ποιήσειαν οἱ θεοὶ
τοσαύτην ἐμοὶ γενέσθαι μανίαν, ὥστε τὴν τῆς
Ἀσίας βασιλίδα δούλην ἔχειν, ἄλλως τε καὶ ξένην
γεγενημένη. εἰ δέ μοι θέλεις χαρίζεσθαι, βασιλεῖ
πέμψον αὐτήν· καὶ γὰρ αὕτη μέ σοι διεφύλαξεν ὡς
3 ἀδελφοῦ γυναῖκα παραλαβοῦσα." "οὐδέν ἐστιν" ἔφη
Χαιρέας, "ὃ σοῦ θελούσης οὐκ ἂν ἐγὼ ποιήσαιμι·
σὺ γὰρ κυρία Στατείρας καὶ πάντων τῶν λαφύρων
καὶ πρὸ πάντων τῆς ἐμῆς ψυχῆς." ἥσθη Καλλιρόη
καὶ κατεφίλησεν αὐτόν, εὐθὺς δὲ ἐκέλευσε τοῖς
ὑπηρέταις ἄγειν αὐτὴν πρὸς Στάτειραν.

4 Ἐτύγχανε δὲ ἐκείνη μετὰ τῶν ἐνδοξοτάτων Περσίδων ἐν κοίλῃ νηΐ, ὅλως οὐδὲν ἐπισταμένη τῶν
γεγενημένων, οὐδ' ὅτι Καλλιρόη Χαιρέαν ἀπείληφε·
πολλὴ γὰρ ἦν παραφυλακὴ καὶ οὐδενὶ ἐξῆν προσ-
5 ελθεῖν, οὐκ ἰδεῖν, οὐ μηνῦσαί τι τῶν πραττομένων.
ὡς δὲ ἧκεν ἐπὶ τὴν ναῦν, τοῦ τριηράρχου δορυφο-
ροῦντος αὐτήν, κατάπληξις εὐθὺς ἦν πάντων καὶ
ταραχὴ διαθεόντων. εἶτά τις ἡσυχῇ πρὸς ἄλλον
ἐλάλησεν "ἡ τοῦ ναυάρχου γυνὴ παραγίνεται." μέγα
δὲ καὶ βύθιον ἀνεστέναξεν ἡ Στάτειρα καὶ κλάουσα
εἶπεν "εἰς ταύτην με τὴν ἡμέραν, ὦ Τύχη, τετήρη-
κας, ἵνα ἡ βασιλὶς ἴδω κυρίαν· πάρεστι γὰρ ἴσως
6 ἰδεῖν οἵαν παρείληφε δούλην." ἤγειρε θρῆνον ἐπὶ
τούτοις καὶ τότε ἔμαθε τί αἰχμαλωσία σωμάτων
εὐγενῶν.

Ἀλλὰ ταχεῖαν ἐποίησεν ὁ θεὸς τὴν μεταβολήν·
Καλλιρόη γὰρ εἰσδραμοῦσα περιεπλάκη τῇ
Στατείρᾳ. "χαῖρε" φησίν, "ὦ βασίλεια· βασιλὶς

make me so mad," cried Callirhoe, "as to keep the queen of Asia as a slave, especially when she has given me hospitality! If you wish to please me, send her to the king. It was she who kept me safe for you, as though she were looking after her brother's wife." "There is nothing," Chaereas replied, "which I would not do for you. Indeed, you are mistress of Statira and of all the booty and, above all, of my heart!" Callirhoe was delighted and kissed him. Then at once she told her servants to take her to Statira.

The queen happened to be in a ship's hold with the noblest Persian women. She knew nothing whatever of what had happened, not even that Callirhoe had recovered Chaereas, since close guard was kept and no one was allowed to come and see her or report what was going on. So, when Callirhoe escorted by the captain came on board, all were suddenly struck with astonishment and ran about in confusion; then one would murmur to another, "The admiral's wife has come." Statira gave a loud deep sigh. "Fortune," she said, with tears in her eyes, "you have preserved me until today, so that I, a queen, may look upon a mistress! She has probably come to see what sort of a slave she has acquired." Thereupon she broke into a lament, realizing at that moment what captivity means for those of noble birth.

But it was a swift change of fortune that the god brought about. Callirhoe ran in and embraced Statira. "Greetings, queen!" she said, "for queen you are and will

---

3.6  τί Cobet: τίς F.

7 γὰρ εἶ καὶ ἀεὶ διαμένεις. οὐκ εἰς πολεμίων χεῖρας
ἐμπέπτωκας, ἀλλὰ τῆς σοὶ φιλτάτης, ἣν εὐηργέτη-
σας. Χαιρέας ὁ ἐμός ἐστι ναύαρχος· ναύαρχον δὲ
Αἰγυπτίων ἐποίησεν αὐτὸν ὀργὴ πρὸς βασιλέα, διὰ
τὸ βραδέως ἀπολαμβάνειν ἐμέ· πέπαυται δὲ καὶ
διήλλακται καὶ οὐκέτι ὑμῖν ἐστι πόλεμιος. ἀνίστασο δέ, φιλτάτη, καὶ ἄπιθι χαίρουσα· ἀπόλαβε
καὶ σὺ τὸν ἄνδρα τὸν σεαυτῆς· ζῇ γὰρ βασιλεύς,
8 κἀκείνῳ σε Χαιρέας πέμπει. ἀνίστασο καὶ σύ,
Ῥοδογούνη, πρώτη μοι φίλη Περσίδων, καὶ βάδιζε
πρὸς τὸν ἄνδρα τὸν σεαυτῆς, καὶ ὅσας ἡ βασιλὶς ἂν
9 ἄλλας θέλῃ, καὶ μέμνησθε Καλλιρόης." ἐξεπλάγη
Στάτειρα τούτων ἀκούσασα τῶν λόγων καὶ οὔτε
πιστεύειν εἶχεν οὔτε ἀπιστεῖν· τὸ δὲ ἦθος Καλλιρόης τοιοῦτον ἦν, ὡς μὴ δοκεῖν εἰρωνεύεσθαι ἐν
μεγάλαις συμφοραῖς· ὁ δὲ καιρὸς ἐκέλευε ταχέως
10 πάντα πράττειν. ἦν οὖν τις ἐν Αἰγυπτίοις Δημήτριος, φιλόσοφος, βασιλεῖ γνώριμος, ἡλικίᾳ προ-
ήκων, παιδείᾳ καὶ ἀρετῇ τῶν ἄλλων Αἰγυπτίων διαφέρων. τοῦτον καλέσας Χαιρέας εἶπεν "ἐγὼ <μὲν>
ἐβουλόμην μετ' ἐμαυτοῦ σε ἄγειν, ἀλλὰ μεγάλης
πράξεως ὑπηρέτην σε ποιοῦμαι· τὴν γὰρ βασιλίδα
11 τῷ μεγάλῳ βασιλεῖ πέμπω διὰ σοῦ. τοῦτο δὲ καὶ σὲ
ποιήσει τιμιώτερον ἐκείνῳ καὶ τοὺς ἄλλους διαλ-
λάξει." ταῦτα εἰπὼν στρατηγὸν ἀπέδειξε Δημήτριον
τῶν ὀπίσω κομιζομένων τριηρῶν.

Πάντες μὲν οὖν ἤθελον ἀκολουθεῖν Χαιρέᾳ καὶ
12 προετίμων αὐτὸν πατρίδων καὶ τέκνων. ὁ δὲ μόνας

always so remain. You have not fallen into the hands of
enemies, but rather of your dear friend whom you have
treated so kindly. It is my Chaereas who is the admiral:
what made him admiral of the Egyptians was his anger
with the king for delaying his recovery of me. But his
anger is now past, he is reconciled and no longer Persia's
enemy. So get up now, dear friend, and go your way safe
and sound. You, too, shall get your husband back. The
king is alive and Chaereas is sending you to him. You, too,
Rhodogune, my first friend among the Persians, get up
and go home to your husband. So too with all those the
queen wishes, and may you all remember Callirhoe."
Statira was astonished to hear these words and could neither believe nor disbelieve. Callirhoe's nature, however,
was not such as to suggest that in serious circumstances
she would be jesting. But the crisis called for immediate
action. Now among the Egyptians there was a certain
Demetrius, a philosopher and an acquaintance of the
king, advanced in years and the superior of the other
Egyptians in education and character. Chaereas summoned him and said, "I had wanted to take you with me,
but instead I am making you my agent in an important
matter; I am sending the queen back to the Great King in
your care. This will both raise your standing with him and
restore the others to favor." Upon this he appointed
Demetrius commander of the ships being sent back.

Now everyone wanted to go with Chaereas, and
thought more of him than of their countries and children.

---

3.10 add. Jackson.
3.11 μὲν οὖν Abresch: γὰρ F.

εἴκοσι τριήρεις ἐπελέξατο τὰς ἀρίστας καὶ μεγί-
στας, ὡς ἂν ὑπὲρ τὸν Ἰόνιον μέλλων περαιοῦσθαι,
καὶ ταύταις ἐνεβίβασεν Ἕλληνας μὲν ἅπαντας ὅσοι
παρῆσαν, Αἰγυπτίων δὲ καὶ Φοινίκων ὅσους ἔμαθεν
εὐζώνους· πολλοὶ καὶ Κυπρίων ἐθελονταὶ <συν>εν-
έβησαν. τοὺς δὲ ἄλλους πάντας ἔπεμψεν οἴκαδε,
διανείμας αὐτοῖς μέρη τῶν λαφύρων, ἵνα χαίροντες
ἐπανίωσι πρὸς τοὺς ἑαυτῶν, ἐντιμότεροι γενόμενοι·
καὶ οὐδεὶς ἠτύχησεν οὐδενός, αἰτήσας παρὰ
Χαιρέου.

Καλλιρόη δὲ προσήνεγκε τὸν κόσμον ἅπαντα τὸν
13 βασιλικὸν Στατείρᾳ. ἡ δὲ οὐκ ἠβουλήθη λαβεῖν,
ἀλλὰ "τούτῳ" φησὶ "<σὺ> κοσμοῦ· πρέπει γὰρ τοιούτῳ σώματι κόσμος βασιλικός. δεῖ γὰρ ἔχειν σε
ἵνα καὶ μητρὶ χαρίσῃ καὶ πατρίοις ἀναθήματα
θεοῖς. ἐγὼ δὲ πλείω τούτων καταλέλοιπα ἐν Βαβυ-
14 λῶνι. θεοὶ δέ σοι παρέχοιεν εὔπλοιαν καὶ σωτηρίαν
καὶ μηδέποτε διαζευχθῆναι Χαιρέου. πάντα πεποίη-
κας εἰς ἐμὲ δικαίως· χρηστὸν ἦθος ἐπεδείξω καὶ τοῦ
κάλλους ἄξιον. καλήν μοι βασιλεὺς ἔδωκε παραθήκην."

4. Τίς ἂν φράσῃ τὴν ἡμέραν ἐκείνην πόσας ἔσχε
πράξεις, πῶς ἀλλήλαις διαφόρους—εὐχομένων,
συντασσομένων, χαιρόντων, λυπουμένων, ἀλλήλοις
ἐντολὰς διδόντων, τοῖς οἴκοι γραφόντων; ἔγραψε δὲ
καὶ Χαιρέας ἐπιστολὴν πρὸς βασιλέα τοιαύτην·

3.12 add. Jackson.

But he chose only twenty ships, the best and the biggest, since he was going to cross the Ionian Sea, and on board he put all the Greeks present, and those Egyptians and Phoenicians of whose prowess he was sure. Many of the Cypriots too embarked as volunteers. All the rest he sent home, giving them a share of the spoil, so that they could return to their families happily and with greater prestige. No one who made a request of Chaereas failed to get it.

Callirhoe brought all the royal adornments to Statira. But she refused to accept them, saying, "You must wear them yourself; beauty like yours must be royally adorned. You need presents for your mother and offerings for your ancestral gods. I left more than these behind in Babylon. May the gods grant you a safe voyage, and may you never again be parted from Chaereas. You have behaved decently to me in every way. You have shown a nature that is noble and worthy of your beauty. It was a fine charge which the king deposited with me."

4. Who could describe that day with its many contrasting scenes? Men were praying and saying good-bye, were sad and were happy, giving each other instructions and writing letters home. Chaereas, too, wrote this letter to the king:

---

3.13 add. Cobet.
4.1 ἀλλήλαις D'Orville διαφόρους Reiske: ἄλλοι διάφοροι F | ἔγραψε Hercher (cf. 4.4): ἔγραφε F.

2  Σὺ μὲν ἔμελλες τὴν δίκην κρίνειν, ἐγὼ δὲ
ἤδη νενίκηκα παρὰ τῷ δικαιοτάτῳ δικαστῇ·
πόλεμος γὰρ ἄριστος κριτὴς τοῦ κρείττονός
τε καὶ χείρονος. οὗτός μοι [Καλλιρόην]
ἀποδέδωκεν οὐ μόνον τὴν γυναῖκα τὴν
3  ἐμήν, ἀλλὰ καὶ τὴν σήν. οὐκ ἐμιμησάμην
δέ σου τὴν βραδυτῆτα, ἀλλὰ ταχέως σοι
μηδὲ ἀπαιτοῦντι Στάτειραν ἀποδίδωμι
καθαρὰν καὶ ἐν αἰχμαλωσίᾳ μείνασαν
βασιλίδα. ἴσθι δὲ οὐκ ἐμέ σοι τὸ δῶρον
ἀλλὰ Καλλιρόην ἀποστέλλειν. ἀνταπαι-
τοῦμεν δέ σε χάριν Αἰγυπτίοις διαλλαγῆ-
ναι· πρέπει γὰρ βασιλεῖ μάλιστα πάντων
ἀνεξικακεῖν. ἕξεις δὲ στρατιώτας ἀγαθοὺς
φιλοῦντάς σε· τοῦ γὰρ ἐμοὶ συνακολουθεῖν
ὡς φίλοι παρὰ σοὶ μᾶλλον εἵλοντο μένειν.

4  Ταῦτα μὲν ἔγραψε Χαιρέας, ἔδοξε δὲ καὶ Καλλιρόῃ δίκαιον εἶναι καὶ εὐχάριστον Διονυσίῳ γράψαι.
τοῦτο μόνον ἐποίησε δίχα Χαιρέου· εἰδυῖα γὰρ
αὐτοῦ τὴν ἔμφυτον ζηλοτυπίαν ἐσπούδαζε λαθεῖν.
λαβοῦσα δὲ γραμματίδιον ἐχάραξεν οὕτως·

5  Καλλιρόη Διονυσίῳ εὐεργέτῃ χαίρειν· σὺ
γὰρ εἶ ὁ καὶ λῃστείας καὶ δουλείας με
ἀπαλλάξας. δέομαί σου, μηδὲν ὀργισθῇς·
εἰμὶ γὰρ τῇ ψυχῇ μετὰ σοῦ διὰ τὸν κοινὸν
υἱόν, ὃν παρακατατίθημί σοι ἐκτρέφειν
τε καὶ παιδεύειν ἀξίως ἡμῶν. μὴ λάβῃ δὲ

You were intending to decide the case, but I
have already been declared the victor by the
most impartial judge: for war is the best arbiter
between stronger and weaker. It has awarded
me not only my wife but yours too. I have not
imitated your slowness, but at once, even before
you ask, I return Statira to you, untouched and
even in captivity treated as a queen; but you
should know that it is not I who send you this
gift, but Callirhoe. In return we ask a favor of
you, that you will pardon the Egyptians, for
even more than other men it becomes a king to
show forbearance. You will have good soldiers
who love you, for rather than follow me as
friends they preferred to stay in your service.

Such was Chaereas' letter. And Callirhoe, too, felt
that it was proper to show her gratitude by writing to
Dionysius. This was the only thing she did without telling
Chaereas, for she was aware of his innate jealousy, and so
took pains to keep it from him. Taking a writing tablet,
she wrote the following:

Callirhoe greets Dionysius her benefactor (for
you are the one who freed me from pirates and
slavery). Please, do not be angry. Indeed, I am
with you in spirit through the son we share, and
I entrust him to you to bring up and to educate
in a way worthy of us. Let him have no experi-

---

4.2 del. Beck.

πεῖραν μητρυιᾶς· ἔχεις οὐ μόνον υἱόν,
6   ἀλλὰ καὶ θυγατέρα· ἀρκεῖ σοι δύο τέκνα.
ὧν γάμον ζεῦξον, ὅταν ἀνὴρ γένηται, καὶ
πέμψον αὐτὸν εἰς Συρακούσας, ἵνα καὶ
τὸν πάππον θεάσηται. ἀσπάζομαί σε,
Πλαγγών. ταῦτά σοι γέγραφα τῇ ἐμῇ χειρί.
ἔρρωσο, ἀγαθὲ Διονύσιε, καὶ Καλλιρόης
μνημόνευε τῆς σῆς.

7   Σφραγίσασα δὲ τὴν ἐπιστολὴν ἀπέκρυψεν ἐν τοῖς
κόλποις καὶ ὅτε ἔδει λοιπὸν ἀνάγεσθαι καὶ ταῖς
τριήρεσι πάντας ἐμβαίνειν, αὐτὴ χεῖρα δοῦσα τῇ
Στατείρᾳ εἰς τὸ πλοῖον εἰσήγαγε. κατεσκευάκει δὲ
Δημήτριος ἐν τῇ νηὶ σκηνὴν βασιλικήν, πορφυρίδα
8   καὶ χρυσοφῆ Βαβυλώνια περιθείς. πάνυ δὲ κολα-
κευτικῶς κατακλίνασα αὐτὴν Καλλιρόη "ἔρρωσό
μοι" φησίν, "ὦ Στάτειρα, καὶ μέμνησό μου καὶ
γράφε μοι πολλάκις εἰς Συρακούσας· ῥᾴδια γὰρ
πάντα βασιλεῖ. κἀγὼ δέ σοι χάριν εἴσομαι παρὰ
τοῖς γονεῦσί μου καὶ τοῖς θεοῖς τοῖς Ἑλληνικοῖς.
συνίστημί σοι τὸ τέκνον μου, ὃ καὶ σὺ ἡδέως εἶδες·
νόμιζε ἐκεῖνο παραθήκην ἔχειν ἀντ' ἐμοῦ."

9   Ταῦτα λεγούσης δακρύων ἐνεπλήσθη καὶ γόον
ἤγειρε ταῖς γυναιξίν· ἐξιοῦσα δὲ τῆς νεὼς ἡ Καλλιρόη, ἠρέμα προσκύψασα τῇ Στατείρᾳ καὶ ἐρυθριῶσα
τὴν ἐπιστολὴν ἐπέδωκε καὶ "ταύτην" εἶπε "δὸς
Διονυσίῳ τῷ δυστυχεῖ, ὃν παρατίθημι σοί τε καὶ
βασιλεῖ. παρηγορήσατε αὐτόν. φοβοῦμαι μὴ ἐμοῦ

ence of a stepmother. You have not only a son,
but a daughter[a] as well; two children are
enough. Marry them to each other when he
becomes a man, and send him to Syracuse so
that he may also see his grandfather. My greetings to you, Plangon. This I have written with
my own hand. Farewell, good Dionysius, and
remember your Callirhoe.

Sealing the letter, she hid it away in her bosom, and
when the time to sail came and everyone had to embark,
she offered her hand to Statira and herself helped her
into the boat. Demetrius had put up a royal canopy for
her on the ship, surrounding it with Babylonian tapestries
of purple and gold thread. Escorting her deferentially to
the couch within, Callirhoe said, "Good-bye, Statira.
Remember me and write to me often in Syracuse, since
all things are easy for the king. I shall acknowledge my
gratitude to you to my parents and the gods of Greece. I
commend my child to your care, since you, too, were fond
of him. Think of him as a trust which you have to take in
my place."

At these words Statira burst into tears and started her
attendants sobbing. Then Callirhoe, as she was about to
leave the ship, leaned unobtrusively towards Statira and,
blushing, handed her the letter, saying, "Give this letter to
poor Dionysius; I trust him to your care and the king's.
You must both comfort him. I fear that he may kill him-

[a] The daughter by his first wife mentioned in 1.12.8. Half
siblings with different mothers could marry and often did.

385

CHARITON

10 χωρισθεὶς ἑαυτὸν ἀνέλῃ." ἔτι δὲ ἂν ἐλάλουν αἱ
γυναῖκες καὶ ἔκλαον καὶ ἀλλήλας κατεφίλουν, εἰ μὴ
παρήγγειλαν οἱ κυβερνῆται τὴν ἀναγωγήν. μέλλουσα δὲ ἐμβαίνειν εἰς τὴν τριήρη ἡ Καλλιρόη τὴν
Ἀφροδίτην προσεκύνησε. "χάρις σοι" φησίν, "ὦ
δέσποινα, τῶν παρόντων. ἤδη μοι διαλλάττῃ· δὸς
δέ μοι καὶ Συρακούσας ἰδεῖν. πολλὴ μὲν ἐν μέσῳ
θάλασσα, καὶ ἐκδέχεταί με φοβερὰ πελάγη, πλὴν
11 οὐ φοβοῦμαι σοῦ μοι συμπλεούσης." ἀλλ' οὐδὲ τῶν
Αἰγυπτίων οὐδεὶς ἐνέβη ταῖς Δημητρίου ναυσίν, εἰ
μὴ πρότερον συνετάξατο Χαιρέα καὶ κεφαλὴν καὶ
χεῖρας αὐτοῦ κατεφίλησε· τοσοῦτον ἵμερον πᾶσιν
ἐνέθηκε. καὶ πρῶτον ἐκεῖνον εἴασεν ἀναχθῆναι τὸν
στόλον, ὡς ἀκούεσθαι μέχρι πόρρω τῆς θαλάσσης
ἐπαίνους μεμιγμένους εὐχαῖς.

5. Καὶ οὗτοι μὲν ἔπλεον, βασιλεὺς δὲ ὁ μέγας
κρατήσας τῶν πολεμίων εἰς Αἴγυπτον μὲν ἐξέπεμπε
τὸν καταστησόμενον τὰ ἐν αὐτῇ βεβαίως, αὐτὸς δ'
2 ἔσπευδεν εἰς Ἄραδον πρὸς τὴν γυναῖκα. ὄντι δὲ
αὐτῷ περὶ <παρα>λίαν καὶ Τύρον καὶ θύοντι τῷ
Ἡρακλεῖ τὰ ἐπινίκια προσῆλθέ τις ἀγγέλλων ὅτι
"Ἄραδος ἐκπεπόρθηται καί ἐστι κενή, πάντα δὲ τὰ
ἐν αὐτῇ φέρουσιν αἱ ναῦς τῶν Αἰγυπτίων." μέγα δὴ
πένθος κατήγγειλε βασιλεῖ, ὡς ἀπολωλυίας τῆς
βασιλίδος. ἐπένθουν δὲ <καὶ> Περσῶν οἱ ἐντιμότα-
τοι

Στάτειραν πρόφασιν, σφῶν δ' αὐτῶν κήδε' ἕκαστος,

386

self now that he has been parted from me." The women might have gone on talking and weeping and embracing, had not the pilots given the signal for putting to sea. On the point of boarding the warship, Callirhoe knelt in homage to Aphrodite. "Lady," she said, "I thank you for my present blessings. Now you are reconciled with me; but grant me also to see Syracuse. A vast sea lies in between and daunting waters await me; but I shall not fear, if you are sailing with me." Not one of the Egyptians boarded the vessels of Demetrius without first saying good-bye to Chaereas and kissing his head and hands, such great affection had he inspired in them all. Moreover, he allowed Demetrius' fleet to set sail first, so that they could hear mingled cheers and prayers until they were far out at sea.

5. So off they sailed. But the Great King, having overcome his foes, sent a governor to Egypt to restore stable government in the country, while he himself hurried on to his wife in Aradus. When he had reached the coast and Tyre, and was sacrificing to Heracles to celebrate his victory, a messenger arrived with the report, "Aradus has been sacked and is deserted and the Egyptian ships are carrying off all that was in it." This news, implying the loss of the queen, caused the king great anguish. Then the Persian nobles too began to mourn,

seemingly for Statira, but in fact each for his own sorrows,[a]

---

[a] *Iliad* 19.302 (women weeping for Patroclus; adapted).

---

5.2 παραλίαν Naber: Χίον F | δὴ Zankogiannes: δὲ F | add. Coraës.

ὁ μὲν γυναῖκα, ὁ δὲ ἀδελφήν, ὁ δὲ θυγατέρα, πάντες δέ τινα, ἕκαστος οἰκεῖον. ἐκπεπλευκότων δὲ τῶν πολεμίων ἄγνωστον ἦν διὰ ποίας θαλάσσης.

3 Τῇ δευτέρᾳ δὲ τῶν ἡμερῶν ὤφθησαν αἱ Αἰγυπτίων ναῦς προσπλέουσαι. καὶ τὸ μὲν ἀληθὲς ἄδηλον ἦν, ἐθαύμαζον δὲ ὁρῶντες, καὶ ἔτι μᾶλλον ἐπέτεινεν αὐτῶν τὴν ἀπορίαν σημεῖον ἀρθὲν ἀπὸ τῆς νεὼς τῆς Δημητρίου βασιλικόν, ὅπερ εἴωθεν αἴρεσθαι μόνον πλέοντος βασιλέως· τοῦτο δὲ ταραχὴν 4 ἐποίησεν, ὡς πολεμίων ὄντων. εὐθὺς δὲ θέοντες ἐμήνυον Ἀρταξέρξῃ "τάχα δή τις εὑρεθήσεται βασιλεὺς Αἰγυπτίων." ὁ δὲ ἀνέθορεν ἐκ τοῦ θρόνου καὶ ἔσπευδεν ἐπὶ τὴν θάλασσαν καὶ σύνθημα πολεμικὸν ἐδίδου· τριήρεις μὲν γὰρ οὐκ ἦσαν αὐτῷ· πᾶν δὲ τὸ πλῆθος ἔστησεν ἐπὶ τοῦ λιμένος παρεσκευασμένον 5 εἰς μάχην. ἤδη δέ τις καὶ τόξον ἐνέτεινε καὶ λόγχην ἔμελλεν ἀφιέναι, εἰ μὴ συνῆκε Δημήτριος καὶ τοῦτο ἐμήνυσε τῇ βασιλίδι. ἡ δὲ Στάτειρα προελθοῦσα τῆς σκηνῆς ἔδειξεν ἑαυτήν. εὐθὺς οὖν τὰ ὅπλα ῥίψαντες προσεκύνησαν· ὁ δὲ βασιλεὺς οὐ κατέσχεν, ἀλλὰ πρὶν καλῶς τὴν ναῦν καταχθῆναι πρῶτος εἰσεπήδησεν εἰς αὐτήν, περιχυθεὶς δὲ τῇ γυναικὶ ἐκ τῆς χαρᾶς δάκρυα ἀφῆκε καὶ εἶπε "τίς ἄρα μοι θεῶν ἀποδέδωκέ σε, γύναι φιλτάτη; ἀμφότερα γὰρ ἄπιστα καὶ ἀπολέσθαι βασιλίδα καὶ ἀπολομένην 6 εὑρεθῆναι. πῶς δέ σε εἰς γῆν καταλιπὼν ἐκ θαλάσσης ἀπολαμβάνω;" Στάτειρα δὲ ἀπεκρίνατο "δῶρον ἔχεις με παρὰ Καλλιρόης." ἀκούσας δὲ τὸ ὄνομα

one for his wife, another for his sister, another for his daughter, each of them for someone of his own. Their enemies had sailed away, but they did not know in which direction.

The next day the Egyptian ships were seen approaching. Not knowing the true state of affairs they were surprised at the sight. Their perplexity was intensified, moreover, by the raising of the royal flag on Demetrius' ship, which by custom is only flown when the pharaoh is on board; and this move, suggesting the presence of enemies, caused a panic. They ran at once to Artaxerxes and said, "Perhaps it will turn out to be a new pharaoh!" He started up from his throne and hurried to the shore, where he gave the signal for battle. To be sure, he had no warships, but he stationed all his forces on the seafront ready to fight. They were already bending their bows and were on the point of launching their spears, when Demetrius took in the situation and reported it to the queen. Statira then came out from the tent and showed herself, and at once they threw down their arms and knelt in homage; the king did not hold back, but before the ship had been firmly moored, he was the first to leap on it. Throwing his arms round his queen, he wept with joy. "Which of the gods has restored you to me, my darling wife!" he said. "Both things pass belief: that my queen should have been lost and that, once lost, she should have been regained. How is it that when I left you on the land, I get you back from the sea?" "You have me as a gift from Callirhoe," replied Statira. On hearing that name, the

---

5.3 μόνον Reiske: μόνου F.

# CHARITON

βασιλεὺς ὡς ἐπὶ τραύματι παλαιῷ πληγὴν ἔλαβε
καινήν· βλέψας δὲ εἰς Ἀρταξάτην τὸν εὐνοῦχον
"ἄγε με" φησὶ "πρὸς Καλλιρόην, ἵνα αὐτῇ χάριν

7  γνῶ." εἶπε δ' ἡ Στάτειρα "μαθήσῃ πάντα παρ'
ἐμοῦ," ἅμα δὲ προῄεσαν ἐκ τοῦ λιμένος εἰς τὰ βασίλεια. τότε δὲ πάντας ἀπαλλαγῆναι κελεύσασα καὶ
μόνον τὸν εὐνοῦχον παρεῖναι, διηγεῖτο τὰ ἐν
Ἀράδῳ, τὰ ἐν Κύπρῳ, καὶ τελευταίαν ἔδωκε τὴν ἐπι-

8  στολὴν τὴν Χαιρέου. βασιλεὺς δὲ ἀναγινώσκων
μυρίων παθῶν ἐπληροῦτο· καὶ γὰρ ὠργίζετο διὰ τὴν
ἅλωσιν τῶν φιλτάτων καὶ μετενόει διὰ τὸ παρασχεῖν
αὐτομολίας ἀνάγκην, καὶ χάριν δὲ αὐτῷ πάλιν ἠπίστατο ὅτι <τὴν βασιλίδα ἀπολάβοι· ἐλυπεῖτο δὲ
ὅτι> Καλλιρόην μηκέτι δύναιτο θεάσασθαι.
μάλιστα δὲ πάντων φθόνος ἥπτετο αὐτοῦ, καὶ ἔλεγε
"μακάριος Χαιρέας, εὐτυχέστερος ἐμοῦ."

9      Ἐπεὶ δὲ ἅλις ἦν τῶν διηγημάτων Στάτειρα εἶπε
"παραμύθησαι, βασιλεῦ, Διονύσιον· τοῦτο γάρ σε
παρακαλεῖ Καλλιρόη." ἐπιστραφεὶς οὖν ὁ Ἀρταξέρξης πρὸς τὸν εὐνοῦχον "ἐλθέτω" φησὶ "Διονύσιος."

10  καὶ ἦλθε ταχέως, μετέωρος ταῖς ἐλπίσι· τῶν γὰρ
περὶ Χαιρέαν ἠπίστατο οὐδέν, μετὰ δὲ τῶν ἄλλων
γυναικῶν ἐδόκει Καλλιρόην παρεῖναι καὶ βασιλέα
καλεῖν αὐτόν, ἵνα ἀποδῷ τὴν γυναῖκα, γέρας τῆς
ἀριστείας. ἐπεὶ δὲ εἰσῆλθε, διηγήσατο αὐτῷ βασιλεὺς πάντα τὰ γεγενημένα. ἐν ἐκείνῳ δὴ τῷ καιρῷ
μάλιστα φρόνησιν Διονύσιος ἐπεδείξατο καὶ παι-

5.7 εἶπε δ' Gasda: εἶπεν F.     5.8 add. D'Orville.
390

king felt, as it were, a fresh stab upon an old wound; and, with a glance at the eunuch Artaxates, he said, "Take me to Callirhoe so that I can thank her." But Statira said, "You will hear the full story from me," and with that they went from the harbor to the palace. Then, after telling the rest to withdraw and only the eunuch to stay, she described what had happened in Aradus and Cyprus, and finally gave him Chaereas' letter. On reading it, the king was overcome with a variety of emotions. He was angry at the capture of what he held most dear and he regretted forcing Chaereas to desert him; then again he was grateful to him for recovering the queen, but he was grieved that he should not be seeing Callirhoe any more; and, above all, he was filled with envy, and muttered, "Happy Chaereas, he is luckier than I!"

When they had fully related their experiences, Statira said, "King, comfort Dionysius, for that is what Callirhoe wants you to do." So Artaxerxes turned to the eunuch and said, "Have Dionysius come here." He came at once in high hopes, knowing nothing of Chaereas' doings, but thinking that Callirhoe had accompanied the other women, and that the king's summons was to give him back his wife as a reward for his valor. When he came in, the king told him all that had happened. At this moment especially Dionysius showed his good sense and fine

---

5.9 φησὶ] T begins.

5.10 οὐδὲν ἠπίστατο Τ | ἐδόκει καὶ Καλλ. Τ | ἦλθε Τ | πάντα] ἐξ ἀρχῆς ἅπαντα Τ | δὴ Τ: δὲ F | μάλιστα Τ: om. F | φρόνησιν ... παιδείαν] Διονύσιος ἐπεδείξατο παιδίαν τε καὶ φρόνησιν Τ.

11 δείαν ἐξαίρετον. ὥσπερ γὰρ εἴ τις κεραυνοῦ πεσόν-
τος πρὸ τῶν ποδῶν αὐτοῦ μὴ ταραχθείη, οὕτως
κἀκεῖνος ἀκούσας λόγων σκηπτοῦ βαρυτέρων, ὅτι
Χαιρέας Καλλιρόην εἰς Συρακούσας ἀπάγει, ὅμως
εὐσταθὴς ἔμεινε καὶ οὐκ ἔδοξεν ἀσφαλὲς αὐτῷ τὸ
12 λυπεῖσθαι, σωθείσης τῆς βασιλίδος. ὁ δὲ Ἀρταξέρξης "εἰ μὲν ἐδυνάμην" ἔφη, "Καλλιρόην ἂν ἀπέ-
δωκά <σοι>, Διονύσιε· πᾶσαν γὰρ εὔνοιαν εἰς ἐμὲ
καὶ πίστιν ἐπεδείξω· τούτου δὲ ὄντος ἀμηχάνου, δίδωμί σοι πάσης Ἰωνίας ἄρχειν, καὶ πρῶτος εὐεργέτης εἰς οἶκον βασιλέως ἀναγραφήσῃ." προσεκύνησεν ὁ Διονύσιος καὶ χάριν ὁμολογήσας ἔσπευδεν
ἀπαλλαγῆναι καὶ δακρύων ἐξουσίαν ἔχειν· ἐξιόντι
δὲ αὐτῷ Στάτειρα τὴν ἐπιστολὴν ἡσυχῇ δίδωσιν.

13 Ὑποστρέψας δὲ καὶ κατακλείσας ἑαυτόν, γνωρίσας τὰ Καλλιρόης γράμματα πρῶτον τὴν ἐπιστολὴν
κατεφίλησεν, εἶτα ἀνοίξας τῷ στήθει προσεπτύξατο
ὡς ἐκείνην παροῦσαν, καὶ ἐπὶ πολὺν χρόνον κατεῖχεν,
ἀναγινώσκειν μὴ δυνάμενος διὰ τὰ δάκρυα. ἀποκλαύσας δὲ μόλις ἀναγινώσκειν ἤρξατο καὶ πρῶτόν
γε Καλλιρόης τοὔνομα κατεφίλησεν. ἐπεὶ δὲ ἦλθεν
εἰς τὸ "Διονυσίῳ εὐεργέτῃ," "οἴμοι" φησὶν "οὐκέτ᾽

5.11 εἴ τις T, Richards: τις F | ταραχθείη F: ταραχθῇ T |
οὕτως T: om. F | λόγους . . . βαρυτέρους T | ἀπάγει] after
Συρ. F: after Χαιρ. T | αὐτῷ Jackson: αὐτῷ F: [T].

5.12 καὶ Καλλ. T | ἀπέδωκα ἂν T | add. Hirschig | εἰς ἐμὲ]
om. T | ἀμηχ.] ἀδυνάτου T | πρῶτον εὐεργέτην εἰς τὸν οἶκον

training. Like a man unperturbed by a thunderbolt falling at his feet, so he, on hearing words more shattering than any thunderbolt—namely that Chaereas was taking Callirhoe back to Syracuse—nevertheless stood there without flinching, deeming any expression of sorrow unsafe, since the queen had been rescued. "If I could," said Artaxerxes, "I would have restored Callirhoe to you, Dionysius, for you have displayed the utmost devotion and loyalty towards me. But this being impossible, I appoint you governor of all Ionia, and you are to have the title of Chief Benefactor of the Royal House." Dionysius knelt in homage and, after expressing his thanks, hastened to leave, so as to be able to give way to his tears. As he went out, Statira quietly handed him the letter.

He went home and shut himself up. Recognizing Callirhoe's handwriting, he first kissed the letter, then opening it, clasped it to his heart as though it were Callirhoe in person, and held it there for a long time, unable to read it for his tears. After his weeping had finally abated, he began to read it, and the first thing he did was to kiss the name "Callirhoe." When he came to "Dionysius her benefactor," he groaned. "Alas, it is no longer 'her husband.'"

---

τοῦ βασιλέως ἀναγραφῆναι T | ὁ om. T | ἔσπευδεν T, Hercher: ἔχειν ἔσπευδεν F | ἡσυχῇ τὴν ἐπιστολὴν T | ἐπιδίδωσιν T.

5.13 εἶτα] καὶ T | προσεπτύξατο T: προσετίθει F | καὶ ἐπὶ . . . ἀνδρί] ἐπὶ πολὺν δὲ χρόνον κατέχων κατέχων αὐτὰ [here a loss by homoeoteleuton has occurred] ἀναγεινώσκι Καλλιρόη κατεφίλησε τοὔνομα Διονυσίῳ εὐεργέτῃ οἴμμοι τῷ ἀνδρὶ οὐκ ἔχω χαίρειν πῶς δύναμε σοῦ διεζευγμένος T.

14 ‘ἀνδρί·’ σὺ γὰρ εὐεργέτης ἐμός· τί γὰρ ἄξιον ἐποί-
ησά σοι;” ἥσθη δὲ τῆς ἐπιστολῆς τῇ ἀπολογίᾳ καὶ
πολλάκις ἀνεγίνωσκε τὰ αὐτά· ὑπεδήλου γὰρ ὡς
ἄκουσα αὐτὸν καταλίποι. οὕτω κοῦφόν ἐστιν ὁ
15 Ἔρως καὶ ἀναπείθει ῥᾳδίως ἀντερᾶσθαι. θεασάμενος δὲ τὸ παιδίον καὶ ‘πήλας ταῖς χερσὶν’ “ἀπ-
ελεύσῃ ποτέ μοι καὶ σύ, τέκνον, πρὸς τὴν μητέρα·
καὶ γὰρ αὐτὴ τοῦτο κεκέλευκεν· ἐγὼ δὲ ἔρημος βιώ-
σομαι, πάντων αἴτιος ἐμαυτῷ γενόμενος. ἀπώλεσέ
με κενὴ ζηλοτυπία καὶ σύ, Βαβυλών.” ταῦτα εἰπὼν
συνεσκευάζετο τὴν ταχίστην καταβαίνειν εἰς
Ἰωνίαν, μέγα νομίζων παραμύθιον πολλὴν ὁδὸν καὶ
πολλῶν πόλεων ἡγεμονίαν καὶ τὰς ἐν Μιλήτῳ
Καλλιρόης εἰκόνας.

6. Τὰ μὲν οὖν περὶ τὴν Ἀσίαν ἐν τούτοις ἦν, ὁ δὲ
Χαιρέας ἤνυσε τὸν πλοῦν εἰς Σικελίαν εὐτυχῶς
(εἱστήκει γὰρ ἀεὶ κατὰ πρύμναν <τὸ πνεῦμα> καὶ
ναῦς ἔχων μεγάλας ἐπελαγίζετο), περιδεῶς ἔχων μὴ
πάλιν αὐτὸν σκληροῦ δαίμονος προσβολὴ κατα-
2 λάβῃ. ἐπεὶ δὲ ἐφάνησαν Συρακοῦσαι, τοῖς τριηράρχαις ἐκέλευσε κοσμῆσαι τὰς τριήρεις καὶ ἅμα
συντεταγμέναις πλεῖν· καὶ γὰρ ἦν γαλήνη.

5.14 εὐ. ἐμ. ] ἐμ. εὐ. T | σοι] σοῦ T | ἥσθη] ἄσ[θ]ετο T | τῇ
ἀπ.] πρὸς τὴν ἀπολογίαν T | τὰ αὐτὰ] [ταῦ]τα τὰ ῥήματα T,
Blake | ὑπ. γὰρ ὡς] ἐ[πίσ]θη γὰρ ὅτι T | αὐτὸν om. T | [κα]τέ-
λιπεν T | οὕτω [ . . . . . . κο]ῦφόν T.

In fact you are the one who is my benefactor. What have I done for you, to deserve that name?" Nevertheless he was pleased with what she wrote in her defense and read the passage again and again, for they suggested that she had left him unwillingly. Love is such a feckless thing, and can easily convince a lover that his love is returned. Looking at his little son, he rocked him in his arms[a] and said, "One day, my child, you too shall leave me and go to your mother; she herself has asked you to. And I shall live all alone, with no one to blame but myself. Baseless jealousy has ruined me, and so have you, Babylon!" With these words he prepared to return to Ionia as quickly as he could, for he found much comfort in thinking of the long journey, his authority over many cities, and the statues of Callirhoe in Miletus.

6. Such, then, was the situation in Asia. Meanwhile, Chaereas safely accomplished the voyage to Sicily (for the wind stood behind him all the way and with large ships he was able to cross the open sea), in spite of his fear that an attack by some malign deity might again strike him down. When Syracuse came in sight, he ordered the captains to decorate the warships and to sail in close formation, for the sea was calm.

---

[a] Quoting an apt phrase from Homer, *Iliad* 6.474 (Hector rocking Astyanax).

---

5.15 θεασάμενος ... χερσὶν] θεασάμενον δὲ τὸ παιδίον τὸν πατέρα [κ]λάοντα προσῆλθεν αὐτῷ καὶ πού μοι πάτερ εἶπεν ἡ μήτηρ ἀπίωμεν πρὸς αὐτήν T | ἀπελεύσῃ ... μητέρα] σὺ μὲν ἀπέλευσαι τέκνον εὐτυχῶς T | συνεσκ- F: παρεσκ- T | καταβαίνειν ... μέγα] μενθαγαν T | πολλῶν : om. F | εἰκόνας T, D'Orville: οἰκήσεις F.

6.1 ἤνυσε τὸν] T breaks off | add. D'Orville.

Ὡς δὲ εἶδον αὐτοὺς οἱ ἐκ τῆς πόλεως, εἶπέ τις
"πόθεν τριήρεις προσπλέουσι; μή τι Ἀττικαί; φέρε
3 οὖν μηνύσωμεν Ἑρμοκράτει." καὶ ταχέως ἐμήνυσε
"στρατηγέ, βουλεύου τί ποιήσεις· τοὺς λιμένας ἀπο-
κλείσωμεν ἢ ἐπαναχθῶμεν; οὐ γὰρ ἴσμεν εἰ μείζων
ἕπεται στόλος, πρόδρομοι δέ εἰσιν αἱ βλεπόμεναι."
καταδραμὼν οὖν ὁ Ἑρμοκράτης ἐκ τῆς ἀγορᾶς ἐπὶ
τὴν θάλασσαν κωπῆρες ἐξέπεμψε πλοῖον ἀπαντᾶν
4 αὐτοῖς. ὁ δὲ ἀποσταλεὶς ἐπυνθάνετο πλησίον ἐλθὼν
τίνες εἴησαν, Χαιρέας δὲ ἐκέλευσεν ἀποκρίνασθαί
τινα τῶν Αἰγυπτίων "ἡμεῖς ἐξ Αἰγύπτου πλέομεν
ἔμποροι, φορτία φέροντες, ἃ Συρακοσίους εὐφρα-
νεῖ." "μὴ ἀθρόοι τοίνυν εἰσπλεῖτε" φησίν, "ἕως ἂν
γνῶμεν εἰ ἀληθεύετε· φορτίδας γὰρ οὐ βλέπω ναῦς
ἀλλὰ μακρὰς καὶ ὡς ἐκ πολέμου τριήρεις, ὥστε αἱ
μὲν πλείους ἔξω τοῦ λιμένος μετέωροι μεινάτωσαν,
μία δὲ καταπλευσάτω." "ποιήσομεν οὕτως."
5 Εἰσέπλευσεν οὖν τριήρης ἡ Χαιρέου πρώτη. εἶχε
δὲ ἐπάνω σκηνὴν συγκεκαλυμμένην Βαβυλωνίοις
παραπετάσμασιν. ἐπεὶ δὲ καθωρμίσθη, πᾶς ὁ λιμὴν
ἀνθρώπων ἐνεπλήσθη· φύσει μὲν γὰρ ὄχλος ἐστὶ
περίεργόν τι χρῆμα, τότε δὲ καὶ πλείονας εἶχον
6 αἰτίας τῆς συνδρομῆς. βλέποντες δὲ εἰς τὴν σκηνὴν
ἔνδον ἐνόμιζον οὐκ ἀνθρώπους ἀλλὰ φόρτον εἶναι
πολυτελῆ, καὶ ἄλλος ἄλλο τι ἐμαντεύετο, πάντα δὲ
μᾶλλον ἢ τὸ ἀληθὲς εἴκαζον· καὶ γὰρ ἦν ἄπιστον ὡς
ἀληθῶς, ἤδη πεπεισμένων αὐτῶν ὅτι Χαιρέας
τέθνηκε, ζῶντα δόξαι καταπλεῖν καὶ μετὰ τοσαύτης

When people from the city saw them, they said, "Whose warships are these approaching? Surely not from Athens? We had better inform Hermocrates." This was done at once. "General," they said, "consider what you wish done. Are we to close the harbors or put to sea against the intruders? We do not know if a larger force is following behind and if what we see is only the advance guard." Hermocrates then hurried down from the marketplace to the shore and sent a rowboat to meet them. The man sent drew near and asked who they were. Chaereas got one of the Egyptians to answer, "We are traders from Egypt with a cargo which will delight the Syracusans." "Well, do not all enter together," he said, "until we confirm that you are speaking the truth. Those are no cargo boats which I see, but naval vessels, apparently warships which have seen action, so most of you must stay at sea outside the harbor; only one may sail in." "Very well," they replied.

So it was the warship of Chaereas which sailed in first. On the upper deck it had a tent covered with Babylonian tapestries. When it dropped anchor, the whole harbor was full of people. Now crowds are naturally curious, and on this occasion they had many reasons for gathering. On seeing the tent, they thought it contained not people but some valuable cargo, and they made various guesses, suggesting everything except the truth. Indeed, now that they were convinced that Chaereas was dead, it passed belief that he could be sailing home alive and amid such

7 πολυτελείας. οἱ μὲν οὖν Χαιρέου γονεῖς οὐδὲ προ-
ήεσαν ἐκ τῆς οἰκίας, Ἑρμοκράτης δὲ ἐπολιτεύετο
μέν, ἀλλὰ πενθῶν, καὶ τότε εἱστήκει μέν, λανθάνων
δέ.

Πάντων δὲ ἀπορούντων καὶ τοὺς ὀφθαλμοὺς ἐκ-
τετακότων αἰφνίδιον εἱλκύσθη τὰ παραπετάσματα,
καὶ ὤφθη Καλλιρόη μὲν ἐπὶ χρυσηλάτου κλίνης ἀνα-
κειμένη, Τυρίαν ἀμπεχομένη πορφύραν, Χαιρέας δὲ
8 αὐτῇ παρακαθήμενος, σχῆμα ἔχων στρατηγοῦ.
οὔτε βροντή ποτε οὕτως ἐξέπληξε τὰς ἀκοὰς οὔτε
ἀστραπὴ τὰς ὄψεις τῶν ἰδόντων, οὔτε θησαυρὸν
εὑρών τις χρυσίου τοσοῦτον ἐξεβόησεν, ὡς τότε τὸ
πλῆθος, ἀπροσδοκήτως ἰδὸν θέαμα λόγου κρεῖττον.
Ἑρμοκράτης δὲ ἀνεπήδησεν ἐπὶ τὴν σκηνὴν καὶ
περιπτυξάμενος τὴν θυγατέρα εἶπε "ζῇς, τέκνον, ἢ
καὶ τοῦτο πεπλάνημαι;" "ζῶ, πάτερ, νῦν ἀληθῶς, ὅτι
σε τεθέαμαι." δάκρυα πᾶσιν ἐχεῖτο μετὰ χαρᾶς.

9 Μεταξὺ δὲ Πολύχαρμος ἐπικαταπλεῖ ταῖς ἄλλαις
τριήρεσιν· αὐτὸς γὰρ ἦν πεπιστευμένος τὸν ἄλλον
στόλον ἀπὸ Κύπρου διὰ τὸ μηκέτι Χαιρέαν ἄλλῳ
τινὶ σχολάζειν δύνασθαι πλὴν Καλλιρόῃ μόνῃ.
10 ταχέως οὖν ὁ λιμὴν ἐπληροῦτο, καὶ ἦν ἐκεῖνο τὸ
σχῆμα τὸ μετὰ τὴν ναυμαχίαν τὴν Ἀττικήν· καὶ
αὗται γὰρ αἱ τριήρεις ἐκ πολέμου κατέπλεον ἐστε-
φανωμέναι, χρησάμεναι Συρακοσίῳ στρατηγῷ.

6.7 μὲν οὖν Blake: τε τοῦ F.

magnificence. Chaereas' parents did not even leave their house, but Hermocrates still held office, though he was in mourning, and was present now, but in the background.

All were puzzled and straining their eyes when suddenly the tapestries were drawn aside, and Callirhoe was to be seen, clothed in Tyrian purple and reclining on a couch of beaten gold, with Chaereas sitting beside her in the uniform of a general. Never did thunder and lightning so startle the ears and eyes of witnesses! Never did anyone who had discovered a treasure of gold shout so loudly as the crowd did then at this unexpected sight too marvelous for words. Hermocrates leaped on board and rushed to the tent; embracing his daughter he cried, "My child, are you really alive or am I deceived in this, too?" "Yes, father, I am, and really so now that I have seen you." Everybody wept for joy.

Meanwhile Polycharmus sailed in with the other ships. He personally had been entrusted with the rest of the fleet when it left Cyprus, because Chaereas could no longer spare time for anything else but Callirhoe alone. Quickly, then, the harbor was filled and took on the appearance which it had after the victory over the Athenians; indeed, these vessels, too, were sailing home from battle, wreathed in victory and under the command of a

---

6.8 Ἑρμ.] T recommences with a baffling sequence, φιλαργ and 17 letterspaces | δὲ] om. T | εἶπε ζῆς F: ζῆς εἶπε T | ἢ om. T | νῦν] εἶπεν T | after σε] ζῶντα add. T | ἐχεῖτο μ. χ.] μ. χ. ἐξεχεῖτο T.     6.9 ἄλλον om. T | μηκέτι] μὴ T | σχ. δυν.] δυν. σχ. T | Καλ. μον.] μόνῳ τῷ Καλλιρόης κάλλει T.     6.10 οὖν T: δὲ F.

συνεμίχθησαν δὲ αἱ φωναί, τῶν μὲν ἀπὸ τῆς θαλάσσης τοὺς ἐπὶ γῆς ἀσπαζομένων, τῶν δὲ ἀπὸ τῆς γῆς
τοὺς ἐν ταῖς τριήρεσιν, εὐφημίαι τε καὶ ἔπαινοι καὶ
συνευχαὶ πυκναὶ παρ' ἀμφοτέρων πρὸς ἀλλήλους.
ἧκε δὲ καὶ ὁ Χαιρέου πατήρ, λιποψυχῶν ἐκ τῆς
11 παραδόξου χαρᾶς. ἐπεκυλίοντο δὲ ἀλλήλοις συνέφ-
ηβοι καὶ συγγυμνασταί, Χαιρέαν ἀσπάσασθαι
θέλοντες, Καλλιρόην δὲ αἱ γυναῖκες. ἔδοξε δὲ ἔτι
καὶ αὐταῖς Καλλιρόην <καλλίω> γεγονέναι, ὥστε
ἀληθῶς εἶπες ἂν αὐτὴν ὁρᾶν τὴν Ἀφροδίτην ἀνα-
δυομένην ἐκ τῆς θαλάσσης.

Προσελθὼν δὲ Χαιρέας τῷ Ἑρμοκράτει καὶ τῷ
πατρὶ "παραλάβετε" ἔφη "τὸν πλοῦτον τοῦ μεγάλου
12 βασιλέως." καὶ εὐθὺς ἐκέλευσεν ἐκκομίζεσθαι ἄργυ-
ρόν τε καὶ χρυσὸν ἀναρίθμητον, εἶτα ἐλέφαντα καὶ
ἤλεκτρον καὶ ἐσθῆτα καὶ πᾶσαν ὕλης τέχνης τε
πολυτέλειαν ἐπέδειξε Συρακοσίοις καὶ κλίνην καὶ
τράπεζαν τοῦ μεγάλου βασιλέως, ὥστε ἐνεπλήσθη
πᾶσα ἡ πόλις, οὐχ ὡς πρότερον ἐκ τοῦ πολέμου τοῦ
Σικελικοῦ πενίας Ἀττικῆς, ἀλλά, τὸ καινότατον, ἐν
εἰρήνῃ λαφύρων Μηδικῶν.

6.10 μὲν T: om. F | ἐπὶ Reiske: ἀπὸ F: T not extant | τῶν δὲ
. . . τριήρεσιν] so T: καὶ πάλιν ἐκείνων τοὺς ἐκ θαλάσσης F |
συνευχαὶ] εὐχαὶ T | πυκναὶ παρ' ἀμφοτέρων om. T | after ἧκε
δὲ] μεταξὺ φερόμενος add. T | λιπο- T, Cobet: λειπο- F.
6.11 ἐπεκυλίοντο T, D'Orville: ἐπεκλύοντο F | add. Reiske
(ἔδοξεν δὲ ὡς ἀλη[θῶς ἔτι] καλλείων [παρ' ἐκείν]ην τὴν ἀνα-
δυομένην T) | ἔφη] φησι T.

Syracusan leader. The voices of those from the sea hailing the people on shore were blended with these welcoming the arrivals from the sea; both exchanged endless blessings, cheers, and prayers with each other. Chaereas' father also came, fainting from unexpected joy. Clubmates and fellow athletes jostled with each other in their eagerness to welcome Chaereas, as the women to welcome Callirhoe. To them it seemed that Callirhoe had become even lovelier; you would really have said that you were looking at Aphrodite herself rising from the sea.[a]

Chaereas went up to Hermocrates and his father and said, "Accept from me the wealth of the Great King." At once he ordered the unloading of a vast quantity of silver and gold; next he showed the Syracusans ivory and amber and clothing and all kinds of valuable material and artwork, including a couch and table of the Great King, so that the whole city was filled, not as previously after the Sicilian war with the poverty of Attica, but, paradoxically, with the spoils of Media in time of peace.

[a] The usual etymology of the goddess's name is 'born of seafoam,' and the most famous painting in the ancient world was Apelles' *Aphrodite Rising from the Sea*.

---

6.12 ἄργυρόν T, Hercher: ἀργύριον F | τε καὶ T: καὶ F | εἶτα] καὶ T | ὕλης τέχνης τε] πλούτου T | after βασ.] καὶ εὐνούχους καὶ παλλακίδας add. T.

7. Ἀθρόον δὲ τὸ πλῆθος ἀνεβόησεν "ἀπίωμεν εἰς τὴν ἐκκλησίαν·" ἐπεθύμουν γὰρ αὐτοὺς καὶ βλέπειν καὶ ἀκούειν· λόγου δὲ θᾶττον ἐπληρώθη τὸ θέατρον ἀνδρῶν τε καὶ γυναικῶν. εἰσελθόντος δὲ μόνου Χαιρέου πᾶσαι καὶ πάντες ἐπεβόησαν "Καλλιρόην

2 παρακάλει." Ἑρμοκράτης δὲ καὶ τοῦτο ἐδημαγώγησεν, εἰσαγαγὼν τὴν θυγατέρα. πρῶτον οὖν ὁ δῆμος εἰς τὸν οὐρανὸν ἀναβλέψας εὐφήμει τοὺς θεοὺς καὶ χάριν ἠπίστατο μᾶλλον ὑπὲρ τῆς ἡμέρας ταύτης ἢ τῆς τῶν ἐπινικίων· εἶτα ποτὲ μὲν ἐσχίζοντο, καὶ οἱ μὲν ἄνδρες ἐπήνουν Χαιρέαν, αἱ δὲ γυναῖκες Καλλιρόην, ποτὲ δ' αὖ πάλιν ἀμφοτέρους κοινῇ· καὶ τοῦτο ἐκείνοις ἥδιον ἦν.

3 Καλλιρόην μὲν οὖν, ὡς ἂν ἐκ πλοῦ καὶ ἀγωνίας <κεκμηκυῖαν>, εὐθὺς ἀσπασαμένην τὴν πατρίδα ἀπήγαγον ἐκ τοῦ θεάτρου, Χαιρέαν δὲ κατεῖχε τὸ πλῆθος, ἀκοῦσαι βουλόμενον πάντα τὰ τῆς ἀποδημίας διηγήματα. κἀκεῖνος ἀπὸ τῶν τελευταίων ἤρξατο, λυπεῖν οὐ θέλων ἐν τοῖς πρώτοις καὶ σκυθρωποῖς τὸν λαόν. ὁ δὲ δῆμος ἐνεκελεύετο "ἐρωτῶμεν, ἄνωθεν ἄρξαι, πάντα ἡμῖν λέγε, μηδὲν παρα-

4 λίπῃς." ὤκνει Χαιρέας, ὡς ἂν ἐπὶ πολλοῖς τῶν οὐ κατὰ γνώμην συμβάντων αἰδούμενος, Ἑρμοκράτης δὲ ἔφη "μηδὲν αἰδεσθῇς, ὦ τέκνον, κἂν λέγῃς τι

7.1 ἀπίωμεν Beck (cf. 3.4.3): ἀξιοῦμεν F | βλέπειν καὶ ἀκούειν T: ἰδεῖν καὶ ἀκοῦσαι F | λόγου δὲ θᾶττον] ἐπὶ δὲ T | δὲ (before μόνου) om. T | καὶ πάντες καὶ πᾶσαι T.

7. With a single voice the crowd shouted, "Let us go to the assembly!" for they were eager to look at them and hear them speak. Sooner than it takes to tell the theater was filled with men and women. But when Chaereas entered by himself, all clamored, women as well as men, "Bring along Callirhoe!" In this too Hermocrates gave in to the people, and brought in his daughter as well. First of all the people lifted their eyes to heaven, and blessed the gods, more thankful for that day than for the one of their victory. Then first they divided, with the men cheering Chaereas and the women Callirhoe, next united again to cheer them both together; and that pleased the couple more.

Since Callirhoe was worn out by her voyage and sufferings, as soon as she had expressed greetings to her native city she was taken home from the theater. But the crowd detained Chaereas, wanting to hear all he had to tell of his adventures abroad. He began with the end, reluctant to distress his audience with the grim events at the beginning. But the people insisted, "Start from the beginning, we beg you. Tell us everything; leave nothing out." Chaereas hesitated, naturally somewhat embarrassed at much which had not turned out as he wished, but Hermocrates said, "My son, do not be embarrassed,

---

7.2 εἰσαγαγὼν T: εἴσαγων καὶ F | ἀναβλέψας Hercher: ἀπο- FT | ἢ τῆς F: ἢ T | ἐσχίζετο T | ποτὲ T, Reiske: ὅτε F | ἥδιστον T.

7.3 Καλλιρόην T: -όη F | ἀν om. T | πλοῦ] T ends | add. Hercher.

λυπηρότερον ἢ πικρότερον ἡμῖν· τὸ γὰρ τέλος λαμπρὸν γενόμενον ἐπισκοτεῖ τοῖς προτέροις ἅπασι, τὸ
δὲ μὴ ῥηθὲν ὑπόνοιαν ἔχει χαλεπωτέραν ἐξ αὐτῆς
5 τῆς σιωπῆς. πατρίδι λέγεις καὶ γονεῦσιν, ὧν ἰσόρροπος ἡ πρὸς ἀμφοτέρους ὑμᾶς φιλοστοργία. τὰ
μὲν οὖν πρῶτα τῶν διηγημάτων ἤδη καὶ ὁ δῆμος
6 ἐπίσταται, καὶ γὰρ τὸν γάμον ὑμᾶς αὐτὸς ἔζευξε.
<πῶς δὲ ἐμπεσὼν διὰ> τὴν τῶν ἀντιμνηστευομένων
ἐπιβουλὴν εἰς ψευδῆ ζηλοτυπίαν ἀκαίρως ἔπληξας
τὴν γυναῖκα πάντες ἔγνωμεν καὶ ὅτι δόξασα τεθνάναι πολυτελῶς ἐκηδεύθη, σὺ δὲ εἰς φόνου δίκην ὑπ-
αχθεὶς σεαυτοῦ κατεψηφίσω, συναποθανεῖν θέλων
7 τῇ γυναικί. ἀλλ᾽ ὁ δῆμός σε ἀπέλυσεν, ἀκούσιον
ἐπιγνοὺς τὸ συμβάν. τά τε τούτων ἐφεξῆς [ἡμῖν
ἀπάγγειλον]· ὅτι Θήρων ὁ τυμβωρύχος νυκτὸς τὸν
τάφον διασκάψας Καλλιρόην ζῶσαν εὑρὼν μετὰ τῶν
ἐνταφίων ἐνέθηκε τῷ πειρατικῷ κέλητι καὶ εἰς
Ἰωνίαν ἐπώλησε, σὺ δὲ κατὰ τὴν ζήτησιν τῆς
γυναικὸς ἐξελθὼν αὐτὴν μὲν οὐχ εὗρες, ἐν δὲ τῇ
8 θαλάσσῃ τῷ πειρατικῷ πλοίῳ περιπεσών, τοὺς μὲν
ἄλλους λῃστὰς τεθνεῶτας κατέλαβες ὑπὸ δίψους,
Θήρωνα δὲ μόνον ἔτι ζῶντα εἰσήγαγες εἰς τὴν ἐκκλησίαν, κἀκεῖνος μὲν βασανισθεὶς ἀνεσκολοπίσθη,
τριήρη δὲ ἐξέπεμψεν ἡ πόλις καὶ πρεσβευτὰς ὑπὲρ
Καλλιρόης, ἑκούσιος δὲ συνεξέπλευσέ σοι Πολύχαρμος ὁ φίλος—ταῦτα ἴσμεν· σὺ δὲ ἡμῖν διήγησαι
τὰ μετὰ τὸν ἔκπλουν συνενεχθέντα τὸν σὸν ἐντεῦθεν."

even if you have something painful or shocking to tell us. The brilliant conclusion overshadows all that has gone before, but saying nothing means that we will suspect even worse from your silence. You are speaking to your native city and your parents, whose affection towards you both is equal. The people already know the first part of your story. In fact they themselves brought about your wedding. How through the plot of rival suitors you conceived an unfounded jealousy and impetuously struck your wife, that we all know; as also that after her seeming death she was given a splendid funeral, and that, when brought to trial for murder, you condemned yourself since you wanted to die with your wife. Nevertheless, the people acquitted you, realizing that what had happened was not deliberate. And likewise what followed: how the grave robber Theron dug his way into the tomb at night, and found Callirhoe alive among the funeral offerings, put her on his pirate cutter, and sold her in Ionia; how you set out in search of your wife and failed to find her but, falling in with the pirate ship at sea, found the other brigands dead of thirst and Theron alone still alive; how you brought him before our assembly and he, confessing under torture, was crucified; how the city dispatched a warship with envoys to search for Callirhoe, and your friend Polycharmus voluntarily joined the expedition: these things we know. Tell us what happened after you sailed off from here."

---

7.4 μικρότερον F, corr. Reiske | ἡμῖν Salvini: ἡμῶν F.
7.6 add. Jackson.
7.7 τε Cobet: δὲ F | del. Hirschig.

9 Ὁ δὲ Χαιρέας ἔνθεν ἑλὼν διηγεῖτο "πλεύσαντες τὸν Ἰόνιον ἀσφαλῶς εἰς χωρίον κατήχθημεν ἀνδρὸς Μιλησίου, Διονυσίου τοὔνομα, πλούτῳ καὶ γένει καὶ δόξῃ πάντων Ἰώνων ὑπερέχοντος. οὗτος δὲ ὁ παρὰ

10 Θήρωνος Καλλιρόην ταλάντου πριάμενος. μὴ φοβηθῆτε· οὐκ ἐδούλευσεν· εὐθὺς γὰρ τὴν ἀργυρώνητον αὐτοῦ δέσποιναν ἀπέδειξε, καὶ ἐρῶν αὐτῆς βιάσασθαι οὐκ ἐτόλμησε τὴν εὐγενῆ, πέμψαι δὲ

11 πάλιν εἰς Συρακούσας οὐχ ὑπέμεινεν ἧς ἤρα. ἐπεὶ δὲ ᾔσθετο Καλλιρόη κύουσαν ἑαυτὴν ἐξ ἐμοῦ, σῶσαι τὸν πολίτην ὑμῖν θέλουσα, ἀνάγκην ἔσχε Διονυσίῳ γαμηθῆναι, σοφιζομένη τοῦ τέκνου τὴν γονήν, ἵνα ἐκ Διονυσίου δόξῃ γεγεννηκέναι, καὶ

12 τραφῇ τὸ παιδίον ἐπαξίως. τρέφεται ἄρ' ὑμῖν, ἄνδρες Συρακόσιοι, πολίτης ἐν Μιλήτῳ πλούσιος ὑπ' ἀνδρὸς ἐνδόξου· καὶ γὰρ ἐκείνου τὸ γένος ἔνδοξον Ἑλληνικόν. μὴ φθονήσωμεν αὐτῷ μεγάλης κληρονομίας.

8. "Ταῦτα μὲν οὖν ἔμαθον ὕστερον· τότε δὲ καταχθεὶς ἐν τῷ χωρίῳ, μόνην εἰκόνα Καλλιρόης θεασάμενος ἐν ἱερῷ ἐγὼ μὲν εἶχον ἀγαθὰς ἐλπίδας, νύκτωρ δὲ Φρύγες λῃσταὶ καταδραμόντες ἐπὶ θάλασσαν ἐνέπρησαν μὲν τὴν τριήρη, τοὺς δὲ πλείστους κατέσφαξαν, ἐμὲ δὲ καὶ Πολύχαρμον

2 δήσαντες ἐπώλησαν εἰς Καρίαν." θρῆνον ἐξέρρηξεν ἐπὶ τούτοις τὸ πλῆθος, εἶπε δὲ Χαιρέας "ἐπιτρέψατέ

7.12 ἄρ' Naber: γὰρ F.

Taking up from this point,[a] Chaereas proceeded with his story. "We sailed safely across the Ionian Sea and put in at the estate of a Milesian named Dionysius, who is the foremost of all Ionians in wealth, lineage, and reputation. He was the man who had bought Callirhoe from Theron for a talent. Do not be alarmed! She did not become a slave; in fact, immediately he bought her he made her the mistress of his heart and, although in love with her, was not so bold as to force his will upon a wellborn girl; on the other hand, he could not bear to send the woman he loved back to Syracuse. When Callirhoe discovered that she was pregnant by me, wishing to preserve your future citizen, she felt compelled to marry Dionysius, and disguised the parentage of the child so that this might seem to be the son of Dionysius and thus be brought up in a worthy manner. Take note, men of Syracuse, in Miletus a fellow citizen of yours is being brought up to a wealthy station by a distinguished man, for Dionysius' family is a distinguished Greek one. Let us not begrudge him his great inheritance.

8. "Naturally I only discovered this later. At that time, when I had landed on the estate, just seeing Callirhoe's statue in a shrine gave me high hopes. But in the night some Phrygian[b] brigands raided the coast and set fire to the warship: they killed most of us, but bound me and Polycharmus and sold us as slaves in Caria." At this a groan burst forth from the crowd, and Chaereas said, "Let

[a] See note on 1.7.6.

[b] Phrygia was a region in the interior of Asia Minor. But there is a slight inconsistency here: at the first mention (3.7.2) the marauders were specified as an oriental garrison (i.e. Persian troops), here they are represented as free-lance brigands.

407

μοι τὰ ἑξῆς σιωπᾶν, σκυθρωπότερα γάρ ἐστι τῶν
πρώτων·" ὁ δὲ δῆμος ἐξεβόησε "λέγε πάντα." καὶ ὃς
ἔλεγεν "ὁ πριάμενος ἡμᾶς, δοῦλος Μιθριδάτου,
στρατηγοῦ Καρίας, ἐκέλευσε σκάπτειν ὄντας πεπε-
δημένους. ἐπεὶ δὲ τὸν δεσμοφύλακα τῶν δεσμωτῶν
ἀπέκτεινάν τινες, ἀνασταυρωθῆναι πάντας ἡμᾶς Μι-
3 θριδάτης ἐκέλευσε. κἀγὼ μὲν ἀπηγόμην· μέλλων δὲ
βασανίζεσθαι Πολύχαρμος εἶπέ μου τοὔνομα καὶ
Μιθριδάτης ἐγνώρισε· Διονυσίου γὰρ ξένος γενόμενος ἐν Μιλήτῳ Χαιρέου θαπτομένου παρῆν· πυθομένη γὰρ Καλλιρόη τὰ περὶ τὴν τριήρη καὶ τοὺς
λῃστάς, κἀμὲ δόξασα τεθνάναι, τάφον ἔχωσέ μοι
4 πολυτελῆ. ταχέως οὖν ὁ Μιθριδάτης ἐκέλευσε
καθαιρεθῆναί με τοῦ σταυροῦ σχεδὸν ἤδη πέρας
ἔχοντα, καὶ ἔσχεν ἐν τοῖς φιλτάτοις· ἀποδοῦναι δέ
μοι Καλλιρόην ἔσπευδε καὶ ἐποίησέ με γράψαι πρὸς
αὐτήν.
5 "'Αμελείᾳ δὲ τοῦ διακονουμένου τὴν ἐπιστολὴν
ἔλαβεν αὐτὸς Διονύσιος. ἐμὲ δὲ ζῆν οὐκ ἐπίστευεν,
ἐπίστευσε δὲ Μιθριδάτην ἐπιβουλεύειν αὐτοῦ τῇ
γυναικί, καὶ εὐθὺς αὐτῷ μοιχείαν ἐγκαλῶν ἐπέστειλε
βασιλεῖ· βασιλεὺς δὲ ἀνεδέξατο τὴν δίκην καὶ
πάντας ἐκάλεσε πρὸς αὐτόν. οὕτως ἀνέβημεν εἰς
6 Βαβυλῶνα. καὶ Καλλιρόην μὲν Διονύσιος ἄγων
περίβλεπτον ἐποίησε <καὶ> κατὰ τὴν Ἀσίαν ὅλην
θαυμαζομένην, ἐμὲ δὲ Μιθριδάτης ἐπηγάγετο· γενόμενοι δὲ ἐκεῖ μεγάλην ἐπὶ βασιλέως δίκην εἴπομεν.
Μιθριδάτην μὲν οὖν εὐθὺς ἀπέλυσεν, ἐμοὶ δὲ καὶ

408

me pass over in silence what came next; it is grimmer than what happened at the start." But the crowd shouted, "Tell us everything!" So he continued, "The man who bought us, a servant of Mithridates, governor of Caria, gave orders for us to be chained and put to digging. After some prisoners murdered the guard, Mithridates ordered us all to be crucified. I too was taken away. As he was about to be tortured, Polycharmus spoke my name,[a] which Mithridates recognized: he, as a guest of Dionysius, had been present at the funeral of Chaereas in Miletus—for Callirhoe, hearing of the warship and the brigands, thought I had been killed and built an expensive tomb for me. So Mithridates quickly had me taken down from the cross—I was pretty well done for by then—and treated me as one of his closest friends. He was eager to restore Callirhoe to me and got me to write her a letter.

"Through the negligence of the carrier Dionysius himself got the letter. He could not believe that I was alive, but believed instead that Mithridates had designs on his wife and immediately sent the king a complaint, accusing him of adultery. The king accepted the case and summoned us all to trial. So we went up to Babylon. By bringing Callirhoe with him Dionysius made her famous and the idol of all Asia; I was taken along by Mithridates. When we got there, we argued the case in a great trial before the king. Well, he acquitted Mithridates immediately and promised an arbitration between Dionysius and

[a] Another inconsistency: it was actually Callirhoe's name (cf. 4.2.12).

8.5 αὐτὸς Hercher: αὐτὴν F.     8.6 add. D'Orville.

Διονυσίῳ διαδικασίαν περὶ τῆς γυναικὸς ἐπήγγειλε,
Καλλιρόην παραθέμενος ἐν τῷ μεταξὺ Στατείρᾳ τῇ
7 βασιλίδι. ποσάκις, ἄνδρες Συρακόσιοι, δοκεῖτε
θάνατον ἐβουλευσάμην ἀπεζευγμένος τῆς γυναικός, εἰ
μή με Πολύχαρμος ἔσωσεν, ὁ μόνος ἐν πᾶσι φίλος πισ-
τός; καὶ γὰρ βασιλεὺς ἠμελήκει τῆς δίκης, ἔρωτι Καλ-
8 λιρόης φλεγόμενος. ἀλλ᾽ οὔτε ἔπεισεν οὔτε ὕβρισεν.
Εὐκαίρως δὲ Αἴγυπτος ἀποστᾶσα βαρὺν ἐκίνη-
σε πόλεμον, ἐμοὶ δὲ μεγάλων ἀγαθῶν αἴτιον. Καλλιρόην μὲν γὰρ ἡ βασιλὶς ἐπήγετο, ψευδῆ δὲ ἀκούσας ἀγγελίαν ἐγὼ φήσαντός τινος ὅτι Διονυσίῳ
παρεδόθη, θέλων ἀμύνασθαι βασιλέα, πρὸς τὸν
Αἰγύπτιον αὐτομολήσας ἔργα μεγάλα διεπραξάμην·
9 καὶ γὰρ Τύρον δυσάλωτον οὖσαν ἐχειρωσάμην
αὐτὸς καὶ ναύαρχος ἀποδειχθεὶς κατεναυμάχησα
τὸν μέγαν βασιλέα καὶ Ἀράδου κύριος ἐγενόμην,
ἔνθα καὶ τὴν βασιλίδα καὶ τὸν πλοῦτον ὃν ἑωράκατε
10 βασιλεὺς ἀπέθετο. ἐδυνάμην οὖν καὶ τὸν Αἰγύπτιον
ἀποδεῖξαι πάσης τῆς Ἀσίας δεσπότην, εἰ μὴ χωρὶς
ἐμοῦ μαχόμενος ἀνῃρέθη. τὸ δὲ λοιπὸν φίλον ὑμῖν
ἐποίησα τὸν μέγαν βασιλέα, τὴν γυναῖκα δωρησά-
μενος αὐτῷ καὶ Περσῶν τοῖς ἐντιμοτάτοις μητέρας
τε καὶ ἀδελφὰς καὶ γυναῖκας καὶ θυγατέρας πέμψας·
11 αὐτὸς δὲ Ἕλληνας τοὺς ἀρίστους Αἰγυπτίων τε τοὺς
θέλοντας ἤγαγον ἐνθάδε. ἐλεύσεται καὶ ἄλλος στόλος ἐξ Ἰωνίας ὑμέτερος· ἄξει δὲ αὐτὸν ὁ Ἑρμοκράτους ἔκγονος."
12 Εὐχαὶ παρὰ πάντων ἐπὶ τούτοις ἐπηκολούθησαν.

me over Callirhoe, whom in the meantime he placed in the care of Queen Statira. Men of Syracuse, how many times do you suppose I resolved to kill myself, parted from my wife—and would have, if Polycharmus, my only loyal friend among them, had not come to my rescue! In fact the king was not interested in the case at all, being ardently in love with Callirhoe. However, he neither seduced her nor used force upon her.

"At this timely moment Egypt revolted and started a fearful war, which however brought me great benefits. The queen took Callirhoe along with her, but I heard a false report from someone who said that she had been handed over to Dionysius; so, wanting to revenge myself on the king, I deserted to the pharaoh and performed some notable feats. I stormed the impregnable Tyre myself, and then, after being appointed admiral, I defeated the Great King on the sea and became master of Aradus, where the king had left the queen and the riches which you have seen. So I could even have made the pharaoh master of all Asia, if he had not joined battle without me and been killed. To conclude, I have gained you the Great King's friendship by returning his wife to him, and by sending back to the Persian nobles their mothers, sisters, wives, and daughters. I myself have brought here the pick of the Greek troops and all Egyptians who wanted to come. Another fleet of yours will also come from Ionia and its leader shall be the grandson of Hermocrates!"

Upon this congratulations burst forth from the lips of

CHARITON

καταπαύσας δὲ τὴν βοὴν Χαιρέας εἶπεν "ἐγὼ καὶ
Καλλιρόη χάριν ἔχομεν ἐφ' ὑμῶν Πολυχάρμῳ τῷ
φίλῳ· καὶ γὰρ εὔνοιαν ἐπεδείξατο καὶ πίστιν ἀληθεστάτην πρὸς ἡμᾶς· κἂν ὑμῖν δοκῇ, δῶμεν αὐτῷ
γυναῖκα τὴν ἀδελφὴν τὴν ἐμήν· προῖκα δὲ ἕξει μέ-
13    ρος τῶν λαφύρων." ἐπευφήμησεν ὁ δῆμος "ἀγαθῷ
ἀνδρὶ Πολυχάρμῳ, φίλῳ πιστῷ, ὁ δῆμός σοι χάριν
ἐπίσταται. τὴν πατρίδα εὐηργέτηκας, ἄξιος Ἑρμοκράτους καὶ Χαιρέου." μετὰ ταῦτα πάλιν Χαιρέας
εἶπε "καὶ τούσδε τοὺς τριακοσίους, Ἕλληνας
ἄνδρας, στρατὸν ἐμὸν ἀνδρεῖον, δέομαι ὑμῶν, πολίτας ποιήσατε." πάλιν ὁ δῆμος ἐπεβόησεν "ἄξιοι
μεθ' ἡμῶν πολιτεύεσθαι· χειροτονείσθω ταῦτα."
14    ψήφισμα ἐγράφη καὶ εὐθὺς ἐκεῖνοι καθίσαντες
μέρος ἦσαν τῆς ἐκκλησίας. καὶ Χαιρέας δὲ ἐδωρή-
σατο τάλαντον ἑκάστῳ, τοῖς δὲ Αἰγυπτίοις ἀπένειμε
χώραν Ἑρμοκράτης, ὥστε ἔχειν αὐτοὺς γεωργεῖν.
15    Ἕως δὲ ἦν τὸ πλῆθος ἐν τῷ θεάτρῳ, Καλλιρόη,
πρὶν εἰς τὴν οἰκίαν εἰσελθεῖν, εἰς τὸ τῆς Ἀφροδίτης
ἱερὸν ἀφίκετο. λαβομένη δὲ αὐτῆς τῶν ποδῶν καὶ
ἐπιθεῖσα τὸ πρόσωπον καὶ λύσασα τὰς κόμας,
καταφιλοῦσα "χάρις σοι" φησίν, "Ἀφροδίτη· πάλιν
γάρ μοι Χαιρέαν ἐν Συρακούσαις ἔδειξας, ὅπου καὶ
16    παρθένος εἶδον αὐτὸν σοῦ θελούσης. οὐ μέμφομαί
σοι, δέσποινα, περὶ ὧν πέπονθα· ταῦτα εἵμαρτό μοι.
δέομαί σου, μηκέτι με Χαιρέου διαζεύξῃς, ἀλλὰ καὶ
βίον μακάριον καὶ θάνατον κοινὸν κατάνευσον
ἡμῖν."

Τοσάδε περὶ Καλλιρόης συνέγραψα.

412

all. Chaereas checked the shouting and said, "Before you all I and Callirhoe offer our thanks to our friend, Polycharmus. He has shown us true devotion and loyalty, and if you consent, let us give him my sister[a] as his bride, and for a dowry he shall have a share of the spoils." The people acclaimed the proposal. "Noble Polycharmus! Faithful friend! The people are grateful to you. You have served your country well, and are worthy of Hermocrates and Chaereas." After this Chaereas continued: "As for these three hundred Greeks, my valiant company, I ask you to make them your fellow citizens." Again the people shouted assent, "They are worthy to be citizens with us: be it put to the vote!" A decree was passed, and the three hundred at once took their seats in the assembly. Chaereas also made each a present of a talent, and Hermocrates distributed land to the Egyptians for them to farm.

While the crowd was in the theater, Callirhoe, before going home, went to Aphrodite's temple. She grasped the goddess's feet, placed her face upon them, let down her hair,[b] and kissing them said, "I thank you, Aphrodite! You have shown me Chaereas once more in Syracuse, where as a girl I set eyes on him as you desired. I do not reproach you, Lady, for what I have suffered: that was my fate. I beg you, never again part me from Chaereas, but grant us a happy life, and death together."

So ends the story I have composed[c] about Callirhoe.

---

[a] We have heard nothing of a sister of Chaereas, but in New Comedy a double marriage was a most satisfactory ending (e.g. in Menander's *Dyscolus*).   [b] As women regularly did before praying to the gods.   [c] The precise word used by Thucydides in his opening sentence.

# INDEX

References consisting of single numerals are to pages; those of three numerals to book, chapter, and section of the Greek text. Lowercase letters refer to the English footnotes. Entries in capitals denote the characters of the novel. C = Callirhoe; Ch = Chaereas; D = Dionysius. A plus sign should be read as "and elsewhere."

abortion considered: 6,
  2.9.2–2.11.4
Abradates: 245a
Achilles: 295a
Achilles Tatius: 4, 15f
Acragas: 37a
ACRAGAS, RULER OF, disappointed
  suitor, schemes to play on Ch's
  jealousy: 1.2.4; foiled, adopts a
  more drastic plan: 1.4.1; his
  crony: 1.4.1; abuses Ch: 1.5.3
Actaeon: 147a
ADRASTUS, an experienced lawyer:
  2.1.6
Alcinous: 109a
Alexander the Great: 12
Alexander Paris: 361c
Alexander Romance: 10
Amphion: 123a
Anchises: 103a
ancient light fiction: 8f
Antonius Diogenes: 9
Apelles: 401a
Aphrodisias, Chariton's home
  town: 1.1.1; possibly the
  residence of Mithridates (then
  called Ninoë): 215a

APHRODITE, C's prayers to: 1.1.7,
  2.2.7f, 3.2.12f, 3.8.7ff, 7.5.2ff,
  8.4.10, 8.8.15f; C compared to:
  1.1.2, 2.2.6, 2.5.7, 3.2.14,
  3.2.17; C mistaken for: 1.14.1,
  2.3.6, 5.9.1; her festival in
  Syracuse: 1.1.4; her temple in
  Syracuse: 1.1.4, 5.5.5; rumored
  to appear to mortals: 1.14.1,
  2.2.5; her shrine near D's
  country house: 2.2.7, 3.6.3;
  plans another marriage for C:
  2.2.8; D calls to witness: 2.5.12,
  3.2.5; D prays to: 5.10.1, 6.2.4;
  her shrine on Aradus: 7.5.1;
  takes pity on Ch: 8.1.3; her
  temple at Paphos: 8.2.7; Ch
  sacrifices to: 8.2.8; born of
  foam: 401a
Apollodorus: 147a
Apuleius, Met. 7.5: 55a
Aradus: 345b; tiny compared with
  Sicily: 7.5.2; captured by Ch:
  7.6.2; abandoned by Ch: 8.2.6
Areopagus: 69a
Ariadne, beautiful in sleep: 53a;
  stolen from Theseus: 147a; her

fame excelled by C: 4.1.8; married by Dionysus: 8.1.2 and note

Aristides, *Milesiaca*: 9

ARISTON, Ch's father and rival of Hermocrates: 1.1.3; has accident: 1.3.1; at C's funeral: 1.6.3; at Ch's departure: 3.5.4; at his return: 8.6.10

Ariston of Corinth, model for Ariston: 31a

Aristophanes, *Frogs 792*: 4.4.1

Armenian route to Babylon: 5.2.1

Artaxares, the model for Artaxates: 11

ARTAXATES, most trusted of the King's eunuchs: 5.2.2+; comforts his master: 6.3.1ff; offers advice about C: 6.4.7; attempts to win C for the King: 6.5.1ff; his emotions on failing: 6.6.1f; attempts to cool the King's ardor: 6.6.6–8; his second approach to C: 6.7.5–13

ARTAXERXES Memnon II: 11; admirer of Hermocrates: 2.6.3; learns of C's beauty: 4.1.8, 5.2.6; Pharnaces' letter to him: 4.6.3; summons Mithridates, D, and C to trial: 4.6.8; announces festival and postponement of the trial: 5.3.11; acquits Mithridates: 5.8.8; postpones trial again: 5.8.9; the King in love with C: 6.1.6–12; again announces a sacred month: 6.2.3; recognizes the power of Love: 6.3.2; goes hunting: 6.4.1ff; learns of the revolt of Egypt: 6.8.1; calls council of war: 6.8.4; marches from Babylon: 6.9.1; takes C with

him: 6.9.7; leaves women on Aradus: 7.4.12f; grieves over the capture of Aradus: 8.5.2; reunited with Statira: 8.5.5; appoints D governor of Ionia: 8.5.12

Artemis: 3.8.6

Asia, riches of flow into Ionia: 1.11.7; is huge: 3.6.2; C's fame fills: 4.1.8, 4.7.7, 5.5.3, 8.8.6; Rhodogune's fame in: 5.3.4; King declares a sacred month for: 6.2.3; in a mighty ferment: 6.8.4; Tyre a wall of: 7.3.2; Statira the Queen of: 8.3.2

Asianic style: 265b

Astyages: 123b

Athena: 3.8.6

Athenagoras, lawyer, Chariton's employer: 1.1.1

Athenians, defeated: *see* Syracuse; talkative and litigious: 1.11.6; victors over Persia: 6.7.10, 7.5.8

Attic style: 265b

*Atticismus*: 1f

authorial comments: 363a

Babylon, eagerly awaits C: 5.3.6; a law court: 5.4.4, 6.1.5; support for Ch or D: 6.1.1ff; gloom descends upon: 6.8.3; close to Syria: 6.8.6; Ch hopes to take: 7.3.4

Bactra: 235b, 6.8.6; Mithridates' home: 5.4.1

*barbaroi*: 83a

*Barlaam and Ioasaph*: 9

bee, the queen: 97b

Benefactor (title): 353a

Bias, one of the Seven Wise Men: 217a

BIAS, chief magistrate of Priene,

# INDEX

intercepts Mithridates' slaves: 4.5.5f; his letter to D.: 4.5.8, 5.6.8

Brasidas: 8.2.12

*Callirhoe*, popularity of: 3ff; title: 3f; synopsis of: 5ff; a historical novel: 10ff; a love story: 12ff; text of: 18; recapitulations: 230a; perhaps published in two papyrus rolls: 230a

CALLIRHOE, the protagonist: 4, 14; daughter of Hermocrates: 1.1.1+; falls in love with Ch: 1.1.6f; all but dies: 1.1.14; her wedding: 1.1.16; unjustly accused: 1.3.5; apparently dies: 1.4.12; her funeral: 1.6.2ff; revives in tomb: 1.8.1ff; taken from tomb by Theron: 1.9.5ff; conveyed overseas: 1.11.1ff; represented by Theron as a slavegirl: 1.12.8; sold to Leonas: 1.14.2ff; in the bath: 2.2.2; Dionysius falls in love with her: 2.3.6ff; learns she is pregnant: 2.8.4ff; considers abortion: 2.10.5ff; decides to marry D: 2.11.5; dresses for the wedding: 3.2.16; bears a son: 3.7.7; arranges funeral for Ch: 4.1.6; attracts Mithridates' love: 4.1.9; Pharnaces in love with: 4.6.2; summoned to Babylon: 4.6.8; eclipses Rhodogune in beauty: 5.3.9; an encouraging dream: 5.5.5ff; appears in court: 5.5.9; sees Ch in court: 5.8.1; Artaxerxes in love with: 6.3.3; encounters with Artaxates: 6.5.1ff, 6.7.5ff; accompanies the King to war: 6.9.8; left on

Aradus: 7.5.2ff; unwittingly rejects Ch: 7.6.7; reunited with Ch: 8.1.8; tells Ch to return Statira: 8.3.2; shows gratitude to Rhodogune: 8.3.8; writes to D: 8.4.5f; restored to her father; 8.6.8

Callirhoe's journeys, map of: after 7; Syracuse to Miletus: 1.11.1–8; Miletus to Babylon: 4.7.3–5.3.11; Babylon to Aradus: 6.9.8; 7.4.11ff; Aradus to Syracuse: 8.2.6–8.6.5

Callisthenes: 10

Caria: 195a

Cephallenia: 153a

Chabrias; 12

CHAEREAS, son of Ariston: 1.1.3; falls in love with C: 1.1.7ff; marries her: 1.1.16; kicks C in jealousy: 1.4.12; on trial: 1.5.4ff; discovers C missing from tomb: 3.3.3; captures pirate ship: 3.3.14f; learns C still alive: 3.4.14; sets out for Miletus: 3.5.4ff; sees statue of C: 3.6.3f; learns C married to D: 3.6.5; becomes slave of Mithridates: 3.7.3; sentenced to crucifixion: 4.2.7; saved from the cross: 4.3.5f; writes to C: 4.4.7ff; accompanies Mithridates to Babylon: 5.2.4; produced in court: 5.8.1; verbal fight with D: 5.8.5; flees to Pharaoh: 7.2.2; welcomed by Pharaoh: 7.2.5; undertakes to capture Tyre: 7.3.4; and does so: 7.4.9; put in charge of Egyptian navy: 7.5.9; defeats Persians: 7.6.1; captures Aradus: 7.6.2ff; recognizes C: 8.1.8; sails to Cyprus: 8.2.7ff;

arranges return of Statira: 8.3.10; sends letter to King: 8.4.2f; returns to Syracuse: 8.6.1; delivers Persian spoils: 8.6.11f; gives account to the Syracusans: 8.7.9–8.8.11; betrothes sister to Polycharmus: 8.8.12; asks citizenship for his 300 Greeks: 8.8.13; an unsatisfactory hero: 14; wishes to die: 1.4.7, 1.5.2, 1.6.1, 3.3.1, 3.3.6, 3.5.6, 4.2.1, 4.3.9, 5.10.6ff, 6.2.8ff, 7.1.6

Chariton, date of: 1f; his style: 13f; his successors: 14ff; his text: 16ff; inconsistencies in: 407b, 409a

Chinese contact with west: 297e

Cilicia, Greek spoken in: 5.1.3

clausulae in Chariton: 23

codex Florentinus: 16ff

codex Thebanus: 16, 18

Coele Syria: 333a

Concord, temple of: 3.2.16

Corinthians: 7.3.7

Cornelius Nepos *12.2*: 12

courtroom in Babylon: 5.4.5

Cretan, Theron feigns to be: 3.3.17, 3.4.14

Crete, tomb-robbers make for: 3.3.9, 3.4.14

Croesus: 339c

Ctesias, *Persica*: 8f, 11

Cyprians: 8.3.12

Cyprus, Ch leaves Aradus for: 8.2.7

Cyrus = Sun: 285a

Cyrus the Great: 123b

δαίμων ἀγαθός: 235a

Demeter, great festival of: 249a

DEMETRIUS, Egyptian philosopher: 7.3.10; put in charge of a fleet: 7.3.11; sets up pavilion for Statira: 8.4.7

Demetrius, false identity given by Theron: 3.4.8

Demosthenes echoed, *De Corona 169*: 1.3.1+; *Olynthiacs 3.19*: 3.9.3+

Diodorus *15.92*: 12

DIONYSIUS, based on Dionysius I of Syracuse: 10; most important man in Ionia: 1.12.6; in mourning for wife's death: 1.12.7; has a happy dream: 2.1.2; visits his estate: 2.3.3f; takes C to be Aphrodite: 2.3.6; smitten by love of C: 2.4.1, 2.4.4f; asks C about herself: 2.5.5ff; promises to treat C as a lady: 2.5.12; C's kiss inflames him: 2.7.7, 2.8.1; C agrees to marry him: 3.1.3; swears to marry C as his lawful wife: 3.2.2; learns about Ch: 3.7.4; gives thanks to Aphrodite: 3.8.3; hears warship arrives from Syracuse: 3.9.10; tricks C into thinking Ch is dead: 3.10.1; builds cenotaph for Ch: 4.1.5f; suspects adulterous plot by Mithridates: 4.5.9f; summoned to trial in Babylon: 4.6.8; journey to Babylon: 4.7.5ff; tries to keep C concealed: 5.2.9; popular support: 5.4.1; speech at trial: 5.6.1–10; verbal fight with Ch: 5.8.5; would send his (supposed) son to intercede for him: 5.10.2ff; accompanies King to war against Egypt: 6.9.1f; has someone tell Ch that

the King has awarded C to him
(D): 7.1.4; defeats Egyptians:
7.5.14; the King promises him
C: 7.5.15; daughter by his first
marriage: 8.4.5 and note;
appointed governor of Ionia:
8.5.12; receives C's letter:
8.5.13f; returns to Miletus:
8.5.15

Dionysus, the god: 8.1.2 and note

Discord (Eris): 37a

Docimus, harbor of: 141a

Ecbatana: 6.8.6

editorial principles: 18f

Eleusis: 249a

*ephedros*: 209a

Epirus: 1.1.2

Euphrates river, starting-point of
the King's empire: 5.1.3;
addressed by C: 5.1.7, 6.6.3;
King assembles forces on its
banks: 6.8.6, 7.2.1

Europe, C the gossip of Asia and:
5.5.3

Flavius; *see* Philostratus

FORTUNE, (Τύχη), produces
better than expected: 1.10.2;
guides Theron and C to
Dionysius: 1.13.4; reproached
by C: 1.14.7ff, 2.8.6, 4.1.12,
4.7.3, 5.1.4ff, 5.5.2f; human
reason powerless against: 2.8.3;
attacks C's chastity: 2.8.4; no
work completed without: 3.3.8;
fickle: 4.4.2; contrives the
unexpected: 4.5.3, 6.8.1; plans a
grim blow: 8.1.2; reproached by
Statira: 8.3.5; funerals: 1.6.2ff,
4.1.7ff

goddesses with mortal lovers: 103a

gods associating with mortal
women: 181a

Greek, custom of building a
cenotaph for the missing dead:
4.1.3; language heard in Cilicia
and Syria: 5.1.3; marriage for
the begetting of children: 137a;
mercenaries in Egypt: 7.3.7;
one who can speak Egyptian:
7.2.2; pride and nobility: 6.4.10

Greeks, difference between
Phoenicians and: 7.3.10;
braggarts and beggars: 5.3.2;
complainers and chatterers:
6.6.7

Hebe: 195d

Helen: 5.2.8

Heliodorus, *Aethiopica*: 4, 11, 16

Heracles, Tyre dedicated to: 7.2.7;
King sacrifices to: 8.5.2

HERMOCRATES, ruler of Syracuse,
victor over Athenians, father of
Callirhoe: 1.1.1; rival of
Ariston: 1.1.3; reluctance to
accept Ch as son-in-law: 1.1.9;
yields to Syracusans: 1.1.12;
comes to C's defense: 1.5.6f; at
C's funeral: 1.6.3; receives
annual presents from the King:
2.6.3; C's child will be like him:
2.11.2; searches Sicily for C:
3.3.8; convenes Syracusans:
3.4.3; vetoes a reprieve of
Theron: 3.4.16; his prowess
invoked by the pharaoh: 7.5.8;
meets Ch's returning fleet:
8.6.3; embraces C: 8.6.8; takes
her to the assembly: 8.7.2; tells
Ch not to omit anything: 8.7.4;
distributes land to the
Egyptians: 8.8.14

Herodotus, quoted or echoed, *1 pref.*: 1.1.1; *1.11.2*: 6.7.7; *1.82*: 7.3.11; *1.107ff*: 2.9.5; *3.106*: 6.4.2; *7.1.1*: 6.2.1; *7.186*: 7.3.9; *8.85*: 7.5.15

hiatus in Chariton: 23

Hippolytus: 1.1.3

Homer, makes Patroclus Achilles' closest friend: 1.5.2;
    *Iliad* quoted or echoed, *1.55*: 4.1.8; *1.317*: 6.2.4; *3.146*: 5.5.9; *4.1*: 5.4.6; *5.696*: 2.7.4+; *6.474*: 8.5.15; *6.479*: 3.8.8; *10.483*: 7.4.6; *13.131*: 7.4.3; *16.215*: 7.4.3; *18.22–24*: 1.4.6+; *19.301f*: 2.5.12+; *21.114*: 3.6.3+; *22.82f*: 3.5.6; *22.304f*: 7.2.4; *22.389f*: 5.10.9; *23.66f*: 2.9.6; *23.71*: 4.1.3; *24.10f*: 6.1.8
    *Odyssey* quoted or echoed, *1.366*: 5.5.9; *4.703*: 1.1.14; *5.33*: 4.1.8; *6.102–4*: 6.4.6; *8.500*: 1.7.6+; *9.34*: 2.11.1+; *11.603*: 4.1.8; *15.21*: 4.4.5; *16.11*: 3.4.4+; *17.37*: 4.7.5; *17.485*, 7: 2.3.7; *18.213*: 5.5.9; *19.54*: 4.7.5; *23.296*: 8.1.17; *24.83*: 4.1.5

homosexuality: 41a

Horace, *Carm. 1.29.9*: 297e

hunting: 297b

HYGINUS, servant of Mithridates, charged to deliver letters to C: 4.5.1; can speak Greek: 4.5.2; reports letters have been intercepted: 4.7.1

Iamblichus, *Babyloniaca*: 15

Ino Leucothea: 195d

*Iolaus*-author: 9

Ionia: 195a; riches flow into: 1.11.7, 5.10.7; enthralled by C's
beauty: 2.7.1; Theron feigns brother in: 3.3.17, 3.4.8; Ch arrives in: 3.6.1; Pharnaces governor of: 4.6.1, 5.6.8; D leaves: 4.7.5; regarded by C as foreign: 5.1.5; D appointed governor of: 8.5.12

Ionian sea: 3.3.8+

Ἰόνιος/Ἰωνία: 149b

Isocrates *6.45* echoed: 4.7.2

Italy, C sought by suitors from: 1.1.2; Theron feigns to have traveled from: 1.12.8; searched for C: 3.3.8

Jackson, John: 23

JEALOUSY (Ζηλοτυπία): 1.2.5

killing an adulterer legal: 47a

lacunas in the text: 6.4.7, 7.6.2, 7.6.7

Laodamia: 275a

Leda: 195b

LEONAS, D's steward: 1.12.8; wishes to see C: 1.13.3; his reaction: 1.14.1; deposits a talent for her: 1.14.5; reports to D: 2.1.3f; vainly seeks Theron: 2.1.6f; invites D to meet C: 2.3.1f; struck by D: 2.3.6; tries to console D: 2.4.9, 2.6.2; tells C to reveal truth: 2.5.3; told to prepare wedding: 3.2.10

Leonidas: 339c

letters in the text; 4.4.7, 4.5.8, 4.6.3, 8.4.2, 8.4.5

Lollianus: 8f

Longus: 4

LOVE (Ἔρως): 29e; likes winning: 1.1.4; prompts C's presence at temple: 1.1.5; spokesman for

# INDEX

the Syracusans: 1.1.12; ally of
Jealousy: 1.2.5; Aphrodite his
mother: 2.2.8; inflames D's
heart: 2.4.5; D hated by him:
2.6.1; naturally optimistic:
2.6.4; maker of brides: 3.2.5;
naturally curious: 3.9.4; cruel
tyrant: 4.2.3; delights in deceit:
4.4.5; dispatches expedition:
4.7.5; depicted by artists: 4.7.6;
as counselor: 6.1.9; the King
sacrifices to him: 6.2.4; rules
the gods: 6.3.2; remedy for:
6.3.7, 6.3.8; fond of adornment:
6.4.3; maddened by noise:
6.4.4; reminds the King of C's
beauty: 6.4.5; 6.7.1; Ch has
made amends to: 8.1.3;
feckless: 8.5.14
Lucian, *Anacharsis 9*: 287a
Lydia: 195a

MALICE (Φθόνος): 1.2.1
marriage formula: 137a
Medea: 121a
Medes and Persians: 7.1.6, 7.5.12
Media, spoils of: 8.6.12
Median ships: 7.6.1
MEGABYZUS (reflects the historical
M., son of Zopyrus, Her. *3.160*;
Thuc. *1.109*): 11; Rhodogune's
husband: 5.3.4, 7.5.5
Melkart = Heracles: 333b
Memphis: 317a
Menander quoted or echoed,
*Arrephorus fr. 59.4* K-T: 55b;
*Dyscolus 841ff*: 413a, *842*: 137a;
*Halieus fr. 18* K-T: 149c; *Heros
fr. 1* K-T: 293a, *fr. 2* K-T: 87a;
*Nauclerus fr. 290* K-T: 43a;
*Periciromene 435f*: 137a; *Samia
727*: 137a; *fr. 542* K-T: 43b

Menelaus: 5.2.8
MENON, of Messene, pirate: 1.7.2
Messene; 55d
*Metiochus and Parthenope*: 10
Milesian warship: 2.11.2
Miletus, home of erotica: 9;
harbors: 87b; wool trade: 145a
MITHRIDATES, satrap of Caria,
historical: 11; Ch enslaved on
his estate: 3.7.3; at Ch's funeral:
4.1.7; falls in love with C: 4.1.9;
returns to Caria: 4.2.4; saves Ch
from the cross: 4.3.5; informs
Ch that C is D's wife: 4.3.8;
advices Ch not to go to Miletus:
4.4.2ff; gives Ch's letter to
Hyginus: 4.5.1f; suspected by
D: 4.5.10; denounced to the
King: 4.6.4; summoned to trial:
4.6.8; his angry reaction:
4.7.1ff; sets out for Babylon:
4.7.4; route through Armenia:
5.2.1; reports to Artaxates:
5.2.2; advises Ch to stay out of
sight: 5.2.4; supported by
governors' faction: 5.4.1;
demands C appear in court:
5.4.9; speech at trial: 5.7.1–7;
produces Ch alive: 5.7.10;
acquitted by the King: 5.8.8;
returns to Caria: 5.8.10
Mysia, kingdom in NW Asia
Minor; 295a

Nemesis: 177b
Neptune: 3.5.9
Nile: 7.3.3
*Ninus fragments*: 10
Nireus: 29f
Nisaean horses: 297c

Odysseus' yarns: 153a

# INDEX

Olympic games; 5.4.4, 287a
Othryades: 339c
Ovid, *Tristia 2.413, 443*: 9

Panthea: 245a, 356a
Paphos: 371a
papyri of *Callirhoe*: 16ff
Parthenius: 6
Pelusium: 6.8.2; strongly fortified:
  335a; pharaoh tries to escape
  to: 7.5.12
Persia, how mobilized: 6.8.7
Persius *1.134*: 4f
Petronius: 8f
PHARAOH (ὁ Αἰγύπτιος): 315b,
  324a; Chaereas escapes to:
  7.2.2; treats Ch as an intimate:
  7.2.5; summons council about
  Tyre: 7.3.1ff; puts Ch in charge
  of navy: 7.5.8f; defeated: 7.5.14
PHARNACES, the name historical:
  11; satrap of Lydia: 4.1.7 and
  note; approached by D: 4.6.1;
  also in love with C: 4.6.2;
  brother of Rhodogune: 5.3.5
Philostratus, Flavius, *Ep. 66*: 3;
  *Life of Apollonius*: 9
PHOCAS, estate manager of D,
  given charge of C: 2.1.1;
  husband of Plangon: 2.2.1;
  threatened by D: 2.7.2; C
  pleads for him: 2.7.6; plots
  destruction of Ch's ship: 3.7.1ff;
  prepares banquet: 3.8.3; cross-
  examined by D: 3.9.6–11
*Phoenicia*: 6.8.2, 7.1.10, 7.2.6
*Phoenicica*: 8
Phrygia: 407b
Pindar, *Isthm. 8.26ff*: 103b
PLANGON, wife of Phocas: 2.2.1;
  takes C to Aphrodite's shrine:
  2.2.5; ordered to look after C:

2.6.4f; asks C to intercede for
  Phocas: 2.7.2; pushes C into D's
  arms: 2.7.7; reveals C's
  pregnancy: 2.8.6; suggests
  abortion: 2.8.7; tells C that D
  will not let her rear Ch's child:
  2.10.1f; suggests passing off
  child as D's: 2.10.5; informs D
  of C's willingness to marry him:
  3.1.3ff; C asks that she be freed:
  3.8.1; comforts C: 5.5.6f
Plutarch, *Artaxerxes 2.2, 5.3*: 11;
  *Crassus 32*: 9; *Dion 3.2*: 11
POLYCHARMUS, Ch's bosom
  companion: 1.5.2; prevents Ch
  from killing himself: 1.5.2,
  1.6.1, 5.10.10, 6.2.8, 6.2.11;
  comforts Ch: 3.6.8, 4.4.1, 5.2.6;
  contrives to leave Syracuse with
  Ch: 3.5.8; visits Aphrodite's
  shrine with Ch: 3.6.3; stops Ch
  from saying too much: 3.6.5;
  enslaved with Ch: 3.7.3;
  relieves Ch of his servile tasks:
  4.2.2f; condemned to
  crucifixion: 4.2.7; brought to
  Mithridates and tells his story:
  4.2.8, 4.2.11–4.3.4; pleads not
  to be separated from Ch: 4.3.5;
  Mithridates looks after him and
  Ch: 4.3.7; shares Ch's room in
  Babylon: 5.2.4; proposes
  glorious death, fleeing to
  pharaoh: 7.1.7ff, 7.1.11; Ch's
  aide in the war: 7.3.5f, 8.2.2;
  reminds Ch and C of crisis:
  8.1.9; arrives in Syracuse: 8.6.9;
  Ch betroths his sister to him:
  8.8.12; acclaimed by
  Syracusans: 8.8.13
Poppaea Sabina: 48a
Priene: 215a

# INDEX

prizes at games: 287a

προσκύνησις: 35e

Protesilaus: 275a

PROVIDENCE (Πρόνοια), pursues
  pirates: 3.3.10; and punishment
  for Theron: 3.3.12, 3.4.7


recognition by breathing: 47b,
  8.1.7

Rhegium: 37b

RHEGIUM, PRINCE OF,
  disappointed suitor: 1.2.2

RHODOGUNE (historically a
  daughter of Artaxerxes II): 11;
  most beautiful of Persian
  women; 5.3.4ff; sister of
  Pharnaces: 5.3.5; acknowledges
  defeat: 5.3.9; daughter of
  Zopyrus, wife of Megabyzus,
  she comforts C: 7.5.5; restored
  to her husband by C: 8.3.8

Richardson, Samuel: 14

RUMOR (Φήμη), reports C's death:
  1.5.1; swiftest of all things:
  3.2.7; reports the tomb-
  robbing: 3.3.2; anticipates Ch's
  return: 3.4.1; arrives in Babylon
  before C: 4.7.5, 5.2.6


sacred month: 287b

Sappho echoed, *fr. 44* LP: 1.1.13;
  *fr. 44A* LP: 1.1.16

satrap = governor: 101a

*Scheintod*: 11

Scythian (Medea): 121a

*Secundus the Silent Philosopher*: 9

sexual fidelity: 15

Sicily, C the idol of: 1.1.1;
  Hermocrates the ruler of: 2.6.3;
  C's child will one day return to:
  2.9.5

Sidon: 345a

Sisenna: 9

Sisennia: 9

slaves, ownership of: 81a; price of:
  81b; state: 157a; torture of: 49b

soliloquies, of Artaxerxes: 6.1.8ff;
  Callirhoe: 1.8.3f, 1.9.3, 1.11.2f,
  1.14.6ff, 2.9.2ff, 2.11.1ff,
  3.10.4ff, 5.1.4ff, 5.5.2ff, 5.9.4f,
  6.6.2ff; Chaereas: 3.6.6ff,
  5.2.4f, 5.10.6ff, 7.1.5f, 7.4.10;
  Dionysius: 2.4.4f, 3.2.7ff,
  5.2.7ff, 5.10.1ff, 6.2.5ff,
  8.5.13ff; Mithridates: 4.7.2,
  4.7.3f; Theron: 1.7.1f, 1.12.2ff

Sophocles *Ajax 550f* echoed:
  3.8.8

Sparta, respectable: 5.2.8

Spartans: 7.3.7

state slaves: 157a

STATIRA, wife of Artaxerxes: 11,
  5.3.1; on beauty of Persian
  women: 5.3.2; C entrusted to
  her care: 5.8.9, 5.9.1; her kind
  treatment of C: 5.9.3; unhappy
  at her husband's attentions to
  C: 6.1.6f; her beauty: 6.3.4; her
  anger feared by Artaxates:
  6.6.2; submissively obeys the
  King: 6.7.5; left behind on
  Aradus: 7.4.12f; comforted by C
  on the capture of Aradus: 7.6.5;
  restored to the King: 8.3.2;
  weeps at prospect of slavery:
  8.3.5; gives royal adornments to
  C: 8.3.13; royal pavilion on
  board ship: 8.4.7f; reunited
  with the King: 8.5.5; gives King
  Ch's letter: 8.5.7; gives C's letter
  to D: 8.5.12

stichomythia (D and Mithridates):
  13, 5.8.5

# INDEX

Strabo *11.13.7*: 297c; *14.1.6*: 87b; *14.1.12*: 217a

Struangarus: 9

Sun, invoked by D: 3.1.8; ancestor of the King: 6.1.10

Susa: 235b

Sybaris: 73c; Theron claims C a slave of: 1.12.8, 2.1.9, 2.5.5; C never in: 2.5.5

Syracusans, hasten to C's tomb: 3.3.2; see Ch off: 3.5.3; often visit Miletus: 4.1.5; of Dorian stock: 7.3.8; welcome the return of Ch and C: 8.6.5ff

Syracuse, its assembly: 1.1.11ff, 3.4.4ff, 8.7.1ff; its defeat of Athenians: 1.1.13, 1.11.2, 7.5.8; seems near to C in Miletus: 4.7.8

Syria, invaded by Egypt: 6.8.2; Babylon near: 6.8.6; promised by pharaoh to Ch: 7.5.7

talent (τάλαντον): 81b

Telephus: 295a

Thermopylae: 7.3.9

THERON, pirate chief, possibly historical: 11; 55a; his plan to plunder C's tomb: 1.7.1ff, 1.9.1ff; finds C alive and abducts her: 1.9.7; decides to sell her into slavery: 1.10.8; his reasons for avoiding Athens: 1.11.6f; sails to Miletus: 1.11.8; seeking a buyer, encounters Leonas: 1.12.8f; tells C he is leaving her with friends: 1.13.9; hands C over to Leonas: 1.14.3; returns to ship and flees: 1.14.6; vainly sought by Leonas: 2.1.6f; in a tempest he alone survives: 3.3.12; found half-dead by Ch:

3.3.16; his false story: 3.3.17f; tried before the Syracusans: 3.4.7ff; recognized by a fisherman: 3.4.11; reveals truth under torture: 3.4.12ff; is convicted and crucified: 3.4.18

Thetis: 103ab

Thucydides, quoted or echoed, *1.1.1*: 1.1.1, 8.8.16; *1.129.3*: 7.5.15; *2.8.1*: 7.5.11; *2.35ff*: 7.3.8; *2.37.1*: 7.3.9; *2.97.1*: 1.11.1; *3.30.1*: 1.14.6

Thurii: 73c

travel by brides: 39b

turban: 297d

Tyre, did not fall to Egyptians: 7.2.6; dedicated to Heracles: 7.2.7; topography of: 7.2.8f; a wall of Asia: 7.3.2; capture of: 12, 7.4.3ff; King sacrifices to Heracles there: 8.5.2

Tyrian purple: 6.4.2, 8.1.14, 8.6.7

Tyrians, most warlike: 7.2.7; loyal to Persia: 7.3.1; boastful: 7.3.9

waterclocks: 49c

weddings: 1.1.15ff, 3.2.14ff

women let down hair: 413b

Xenophon of Athens: 8; *Anabasis* summaries a model: 230a; *Cyropaedia* quoted or echoed, *2.1.9*: 5.2.2; *4.1.3*: 4.5.3; *4.2.2*: 6.9.6; *5.1.6*: 356a; *5.1.24*: 2.3.10n; *6.1.30*: 6.8.7; *6.4.3*: 2.5.7; *6.4.6*: 4.1.12; *6.4.10*: 5.3.10; *6.4.11*: 5.2.9; *7.1.32*: 6.9.5+; *7.5.53*: 6.3.9; *8.3.13*: 6.4.2; *Symposium 2.24* echoed: 1.1.15

Xenophon of Ephesus: 4, 15

Xerxes: 7.3.9

# INDEX

Zarina, queen of Sacae: 9
ZENOPHANES of Thurii, pirate:
   1.7.2
Zethus: 123a

ZOPYRUS (reflects the historical Z.,
   father of Megabyzus, q.v.): 11;
   Rhodogune's father: 5.3.4, 7.5.5